ME AND SARA-LEA

ME AND SARA-LEA

When hearts hold lifetimes of secrets,
solving a mystery can be murder

A novel based on a true story

Charlie Trebla

Library of Congress Control Number: 2011961160
ISBN: Hardcover   978-1-4653-0776-7
                 Softcover   978-1-4653-0777-4
                 Ebook   978-1-4653-0778-1

To order additional copies of this book, contact:
Xlibris Corporation
0-800-644-6988
www.xlibrispublishing.co.uk
Orders@xlibrispublishing.co.uk
303041

CONTENTS

PART I: The Other Man

CHOKE IT OFF

ECSTASY OF BETRAYAL

KILLING-OFF CALIX

WHAT IS, IS

PART II: The Other Woman

RAINBOW PROMISE

EQUIFINALITY

EPILOGUE

DEDICATION

For my boys—
Who look at me each day with the
soundless challenge:
'Who are you, really?'

No one would fall in love if he hadn't read about it first.

(Rochefoucauld)

Seduce my mind and you can have my body
Find my soul and I'm yours forever.

(Unknown)

Marriage is against nature.
You can be certain only of this moment that is in your hands.
All promises for tomorrow are lies,
  and marriage is a promise for your whole life,
    that you will remain together,
      that you will love each other,
        that you will respect each other till your last breath.

(Osho)

INSPIRED BY A POEM
BY NANCY WOOD

My help is on the mountain
Where I take myself to heal
The earthly wounds
That people give to me
I find a rock with sun on it
And a stream where the water runs gentle
And trees which one by one give me company
So must I stay for a long time
Until I have grown from the rock
And the stream is running through me
And I cannot tell myself from one tall tree
Then I know that nothing touches me
Nor makes me run away
My help is on the mountain that I take away with me.

AUTHOR'S NOTE

This is my first novel. It was inspired by my children, who seem to look at me every day with the soundless challenge: 'Who are you, really?' I needed to discover (or create) who I really am.

It was a demanding task, self-inflicted, to write this book. Not only was it my first attempt to complete a full-length novel, but the very personal nature of it was, at times, gruelling in the extreme. When I felt overwhelmed by the revelations of last year, I started emptying my heart and mind in a personal journal. I don't know at what moment it turned into a novel, or why. It was initially intended, I suppose, as an instrument of cathartic release from the turbulent emotions and events that seemed to threaten to annihilate me and forever undo life as I knew and imagined it to be. And, to some extent, this purpose was accomplished as I narrated my journal entries and the story found its own path.

Engrossed in the ecstasy of self-pity, then later the burden of self-awareness, at some stage I wanted the story to come to an end so that I could put it away. I forget how often I typed 'Final Version' but then had to reopen the document a few days later. When it seemed that an ending of sorts had presented itself, I found that I had over 500,000 words. But that was my story; it contained everything I needed to say. Her story would be another novel entirely.

So it was a tough day, the day I decided to publish it—I would have to rewrite my story. How would I represent what happened but not all I had to tell? How deep should I go psychologically? Do I keep it firmly anchored in reality? Threaded between the embroidered storyline, I was sharing the secrets of other people, many of whom I hold dear and others not so but nevertheless felt a profound desire to respect their integrity and to honour how life has chosen our paths to cross in this way. I soon realised that because it was written in real time, as this period of our lives unfolded, I had to relinquish any desire to prescribe the twists and turns in the plot. But I cannot claim I did not have a say in the outcome. My thoughts and feelings, my intentions and choices, conspired with that of others to co-create this future from all possible futures.

I think someone once said: 'There is my version of the truth, and your version, and there is the truth. And then there is what actually happened,' or words to that effect.

So this is my story, my version of (not) the truth. And so, while what you read in this novel is based on a 'true' story, or should I say actual events, I cannot be sure they really took place. Some parts I am more certain of because I was there or I found out about it and could confirm it for myself; yet others would have a different version of events. For the rest, I relied on hearsay, conjecture, and my imagination—dramatising and fictionalising, even if it was only to justify what I was feeling and experiencing, and I needed to explore and share with you some of the issues that have emerged for me from this experience.

And in the end, it took on a life of its own, fuelled by my imagination, and I dedicate it to the pursuit of wholeness and the spirit of love.

I can confidently claim that any resemblance to actual persons, places and events is purely coincidental and a figment of the active imagination of the reader. If you think you see yourself or someone you know in one of the characters, as is the case with most novels, you're probably right, and wrong. How I experienced it is all that matters to me. You, the reader, can choose to decide for yourself what actually happened. It probably doesn't matter because where it resonates and speaks to you, carries weight for you, and causes you to contemplate yourself, your life, and your choices, is what should matter to you.

I publish under a nom de plume out of respect for our young children who will, when they choose, come across the truth and decide for themselves what really happened.

Charlie Trebla

11 November 2011

PART I

The Other Man

This is not the truth . . .

it's what actually happened

Part I: The Other Man—'This is not the truth . . . it's what actually happened'

Prologue: Thursday, 9 December 2010

Dead, or deeply buried

Callous bitch

Terminal descent

Choke it off

Ecstasy of betrayal

Killing off Calix

What is, is

End of Part 1

PROLOGUE

Nothing is so oppressive as a secret:
women find it difficult to keep one long;
and I know a goodly number of men who
are women in this regard.

(La Fontaine)

Thursday December 9, 2010

I am late, and Jim is never inclined to hide his irritation at this. He is nursing a cappuccino impatiently at the delicatessen, where I spend most of my days writing. As I unhook the gate leading to the deli courtyard, my two Bernese Mountain Dogs, Harry and Sally, impatiently needle through the gap and I stumble and nearly drop my prized possession. Taking in the pair of animal horns I carry in front of me like a sporran, Jim's expression is instantly transformed into a comical blend of mute suspicion and perplexed inquiry.

'And now?' he says, finding the perfect intonation to match his rhetorical question, 'I know you're patriotic, but the World Cup only starts next year.'

'It's not a Springbok,' I say, referring to the diminutive antelope worn as an emblem by our nation's rugby team, revered by many as the definitive icon of the current world champions and abhorred by others as a symbol of Apartheid.

'Then what's with the laptop?' he says, brushing off the dogs'
effervescent greeting. 'Are you having an identity crisis, trying to bridge
the gap between homo sapiens and our crusty-knuckled ancestors? At
least you're walking upright. But barely, I might add.' He picks at his
shorts, plucking imaginary dog hairs.

'I have something to show you.'

'I can see that. Did you grow them overnight? Useful for a threesome,
I guess.'

Whatever blows your hair back, Jim. 'This,' I say, shoving the
horns in his face, 'I found on the bonnet of my car this morning. It
left scratches.' Jim turns up his nose and holds up his hands, declining
to take the proffered pair of ringed phalluses bound together by the
remains of skull and hair, as it was in life. 'And before you ask, it's a goat.
Or was.'

'How thoughtful; your star sign.'

I sit down and log on. 'What do you know about the Middle
Ages?'

'Middle age? You probably know more about that than me.'

'The Middle *Ages*, Jim. I'm talking about that period of history
characterized by a general state of carnage and disorder and the
disintegration of infrastructure and the proliferation of warring tribes.
And when security fears birthed feudal enclaves protected by lords and
masters and pledged allegiance to the crown. You know, much like our
country today.'

'That time was preceded by the collapse of Roman society, which
paved the way for the Early Middle Ages. There was a superfluity of civil
wars and the better-known Crusades, followed by the Hundred Years'
War.' Jim was a History major, and still reads widely on the topic to
garner business strategies from the principles of ancient warfare.

I say, 'Yes, and bloodshed was made respectable by the tradition of
chivalry which ritualized violence.'

'Are you considering a new approach to Calix? You'd have my full
support, from a respectable distance, of course, purely in an advisory
capacity.' Jim is fixated by Calix, Sarah's lover.

'Just tell me more, Jim.'

'Well, in the 1400s the Black Death, or the Plague, paradoxically sparked an intellectual revival and a series of technological innovations that heralded the High Middle Ages. The resurgence of religious movements probably reflected a desire to extract sanity from chaos, and to find purpose in the afterlife which would make more bearable the hell on earth. Perhaps that's another option for you? Anyway, then came the calamities and upheavals of the Late Middle Ages, and dramatic climate change set off intervallic rounds of famine. In fact, you're right, it sounds not entirely unlike the world today. Or your own circumstances— intellectual revival aside, chaos and sexual drought come to mind.'

Samantha, who owns the deli, comes to greet us and she inquires about the pair of horns and suddenly we are at the center of the deli universe and the target of impolite but well-meaning jokes about dildos and swinging and battery packs. Impatient to continue our conversation, I put the goat's horns down on the brick paving but Harry barks and growls at it and Sally backs off, so I put it back on the table.

'That's not very hygienic,' Azura says unhelpfully as she walks past, and I wave to her. She has a professional and intimate knowledge of sex aids, hygienic or not. And I am not unaware of the syncronicity in this moment as it was Azura who blew the whistle on Sarah's affair.

'Thanks for your unsolicited opinion,' I say with a smile to mask my 'it's none of your business' and Samantha brings two plastic grocery bags which I impale on each horn in a gesture of respectability, like 'willy-warmers'.

'So what's this about?' Jim says. 'Have you unearthed a medieval horn?'

'My learned friend, I ask the questions today, and what I'm interested in are the morals and social codes of that time. As I understand it, loyalty was the key. The glue that held together the feudal system was unquestioned devotion and duty, whether it was of the peasant to their landowner benefactors, or of mercenaries to their lords, or of wife to husband, and so on. So, professor, what was the norm of the day regards sexual or marital infidelity?'

'Ah, straight to the issue, are we? I guess you will forgive me for saying that's a pointed question?' he says, looking over at the plastic bags. 'Okay, never mind. Other relationships were not permitted, but furtive infidelity was no doubt rife and became a fine art. There was some pushback, though, along the lines of "neither continence nor virginity was more pleasing in the sight of God than married chastity and fidelity", but there was little equality of the sexes and women who strayed were ruthlessly treated. Adulteresses were sometimes expelled from their homes, or had their heads shaven and were forced to parade in public for the disgrace they had brought to their husbands. My word, how things have changed.'

'You think so?' I say, not sure whether he is bemoaning the liberation of women and the insipid rebuke he believes they now receive for adultery or the perceived incidence of infidelity.

'Anyhow,' he says, 'serfs suffered the ignominy of their wealthy landowners sleeping with their wives whenever they chose.'

Right on the button. 'I remember that my perception of horned animals was forever altered in History 101 when I read that aristocrats would display a set of horns on the front door to signify the nature of their visit and advise the peasant husband to stay away.'

'And I think it was the Arab aristocracy,' he says, 'when they ruled Sicily, who apparently went deer hunting and then demanded a bed for the night from local peasants. This included the sexual services of the peasant's wife, the humiliation of which would be offset by the gift of the deer's antlers. Puts a whole new dimension to the term "horny", hey?' The rim of his cup rests on his lower lip, frothy, his taste buds' desire for cappuccino unrequited. Jim looks at the plastic bags with abrupt recognition of the relevance of their contents. 'The fucking bastard,' he says too loudly, spewing cinnamon froth and getting the sudden attention of the other patrons.

'Let's leave Calix out of this for a moment, Jim.'

But he is obdurate, and leans close to me with a pretense of confidentiality. 'Fuck it, Clive, he's really testing you now. Surely even you have your limits?' Then, drawing on the scenarios he sketched the other day about whether their relationship still persists, he says, 'He's still fucking her, brother, and now he's letting you know in no uncertain terms because you have not gratified his sick mind by reacting in the way he needs you to and he needs to get his kicks. And that time he stuck two fingers above his head when you drove past? You thought the gesture was of a horned devil, but you were wrong. Wake up, peasant!'

Ignoring him, I say, 'What's the modern day equivalent of these horns?' But he is looking at me with fury in his scowl. 'Come on, Jim.'

Shaking his head, he says, 'I don't think there is one. Back then it was based on status, nobility, but today your wife could be fiddling with the muscle-bound handyman's toolbox and what's he going to compensate you with? A screwdriver? A variable-speed drill and drill bits? A ball-and-socket? Maybe a toilet plunger?'

'Fuck sakes, Jim, come back to the point.'

'The point is you're getting screwed. Okay, okay,' he says, surrendering to my look. 'The answer is it's gone underground again. So the infidelity still takes place but we husbands are not compensated for the indignity of it. Women, except my wife of course, are no longer considered to be possessed by us. Crazy notion, isn't it? That's why we men are so fucked up . . .'

'They might be possessed, Jim, but not by us.'

'In your specific case, oh unwashed peasant, the corresponding symbol might be a red sweater or heart-shaped stones. Have you ever counted how many Sara-lea has?'

'You have an amazing ability to boost my ego, Jim,' and I tell him about what Sarah revealed of one of her past lives and the relevance of my earlier interest in the Medieval period.

When I am done, with a disparaging gesture Jim says, 'I rest my case. I'll stick with "possessed". She's fucking crazy. And he's fucking her.'

'I quickly want to show you this, Jim. I did some research about the origin of this metaphor and found a few versions. The legend of the Minotaur came up . . .'

'When King Minos of Crete was betrayed by his wife, Queen Pasiphae. The most prominent proof of her infidelity with a white bull was the horned offspring, and this was taken as its symbol. It's always the Greeks, isn't it?'

'Yes, the irony in that has not escaped me.' Calix's Greek heritage.

'I'm telling you, it's Calix who gifted you those horns. Given your little Jack a haircut lately? Checked for signs of unusual growths?'

'Jim, please, leave my boys out of this. Another possible origin of this symbol comes from Roman times. It seems that horns were given to soldiers returning from battle, and came to imply that they had been victorious in battle in faraway places but not so with their wives who were satisfied by others while they were absent.'

'Just like you, a returning hero, triumphant in modern-day business warfare traipsing through the Middle East and around the country to protect and provide for your family I might add, while he's fulfilling her needs at home. Fucking jerk. Even Shakespeare's yarns are sprinkled with references to cuckolds and horns. Actually, I think it is a metaphor for infidelity in many countries. I think it's because just like a horned animal you cannot see your own horns, and the cuckold is usually the last to know about his wife's infidelity. But it's also an insulting gesture, the horned hand, to slur the injured party. The English expression "cornuted" has its Italian equivalent in "cornuto". And in other European countries, like Spain, they use the horns to symbolize infidelity. In French it has the same connotation—"Avoir des cornes", meaning to have horns. Even in some Eastern European nations, such as Slovenia and other ex-Yugoslav countries it is used exclusively for women cheating on their husbands.'

'I bow to your superior knowledge, Jim.'

'Perhaps it's particularly relevant to mention the Greek term 'κερατάς' which is also the anthroponymic of horns.'

'Where, or more importantly, why, do you keep all this obtuse stuff filed away in your head?'

'Oh, purely for its entertainment value.'

'I put the question to the universe today, or at least let it waft through the internet ether, and got some takers already.' I turn the computer towards him. 'Look at the thread of responses on this blog.' There is some confirmation of what Jim has said and other examples.

'Perhaps he was provoked by the calm way you converse with him?'

'Calix? Assuming it was him.'

'Jesus, Clive, you're infuriating. I think this is good enough motive to break his kneecaps; that's if you need more justification. Or if you're squeamish, push him off that mountain of yours and let the rocks do the work for you.'

'I get the sense that he will simply be replaced by another.'

'Then it's Sara-lea you have to get rid of. Eliminate her from your orbit. Or both of them.'

Dead, or Deeply Buried

1

Only the broken-hearted know the truth
about love.

(Mason Cooley)

Sunday, 12 December 2010

I sit back and light another cigarette.

My wife has gone. She has disappeared, vanished. Two days now.
Forty-eight hours.

She is missing, and I am trying to find her, or find out what has
happened to her. She might be dead or in harm's way or lying in a coma
in some hospital; I have no inkling of what has happened to her. Or she
might be with him, freshly returned after eloping for the weekend and
just a few meters down the road or far away. I really don't know. This
last option I prefer as it means she is safe, but it is almost more painful
because it speaks of me and what I have become to her.

My mind houses bulging files and folders that I no longer open but
cannot delete, of descriptors of Sarah's behaviour. In just last week I could
find an example of each, and together they conspired to push me over
the edge. Folder One: Title 'Judgemental' with files—hypercritical and
finicky fault-finding, expresses unnecessarily nasty, harsh views and bitter
accusations, quick to attack others and defend herself, makes negative
moral judgments of a person and their motives, mostly vitriolic but at
times a silent punisher, and so on. Folder Two: Title 'Temperamental'

with files—volatile moods and unpredictable explosive outbursts, highly strung and anxious, obnoxiously confrontational and antagonistic, incessantly argumentative and oppositional, aggressive and may threaten violence that spills over with rage-filled resentment or a fury that smoulders in silence. Folder Three: Title 'Manipulative' with files—secretive and misleading, deliberately vague with occasional outright untruths, poses disturbing riddles and tests, controlling, devious, scheming and game playing, a talented blamer and guilt-peddler who bullies, coerces and threatens or turns her coercion inwards by threatening to harm herself if she does not get her way, and pledges wonderful things if her demands are met but seldom delivers on the tantalizing promise.

In short, she gained my compliance with the underlying threat—'If you don't behave the way I want you to, you will suffer the consequences'. She always went for the emotional jugular, where she could inflict the most hurtful damage, as she knew my deepest secrets and vulnerabilities since I repeatedly disclosed them to her—'These are the things about you that I tell other people,' she often said, knowing that would stop me in my tracks. Her well-timed disparaging labels were the real killer. And she was clever enough to do it; in fact, so skillful that, outwitted, outmaneuvered and ambushed, I always questioned my perceptions of what was happening and started to believe I was at fault. At times subtle and insidious, like ivy, its coiling tendrils still cling to me, eating away at me. My self-worth eroded and my integrity in shatters, I began to doubt myself. And so, swimming in a cauldron of rage at both her and myself, I took drastic steps to break free from the fear, obligation and guilt she imposed. So now she is 'gone'.

There are also two relatively new files (yes, I know, I've become just like her—labelling *her* behaviour now; live with someone long enough and I guess it's a foregone conclusion). One is branded 'Infidelity' which is chunky and burdensome and therein lodges much of me, the account of a man's virtual disintegration and subsequent struggle to regain his self-esteem and learn to trust again. Recently I had cause to reopen this file and append new developments. I am not sure what to call the other one; it is temporarily tagged 'Suicide Attempts' but 'Murderous Intent' may better cover it. The boys—Joshua, Jeremiah, and little Jack—if they peeped, would find they have not been overlooked as reluctant accomplices. I hope I never have to reopen this file because I will likely have to rename it 'Homicide' and create a sub-folder 'Infanticide'– but a cold shiver knowingly zig-zags my body's intuitive response to that. Perhaps I should add a file labelled 'Psychoses and Mental Illnesses', but this subject matter already seems to be well represented across the board.

Just last week, in the midst of quarrelsome times, Sarah came to me and said something that was not very nice. I started to say something about—'I wonder if we can find another way to have conversations to prevent one of us being ugly with the other, especially in front of the boys' but got no more than four or five words into the sentence when she stuck her fingers in her ears and walked away. I thought—I rest my case. Then she came back and said, 'Are you finished yet?' and I said, 'Sarah, I have barely started to . . . ' but found I was again talking to myself as she headed away down the passage.

So there are other terms that come to mind, like rude, disrespectful, and dismissive; oh, I nearly forgot—selfish, deceitful, fearful, suspicious, fraudulent, and inauthentic—it's such a long and shockingly repugnant list of characterisations I feel embarrassed to even think about it. They filled my mind so in recent weeks that, try as I might, I could not access even brief experiences of her where the antonyms would come into play. They so besieged me that just days ago I was shocked by the realisation that I wished her dead or gone. No, it's not that but rather I imagined life without her; I imagined her dead to me. Incarcerated, in another dimension, the capacity for judgement and vitriol and injury to others somehow wiped off her hard drive. In some way out of my life, out of my way, but not out of my heart. Accessible, but on my terms, where I can choose when to enter her physical space, visit her heart, stroke her hair, love her, and then leave with joy and energy intact and brush any potential contaminants off my shoulders. It seems I wished too hard.

For tonight I wish her back no matter the circumstances even though I still think of her this way and feel the effects of her psychotic madness etched into the whiteness of my bones such that at times I have questioned my own sanity. I really wonder about myself, about how much I respect myself because I am still here, forgiving (with difficulty) and trying again.

So I am sitting in my study, trying to make sense of what has happened and decide what I should do next. I haven't sat here at my desk for any length of time for many years now, since long before the children were born. It used to be a haven: my space, my den. Everything had been arranged as I needed it to be, busy and full but uncluttered, and I could always find what I needed. At some point on Friday night, when I did not know what else to do but wait for her as I had searched the house and her car and all her personal paraphernalia mysteriously left behind and made that rage-filled excursion to Calix's house across the road expecting to find her there, I had thrown on to the floor the piles of unwanted stuff that had accumulated on the desk—papers and articles of all description, magazines, three Lever Arch files containing information about my last project, a pile of overdue library books, some art drawings and pottery the boys had done (others of which were randomly distributed around the house and piles of it lay exposed under the glass-topped coffee table in the lounge and on the tiled kitchen floor), a cardboard box spilling out paint materials and other miscellaneous things, one of the boys' sandals (I wondered where its twin is?), a damp, chlorine-infused beach towel, and what appeared to be one of Joshua's latest frightening science experiments. This exercise had exposed other things, objects that had always been there because I had considered them useful and had put them there. But that was when this was my study.

And this is where I have spent the last two nights. Slothfully, I move the candle I light each evening and place it before me on the desk to invoke her presence, as it is starting to cough and splutter in the melted wax and is bothering my eyes, but I am too lazy to rummage around for another one.

Seeking clues to her whereabouts in recent defining moments, my thoughts skip and jump through the build-up to her disappearance on Friday, preceded by a week of mounting discord and culminating in catastrophic encounters. But the memories of this past week are too raw and my mind is locked into the past, and I stare out the window at the valley below, resenting how I had wrestled my way out of despair the past six months only for it to come to this—for her to leave.

Memories flit around and then settle on the conversation of last Saturday, probably because it felt so dark and pressing that it still perturbs me beyond its apparent significance. Travelling out of the village in the Jeep that day, on our way to a children's birthday party at a play park, we were mid-argument when her lover, Calix, came into view around a bend on the twisting mountain pass, driving his impossible-to-miss vehicle that looks like 'Luigi' of animated Lightning McQueen fame. The boys, feeding on the vibe between us, were irritating each other in the rear seats and fraying our nerves, and still seething from her earlier bitter outbursts, I was struggling to contain myself. On the basis that I always greeted him, I said, 'Oh, hello there,' but loudly and somewhat caustically with an impulsive wave through the windscreen, and Sarah berated me for acknowledging him, as if I should have pretended he didn't exist or their affair never happened. 'When you speak to me like that,' I said, 'I sometimes wonder whether there's an ounce of sensitivity in your heart, whether you consider for a moment what I'm feeling,' and that served to embed the tension which swirled between us in acrid silence as we left the city limits.

We arrived at the venue none-too-soon and spilled out of the vehicle in all directions, desperate to dissociate ourselves from the vibe that pursued us in the confines of forced proximity in the Jeep for so long and to secure enough distance between us and whichever person we felt was responsible for this contamination. Sarah stewed silently all afternoon at the play-park, which had an assortment of children's rides, activities, and games to keep even the most spoilt and disenchanted children busy for hours, for the most part avoiding any contact with me. Whenever I quietly sidled up to her while she chatted to other parents, offering her unsolicited views on their health and relationships and characters, she would immediately move off and take up residence somewhere else. I persisted for a while, but she has done this time and time again at social occasions over recent months, and I eventually gave up before becoming crestfallen and hitched myself to the only other parent I knew by name. Soon we grew tired of each other, and feeling strangely lost and out-of-place, I moved away to the fringe of the boisterous pre-schooler activity and slumped down on a bench with a beer and tried to assume an 'I'm okay with this' disposition, but my heavy energy probably attracted nobody to join me there. Then I noticed two other fathers, perhaps feeling that my actions gave them the permission they were longing for, also claim a bench each, but not near me, and by being motionless, perfect the art of being invisible to their demanding children.

Just as I was finally relishing the solitude, Sarah strode briskly towards me, and I steeled myself. She sat down emphatically next to me and seemed to come to a decision. 'Do you want to hear about what came up in my transformative kinesiology session last week?' she said in a way that saying 'no' was not an option. She had taken along her best friend Angela for support to this appointment with one of the gurus in the field, who worked in a way not unlike her. I realised I hadn't the faintest idea what it was about and was intrigued yet apprehensive about what it may have revealed. The reverberating force field created by our proximity almost jettisoned me off the bench but I failed to locate the source of my foreboding. I could not gauge how she was feeling although she was definitely restless and distant, thoughtful perhaps, but as she was volunteering to share it, my curiosity won out over my anxiety.

I said, 'Yes.'

And she said, 'I know you don't believe this stuff, but I do.' This firmly underscored the vastness between us, and I opened my mouth to protest, but I realised that I didn't even know what she was about to say and thought better of it. Maybe she needed the detachment from me that this comment served to create. Besides, with an opening remark like that, she was probably right. There was a void between us vast as The Rift Valley, like a no-go demilitarised zone, alternately vacant and looming then buzzing with frenzied static as if we just could not tune in to each other's wavelengths. So I sent in my imaginary drones, my trouble sensors, hopefully just below her radar, to try and get a sense of what this friction was about, me or her or someone else, past or present or future, real or imagined? But they returned to base none the wiser. Perhaps her counter-intelligence unit was just too skilful? Sitting next to her on the bench, we were both facing the playing children, so I turned more towards her to show her I was giving her my full attention, crossed my legs, and draped one arm over the back rest. Better than folding my arms, I thought. Without further preamble, she said, 'Turns out we were in a relationship before, in 1303. I was the man, you were the woman.'

Wait, this was too quick for me to take in. Was this something like past-life regression? Was she hypnotised and fed suggestive questions? I have always been sceptical about this as her belief in reincarnation and any biased suggestions by the hypnotist, I felt, were likely to prejudice the memories she recalled. Had he or she locked onto something which may have produced apparent memories which became indistinguishable from reminiscences based on events that actually occurred during her life or lives?

Then Sarah said, 'You were pregnant through infidelity, with my brother, actually, and I got violent and attacked you with a knife, and you lost the baby.' She paused and stretched her neck to glance in the direction of the jungle gym, anxious about one of our boys precariously perched on the top on the 'monkey bars', which rather inconsiderately looped and levitated too close to pointy-topped metal railings, which gave me the chance to think.

I was not sure I had heard her right. Did I lose the unborn baby, brutalised in my womb, or was it violently butchered after it was born? Was it incest? No, that's not what you call it if it was with her, I mean, his, brother, is it? Or was it rape, or was I in love, and where were we, and . . . ? But I did not dare interrupt to ask her questions.

'Thirteen-oh-three,' I thought to myself while her attention was diverted. I must Google this, but drawing deep on my undergraduate studies, if memory serves, wasn't this the time of the Dark Ages of economic and cultural impoverishment and a deeply illiterate population who lived in a state of nature with a quality of life barely exceeding that of their livestock, and where men held sway over their women? My word, how things have changed, I thought. And the latter perception held an unnerving undertone for me, given the alleged he-she inversion of our previous incarnation.

So I am actually a middle-aged woman!

Sitting there next to Sarah, I knew myself well enough to understand that this weak play on words was my attempt to deflect rising thoughts, not yet made conscious because ancient self-protecting brain programming swiftly cut in, aware that they would be too unbearable if given the chance to surface. And to buy time for me to take it all in, this stuff she was spouting. I was just grateful that I had the foresight to not say it out aloud as her retribution would have been swift and definitive. Being so cynical about these things, I was reluctant to admit even to myself that I was struck by the hint of karmic payback in the infidelity. The apparent imbalance of masculine-feminine energy within Sarah and me also seemed to find form in the revelation she had shared. In more than our display of the emotional characteristics of these archetypes, Sarah has not only hardened her mind but also intentionally strengthened her physique to ensure that she is impervious to abuse. Not to mention the interminable struggle we have had to conceive, suffering nine lost pregnancies, and I fought down the rising anger at the memory of her unilateral decision to abort a pregnancy when I was in the Middle East, which subsequently left me wondering whether that foetus was part-mine or part-Calix's. We have never discussed it, but deep within me I know I have never forgiven her; I knew that was our last chance to have a baby girl. And if she had given it up because she was in love with Calix, I want to kill him . . .

This thought lifted other memories I had buried deep, of us terminating a sixteen-week pregnancy when we had yet to have a successful birth on the medical view that the foetus was not viable but which said 'expert opinion' later turned out to be erroneous after chromosome testing. That was in 2003, precisely 700 years later; and Calix first laid eyes on Sarah on the date she and I first made love, seven years later to the day. Sevens everywhere . . . It left us with the knowledge that we had pulled from Sarah's womb, silently screaming as we dismembered it limb from limb and placed its fragments in a cold silver pan under bright theatre lights, a forming body the resident soul of which had chosen us to be the parents of its earthly female form, and dumped it in the hazardous medical waste dump. Afterwards, we called her Angelique and buried something claiming to be the placenta which the gynaecologist presented to us in the hole I dug with my hands in what we call 'the secret garden' outside the French doors of our bedroom, on my knees as tears streamed a river while Sarah watched from behind my stooped back, and from which a purpose-purchased red berry tree now flourishes. Then I recalled that she had also fallen pregnant a few weeks before we got married, and I made a mental note to ask her one day whether we had terminated that pregnancy too, as I could not remember, but I knew this was certainly not the time to inquire.

Jeremiah had dismounted his risky refuge atop which he had seemingly sought to escape the jaunts and jeers of his peers who seemed to find this unnecessarily ugly behaviour entertaining and was again swinging dexterously arm over arm on the relative safety of the 'monkey bars'. I quickly scanned the playground apparatus for his big brother, Joshua, and little Jack, and located both of them. Absorbing their joyful explorations saddened me so when I considered their likely future of which they had no inkling, now rushing at them like a steam locomotive about to exit a darkened tunnel and overrun them. With her anxiety temporarily tucked away, Sarah held her gaze in the direction of the playing children and said. 'I went with the question, "Why can't I accept love?"'

I didn't want to push her too hard to reveal more of what she had experienced as things were so tenuous between us and she would likely close down, so when she followed this with silence, I just said, 'What meaning does it have for you?' not quite sure myself to what I was referring.

'It helps me understand why I have invited abuse into my life this time around—all those abusive male figures!'

How easily I have become a stand-in for these abusive figures from her past. I could not help but feel offended that she was including me in that category, but I thought that she had not only received abuse but now exacted it too. So of the abuse, I didn't recognise this behaviour in me but rather in her, or at least, the person I more and more frequently experienced her to be—those invectives and verbal outbursts and name-calling, that cruelly dismissive manner of hers and lack of compassion when I was needy and reaching out to her and that soul-crushing impenetrable hardness when I was trying to console her; that manipulative emotional toying and general maltreatment that seemed to exploit the weaknesses in my personality as is the modus operandi of a seasoned manipulator, especially my feminine passivity and submissiveness and concerned consideration for her feelings that gave her the power to parade the gifts of love that Calix had given her despite the ego-defensive pain I felt; and the general sense I have of years of emotional neglect and physical aggression, which accompanied many of our interactions. And what about attempting to exterminate your young children? That's hardly covered by 'abuse'; it sounds like attempted murder to me, and psychotic madness is a poor defence.

I looked away, stunned by my own harsh descriptors of her. Was this how I still felt today about her or lingering resentments from the past that I have unfairly embroidered? Was it even from this lifetime? Either way, what did I need to do with the answer to this question? Silence was the only way through which I could subdue the intensifying thoughts threatening to disrupt this moment of sharing, and when that appeared inadequate, I excused myself to check on the boys and take them for a ride on the train.

I go to the kitchen and fix myself more coffee. On the long drive home that day, drawn out not by time and distance, but by mood, I was aware of just how disturbed I was by the story of thirteen-oh-three, and it haunts me still even though I could chose to view it as fairly innocuous. Recalling Sarah's story now, a quiet knowing surfaces that in AD 1303, I conceived out of love and that this love has been reignited through other lifetimes but, out of necessity, always covertly. And I know, quite simply, that he or she is waiting now for the opportunity to reconnect, to be recognised by me. I wonder whether I should open another folder, one that is more abstrusely esoteric and mystical. What might be a suitably cryptic label?—'Past Lives' or 'Other lifetimes' or 'Love of my Lifetimes'? That would intrigue anybody, no? It promises to be a good read.

Back in the study, I half-sit, stooped over my desk, with my head in my hands, smoking and drinking coffee, rummaging through my mind for what I have overlooked, for what I haven't yet done and who I haven't yet contacted to inquire about whether they saw her last Friday or whether they have any idea where she might be. Trying to simplify the situation and reduce the options I need to consider, looking for the simple, obvious explanation, rather than the complex or the inexplicable. Or worse, the unthinkable!

I look towards Jim's house. I cannot quite make it out, but I know it nestles amongst the towering trees beyond the twinkling lights of the valley of smallholdings picture-framed by the study window. I recall being submerged to my chin in his Jacuzzi in the freezing winter evenings all those months ago when I had moved out of home for a while in the numbing wake of discovering the protracted betrayal, our thoughts propelled by beers in hand. This was a ritual we called 'Jacuzzi therapy'. I was wallowing 'on the couch', heavy with anguish and self-pity and wanting to ride these feelings rather than emerge prematurely from depression in the wake of the infidelity and be forever destabilised by it. I was, I resolved, grappling with a double betrayal—the infidelity and what seemed to be its insurmountable proportions as I uncovered more of the truth, but riding pillion were the sickening untruths that seemed to persist in present time, and which suggested a relationship already sick to its core. I sensed that this was a defining moment for me, and I was desperately trying to comprehend what was happening and figure out how to respond. Jim was trying to get me to see the writing on the wall.

On one occasion, tired of him badgering me with his philosophy on life and frustrated by the differences in approach between us that were becoming all the more apparent, I said, 'Are you a "what" or a "how" person?'

'That's so infuriating. Why do you always ask questions,' he said, 'and something completely unrelated to the topic?'

'That's just me. As a colleague of mine once said to a shifty CEO of one of our client companies, who was growing evermore embarrassed by my persistent probing, "Clive is one big question mark. But his spine is straight".'

'You liked that, didn't you? It's quite a fucking endorsement,' Jim said, seamlessly blending profane exclamation with rhetorical question. He is quick; I will give him that.

'I don't know. I thought it made me look more like a misprint, a surprised and rigid exclamation mark.'

'You're so sensitive,' he said. 'Anyway, describe these characterisations.'

'Okay. I think you're a "what" person. You always start with a strategy. You want to decide the result of what you're trying to achieve—the endgame. Only then you want to know "how", so you plan the steps to get there: first do this and then do that. You formulate the problem and then you implement your chosen solution. Like managing a project, and as if you can control all the variables. Relinquishing the illusion of control is a huge challenge, especially for you.'

'So which one are you?' he said, refusing to let my last words stick to him.

'I think I'm a "why" person.'

'For fuck sake, is there also a "who", "where", and "when" person?'

'Just listen,' I said. 'I want to know *why* we are doing this particular thing, *why* we are using this approach, *why* this is happening to me, *why* we are asking this specific question—even whether we are asking the right question?'

'And just how does that help you now? You're in a very shit place. Your neighbour is screwing your wife and you're about to lose your family.'

'Not sure. But I am asking myself why I have invited this situation into my life.'

And then we sparred at length about the relative value of these approaches until Jim said, 'That's the problem I have with you. You get so caught up in "why" that it leaves you indecisive and unsure of yourself. You never get to act. I would rather take action even if it turns out I'm doing the wrong thing.'

'That's why, if you'll excuse the expression, I think you get it wrong sometimes and around the wrong way—like "aim-fire-ready". That's like choosing "how to respond" followed in rapid succession by "act", at times with "what is the situation I'm dealing with" as an afterthought. But what's the use of neatly solving something if it's the wrong problem or question, or if by the time you've solved it the context has changed? You might be doing something right, but are you doing the right thing? And anyway, not everything needs a solution.'

'But you have to do something, Clive, even if you feel like you're not quite ready.'

'Like I said earlier, I prefer to scan, as in "scan-converge-be", with the emphasis on scanning to absorb enough of the picture, all the relevant variables, especially the grey areas or things that have their own momentum. You have to understand or at least consider and assimilate what you're dealing with first, at least, sufficiently to choose a path forward. And to do that, you have to know who you are and that you are in everybody around you. So if you don't understand your external world, you will never understand yourself.'

'You speak so eloquently,' Jim said, 'that I can't understand a thing you've said,' and he buried his nose into his beer either seeking inspiration or wishing to sedate himself.

'It's a firm belief in the art of trusting the process,' I said, showing him my empty glass. 'What you need to focus on tends to emerge, seemingly of its own accord, and you'll find that much of what you need to do, to act on, is already done.' He pointed to the stockpile of beers just out of reach, and I had to clamber out the Jacuzzi to pull them closer. 'The process of scanning until you find your attention focusing or converging on certain elements has already taken you halfway there. And as my physics teacher used to say—"the rest is easy". You may still need to consciously choose a path, make a decision, or act in some way, but less so than you realise. You just need to "be". The trick is to feel comfortable to relinquish control, or the belief that you need to or should be able to control everything.'

'Except that I'm still convinced you must be in control of the decision you make here, otherwise you will be left sucking the hind tit.'

'Those are your fears, Jim, your insecurity. You are always desperate to do something, anything, so long as you can escape the pain you are feeling.'

'Don't give me that psycho-babble,' Jim said. 'Not everything originated in my childhood.'

'Look, Jim, let's agree to disagree. We all have a way of seeing the world. We all have subjective experiences, our perceptions of the objective reality. How we choose to be or act in a particular situation is a result of this perception, this lens through which we see our environment.'

But I know the weak link in my thesis is that I live in my head, asking 'why?' and observing myself and what is around me, and seldom get around to 'being in the moment' or understanding who I really am.

The makeshift paper ashtray is alight in heated fury and foolishly I blow at it and spread glowing ash across the desktop as it loops into the air and comes to rest against the framed photograph of Sarah, then slides ragdoll-like down the glass to a standstill, concealing her face.

I cannot beat the words of this song out of my head:

<blockquote>
So long
Bitch, you did me so wrong
I don't want to go on
Living in this world without you
</blockquote>

'Sorry, Jim,' I say aloud towards his house. 'I need to have the last word and say "you were right". Despite your wise words and dire warnings, I got scared and returned to my defunct marriage, irrevocably tampered with and broken, on a wing and a prayer, and I still haven't figured out why. And every night for nearly six months, I have paced the kitchen courtyard after midnight, cigarette and cappuccino in hand, in tormented grief and self-diminishment as I watched my masculine potency bleed out of my pores and seep into the storm-water drains, forever lost to me.'

2

We always deceive ourselves twice
about the people we love—first to their
advantage, then to their disadvantage.

(Albert Camus)

Sunday, 12 December 2010 (continued)

I am perplexed and have absolutely no idea of what to do other than to sit it out. My mind seeks respite in more pleasant memories than those which have frazzled its synapses all evening. So I venture on to the balcony again. It is so uncomfortably muggy I remove the board shorts I am wearing and stand naked against the balustrade imploring it to cool me. It is even warmer outside than inside, and very still, a clue that before sunrise low-hanging mist will roll in from the Atlantic Ocean and blanket the valley below me, and above which the loop of mountains will proudly parade their highest rocky peaks, motionless as leathery alligators in waiting. I hear Harry and Sally pour their lethargic frames off the couch in the entrance hall, and they saunter on to the balcony, greet my hand with their noses and then collapse heavily on the cool tiles, panting and drooling. Perhaps I should let them dip in the swimming pool? I should too. I light a cigarette.

I look out at the mountains crisply edged and silhouetted by the city lights. Infused by the natural beauty before me, I time-machine back to twenty years ago when, while married to my first wife, over the course of two years I had looked at more than fifty properties in the village with the intention to purchase our first home. Someone, on the off-chance, mentioned that this property was available, and when I arrived, I parked the car on the road and walked down the precariously steep hairpin driveway and the more-than-twenty steps leading to the wide, twin-door entrance. Ignoring the realtor's verbosity, as people of her ilk I had by then come to treat with disdain, I found myself moving quickly through the living areas to the balcony, lured, it seemed, by the magnetism of the panoramic views and the sensation of complete solitude. On that day, I stood exactly where I stand right now. The erven on both sides were as yet undeveloped, and I could see no sign of neighbours' houses such was the preservation of indigenous vegetation although this blissful sense of space has since gone. Behind me, the property where Calix now lives was nothing but a demarcated plot intended for future development in a deeply buried file in the town planner's office, and the top-end of our driveway was effectively the start of the mountain path. I looked down at the pool and garden which was somehow levelled by meticulous 'cut-and-fill' despite also staying true to the steep natural gradient of the mountainside. When I left, I signed the offer to purchase, even though I could not recall how many bedrooms or bathrooms there were nor the condition of the plumbing or whether the roof was tiled.

Over the years, life had occasionally dictated that I move for a few months or years to other cities and countries, but I kept the house and always returned after each sojourn grateful that I had never considered selling this place where I believed my soul found eternal stillness and serenity. In more recent times, I had a job that required me to commute to another city almost every other week while I stubbornly refused to relocate my family from my beloved city and home; such is the connection I feel for this place. I recognised immediately that this was home, and this was how it had felt to me since then until a few months ago when I found out what had been going on here during the last three years.

That thought propels me from the balcony, and I collapse on to the couch, where I lie down and close my eyes. Question marks float and bounce off the walls of my mind like a screensaver. *Why? Bump—Why?*

Bump—Why? I don't want to just float around here like a puppet and wait for somebody to pull the strings to determine my tomorrow, but I don't know what else to do. I know I am in the midst of a life-defining moment. My future is wide open, again, and from all my possible futures, I need to choose a path forward. Perhaps I already have, and it feels like there is a story emerging out of this that is worth telling, but I am not sure what it is. I guess it is about me, falling apart and trying to reinvent myself. Oh, and Sarah, of course. I think I will call it—'*Me and Sara-lea: AD 1303*'. That's as good a working title as any. So let me start somewhere and see where it goes.

My name, Clive, derives from Cliff and denotes 'cliff-side dweller'. My parents were wise; perhaps they know me better than I give them credit for.

The need for solitude and elevation are indelibly etched in my soul. Mountains heal my wounds, where the luxury of detached perspective nourishes my being. I seem to live my life on the fringe of something, habitually placing myself at some vantage point, looking in. I thrive on altitude, even if only metaphoric; when I find my physical self on the same contour plane as others, at best I can be 'in but not of' whatever is happening around me. But even then, it's not long before I feel the compulsion to extricate myself as I don't have a great affinity for the frivolity of joyous celebrations, crowded events, and social gatherings. You will seldom find me partaking of relaxed and perky banter and more likely observe me on the outskirts immersed in deep dialogue with someone, or on my own, and at ease with either. I am often considered to be aloof and detached and deep in conversation with myself. This perception is not entirely wrong.

The one-acre property I call home is pin-holed against the mountainside surrounded by glorious towering peaks where some say two of the world's oceans collide and overlooking the valley of small-holdings and vineyards. To the south, the calm bay visible from the garden and balcony is capped by the crescent of beach, which is peppered at dawn and dusk by strollers and their dogs traversing the river that bisects it and empties into the bay. The beach is buffered at one end by the fishing harbour, fishing village, and headland, in that order, and at the other by a monolith promontory of rock with precipitous cliffs, which caters both for intrepid hikers and occasional suicides, depending on your fancy. I think of these buffers as protective telomeres, which safeguard the white sands from further deterioration and fusion with invasive human development, like repetitive DNA sequences at the end of a chromosome, which gives me cause to wonder at the condition of my telomeres as I have aged a lifetime these past six months.

Encased as it is by mountains and sea and accessed only by scenic, twisting mountain passes, one can still imagine the original reason people visited here, and this village was born. And why calving Southern Right whales journey here each year to birth and suckle their young in the calm waters and provide viewing joy for children and adults alike. The protective inlet proffered the safe haven of still waters in tumultuous 'Cape of Storms' seas, and from this, the fishing village character emerged. Long ago the glorious sand dunes stretched from the rolling waves up beyond the hourglass waistline between bosom and hip of adjacent mountain peaks that amphitheatre the valley they tenderly embrace, poured over, and descended again towards the setting sun where they were decanted on a secluded nudist beach at the foot of 'my mountain'. Although they have long since been reclaimed for human settlement, pockets remain scattered above the building line near our home, waiting to be wind-borne to the ocean beyond. From where I sprawl on the couch, I turn my head and look east across the valley and, with appreciation, note the profusion of night-time lights below me, which nonetheless hints at large swaths of land here and there still dedicated to smallholdings and grazing pastures. The leopards, mountain goats, and antelope are no more, and nomadic, marauding baboon troops visit infrequently, yet still the vineyards that cling to the slopes across the valley whisper of another life and time of the early settlers.

The fifty or so residents of this cliff-side enclave that hovers above the valley and the village, precariously slapped like a fridge-magnet afterthought on to near-vertical east-facing slopes as the village expanded, undoubtedly squint into the first hint of sunrise now less than two hours away before any other inhabitants of this city. Hence the name 'Mount Mpumalanga'—place of the rising sun, for this cluster of properties, cordoned off with electrified fencing and security guards at the only vehicular access road since a spate of housebreakings and a murder-robbery, just two doors from us nearly five years ago. I have come to think of this as 'my mountain'. From the shoulder of this rock-strewn mound, which arrogantly interrupts the rolling ocean to the west, above the house and just beyond the uncertain firebreak which demarcates the upper limits of legal residential intrusion, indigenous fynbos clings to plunging cliffs at the base of which waves relentlessly expend their energy, tirelessly at pains to fulfil their mission. My soul is infused with the beauty of this rocky peak to which we cling, where it has endured both peace and torment, both the excruciating bliss of a peace so intolerable it made me want to scream and the tormented ecstasy of betrayal so indelible I was driven beyond madness and capable of wanting someone dead.

But I get ahead of myself.

I have had three long-term relationships with three very different women during the nearly twenty years I have lived in this house. My first wife, Kimberly, seemed to want to be somewhere else all the time, usually on another continent, and in my efforts to be in a relationship with her, I had to endure long absences that eventually proved all too much, even for me. The night we returned from our honeymoon, lying in our bed, she had said, 'I don't like this, being married. Let's pretend we are having an affair,' and this should have been fair warning to me of what was to come. But I loved her, or loved the idea of her, as I once told somebody when I was trying to figure out why it seemed I was happier and more relaxed when she was away, for some or other reason, than when she was at home and why I felt my energy drain from me when in close proximity to her, especially when I climbed into bed next to her.

Still burning in the decaying embers of my first marriage, I met Lisa who was just what I desperately needed then: loving, gentle, quietly supportive, and understanding. The Libran in her created a peaceful home with clustered corners complemented by free space. But as I gradually found my feet, this much-needed comforting relationship became uninspiring over the years and so we drifted aimlessly until our relationship practically ground to a halt.

But separation required a catalyst, and this came in the form of Sarah, with whom I fell in love the moment we met. It was 10 August 2000, which made that date earlier this year a significant one as it was the tenth anniversary of our first date over a cup of coffee, and our first kiss, when she unfastened her brassiere and took my hand, and cupped it over her breast. This 'special date' came and went this year with us living in separate homes. Sarah had made no reference to it as a special day, and I remember now my devastation at the plight in which we found ourselves ten years later and how that differed from the chemistry of the moment that day our lips first touched. I could not help but mention it to her, of course, probably toned with sullen resentment, and her response was mind-bogglingly dismissive.

Anyhow, the first contact we had lasted about thirty seconds outside a gym some weeks before our first kiss, flirty flattery by Sarah, which I recall as her saying, 'Great legs', to which I could not think of anything apt to say, overwhelmed by so many of her body parts deserving of appreciative commentary and concerned that I would choose one and a descriptor that might offend her and aware of what I was really thinking and sure that would certainly offend her. So I retreated hastily in the fading light to find my car cursing my ineptitude and regretting a lost opportunity to at least bolster my self-esteem by holding the gaze of this beauty for a few short seconds longer.

Then I encountered her three days before our first kiss, when I had shuffled grimacing into the nearest pharmacy urgently seeking painkillers to subdue the throbbing spasms racking my body as the anaesthetic abruptly wore off after a small operation on my back. As I passed under the air-conditioned blast of the pharmacy entrance, eyes imploring almost anyone, customer or staff member, to notice me, she floated like an angel from behind the dispensary, eyes laughing and full lips parted in what I fleetingly chose to register as delight at my arrival. She held me gently and said, 'You're sore.' In that single eternal moment I had a vision, which is as clear to me now as it was then—an image of rolling green fields of undulating grass in the foreground safely amphitheatred by an enchanting forest of trees, and of a beautiful, graceful, mysterious, dark-haired woman with three young children cavorting with irrepressible glee, and the most serene calmness came across me.

Ten days later, we made love, and I was well and truly in love. In the months that followed, we made love at least twice a day, and Sarah was more responsive than any woman I had been with. At first, I was in awe of the endless multiple orgasms that seemed to erupt from the deepest core of her and its lava cascaded from her and enveloped me and sealed our soul-bond as we lay intertwined for many hours, with me still inside her. It was not so much her 'sexual' response, but the deepest vulnerable connection we always shared that fed our lovemaking. She was often overwhelmed to tears and always held me close and said, 'Oh, how our bodies sing together' or 'How beautifully our souls dance!' And I remember, in the weeks that followed our first kiss, wary of my neediness, how I carefully observed her and tried to ascertain how I really felt about her, and I came to the following conclusions. Her physical beauty astounded me, and I felt I would never tire of the wonder of it. But her inner beauty, the loving tenderness which seemed to ooze in abundance from her, and how she seemed to understand and accept me and my past because of what she had experienced in her life, left me feeling that I could be myself with her—that my heart was safe with her.

At the first opportunity I got, I told Lisa I had met somebody else and I wanted to marry her. Lisa stumbled and crumbled and it was a few weeks before we parted ways as she was traipsing around the country for her work. Declaring my intentions sparked the demise of my second meaningful relationship the distant memories of which lay embedded in these house walls. Four months later, Sarah and I were married on a wine farm in what was, centuries ago, an eight-seater slave chapel, which accommodated ten seated well-wishers as two of them thoughtfully brought their own wheel chairs. The 'wheelchairs' and the 'slave chapel' are vying for top spot as meaningful indicators of our future.

I later learnt that Sarah had been accosted in her apartment and all but gang-raped shortly before we met. I can only imagine how that must have resurfaced the childhood physical, emotional, and sexual exploitation she had deeply tucked away. Years later she told me that she was suffering from post-traumatic stress and believed that, with me, life would take on new meaning, and she would feel safe, loved, and whole again. But the import of all this only revealed itself much later.

I soon acknowledged to myself that Sarah came with 'trouble' and that the turbulence would likely challenge me and shake me to the core. I had a taste of this in those early, heady months; it certainly showed itself, flickering brightly and briefly before, I guess, the love I felt extinguished it. I thought hard about it, and I decided that my love for her was deep and that I could love her through it, no matter what it brought. I just didn't know how hard it would hit me, being worn down for months, years really, by a personality that challenged all my wounds and deficiencies, and that when I was at my lowest ebb, when we really could no longer truly 'see' each other, I would discover a deep betrayal that would devastate me and question everything I believed in and held dear.

Lying here on the couch, a sound finds voice in my throat, trying to vent itself through my mouth in the form a sardonic laugh, but it is forced back down emitting only a 'hah,' as I remember my crazy notion that the truth would be revealed before I took a few days out to gather myself, and I would be able to return home a mere two months after I found out about the affair, healed and happy in an honest and open, though flawed, marriage. And how I relentlessly fought this losing battle while we were separated for those few weeks and have never really let go of its promise. Suddenly aware that this was where they had lain together, entwined, and made love, I fling myself off the couch and light a cigarette and pace the balcony which does not feel long enough for me to create distance between myself and those thoughts.

This story, if it were written, is really about me—about my journey, my 'fire-walk'. But it may at times sound like it is about her, so let me tell you a little about Sarah. A few years ago, she insisted she must be called by her full name, Sara-lea, but this sounded to me like calling my mom 'mother', and I still cannot get used to it. So I persisted in calling her Sarah or 'my love' or 'angel', and she seems to have relented to this except when she is angry, which is often.

Sarah was an abandoned and abused child. Barely out of toddler's diapers, Sarah and her younger half-sister, Roxanne, were handed over to the child-welfare system. Sarah's biological father had tried to hurl them off the balcony when he learned that his wife was sleeping with their neighbour, his best friend, and father of Roxanne. Some minor details aside, notch up one for 'history repeats itself'? But she did not escape the abuse of her stepfather, other family members, and temporary foster parents.

The man she chose, when five years old, to call 'Dad', who was neither her biological, adoptive, nor foster father, died the week we first laid eyes on each other, and since a 'true daddy' was never really in her life she has continued this search for a father-figure for over forty years. Yet again, just weeks ago, this backfired on her. She found a man (let's call him Eric), apparently huge and larger-than-life, encouraging and supportive, a shoulder to cry on, offering promisingly protective bear-sized hugs. But, sadly, it was not unconditional, fatherly love. Making full use of her vulnerability and the information she had confided in him, and in full knowledge that we were in the midst of an extremely sensitive time in the wake of her affair, Eric started to come on to her. At first it was endearing and supportive, the innuendos subtle, and must have been enticing for her, this fatherly, big-brother appreciative nurturing of her, I can see that. But when he overstepped the mark, time and again, she seemed to be at a loss how to cope with it, feeling helpless as she must have been as a child. Or maybe she found that she wanted it, and I shudder at the guilt this must have engendered. I will probably never know. This father-figure who desired her sex, skewered all Sarah's ancient wounds—just as those who, in her youth, she had trusted but they touched her or wanted to and let this be known through their behaviour and words. When I discovered the gist of what was happening I accused her of nothing, but I had a go at him by email, to keep a respectful distance but let him know in no uncertain terms to back off.

My reaction was read by both as 'ego', *my* insecurity, which of course it also was. My ego did contaminate my view as what I saw mimicked how her relationship with Calix began—from client to trusted friend to declarations of desire to . . . To them, it was all a matter of how innocent and wonderful their special friendship was. They quickly formed a defensive silence around it and tried to belittle me for my audacious indignation, and this also triggered memories of secrets and lies around Calix and stoked my ego's outrage. That Eric was playing with a married woman aside, neither were willing to see or admit that Eric was meddling with the sacred—her deepest wounds. I will never know how far this infatuation had progressed nor Sarah's complicity in it, but Sarah's response to me, her attack on my character, hurt the most and this provoked my anxiety about her ongoing relationship with Calix and gave me cause about two weeks ago to try and expose it.

Sarah survived her childhood by adopting an air of invincibility and 'acting strong' to cope with the most traumatic and uncertain situations. To declare her true self, occasionally weak and lost, would have put her at risk of crumbling, she said. So she presented carefully constructed parts of herself to each person, but never all of her, as if she suspected a child-welfare official might arrive unannounced and remove her to another home, where she would put together a fresh personality by being whatever was required of the new circumstances. 'She's been a Barbie doll all her life,' Roxanne once told me. 'She knows herself so well that she can choose when to hide or show aspects of her and become what she wants to appear. She'll never show her complete self to you, Clive, it would be too risky for her to do that.'

'It's not that she pretends to be someone she is not but that you only see the side she wants to show you?' I said.

'Somewhere deep inside of her she sees it all,' Roxanne said. 'Her calculating intellect surveys all of her and can extract and exhibit the persona of her choice to suit the moment, usually to counter her biggest fears vented by each situation.'

So too, in adulthood, she exhibited this side of herself for one person, that side for another. She was flamboyant, light, and entertaining in these circles, yet deep, engrossing, and intense in others. And altogether something else alongside people truly close to her, who could 'see' her, for fear they might hurt her or abandon her. No-one outside this closed circle would believe you if you told them of her fear-filled psychotic rantings, as they never saw it. With new acquaintances, she quickly ascertained from their star signs and numbers and other information whether she believed they could hurt her, and assigned them a place in some hierarchy in her mind and treated them accordingly. In my time with her, she dipped and weaved so much that I never felt like I could see the real, authentic whole of her. When I asked her about it, Sarah said, 'It leaves me feeling too vulnerable.' Come to think of it, the lyrics from the song I selected for our wedding were wisely chosen: 'She's like a new girl every day, and now the rest don't bother me, I'm far too busy loving her.'

Sarah's background had consequences. While living with my first two wives in this house, personal space was never an issue, and I would never have thought to use the term 'my space'. Sarah moved in with next-to-nothing; in a short period of time, she began to accumulate things, yet I don't think I noticed it, or I pretended it didn't bother me. But at some point, it did begin to gnaw at me. I suppose I could say I prefer a minimalist look and feel, at least, by comparison to her. Gradually, or so it seemed, every open space and flat surface around the house was filled with something: big things, small things, and apparently meaningless things. It wasn't so much that there was stuff everywhere, but rather what kind of stuff was there and how it was arranged or displayed. Once every available horizontal space was filled, then things were put on top of other things. Any attempt on my part to surreptitiously move things around so as to free up some space was met with a sharp rebuke. Perhaps to someone who possessed a very different mind to mine, there would appear to be a sort of calming order to all this simply disguised as chaos and viewed as such by the uninitiated: a good reason why this thing should be put with that thing, and why everything needed to be visible and almost nothing packed away or discarded when it had outlived its purpose.

But I just could not see it. And nor could Jim. 'The hallmark of a frenzied and disordered mind,' he always said.

So her early trauma and nomadic experiences had bothersome repercussions, at least for me—she became a hoarder of all things. There was nothing she could throw away, discard or hide at the back of a cupboard. Mild suggestions of a clean-up and throw-out sent her into rage and despair. Even in her young adult life, Sarah had experienced catastrophic losses of almost all the property she owned at a particular time. The theme of loss was huge for her—loss of material belongings, loss of people close to her, loss of her family and a true childhood, loss of innocence and self-respect, and, of course, loss of unborn babies.

It was all quite extreme and probably had some deep psychological undertone, and I endured the last ten years with a mixture of irritation and an attempt to be sensitive to something I realised I would never truly understand, nor be able to change. I had asked her a number of times what her need to fill every space was about, sometimes with annoyance in my voice, but usually with a genuine tenderness as I tried to understand her better. Her standard response had something to do with how it made her feel—that it made her feel rich, that she belonged, that it acknowledged her existence, and that it helped her to find order in the chaos of her mind. She said that she needed to fill the space with things that helped her feel whole again, a real person worthy of respect and admiration, a person whose life was not to be ashamed of, and who could own her space. Every now and then, she would elaborate and reveal that because she was an abandoned child, she went through childhood with very few personal possessions and very little she could call her own, and she seldom stayed long enough in one place to feel she belonged there. She moved so often between children's homes and foster homes and places of safety with her meagre possessions, her younger half-sister in tow, that she attended thirteen different schools. With me, she said, for the first time in her life, she had put down roots and at last discarded the gypsy-existence to which she had become so accustomed.

She had no more than a handful of treasured photographs to recollect her youth and clung with a mixture of glee and melancholy to them when they gradually surfaced from somewhere or another. Her official child welfare records have gone missing or were destroyed, and her mother was reticent to reveal what happened all those years ago, lying and changing the story or clamming up in tears whenever Sarah broached the topic or tried to discover the origin of long unsightly scars and healed fractures and mottled burns her otherwise immaculate skin displayed. I always imagined she suffered these at the hands of others, but given her recent behaviour I now wonder whether it was self-inflicted, and I feel equally sickened by the fact that she could do such things to herself as I am that others could have caused her such harm that she would want to. So these things also helped her to chronicle her life, to remember her experiences during these past ten years and before that; where she was and when, who she was with, what they were doing, and how she was feeling. It helped her feel that she had a past, even though I sometimes wondered why she would want to, given her experiences. So a heart-shaped stone placed here recalled her feelings about a special person, a leaf put there was reminiscent of some experience, a candle on the cabinet reminded her of someone now departed, the smell of a sandalwood basket on the floor evoked memories of a meaningful encounter, and so on. As she tried to make sense of her life, of her past, and accept who she was, these things were critically important to her, as much of her early history was unclear or the horrors therein were erased or deeply buried by her design.

Mostly it kept her sane, a counterfoil to the terrors of her past.

Mostly it drove me insane.

I think I have finally developed some understanding of how it works for her, and where it comes from. Most of it seemed to stem from that most elementary of fears encountered in the helplessness of infancy—abandonment—real or imagined. I simply had to request some time for myself or ask her a question or disagree or reject an idea or demand of hers to set off the chain of abandonment fantasies and the rush of fears that accompanied it.

She always said that she 'felt' everything around her, as if she suffered some sort of sensory hyper-sensitivity or lacked an 'emotional skin'.

She felt anguish and agony at the slightest caress, like someone with third-degree burns over ninety percent of their body, permeated by energetic vibrations unnoticed by most that induced a constant state of high alert. Blinded by the intensity of her own fears and needs, she seemed oblivious to my feelings and not very introspective about her own behaviour; if she was, then it was readily justified with the irrefutable 'it is not my fault, these are the wounds from my traumatic childhood'. Accumulated and now overwhelming fear stoked her manipulative behaviour, and so in her morbid desire to avoid emotional pain, she lived outside of herself and never in-the-moment. She always imagined she'd rather be in a better tomorrow, even if today wasn't actually that bad, and she busied herself with other people and other things, making sure she was safe with them, and so that she would not have to suffer her real feelings. At times she dissociated to such an extent that her memory of a shared situation was quite different to mine.

If the ebb was a fear of 'abandonment', the flow was the terror of 'engulfment', and as inexorably as the tides she seamlessly made them her reality. The key to this element seemed to be about 'control'—again, instilled by her insufferable childhood at the mercy of the sick minds of others. Uncertainty heightened her anxiety levels, and if she began to feel that she was not in control, that her world was no longer predictable and manageable, it raised her childhood memories, and her impulse to engage in hoarding and obsessive-compulsive habits was amplified. She endeavoured to moderate this by indulging in compensatory behaviour, little 'tricks' she had learnt to still her mind. But the more her sensory system became saturated, the more bizarre the routines she adopted, and overload provoked diabolical outbursts and brief psychotic moments. She viewed even mild frustration as potentially catastrophic and every minor discord between us coloured her view of our whole relationship, and it led quickly to more manipulative pressure and threats and outbursts. Being fair, considering my feelings, talking things through and keeping my trust did not feature high on her list. And it often felt like her goal was to win rather than to find a suitable solution to a problem.

Her emotional memories kept her locked into old fears and her most common reflex was anger, usually designed to hurt, and when she got upset I tended to assume responsibility for it. Then she resorted to obligation and duty, emphasizing her self-sacrifice and how much she did and how busy she was and how I owed her, and that I 'must' do this or 'have to' do that. Often she invoked higher 'authority, like her therapist, or she enlisted indistinct allies like 'other married couples'.

Childhood abuse, fears, anxieties and insecurities—a potent cocktail. And I carried such vengeful hatred for the original perpetrators in her youth. I tried to understand that her history, her profound sense of childhood helplessness, caused a meteoric spike of anxiety and insecurity that gave rise to a sweeping sense of deprivation, and that as an adult she tried to compensate for it by developing elaborate strategies to avoid ever experiencing pain of that magnitude again. She became a seasoned manipulator and blamer and preferred to activate my strong feelings towards her, albeit negative ones, as this created the semblance of a bond between us and kept the focus on her, which I guess confirmed for her that she had not been abandoned or discarded—like the bored and overlooked pet dog left in the yard all day who behaved badly in order to get the whip rather than wallow in neglect, any feedback was desirable.

So she clung fiercely to everything, and if I wanted to spend time on my own or with someone else she saw this as a sign that I might abandon her, that to be alone was to have to be faced with the 'nothingness' she felt inside her. Then she reverted to old patterns in an attempt to provide for herself a reassuring structure and predictability. But if you think I have got her all worked out, you'd be wrong. After ten years I could still not get a handle on her. And it was an ever-growing burden perfectly sculptured for my personality to absorb; it pressed all my hot buttons. Reluctant to hurt her feelings and fearful of her rage-filled reaction, the more she peddled guilt and blame, the more resentful I became—until I could no longer silence that inner voice that kept telling me the truth and the self-loathing that built up in me was corrosive and eventually, explosive.

And so it happened that what I had thought of as my house became our house when I married Sarah, ten years ago, and then her house. She soaked the space with all of herself, in a similar way, I suspect, that I saw how she touched every person within a certain radius of her and left an indelible mark on them, even if she did not actually speak to them. She believed that every person she encountered, all the incidents and chance meetings and coincidences, were there because she had drawn them to her, to learn and grow. She said that a part of her was reflected in all of them, that she could only get a sense of herself by getting a sense of others. So she set about each interaction to learn about herself, and she would butterfly around at every social situation and leave others with something to think about after the encounter. She felt she did not exist without seeing herself in others, leaving a part of her with them in exchange for a slice of them.

This was her appeal, her charm, the goddess-gift she possessed. This enigmatic allure, under which enchantment I no doubt fell and still languish, attracted people who felt their lives were fuller for having met her. Many people felt better after engaging with her, lighter and more centred, healed and balanced somehow, and continued to seek her out, perhaps without even knowing why. Countless people were in awe of her; they worshipped her for the joy she brought into their lives and her magic healing powers. Some were sufficiently moved to convey to me how they admired and respected her rare qualities, that they found her to be truly gifted in her healing work, outrageously generous, vibrant and optimistic, powerful yet vulnerable, compassionate and sensitive, gentle yet intense, and much more. And I so wanted to get to know this side of her.

But I came to discover that not everybody felt this way about her.

Her lifelong endeavour to establish her own boundaries paradoxically appeared to leave her oblivious of the personal limits of others—where she ended and they began. So Sarah had the habit of walking up to people and telling them who they really are and what she saw in them. I always tried to tell her that she needed to be welcomed in, to be given permission to do this. Sometimes her comments were received with amazement, and the recipient elevated her to goddess-healer. But it was not always flattering, particularly when she did not like them or felt unsafe with them, and she told them so but with such conviction and confirmation, she averred, by her instruments of magic that they were repulsed by her, complaining that she invaded, uninvited, their personal space. These individuals spoke of how uneasy she made them feel with her lack of boundaries and personal space and her sense of entitlement to crash into their psyches. They derided her eternal repertoire of party tricks, from star signs to palm reading, swinging pendulums, and divining rods as insecure attention-seeking routines. When she started on this stuff, I noticed some of them dig their hands into their pockets and if only they could do the same with their irises, they would have. They saw her dark side (or was it the reflection of their own?), her 'malevolent energy', they said, and felt that she used her intuitive powers to do harm. Some people felt this so strongly they thought she was evil.

But more about that later!

I was saying that she heals people; she is an intuitive healer. Or as she might say when asked, 'a holistic therapist, using multiple modalities', some of which I could sprout forth but with much less elegance than her when asked what my wife does, and only by throw-away labels, usually not getting much further than 'live blood analysis and kinesiology and homeopathy and that sort of thing, but perhaps you should ask her if you are really interested'. She had an astute ability to read others and uncover their vulnerabilities. I was in awe of her healing gifts, as were many others, and knew that genius does not come without personal pain. She always assumed this helper-healer role, even when not working, as if it provided for her an identity, a form of interacting with people that allowed her to feel in control and lessen her feelings of emptiness. She frequently felt the need to point out that she was not stupid, which seemed to be one of the insults hurled at her by her stepfather.

So if I wrote this story, I would be careful to add that Sarah is a qualified beauty therapist, who gravitated towards the complementary health profession, and when I met her, she was studying to be a doctor of natural medicine. But her most valuable skills emanated from deep within. She could act as the instrument, the medium, through which you restored your well-being by provoking your body to heal itself using these skills and other more esoteric means, but mostly her innate talents. She could even help you heal yourself remotely, from a distance. Clearly not one of her disciples, Jim thought this rather funny. 'Does this mean that the further you are away from her, the better you feel?' he would say.

Jim was lined up to be my best man when I married Kimberly, but as he lived overseas, when we changed the date, my other life-long friend Matthew stood in. So Jim got his chance when I married Sarah, but it became such a problem for him to spend time with me that we barely saw each other for the next ten years, and he said he just could not cope with the chaos in our home and the 'ill-disciplined' free expression of our boys, and he was unable to relate to Sarah's esoteric mind; he found unbearable her manner and her critical, controlling, and irrational energy. Some months ago, I had told him what had happened in our marriage, and he and his wife granted me the temporary sanctuary of their home while I fought my way back to wholeness again, and since then we have spent a lot of time together, but never with Sarah present. Most of the time he tried, head shaking from side to side, to understand why I was still with her and to get me to acknowledge the real reasons for staying.

Anyhow, when little Jack, the third born, arrived, we started to run out of space, and we moved out the house while we endured the mishaps and frustrations of extensive alterations. But it proved to be worth the effort in the end; our new home was spacious and bright and child-friendly. I did not know at the time that we would only enjoy this home we had created together for two months before I went to work in the Middle East, without my family. And I had no idea of what would take place in our sanctuary in my absence. In fact, the seed was planted, so to speak, before I even departed, and it would continue to grow even after my return, secretly nurtured and unnoticed by me, from every crevice and corner in this house and seep through the walls like latent rising damp. I can still not expunge its pungent odour.

As the physical and psychological spaces became more filled and cluttered over the years, so I began to feel less at ease in the house, less inclined to spend time there, and less peaceful when I had to spend time there. It became her house. So I would head out whenever I could, even when no one else was home, and often when they were, much to her dismay and annoyance. In truth, this was also because I needed to escape the anxiety-laden tension that increasingly permeated our space. And this played right into her deepest wounds. It seemed that if I was not physically present with her, I did not exist on an emotional level. So she would contact me frequently, obsessively, to reassure herself that I still cared for her. When this proved insufficient, she would set little tests of my love, typically ones that were near-impossible to meet. 'Pick up Jack for me and meet me half-way,' she might say even if she knew I was in a meeting with a client. If I declined, I was devalued to sinner from saint, to villain from hero, in a heartbeat, as all the real or imagined 'negatives' she collected and stored away assumed centre-stage for weeks or months until something prompted her to change the lens through which she saw me. Then suddenly, I was her 'Greek God' again, perfect in every way. Perhaps she tired of me when she found the genuine article, of Greek heritage?

Anyhow, this habit became particularly prevalent in recent years, and with the revelation of the affair, with the knowledge that he lives next door and had been in our house, that she had made love with him here, it felt like this house, once our home, was irrevocably and emphatically no longer mine. And more recently, her increasingly obsessive and bizarre behaviour, peppered with brief psychotic episodes and self-mutilating cries for help, conspired to create a space the energy of which was tainted forever in my mind. And so the sanctuary of our home, and the relative tranquillity I had found in favourite spaces here and there, like a cat on its much loved chair, was no more.

So now my study, which I should call 'the study', feels like it is no longer mine. It had been the one room in the house where I had permitted myself to smoke behind a closed door during my first two relationships, and I would exit the room hours later, my hair and clothes and breath, reeking of nicotine.

But that was many years ago; I had stopped smoking inside the house over ten years ago. Come to think of it, I should really stop smoking, full stop. But not tonight! Tonight I smoke in the study.

3

Blame keeps wounds open. Only
forgiveness heals.

(Willa Cather)

Monday, 13 December 2010

The boys are asleep and I am now sitting motionless in the lounge staring unfocused at the lights in the valley; just waiting. I had thought she would reappear first thing this morning, her unannounced desertion somehow encapsulated within the weekend, but now I no longer expect her to come home.

We got through the weekend, the three boys and I, pretending it was entirely normal that she was not here, as if she was attending a residential weekend workshop or something. At least, this was what I told the boys, who seemed to accept the explanation but from time to time still asked where she was. By the time we left on Saturday morning for the first of two children's parties, there was still no sign of Sarah. I had texted her half-sister, Roxanne, incarcerated at a drug dependence clinic, to let her know, and it seems that Sarah's closest friend at work could also shed no light on the situation. As we left our house and drove slowly past Calix's, I checked it for signs of occupation. I have driven past that house every day for nearly three years since he has been staying there, but for only the last six months with the knowledge the he was sleeping with my wife.

I stopped and reversed and got out the car to ring the doorbell, fighting away the recent memory of how I had dashed over here on Friday evening, emboldened by false bravado yet sickened with wrath and convinced that she was here, and had tried in vain to gain access to his property or force them to reveal that they huddled together in the darkened interior. This morning I stood yet again at his front door and tried his cellphone number and listened intently for its telltale ring from inside; but I could not hear it. There was no response from inside his house, and under normal circumstances, I would have guessed he has gone away for the weekend, or was sleeping over somewhere, perhaps with someone else's wife. I felt cynical and angry; no, absolutely livid. Over the past months, I have alternately thought of him as a fallible man, no better or worse than me, or a real cunt, a serial philanderer who sleeps with other men's wives and tries to get as close as he can to them and their families according to what I have heard. Today it was the latter view, and I felt relieved and vindicated in having felt this way about him.

I returned to the boys whose boredom had given rise to teasing each other in the cramped proximity of the three-in-a-row rear seat, and they wanted to know what was going on.

Jeremiah said, 'What were you doing, Dad?'

Joshua said, 'That's Calix's house.'

Jack said, 'No, it's not,' looking at the wrong house.

'Yes, it is,' Joshua said, in 'I'm cleverer than you' fashion. 'We played with him there in the attic and had pillow fights.'

'And we raced him down the mountain road on our bikes,' Jeremiah said, mediating the conflict brewing and distracting Jack with a joyous memory to pacify him.

'On our big bikes?' Jack said, trying to recall.

'You were on your pink Y-bike. I fell off and hurt my knee, you remember? Mom told us to be careful all the time. Calix carried me home on his shoulders. You know, Dad, . . .'

Jack said, 'Dad, is Mom there?' And at that, I had accelerated away, a little too quickly for their liking, but at least it changed the subject.

So this evening, once the boys are deeply asleep after the excesses of the day's activities, I again feel the rush of panic course through my veins as twilight fades and seek relief by following up the calls I had made on Friday night to the police station and the hospital; they say, 'Come in and file a missing person's report,' and 'no person of that description has been admitted in the last forty-eight hours,' in that order. So I phone Sarah's biological mother who lives a half-day's drive away, and try and reassure her that everything is fine and that Sarah just needs some space to sort herself out. She has done her own time in state mental institutions, and in recent years, I have come to discover this seemed to be a favourite family pastime. So I did not want to tell her that her daughter has disappeared, but Roxanne has phoned her and filled her in, and she has left a message for me today beseeching me to get hold of her.

'Keep it to yourself,' I say to her, knowing she will not, 'and out of the social media and that obnoxious Facebook you are so gripped by.' In her self-absorbed way, she seems more concerned about the inconvenience that her river-fronted house has been flooded by unseasonal heavy rains. I hurriedly mutter some words of consolation and disconnect.

I really don't want to alert more people to the situation than I absolutely have to as I will then have to deal with their distress as well, so I scroll through my cellphone contacts list, searching for Sarah's friends' numbers I happen to have. I pick out who I think are her three closest friends and her psychotherapist. Only one of these friends, her current closest girlfriend Angela, I know for certain is privy to the affair, although apparently after the fact. But I realise that there is absolutely nothing of which I can be entirely certain as Sarah has been secretive and dishonest and vague about so much. Anyhow, I tell Angela that I don't know where Sarah is and ask her if she thinks Sarah could be with Calix. She is very distressed to hear about Sarah and offers with pride at her deduction that this explains why Sarah has not responded to her calls to get together over the weekend, but she appears to know nothing more and voluntarily confides that as far as she knows Sarah is no longer seeing Calix.

I am about to say that Sarah was sleeping with him for three years and she apparently never knew, when Angela says, 'It's very worrying, Clive. Sarah would never just leave, especially not without the boys. And you must be so worried after what she did to herself before. What are you going to do?'

'Keep looking' and 'I will keep you posted' seem like the only appropriate responses to that question. To the others, I don't let on that she has been missing for two days; I just say I can't get hold of her this evening and leave out all the other details so they are not overly concerned by my questions, and they say, 'I'm sure she is just running a little late' or words to that effect.

To her psychotherapist I am more forthcoming, though we struggle a bit, fencing duel–like, getting around the patient confidentiality issue. At first, she is wary; she seems mistrustful of the reasons for my call, and her responses are guarded and circumspect. I explain how it took me a while to find her phone number and that I understand there may be things she cannot reveal, but that the circumstances are such that I simply have to speak to her. I tell her that I haven't seen or heard from Sarah since Friday and that I am, for obvious reasons I thought, concerned.

'Catherine, I know that Sarah has been in a particularly bad place for a few weeks, for a few months really, maybe since September, when you sent her to a psychiatrist. Or her doctor did, I can't remember now. You know, when she hurt herself and the boys.'

No response.

'She was in a state of high anxiety,' I continue, 'and really not coping with the situation and her feelings about herself. It just became all too much for her, and she was hospitalised for a few weeks.' She knows all this; we are wasting time. But I need her to say something, for her to feel we are on the same side and have the same interests at heart, and I am stalling while I figure out how to extract information from her, if she has any. 'The psychotherapy and medication really seemed to help. Once they established the appropriate dosage, she seemed fine after that, but a few weeks later, she seemed to go backwards again, like a relapse.' I feel like I'm reading from a medical report. 'Actually, I suppose she was very up and down since then, although she seemed stable enough to manage, but obviously she wasn't, and lately things got really bad again, especially in the last few days.'

I am telling her this to try and convince her that I am aware of Sarah's recent state of mind and that I know Sarah is discussing it with her, as if to let her know I am up to date with it, and she is not contravening any confidentiality by responding candidly to me. Wanting to end the monologue, I say, 'Why else would she disappear, Catherine, without trace or any explanation?'

'What makes you think she has disappeared?' Catherine says.

'For fuck sake,' says the voice in my head. 'Look, she has either vanished of her own accord, or something terrible has happened to her.' I feel quite annoyed now and can hear the exasperation in my own voice. I explain in detail what I came home to on Friday evening and make it clear why it does not make sense to me that all her personal belongings were here but she was not. 'I have tried the police, the hospital, nothing. Even some of her friends . . .' Hang on what is she saying to me? Is she trying to tell me something, that Sarah has not disappeared?

'Please, Catherine, do you know anything? I am really worried about her, after what she did to herself. Do you think she has hurt herself again?' I know that I am not in a strong bargaining position and am losing ground. 'If she is okay, but just needs some space, that's fine. I will let her be. Otherwise I have to think the worst.'

'Are the boys safe?' Ah, does she finally comprehend the reality of this moment?

'They're with me.' What will it take to get her to open up? 'She started cutting herself again last week. Has she told you that?'

A long pause; she is thinking about it. 'Sara-lea came to see me early last week. She was not in a good way, and I was worried about her. Her anxiety was peaking, and I thought she might be fragmenting a bit. But all I can say is that there was no indication that what you are describing would happen.'

What the hell does 'fragmenting' mean? Does she know what happened on Thursday? I say, 'Did she see you on Friday? We had an incident on Thursday that seemed to leave her in a really bad way. I think it completely freaked her out. It tapped into her worst fears and shame and childhood issues of being abandoned, and I'm afraid it's tipped her over the edge.'

Silence.

'Catherine, I'm sure she has hurt herself again. She hid her arms from me the day before she disappeared, covered them up even though it was so hot.' Will that inspire her to help me? 'Did she speak to you or try to contact you?'

'I cannot say.' You don't know? Won't say? Why are you making this so hard for me?

'Okay. Then can you give me the phone number of her psychiatrist? I don't even know her name as Sarah kept it secret from me, which is fine, but I need to reach her now. Maybe she stopped taking the tablets? She wouldn't let me ask as she felt I was linking it to her mood whenever I inquired. But that would seem to fit with her recent behaviour that was becoming more . . . more bizarre and obsessive.' I really struggled to spit out the labels.

Catherine seems to come to a decision or maybe just wants to fob me off. She says, 'I will phone her psychiatrist and get back to you if there is anything I can convey to you.'

Back in the study, I am fidgety, and the desk still appears disorderly, a mirror of my mind which is bursting with the chaotic collection of my thoughts and unconfirmed conclusions about her disappearance, riddled with unanswered questions to an unfathomable conundrum, like an obscure 5,000-piece jigsaw puzzle with more than 5,000 pieces, which was my way of distinguishing between the terms 'complicated' and 'complex'. I had left on the desk only the photographs of Sarah and the boys and our dogs and cats, some of which had passed on. And this is where I had spent the last three nights.

I extinguish my cigarette in a makeshift ashtray I mould out of a sheet of used A4 paper lying in the printer as the other one is overfull. Looking for something else to do with my hands, I rearrange the photo frames directly in front of me, placing them in equal numbers around a large silver-framed sepia photograph of us on our wedding day. It works out well because there are pairs of approximately the same size, and I can position one of each matching pair on either side of the wedding picture. Right now, my intellect needs this appearance of symmetry as if I might mimic it in my mind and more easily locate the redundant pieces of the puzzle I can discard.

But there remains one photograph that does not have a matching pair, neither in size nor subject. It is one of those sublimely beautiful pictures you can seldom create by design, no matter how good a photographer you are. The light and composition is just awe-inspiring, but mostly it's the depth of emotion captured in the moment, almost transcendental. A full-face close-up of Sarah caught unawares by the photo opportunity, her chin resting on her knuckles, gazing wistfully into the middle distance I imagine at nothing in particular but an image or thought in her mind. She is mesmerising, even in two-dimensional flatness. Four decades, perhaps many lifetimes, coalesce in her face, the depth of her eyes and the out-of-frame time-travel of her gaze. I hold this picture in both hands and run my fingers lightly over her face. I realise that I don't know who took the photograph.

I feel that I can claim to anyone that asks that I have done everything I can to find her, or to find out where she is and what has transpired to bring about her apparent disappearance. Again, my mind goes back to Friday, and for the umpteenth time, I recollect the events of that day. I can recall everything clearly and chronologically; my mind just works like that, like a motion picture . . .

The last image I have of her, on Friday morning, fills my mind: I was standing at the front door. I watched her ascend the steps at a trot towards the driveway and turn towards the carport which provides our cars a modicum of shelter from the summer sun and marks the start of her workday. The words we shared the previous day, before she went out for the evening, were about separating, sparked by a calamitous week, but she would have none of it. If the goat-horns had not already tipped me over the edge, torturous recollections of what I read the prior evening in her journal festered, oozing putrid green and spewing shards of stalactites and stalagmites which impaled me, my eyelids tooth-picked open to ensure that no matter which way I turned a vivid view of her infidelity, past and present, was in full view. She was wearing one of her favorite outfits; a long, black lace skirt the style of which accentuates her long legs and a few thin layers of tops, the outermost of which is turquoise, one of 'her' colours. Despite the early morning already predicting a stifling hot, sticky day, the long-sleeved blouse extended beyond her wrists and again I feared she had marked them with her pain. It had been weeks since we last shared any physical affection. She looked beautiful and sexy with her hips swaying and her curves emphasized with just the right amount of tantalizing hint of what lies beneath, and I wanted to reach out to her and hold her and tell her so, but I didn't as I have learnt that anything that gets in her way now as she rushes to work will likely be unceremoniously thrust aside. I waved goodbye as she accelerated off, turning left instead of right at the end of the driveway which, as it has the last six months, twisted a knot in my stomach and I wondered if it will ever not be so. But there was nothing noticeably untoward when I closed the front door on her departing car that warned me that it would be any different to any other day.

Calm filled the space, but I felt sad. I took a deep breath, and let it out through my teeth. I sensed a collective sigh from the boys as the tension evaporated. I fed the dogs and the cats, coaxed the boys to finish their breakfast while I sat with them and ate mine, got them dressed and brushed their teeth and hair while I mediated a few incidents of sibling rivalry. About half an hour after she departed, I grabbed my stuff and the boys' bags, the antecedent to departure which provoked Pavlov-like barking and prancing from the dogs keen to leap into the rear of the car and accompany me for the day. Then I ushered the boys, their smiling faces shiny with suntan lotion, out of the house and into the car and off to their last day of school for the year. Then I went to work.

I wondered whether I would truly ever 'see' her again.

4

How unhappy is he who cannot
forgive himself.

(Publilius Syrus)

Tuesday December 14, 2010

My eyes keep wandering towards my journal. I had started writing just after I found out about the affair, to escape the vortex of conversations in my head, as if putting it out there would objectify it, so that it would not retain its maddening grip on me with its endless repetition as I paced around outside at night, unable to sleep. I can draft short manuscripts in my head, and seamlessly recap it over and over again, word for carefully-chosen word, sometimes editing by copying and pasting or scrolling through a mental thesaurus for the perfect phrase that evokes the intended emotions and emphasizes a key point. It is a maddening ability that serves so well in certain aspects of my work, but was surely a sign of near insanity or would soon lead to it. I get up and sit down again, not sure what to do with myself.

What is driving me to remember that time is my fascination with how obsessed I was about the 'facts' of what had happened. My pain sought a vent for the pain of betrayal as I felt I might otherwise implode, and my savior, I thought, was more information. But actually it was the sensation of unbridled fear, that perpetual irrepressible physiological upsurge from which there was no relief. So I went after 'facts' and what

I thought I needed was honesty, and it is only with the hindsight of my increasing torment as the months wore on that I understood the impact of trust broken. But what did this do for her state of mind? Before this she was evasive, trying to protect herself or me from the truth, but then she seemed to close down completely.

I snatch at the bitter-pill journal and flip it open to a random page. It is dated 'Sunday, August 1', around the midpoint of the four weeks I had moved out of home and stayed with Jim's family. It starts like this:

> *Ok, I am sitting here in the early evening in shock and desperation. Here's how the day went . . . .*

The entries for the next few days are long and detailed, horrific accounts of our physical and verbal clashes in front of the boys. One portrayed how Sarah completely lost her composure in public and accused me of having an affair when she found me sitting at the hotel pub with Jim and a couple of female acquaintances of his one evening. Another scripted a cop-movie-like car chase with her enhanced-performance sports car pursuing my three-ton SUV while the boys screamed wild-eyed in the seats behind me. On one particular night, and I still remember it clearly, I was convinced he was with her, and I wrote how I was driven to distraction in the early hours until I drove across the valley to our house, and parked in the shadows around the corner from our house and sneaked around the garden looking and listening for tell-tale signs of them cuddling up inside, but not brave enough to peak through a window for fear that she might see me or the dogs would hear me.

It seems I spoke with few people during this time, and my journal was my daily confidant. I conversed with myself at length about what I viewed as her abominable behaviour towards me, her dismissive utterances and her vengeful habit of limiting my time with the boys as if we were already formally separated. There are recordings of interminable late-night arguments on the telephone, pain-fueled and blame-encrusted, and transcripts of endlessly severe and snappish text messages. Scattered throughout are depictions of my self-righteous indignation as I uncovered more truths about their affair and imagined others. Every so often I wrote how I pleaded with her to sit down and talk to me, to meet with me so that we could try to find a way forward, but she would have none of it. And then, towards the end, the details of a long and tempestuous telephone conversation, alternately throbbing with loving tenderness and spiked with anguish and heartache while she drank too much until she vomited while I stayed on the phone-line out of concern for her wellbeing and wondered whether I should get in my car and go to her.

There are so many anecdotes of boys in tears asking when Daddy will come home.

And of tremendous pain on both sides.

But most of all, the impression I am left with as I finally close the journal is about my own deterioration, of my emotional collapse (which I felt but mostly denied) and physical decline (which I refused to acknowledge but stared back at me in the mirror). The last entry is dated August 10, 2010 and reads:

The sky is starting to show itself, and the new day has begun. Another chance to make it work.

Ten years ago we shared our first kiss, but I doubt we will celebrate that today. I have been awake for hours, sitting on the balcony and smoking. Jim's comment to me last night as we languished in the Jacuzzi with a beer was—'Have you taken a good look at yourself lately? You look awful. And I'm scared you're going to collapse with a heart-attack when we play beach bats. You have to start focusing on things that will help you feel good about yourself and get your strength back. Only then will you be able to deal with this situation.'

So before I take a shower I look at myself in the mirror. A friend's comment yesterday about my beard also makes me think. I had stopped shaving when I left home, and my beard is full but neat. What shocks me, though, as I peer through thick, grainy eyes at myself in the mirror, is that my hair seems to have turned ash-grey overnight, almost white, in places. I could choose to view it as distinguished, I guess, but my rheumy, bloodshot eyes give me away.

People are commenting about how thin I have become, so I get on the bathroom scale, and I see I have lost about seven kilograms in the last six weeks—is that possible? I look and feel terrible, and am worried that there is something really devastating going on in my body of which I am unaware. I have tried not to pay too much attention to the obvious signs, the permanent thick cough and shortness of breath; the headaches and pain in my chest I put down to anxiety and stress and panic attacks for which I swallow tablets for anxiety. My chest spasms as I cough again and try and convince myself it is just a mid-winter chest infection and exhaustion from lack of sleep and the emotional toll.

I am suddenly aware that I have never been so traumatized in my entire life. I have never before felt that my whole world is falling apart; even in bad times, there always seemed to be something to hold onto, something that was okay. But now there is nothing.

I can hear Harry whining at the door, so I let both the dogs out and refill my coffee and take the journal with me and sit on the barstool at the kitchen counter. I turn to the front and page through the first few entries in my journal. I remind myself I am trying to unearth possible reasons for her disappearance, but reading a selection of the first few entries in my journal, going back in time like this, is going to kill me, I am convinced of that. I must not let this exercise take me back to that time, just a few months ago but what seems an eternity, when it felt like my life was falling apart. When I felt so weak, small, confused, and desperate, scrambling around for anything to hold myself together, so sad and hurt and hardly sleeping, but not really caring about myself. But is this any different to how I feel now—scared, forlorn, inadequate and desolate? All the work I have done on myself these past few months, to deal with the revelation of infidelity and the sense of deceit and betrayal that accompanied it, and to show her as best I could that I love her and would not abandon her no matter what, seems to have instantly evaporated. I would now just add mystified and powerless.

When I had confronted Sarah about the affair it was with a naive trust that all would be revealed. When we sat with Vincenzo, our couple therapist, I had expected her to say she has been involved with someone for a few months; I could probably manage something in the order of three to six months. But slowly her selective honesty and general unwillingness to divulge the truth became more and more apparent to me and as I discovered the full extent and depth of their relationship I sank into deep despair. It was more than I could take. Until then, I had attempted to transform my anger and pain through words on a disembodied computer screen, which morphed into a letter not intended for her eyes, because I was too afraid to unravel the hope I was feeling as we seemed, at least, to be talking during the first few weeks. This letter I had printed out and inserted into the front cover of my journal, and I pleaded with her that my compassion and understanding were being tested to the limits. Then, compelled by her persistent secrecy to find out information for myself, I crossed my own boundaries of respect for privacy and what I began to unearth had enraged me and brought into stark relief my true feelings of deceit and betrayal, of lies and secrets, and mostly complete disregard for me. And after this my compassion and patience turned to anger and bitterness, and our communication deteriorated rapidly into daily full-blown fights. So in frustration I had regretfully emailed that letter to her.

Sarah did not respond and would not let me speak to her about these things, so I wrote her more letters. I can remember almost every word, but sitting here I feel compelled to read them through again. Taped to the back of one of the pages are two of these letters—the first was about her itemised cell phone account, the second was about the incriminating information I found on her cell phone, computer and in her diary and journal. She had insisted that their relationship had ended ten months earlier, but I learned this was not the case and the intensive contact she still had with him, and then lied about, sickens me still. Likewise, how long he has lived next door and all the other 'untruths'. At the time, I thought these letters were intended to show her that the ongoing deceit she seemed inclined to persist with would not permit me to get over it, and would prevent me from learning to trust her again and start the process of grieving and letting go, of rebuilding our relationship. I also thought that my confessions that I had invaded her privacy would encourage her to open up and work together with me on the situation that confronted us.

But they were, I guess, really direct attacks on her integrity; a black-and-white 'caught-in-a-lie' exposure that hopelessly belittled and cornered her. It was an attempt by me to regain some control of the situation by revealing to her that I knew stuff and she could not deceive me like that again, and to prove to myself that I was not completely disempowered by the situation. It probably also gave me something to focus on—if she would not help me make sense of the state of affairs, so to speak, then I would do so myself. I glance at the letters and then close my journal. I don't need to read them; I remember what I had said.

I can see now, with the perspective of time and healing, how I had crossed the line from reasonableness to closed-mindedness—how my initial disbelief and denial of the full reality had morphed into rage and resentment. Once I had lost faith in her willingness to be open and honest, I did not want to hear or see or believe in anything that gave some balance to what had happened. I considered only the facts or suspicions that confirmed for me the worst about her, to justify my pain. I tended to look for and notice only what reinforced my beliefs of her and to gloss over and undervalue everything else. In the process, I selected out and focused on damning evidence to substantiate my victim mentality and held it up in remembrance while ignoring contrary indications of my role in it or her professed love for me.

I hold my head in my hands and rub my eyes. I feel sick, a deep nausea emanating from my gut, bile rising in my throat. In these letters I seemed to ramble on and on, saying the same thing in many different ways, really rubbing it in. I just can't believe how pedantic I was (or am?) and how this tactic of shoving things down her throat must have sickened her and left her feeling anything but good and whole, both necessary requirements for her own salvation and her ability to face up to what has happened. I can see now it was the last thing she needed, but at the time it was the only way I knew how to try and provoke her into telling the truth and deal with the pain that engulfed me. Now I sit here and wonder just what role this had played in her sudden decline and her poor state of mind in recent weeks.

I check the time; it's after midnight. My hands are trembling, and I am not sure whether it is the emotion I am feeling as I read this short history of our recent months or my desperate need to have her back, to hold her in my arms and tell her 'It's okay. I love you'. Or too much caffeine and nicotine. I know that sleep will not come if I close my eyes, certainly not on that mattress indelibly stained with their lovemaking, as images of them together in ecstatic intimacy will fill the void in my head. So I lumber down the passageway to check on the boys. I kiss each of them and whisper—'I love you. Sweet dreams.' Jack has discarded his duvet and lies naked on the sheet, his dysentery-induced fever on the rise again, and in anticipation that he will call out for me within the hour I prepare his medication and then step out onto the lounge balcony and look across the valley towards Jim's property. Irritation swells and envelops my sense of hopelessness at his 'I told you so' self-congratulatory smugness when I saw him this afternoon.

With these thoughts meandering through my mind, I finally drift off into an uneasy sleep on the couch . . .

. . . Little Jack is screaming, stumbling down the dimly lit passage, having given up on the hopeful expectation that his calls will be answered by my slipping gently into bed with him with a 'Hush, Daddy's here. Go back to sleep.' In my exhausted confusion and haste to reach him, I crash to the floor before I register that I am on the couch and not in bed.

I am fearful he will wake the others with his anguished cries, so I take him to our bedroom further away from the other boys. He needs to wee and then, thankfully, with the apparent reassurance of my presence and heavily medicated, lies motionless in bed and drifts off to sleep, holding my hand.

I lie here, suddenly realising I would prefer to be in his room, as I am surrounded instantly by distressing images of her in this room, and then the gaping absence of her. I am crying, unable to sleep, eyes fixed on the shadow of the ceiling. I know it is exhaustion and that things will feel better in the light of a new day, and I will be distracted by the demands of the boys.

CALLOUS BITCH

5

Thursday, 16 December 2010

I am hiking with the dogs across the valley from our house, a couple hundred metres above sea level. To my left, looms an expanse of rock, gorges, and ravines gouged by giant-fingernails out of what appears to be a vertical wall of granite. There are many hiking trails here, but since the huge fire some years ago, they have become 'Oh fuck zones' when you look at a climb or drop-off with gut-churning trepidation. In the distance awaits our goal, the crest of the mountain and below us, to our right, the bay extending to an expanse of ocean doing its best to imitate whipped cream. Almost the entire ocean surface in view is white, beaten mercilessly by the gale-force winds. All around us, the re-emerging flora on the mountainside appears to sway and weave and if I focus on it, I feel the onset of vertigo. So I watch my booted feet, which precede me along the stony path or squint at the steadfast peak in the middle distance towards which we advance. The durability suggested by its virtual eternalness brings into stark relief the transience of this moment in my life and the relative insignificance of the physical vessel chosen by my soul to experience the journey.

It is also potentially dangerous, I think, as I remember how a fit young paramedic was recently brushed off this mountainside by a wind of this magnitude, not far from here, and deposited lifeless some two hundred metres below. Still others, as was the case yesterday, choose this as the setting for their final conscious act and rather inconsiderately take their vehicles with them over the edge, like the ancient pharaohs of Egypt mummified with their worldly goods as if they think they might need wrecked transport in the afterlife and have lost faith in earthbound panel beaters. Not long ago it had enticed Roxanne, and I wonder how this lump of rock feels about the role it plays in such events.

We have not yet encountered any other hikers, and I am not surprised as the strong wind would have discouraged many outdoor nature lovers. From where I parked the car, we trudged up the diagonal overgrown path and negotiated the steep, narrow shaded gully with its terraced exposed roots where we lingered to take in the ruggedly magnificent views. Using the plastic pipe I carry to sip water from otherwise inaccessible alcoves and fissures, I drank from the unadulterated stream that still trickles despite the summer drought and tried to siphon some into the dogs' mouths but they were not impressed by the indignity of it. Then we were exposed to the full force of the gale as we traversed the buttress, but the contour which we now follow weaves in and out of ravines which provide brief respite from the sun. This turns me at an oblique angle to the wind, which seems hell-bent on ramming me into the rock face, and I have to aim to walk myself off the opposite edge in order for our combined vectors to keep me on the path. But in the succinct and unpredictable lulls of the variable gusts, my body suddenly finds itself ahead of my feet and about to freefall to oblivion. Coming out of each shady ravine, the challenge is reversed, and for this reason, the going is laborious as I shuffle along Sherpa-like.

The wind is ripping at my exposed skin, but it helps to cool me, and its unpredictable volatility demands concentration and helps convince me that my mind is, for once, more placid than my surroundings. It is exactly what I need right now, and I taunt it, goading it to give me all it's got. Trudging along and comforted that no one can hear me as I am 'farting against thunder', I sing out aloud, 'Crazy skies are wild above me now, winds are howling at my face, and everything I held so dear, disappears without a trace . . .' unconcerned that I twist the words to match my surroundings. But the thoughts I have so far evaded inevitably fill my mind soon after we have ascended to the contour which takes us to the peak.

The anniversary of the day she first treated Calix as a client three years ago, I asked Sarah if I could move back into the house. I had been living with Jim and his family for a month, much longer than I had intended. Two months had elapsed since I found out about the affair, and I had not anticipated that a reasonable level of disclosure, really just lucid and direct answers from her to my basic questions, would be so elusive and that I would feel that insincerity and disrespect would still fill the broken space between us.

We were sitting on less-than-comfortable bar stools at a coffee counter overlooking the main road. She had declined my offer of something to drink, as if she did not plan to stay long.

'You can stay tonight, but sleep in Jack's room,' Sarah said, looking the other way and needing to assert some control over the situation.

'I think all the uncertainty is not good for the boys, Sarah. They've been through hell and need something more stable. We need to decide what to tell them. I can't be there one day and not the next.'

'One day at a time,' she said, standing up. I could almost see her heels firmly embedded in the concrete in case I thought to dissuade her of her view. I felt, again, like it was me who has had the affair. I felt no desire from her to reconcile, to be understanding, kind, and gentle with my pain. I tried to reason with her.

'Sarah, it was you who suggested that I should go away for a while so that . . .'

She stabbed her finger at me and said, 'You left, and you left me with the children and a house to look after. I'm not having you back after what you've done!'

What I've done? 'That wasn't . . .'

'You can stay tonight. We will talk about it again tomorrow.' And I watched her as she walked away, across the road and along the sidewalk past her car, until I could no longer pick her out.

I swallowed my annoyance that I had to negotiate my way back into my own home, when the last few weeks were meant to be time out away from her, to heal and for us to get some perspective on the situation, and to stop our bitter angry words in front of the children. It was Sarah who had suggested I do this, prompted by Angela, but it seems she has forgotten this or chose to make out that I had left and abandoned her.

But I was back in the house, at least for one night.

And I remember a conversation I had with Azura just days after I had returned home. Still shell shocked by Sarah's non-reconciliatory response to me these past two months and pouring over my struggle with the 'moving target' of different versions of the truth Sarah had presented to me, I was sitting at the deli, writing in my journal and nursing a cappuccino when she came by. By then I had decided that I would no more test the veracity of the little Sarah had revealed, as the more I surreptitiously dug up the more horrified I was, even more so by the extent of her ongoing lies than the depth of what had actually been happening right under my nose. But my intellect waged battle with my integrity and self-respect and try as I might, I remained intensely unsettled by what might still be going on between her and Calix and knew that I could not rely on her to pacify my disquiet as I no longer had faith in her willingness to be candid. I knew this would remain my personal challenge, to learn to trust someone who continued to defy my desire to do so.

Azura had been a catalyst in 'outing' the affair, or more like a conduit, as some of the stories I heard came via her out of concern for me. People seemed to decant their observations and gossip into the receptacle which is how she somehow presented herself. She sat down with me and asked how things were going, so I filled her in. She listened, and then she put her hand on my arm, 'You are a good man, Clive.'

'Why do you say that?' I was half-challenging, half-needy of an ego boost.

'Because you haven't left her. Most men would have.'

'Really?' Why am I not like them?

'Three friends of mine have just gone through exactly the same thing. And a while ago, another two couples. In each case, the men have left; no question of trying to work it out.'

This reminded me of all the conversations I'd had in the previous few weeks with other people. I had heard and overheard so many stories about affairs that I felt overwhelmed by just how much it was taking place right here in the village. And they all confirmed Azura's assertion; it seemed unusual to hang in and try to save the relationship. It made me feel stupid and emasculated.

'And I must tell you, Clive, I am totally flabbergasted with women,' Azura said, despite being one herself, and I wondered whether her opinion carried more weight as she swings both ways. 'I have so many friends who are just playing their men, and the guys put up with it. Why can't Sara-lea just sit with you and have an honest conversation? It should be non-negotiable; can't she see that if nothing else, she owes you that?'

'It's too difficult for her.'

'If she is feeling bad about it, and let's not forget that she probably should, that's no excuse for being dishonest and to leave you with uncertainty about what happened. It just keeps you guessing whether anything she says now is truthful, and you're no doubt wondering whether they are still seeing each other.' It was as if she knew what was preoccupying my mind before she sat down, and she was genuinely getting quite worked up. 'Fuck it, Clive, who does she think she is? Does she not even have enough respect for you to get rid of the gifts of love he gave her? She seems to parade them in front of you. Hasn't she hurt you enough?' Her hands were flapping, trying to pluck from the air strong enough words to match how she was feeling. 'She . . . it . . . it's completely unreasonable,' was the best she could do.

'She thinks differently to most people, Azura.'

She shook her head and glared her disbelief at me. 'Clive, you are so much more than she sees in you.' We sat quietly for a while, and then she said, 'Why don't you go on an adventure? With yourself. Somewhere, anywhere, it doesn't matter.'

I was tempted but felt I was not yet ready for that. Besides, I could stay right where I was and embark on that adventure. Doesn't everything happen in your heart and mind, no matter where you are?

'Maybe that time will come,' I said, brushing it aside as the truth of it was I was feeling so devastated that I feared I would disintegrate entirely if I took off on a personal venture of self-discovery. I preferred to pretend that everything was okay, that none of this had taken place, and that we would be better off as a result of what has happened. No, that was not it; what I needed was to feel our togetherness, that we were closer now than ever before. And that reassuring sense I did not feel.

And now I think of what I had in recent years experienced as Sarah's complete emotional detachment from me, of how her reaction to a situation seemed disproportionate and misdirected, expressed as anger and criticism and disappointment in me, rather than support and understanding. Like when we could have lost the boys in that car accident the week before I moved back into the house; a moment when one expects support from your loved ones, when everything else, no matter how irritating, is put aside in favour of gratitude that they are okay and an appreciation that everybody is in shock and what they need the most is gentleness and tenderness.

On that Friday, in keeping with our now-established pattern, my parents collected the boys from their schools for the usual Friday afternoon programme at their house. This was the only weekday afternoon I had at my disposal, and I have come to relish it as the weekend loomed and, with it, very little time to do as I wish. As luck would have it, I had switched off my cellphone while playing tennis with Matthew at two o'clock. When we were done, we settled down at a restaurant for a cool-down drink, and I checked my phone and saw that I had eight voice messages. I instantly knew that something was wrong, and I listened to the first message—'. . . the boys have been in a car accident . . . ' and I immediately disconnected the message service and phoned Sarah. My mind went into overdrive, and my body started to shake uncontrollably to an extent I think would only be induced by some calamity around the boys. I could not keep still, so I stood up, with Matthew looking at me concerned but patient enough to wait for me to explain to him what was going on.

'Why wasn't your phone on?' were Sarah's first words.

'I was playing tennis. Are they okay?'

'No, you weren't. We looked for you at the courts.'

'I was playing tennis with Matthew. We have just finished.' I needed to know whether they were okay.

'Where were you really? Why were you not contactable?'

I was shaking so badly I had to hold the cellphone in both hands. 'Sarah, I was playing tennis. My phone was in the car. It's too hot to leave it on the court. Now I am with Matthew at the deli.'

'Nobody could get hold of you.'

'I'm really sorry,' I said. 'Where are they? Are they okay?'

'You have to keep your phone on.'

'Sarah, please, this is not the time for that. We can talk about that later. What happened? Is everybody all right?' But she had put the phone down.

My body hadn't stopped shaking since I listened to that first voice message a few minutes earlier. Matthew looked at me and said, 'Sit down.'

'I must go,' I said.

'Sit down,' he said, firmly. 'Take five minutes. They're okay,' but I stood at the table and smoked a cigarette while he shook his head and bit his tongue to avoid having a go at Sarah's attitude on the telephone. I could see he was beating down the things he wanted to say.

But my concern for the boys would not dissipate. 'Matthew, she is obviously in a state and that's why she says these things.'

'Stop making excuses for her.'

'But the problem is, she files it away and whips it out when she wants to tell me what a shit I am. That's what gets to me.' And she uses this to justify why she had an affair, but I don't tell him this; he does not know about it.

All he said was, 'She is just trying to control you.'

Twenty minutes later I discovered that nobody was at home and tracked them down at the hospital. The delay in seeing them was

unbearable as she knew it would be and that spite from her felt most
grotesque. By the time I arrived at casualty, Sarah had easily persuaded
other family members of my wrong-doing, and I faced a firing-squad
of guilt-trip bullets which found their mark. I wanted to hug Sarah in a
show of support and gratefulness that everybody was okay, but it was as
if there was a force-field between us and I felt I would be exterminated
if I got within metres of her. So I held the boys close, and only then,
when I saw they were okay, did the tremors subside. It took days for her
to calm down and speak to me but even then with pent-up resentment
and broiling anger.

The next weekend, the last of August, we joined our close friends
Matthew and Jordan at our favourite getaway in the mountains, which
caters for almost any outdoor fancy, in our case, rock climbing and
abseiling, hiking and swimming and cycling, and your choice of extreme
off-road trails almost custom-designed for the Jeep's as-yet untested
adroitness, in a wilderness sprinkled with extraordinary rock formations.
They were married shortly after us and now have two boys bridging the
age bracket between our eldest and youngest. I have known Matthew
practically all my life, and Jordan is one of Sarah's closest friends. We
borrowed a camping trailer, partly as a treat for the boys, partly as a
gentle introduction to a way of life of which we have often dreamt.

This weekend stood out for a number of reasons. The day we arrived,
and after Sarah and Jordan returned from a late-afternoon hike, we had
dinner with our friends and then went to bed. Sarah cuddled close to me,
her thigh draped across my stomach, her arm encasing my chest, and her
face buried in my neck. She nibbled and kissed my earlobe. I was almost
paralysed by the intensity and promise of it, and we made love for the
first time in many months. It was beautiful and gentle, yet intense. The
sensations were almost too much for me to bear, and my emotions were
overwrought with mixed feelings and ugly images. It seemed to go on
forever, then suddenly I lost control and was unable to withdraw, and I
came inside her such was the intensity but polluted by thoughts that she
allowed him to do this. In that moment she held me and repeated, 'You
can't, you can't,' and all I could think was 'he did!' But I was grateful for

the bond it seemed to reseal, the fresh scar it kissed, and wondered what it meant for her and for us. I thought that the moment was well-chosen, away from him, our home, and our bed.

The next day as Sarah prepared to take a shower, emboldened by the previous night's communion, I ventured as far as the kitchen and kept the space afforded by an adjacent room between us and said, 'Can I join you in the shower?'

'No, this is my time,' she said, looking the other way.

'Oh, I just thought . . .'

She swung round and somehow managed to lurch at me, chin jutting, while hanging on to the bathroom door handle—'You can't! This is my quiet time. You need to respect my space.' I extended a palm in retreat. 'Get away, get away from me!' she said and slammed and locked the bathroom door.

Momentarily stunned, I didn't know what to say next, and I just stood there, hesitant and hurt. I had not allowed for this response, or maybe I was too accustomed to it. 'I just . . .' I said to the door. There must be something apt to say, I thought, more for my sake perhaps than hers, but it did not occur to me. Matthew, who was standing nearby in the kitchen, came over and put a hand on my shoulder and squeezed gently and then moved off towards Jordan in the lounge.

I followed Matthew's lead for breakfast, muesli and fruit, and a while later, he said, 'You ready, yet?'

Looking more professional in my cycling kit than I felt but deciding I should perhaps enjoy that illusion alongside Matthew's authentically scarred extreme endurance physique, I kissed the boys and waved to a cheery Jordan. She gave me an appreciative look and said I look great and should really think of modeling again. 'He still has a great six-pack,' she said to Matthew. Courtesy of a strenuous weight-loss regime of caffeine and nicotine and dysphoria—depression, anxiety, rage and despair in equal measure; side effects include dire emotional collateral damage and permanent scarring—not for the faint-hearted, I thought. 'What about Clive being the forty-something model for our website?' Jordan said.

'The make-up artist will have her work cut out to make me look that old,' I said, and gave her a 'thanks for the confidence boost' hug.

I instructed the dogs to 'stay' as they were not allowed to wander around this protected reserve where livestock coexisted with elusive leopards and caracal and may find themselves the recipient of a farmer's rifled bullet or severely chastised by the resident hound, an Anatolian Shepherd who, like them, was mostly placid as a puppy but dispatched of leopards that ventured near his herd of cattle. The cloud of dust kicked up by our 'knobblies' on the dirt roads hung behind us in the stillness as we cycled through the farms at high altitude, on a plateau encased in peaks snow-capped in winter, and as I took in this splendour, I wished I had brought my camera with me.

Cycling with my friend of nearly forty years seemed an opportune moment, and I revealed the situation that threatened to destroy our marriage. Matthew is impartial and wise and always seemed to make choices and decisions with good reasoning yet in a way that best suits him. It flowed easily from me while he listened and shared some of his views. He offered that he probably did not know whether his wife, Jordan, has had an affair and that if she has, he could only hope that it was a brief fling that passed by and made no material difference to their relationship.

'Actually, I saw her with a guy once, a few months ago.' Matthew recalled of Sarah, as if he was just making small talk to pass the time. He described this person to me; it was Calix. 'I was on a training ride up the mountain pass in your neck of the woods. They were not holding hands or kissing or anything, but it was obvious to me they were together.'

'What do you mean?' I said, aware that this sounded just like the story I had heard from my other long-standing friend, Jim, and I wondered just how many people who knew us had seen them together and drawn their own conclusions but not conveyed their concerns to me.

'I could just tell. They were acting like a couple.'

Matthew knew all the short-cuts to get to where he wanted to go as this was his pre-season training ground, and I was grateful for the fact that he just wanted time in the saddle rather than endurance or speed training or, perhaps even worse for me, the technical sections. We dismounted to scramble across a rocky riverbed, Matthew somehow managing to do this without slowing down. When I caught up with him, he said he did not judge Sarah for the affair, though, in possession now of some of the specific circumstances, he admitted that, if it were him, he did not think he could cope with it and stay in the marriage as it was not a fleeting relationship, and the ongoing proximity of her lover would be intolerable. But he really wanted to talk about something else that was bothering him, and as I struggled to keep pace with him on the single tracks, he told me what had troubled him and his wife over the years about Sarah's behaviour and attitude towards me.

'It's the way she is with you,' he said, the gap between us widening as I battled to get traction on the loose stones on the ever-increasing gradient. 'It seems to have left you smaller than you were, like you're not a whole person any more. It's not at all how I remember you. Every time we have come away with you here, it gets worse, and you just sit on the fringes, smoking and drinking coffee. The rest of us would be out for hours each day on our mountain bikes, or hiking or climbing, but you never joined in with any activities that would take you away from the house or your children as if you were not allowed to be independent. And she would put you under tremendous pressure if you had wanted to go for a walk or a swim. Anything you wanted to do, she slated as selfish, I heard her. Even if you offered to take your boys with you, she would place limitations around this and effectively prevent it from happening.'

I was unable to clearly hear what he was saying with the crunching under tire and my laboured breathing and was almost at a standstill as the chain kept jumping a gear under pressure of the torque, and I wondered if this was not worse for my knees than running up this hill.

'Wait for me at the top. I can't hear you,' I said as I lost all forward momentum and toppled sideways into a considerate cushioning bush, unable to release my new cycling shoes from the pedal cleats in time. It was not particularly elegant, and I trust nobody in this wilderness saw me except the local wildlife, but I looked around in self-conscious embarrassment anyway.

I was unable to get going again up the incline and realised I was probably in the wrong gear. As I arrived at the top, pushing the bicycle and drinking the concoction he had mixed for me from the water bottle and which thus far was not proving noticeably beneficial to my stamina, Matthew was grinning and stretching his calves, and I then recalled that he had only promised it would help tremendously with my recovery afterwards. I was using his spare mountain bike, and between gasps I said, 'This is such a great bike, but I think the chain or the cogs or the gears or whatever they're called need adjusting.'

But he ignored my excuses, and with no hint of being short of breath, he said, 'Whenever you tried to step up, it seemed like you were pushed down again, and perhaps in the end, you were just too terrified to move, to say what you wanted or do what you needed. When it got too much for you, you would pitch in with a sarcastic comment, which was not helpful, but I saw it as an attempt to hide your resentment and helplessness. My cycling friends who were here last year commented on it; in fact, we were all quite concerned about you. They would joke that you needed therapy. They were just seeing a single moment of it, and it was very apparent to them. They didn't really know, as I do, how deep seated it is.'

Getting ready to set off again, he looked back at me as if to establish how I was coping with his description of things. I had been holding on to what was different and better about this weekend away than previous times. Sarah had not objected to towing the camping trailer; that was a good start, and her anxiety was manageable as the Jeep hauled its load up the mountain pass to this plateau. Nor the boys' bicycles—that was unusual. And when we arrived the previous day, Sarah had gone hiking and now I was cycling. But Matthew was right about the other occasions, and I felt mildly embarrassed by what he had witnessed but also embittered.

Then Matthew said, 'I just wonder what you do with it, all your anger?' I was not sure if he expected an answer to his question because he was off, hopping his bicycle across boulders and crevasses as if it was an appendage he had been born with, before he disappeared over the top and started the descent and bellowed, 'See you at the bottom.'

'I thought we were not doing anything technical today,' I said to the local fauna and flora as I set off. We were on a section of the hiking trail I would have been wary of to walk on, never mind cycle, what with the precipitous drop off and hairpin bends and metre-high steps, and I swallowed my pride and dismounted whenever fear overcame me, swearing at the sticky cleats. Suddenly I hit a jeep track of sorts, wide and winding and with loose gravel and, encouraged, I flung myself and my expensive borrowed steed down the hill as I thought this was where I could make up some ground. It was exhilarating. But around the last bend, I also discovered, too late, that treacherous patches of soft sand made an unannounced appearance and as the front wheel dug deep, I flew over the handlebars and landed in disarray with my helmeted head cracking distinctly against an unflinching rock, loud enough for Matthew to retrace his tire tracks and find me trying to disentangle myself from a bush. So that's how to quickly unclip from the cleats, I thought.

'You okay?' he said.

'Sorry about your bike.'

'I'm sure it's fine. It already has a crack from when I landed on a rock. In fact, it broke completely in half and is just welded together.' That made me feel much better, and if he was not there, I would have taken a lot longer to get up. My knees hurt. In fact, everything hurt.

'Anything broken?' Matthew said, as I tenderly pressed on the welts that quickly formed and tried in vain to brush grit from the cuts and recognised the benefit of shaving one's legs. He has so many metal pins and staples in him from spectacular falls in podium-placing successes around the world that he needs to present a medical certificate when passing through airport X-ray machines.

'Me or the bike?'

'Let's head back. It's a doddle from here,' he said, evidently reassured there was nothing to be concerned about. Shaken, I focused on the terrain, the initial elation I felt cycling with Matthew now wearing off. We were at pace on the flat, my lungs were struggling for oxygen, and I could not respond to him as he nattered on even if I could think of something to say. I was aware of a niggling need to return to the house, of preparing myself to handle the expected onslaught from Sarah, yet knowing that arriving back sooner or later would make no difference as I was already feeling defensive which would only strengthen her resentment at my absence and for not carrying the load with the children. In an instant, I was struck by the role I have played in creating this pattern we fall into.

Matthew pulled back again so that I could draw level with him. 'Jordan and I have often discussed it,' he said, back on the topic of Sarah's behaviour towards me and expelling my self-defeating reflections from my mind.

'So why don't you say something to Sarah?' I said, feeling isolated and like I could do with some support. And tiring a bit with how effortlessly other people spout forth their views on this intractable quandary.

'It is pointless to raise it with Sara-lea as a one-off indictment,' he said. 'In fact, Jordan has gently tried to approach these issues with her—how she treats you and the boys, but she says Sara-lea is always quick to pull down the shutters, and she just won't engage the topic. The only way would be to work on it relentlessly and see who cracks first because that is probably what will happen. It would simply ruin our friendship. I can understand that's the predicament you have being married to her, and there's probably nothing you can do. So my main concern is for you, and how you choose to respond to it.'

'She has issues from her early life,' I said, but I already knew it did not sound convincing, and Matthew squinted at me. 'Look, Matthew, you're right. I thought I could rescue her, be her knight in shining armour. But I'm just not strong enough to deal with all the shit.' I tried to pull ahead of him as if this would disinvest me of my troubles, but without any noticeable change in cadence, Matthew kept alongside me.

'You are languishing in no-man's land, like a frog in slowly boiling water, unsure of your own needs and feeling guilty about whatever it is she is going through and even believing that you are to blame for the affair,' Matthew said. 'You're actually filled with more fear than she is—afraid of hurting her, dancing on egg-shells to avoid her anger and disapproval, scared she will leave you. And now that you have learnt that she has all but done that, I'm sure you are petrified. Your nature is to always be reasonable, talk things through and accommodate her needs. But you are too desperate for her to like you and I guess you don't want to break the tacit promise you made to love and protect her forever. But trying to be nice and gentle won't earn you her admiration as you will never be able to do enough. But standing your ground will.'

I avoided the glance he cast at me. 'You need to do things that will make you feel good. Other men in this situation go out and have a good time, have some drinks with the boys or have one-night-stands or an ego-boosting affair. Anything, really, that will tuck away the feelings they have that diminish them and keep them lingering in victim mode with the doubts and questions of self-worth brought on by an affair. I know many men in unhappy marriages who hang out at escort and strip clubs, just to affirm that they are attractive, desirable, and appreciated. It is not about the sex, and sometimes the interaction does not even include the physical act but is about spending time in company that leaves them feeling good about themselves . . .'

I have heard so much well-intentioned advice lately, and from what I can make of it, it has to do with my masculine energy. Their intentions always felt well-meaning, and they made it sound like these activities were the norm, even acceptable. When I baulked at this, or so it must have appeared to others, some tried to help me see that I could play this out in other ways, like bury myself in my work or career or some creative outlet or endurance sport, depending on how they knew me and judged my talents. Hearing these approaches to my situation did throw me into turmoil—yet I stayed in the marriage; I had returned to the house, suppressing my feelings and with my needs unmet, and I immediately got caught up in the tumultuous tornado of Sarah's emotional demands *and* a broken relationship. I could literally feel my potency evaporate; the ebb of that deeply intrinsic power as my life force waned and gushed, free-flowing across the paved kitchen courtyard where I paced after midnight, smoking, and seeped into the garden soil beyond the gate, forever squandered.

As I recall now my conversation with Matthew, I also hear my psychotherapist, Vincenzo, who used a much stronger word than male energy—'masochism'. He felt that I needed to explore why I always found myself in this type of relationship with women, and why I could not assert my needs more strongly or why I accepted things that were excruciating to me, things that were clearly beyond the pale, and why I always relinquished my needs. He picked up on it when he heard me apologising to Sarah, trying to make her feel better about the affair, or at least not feel bad about it. He said it was already clear to him all through therapy the previous year, and had wanted to delve into my upbringing and my parents and said it would take a few years of in-depth therapy to work through it, so I said, 'No thanks, I am in a crisis. I need help now.'

I thought I knew what 'masochism' meant, but of course, I looked it up anyway: I was informed that it refers to the tendency to derive gratification from experiencing mistreatment in the form of (physical) pain, suffering, humiliation, deprivation, degradation, domination or offence by another person, and a propensity to find pleasure in self-denial and submissiveness, and to actually seek out this form of gratification. The last words sounded particularly sick and ominous. At the time, reeling from the discovery of the affair, it either did not resonate with me or I was too fearful of exploring it further.

And I now have an interesting take on this inversion of masculine-feminine energy—'thirteen-oh-three'. Now my new therapist talks of my wounded child, and how Sarah, while possibly inclined towards excessive masculine energy due to her own childhood, is further encouraged to emphasise this for fear of crumbling if she acknowledges weakness and in an attempt to compensate for my disproportionate levels of feminine energy, the origins of which, in turn, is located in my upbringing. How I wish I had had a father or a father-figure from whom to learn this life skill!

So while I listened intently and found it difficult to disagree with Matthew, I guess I remained sceptical about how much of this so-called advice was really to do with him rather than me.

Matthew interrupted my thoughts, 'Clive, listen to me because you're infuriating. You really need to decide what you want and look to your own needs. I'm not just referring to the affair, but also how she is with you. I go cycling every day. Some people think I am selfish and maybe I am, but that's the deal, and Jordan knows it. Remember this morning when she asked me how much time she has to exercise tomorrow before we leave here, I said she can have as much time as she needs as long as it does not interfere with my training programme. It was a very straightforward discussion and both our needs will be accommodated somehow. I can't imagine that happening with you and Sara-lea.'

He was right; Sarah has already decided that tomorrow she is cycling out of here with Jordan and I have to watch the boys and pack the car.

'Matthew, a few weeks ago she held a knife to her throat.'

He looked across at me. 'When are you going to admit to yourself that her behaviour is outrageous? That she is ill, that she has a personality disorder?'

'It's like she's completely out of control when she reacts to a situation,' I said.

'Don't concern yourself with her melodramatic threats. It's emotional blackmail.'

'You would not believe some of the things I could tell you, and each time I question whether I should not be able to handle it better, as if it is my fault. It feels as if a hundred things I don't even know about, and that are much bigger than me anyway, pour into her head, and her reaction is completely disproportionate, and I feel completely helpless.'

'She is a master of manipulation in those moments, Clive. The only thing that concerns me is what you are going to do about it. You need to make a choice for yourself: get out of there real quick or learn how to stand up for yourself. And that situation in the shower this morning? Well, I went absolutely cold, the hairs on my neck stood up. It was not even about me, but the frostiness in the tone of her words and body language stuck to me like Teflon and even I felt disembowelled by her response to you. Jordan overheard it; she was not even nearby, but she was so disturbed by how it made her feel she had to go for a stroll to get rid of it. When she came back she said to me that she's had enough of this treatment you get from Sara-lea, which was also fuelled by how Sara-lea was instructing her last night how to look after our boys properly. But I managed to calm her down. She said Sara-lea could have approached it in so many other ways to let you down gently but with feeling, and leave you knowing that she appreciates your desire to be close. It just made me see how cruel people can be in a relationship.'

When we got back, Sarah went crazy and started screaming and throwing things around. I still have not figured out what it was all about, though she seemed to have had words with Jordan and demanded that I support her point of view. When I said I don't even know what they spoke about, I was demonised in an instant. Matthew and I retreated hurriedly and formed a protective huddle around our boys, but Jordan, unable to restrain herself any longer, took her on and then Sarah disappeared for hours and returned long after dark.

Next morning, she was cheery as ever while the rest of us walked around on eggshells.

Before we left on the long drive home, Matthew came over to me and said, 'I'd go insane within a week if I was you.' Which was quite an admission, coming from Matthew, whose steely resolve and sense of self was flustered by nothing.

The dogs, Harry and Sally, make me laugh, and this breaks my train of thought. They run ahead as always, just like the boys with their 'me first' excitement, pushing and shoving each other to be first out the front door, or whatever the challenge of the moment is, and usually ending in tears and accusations. Running ahead and away from me, the tail-wind whips the dogs' tails relentlessly on the left and right of their rumps as if encouraging them to squeeze an extra second off their record time for the long-distance steeplechase, and their hair lies unaccustomed and awkward against the grain. The strength of the gusts of wind propels them moonwalk-like in ungainly fashion to the imaginary finish line. They turn around frequently and face into the wind to check my progress, their eye sockets pulled wide by the wind as if struggling to expel their cannon-ball eyes, and their hair undulating in waves against their bodies. Like this, they look rabid and near hysteria, but they love it. I acknowledge them with a smile and a wave, and with a yelp and a bound, they are off again.

Struggling through the gale, I find myself ruminating about Sarah's mental deterioration, though I am immediately uncomfortable with that description. Her 'mental state' sounds, perhaps, more neutral. Since I moved back into the house, I had managed, to a large extent, to still my mind and keep my frenzied thoughts about their affair in the background, at least to the extent that I could prevent spewing these damning imaginings at her, though I was never truly free of it, and it occupied my mind day and night. I had even resigned myself to concede defeat and gave up expecting a degree of openness from her, at least for a while yet. I tried hard to accept her reasoning. 'In time,' Sarah had said, 'all will be revealed, and you will have all your questions answered.' But mostly, I was completely thrown by the hard line she had taken and her apparent disregard for opportunities to help put me at ease and bridge the gap between us. In retrospect, I was still tortured by what had happened and the possibility that it was continuing, and I had long conversations with myself while I paced the courtyard at night. I challenged myself to overcome my now deep-seated fear of rejection and swallowed my resentment around the sexual issues and our occasional physical affection was reassuring and perhaps the only light I saw.

The only times my obsession with what had happened floated gratefully into the background was when Sarah's current behaviour, ever-demanding, disapproving, and constantly on edge, demanded all my energy to withstand. I became, to her, the most inconsiderate person to share a home with, and every morning she complained in accusatory tones disproportionate to the transgression about how I disturbed her sleep with my nocturnal meanderings. I regularly asked her to stop censuring me unnecessarily, and one day she eventually said, 'I will try not to criticise you so much.'

But I didn't notice any real change in this pattern. If it felt any different to the last three years, it was simply a matter of intensity. My ego, obsessed with insecurity and fears and details of the affair that I knew or imagined as I tried to hold my own world together, and bombarded by aftershocks—the things I continued to find out and piece together—fought for headspace with the turmoil unleashed by my struggle with her daily behaviour. Notwithstanding the well-meaning advice from Jim and Matthew and others, after the madness and anger between us during July and August, I convinced myself that it was just the way things were. Vexed by my own torment, I did not really notice the stark signs of a person falling apart like continental drift in front of my eyes, a psyche fragmented since early childhood now drowning as oceans of personal issues and questions of self flooded in. What were the signs that I had missed or chose to ignore?

After nearly two hours' walking, we seek respite from the wind and sun in a small cave hewn out of the rock in a ravine, which in winter would supply hikers with running waters from the seasonal rains but is now dry. I take the water bottles from my backpack and pour water into the tiny bowls, which the dogs lap up and then give me a perfunctory gesture of thanks before collapsing heavily in the shade. This is a necessary rest-break, and the change of activity interrupts my thoughts, but no sooner we set off again, and the memories I have been avoiding the most find traction in my mind. I still cannot shake off the notion that I was responsible for provoking her sudden state of mental collapse that required psychiatric care, as the feelings I had bottled up since she refused to engage the topic of 'us' could no longer be contained. And for that reason, I have been avoiding recollecting what took place that week in September; such are the feelings it evokes in me. I was as distressed about my own decline as I was at what had precipitated hers, but in the relative solitude on this wind-swept walk, my mind engages with trepidation the days leading up to her hospitalisation.

6

He who gives up the smallest part of a
secret has the rest no longer
in his power.

(Jean Paul Richter)

Friday, 10 September 2010

Sarah has just presented me with a little heart-shaped stone. She has a bit of space in her workday, and we are strolling along the contour path which snakes through occasional pine tree forests, condemned as non-indigenous vegetation but which has not yet been cleared. I grew up in my parents' house nestled on the slopes just below us, and running with my Border Collie dogs along this track was a daily routine as a teenager. On occasion, I had sneaked a mountain bike up here even though it was not allowed and challenged myself on the more treacherous sections where steep, rocky dongas had carved the direct up-down route, instead of the hiking track, which cut into the deep ravines but makes for easy walking.

It is hot, and if the afternoon sun's shimmering reflection off the Atlantic Ocean was not prohibitively dazzling, the fierce squinting frown that already furrowed my brow would only now have appeared to mirror my emotions. She has picked up the stone at the turnaround point, marked by a timber-slated bench in the shade of a single pine tree, beyond which a steep descent has the path to meet the road.

By an act of providence, perhaps, this was the spot we had clambered up to on a scorching December day ten years ago, legally married. Having extricated ourselves from the rear of the chauffeur-driven vintage car, not blessed with air-conditioning, and trailed by our two photographers, Sarah laughingly struggled in her heeled shoes and tapered wedding dress as we scrambled up from the road, which twists and turns in the waist between two mountains. On our way to the wedding reception, where guests drank champagne and dutifully awaited our arrival, we had endured the hour-long trip from the small chapel where we had exchanged vows, but could no longer bear the stifling heat, and this spontaneous pull-over en route produced marvellous photo-opportunities as we giggled and danced in euphoric love and drank Red Bull and champagne from the bottle.

I wonder if it is only me who feels sentimental right now or if she has the same fond memories? I stare at the stone but cannot bring myself to accept it from her.

'I noticed you gawking at the stones in my consulting room the other day,' Sarah says. 'Here, take this. It represents love.'

The other day Sarah had offered to give me a massage treatment. I knew this was one of those break-through moments I had to face, but at first, I could not stop imagining her treating Calix like this. I knew from having sneaked a look at her appointment diary that he had 'consulted' her about twice a month since the start of this year, or at least these were the appointments she was brave enough to diarise, and who knows at what frequency in the preceding years of their affair. There was a time when Sarah said she was not comfortable to massage men, and by some strange coincidence, that morning Joshua had asked me if Mom also treated male clients, and whether it was more often women or men that she saw at her work. His use of the word 'treat' sounded like 'give pleasure or delight' rather than 'make well or administer healing', such was my state of mind at the time. It was difficult to release those thoughts and to relax into the massage, yet I was appreciative of being with her and wanted to watch and touch her gently while she worked. I tried to feel her love through her touch but nothing was untainted, and it seemed almost everything could propel thoughts of him and them into the moment. It seemed she also struggled for a while to loosen up. I was naked, as always, for the massage, and I wondered whether he was when she treated him? Working on my thighs and buttocks, her hands moved close to my groin, her fingers sometimes brushed against my scrotum. For a moment I found myself aroused. Was he too?

Afterwards, she asked me to blow out the candles. There were three single candles, a representation I now detested, plus the big grey one we had used in couple therapy last year with Vincenzo. Some weeks into that therapy process, she had asked if we could burn a candle during sessions, so I had gone out and found one, a beautiful large one with three wicks. I remember that at some point one of the wicks no longer worked and lay in the wax, so we just lit two of them. She had seemed okay with this. As I blew out the flames, the symbolism of it detonated in my brain. To think that he sat there, symbolically, with us all that time in therapy while we tried to fix our relationship! I acknowledged my feelings by simply saying to Sarah that she must have been faintly amused at this a year ago in therapy.

Sarah is still standing next to the bench and holding the heart-shaped stone in her palm, offering it to me. I think of the candle and of where we are standing and all the other things that happened these past three years the significance and import of which I am no longer unaware. It's these little things that still torment me.

'You have to move on from that,' Sarah says, breaking into my thoughts, and I wonder if she can read my mind as for a moment I am confused whether her words came from my memory of that time, or she is saying them now.

I say, 'What it represents for me is your love for him, and his for you,' digging my hands into my pockets. 'It makes me think of deceit and betrayal, and it hurts to see them lying all around you, at home and in your consulting rooms. What we have to do is find our own rituals, our own symbols, things that are unique to us.'

She tosses the stone away and walks on, ahead of me, back towards our cars.

'Are you expecting it to be one hundred percent gone, ever? Like it never happened,' I say, talking to the back of her head and trying to keep up. 'Because I think that's asking too much. I can't avoid the triggers I react to, the things that remind me of what took place. I just have to cope with the way I feel about it, and I think I am getting better at that every day.'

'But you have to let it go. I can't stand this.'

'You are absolutely right, Sarah, but the reminders of what happened are all around us, and we have to deal with these moments gently. I am sure you have them too, even though you seem to say you have completely cut yourself off from thoughts of him. I still don't quite understand what that means or how you think you do it. Having said this, I think we are barking up the wrong tree because we will both feel that things have moved on when we feel safer with each other, when we can entrust our hearts to each other.' I am struggling to keep pace with her and I am not sure whether my words are carrying to her. 'So it's not just what you think is happening in my mind, that I am not letting go of things. Take the other day, for instance, when I wanted to use your car to go somewhere, and you said I couldn't because your journal and other personal stuff are in your car. You felt you could not trust me and that I might read your journal you keep there. And who knows, you . . .'

'You have read my journal.'

' . . . could be right, so I am not judging your reaction, but it struck me because I then wondered whether there is information in your journal that you don't want me to see, not just for privacy reasons but because it's incriminatory. This was never an issue before.' Her journals lay around the house, and it never occurred to me to take a look, even after I returned from the Middle East and I was certain she was having an affair. Now I am not so sure I would be so well behaved. So maybe the boundaries we had implicitly believed in have been moved, I just don't know. 'All I am trying to say is that you also have to let go of what happened, and perhaps allow for some of the things that occur between us now as frustrating as they are at times. We have to see them in a positive light as indicators of how much we trust each other and take some risks.'

'I am glad you can hear that you are talking to yourself,' she says. She has listened intently, or so I thought, but she says this rather than something about what I am saying. Something, anything, I can build on so that we can actually get somewhere with the topic.

'I'm trying to say something positive, Sarah. That I want to return to that level of trust, and it has to start somewhere. At the same time, I know we need to be more patient and that things will not be resolved overnight.'

'You need to trust yourself,' she says.

I am walking behind her on a track wide enough for two, but this is how she seems to want it. I cannot see her face and have to strain to hear her responses. The other day, when I was looking for some library books we could not find, I wanted to look in her bedside cabinet. But she would not let me. That was just after I crept up behind her to give her a cuddle and she freaked out because she was texting someone on her cellphone and accused me of trying to read the messages over her shoulder.

'It's a horrible way to live for both of us. I want to change that—the little things, trust with a small 't'. Trust with a big 'T', that will take longer. But we have to start somewhere.'

But she keeps throwing it back at me. 'You will have to stop behaving like that first.'

'This is ridiculous, Sarah.' I am struggling to keep my temper in check; can't she just acknowledge some of the reality? 'Back then, I had every reason to look. You were denying an affair that I knew had happened and then lying about things that I already knew about. What did you expect me to do, just let it go? I had to show you proof that I knew, to get you to admit the affair and to open up. And you have done the same thing, looking into my stuff, but in your case, dare I say, without good reason.'

We lapse into silence and soon reach our cars. 'Let's pick this up later,' I say.

Soon as the boys are asleep this evening, I find her smoking a cigarette in the courtyard, and say, 'Can we finish that conversation we started?'

'What conversation?' she says.

'We were talking about the things that trigger me.'

She does not seem keen at all, but I am determined. So without waiting for permission, I say, 'At the risk of irritating you, let me say this, so that you know where I am at, because I need you to know what it's like for me. I think I have come a long way in accepting what happened and trying to understand why. So I want to focus on how we are today.' As for forgiveness, well, I thought that was there from the start, but I've come to realise that it takes longer and seems to come in waves. But only when she stops loving him. 'What I was saying earlier is about the hurt and the anger, the feelings of insecurity and the sense of betrayal that are triggered from time to time. They are perhaps more muted but have not gone away, especially as it seems you still have contact with him that you keep hidden from me.'

She looks ashen-faced, and I have the sense that I should just walk away as I am treading on her sacred ground. I am also not relishing this discussion, but I am feeling on edge and really need to off-load stuff I have not yet said to her. I have been silent with my feelings for too long. I have not raised the topic since she held that knife to her throat and threatened to use it if I mentioned another word about her affair. I cannot tolerate her evasion-lies-shutdown; not with what I have discovered and not with him living next door. I need her to see that I cannot take it any more, that the last few weeks have been too much for me with all that's been going on, and that I need her help. Is it too much to ask her for support and understanding?

She offers no response; just lights another cigarette. So I say, 'But it is not like that. It is all around us. He lives over the road, we both see him frequently, and that is a trigger for me. I am sure the synapses are firing like crazy in my head, arousing the deepest, ugliest stuff even if I don't consciously register it or dwell on it. And I always find you on your cellphone when I come out of the boys' bedrooms after putting them to sleep. This was when you always texted or phoned him, and that's such a huge trigger for me; it was an accomplice to your deceit, and it's like showing a red flag to a bull.'

I pause, needing a response from her, but then something occurs to me.

'Actually, I never realised before now just how pervasive this stuff is at an unconscious or instinctive level, and how it constantly undermines how we are trying to move forward in the spirit of reconciliation. I am getting a real appreciation for how this works now. Just last Friday evening, for instance, something happened as I turned into the driveway that I am sure has played itself out in the vibe between us that evening. These triggers, like when I see Calix, I always try to hide from you, but I can see now that this is not possible as something inside me is different, even if just for a while.'

'What happened now?' Her tone is not inquisitive and her body language is closed off to hearing my response, like she is finding this tiresome.

'I don't really want to talk about it, but that would be silly as it is actually between us right now. Do you want some tea?' I say, and without waiting for a response, I go into the kitchen, and she follows me there. I have been feeling vulnerable and suspicious this week, still reeling from the culmination of the tension since I moved back into our house, and have been replaying the time of their affair in my mind. I realise I am breaking the promise I made with myself to never again raise anything about him with her; not since she used the knife.

'What happened?' she says again, angry now and more demanding.

'Okay. So . . . as I was turning into the driveway, he was walking past our house. I didn't wave a greeting to him as I often do, but then as we passed him in the rear-view mirror, I saw him doing this extravagant windmill wave, as if mocking, taunting me, and then extending his arms to the sky and looking down at our house. I'm sure I didn't imagine it. Then he turned towards the car and stuck two fingers above his head, like the horns of a devil or a goat. The dogs started growling at him from the back of the car, which they never do; they must really hate him, or perhaps they picked up my feelings, I don't know. Their barking woke Jack up, which infuriated him, and he started screaming. Then Joshua said, "Why didn't you say 'hello' to Calix?" When I did not respond, Jeremiah said, "He is not Daddy's friend, he is Mommy's friend." It just took the whole thing with him to another level of respect for me, and whether he will let us move on with our lives.'

'He is not like that,' she says as she steps outside and lights another cigarette. I follow her into the courtyard with our tea. 'He would not be malicious or disrespectful. You think those things because that's what you are.'

My ego recoils at the tacit comparison. 'Of course not, he is perfect. It is only me who behaves like that in your mind.' Here is the sarcasm that Matthew was speaking about.

Sarah says nothing; she just looks at the ground, and I think—'How much more malicious and disrespectful could he be of me than to come into my house and sleep with my wife and gloat at me and still want her even though I know? He . . .' Oh fuck, we are back in this space, back on this topic, and all the repressed thoughts I have stifled jostle for airtime. I have opened Pandora's Box, and the words flow with a sickly aftertaste from my constricted throat.

'Not only that, but he moves in next door,' I say, following her around the courtyard, hemming her in. 'That is a very calculated move. It's so disturbing for me as he surely knew that this meant we would cross paths often and greet each other while walking on the mountain, and we would drive past him together in our car. It not only dramatically increased the risk you both were taking but was also cruel and menacing. Or maybe it just made things easier for you; actually I've never thought of it that way. And . . . and,' I raise my index finger and shake my hand at her, to show her that there is much more to say, 'he wanted to meet with me and get to know me while you were sleeping with him, isn't that sinister? Don't you wonder about it? And he has apparently followed you around and, if I am to believe you, it is him who won't leave you alone. He's trying to get you back, isn't he?' I turn away, but I am not yet done and reel around to face her again and say, 'So no matter what you say, I really don't think this is over yet. You are still in love with each other.'

I light a cigarette and pretend to show a sudden interest in the condition of our fledgling vegetable garden. She comes up behind me and puts her arms around me. 'I am sorry for your troubles,' she says. And in this moment I register that there is nothing she can say or do that will make it any easier for me to climb this mountain.

I feel tense as a tightrope, but that is how I have constantly felt for a few weeks now. I want to walk away from this moment and come back inside in a better space. I say. 'Give me a few minutes, I am going to backwash and clean the pool.'

I know what is fuelling this conversation for me. Walking up the mountain yesterday evening, I had my first full conversation with Calix, just the two of us, just short of the summit. In fact, it was hardly a conversation; innocuous words were given the task of holding the line between us and they performed admirably for almost half-an-hour. He was wearing, as always, the red sweater, the twin of which she openly wears but denies it was connected to him, and my irritation flared at her lies. So this time I placed myself deliberately on his path to the top in such a way that he would have to make an effort to avoid me.

'Hello, Calix,' I said, looking at the top of his bowed head as he ascended the steep path towards me. He looked up, and I got the sense that he knew I was there.

'Hello,' he said, stopping short of me, lifting a foot to a boulder and resting an elbow on his knee. I didn't really know what my plan was (sorry Jim, you try so hard to convince me I need one), or what I was trying to get out of a conversation with him. I thought that a neutral place to start was to ask him about his vintage car, feigning fascination in its origin and hoping to stoke a passion of his while we mentally manoeuvred ourselves for what might happen. I was not feeling in the least anxious, and the dogs picked this up and acknowledged him and he fussed over them while he talked, perhaps for something to do. It irritated me intensely when he used affectionate diminutives of their names, and the familiarity this suggested cut deep. Then we moved on to talking about nature and the mountain and eco-friendly construction.

His eyes were cold blue, etched and earnest, but his lips seemed to sneer at me. I could feel his mind was working overtime; mine was paralysed—it had stuff to say but while pain and accusation jostle in the queue my tongue and lips have no words to form. 'I am amazed that so few people seem to take the opportunity to walk up here. It's just so accessible and is really rewarding for so little effort,' he said. 'I've been doing it for years.'

Was he taunting me about how long he has been here? 'Do you always go to the top?' I said.

'Always. I like to come up here at full moon. I feel like this is my mountain.' I stopped myself just in time from saying that I felt the same way, and that, by the way, that was my house down there and that was my wife. Then I remembered that I had told Sarah that he sometimes seemed to follow me up 'my fucking mountain', and I wondered if she had told him this, and he was trying to stake his own claim to it.

Come on, Clive, dialogue is your precision tool, so what on earth should one say in a moment like this? I said I don't want to hold him up and gave him the opportunity to continue climbing, but he opted to stay and talk. We spoke for about half an hour, and it would have been fairly disappointing for an interested observer hoping for fireworks. I watched him intently while he spoke, but he seldom looked at me, and I could not help but wonder what he was really thinking and feeling. Was he relishing this, or was it awkward for him?

I remained seated on a rock, and he remained standing. I could not help but look at him and wonder what she saw in him; what did it for her? But I was appraising him as a man, not as a woman would. And I did not get very far, as trying to imagine the deep love they shared soon took me to images of her touching his cheek, holding his hand, kissing his lips, probing his mouth, and taking him inside her. And I felt my body stiffen and shudder, trying to wrench itself free from the overwhelming, uncontrollable surges of stomach-turning images. I wanted to vomit. I felt eviscerated, no, castrated, like I had taken a knife to my scrotum while his manhood shone proudly like a totem pole. Is dialogue appropriate to these circumstances? Or should we settle this once and for all by whipping out and measuring up our manhood? Confronting him, going 'head-to-head' with him, so to speak, will just confirm I am the jerk she says I am. If I insist they never see each other again, then he might refuse to abide by this or agree but I will never know and will always be trying to find out. It was a Catch-22—they would act as they wished and there was nothing I could do about it. I decided the best option was to give away as little as possible.

All this juxtaposed the conversation we pretended to have. We talked about the houses we could see below us, including the ones in which we were living, and I guided the conversation to where he was staying. After he said that he had been living there for 'about three or four years now', which would make it from 2007 or early 2008, I barely heard the other insignificant things he said until he mentioned that he had no intention of moving soon. It was now much later than I had expected to return home. It felt like a good time to go, and I took my leave saying, 'I think I will be going now before I cool down too much.'

I don't do a good job with the swimming pool, and when I get back, I am not really in a better space. After talking with Calix I realized I could do nothing about the situation; my only recourse was to rebuild the loving trust with Sarah with acts and words. We take our tea, reheated in the microwave, and sit on the paving in the courtyard. I want to clear the space between us but don't know how to do it except to say something to her. We always seem to leave our conversations hanging, incomplete, somehow in a worse state than before we started, creating a distance between us when they should bring us closer.

'I have said this much, so let me finish it as I don't really want to say this stuff again. What happened stays with us because he does. He is present, in spirit, in our home, not just because he was often here, and you experienced him here, but because you won't let him go. The intimate and erotic gifts and keepsakes you hold on to, keep him here, and so do the love poems and whatever else you refuse to delete from your email or throw away or return to him.'

'Just get over it,' Sarah says.

'And I even had to ask you to stop typing "XXX" for kisses on your text messages to me. It's infantile but it's my desperation showing, trying to show you that there are so many things that hurt. That it's all over the place. It's as though nothing we had built up is ours and ours alone. Even the act of finding you those stone hearts you so love is now contaminated because that is what he did.' I hate what I am saying; I sound so . . . stupid.

'They mean nothing to me now.' She wanders inside the kitchen and I follow her.

'Sara-lea,' I say, poking my finger at her and hoping that the unusual usage of her preferred name will draw her attention to what I am saying, 'just because you say you have neutralised his energy with your magic muti does not mean it's okay for me. How do you think I feel about these things? I'm trying to be open-minded about this, but do you have to wear the fucking underwear he gave you? Do you have any idea how much it hurts?' Anger feels better than stupid.

'I can understand that . . .'

'No, you don't. You have no idea! If you did, you would, at least, do the right thing for me and for us. Just honour our relationship, Sarah. Can't you tuck those things away, just until we're over the worst of it?' I find that I have shuffled over to where the steak knives lie inviting you to unsheathe them, and behind my back I run my fingers across the wood grain of their housing.

Sarah stands rigid and controlled, batting everything back at me. She says, 'Those are your needs. It's just your ego.'

Yes, my ego is now fully engaged. I need her to acknowledge my feelings and experience of this as real. 'It's because you integrated him into every aspect of your life that there is just no escaping him. This week in therapy Vincenzo thought he should warn me that I may bump into Calix there as he is best friends with his neighbour who lives on the same property. And guess what? On my way out I walked slap-bang into Calix. Therapy should be a safe haven, just like our home and the street we live in. He's fucking everywhere, Sarah! And it took me a while to realise that you wouldn't let me take the boys to ride their bikes on the street because you feared we might bump into him, and I might learn something from what they say.'

Expressing all my bottled-up feelings to her now makes it seem all too much for me; the list of peeved allegations is endless, and I realise that I actually want her to say these things, to admit just how difficult this is for me, to tell me that it is unfair that I have to deal with these circumstances. I want to hear it from her. I want the impossible. I am asking her to save me from the pain, which rears up everywhere I look, but she can't; she would have to roll back the wheel of time, undo everything. But even with her magic powers, she can't do that.

Sarah blocks her ears and says, 'You can't do this to me! You are not allowed to say these things. I'm not listening anymore.'

I want to scream. Fighting hard to hold onto the belief that I have the right to be heard and to be responded to with courtesy, I talk right over her. 'In any event, the boys are conscious of your relationship with him too because you spent time together almost as a family. The other day, when I was with the boys and for some reason Calix was in the conversation, I think we had just driven past him again, little Jack said, "Is he bigger than you, Daddy?" I said, "I don't know. What do you think?" Then he said, "Is he older than you, Daddy?" So I said, "I don't know, he is not my friend." Then after a long silence, Joshua said, "Don't worry, he is just a friend of Mommy's. You will have to ask her," as if he was trying to make it all right for everyone, or for himself. He has said this a few times now, and I am beginning to worry that he is making something of this situation even if he does not yet have the adult words for it, like he can feel there is something wrong with the whole setup. I just don't really know what to do in these situations, whether there is a more appropriate way to deal with it.'

I am standing close to the kitchen door with another cigarette. Sarah says nothing; she has removed her fingers from her ears and just keeps herself busy as if she does not want to show that she is giving her full attention to the conversation. Did she hear any of that? I measure the distance between her and the steak knives threaded into their wooden block, but I suspect she can telepathically call on them to make the journey to her hand.

After a long pause, without turning to face me, she says, 'Is that all?'

'No, but it's enough, isn't it?' I say. I sense that she is about to excuse herself from the conversation. Before now, if I tried to raise something, she would tell me I am abusing her and that I must take all my shit to therapy as she does not want to hear it. I can see how I swing between accusation and pleading with her. I feel prone to losing it in my current state and know that I should probably stop now as this is just the same old story, but I can't. If just for my own sake, I need this summary of how things stand.

'Sarah, the point is that none of this is within my control, and what I am saying to you is not new. I am sure I have said it all before, one way or another. But it really is easier to deal with now and if it affects me for a moment here and there, I really can't help that. I try not to make it an issue for us, but I have to accept that it impacts me in some way that may be tangible for you, and you don't like that. You get irritated with me; you just want it gone. What I'm trying to emphasise is that because it is all around us, your expectation that it should be dealt with by now is unrealistic. We need to be more patient. All I'm asking of you is to do what you can to put me at ease and get him out of your heart, but you seem to be doing the opposite.'

I look at her, but she is staring at her hands, fingers tapping the countertop. It feels like she has removed herself from the discussion. I say, 'In particular, the thing that lingers between us, that gets in the way of us both feeling that we are in a relationship in which our hearts are safe with each other and we can trust, really trust and believe, is the sense of honesty and respect connecting us. That is what is holding us back, not the bad thoughts and memories of the past; in fact, those are to be expected and are natural and healthy.' I realise I have come full circle in the conversation, which seems more and more like a monologue now, that we had this afternoon when walking together. Right back to the respect and honesty that breeds trust. 'So I am not talking about the deceit and betrayal that took place during the last three years. What I am talking about is the honesty and openness since then and the concern and compassion we show for each other now.'

'There's nothing going on. We have no contact whatsoever,' she says.

I am convinced this is not true, and for a moment, I am stuck, flabbergasted by her barefaced lie when she knows, at the very least, that I can get access to her telephone records. How can she do this, this blatant falsity? My frustration results in an ultimatum. 'Have you come across anybody, husband or wife, who has stayed in their marriage after an affair of this magnitude? Because I haven't.'

I wait for her to respond. It squeezes out a reticent 'No.'

'And you are cagey and secretive about your contact with him, which means that whatever's going on there, you are keeping outside of our relationship. Some people define that as having an affair. So if you want to still see him or have some sort of contact with him, I need you to be open about it, and the least he can do is come and speak to me and make things okay with me. Let me see who he really is.'

'He won't do that. He doesn't like confrontation.'

'Well, I don't like him sleeping with my wife, so he should have thought about that.' Perhaps I should be saying this to Calix?

'He's not responsible. It happened because you were not there for me.'

The flaming arrows of blame find their target. 'How can he not be responsible?'

'You won't get anything out of him.'

'You are so protective of him,' I say. 'You defend him all the time.'

'There is nothing else to tell you. I have told you the truth,' she says.

'That's not true! There is a lot you haven't told me, but that is not the point right now, and I don't want to know any more.' Because I won't believe a word she says. 'The issue is that what you have told me includes so many lies, that's what I'm talking about. And you're still doing it.'

'Like what?' she says.

'Let's not go back there.'

'Tell me,' she says in that way that will not accept 'no' for an answer.

Fuck this. We have come this far in the conversation, it does not really matter whether I say it or not, I tell myself. But I know it is a test, to find out what I know, especially which lies I have not picked up. My mind silently rattles off the list.

I say aloud, "There are so many examples, Sarah. You know what they are. I just don't know why you do it?' She stares at me, defiant.

I take a deep breath. 'Let's leave the past in the past, Sarah. What I need today is your honesty about things to do with Calix. That's the only point I'm trying to make. No more "red sweater" lies. Please, just be transparent about what is going on now.'

'If I was inconsistent or vague about certain things, it was because of the shame I felt,' she says, leaning forward and practically spitting it at me. 'That's why I'm reading about guilt and shame, don't you get it?'

I did not know that, and I want to steer the conversation away from here. We should be talking about our relationship today, something we can have an influence over. After all, she said that this is what she deals with in therapy.

'Sarah, I understand that now.' In fact, I think I knew it from the start, that it was just too difficult for her to even tell herself the truth, never mind me. That's why I tried to give her time. 'But some time has elapsed, so don't you think that if you spoke about it now, just said the honest words to me, this would reduce the shame that clings to you? And if you feel so much shame, then why wear the twin red sweater and his other gifts, especially the lingerie? That's what makes no sense.'

I wonder if she is even listening. Not expecting her to answer, I say, 'Anyway, our experience of this thing that happened leaves each of us in a very different place. One of the things I know is that you are capable of keeping a parallel relationship secret for so long under these incredible conditions, right next door and in our house. That's quite a skill. And I have to admit that it is difficult to let go of this, to believe that the person you were then, able to do that, is now faithful and honest and holds no secrets. As I have always said, you had the opportunity to alleviate my distrust right at the beginning by being truthful when we first spoke about it.'

I know I am insulting her character, but my frustration has brought about an escalation. What started, I thought, as a reasonable sharing of how I'm feeling has become a venting of all my hurt and frustration. She flings her arms into the air and sighs and mumbles something under her breath. Then she says, 'What I have to live with now is someone who is insecure.'

'Sarah, that's why I'm astounded that you still allow any room for doubt about your total honesty.' The words spit from between my clenched teeth; can't she get it? 'That was the critical moment for us, but the opportunity has been lost to take our relationship to a higher place, where I could look you in the eyes and see your soul, and you could touch mine. I would have sat with you and listened, no matter what you said. I would have held you in my arms and cried with you.'

But just then, little Jack wakes up crying out for us as if he is moved to tears by the desolate picture fashioned by these words and what it might mean for his future. Two at a time, Sarah takes the stairs that split the levels and clean lines of our house. To her departing back, I say, 'I would have picked you up and carried you across the bridge if it seemed too far. Together, on the other side, I would truly know you, and you would truly know me. Our souls would have touched.' But I doubt she hears much of this. I have little doubt in my mind that she will spend the night in Jack's bedroom. I don't want to be near her anyway, and more frustrated than I was to start with, I make coffee and wander into my study.

7

Much of your pain is the bitter potion
by which the physician within you heals
your sick self.

(Kahlil Gibran)

Sunday, 12 September 2010

It's lunchtime. Sarah has just arrived home. I barely heard her 'hello', and she has not glanced my way yet, perhaps not surprising after last night's debacle. She said she was going to the gym, but I know she would never spend four hours there. To ask where she has been would appear to her to be coming from my fragile ego which doubts her faithfulness, which I guess it does, and invite her scorn. That is the absurd reality of our situation. With Vincenzo's advice ringing in my ears, it occurs to me that what I need most right now is some personal space as I have looked after the boys all morning. When I say to her, 'I would like to go out after lunch to write and get some exercise, is that okay?' I can sense her hostility before the words, 'You are always out,' even reach my ears. But I have been anticipating it and am already boiling over with tension.

'Sarah, I've been with you or the boys almost the whole weekend.' We have had this conversation so often, I might as well just depress the playback button.

Still turned away from me, she repeats her mantra she stores for these moments. I am tempted to mouth it as she speaks, but she would hit the roof. 'Do whatever you want, that's what you always do.'

Then, because she thinks I always want to get away from her, I say, 'Actually, I like to spend enjoyable time with you and be with the boys. But sometimes I also want to write, get some exercise, run some errands, or even chat with a friend over a cup of coffee once in a while.'

'You always go out,' she says again, carrying the chicken pie and walking away from me towards the lounge. I know I should stop right here and just leave it alone. I have repeatedly told myself this, but her response infuriates me.

'Please don't walk away from me while we are talking,' I say.

'These plates are hot,' she says.

'Then put them down on the counter, you've accidentally burnt yourself so often lately.' I reach out to her. 'Here, let me take them.'

She somehow holds on to the plates while pointing her finger at me. 'Don't you dare speak to me like that! It's disrespectful. Say "please".' I start to explain that in emergency situations, like blistered fingers, there is no need for niceties, but she says, 'You just want to blame me.'

'Sarah . . . ,' I say, wondering how she made the leap to blame.

'It's Sara-lea!'

'Okay, Sara-lea. Let's take blame out of the equation for a moment. Let's say that nobody is to blame for the affair, if that's what you're referring to, or that we are both equally to blame for the fact that an affair took place. We could even say, for sake of argument, that it is acceptable to have an affair, that we have freedom to express our love connection with others. Jesus, Sarah, put down the plates, I can almost smell your fingers burning.'

I am still thinking of all the things that seem to keep the affair alive with constant reminders of what happened, mainly brought on by the fact that she invited him right into our lives. I vented much of that the other night, yet it seems that outburst opened the floodgates, and I am angry with myself for not letting this out earlier, weeks ago or before I had returned home, as it now feels less valid to do so. I feel that I have undermined myself, and this just compounds my frustration standing here in front of her. We should be talking this through with compassion, seeking to understand; we should be holding each other. Why are we not doing this? Am I still too enraged and hurt? Is it because she is just so adept at expertly deflecting my attempts to talk that I feel the need to raise these points in angry desperation? She has been so defensive, closed off to me, and secretive. Protective of him and blaming me and telling me I must change.

The suppressed anger and deep hurt boils over, and months of unresolved issues and all the resentment that has swirled unabated around my mind for months queues up and jostles for pole position in the front of my mind like a bubble-gum dispenser, hoping to be the lucky one to fall through the slot and be ejected from my mouth to be devoured by her ears, fearing that if they do not find voice now, they will forever be abandoned and left to rot in my head. I am not sure this will get us anywhere; I am at risk of repeating the conversation of the other night and getting worked up. So the intended conversation happens only in my head, for fear that it will be rejected by her.

'Please Sarah, there's stuff I just need to say to you,' I say in my imaginary conversation with her. 'Did you even think about respect for me, for our marriage? Did you, or he, ever wonder aloud about what you were doing to me? Even if I never found out—you know, it's like people who say you are only guilty of something if you get caught.'

I imagine Sarah would interrupt me and say, 'You abandoned me!' as this is how she justifies it and her recollection of the facts seem to bear no resemblance to my reality.

We stand there, she suspended midway out of the open-plan kitchen, me centre-stage in the kitchen as if I want to be close to all the exits and keep all my options open. Aware that I have folded my arms, and wanting to deny her the opportunity to say that I have adopted an aggressive stance, I quickly unfold them but don't quite know what to do with them. I cannot smoke in the kitchen. But I am not done with my internal dialogue, and I try a different tack.

'What really amazes me is how you can admire and respect someone who does this, who actually makes a habit of sleeping with the wives of close friends and business partners, or, in this case, a neighbour? Is he the sort of person who doesn't care less if he is breaking up a marriage and ruining the lives of three children? Did he even consider this?'

Sarah's voice in my head says, 'He's a wonderful man; you're not!' And I realise with a start that I am now attacking him or running her down by trying to undermine him. I'm trying to talk about respect, aren't I? Doing things that honour our relationship. How do I do that?

Clunk—another topic drops into a slot and screams its silent pain: 'How did you make it okay in your mind to take him into our bedroom and make love with him in our bed, even though you insist on denying that you did? No matter what you felt about me at the time, how could you feel so . . . completely nothing for me. Even if I never found out . . . What have I become to you . . . ?'

Sarah, probably wondering where I have gone to in my head, cuts into my made-up conversation and says, 'What I did to you was terrible. It is probably the most terrible thing I could do.'

Flummoxed, I suddenly don't quite know how to continue. I wish the ulcerated issues would behave and present themselves in a more orderly fashion in my mind, alphabetically perhaps. I could not have made it easier for them; I have a neat sentence for each of them with simple words which should not constrict my gullet. I cannot remember what the point of this conversation is. Oh yes, I want to talk about now, not then; it is actually my bitterness at how she has responded to my needs since I found out. It has been in my head for ages, but it now occurs to me that this is the wrong time to address it. It's just that we never do, and now I don't know how to back out of it. She turns away from me; she is about to make her getaway.

I say aloud to her, 'What I'm actually trying to get at is how I think you have responded to me since I found out, that you don't seem to go out of your way to put me at ease. You continue to lie to me and refuse to be open about what happened.'

The dispenser holding the topics malfunctions, releasing too many issues at once through the slit now hopelessly stretched and deformed, and they tumble into a heap at the back of my throat and scratch and kick and claw their way out, the pain referred from my heart raking bloody tracks on my tongue which feels thick and cumbersome. Sounding ridiculously pitiful to myself, I say, 'There are just so many examples of you not being sensitive to how I might feel.'

'These things don't occur to me.'

'Well they should,' I say, with a heavy dose of disgust. 'So I am waiting for you to show me, give me a sign, that you really want us.'

This is a debacle; I have thrown together so many issues that sit in my mind like keywords or sub-headings under the title 'Infidelity'—respect, honesty, secrecy, reconciliatory behaviour, putting me at ease. I cannot even recall what I have said to her and what I said to myself.

'We can't rebuild, Sarah, unless we put some effort in, to talk and be together.' I am shouting now, sounding demented. 'Look at what happened last night when we went out, how you tore me down. Actually, I don't find your behaviour reconciling at all, so much so that it's as if I am the one who had the affair.'

'Those are your feelings,' she says, as if she has had no role in how betrayed I feel. But I also realise it is a tactic I should employ with abandon when she unleashes her demeaning missiles at me.

She follows it up with, 'You are insecure.' No kidding? Is she surprised that I am? She manages to convey this with bitter accusation in her voice, and the demeaning indictment sticks like industrial-strength Bostick, and I have to keep going to get myself unglued. I have suppressed these thoughts and feelings for weeks, having given up after that initial flurry when I had tried to persuade her to talk about things. Why have I gone back to this place with her? What has happened to take me there? I am afraid that she will adopt her normal response and end the conversation by sticking her fingers in her ears or walking out or by telling me I am not allowed to say these things.

'Sarah . . .'

'It's all your ego, Clive. You are not balanced; you need a homeopathic remedy.' With a single sweeping statement she seems to nullify what I have said, to invalidate what I am feeling. It works as intended, and I am incensed yet doubt myself—Maybe it's not the way I see it? Would a 'real' man be able to accept this? To get out of this situation, I decide I need a parting shot, one that is really ugly. 'I'm actually not that concerned about the affair, Sarah. I mean, of course it's an issue, but what distresses me the most is that it seems nothing has changed. The way you speak to me today is the same as it always was. Harsh.' Is that the worst I can do?

'I say what I feel,' she says.

'But there is so much animosity in your words, and very little indication that you understand that I am struggling to deal with this situation, that you are willing to give me some leeway. That's why I feel the need to tell you these things.' Am I pleading for mercy with the woman that tortures me? Asking her to make it right, take it away?

'What the hell does that mean?' she says, lurching at me, her anger flaring. The boys are pretending to occupy themselves, but are listening to every word. I must pull back now, but I can't.

'That's exactly what I'm talking about. Those are strong words, just short of a full-frontal attack.' My voice sounds desperate, high-pitched. We glare at each other. I feel stupid, humiliated, vulnerable, and angry with myself for exposing my feelings to her.

'I'm going now,' I say.

'This is what you always do, create a problem and then leave. So what time will you be back?'

'I don't know exactly, around mid-afternoon, does it matter?' I know I am being vague but right now committing to being back soon is too much for me.

'Catherine says you need to give me a time.'

Fuck Catherine. 'Sarah, it's not useful . . .'

'Give me a time. I need the structure, the containment.' Her anxiety is palpable.

I am fighting in my corner to change things, to have her see that I can't go on like this in the vise-grip of her obsessive controlling behaviour. Why can't I just tell her to 'fuck off'? I don't even have to say it with aggression or anger, if that's what I am worried about. Just tell her we have discussed this topic a thousand times, and I will no longer engage with her on it; it is no longer a subject for discussion.

Instead I say, 'Sarah, this issue with time and structure has bothered you for a long time. We both know that it doesn't work, unless we have to get somewhere and time is important and . . .'

'It's important to me,' she screams.

' . . . you need to know.' My hands are open, palms up, flapping up and down in front of me like I am fanning her to cool her down.

'Sarah, I'm not going to do it.' It's just a setup. 'If I'm five minutes late, you go ballistic.'

We are now in the lounge and in front of the boys, and they react as they have of late to our public spats. With Jack leading the way, they physically push us apart and produce unbearable high-pitched screams, their version of 'white-noise', and shout, 'Stop, stop it.'

'You're so inconsiderate!' she says. I metaphorically duck to avoid the label which fizzles out above my head like a tracer bullet. I can feel my resolve weakening, the way it always does, and probably always will. I lose heart, and think, again, of giving up, of leaving her for good.

Fending off little Jack, who is pounding at my thighs in rage, and lowering my voice but not the venom in the words, I say, 'I will see you later.' I kiss the boys goodbye and have to fight my way out of the front door as they tear at my jeans and block my path and plead with me to stay. I feel like a leopard caught in a gin-trap, prepared to chew off my own paw to escape. Their screams ringing in my ears, I drive down to the village and phone Jim and ask him to meet me for a beer. He wastes no time getting there.

8

He who cannot forgive breaks the bridge
over which he himself must pass.

(George Herbert)

Wednesday, 15 September 2010

Sarah arrived home at about eleven o'clock this evening, and found
me sitting in the kitchen courtyard drinking coffee and smoking. She
paced around and had a cigarette and I found myself waiting for her
to say something significant, as she seemed to be working towards
something, but then she said she was going to get ready for bed.

I climbed into bed while she washed her face and now I am lying
under the duvet, propped up against the continental pillows, reading a
novel, hoping its content can lull me to sleep. But my pores ooze the
pain of what I observed this evening. Harry and Sally have jumped onto
the bed; I gave in and nodded to them after they stood alongside it with
their chins on the mattress, their doleful eyes pleading with me and
emitting occasional 'meeps' while Sarah competed her ablutions in the
bathroom. The cats sit on the headboard behind me, waiting for Sarah.

Sarah sits down tall and straight and still fully clothed on the bottom
edge of the bed, and says, 'There are four things I want to discuss with
you. I find them totally unacceptable.' Here we go again, I think, but it
is okay because talking, any talking, is good, isn't it? 'We cannot let your
parents babysit the boys on Saturday nights. I'm not having it.'

I put the book down on the bedside table and give her my full attention. Last Saturday was our second attempt at a night out together, and the boys stayed with their grandparents as arranged. It was tragic how it turned out.

'Sarah, they are happy to do it, they want to do it. And it's such important time for us. So let's give it a chance and if it becomes a problem we will try something else.'

Then we go around in circles, as I try every justification I could think of.

'You're not hearing me,' she says, stretching her neck towards me and raising her voice with exaggerated pronunciation of each word that follows causing the dogs to lift their heads, disturbed by the aggression in her voice. 'The boys cannot sleep over there until they are older.'

'Sarah, is this about us spending time together on Saturday nights?'

After the affair, I had asked her for two things, practical things I thought we could do that would begin to help rebuild our relationship. The first request I had was to find a couple of unrushed hours during the week for us to meet, to have lunch, go for a walk on the mountain, sit on the beach, it didn't really matter what we did as long as it was time alone together. But Sarah seemed very resistant to it and so far it proved impossible to coerce her, for that is what it felt like, to build it into her week. I had some compassion for this, as almost any conversation between us was argumentative and virtually any topic quickly became contentious, heavy and simply locked-in our animosity.

The second request was to spend one evening a week together, a night liberated of children waking up and demanding our presence in their beds, so that we could actually wake up in the same bed together. It did not feel like too much ask, yet it meant that the boys needed to sleep over somewhere. But having finally accomplished it, was she now busy working against it? We had somehow managed to organize these nights together two weekends in a row now, and I should have been more observant of the forewarnings of her emotional breakdown. Last

Saturday, as we drove towards my parents' house to drop the boys for a sleepover, one of them said, 'Look, there's a car just like Calix's.' I don't think this caused the evening to turn out as it did, but it was surely a sign of things to come.

As if terrified of what might transpire during our time together, Sarah started criticizing me the minute we left my parents house, and by the time we arrived at what was meant to be an early pre-theatre dinner, there was a complete breakdown in our ability to interact. Whenever I tried to say something, not more than four or five words into a sentence, she would interrupt and tell me I can't say it like *that*, I must say it like *this*. While she ate a salad and I passive-aggressively smoked cigarettes in the open-air section of the theatre's restaurant facing the palm trees that lined the beach, we spent an hour in this manner not actually accomplishing anything, but with a lot of words, until I withdrew and sulked. This continued after the show, when we went for a drink just because it felt too depressing to go home early on our night out. I simply could not say anything without her instructing me what I can say and how to say it. I felt humiliated, but was so wrapped up in my own regression that I failed to take heed of her degeneration, of how her bizarre behaviour that evening should have alerted me to the fact that she was literally on the edge of breakdown.

Sarah picks at another two issues while I lie there on my side of the bed recalling these recent events, feeling more and more disconsolate and at war with her. She has not moved from the bottom corner of the bed, and I still slouch against the pillows diagonally opposite her. Harry has imperceptibly leopard-crawled towards me as the accusations persisted, and only now I notice his head and shoulders lie across my thighs, such is his stealth, and he watches me intently with slowly-blinking eyes and furrowed brow. Sally, closer to the bottom of the bed, rests her head on his back and looks at me.

'And the fourth issue,' she says, although we have not yet resolved the first issue and I don't really understand her point on her other concerns, 'is I will never again let you treat me the way you treated me this evening. Never again will you do that to me. I will not put up with it. It's exactly the kind of behaviour I will not accept from you.'

Sarah had gone out at six thirty this evening for the third Wednesday in a row. I thought that its recent introduction was a way to establish some independence and of getting some space to unwind from the tension that infiltrated our evenings together. In a flash, I trace the events of the evening to try locate where she is going with this.

I had arrived home just after six o'clock, late as far as she was concerned, but I was in no particular rush as recent days in her presence have been energy-sapping. She was preparing dinner for the children, and for me I assumed, but the heat and steam was emanating more from her than the stove. She was clearly in a black mood, maybe still about last Saturday evening or because I had given her little time to get ready to go out or for some other reason unknown to me. I think I have generally given up establishing the cause of her frame of mind, which I suddenly found very sad.

I was feeling shattered from lack of sleep and the perpetual emotional turbulence. We barely greeted each other, and I didn't disclose what I had inadvertently come across today nor the fact that I had just driven past Calix as he reversed out his driveway, in such great haste that I had to come to a halt to avoid colliding with him. I acknowledged him, as had become the norm, with a wave and a nod, but he looked away and seemed to fold his tall frame and huddle down behind the steering wheel of his cramped vehicle as if he wished to go unnoticed. Crossing paths with him was not unusual, but I was abruptly in the grip of irrational thoughts as I speculated whether he was rushing off to meet her; after all, this was what they had done just a few short months ago—meeting secretly at some event. Within ten minutes, she walked out the door. She had said nothing about her plans for the evening. 'Where will you be tonight?' I said, talking to her retreating back as she walked up the front steps to her car.

'I'm going to a talk and then out to drinks. I don't know what time I will be home.' And she was gone. Although she did not say, I had no doubt she was going to a monthly event at a venue the two of them used as a cover to meet in public.

Paranoia seeped through my pores as she drove down the road. I just had to speak to her, but I didn't know what to say. I knew it was unfair for her to carry the burden of my insecurity and anxiety. And little Jack was feeling ill with tummy cramps and a headache. Typically Sarah would have left me precise instructions—if he is feeling this, then give him this medicine; if he is feeling that, then give him the other medicine. And don't give him this one with that one, leave so many hours between these ones, and if that happens, take him straight to hospital. I suppose I should be more up to speed on these things, and I imagine given the chance or the imperative I would work it out for myself, but I was often left more concerned that I followed her guidelines to the letter than for the well-being of the sick child. And she always said that if anything happened, to call her; even if nothing happened, to call her. She had done none of this tonight, which is probably the way it should be, but tonight it did not suit me. I needed her to be concerned, to be close; I needed the familiarity of old patterns.

So I thought I would call her before she arrived at the venue. 'Hi love, sorry to bother you, but will you have your phone on, just in case, for Jack?' My voice was weak, and I could smell the desperation and fear. I imagined it travelling to her ear and met with derision.

'I'm not going to have my phone on. It's my night out! How dare you do this, you creep? My therapist said you would do this and that it's not okay.' Her voice was snappy, biting, and full of antagonism.

'But, Sarah, I just need to be sure I can contact you if I need to.'

'Why?'

'Little Jack is sick, and I might need to get hold of you if he gets worse. And you didn't tell me what medication he has taken in the last few hours, so I don't know . . .'

'Just leave me alone, I need my space.'

'I understand that, but, Sarah . . .'

'You can't do this to me! I don't want you phoning me. I will not have my phone with me.'

'Sarah, what if . . . ' But she had disconnected.

In an instant, I became convinced that this was a sign that something was going on, that they were meeting there tonight. I just could not believe they would run the risk of that, even though they had taken so many chances over the years. The fact that she had chosen to be incommunicado left me shaken instead of reassured. And her reaction did not help me feel at ease, to counteract the doubts and insecurities I was experiencing for the first time in our relationship, and for which I guess I held her accountable.

Sarah is glaring at me from the far corner of the bed. Why she is in such a state, I don't know. Is this her guilt about this evening? What has preceded this? She has been on about forgiveness, lately, asking me, 'Have you forgiven me?' to which I said, 'Every day we forgive each other for things. I mean, forgiveness is ongoing and should include things other than the affair, every day. So yes, I continue to let it go. However, it is less important whether I have forgiven you, but rather whether you have forgiven yourself. Then my forgiving is less critical and you will accept it. You will have to forgive yourself, stop feeling shame and guilt before you will feel strong enough for honesty.'

'I just called you to know what to do with Jack,' I say.

'You're not being authentic,' she says, her eyes burning into me, leaning aggressively towards me with her long slender index finger waving disapprovingly as if she is casting a spell, and I feel like I will explode in a puff of smoke and nothingness. Authentic? This is her new word, and it immediately irritates me as she makes it sound like nirvana, like it is the only thing that matters. I remember now that she has a handwritten note pasted on the built-in cupboard at the entrance to the en suite bathroom: 'Authenticity', and below it, a definition is scribbled, 'doing it for me, not for them.' That is exactly how this whole thing feels to me: my pain, her gain. As these thoughts flash through my mind, I feel myself sinking deeper into the pillows that prop me up, smothered by the g-force of her rage-filled energy.

I say, 'Okay, Sarah, I was feeling insecure, but the way you spoke to me on the phone was unnecessary.'

But she does not want to hear about the conversation on the phone and how she spoke to me. She wants me to speak about me and my insecurity, my smallness, my faults. 'You're lying. You're not being authentic!' she says again, more forcefully.

She's half-right. But surely she knows how insecure I feel and understands that feelings of insecurity are triggered daily for me, as I have recently told her that they would be when she goes out at night as she has just done. She only seems to 'see' her own feelings. 'Okay,' I say, relenting, 'let me say it. When you left to go out, I felt insecure because . . .'

'You can't say that. You must say how you feel.'

'But I'm trying to.' And I start again. I try to say it four times, and each time she cuts me short and tells me how I must say it. It feels like a replay of last Saturday night, when she would not let me speak as I felt, and I start to feel ill, physically ill. I think I am going to vomit, the accumulation of the evening's self-inflicted paranoia now tested by her poison tongue and brewing a concoction so vile it must be expelled. 'Please, Sarah, please stop. Why are you doing this?'

'Say it!' she says, spitting out her command, riling me.

'Please, I feel like I am going to vomit.'

'Say that . . .'

'Stop telling me what to say!' My upper body shudders and lurches upright off the pillows in a spasm to contain the bile rising in my throat.

'Just . . . ' But that is as far as she gets.

'You're callous,' I say, the sibilant hissing between clenched teeth. And the dogs are off the bed in an instant. And then I lose it. I throw off the duvet, stagger to the other side of our double-volume bedroom, where I throw on my clothes from yesterday that lie over the armchair ready for my post-midnight pacing around the courtyard. All the while I am shouting, 'You callous bitch, you fucking callous bitch.' I am aware that she has left the room, that Jack is crying, probably woken up by my tirade, and I think she is in his bedroom. I have enough sense to grab my warmest jacket and scarf and find myself at the front door, still screaming, 'You callous bitch. You're still fucking him.'

Down in the village, I wander around aimlessly with Harry and Sally, huddled against the cold wind. Eventually I find myself at the deli that seems about to close, but I order a cappuccino and opt to sit outside in familiar surroundings where there are no patrons due to the wind. I want it this way, the solitude, the cool night air, comforted by the chilly discomfort and aloneness of it. I sit there for an hour while they are cashing up and cleaning the tables around me, my mind foggy while I try and decide what to do. The awareness that our relationship seems so broken is there but almost seems beside the point and is superseded by the sheer ugliness I experienced. Not for the first time, I try to persuade myself that I need to leave this relationship. But I am aware of how angry I am with myself, for not being able to draw the line before it is well crossed and for allowing Sarah to trample over my personal boundaries, if only I could establish them. Then she phones, but I stare at the phone and cannot answer it. I just can't take any more, and it feels like the end of the road. How often I have reneged after reaching that conclusion; what is this hold she has on me? Her third call I take.

'You scared me, you bastard!' she says, 'How dare you do that to me? I am shaking.'

I feel I need to be on the offensive. 'I cannot deal with what happened this evening, Sarah. We need to separate for a while. My heart is not safe with you at all.' This is the thought that keeps circling my head without finding an exit. And how 'callous' sounds like his surname.

'And I am not safe with you!' she says. 'You frighten my being, so right now it's back to emergency measures. So I have bolted the door and I have called the police and security. Don't come home tonight, I don't feel safe around you now, and your aggression is scary. I want you out of my house and out of my life!! Jack is crying again.' And she disconnects. I wonder if she has called Calix; just next door, he would get there quicker than anybody.

I know what is going on in her mind. Countless times before she has told me that I physically abuse her and that she fears my physical aggression. And I recall that she told me the first thing she did when I said I know about the affair was to contact Calix to tell him to be careful of me and that I was likely to do something vicious. She has even told her friends that I have hurt her, which so perturbed me that I took it to therapy, wondering if it was true. But questions of my potentially violent nature have been summarily dismissed by the psychologists with a, 'Those are her issues' or a categorical, 'That is not abuse.' These incidents, I think, are embroidered in her mind, and I am construed as a violent character ready to physically batter her to get my way. I have come to think that she actually believes this, and it has troubled me so. But I understand, given her history, just how freaked out she is after I shouted at her earlier this evening. I know that her stepfather and other significant males performed all manner of abuse on her, and she has told me how their otherwise calm demeanour transformed abruptly into verbal outbursts and physical assault. Deep down, I believe that this is what she has transferred on to me, as if I am the cumulative reincarnation of all men who have caused her to fear real or imagined violence. It eviscerates me—whenever I try to stand firm she just has to hint that I am abusing her for the rug beneath my feet to upend me. The problem is that I think my reaction was abusive, no matter how she incited me. Perhaps if she had come at me I would have hurt her?

The staff at the deli can see from my demeanour that I am not all right, but they leave me alone outside until there is nothing else to pack away and take indoors and tidy up, and they have long since done the cashing up. And still, despite their long day, still to be followed by a long ride home and that some of them had no doubt worked double shift, they do not ask me to leave but invite me inside for a drink, where I stand behind a chair near them, afraid to sit down and baulking at conversation and company.

Back outside, the night is cool and gusty. I pass as much time as I can, wandering around and strolling along the darkened beach front with Harry and Sally. Then I get in the car and drive, aimlessly, and an hour or so later, I find that I have circumnavigated the peninsula which is the bedrock of our city, an isthmus once effortlessly separated from the continental mainland by the ocean and which may, in due time, again enjoy the solitude of severance. I reflect on how it encapsulates who I am, occasionally distant and unyielding but, I like to think, always there when you look for it. But I have a gnawing need to be near to Sarah and the children as the fear that she might do something terrible now is very tangible. I am suddenly edgy as I pass through an unfamiliar suburb and seem to catch every second traffic light on what seems to be the main road, probably due to the speed at which I cruise. At this hour, there is not another moving vehicle in sight. On another one of these interminable waits, while I turn my head to talk to the dogs to boost my confidence and feel that I am not alone, the passenger door opens and my heart rate doubles, though I am not sure whether it is anxiety or anticipation. Harry barks, startling my uninvited guest, and I tell him it is okay and her too. The traffic light finally stirs and gives me right of way as she climbs in, and as the song goes 'I took some comfort there'.

Afterwards, I seek out an all-night garage and lock myself in the public toilets until the desperate knocking on the locked door forces me to take one last pitiful look at myself in the cracked mirror and return to the Jeep. Then I park the SUV on the road leading to our house and sit next to the dogs on the grass verge and smoke a couple of cigarettes while I contemplate the silhouette of the surrounding mountain peaks. I guess I could knock on the front door just now and try to negotiate my way back into the house. But the thought of standing outside the front door and arguing with her, reasoning and pleading with her to let me in, persuading her that I am not violent and will not hurt her, when she holds all the cards, prevents me.

Suddenly, everything seems wrong. Panicked, I find myself at our front door, but it is bolted from the inside. Harry and Sally are instantly alert, soaking up my anxiety. Shaking the door, pounding at it, I call out Sarah's name. I cannot see through the security shutters that protect the boys' bedrooms, and call for them too into the darkness beyond. No response; how should I interpret that? I tear at the shutters, trying to pull them off their runners, cursing my fingers now running with blood. I run down to the pool garden and get access through the pool room, frantically yelling out their names while I am fighting with the tacky double locks of the security gates and take the stairs three at a time.

9

Life is like an hourglass, eventually
everything hits the bottom.

(Unknown)

Wednesday, 15 September 2010 (continued)

I yell at my cell phone, 'Doctor Webb, I found Sarah in the bath, and there's blood all over the walls . . .'

'Who?'

'Sarah . . . Sara-lea, please, Doctor Webb, this is Clive. It's Sara-lea. She's lying in a bath full of blood . . . ' I struggle to find a way to keep the cellphone to my ear while I hold Sarah, cradling her, pleading with her, shaking her..

'Slow down, Clive. Has she hurt . . .'

That must be Doctor Webb's voice, the Doctor-on-call. But it does not sound panicked enough; I am obviously not making myself clear. 'You don't understand. This is a fucking emergency. I just got home, and she's bleeding out in the bath. I've pulled her out, and I don't know if she . . . fuck . . . there's blood *everywhere*.' I know it is my voice I hear, but it sounds like somebody else's as it echoes and ricochets off the bathroom walls and causes delayed feedback, which is confusing my brain.

'Was she attacked? Are there any injuries you can see?'

'I don't know. I can't see. I mean no, she wasn't attacked. Just her wrists . . . her wrists are bleeding. She's slit her wrists, and she's covered the walls with her blood. Please, I don't . . .'

'Is she conscious?'

'What?'

'Is she . . .'

'Fuck, come on, Sarah, come on. I mean, I don't know. I think so, but she's just lying there. The bath's all red . . . Wait . . . I think I can feel a pulse. I'm not sure.'

'Clive, is she responding to you?'

'Sarah, don't do this! No, nothing, she had almost slipped under the water when I found her.'

'Okay, Clive, I need to know if she's breathing.'

'I already told you she's bleeding everywhere.'

'Is she *breathing*, Clive?'

'Oh, I don't know. How do I know that?' What a fucking waste of time and money that emergency first aid course was.

'Is her chest moving up and down?' So logical, Doctor Webb is.

'Um . . . No, I don't think so.' I really can't tell. 'Breathe, Sarah, for fuck sake . . . Jesus, she slit her throat . . . no, wait . . . It's just a superficial cut. Maybe she tried and lost her nerve?'

Doctor Webb says, 'Then put your cheek next to her nose and see if you can feel her breath. And listen for it. I'll give you ten seconds.'

I count to ten, too quickly. 'Doctor Webb? Yes, I think she is breathing. How do I stop the bleeding?'

'Is it spurting?'

'Not really, just oozing now. Wait, I'm putting you on "speaker" . . . Okay, go ahead.'

'You need to apply direct pressure to the wounds to control the bleeding. Wrap something, anything, around her wrists and don't remove it. Where are you?'

I shout, 'At home, in our house,' because Doctor Webb's voice is so faint.

'No, I mean . . .'

'Oh, in the bathroom. Our bathroom . . . Jesus . . . the boys! Where are they? Doctor, I can't see the boys.'

I'm running up the stairs to their bedrooms, screaming, 'Get the fuck out the way' at Sally who is under my feet in deep mothering concern, and I realise she has been trying to get my attention. I just about hear Doctor Webb's voice imploring me, 'Clive, stay with her. You need to attend to Sara-lea, don't leave her. You need to stop the bleeding and then get her to the emergency unit as quickly as possible.'

I take the first door to the left to Jack's room and switch on the light.

'Clive, are you there? Stay on the line . . . Clive?'

I'm already on my way back down the stairs to Sarah. 'The boys are fine. They're asleep,' I say.

'You need to wake them up.' There is a concern in her voice that I cannot interpret.

'What? Why? I don't want to. I'm going back to Sarah.'

'Just wake them up, now,' Doctor Webb says.

'Fuck it!' Twenty seconds pass.

'Clive? Are you there? What's happening?'

The cellphone back at my ear, I say, 'Doctor Webb? Come on, Jack. Jack! Wake up! I can't get them to wake up! Jesus! Doctor, I don't know what to do. They won't wake up, none of them.'

'Any signs of injury? Blunt trauma?' Doctor Webb's voice shrieks in my ear because I forget the cellphone is on 'speaker'.

'What?'

'Never mind. Do you see any pills? Pill boxes?'

'No. I mean, wait. Actually, I think there was something on the floor with Sarah, you know, in the bathroom, on the floor where . . . come on, Josh, wake up! . . . fuck . . . Sorry, I dropped the phone.'

'Can somebody assist you or are you alone?'

'I'm alone. Come on, we're wasting time.'

'Okay, Clive. Stop for a moment and listen to me. Go and get the pill box. Actually, never mind, here's what you need to do. Jack's the smallest, right? So start with him. You need to keep him moving. Start with thirty seconds each. Jack first, then the others, just keep rotating . . .'

'Jesus! I can't, please, what's wrong with them?'

'Clive, listen. Pick them up, try to get them to walk around. You have to keep them awake.'

'What's wrong with them?' I am screaming, demanding clarity.

'It's probably sleeping tablets, an overdose. You must start now. Somebody will be with you shortly.'

'What about Sarah?'

'Hang in there. Help is on its way.'

TERMINAL DESCENT

10

If you have integrity, nothing else
matters. If you don't have integrity,
nothing else matters.

(Alan Simpson)

Thursday, 16 December 2010 (continued)

That was an interminable night, Wednesday, 15 September. At the emergency unit, I gave the medical staff a tough time while they all-too-calmly, I thought, administered intravenous fluids and set about pumping the boys' stomachs. But when little Jack was hooked up to a respirator to help him breathe, I went crazy. I insisted that I was just urging them on while running between curtained-off beds, but they seemed to have a different view and the security staff physically removed me and I was sedated. As a result, I cannot remember who was force-fed which medicines and charcoal to absorb the drug, but I recall something about a dialysis machine being used to clean the blood. I was barely aware of Sarah's progress and can only assume that the paramedics who responded to the call-out to our house relayed the little information I could give them.

Next thing, the boys were taken off to a 'temporary place of safety'—I had my doubts about how appropriate that term was given what I had learnt from Sarah's experiences, and I feared for them. I was arrested, then released, on suspicion of attempted murder, I think they said, but in the turmoil and puzzlement of the time everything was vague afterwards and nothing got traction in my mind which was saturated with the terror images of that evening. Far as I can remember, I was not actually charged. From what I could make out, it seems that Sarah had spun a convincing story as the victim that night, and the calls she made to the police and security and others after I fled the house must have supported her claim that she was being terrorized by me. And as I could not account for the intervening hours between leaving the deli and phoning the doctor in panic, for reasons of embarrassment, the inkling of doubt she had seeded was enough. I could understand if, as she lay there in the clinic, she was confused about the events that took place that night, but it was more likely she knew exactly what she was doing. And when I saw or imagined skepticism in other's faces and questions, I started to question my own sanity; I wondered what had really happened that night.

Jim's advice was to go on the offensive, but I even began to suspect whether he believed me, such was my confusion. Cold and clammy, my gut nauseous, I replaced the advocate I had retained when even he suggested that I had only phoned the good doctor when I had come to my senses and in remorse for what I had done to the boys. When I got the chance for a private chat with Sarah while she convalesced in the clinic, I said, 'Sarah, I can see what's going on here and to some extent I can understand what you are trying to do, to protect yourself. But if this goes on we are both going to lose the boys, do you realize that?' But she turned away and I quickly realized that she did not want to hear it, especially anything that showed her I could see what she was up to. So I gave her the bottom line, 'Withdraw your statements about me and I will argue that you are fit to be at home and with the children.'

Sarah was hospitalised for a month or so and thereafter sought regular psychiatric care. Contrary to the advice I received, I argued that the boys needed their mother and reached a compromise arrangement that she could continue to live at home and be with them, provided this took place in the presence of two other responsible adults and, if I was present, then with me alone. My new advocate was at a loss to explain how we got away with it; something about a 'technicality' she said, which seemed to cover all eventualities from the inexplicable to the bizarre, and she said it was unheard of for the authorities to release children to the parents in such circumstances.

The boys had to endure twice-weekly interviews with a child-care worker, who reported her findings to the psychiatrist and the court but never to us, and whose accusatory eyes flicked between Sarah and me at each visit as if looking for any excuse to remove the boys from our care. I had to shield Sarah in order to safeguard myself so that the boys would not be taken into the system; once that happened, it was unlikely they would return, just like Sarah and Roxanne. Far as I know the investigation continues and this is the fear I now live with—whether her disappearance will provoke the removal of the boys unless I can play-down the concerns of the detectives investigating her disappearance?

Sarah settled into a cocktail of mood-correcting drugs and the court-stipulated biweekly psychoanalysis in addition to seeing her regular therapist, with the promise of a monthly review of the situation. Tranquilised to the hilt, she became more like the person I thought she was many, many years ago. No, that doesn't sound right; she was never numbed to the world, but now I could describe her as amenable—no more the angry outbursts and battle-ready callous words to pre-emptively attack me or defend herself from imaginary wrongs; gone were the unreasonable demands and unsolicited attacks on my person, the constant tension of expectations not met around the house, the obsessive busyness or self-induced rush of lateness and never having enough time to do everything she felt she should be doing. Sarah was kind and accommodating and her typical behaviour was noticeable by its absence. She was softer and gentler and affectionate and, after the initial few weeks to stabilise, responsive to my loving overtures to engage in physical affection, letting me hold her close at night. In fact, she started to idolise me.

But actually, she was not okay.

As we traverse the final descent, I wonder what pearls of wisdom can I glean from all this?

I still berate myself for not picking up earlier that Sarah was signaling she needed help. I belatedly realized that the burns and lacerations that preceded that 'night of the pink bath' and scarred her hands and arms were not due to her clumsiness opening the tin of tuna or neglecting to wear oven gloves when checking the roast chicken or not realising the stove plate was still hot or the kettle had just boiled or because the candle fell over and the paper caught alight. Self-mutilation was beyond my scope of expertise and experience.

I told Vincenzo that in the preceding weeks as she had searched for redemption, for liberation from her personal history and emancipation from her wounds that compelled her to react to certain situations as she did, the one person (other than herself) who could and should have played a pivotal role through forgiveness and acceptance, was busy trying to crush her with accusations, snuff out her spirit, and preclude her from making sense of what had happened and why. Vincenzo spent many therapy sessions trying to convince me that I was not the cause of her destructive behavior that night, but that what happened when I stormed out of the house simply triggered it; that, in fact, it was probably just one of many triggers that accumulated that day. He said that by the time Sarah came home that evening she needed a target to sponge up all her projections and through which to vent that which was no longer repressible. He said it was a form of brainwashing when Sarah bombarded me with consistent negative messages and I started to believe them, give them credence, and said something about 'projective identification'. I looked it up, but still don't understand it.

In hindsight, one of the first clues to the tectonic shifts rupturing her already fragile sanity, was an almost flippant passing comment she made over dinner one evening the week before she cut herself and fed those pills to the boys. Apparently brought to the fore by the work she was doing in psychotherapy, she mentioned how she had been torn apart as she tried to manage the 'duality' of the past three years, of loving two men. I acknowledged her comment, but did not push her to reveal more, choosing rather to see it as an admission of what had been going on which I realized was one of the unrequited needs of mine. I felt somewhat split myself, living in this ruptured relationship yet having dinner with my family as if nothing had happened, chatting about their day with the boys who were cheerfully naughty and full of energy.

And I remember just how rough our relationship was after my return from the Middle East, and I was travelling out of town every week or two for a few days. In many ways, it just seemed to continue the abrasiveness of the year before my departure (2007), and I remember late-evening phone calls when I was out of town:

'I just can't take this any more!' she had said on one occasion after a long and torturous telephone discussion about our flawed relationship. 'Why don't you leave me?' At the time I could not understand what she was on about; we were arguing, but why did she want me to abscond? Now I imagine that he had just left the house after an evening of loving and that the cognitive dissonance produced by managing parallel emotional and physical relationships was taking its toll, but she was not brave enough to initiate the break-up. What had that one informant said? That the only reason she had not left me was for the sake of the children.

My reverie has brought me almost to the end of the walk. I am feeling physically strong and refreshed by the wind howling at my face. Suddenly too tired to take carefully measured leaps and too emotionally drained to bother, I launch myself incautiously down the oversized boulders and loose gravel to return to the tarred road that zigzags below us, skirting the ocean's waves crashing against the boulders that aeons ago dislodged from the upper cliff-face to be carelessly deposited below . My legs show signs of fatigue and my knees, though well-warmed and doing well on the plateau, throb in protest. Watching the dogs gleefully negotiate the stepped descent, I wonder what half-witted ancestor decided that an upright posture was advantageous to our survival.

11

Three things cannot long stay hidden:
the sun, the moon and the truth.

(Gautama Siddhartha, the Buddha)

Saturday, 18 December 2010

The police services finally feign interest in Sarah's apparent disappearance and honour me with their second visit in as many days. Sarah's mother and sister have been badgering them for days, and I guess they were right to do so as I had lost interest in securing their attention but mostly did not want to for fear of losing the boys. Their unannounced arrival so early today unnerved me. Cursing the unfortunate absence of the boys, who slept over at their grandparents last night, as I could not use their presence as an excuse to avoid certain topics, I welcomed them in and made them tea even though they declined my offer and then primed myself for an awkward interrogation.

It started smoothly enough. I have by now so frequently rehearsed and repeated to others who inquired about the details of the Friday of her disappearance that it slipped off my tongue so sweetly without so much as a deviation sufficient to raise the curiosity of an overworked detective, or so I thought. I didn't have to work hard to feign my sorrow and grief when I insisted on walking them through all my movements that evening in non-dress rehearsal fashion and showing them again all her personal possessions mysteriously left in the house until they got bored or embarrassed by the emotions that welled up and moved back to the lounge with a 'We may need to take a closer look at those,' pointing conspiratorially to the laptop and cellphone.

'You're welcome to them now,' I said, knowing that would commit them to actually doing something with them, and I got the expected response that they would let me know.

Now the two detectives have ensconced themselves in the armchairs, flanking me. I feel hemmed in, with only my cup of tea to hold and strangely self-conscious about lighting a cigarette. I cannot locate any twirly-whirly sugar wrappers in my pockets. Again, we go through my whereabouts that day, and they are forthright enough to say I need an alibi. This time they also want to know about the few days preceding her departure and 'anything else that may be relevant,' and what I have done since to track her down. I think this is a good moment to show them that I have been sleuthing around in distraught-husband concern and have managed to track down two of her clients scheduled in her diary for that afternoon who said that she had 'uncharacteristically' cancelled her appointments with them at the last minute, 'just before lunch time, if memory serves'. Trying to sound confused and helpful rather than arrogant, I proudly declare that one of the staff members at the health store where she worked, when pressed, vaguely admitted rather nervously as if I was accusing her of something that 'Sara-lea seemed to leave well before closing time, but I can't be sure exactly when, and we don't keep tabs on the whereabouts of the consultants working upstairs, and they have a separate entrance anyway'.

'So she might have come home early on Friday,' I proffer to a nodding detective, his brow furrowed as he scribbles this insight into his flip-top notebook.

'Yes, it looks like she left work early that afternoon,' the other one paraphrases, as if wanting to claim the deduction for himself. 'Do you have the names and contact details of these persons?'

I'm confused, which one of you is the bad cop? I want to laugh.

And then, again, 'Let's get back to what happened the day before. That was, um . . .'

'Thursday,' I say, regretting it immediately, as I should have made him sweat, perhaps let him get it wrong. Stop being so helpful, I admonish myself. I need to keep the upper hand.

And so it goes on. Of course, I make no mention of the combative series of arguments that made up the preceding week, and I leave out the torrid details of the affair, but because they will pick it up from my telephone records, I am careful to mention that I had tried to contact one of the neighbours, a close friend and client of hers, in case, I said, he had seen her arrive home and subsequently leave the house. 'But all I got was his voicemail,' I say.

'What's his name, this neighbour?'

'Cunt' probably sums it up—I think, hoping they are not telepathic, and say, 'Calix,' and spell it for them, more than once.

I am wondering what a heart-shaped cunt looks like, when they inquire about her recent state of mind. 'Oh, I think she struggled with herself at times,' I say, 'but then who doesn't?' and they nod and smile, but I am the only one who laughs. Have they already ascertained this? If they check her medical records, this will reveal her psychological health, and if they verify mine, what might that expose? What is disclosed in therapy is confidential, isn't it?

'And she seemed to have a bit of a nervous breakdown some months ago but, lately she's been fine, really.'

They go down that avenue of questioning but I remain impassive and vague and they end up saying they will look into it. And to divert them, I keep asking them whether I should have done something else, whether there is something I have overlooked, and I am smugly proud and satisfied by their vacant responses and placating gestures that I have done everything I could reasonably have been expected to do. It would truly rile me if I have missed something.

But when they say, 'What is your marriage like?' I start to panic.

'What do you mean?'

'Have you had any marital problems?' I stare blankly at them. 'Have there been any incidents of infidelity? What about financial difficulties and behavioural problems with your children? That sort of thing.'

I sweat this one a bit because if they investigate further the history of her telephone accounts or ask pointed questions of others, the truth will likely be revealed, and I will have some explaining to do about their relationship and why I neglected to mention it. And I wonder how Calix, if asked, will respond to this one? I try to recall for myself who else I had phoned; the psychotherapist may prove to be tricky. 'I wasn't thinking clearly, I was so distressed' or something along those lines should cover it. But I realise that if they get anal about this, there will be a lot of awkward questions.

Then they look around the house again and repeat lots of questions as if they are looking for inconsistencies in my responses, but my initial irritation recedes once I convince myself to be curious about the process as this may help me later, and I sit through the remainder of it in good humour. Before they leave, they ask–tell me to present myself at the local police station on Monday morning to fill out forms and make a signed statement to them. As we bid goodbye, they promise to stay in touch, but I have the sense that I will not see or hear from them again until the New Year, as the promise of looming annual holidays should never get in the way of an important investigation.

But their visit does get me thinking about things again. I have been steering clear of the details of that week, of the days immediately preceding her disappearance, as I still feel too traumatised by it. This morning, as I left out most of the details, we only covered in cursory fashion our jarring interactions and the multitude of stressors that converged and precipitated yet another mention of separation between Sarah and me. But troubled now about the detectives' inquiries and future questions they might ask about what preceded Sarah's disappearance, I know I need to run through what happened and decide what to commit in my declaration to the police on Monday and what I can safely leave undisclosed.

12

How can we expect another to keep our
secret if we cannot keep it ourselves.

(La Rochefoucauld)

Saturday December 18, 2010 (continued)

Once the boys are asleep I sit, once again, in the study while my mind trawls through recent months. After the October 'eye-of-the-storm', notable for its calmness and ease between us coaxed by mood pills and intensive therapy, things returned to normal abnormality. And I cannot pretend that our relationship was robust and awe-inspiring. If you like, the 'hygiene' factors were there, and I did not feel grossly dissatisfied, but inspirational, it was not. That harmonious month of October gradually, or perhaps suddenly but unnoticed as such due to my exasperation, gave way to a traumatic few weeks and harrowing incidents that lead up to her disappearance. By November, soaring with mistaken optimism by the reassuring calm that had descended upon our relationship, from time to time I tried to engage her in conversation about us, trying to let her know that we really had to talk about us and what was going on between us.

One day I said to her, 'It seems you are having such a hard time with yourself lately, Sarah. What are you struggling with, let's talk about it?'

'This has been a bad month for me. There are so many anniversaries, so many losses. I'm just so affected by things,' she said.

'I'm sorry you are feeling all of this, and I didn't even know.'

My mind was racing through what November meant for her. The pregnancy we had terminated at sixteen weeks, of a little girl foetus we came to call Angelique, was conceived in this month? The pregnancy she terminated while I was in the Middle East, which may not have been mine? Or something to do with the other relationship she had? Someone died, or something else I don't recall or don't have any knowledge of? I really didn't know.

'Is it Roxanne?' I said, feeling like I was playing a game of 'twenty questions' and that I had to start somewhere.

'A lot of things have come up in therapy recently, and sometimes they're just too hard to deal with,' she said, but left it at that as if I should know how she was feeling and what this was about. I felt so desperate to connect with her but had learnt that she would retract into her shell if I pushed her to be more specific. So I said, 'Strange as it may sound, I so yearn for the illusion of a relaxing, fun-filled afternoon with you and the boys, sharing and playing and laughing together with loving appreciation—joyous in your joy, and you in mine. Lots of touching, eye contact, a real sense of oneness, and a history and a future of togetherness; wanting you and being wanted by you, our love sealed later by meeting that desire.' It was perhaps too poetic for her, and Sarah seemed unmoved, even fearful of this attempt to grow and learn together, to approach our situation as a unit, a team trying to work things out.

And as I recall this time, I am starting to wonder whether my view of 'blissful October' is not just a regressive fallacy, a simple oscillation, albeit dramatic, of the inevitable fluctuations of her emotions and well-being. And of mine, buoyed by an unhealthy dose of self-deception and hope that the catalyst of the affair and its aftermath would bring us together. And I speculate whether what has emerged as factual account in my memory of that time is perhaps simply a confabulation, at best based partly on the fact that we seemed to be getting along. It probably had little to do with her psychotherapy and mood-stabilising drugs or our relationship really improving or any other variable. I think I had to justify to myself that the pain I was enduring and the betrayal I was accepting was for good reason.

And me?

Caught off-guard, perhaps, by the false promises of the month of October, by the beginning of December I had hit rock bottom. As Sarah's behaviour gnawed at me, and mine no doubt at her, a few disconnected things conspired to bring it to a head.

One was work. It was dwindling and had been not more than a trickle since early in the year. Since the mid-year, in truth, I was so swept up in my head about the affair and concern for Sarah's health that I was unable to inspire myself to put much effort in. Since she came out of hospital, I watched her like a hawk but never acknowledged to myself the strain I was under. Everything became too much for me: simple chores, daily tasks, home maintenance, personal grooming—nothing seemed to matter to me. I was caught up in myself and my dark thoughts and became evermore reclusive. My naturally introverted personality came into full force; social gatherings overwhelmed me, and I sought out even more time to be alone and the mindless rigor of physical exercise to provide momentary relief and the illusion of well-being and accomplishment and purpose in each day.

Then two shocking events tipped the scales. The first was the sudden death in October of my brother-in-law after decades of alcohol and drug abuse. The insolvent estate left my sister with huge financial debts, and this had compounded our sense of financial insecurity as a family. This sparked Sarah's fears; her anxiety soared and she put tremendous pressure on me to get my act together

The other was Roxanne. At the end of October she attempted suicide, after many weeks of plummeting desperation at her personal circumstances—still single and childless in her early forties, without the imagined comforts of a fulcrum-family and effectively dislocated from the only familial relationship she knew which was with her half-sister, she had just been retrenched and was in perilous financial difficulties as a result of her addictive nature. And then the realisation that her on-off relationship on which she had pinned such long-term hopes was finally and irretrievably over seemed to tip her over the edge. With a history of addictions and Bipolar II Disorder, it was a quick drop to hell, and she was found unconscious on the floor of her kitchen with a cord, which had been gracious enough to snap, around her neck.

The day before Roxanne tried to end her life she called me, incoherent and sobbing, and said, 'I have just driven past you at the deli. I'm on my way up the mountain pass, and I'm going to drive off the cliff.'

'Come and talk with me,' I said, and she did.

'I only feel okay when I am with you, Clive.' And from that moment, I knew she should be on suicide-watch. I managed to convince her to see her psychiatrist the next day and encouraged her to attend a job interview that had been offered her through a friend, but it was all too much and pushed her over the edge and after that appointment, she went to her apartment and fashioned a noose for her neck. I felt partly responsible.

As it turned out, hospitalisation and weeks of hopeful electro-convulsive therapy for Roxanne proved expensive but futile, and subsequent convalescence at our house was perhaps too much for our already fragile relationship to bear, given that Sarah's relationship with her half-sister was diabolical in the best of times. Roxanne drifted around our house and then shut herself in my study which served as her temporary bedroom. Early mornings I crept through the house to check on her, fretting that I would find that her impending second attempt to do away with herself would be better planned and executed. I wondered how I would explain to the boys why their beloved aunt was no more. And I speculated whether a space clearing for our house would ever manage to cleanse the lingering ghost of death any more effectively than how I doubted it would expunge the protracted memories of infidelity.

The added stress of not letting her out of our sight while she berated herself for her failed attempt on her own life and desired to complete the job frayed our nerves. Sarah could barely manage to deal with her being cooped up with us. Attempts to talk were interspersed with an onslaught of outbursts and interplays between us that ratcheted up both in intensity and frequency as the days progressed. She had a go at me, at Roxanne, and at the boys, and within ten days this contributed to taking Roxanne back to the brink, and we coaxed her into a clinic for observation under high risk for suicide. As our financial situation was unpredictable and Roxanne was in debt, we had to leave her kicking and screaming in a state-funded institution.

At first, the trauma brought us closer, Sarah and me, or so it seemed, but just for a while. I huddled around her in genuine concern for Roxanne and tried to shield her from unnecessary exposure. But her sudden realisation of the possible genetic link to her own sanity gnawed at Sarah, as over the years her mother and uncle and brother had been in and out of psychiatric institutions and frankly, made me wonder whether there was something in this that could explain, at least in part, her erratic moods and errant reactions and hypersensitivity and provide some relief for me that I was not the horrid person she seemed to say I was.

One day, to imbue some levity, we took the boys to the circus. During intermission, I drifted off towards the edge of the hyper-jittery crowd consumed with the aroma of candy-floss and enraptured by clowns on stilts, and was self-consciously smoking a cigarette under a 'No-Smoking' sign. Suddenly this voice alongside me proclaimed that I was born on the day of 'heroic inevitability' and then lapsed into silence. My first thought was, 'Leave me alone, loony', but a serene and unimposing certainty seemed to radiate from within the body that housed this unsolicited voice. I put the wasted fag filter under my shoe and wondered what my chances were of lighting another before Sarah would gesture her irritation at me. I thought, 'What the hell,' and glanced at my new companion through the smoke from the first exhalation of my second fag. Middle-aged, conservatively dressed, and with the air of 'old-fashioned' clinging to her, you would be hard-pressed to find a person more unnoticeable and average-looking.

'She's Pleiadian,' my companion said. For a moment I thought I misheard her. When the word registered, I wondered if she was talking about the constellation of stars that supposedly helped guide Greek sailors or an enlightened being resonating at high frequency.

'Just more Greek mythology,' I thought, irked, and wondered how to alter the association I had with it.

'Look at her beauty; how tall she is. She stands head and shoulders above all those around her. She's here to infuse a higher consciousness, to bring light and knowledge, but many are closed to her pure wisdom and it's difficult for her to blend in.' Following her gaze, I became aware that she was watching Sarah interacting with the boys and wondered how she knew we were connected unless she had watched us for a while.

Perhaps encouraged because I had chosen to stay, still looking at Sarah, the woman said, 'She has the gift. She has seeing eyes.' Yes, I thought, most members of our species have this genetic mutation called eyes. 'She struggles so with this, but she will learn to harness it soon. It's so difficult for others to understand you, to live with you, so we leave.' I flicked away the guilt-trip, but it buzzed irritatingly around my head. It was clear she was now talking about herself as well, and she suddenly appeared sad and lonely. 'Your soul learns and grows through love, and you are connected to her in love by the past and the future, but she knows only pain as the pathway of her growth. Your experiences in this life and other incarnations, past and future, always reveal opportunities for guilt and the gift of shame. Through this pain, your soul learns and grows. So do not linger with them, nor wish them away, nor attempt to undo them or right past wrongs, nor seek or expect absolution. Visit them only for the purpose of understanding your present.' Was she talking to me or Sarah? 'Bear with her but don't lose your essence,' she said. 'She sees your soft, acquiescent, malleable exterior and feels she can take advantage of this, but it belies your inner strength. Inside, you are grounded like a rock. You have a fearless centre. She needs that.'

'It takes one to know one,' I thought, starting to feel a little uneasy and imposed upon. She stood quietly alongside me for a few minutes and then said, 'You are a reluctant hero, for all of them. It is inevitable that you assume this role,' before moving off.

I have not yet decided whether she was a traveller through many lifetimes, or a psychic or a charlatan, and I dismissed this chance encounter as a frivolous chat with a stranger, but it was stored in my memory. Wouldn't it be neat if I could say that Sarah was gifted or not well and could not help herself and then selflessly devote myself to her in the knowledge that this was my chosen role, my gift to humanity, to martyr myself to this purpose?

By late November, our communication was in terminal decline. We evaded the issue of 'us'; in fact, Sarah spurned most conversations and alone time with me. We never addressed her affair or our relationship, for fear that if I pressed her hard and she ducked and dived, I would be unable to reign in my outbursts of frustration, and this would again tip her over the edge. Fuelled by a general irritation and tiredness but more so anchor-dragged in the wake of the infidelity and a now long memory of a challenging and at times desperate relationship, what were perhaps typical relationship spats escalated into hard-currency issues that sat, unspoken and unresolved, between us.

I entered a phase of 'I'm tired of dealing with this, both the affair and her conduct towards me', and I was getting grumpier by the day as I encountered an escalation in her confrontational behaviour and bitter recriminations and more demoralised by our inability to change the pattern of our response to each other. While highly distressing to me, my experience of her behaviour did not feel out-of-the-ordinary. It was how I clearly remember her to be the last few years, brought about perhaps by how she felt about me or, alternatively, how she felt about him, or both.

Grappling with the recent uncertainty around her fatherly-friendship with 'client' Eric, I was completely strung out by the time I heard more whispers that her affair with Calix had not ended. I had no hard evidence and did not look for it, but it plagued me terribly. I found myself obsessing about finding them *in flagrante,* and I played out various scenarios in my mind which sometimes ended in confrontation and violence. The best I could do was to ask her how things were working out with Calix. So one day while driving along the coast road, I asked Sarah about it, fuelled by a fresh run of sleepless nights and dark forebodings and reasoning that with Roxanne temporarily out of our hands and in professional care, it would be opportune to raise the topic. Her reaction was a dead give-away that she was hiding something, although perhaps also the sign of a mind at breaking point.

'There is absolutely no interaction with Calix at all,' she screamed at me. 'Stop the car!'

I did.

'It's just a question, Sarah, and a fair one, I think, under the circumstances.'

'You're abusing me! Why don't you just leave me?' Her voice was shrill, her body language so aggressive I thought for a moment she was going to hit me. And I remember her saying those words three years ago when she was deeply embedded with him and could not cope with the duality, and 'duped' is rapid-fire synapsed in my fear centers.

'Look, I believe that you are still seeing him or at least, making contact with him,' I said. I tried to convince myself that I would not have a problem with that if only she was open about it, but I wanted to get her on the honesty bit, to show her this was the only way forward for us. A loathing for secretiveness and deceit had set up camp in my heart, and an agent of transparency had been sent to the frontlines by the General of Integrity with the mission to dislodge the stays and return with the tent pegs, dragging victoriously the soiled canvass of deception and intrigue. 'Just last month you volunteered to tell me if you had any contact with him of any nature, but I don't think that you have kept your promise . . .'

'You only know because you have been checking my cellphone bills,' she inadvertently let on.

I imagined I had hit pay dirt. 'That sounds like an admission.'

'No, it's not, you bastard!' she said, grabbing her cellphone and slamming the car door. 'My psychiatrist says you can't do this to me—test me all the time.' And she stormed off down the windy, deserted road.

I wondered who was really being tested here and called after her, 'Come on, Sarah, you don't need . . .'

'Why don't you follow me around all day? Why don't you check my phone account?' she said. And then, awkwardly, over her shoulder, 'Walking away is not an admission of guilt,' she said and receded into the shadows.

But it occurred to me that it was and so that was what I did the next day. And when I scanned her telephone account for the past month, I found not the high intensity of multiple daily calls and late night texts as before, but a number of text and phone call exchanges nonetheless, which I could probably safely double as he no doubt contacted her too. So it was true, these stories I had heard, or at the very least something was afoot which she would not disclose, and I tried to isolate exactly why this was a problem for me. If she was interacting with him, even in a friendship of sorts, that would require work on my part, but it was acceptable to me. In fact, I expected it, and if I felt it was honourable, I would have embraced it. I might have wondered: what role was he playing in her life, and what was the nature of their relationship? And depending on the answers to these questions, I might wonder how we were going to make it while he was still in the picture? But the issue was that she was concealing it from me. So I thought about it. I did not want to admit to her that I had fallen into the trap of scrutinising her phone statements, even though she knew I could and had taunted me to do it, but what she was doing hurt me beyond measure and hurled me right back to day one. I was astounded that she would be so blatant, as if she was untouchable. And I was perplexed, not sure what to do with this information, as she would no doubt find justification for each of the communications. I was unsure where I wanted to draw the line, or whether I was prepared to act on the implicit consequence—*that* was really my Achilles' heel.

My tenuous hold on 'okay-ness' faltered after this altercation and the confirmation offered by her telephone statements. I felt . . . What? I felt splintered, like I was fragmenting into millions of pieces of glass shards with the endless stress and tension and discord between us and uncertain of what was and was not happening, and the doubts and fears cascaded and enveloped me. But mostly, the deceit proved too much for my self-respect to shoulder. Only writing seemed to help hold me.

It seems that exposing her furtive contact with Calix was too much for her, and each day from then on, my afternoon homecomings were greeted with her blood graffitied on the bathroom walls. I needed to share my growing concern with Sarah's psychiatrist, but her response was simply to encourage Sarah to consult her daily. 'Sara-lea has developed intricate mechanisms for her survival,' she said, relayed to me by Catherine when I accosted her in the grocer check-out one day.

The fine balance between concerned care for Sarah and overprotection of the boys drove me beyond my limits. Fresh out of ideas, I acknowledged the meltdown that seeped from my pores one night by going on a cocktail of anti-depressants, tranquillisers, and sleeping tablets. And I started intensive psychotherapy with a new psychiatrist. But the medication had apparently not yet kicked in and pent-up emotions and self-doubt had coalesced into a third consecutive sleepless night for me. The previous day's psychotherapy session had aroused my deepest wounds and frustration and, lying in bed, I felt like I was falling apart, literally going crazy. So I made myself a cappuccino-to-go and left the house before sunrise, unable to take it any more, and, in a state of madness, walked for hours with the dogs and did not respond to her attempts to reach me on the cellphone.

Just in time, it seemed, for the final countdown to her disappearance.

That week, my eyes were opened by Jim and Julia, my new therapist. Stark, undeniable revelations, and I fell off the edge and wanted her 'gone'.

Will they get to all of this on Monday's statement-interrogation?

I will say, 'It's not relevant.'

Bad-cop will tap his pen on the metal tabletop and say, 'Everything is.'

I will look up at the swinging naked light bulb and say, 'I don't know where to start.'

Good-cop will walk behind me and place his hand on my shoulder and softly say, 'Let's start at the beginning.'

I will extend my hands in protest and say, 'But that's over forty years ago.' Many lifetimes, actually.

Bad-cop will stop tapping and close in on me and say, 'I'm not going anywhere.'

I will turn to good-cop and say, 'I don't know how to make you understand.'

Good-cop will smile a reassurance and say, 'Just tell us the facts.'

I will examine my fingernails and say, 'Facts are just what you choose to believe in.'

Bad-cop will lean in close and say, 'We will decide what to believe.'

I know I will say too much. And nobody, in the retelling, will ever comprehend why it was more than I could take.

Okay, last week began like this . . . .

CHOKE IT OFF

13

A man can hide all things, excepting
twain—that he is drunk, and that he is
in love.

(Didot)

Sunday, 5 December 2010

Her cellphone alarm breaks the early dawn silence. That means, it must be ten minutes after six, her habitual time to rise for weekday 'quiet time', but she has again forgotten to cancel it for the weekend. I groan and turn over. I have not had much sleep again for the fifth night in a row, but then, none of us have slept well last night, and I am finally luxuriating in a deep and groggy dream and determined not to wake up early.

Then I realise she is not in bed with me, Jeremiah is. This has been the story of the last five days, not entirely unusual in the greater scheme of things but exacerbated by the fact that the boys are at various stages of illness with tummy cramps and fever, with little Jack being the worst with a confirmed case of dysentery. So the nights have been a case of musical beds, and if we had thought of it, we could probably have made some fun of it by betting on which bed each of us would wake up in each morning.

The cellphone has snoozed for the mandatory five minutes and the alarm goes off again. I realise that perhaps Sarah wants to rise early today for quiet time anyway, which she says she finds helpful—'it's absolutely critical to settle myself for my day'—if she is struggling with stuff in her mind, which she no doubt is. So I pick up the phone, holding it gingerly, repulsed by the secrets it holds, and go in search of her in one of the other bedrooms, and I turn left at the top of the stairs and get it right first time and muse that I could have made some money out of that. But it is obvious really; she is asleep in little Jack's bed with him, so perhaps the odds would not have been great, anyway. She seems to want to sleep on, so I take Jeremiah, who was woken up by the alarm and is grumpy, to the kitchen and fix myself a cup of coffee and brew some tea for Sarah.

When she gets up at eight o'clock, and a respectable time has elapsed, I let her know that I was really looking forward to sleeping in and perhaps we can find a different way to deal with the alarm on weekends if she is not going to be able to switch it off or has no intention of getting up early anyway. She is extremely crabby and has a few choice words for me about having the audacity to even raise it. So I wait a while for things to simmer down. Then I say, 'Sarah, would you still like to have some quiet time?'

'I can't do it now! I have been distracted by our conversation, and there are things to do around the house. I wanted to sleep in.' She makes it sound like I was to blame.

'Okay,' I say, although I am wondering what all these things are that are so urgent on the weekend that they cannot wait thirty minutes.

'You are so selfish!' she says, and for a moment, I have no idea what she is referring to. 'This is what I tell other people about you. And they all agree; they think you're despicable!' Yes, I am fully aware of her distortion campaign, and that her fears of my possible desertion have led to paranoid portrayals of my exploitation and abuse. It is a short leap from her disapproval-rejection to intimidation and menacing threats to unveil the worst side of me to people who matter. I have tried to coach myself to just ignore these comments and labels, but maybe I am not yet awake enough to think straight.

'Sarah, if you . . .'

'My name is Sara-lea!'

' . . . wanted to have your quiet time, you could have done it this morning at any time, or you can do it now, if you like.' I am trying to sustain a lilting, cheery tone.

I think, 'Clive, don't get hooked. There is nothing you can do about this, and you don't have to feel guilty for how she feels. And whatever you do, don't try to reason with her. It is a Sunday, after all, and this is how Sundays are, for reasons only she truly knows. It is not your stuff.'

But the selfish demands quickly ramp up to angry, abusive instincts, and she unlocks the chest and buries her head in search of an appropriate weapon from her arsenal of ridicule and sarcasm and devious plots designed to hurt, and she knows the left-right combination of an intentional angry outburst and a shocking global label is her most sophisticated and destructive. Sarah selects a demeaning judgment and says, 'You're sick, you fucking bastard' and turns on her heels, mumbling things about me just loud enough for me to hear but not quite make out exactly what she is saying.

As I empty my lungs to ward off the visceral reaction, which brings on a spell of dizziness, I consider what has happened so far and what role I have perhaps played in bringing about this display of acrimony and antagonism. I know she feels that I have made her unhappy, by not giving her what she thinks she wants; that I am not being fair. And that if she does not get everything she wants, she feels that she is worthless, that I don't love her. For her, it is all-or-nothing, all good or all bad; there is no middle ground. I seem to transform from hero to demon mid-sentence.

I find it impossible to not absorb what she says, to not feel somewhat the way she describes me, even if I try and convince myself that she does not intentionally wish to make me 'bad', or she feels that way about herself. She seems to think that the only thing I understand is punishment and wants to teach me a lesson, or she feels duty-bound to offer me 'guidance' on how to be a better person. I even consider that she may be entirely unconscious of the parts of her behavior that are obnoxious and hurtful. If I mention it later, she certainly seems surprised that it upset me and often claims to have no recollection of the conversation or of saying those things. And heaven help me if, vexed, I go about proving my version of events—what actually happened, she says, does not matter. How can I counter that? But her anger makes me feel unsafe and insecure and too often recently I have taken the bait. My sense of injustice, of being falsely accused, rouses my anger and out of self-protection I feel the need to retaliate or to explain myself for fear she will destroy me. I am trying, these days, to avoid letting my mind go to this place, but I nevertheless wonder just how much more of this I can take.

But there are things that have to be said to each other, just in the normal course of a pre-breakfast early Sunday morning, so I can't entirely avoid her ill-tempered labelling and criticism. I feel hamstrung after confronting her about Calix the other day, fearful of provoking her mental cascade into oblivion, as since then she has taken to mutilating herself and tracing her curses in blood on the bathroom mirror. So I have to practice expelling my likely retorts in a sigh of unvented words, and busy myself with locating the origin of her angst. I wonder whether her anger is a spillover from what happened last night or yesterday, about the party, when I learned that I had, once upon a time, been an unfaithful pregnant woman in the Middle Ages.

A little later, feeling resentful if not battered and bruised, I am relieved when she finally goes off to gym and I play with the boys, creating imaginary stories with the help of their farm trucks and animals, but I remain distracted and unsettled by how the day started. The conversation I had with Roxanne yesterday morning finds traction. She was still attending the residential addictions programme but, being a Saturday it was a free day. She had called me and said, 'I want to come clean with you, Clive. Can we meet for coffee?' Part of the twelve-step programme, I guess, making good your gaffes.

'There's a sardine run,' I said. 'I'd like the boys to enjoy it, so let's rather go for a walk.' We strolled along the beach. A red tide, hanging just off-shore, had herded thousands of hapless sardines into the bay, and schools of dolphins and seals were patrolling just meters from us in the breakers, feasting on nature's gift. Some floated in the shallows and were already dead from the depleted oxygen levels. The boys, wielding their fishing nets, were rescuing the gasping flip-flapping creatures but unwittingly tossing them to the waiting seals.

Roxanne said, 'You're right, Clive, I knew right from the start, when you were in the Middle East.' I had been repulsed by her blatant lie when she had texted me after Sarah had confessed the affair at that first appointment with Vincenzo, pleading her ignorance of the affair and saying how awful it was. But I thought it best to let her speak, though I saw tears brimming and wondered if this was a good idea considering her plight.

I said, 'It's okay, Roxanne. I figured it out a long time ago, that you have been party to this all along.'

'They were just too over-friendly when I saw them together, like once they had a picnic on the beach and I just turned up and I could see it. They tried to keep it away from me and did not want me around when they were together. But I knew for sure what was happening when I slept over at your house one night, just to help Sara-lea with the boys and keep her company. I was sleeping in your study, but I am a light sleeper and use ear-plugs to cut out any noise, and the dogs were going crazy running up and down the passage clearly in distress and they came to me to wake me up. So I followed them down the passage to your bedroom, and I heard them in there. I'm so sorry.'

'How could you be certain?' I knew it was a stupid question, but I wanted her to tell me more.

'I stood outside the closed door and I could hear them, Clive, having sex. Jesus, I'm sorry. I didn't know what to do, so I just went back to bed. The next morning I had a fight with Sara-lea. I told her it has to stop and that I was going to phone you overseas, but I didn't have your number and she wouldn't give it to me.'

'Was Calix still there?'

'No, he had left.'

'And that was the start of the dogs messing in the lounge at night whenever I went away on business. Am I right?' She nodded. 'I just knew it. Their natural sense of pack-hierarchy was disturbed. After I came back from the Middle East, every time I went away on business they crapped in the house. They were trying to mark their territory because another pack-leader male had moved in for the night. And to think I chastised them for it.'

Roxanne said, 'But at some stage I spoke to him too and told him that what was going on was not okay. We really didn't get along and he didn't like me one bit. But I didn't know that the affair continued, Clive. She told me it was over.'

'When?'

'When you came back from the Middle East. And Sara-lea kept saying that she thought you were having an affair overseas, but I told her that she thought that way because *she* was having one. Anyway, that's why I was so shocked when Sara-lea told me that he had come to the house to feed your pets when you were away last Easter Weekend in April. I just told her that I can't believe that he is not out of her life.'

'How could you not know that it was still going on, Roxanne?' I said. 'You are so close to Sarah.'

'Clive, I'm so sorry, but Sara-lea is lying. She has lied to me and she is lying to you. She has always done that.'

'She lies impulsively when she's feeling cornered, Rox. I'm not sure she's even conscious of it, or if she is then it's entirely justifiable to her as her very being feels threatened. I find her dishonesty incredibly difficult to accept, but I don't think she's being intentionally manipulative or malicious, it's just a desperate attempt to cope with fear and loss. So I think she fears losing my love over her affair with Calix and she responds with denial and contempt and outrage as it is easier than fear and makes her feel less vulnerable.'

By then the boys were chest-deep in the small breakers, which meant Jack could barely stand, and we all waded in through the wall of sardines, the mass of which parted and then closed in behind us, shimmering green-blue-silver. The proximity of the boys precluded further talk and I was grateful for this.

But Roxanne had the last word, 'And just the other day I heard from someone that it's still going on. But when I confronted Sara-lea, she hit the roof. And that's the other reason I have come to you now; I'm not going to be a part of this deceit anymore.'

As my thoughts of Roxanne collapse, I think, 'It was a moment of almost biblical proportions, in the shallow waters of the bay, and nobody in the valley went hungry last night. Now I am wishing for a miracle.'

———⬩⬩⬩———

The day passes, and in the evening as the sun is setting, we are up on the road at the top of the driveway saying goodnight to Matthew and Jordan who came over with their young children for a barbeque and a swim to get some relief from the summer heat. After they drive away to our waves and calls of goodbyes, Sarah says, 'Shit, this had to happen now.'

'What is it?' I say, my attention focused on getting the boys into the front seats of my car, which is still parked on the road as they argue with each other whose turn it is to sit on my lap and help me drive it down the driveway.

'Nothing,' she says, but looks like a startled wild animal and quickly walks, scampers actually, to the far side of the car. I feel a swirling energy, disorienting sounds of stampeding beasts, and then I see him. Calix is returning from an evening walk up 'our mountain' and is walking towards us on his way back to his cottage.

I turn to face him, wait a couple of seconds for him to reach me, and say, 'Hello, Calix.'

Pausing mid-stride, hesitant, and unsure of whether to keep moving or come to a standstill, he says, 'Hi.' He stops, half-stumbling as if the confused message gave two different instructions to each foot.

He looks embarrassed and makes as if to take off again when I say, 'Did you go to the top?' I want him to linger, and I can't think of anything else to say while Roxanne's sickening image of them making love in our bed breaks free of its cage in the attic of my mind, and I can't see where Sarah is.

'Always,' he says, and keeps his distance, backing off from me; expecting violence?

His monosyllabic response and more so his demeanour, seem to suggest he is repulsed by me. It feels like a stand-off and that I am his enemy. Or is it just me feeling like this? Where are my troops? Sarah should be by my side, in a show of solidarity. Then the boys run to him and hug him excitedly shouting, 'Calix! Calix!' and time stops for me. I stand where I am, which occurs to me to be at a respectable distance, and I seem to lose my ability to hear as if their connection with him is simply too much to bear. I am not sure if he is still speaking, and there is just a vague background din. Our three energies, or is it six with the boys, vortex into a dark channel, which sucks me in. Images roll at high speed, all out-of-time sync, lifetimes past and future, pain, joy, hatred, love, death, and rebirth, and I feel like my cells have dispersed and are floating free. It seems like an eternity, but then it is gone.

On the road in the twilight, I see Sarah's hand raised and waving over the roof of the car. Roxanne's story machine-guns my synapses, and I look at the woman and man standing in front of me. From the far side of our vehicle, she cannot see me and perhaps thinks I cannot see her and what she is doing. My neck will not turn my head and my eyes rotate to look in that direction, but I can't be sure if or how he acknowledges her gesture; he may have said something. As the boys withdraw, I see Calix smile and wink at her. And then the moment is over, and he is off, and I can hear and move again.

Back inside the house, I wonder whether Sarah's behaviour was just a moment of silliness and awkwardness. If she is behaving in this way out of concern for me, why hadn't she come to stand next to me, to own our space, to show him we are united—are we? Why hadn't she interacted with him in whatever way she would have done if I was not there? To give a clear message that she is no longer affected by him and that this is *our* home and *our* family and the fortress is impenetrable. If I had thought that I might have reaped some gratification from this, that it might have extinguished my lingering insecurity and jealousy of Calix, I would have been wrong. The idea of inflicting my feelings on Sarah leaves me feeling tainted, like a torturer, by this transaction on the roadside. The only thing I am completely certain about after this interaction is that he still loves her. I could see it, sense it. And that she still has feelings for him, the depth of which mean it would be unworkable for them to have the friendship I have often suggested she pursue with him as it seemed to fit with one of her assertions that it is over and has been for a long time, and they are just friends. Too risky, even, while he continues to live so near.

Of all the moments that flashed before me, in an instant, as I stood in the energy triad, one still traverses my mind: the motion of being on horseback, at speed, the visceral drumming of hoofed creatures, endless charred fields stretching before me, wafts of smoke or mist as if a wave of destruction has swept across the countryside, and something lying in a distant field cloaked in burgundy-red. And I am reminded of how often I have seen him wearing that red sweater that connects them, at the top of our mountain at sunrise while I smoke my morning cigarettes and drink coffee in the kitchen courtyard, looking down at us arms outstretched in worship as if to beckon or embrace her. I was certain Sarah was aware of this habit and that it has been one of their greeting routines for ages, just like the fresh flowers he displays in his lounge window for her to drive past every day.

Just last week, standing in the open front doorway, wearing just a G-string and silk camisole which I am convinced he gave to her, she asked me, 'What are you staring at up there?'

I looked at her and then back to the figure dressed in red on the pinnacle of rock. 'If we can see him so clearly,' I said, 'then he can see us.'

And without a word she turned on her heels and put on something less revealing.

14

Selfishness is not living as one wishes
to live, it is asking others to live as one
wishes to live.

(Oscar Wilde)

Monday, 6 December 2010

'You're so selfish!' she says, speaking with her whole body. 'I don't see why I cannot work this morning while you look after little Jack?'

It is early morning and the boys are drifting one by one, still half asleep, into the lounge, and we are multitasking, trying to get everything together to meet the school deadline while meeting their simultaneous demands for instant gratification of their wishes to switch on the television, play with me, make me tea or hot chocolate or juice, I want to watch a video, I am hungry, and sit on the couch with me now—none of which is preceded by 'please' or followed by 'thank you'.

I idly wonder what turmoil will descend upon me next week when the long summer school vacations begin, and I cannot be guaranteed even the morning hours to myself without coming under pressure from her of having to justify why I am not looking after the boys or staying at home. Because my work hours are generally flexible, and I only sporadically experience the demands of having to work a full day and even less often consecutive full days and then only when under deadline for a project, she always feels that I am inconsiderate if I appear unwilling to interrupt what work I am doing at the drop of a hat. She seems inclined to test me on this at regular intervals.

I suspend what I am doing. I generally like to get up early, because if I sleep in I tend to feel drowsy and take a while to be fully functional. This also gives me a chance to make tea for Sarah, a small token of love and consideration but one which I have come to learn means the world to her. To be honest, it probably serves as a poor substitute for a strained couple feeling distant from each other and waking up again in separate bedrooms and makes less awkward our first encounter of the morning with a—'Hi, here's some tea for you.'

My eyes are not yet focusing as I have not yet had a sip of coffee nor a drag of nicotine, after which, and only after which, I usually permit myself to take my first conscious breath of morning air and accept that the day has begun. I feel as if I have unintentionally pushed the 'play' button of the horror-movie video I had thankfully paused last night and vowed to return to the video store of 'life' first thing this morning and insist that they re-rate it 'sensitive viewers be advised, this experience is extremely hazardous for your happiness' and ask for my money back.

Vaguely convinced that I have misheard her, yet feeling that there is something I should do or say in response to her, I try to place her invective in context and am rewarded with fuzzy recollections of recent conversations that seem to relate to the topic.

Late last night Sarah had said, 'Jack is still contagious for another twenty-four hours, so he cannot go to school tomorrow. I have only one client, anyway, a regular for a massage, and he is happy to move his appointment to another day.' By which I had assumed she wanted to stay with Jack for the morning, which meant we would have to call on Naomi the au pair to accompany her. She never refers directly to it, but I can sense that being shadowed by her chaperone feels like a noose around her neck.

'Okay. Then would you like me to take the other boys to school in the morning?' I said last night, thinking this would be a helpful thing to say.

'Yes,' she said, and then, a little later, 'Or I could take them and then go to gym.' Again, she will need a chaperone; did Sarah think that our au pair Naomi was sitting by her telephone just waiting for our call? But I wanted to see where this settles; otherwise I would be raising this impediment at every turn.

'That's also okay,' I said, and we had left it at that.

But this morning she is furious with me, and 'you're so selfish' are the first words we share in the kitchen, instead of 'hello' escorted by a cup of tea. While my mind argues with itself about whether Sarah even understands the concept of 'selfishness', I say, 'Sarah, I try not to interfere with your work and your programme for the day. If you have appointments, or want to go to gym, that's fine, like I said.'

'But you should have said "why don't you go to work, I will look after little Jack".'

She often does this—tells me what I should have said, usually long after I can do anything about it. I think it is part of her preoccupation with her own needs and that anything that does not fit the programme she has determined will upset her balance is worse than intolerable for her as her anxiety escalates. She seems genetically incapable of considering alternatives or other viewpoints; it is not about how valuable they might be; it is just that they are not hers. And then in comes the character assassination supported by the long list of labels disgorged from her mouth without her realising just how hurtful and unfair they are, and how they rupture our fragile bond.

'I don't always get it right,' I say. 'You can do it whichever way you like, I don't mind. You decide,' which is not my normal way of responding to her, but I want to placate her so that I can smoke my cigarette in peace. Is not the only way to respond to someone who is reflexively oppositional, to give them nothing to oppose?

Our communication has been strained this weekend and neither of us are in a good space, and we tentatively say a few things to each other through the kitchen window. We pepper the time with standard questions and statements that only require monosyllabic responses or grunts or the desired action from me which indicates compliance, which is what they get; arbitrary practical things, careful not to raise anything potentially contentious.

I say, 'Do you have a lot of clients today?'

'I have a full day," she says, while in high-speed perpetual motion across the kitchen floor from countertop to refrigerator to cupboard to school bag to countertop in vectors which, if traced, may prove to be highly inefficient but the cumulative equivalent of twenty minutes on the treadmill. That is not what she had said last night.

Then I am outside for a while, my so-called quiet time forfeited to the pressing need to hurriedly clean and backwash the pool and give some water to the pot plants that will not manage the hot summer day that is looming. I return to the kitchen nervously expecting her recrimination, and I am not disappointed as her anxiety builds.

'Where have you been? Come inside now, I can't do all of this on my own. They need to get dressed now, you are going to be late. And don't forget to give Jack his muti.'

There was a time when I used to take her on about talking to me like this, but I manage to keep the conversation I would have with her swirling around my own head. I silently wonder whether she has taken her medication yet, but dare not ask.

Off she goes to gym and work, and I drop the two older boys at school and look after little Jack. Jim tracks us down at the nursery playground, but then thinks better of hanging around—too many children—and he goes to the deli.

Mid-afternoon, looking around the kitchen in a way that shows she knows already that it is not there, Sarah says, 'Where's the avocado?' By her tone of voice I can sense trouble coming.

'Oh, I ate it for breakfast,' I say.

'How could you do that?' The look on her face shows her scorn, that it was so obviously the wrong thing to do.

Keeping my distance offered by the large open-plan kitchen, I look at her and hold on to an overflowing counter top to steady myself or maybe to have handy something with which to defend myself. It occurs to me that it is far too heavy to lift, so I will have to hide under it if it comes to that. 'You offered it to me this morning,' I say. 'You said, "Here's a ripe avo. You can have for breakfast".'

'I can't believe you ate all of it! You did not even leave me some.'

'I'm sorry, I didn't . . .'

'You're so selfish. I would never do that!'

It seems obvious now what her theme is for today. My body feels like it is made of tightly coiled springs, fully compressed, about to unleash from recoil and propel me through the ceiling. I should just walk away; I know this, but the label sticks like a post-it and hooks me and reels me in.

Appealing to logic and reason, I say, 'Sarah, you gave me the avo.'

'It's Sara-lea!'

Let's stick to the topic of the avocado. 'Okay,' I say, relenting. 'It did not occur to me that I should only eat half of it. If you had let me know, I would gladly have done so. Should I go to the shop quickly to get you another one?'

But it seems she does not want a solution to the situation. Perhaps that would leave her without a subject through which to channel her wrath. She says, 'I just don't get you. You're so mean!'

Her words cut through me to the bone. She seems to have an infinite supply of characterisations to write me off, and I feel the stamp indelibly large on my forehead. 'Toss it away if it does not fit,' I say to myself.

Then I say to her, trying my best to maintain my composure, 'Look Sarah, these are your perceptions of me, and if you're going to always express them in such a scathing way, I'd rather not hear your opinion of me, especially in front of the boys. Even if you are unhappy with what I am doing, you have no right to control me. So if you are unhappy with something, tell me about how it makes you feel. That will be helpful. You need to look at the habit you have of criticising me and wanting me to be someone I'm not—of wanting me to change. I think you should focus more on who *you* are and who *you* want to be and leave me to decide the same for myself.'

But self-reflection is the last thing she wants. 'You're the most disgusting person I've ever met!' she says.

Suddenly aware that all this is within earshot of the boys, I go sit with them on the floor of the lounge where they are playing, and they are excited to have me join in with their imaginary story of a wildlife adventure with their favourite animals and toy explorer trucks kitted out with all the necessary accessories. They assign certain toys and roles to me, and I can't help but think how much I would like to bring this fantasy to reality. Nature is not without its hazards, but usually it is not self-inflicted and not the result of wanton cruelty.

15

If you wish another to keep your secret,
first keep it yourself.

(Seneca)

Tuesday, 7 December 2010

'That must have been weird for him,' Jim says, ejecting crumbs from his mouthful of muffin, while speculating about being 'the other man'. I am not sure whether he is wondering how Calix might have felt having sex in our bedroom or bumping into Sarah and me on the road the other evening. He has been saying all along that both Sarah and Calix must still have strong feelings for each other, given the depth of the relationship they had. 'Unless he is a player, of course. Then it gets very interesting.'

I am not sure I want to hear this. 'What do you mean?' I say.

'A player? You know, it's what he does for a living, sleeping with other men's wives. He gets a kick out of it,' he says, as if he was reading from *Extramarital affairs for Dummies*. 'You said he has done this before, apparently at the same time he was seeing your wife. She seemed to be so bothered by it that she even mentioned it to you. In fact, maybe this is why things did not work out between the two of them.'

'You mean . . .'

'Yes, he was also seeing another married woman and that's why she never made the move to leave you. You told me that she said they tried to end it a number of times, but she won't tell you why she did not leave you for him. It's conceivable that she found out and threatened to stop seeing him, so he promised to drop the other one, and then it's on again, but he fools around again, and so on.'

I think of Sarah, concerned for her again. Recently we found out that another married man with whom she had an affair for one year long before she met me, still continues to have these extramarital affairs. She was devastated to hear this as it dawned on her that her relationship with him was not as special and unique as she had thought.

'You're being ridiculous,' I say, but I have a morbid interest in where he was going with this. I empty the contents of a brown sugar sachet into the ashtray and roll myself a twirly-whirly to keep my fingers busy, a habit started just after I learnt about the affair. My dogs, Harry and Sally, meander back into the courtyard of the deli, having relieved themselves on the adjacent grass patch and sniffed around to their hearts' content.

'Am I? If he is a player, then surely this is what he would do, especially if he is getting bored with her, Sara-lea, that is. Maybe he had accomplished everything he could, short of her leaving you. And there is enough evidence of a planned execution here, the way he seemed to know who she was before he set up the situation by making an appointment to be treated by her. I bet he did some research on her and then he shared of himself in those sessions in a way that was appealing to her and talked her language like the astrology and all that mumbo-jumbo new-age stuff. Probably loves to cook too or quickly took some cooking lessons; she likes that in a man, doesn't she?' I wince. 'Then he found out her husband would be absent, working overseas and realised she would be vulnerable and alone with young children, so he moved in next door to get really close. Fuck it, Clive, can't you see it?' I don't say anything, thinking this was his fantasy, not mine. But he is persistent. 'Did she ever tell you how it started, who made the first move?'

'I'm not sure,' I say.

'I bet she said it was him, but it was actually her. She just thought it was him, or wanted to. That's how these guys work—experts at seduction, they are. Very clever too. They take the woman's guilt away, make her feel it is not her fault when she finds herself shagging the neighbour. Then she finds she can't stop seeing him, and it's too late. She talks herself right into it.'

He is right; Sarah had felt compelled to volunteer right up front, under no pressure to do so, that 'he initiated the relationship', as if it was vital to her that this was how it happened. 'I don't think . . . ' I say, but Jim is evidently not curious about what I think. Not yet. He has not finished painting his portentous picture.

Jim leans forward, relishing the moment he can illuminate the bleak details. 'Think of the kick he must have got out of seeing you leave your house everyday for three years naively unaware of what was going on, or of driving past the two of you and sharing a knowing glance with her that you were oblivious to, or of greeting you when you walked past him up that hill you share. Perhaps he was in your bed the previous night, fucking her or would be the next night when you travelled on business or he was sharing sexy thoughts with her on the phone when he walked past you. You can see how this could appeal to him.'

I don't want to see it; I want to go for a walk, anything, to get away from these possibilities. Jim seems to be acquainted with so much about how Calix manipulated this affair into being that I wonder if he is creating a scenario that would appeal to himself. 'And you also said that he wanted to meet with you; how sick is that? Perhaps this was the next step for him, chatting to you, pretending to be a friend or acquaintance of Sara-lea. He even seems to be following her around lately, or at least, that is the story she told you.'

I crane my neck to the laughter coming from the table behind me, which I find seats four women probably in their forties, and the purest blue eyes of a blond-haired woman lock with mine. Soft and endlessly deep, they seem to invite me in, as if my free-fall will be cushioned if I leapt in through the sockets. They are all vaguely familiar, as are all inhabitants of this valley, and I have been tuning in and out of their conversation about infidelity, about the soon-to-be-ex-husband of one who has been 'banging this girl no older than our daughter'. Braver than me, that woman has taken a stand and twenty-five years of marriage has gone up in smoke. Why do I have such self-doubt? Nothing about this situation feels okay for me. My integrity, my wholeness, is being challenged and I feel so perforated I think it is only my tension and anxiety that is holding me together.

'In this scenario,' Jim says as if the film he is rolling in his mind cannot be paused, 'what has now happened with you finding out just ups the ante for him, it makes things very interesting. Can he still lure her and seduce her? And wouldn't this be amazing for him, to be fucking your wife still even though you know about the affair?'

'Stop saying that,' I say.

'What?'

'Fucking her.'

'But that's what he's doing. Or what he did.'

'It's just, you know, disrespectful, especially if that's not what is going on.'

'If he's not fucking her, he's certainly dreaming about it. She fills his fantasies while he's jerking off and I bet it's the same for her.' I blow smoke at him. 'So how would you like me to say it?'

He gazes at me with a sorry look on his face, clear in his mind that I am denying the reality and then shakes his head mournfully, almost but not quite imperceptibly. I try to assume an 'un-sorry-for-myself' look. 'Anyhow,' he says, getting no response, 'I think the alternative scenario is even worse.'

I reach for my sunglasses and sink lower in my chair as if together these actions will make what I am feeling less visible to others. Her blue eyes, filled with grief and compassion, a love so wide it seems I will never find the edge, still float behind my polarized lenses.

'What scenario is that?' I say, not sure I want to hear it.

'That they truly love each other. Still.'

'Fuck you, Jim! You really get off on this stuff, don't you?' I say, annoyed that he has got my full attention now. I think this option sounds more wholesome, perhaps the way I want to think of her, and it is the one I had assumed especially after what I had heard about how intense their relationship was and the few things I had seen that they had written to each other right up till June. But I immediately see there is a catch in this preference. I am thinking of the words that were used by one of the people who knew about the affair—'besotted with each other'—not sure in which of Jim's scenarios this description is more appropriate. Reminded of those loving words, my stomach goes into a knot, and I shift in my chair. My hands need something to do, so I light another cigarette and watch the fingers of my right hand offer the filter to my mouth and twirl at the same time.

He is nonplussed by my outburst and stretches out his legs and finds something in the middle distance to focus on. Not wanting to commit either way, I say, 'Okay, that is the way she seemed to describe it, that they were very close. It was a deep and meaningful relationship. That much we have established. But why is this option even worse?'

'Well, think about it.' He leans forward again and tries to put me in Calix's shoes. 'How does he feel today, assuming she has called it off?' He leaves that possibility hanging. 'After nearly three years of being hopelessly in love with someone, it is suddenly ended by the married woman you are seeing. She has decided to stay with her husband, for whatever reason. She tells you she can never see or speak to you again because her husband has found out. You are bereft, and you can think of nothing but her and all your dreams of being together one day. She may have even promised you this, and you have waited patiently for her to make the move, but now she reneges. And you still live next door and see her driving past each day. You had all that daily contact with her, and access to her, and that is suddenly taken away. And you see him, that bastard of a husband whom she spoke so poorly of, all the time, who seems unruffled by a mountain-top chat with you and he waves and smiles at you when you drive past despite what you have done. If I was him, all this would drive me insane. If it was me I would develop a warped view of the situation and convince myself that the husband has stolen her away from me. I would be even more in love with her now because I can no longer have her.'

'You have quite an imagination,' I say, leaning over to retrieve the twirly-whirly that has slipped from my grasp but finding that it has rolled away beyond my reach. So I take a cigarette out of its box before I realise I am already holding one.

'Yes, I do. Anyhow, is he seeing anyone else now?'

'I don't know. All I can say is that there never seems to be anyone staying over, and he is always walking up the mountain or along the road on his own. And at the very beginning, when I found out, Sarah said something about feeling sorry for him as he will now be all alone.'

'So he is still in love with her, and this is dangerous for you,' Jim says, turning his conjecture into a foregone conclusion. 'Do you think this goes away overnight?' Without waiting for an answer, he says, 'And I bet it's the same for her.'

That supposition I want to ridicule with all my might. 'But Sarah said that she is able to cut things out of her life just like that. Cut-and-run was a matter of survival for her, she has learnt to do that all her life,' I say, even though I have never really believed that she can do this, not when this connection, by her own admission, was so deep.

But I know Jim's right; even if they are not sleeping together anymore they are still in love—their hearts and minds are joined forever in an eternal dance of love and I simply don't know how to deal with this. And when I have tried to coax her to reveal how she is coping with ending the relationship, it was always the same response—denial of the reality and angry indignation that I should have the gall to raise it and cutting insinuations that it is my weakness, my smallness, my ego, that cannot rise to the challenge.

Jim looks at me again as if he fears for my mental health and seems to weigh up how to say the next thing to me in words simple enough for me to understand.

'Clive, old buddy, life does not work like that. You know the situation I have been in for the last few years and the way I still feel about her and that she constantly fills my thoughts and it torments me. And we haven't even slept together. So trust me, I know.' His hand reaches out towards me but halts midair as he thinks better of this show of affection and camaraderie. 'Maybe over a very long time, and if you are very far away, but when you are right next door and the memories linger in your house, your bed, your consulting rooms and other places you still go to and around people you see, it takes a long time to fade. Even your children and her sister . . . what's her name again?'

'Roxanne.'

'Oh yes, Roxanne, who sometimes "puts on her red light" . . .'

'What are you talking about?'

'Never mind. They all occasionally remind her of him as they were involved in it all. Ever thought of whether she still wears the things he gave her? Does she still keep the pictures and love letters and poems?'

Feeling quite ill with all the possibilities, I say, 'I don't want to.' But I do think about it, and I know she does, and it still drives me mad.

'Well, you told me she does. I bet everyday he still puts that fresh flower in a vase that she can see from the road when she drives past, and they both wear those red sweaters. I can't think of a more hurtful thing for her to do to you now, and I bet he just loves to see her in it. He certainly flaunts it in front of you so he clearly feels nothing about your heartache.' I start to say something but Jim won't hear it. 'Fuck it, Clive, it's the least he can do, as he apparently doesn't have enough respect to move out and let you guys work it out without his energy next door. Can't you see it, their total disregard for you?' I blow smoke through the cylinder of the twirly-whirly. 'She can't change what she has done in the past and that she fell in love, but she now has full control over the choices she makes to show her commitment to you and put you at ease. It's vicious, inhuman, completely heartless, and she knows you will just accept it.'

He is getting really worked up, a mere consonant away from telling me I am a 'complete idiot'. 'Talking of cutting things out, have you found an answer to your question yet?'

The sudden change of tack confuses me. 'What question?'

'You know, you said you started going to a new psychotherapist to find a way to cut out the negative feelings you attach to things you think of, things that you are reminded of every day about the affair.'

'Oh, you mean the triggers. Yes, well, no. Actually, I haven't found an answer yet. Except that I have to face them head-on. Like having my first conversation with him and feeling okay afterwards or getting a massage from Sarah in her consulting rooms without being so freaked out by it and the heart-shaped stones lying about. I just have to start doing these things rather than be held hostage by them. The other evening I even took that grey candle with the three wicks and lay in the bath with the two good wicks burning.'

'I don't think this is the right way to describe the problem you have. The problem is that you are not convinced it is over, and she hasn't helped you with that. If you believed it was over, then you would simply say to yourself, "I am having a great massage from Sara-lea, and the history in this room does not matter".'

'You don't know what you are talking about,' I say, irritated with his oversimplification. And I am convinced it is not over. 'I don't think you can say that unless you've been in this situation.'

'My good-looking friend,' he says. 'The only way to deal with this is to change the way you see a situation, to reinterpret it positively, or at least, constructively.' We've been down that road before. 'But you can't do it selectively. You have to deal with the whole.'

'Yes, I realise that now. All these months I have been trying to deal individually with each part of the affair that upsets me. But it's a very long list, and it completely overwhelms me.'

'Because you are dealing with your feelings here, not an event or a fact. So if you cover up all your feelings, then you lose the positive stuff as well.' He speaks with the reassurance of someone who knows exactly what he is talking about.

'Jim, these are the unintended consequences that worry me a bit. I keep telling Sarah that what I need most is for her to fill in the blanks for me about the last three years. Otherwise I have to erase all of it from my memory banks because I can't talk about my time in the Middle East without referring to the experience my family had at home. I can't rub out those formative years from the boys when they refer so often to it. And I cannot pretend not to care how she probably still feels about him.'

'Yes. If you are a top sportsman, and you are nervous that you will lose a match, you can decide to not worry about whether you win or lose, but you have to be careful that you don't lose the passion that keeps you out there fighting for every point.' I am irked by how Jim likes to explain himself with little stories like this, and so aware that my passion for my marriage has at best assumed a holding pattern.

The table-of-four departs amidst much laughter and camaraderie but I am offered only her rear and I cannot descend into the bottomless blue pools of her soul.

'Jim, I get your point but that's the least of my worries right now. I'm much more devastated by the relentless, daily onslaught I get from her.'

Jim looks at his watch, drains his cappuccino, and gets up. 'Then what are you going to do about it? You must leave her before you go crazy. Oh, that reminds me.' He sits down again. 'I spoke to "Mouse" last night.' His wife.

'I'm sure that was a nice change for her.'

'I told her how Sara-lea treated you when you went out last weekend and her shocking accusations of you at the beach the other day and how even I felt guilty even though it wasn't directed at me. I have so frequently seen this kind of interaction between you, and that's why I avoid being near her.' I am only half-listening, wondering whether Jim ever calls his wife by her real name, when my cellphone beeps a text notification.

'Anyway, Mouse thinks Sara-lea is crazy and had a few choice words to say about her. You and me, we talk for an hour. My wife, she gets the point across in three precise sentences. She said that putting the phone down on someone, or blocking your ears in the middle of a conversation, is unacceptably rude, and she went on and on about respect and boundaries and how she is amazed you don't tell Sara-lea to back off when she behaves like this.'

'After what she did to herself and the boys? Get real, Jim. It's a miracle they survived, and I am on edge all the time and so scared I might do something that sets her off again.'

Ignoring my attempt to justify my behaviour, he says, 'Then Mouse asked me what you do with all your anger?'

I have lost count how often I have been asked this. I say, 'Is she also a psychiatrist?' I dial Sarah's cell number, but there is no response.

'And I told Mouse how she pretends to be busy at work but isn't.'

I say, 'Funny thing is, yesterday she was uncontactable.'

'Mouse?'

'The subject is Sarah. Yesterday she phoned to say she was going to collect a client at her house and may be out of cellphone range. But it's a weird thing to say. Not only was it just around the corner from her work, but she never tells me about her day, so why would she think to tell me this?'

'And you believe her? You trust her?' With a dismissive waft of his hand, he says, 'Even Mouse thinks you're crazy.'

'Jim, that was a message from the school. It seems Jeremiah is feeling unwell, and they texted to ask if we could fetch him early. Sarah works just around the corner from the school, and she could be with him till I get there, but I can't reach her. Do you think she could be on her way and her phone is on silent?'

Jim's look needs little interpretation, clear in his mind that I am deluding myself. I continue to try and reach Sarah on the phone, leaving text messages and voicemails.

'Don't you need to go now, Jim?' He mirrors the likely reality too strongly for me.

But Jim says, 'I hope the adult minder is with her,' and then goes on about how Sarah disrespects my feelings and my space and recites endless examples of this, like how I cannot work from home because my home office is continually overrun and used as a dumping ground. He describes what would happen in his house if some of his personal items were disturbed; it sounds like a concentration camp. He says he understands how my personality is one that accommodates and tolerates and allows for her personal history and that because she had nothing as a child she now needs to fill all the space around her to help her feel she exists. Getting no response out of me, Jim turns up the volume and says, 'Anyway, I said something else to Mouse last night. I told her I was scared shitless to even say the words.'

'If you're trying to build suspense and intrigue, it is not working,' I say. 'Just say it.'

His fingers rap the tabletop, and he cannot look me in the eye. 'Even though you are the most tolerant of fellows, I told her that if this goes on much longer, I am really worried that you will lose it, that you will kill her in a fit of rage.' I don't hear him clearly, and he has to repeat it. Then he retracts a little and says, 'Or else you will get really ill.' I just look at him. 'I really must go now, Clive.'

'Good.'

'But I will leave you with this,' he says, leaning towards me and filling my eyes with his face. He wags his index finger at me. 'I would sooner understand quantum physics than the inner workings of women. There's just no way to explain them. And they can be so cruel.' That word hits me in the solar plexus. 'You know, if a man does bad things, plays around a bit, that's what he does. Then he comes home and loves his wife. But women? They will not only do it, but they will make it as painful for you as possible. They will put the knife in and twist it. They are brutal. It's a mystery to me how they do it.'

16

Anger makes you smaller, while
forgiveness forces you to grow beyond
what you were.

(Cherie Carter-Scott)

Wednesday, 8 December 2010

Today we meet for coffee after I dropped the boys at school. It did not start well. She arrived ninety minutes late, and as she swept up to me, I asked her if she was okay and whether something kept her because I was concerned as I could not reach her on the cellphone. And then she lost it, yelling that I have all the time in the world, and there is no reason she needs to rush as I have nothing else of importance to do with my day.

So now, sitting on high bar stools at the coffee counter, there is so much tension in the air, but I don't want to raise it as I expect her to make it all about me. We have been talking about money, our monthly budget, and an expensive piece of equipment she wants to buy for her work but says she cannot because I do not have a regular, stable income—or at least, that is the way I heard it. Although she has always withheld from me how much she actually earns, I calculate that the price tag of this machine probably exceeds her annual income. When she refers to how her friends are helped out financially by their high-income husbands, I wonder why I feel responsible if she wants to purchase a piece of apparatus the cost of which should be covered by the increased earnings it produces for her part-time business. But for some reason I do. Then she clarifies any doubts I have about my inadequacies and I am horrified as I grab her put-down with both hands and realise just how bruised my ego really is.

Our conversation is stilted, the air-space between us reverberating with friction and hostility. She is only half-attentive and keeps checking her phone and looking through her appointment book, and it gets so argumentative that I am relieved when she brings up her psychotherapy schedule, which gives me the opportunity to change the topic and say something I think is hopeful.

'You said last week that Catherine feels you are in a good space, and I realise that I assumed this meant . . .'

It does not feel sustainable for her to continue as she is forever. The boys are feeling the strain and the impact of the restrictions placed on her movement with them. But I know it is actually me who is cracking up, and I want to ask her more directly how she is feeling or even about her psychiatrist's view and prognosis. But I am battling with my choice of words as I know that a direct approach will cause her to scarper, and she lunges at this because I am not just spitting it out as she does.

Sarah says, 'Just say it.'

So I say, 'It's just that I assumed it meant that you had processed things to a point where it had settled in a more comfortable space for you and that you are okay with yourself and with Calix.'

'So?'

'So my assumption was that this meant you have come to understand, for yourself, why it happened.'

'Why don't you tell me why you think it happened?' Is she referring to her affair with Calix or her attempt to take her life?

'I don't want to hypothesise about it,' I say and realise we are both avoiding naming either topic.

Sarah gets off her barstool, and walking away, she says, 'Think about it. I need to make a wee.'

Irritated by how she manages to insinuate a command in her tone, and knowing that on her return she will ask me for a response, I tell myself I will not oblige. But I have wondered about it, of course, and I cannot prevent myself from talking to her in my head as she makes the long trip up the stairs and halfway through the shopping centre to the public toilets. Just last Thursday, I had sat in front of Julia, my new psychotherapist, and responded to her question of what I thought went wrong in our marriage relationship. All the usual stuff came up—that we did not give enough attention to 'us', our dysfunctional communication, unresolved past issues, and so on.

Sarah comes back, and I think that was quick. Without a word, she picks up her cellphone and sets off again, and I wonder whether she wants to make a private call or is afraid I might steal a glance at her phone?

Then my thoughts leap back to therapy last week, when Julia said, 'That was then, Clive. What do you need now?' But I went completely mute; I just froze. So she coaxed me into talking to Sarah as if she was there, sitting on the unoccupied couch on my right. I turned my body towards the deserted couch on Julia's left. 'What would you really like to say to her?' Julia sweet-talked me.

I regretted having opened the topic, and it took a while for her to convince me to do this, to talk to the inanimate couch as if Sarah sat there, but after many false starts, I finally got something out. I took a deep breath and tried to decide which cushion to address. I was having great difficulty putting the appropriate passion into the words that seemed to spew without emotional tone from my mouth. I drank some water to get me going again, and it reminded me of how I used to stutter as a young child when I wanted to say something that the recipient may not like to hear and needed some distraction like an irrelevant but cooperative word beginning with a consonant to propel the errant tongue-tying vowel off my tongue. I told myself I was being ridiculous; she was not even here, and I was talking to a fucking cushion, for goodness sake!

Soon my hands were flapping and my voice was whining. I was afraid to pause in case I could not kick-start my sticky tongue again, but my mouth went dry, and I looked at Julia for help.

'This is so stupid, Julia. I can talk to an inert couch, but I can't talk with Sarah. That's the problem, don't you understand?'

'In therapy, you can say things and feel things that you can't always express elsewhere. It is useful. Why don't you just keep going?' Julia said, directing my gaze back to the unoccupied couch with her hand. I glance at the couch and then back at Julia. 'I wonder whether it will help if you talk to her about yourself, rather than her behaviour. Tell her that you are just trying to explain how you experience her behaviour. Tell her that you're trying to show her that it comes out in unintended ways, and that it puts you in a very negative space.'

'You just don't get it, Julia,' I said. 'This is just relationship trivia, not the real important challenges Sarah and I should be confronting with honesty. It feels so pointless.' No response. 'Fuck it. Okay. This child in me, wounded, if you like, by the guilt he felt by being blamed as the cause of his mother's condition, is still there . . .'

With a nod in the direction of the couch, Julia reminded me again that I was looking at her and not at 'Sarah'. I rubbed my eyes. For a moment I imagined my mother sitting there. Then the floodgates opened, and it all poured out. I had regressed to such an un-centred place, shaken by recent adverse events, that all the wounds from my own childhood were leaking in. I thought that no matter what Julia did now, I would keep right on talking, even if she left the room. I needed to hear myself say these things. They were not particularly revolutionary or ground-breaking insights; on the contrary, they were quite plain and simple truths. But I found, for a change, that I was not stating them in an objective fashion like I was observing and reflecting on someone else. I was really feeling them, with anguish and inner turmoil. Tears filled my eyes and made the couch swim. Suddenly my mother was sitting there again, blurred, and I had to blink rapidly to bring the mirage into focus as Sarah. I leaned forward in my seat, now angry with the couch. I wanted to leap out of my chair and pounce on it and rip the cushions apart.

Eventually Julia said, 'How would you like to conclude with her?' glancing at the clock. But I could not go on. I was shaking. My quivering lips would not cooperate. By then I was over at the couch, bent double, dripping tears on my knees and beating and shaking the cushions. A horrible sound squeezed through my clenched fists pressed against my mouth. It felt like an exorcism.

Julia waited and then said, 'That's enough for today.'

Sarah takes ages to return from the bathroom; I guess she has strolled around a bit before coming back. I ask the waitress for a bowl of water for the dogs, and while we wait, I let them sniff around on the manicured lawn across from the parking lot that buttresses the coffee bar counter at which we sit. I have another cigarette in my hand and have half made up my mind to not return to therapy again when Sarah sits down at our table, and I share none of my thoughts with her.

'So?' Sarah says, and I shrug and scratch Sally's ears. Reliving last Thursday's therapy session in her absence has left me traumatised.

'Well, I'm not going to say. You tell me what you think,' she says again, while these unspoken thoughts linger in my mind, and she gets busy again with her diary and cellphone. 'You have raised it, so you have the need, not me. It is not in my nature to sit down and have big conversations about things. I give you answers to these questions all the time, everyday.'

'Sarah, I'm not actually asking you to tell me why you think it happened. I'm just asking whether you have come to some conclusions for yourself, which may or may not be different from what you originally thought.' Which topic should I go for? I look away and play with my cigarette box. Have I not learnt from the way our discussions have gone the last few days? I am feeling so wound up that it takes an immense effort not to have a go at her. I pick the topic of 'affair' in preference to 'attempted suicide', though I suspect the answers might be similar. 'In fact, I am only raising it because six months ago you said that this was the only thing you were prepared to talk about—*why* it happened. I'm really just asking if you're okay. But you don't have to say.'

'You are always on the periphery. There, that's one answer to your question,' she says, her chameleon-like tongue folding out her mouth to rest its point on her chin, a gesture I have learnt coincides with unkind feelings of one-upmanship and spite. She makes it sound like she narrates the copy on the page and I am a footnote or a comment in the side column, and I think this is a great metaphor of life with her.

Just for a moment I consider again whether to tell her what I think the reasons are, but instead, I say, 'Sarah, I feel like I have to solve a riddle to find answers to this question of why.'

'I am not good at accessing my own feelings,' she says. 'I only feel things through the feelings of others. I feel muzzled because of the life I have had and how I have had to deal with things.'

'I understand that, or try to.' And you are exceptionally skilled at intuiting the feelings of others. 'It's just that I am surprised that the work you have been doing with Catherine has not brought you to this place . . .'

This seems completely out of context, bringing Catherine into it. The reason I raised this to start with seems to be lost and the conversation drifts until we have an excuse to end it because she has to go to an appointment. I walk her to her car, and before she climbs in, she gives me a piece of her mind and tells me how upset she is with me and that I am rude and have abused her by what I said; all the usual labels that just leave me cold. Is she feeling so worthless she needs to debase me? Two vehicles have stopped alongside us, one on the left and the other on the right, like jousting knights-in-armour on their steeds with revving lances at the ready and a 'mine is bigger than yours' declaration, waiting for her to vacate the sought-after parking bay. The drivers are gesticulating to each other arguing over who was there first. But they soon forget their differences when they find the dressing down I am getting to be much more interesting. When it seems like she is finished, as she walks around me and opens her car door, I start to say something but realise I am about to defend myself, and I pause mid-sentence.

'Go on, say it,' she says, wanting something else to have a go at. 'Say it!' she screams.

I lower my eyes and fight the temptation to glance over at our audience. 'It's okay, Sarah, you need to go now.'

'Now you're just trying to control me,' she says, because I won't finish what I started to say, and drives off.

Later, I am busy preparing for a client's end-of-year strategy session scheduled for next week over a belated finger lunch when Sarah phones me after three o'clock. 'The boys are going to a party at four o'clock. Join us. Don't be late.' She puts the phone down.

I call her back. 'Sarah, I did not know about the party. I am working and have a few errands to run, so I will join you after that. I won't be long.' But this does not settle well with her.

I arrive at the party at four thirty and Jordan is the first adult I encounter. Sarah sees me walk through the garden gate, makes a point of looking at her watch, and makes a beeline for me. I know that in her mind she has concocted a story that confirms her belief that I committed to four o'clock and that I am late.

'Here she comes,' Jordan says through lips that don't move, her face locked into a gruesome smile.

Sarah is fuming. 'Why are you so late? You said four o'clock; you might as well not have come! It's almost time to go.'

'Sarah, I said I will come when I can.'

'I'm Sara-lea!'

I ignore it and say to Jordan, 'Where's Matt?'

'He's busy. He'll come later, if at all,' Jordan says. 'The party ends at six, so there's plenty of time.' Foolishly, I thought that strengthened my case. But Jordan does not appreciate being drawn into the fray and heads off in search of a more pleasant conversation, which she is likely to find just about anywhere.

I look at my watch even though I don't want to, as my automatic reaction is to point out that the party only started thirty minutes ago, but I catch myself midstream; this is not about the time of my arrival. Logic and reason have no part to play in this discussion.

'I have to get the kids home to feed them supper. You're always late.'

Actually, it is Sarah who always arrives home later than the time she promises, and this gets a rise out of me, as it always does. I usually resort to establishing the facts and reminding her of them, but her preconceived view always stubbornly remained and continued to influence her reasoning as if the proof was irrelevant for her. I found this frustrating in the extreme. Fortunately Jeremiah has spotted me and runs over to greet me, and Sarah walks away leaving words of disgust in her wake.

As it turns out, the party is a roaring success, and it's me who has to encourage Sarah to leave as it is nearing six thirty, and I can sense a meltdown from all corners. We are about to turn into our driveway, when Calix reverses out of his, and Sarah looks the other way as I have to wait for him. The boys wave to him amid squeals of, 'There's Calix! Please can we say hello to him?'

'Next time,' I say, and smile at him as he drives off. It's bizarre, I know.

Inside now, Sarah opens the refrigerator and removes a Tupperware of leftover pasta from dinner two nights ago. There is perhaps enough for one extra-large single adult helping left. 'Oh no,' she says, making a show of looking deep into the container as if it is difficult to find any food inside and then at me with accusation. 'Who ate the pasta?'

Here we go again. 'Um, I had some for lunch,' I say, red lights flashing, 'Danger—evacuate immediately' in my head.

'I can't believe you. What am I going to give the children for dinner?'

'I'm sorry, Sarah. I didn't know you wanted to give it to them tonight.' I step towards her, trying to keep my voice low so as to not arouse the boys' attention. 'It was in the fridge and would not last another day. I really thought I should eat it. Anyway, they have eaten a lot at the party. Perhaps we should just add something to what's there and make a meal of it?'

'I can't believe you did that. You're so self-centred!' Vapours from her bitterness waft over to me and seep in through my pores.

My mind's command to convince my body to just walk away does not take hold quickly enough. 'Sarah, this is ridiculous,' I plead with open palms. 'How was I to know?'

'You're selfish! I'm going to teach you to be unselfish!'

What I like to assume is my patience with her, fending off her attacks and accusations all day, lets me down, and I cannot let this go without challenging it. 'So now you're my self-proclaimed teacher? Perhaps you've forgotten that you teach what you most need to learn, Sarah.'

'Now you're being rude. Stop trying to control me!'

I don't say aloud, 'Are you talking to yourself, Sarah?'

Ecstasy Of Betrayal

17

```
Pain is inevitable.
Suffering is optional.
```

```
        (M. Kathleen Casey)
```

Thursday, 9 December 2010

'And so his wife says, "Do you think you can be with only one person for the rest of your life?" and he says, "Yes" but is clearly perplexed by the direction of the conversation. This is right at the beginning of the movie, and they are having dinner together at a restaurant. Then she says, "Have you never thought you would like to sleep with somebody else?" And he says, "No, I only want you. I promise". So she says, and this was interesting for me, "It is not a promise. It is a choice".'

I am in Julia's quiet therapy rooms, shrouded by huge milkwood trees, and the birds outside chirp a happy tune, which contrasts sharply with my mood today. It is hot and muggy, and I would rather be swimming in the pool or the ocean. I have kicked off my sandals, and my right leg has found its way over the arm of the easy chair in which I spend this fifty-minute hour every week, each time swearing it is the last one I will attend, and after my 'goat-horn' conversation with Jim I am hardly in the mood.

I am telling my therapist Julia about a movie, a new release on DVD. Sarah did not want to watch it with me, as I had expected; she just emitted a dismissive sigh and tossed her head when I told her last week that I was going to watch this movie sometime. Initially I had wanted

Sarah to see just how much I was hurting because of what she had done and that I was reminded of it everywhere I turned. But now I felt it was high time I risked breaking through some of these barriers that were affecting my life. And that is probably why I was so keen to face that first real encounter with Calix.

'Which is,' I feel I need to remind Julia, 'the point I keep making to Sarah—that we were both unhappy but that it was her choice to sleep with another man. At least, the wife in the movie chose to be unfaithful on another continent, not in their marital bed with the neighbour.'

Julia seems to be waiting for me to go somewhere with this.

'Anyhow, the husband seems to be in possession of his wife's cellphone and checks her voicemail, and there is a message from a man who does not name himself but who says how much he can't wait to see her again. Next thing, the husband is searching through her laptop and comes across some clearly incriminating emails and then he really delves into it and finally manages to crack a password to a folder called "Love" in which he finds pictures of his wife and her lover naked together in a foreign city. So there is his proof, no doubt about it. And he is enraged to murder, so he sets about finding this man and befriends him and plots to kill him. At one stage, he even picks up a hammer to bludgeon him to death, but instead, he decides to trick him and plays him along and finally discloses his true identity as her husband.'

I stop for air.

'What meaning does this have for you?' Julia says.

'Fucking shrinks,' I think to myself, but I have only myself to blame for pitching up here today. I cast a disparaging look at the inanimate couch, which seems to have forgiven me my indiscretions of last week.

I say, 'Well, I think at this stage I wanted Sarah to see just how tormented this man was. It seemed strange to me that he did not take it out on his wife, like I have. Instead, he dropped his entire life to go in search of this man and wreak revenge. And for a moment I wondered if this is the masculine energy you speak of. Because if it is, I am seriously deficient, especially as I had a long friendly chat with Calix some time ago that I still want to tell you about. In fact, I haven't confronted him at all.'

I glance at the clock, anxious that we will run out of time before I have said all the things I think I want to say today. I am completely exasperated and at my wits' end. It is not just the awful day-to-day experience of our relationship, of conversations loaded with repugnant repressions, barbed criticisms slashing away at me, reducing me, each affront accumulating until it fetches a lurching retort from me, but that I feel I am simply not equipped to deal with Sarah's mental state. When I say it like that it seems more hopeful as it can be thought of as temporary, and that is the only optimism that keeps me hanging in there. But if it is her personality, who she really is, then it leaves me in despair because it is the way it will always be, and I have not yet solved the conundrum of how to respond to it in a way that does not leave me so appallingly affected. And I seem devoid of the resolve to leave her.

'And to show her that keeping things he gave her is so hurtful,' I say, 'like the stuff she wears or the "I love you so much" messages and pictures she insists on keeping on her email. This stuff drove the husband completely insane; once he had managed to crack the password, he kept on scrolling through these pictures of them naked together with a mixture of disbelief and outrage. You could just see how it rolled on like a slide show in his mind every hour of the day and night, and I know exactly how that feels; it's relentless, that torment. The other thing, of course, is that the husband seemed to throw any respect for privacy right out the window. From that point on, nothing was out of bounds. And I wanted Sarah to see this as I am still angry with her for being so upset that I had dug into her personal things when she denied the affair and later when she kept being dishonest with me about what had actually happened. And then I was stupid enough to confess this to her and apologise.'

'So you are angry with yourself.'

I look at Julia. Why is this always about me? I need to deflect the discomfort I feel and say, 'What should I make of the fact that another of Sarah's ex-boyfriends has just moved into the area? That would make it four that I know of, including Calix.'

'What do you make of it?'

'Probably nothing. I think that's a good option.'

'Let's divide this into three separate topics,' she says, sensing my feeble attempt to sidetrack the conversation and trying to be helpful. 'We can talk about Sarah and what you think is going on for her, or we can talk about what is going on between the two of you in your relationship today, or we can talk about you.' While speaking, she cups her hands together and places three invisible boxes in the air. 'One of the things you need to think about is whether you want to stay victim to the affair. It serves a purpose for you by giving you something to focus on, and you can direct your anger at her or at him and not really deal with yourself. For months now, you have put much of your life on the back burner. You have become obsessed with the affair and questions about the future of your marriage and, of course, dealing with what she did to herself and your boys. But do you want to stay there? You can choose to if you want, but you must realise that this game has a pay-off for you.'

'Okay,' I say, 'so let's talk about our relationship because it has been a ghastly week in that regard.'

Julia says, 'It seems to me like you feel you have to resort to movies to communicate to her what you feel, so let's talk about your interaction. How is that going this week?'

'It's shocking. We discussed that last week, and I'm sure we don't want to waste time here with examples, but anything that refers to the affair or her feelings, like to ask her how she is doing, is like showing a red flag to a bull. This week I have been guilty of wanting to raise parts of the affair in some way as a way of trying to explain where I am at. What sparked this off is that I heard more stories the other day.' I stop because I don't really want to go there because it makes me feel anxious just to think of the possibility that the affair is still going on.

Julia coaxes me, 'What stories?'

'You know—stories, rumours, gossip, and hearsay. The unpleasant truth. Whatever the fuck you want to call it, depending on your point of view.' The expletive is my way of projecting my hurt and uncertainty on to Julia, but I have no intention of apologising. 'Stories that are no less incriminating than the first ones I heard. In fact, when I think of it now, those ones were more about seeing things that did not fit, that seemed suspicious, and how the two of them acted when they were together or something that was said. These stories, the ones I have just heard, are more direct. People are stating it as fact, saying that she is still having an affair.'

'Clive, I want to try something. Over there, there are about 200 objects of all sorts,' Julia says, pointing to her box of tricks. 'I want you to select three or four items, and then arrange them as you wish in this sandbox. Take all the time you need.'

I am not enthralled by the prospect of this game, but right now it feels like a better option than talking. So I close my eyes and bury my hands in the container, feeling for something that seems to speak to me. I choose a hefty screw, encrusted with rust, a little silver helix that has been bent out of shape, and a little antelope. I avoid anything that resembles a heart-shape to the touch. But I end up with four items as something clings to the antelope's horns; it is a little charm of a fisted hand, the index finger outstretched, pointing, attached to what looks like a key ring with a ball.

I am at a loss to explain my choices to Julia, so she offers her interpretations. 'That corroded phallus,' she says, 'that's the state of your masculine energy and sexual vitality. And you're being screwed, big time.' She pauses, letting it sink in, or maybe wondering how to be a little less brutally direct. 'That misshapen spring over there? It should be infinitely flexible, able to shoulder any burden, but it can no longer work. Why? Because it has been so manipulated that it is bent and twisted and deformed out of shape. It can never return to what it was; no matter how much it tries, it will never be fully functional again and never fit for the purpose for which it was originally designed. There is no elasticity, no bounce or suppleness, or ability to absorb the knocks, and like the ruined suspension of a car, it can no longer soften the bumpy road. The entity it is designed to support, that being, will fall apart from the resultant damage in the long-term. Does that feel like you?' It seems like she is quite enjoying herself. 'And that accusatory finger and the threat of violence promised by the clenched fist . . .'

'Wait, let me have a go now.' I say, her analysis ringing its indictment in my ears. I feel like I am trussed up in a bell tower at midnight, 'gong . . . gong . . . gong' endlessly reverberating through my bones. 'Okay, I can see the image of "a firm grip" on me. It's fierce and brutal, or threatens to be so. It's closed off, too, like it holds closely-guarded secrets never to see the light of day. And now that I see it displayed in the sand tray, I see it's actually attached to a little ball-and-chain, the yoke of bondage and oppression of the type convicts used to haul around. When the chain is slack, there's just a transitory moment of freedom, or the hint, the possibility, the illusion of it, but then it yanks you back and reminds you there's just no escape from it. It's a constant encumbrance on your liberty, your free will. Your spirit can never soar.' I hold my head in my hands.

'And what about the antelope?'

'Well, that's a very interesting one, which has very recently acquired new meaning for me. It's the cornuted cuckold, the last person to know about his wife's infidelity.' And I tell her how I was presented with one this morning, left in anonymity on the bonnet of the Jeep, and how Jim concluded our earlier discussion at the deli.

'So where does that leave you?' I have the impression Julia is quite affected by all of this.

'I don't want to think about it. The gift of the horns could be malicious, and the rumours could be mistaken. All I'm saying is that I think the stories provoked the stuff I said to her recently, so they are obviously niggling me. But I think I have dismissed them, for now at least. What else can I do, without proof? And I just don't have the inclination or the heart to start digging around again.'

'I mean where does this exercise leave you?'

'Oh. I suppose . . . Screwed yet celibate, and um . . . manipulated, blamed, controlled, and hamstrung. And practically dysfunctional.' The words seem such an indictment on me, and I want to hide them away. I want to threaten her if she mentions them to anybody. 'For fuck sake, Julia, it sounds so pathetic! So I ask you again, is the way I have approached this whole thing—the affair, my marriage, Sarah's condition, her behaviour, everything—defeating my masculine energy, my male potency?'

'If it is directed towards a constructive end, rather than coming from a place of insecurity, that is what we are talking about,' says Julia.

'That's totally unhelpful to me, Julia, and convincing myself that I do not feel insecure feels like an exercise in self-delusion; just ignore all the flashing red lights and carry on regardless. I don't know how to do it without it feeling like a semantic manipulation. All I seem to need from her is open and honest conversation, no more secrets and intrigue. But our conversations get all fucked up. The problem is, I'm so torn up about her betrayal *and* our dysfunctional relationship, the way she treats me—it's a double-whammy.'

'If it feels impossible to communicate, why don't you try a technique like holding a talk-ball and only the person with the ball can speak . . .'

I am already shaking my head and cut her short. 'She would rather die than do that.'

'Or like I have said before, you need a mediator or couple therapist to help you have these conversations.'

'I've told you, she has refused to go to therapy with me since the beginning, ever since we saw Vincenzo, which was terrible for her. So what else is there?'

'Without any of these options, frankly, I don't have much hope for your communication improving. And if you can't talk together about these things, then, I hate to say this, but it seems like you feel there is no way forward for you in this relationship. So do you feel you are able to let go of the need to have those conversations about your relationship or the affair for a while?' she says.

'Yes, maybe, I don't know. I haven't raised anything since she closed down and refused to speak further about it, months ago, and certainly not since her attempted suicide. That scared the shit out of me—that I caused her breakdown. Like I said, the rumours brought it up for me again, seeing what transpired with Calix on the road the other evening and now these fucking horns. Until now I have been trying to deal with each aspect separately, like letting the demon out of the cage by fully revealing to myself the entire extent of it, bit by bit. But it has overwhelmed me because there are so many things that it has touched, and it has invaded our whole relationship to the extent that it seems like there is nothing left that is special to us.' I stare out of the glass-fronted door, trying to locate the birds in the trees as I cannot look at Julia; I am so appalled by hearing my own immaturity and confessing it to another.

She says, 'You need to think about reclaiming your space, to continue the rituals you shared that were special to your relationship or build new ones.'

'I know this. I'm just grappling with it at the moment. In fact, we had this huge argument because I don't respond to her when she says to me "I love you". I told her that I don't know what that means any more. That's how bad it is. As a close friend of mine said, their love still lives on in their hearts.'

'What does it mean to you?' she says.

'What?' I bark at her. 'What does "I love you" mean?' Julie nods. 'I don't know and don't care right now. All I know is that I can't say those words to her, and maybe I'm just sulking about everything, and I am scared to put my heart on the line. Anyhow, I think I have come to the conclusion that I need to smother it all with a blanket. Just choke it off at its source so that none of its fucking tentacles can reach out and get a grip on me at any time it chooses.'

'A blanket?'

'Yes, the whole thing, the last three years. Everything! Completely suffocate it. Snuff it out. Even if there is some collateral damage and I lose some of the good memories, that's just too bad.'

Julia has a concerned look on her face. 'So you are denying yourself opportunities to have a good time with her or share intimate moments?'

But I ignore her question and continue, 'Early on, I wrote her a long letter spewing out all my hurt and ugly feelings, and at the time, I was thinking, "How do I kill off Calix?" and I think I have found the answer to that.'

Julia scribbles a few notes in her book and then says, 'How do you propose to do this?'

'I will figure that out.' That is for me to know, and it feels like this is the gift I have been waiting for and I have been searching for all along and that there must be something in it for me at the end of all this pain. The answer to the question—'What's in it for me?'

Julia looks at the clock and leans forward in her chair, indicating that our time is up.

'But I haven't told you the most fascinating part in the movie,' I say, slipping into my sandals. 'When the husband finally confronts the lover and unveils the masquerade, disrobes himself so to speak, to reveal that he is the husband, he also tells her lover that she is actually dead.' Julia looks at me. 'Isn't that absurd—all that over a dead woman?'

18

Never inquire into another man's secret;
but conceal that which is entrusted to
you, though pressed both by wine and
anger to reveal it.

(Horace)

Sunday, 19 December 2010

That Thursday, the day before she disappeared, was the day we shared those ugly words about separating. The goat's horns I showed him earlier that morning safely tucked out of sight in the car, after therapy Jim offered me the release of chasing a flying disc across the beach after which we cooled down at the deli. He kept trying to raise the cornuted issue, wanting me to commit to action. 'What are you going to do about it?' he kept saying, but it felt like this was for his own gratification and I would not allow the topic to get traction. Sarah phoned just after Jim left the deli and I was making friends with another 'red cappuccino'. My mind was settled in its turmoil. Jim would no doubt later pay homage to the gods of choreography that he had evaded her.

'We are coming to say hello. They want to see you,' she said from her car, and I heard the boys yelling in the background, a sibling fight clearly on the rampage. I hoped the au pair was with them, more so for my real fears than the legal requirements.

My mind was still busy with the content of psychotherapy and cornuted cuckolds, so I said to the voice on the telephone, 'Um . . . Okay. Actually, I thought we were meeting at home just now?'

'We are outside the restaurant already,' she said.

'That's okay, then.' Perhaps I can show her the goat's horns? Or does she already know?

I did all the right things, or so I thought. I quickly packed up my stuff so that I could give them all my attention, and then I went outside to her car to greet them all and helped her bring the boys inside. All told, their arrival held little promise. Little Jack was not feeling well again as his morning dose of painkillers had likely worn off by now, and he had an intense headache as his little body tried to ward off the infection. Jeremiah was exhausted after school sports practice. Joshua seemed to be sulking. Saying 'hello' to the au pair, I picked up Jack and Jeremiah and carried them to the restaurant table where I had been sitting. Then I went to the bathroom, and Jack followed me there and asked, 'Whose cappuccino is that?'

'Pardon?' I said, looking for the cappuccino to which he referred and not immediately comprehending what he was asking.

'Mommy wants to know,' he said, and then I understood. Sarah was suspicious or, as she would put it, just needing to join the dots when things seem out of place.

'Oh, it was Jim's.'

'I'm going to tell Mommy,' he said.

I followed him back to the table and overheard him repeat my response to her question. She was bristling with anger.

'But Jim is not left-handed,' Sarah said, eyeing the empty coffee cup he had left behind and then looking at me. The things she notices, that bother her, never cease to astound me.

'No, but that was his,' I said. Is it just me who is tense, or am I imagining that she is pretty freaked out?

'That is not Jim's,' she said, stabbing a finger emphatically at me, as if she has caught me red-handed with something. 'Whose is it?'

'Sarah, it was Jim's, and he has just left.'

She repeated the question, louder.

Regretting that I had not hightailed it out the back entrance when they arrived, I leaned forward, incensed now, hissing, 'It was Jim's,' wishing I could think of another way to put it. 'I do not lie to you.' The insinuation was clear as daylight that I thought she did not extend me the same courtesy.

From that moment on, it just got worse. Everything bothered and agitated her—little imperfections in the music, the cutlery, the people, the traffic, and mostly me. I tried to visualise her senses saturated beyond their capacity. She ignored me and would not respond to my efforts at conversation and, for long moments, just stared at me. Then it escalated and she threw at me everything obnoxious she could think of, and it was with steely determination that I kept my reaction muted. Perhaps this just frustrated her more, unable to deposit her pain on me?

Soon Jack was complaining about his stomach being sore, and I wondered how much of this was psychosomatic. He wanted to go home and insisted on going with me, while the other two hesitated as if they did not want to go with either of us. Despite the heat and humidity of the early afternoon, sticky enough to encourage near-nakedness, I noticed that Sarah was wearing a long-sleeved sweater, the cuffs of which extended to her palms, and with growing concern I wondered what self-inflicted misery it concealed.

Sarah pushed back her chair and said, 'Bye, *Clive*,' with the emphasis on my name, so I mimicked her with, 'Bye, *Sarah*,' in similar fashion.

'Piss off!' she said and walked to her car.

The few patrons sitting around us turned their heads and stared at me with derision. They happened to be females, and I wondered if this was why they seem to have judged me. Driving home behind her, her text message announced that she was going out again that evening. I avoided what she was really asking by responding, 'You deserve some time-out, and it is always good for you to spend time with Angela.' And I dismissed any miserable thoughts from my mind as I was determined to not allow these things to constrain my recovery, but I knew I had to make a move, if not for me, then for the boys.

—◦◦◦—

Later that afternoon, I could not find her anywhere in the house. Calling out her name, I followed the weathervane of the dogs' wagging tails which came to a standstill at the lounge curtains which were drawn closed. Peeking through the gap, I saw her sitting on a chair on the now-shaded East-facing balcony, with a cup of tea in her hands. I knocked on the glass sliding doors she had closed to separate herself from us and gestured a request for permission to join her. She did not respond—just stared into the distance. So I slid open a small gap in the doors I hoped would not prove to be offensive and offered her another cup of tea for which I got no response.

'Sarah,' I said, standing a little distance from her as I thought that was what she would prefer, 'I think we need to consider separating for a while to find a way through this.'

'Then go,' she said to the balustrade.

'We need to talk about how to do this, Sarah. Let's set aside some time. We need to agree how to manage the boys, and who should move out of . . .'

'I am not leaving this house or the children.'

So I grabbed a towel and went outside and jumped in the pool, and Harry and Sally brought their tennis balls for me to throw for them. The shock of cold water brought on an instant headache which I am sure was already there. Then I sat in the garden near the cooling waters of the pool, which reflected rippling colours and smoked a cigarette. And there I stayed until Angela came and collected her, and off they went to some or other event or presentation about natural medicine and health-related concerns or 'green living' in our village.

She did this mid-week from time to time, usually followed by drinks or a meal with her friend Angela, and she usually returned all the better for it, except for that night. But it surfaced harrowing memories of that night she locked me out the house and the shocking scene to which I had returned. The difference this time was that the talk was held at a wellness retreat just below us in the valley. It is called Phakalot (pronounced Pah-kah-lo), which Angela rather disingenuously calls 'Fuck-a-lot', and I wondered whether she was aware of the hurtful irony in this as he, Sarah's other man, had helped to design and build this venue, which is owned by his ex-wife, and it is one of the places they frequented together mistakenly secure in the belief that they could safely interact in the public eye without the true nature of their relationship being exposed.

The children needed their dinner, and I busied myself with final preparations and got them to the dinner table. Much as I tried to distract myself with childlike chatter and playfulness, I struggled to sit through dinner. I just could not bear the thought of them together that evening, even if it was over, and especially if it was not. The shared smiles and knowing glances and sneaked touches that would only be noticed and questioned by the astute, as it was all those months ago, littered my mind. Mostly I was irritated with myself, struck by the amount of insecurity I felt and that I had not really moved on from this in the way I thought I had. But what was coming at me these last few days, was coming thick and fast, relentlessly, and I was porous and had soaked it all up, and I sat at the dinner table heavy and drenched.

I had chosen to be here despite having a good sense of the situation I was in, and I had set myself the task of conquering my ego's response to the betrayal, persuaded that I would learn valuable lessons from it. Sometimes I wondered whether I was afraid of what it would mean to have another failed marriage, or of what people might say—'Clive could not deal with it, what a typical male ego response.' And always, of course, the hope that we could one day find the magic again. So I told myself I was being ridiculous; that even if they were still seeing each other it would come out in time and my decision, the action I needed to take, would be clear, rather than continue to linger in ambiguity as it currently was.

I wanted so badly to put it away, but Jim's scenarios and goat's horns and rusty phalluses and manipulated spring coils lurked and won the day. I felt driven to act, to find out for myself. I think I was looking for the proof I needed to make my decision irrevocable. So I told the boys we were going for a drive before bedtime, to see the stars through the sunroof of the car. Once in the car, I encouraged them to watch the night sky and drift off to sleep while I cruised slowly along the roads surrounding Phakalot, looking for his car, and looking for a couple furtively embracing in the shadows. But the roads were full of cars, and he could have parked anywhere, some distance from the venue if he was wise, especially after he knew I saw him leave his house shortly after Angela collected Sarah, when I had taken the wheelie-bin out. Just like 'Pink Wednesday', I thought. Short of entering the venue and taking a look, I would never actually be sure whether he was there. My car was easily recognizable and I was afraid that Sarah, or someone who knew us, might see me. I started to feel foolish, and the embarrassment of having to explain what I was doing began to override my insecurity.

The boys were tiring of the adventure and wanted to go home. With anxiety growing I retraced my route countless times until, with a sense of almost universal reprieve, I saw what I had come to see, and we could go home. His car suddenly leapt out at us, exposed behind a truck as we paused at the traffic roundabout; him sitting in the driver's seat and our eyes locked and neither of us could move if that is what we wanted to do. I looked for signs of her in his vehicle but could see nobody else there, unless she was crouching low in that undersized excuse for vehicular transport, which only brought on the horror image that she was going down on him and I had misinterpreted his open-mouthed caught-in-the-act expression. Someone behind me sounded a frustrated horn, and I swore at them and him and her and drove home in shock, the artillery in my head firing salvoes trying to reason with itself.

'Sarah is not inclined to perform that act,' Experience said.

'It's only with you she doesn't like it,' Self-doubt responded.

'Crap, it was one of the most demeaning acts of her childhood abuse and she has never been able to bring herself . . .' Pity complained

'How do you know? You've never actually asked her,' Logic questioned.

'She hates what she sees as gratuitous sexual acts, one-sided pleasure-giving,' Sexual frustration argued.

'Well, she's loving it now,' Imagination taunted.

'And she'd never bring herself to do it in a public place, in a car, for goodness sake,' Denial refuted.

'Just how do you think they got their rocks off when you were in town and he lives next door?' That was Jim's voice. 'Fuck off, Jim!'

That was just ten days ago, and I feel like I am reliving that sordid tour of Phakalot's environs. Who knows what may have transpired at that place that night? What was he doing there, in his car? I am not so sure anymore that she was with him; I think I imagined what I wanted or expected to see, but he looked so desperate, so alone, his life force sitting, ghost-like and unkempt, alongside him.

But what I do know are the words I read in her journal that evening while I imagined the interplay at Phakalot.

Perhaps, putting it all together, it was all cumulatively just too much for her, and she had to leave?

Or maybe she is dead?

I have only questions, no answers.

19

Anyone who hasn't experienced the
ecstasy of betrayal knows nothing about
ecstasy at all.

(Jean Genet)

Thursday December 9, 2010 (continued)

I am aware that Sarah has always kept a journal, ever since I have known her, and she said this had started in childhood. In recent months during her morning quiet times I have assumed she maintained this practice. Sarah has gone with Angela to Phakalot and the boys are asleep, somewhat disappointed with our evening tour of the village. I pace around fettered by an imaginary ball-and-chain, and every which way I turn I see goat's horns and rusty phalluses and Calix sitting in his car trying to make himself invisible. So I start rummaging around, everywhere I can think of that I have not yet looked, and even where I have already searched a few months ago. I realize, with some frustration, that it is a fairly superficial search, assuming she really wanted to hide it. Perhaps she has even stored her journals somewhere other than in the house, for safekeeping, especially when she became aware I was on the lookout for incriminating evidence?

My hands are trembling, my lips quivering, and my thoughts, for the first time, are of revenge. Finally I am in our bedroom. I get temporarily waylaid staring at the items she still keeps that I previously identified were most likely from him, and other keepsakes she might associate with him. There are no doubt other innocuous things and not-so-inoffensive cherished gifts of which I am unaware. These are things she had refused to disclose to me or to tuck away out of sight or to discard or return to him. The intimate and erotic nature of some of them send my thoughts down a path of pain and betrayal and I have to fight hard to eradicate it from my mind. I turn my eyes from the lingerie he gave her and remind myself I want to find something that I don't yet know about. Strangely, the things that are not so erotic seem more intimate and really hurt as a reminder of how close they were or are.

Her bedside table is locked and I have a sudden desperation to get access to it even if it just gives me something to focus on. I try to find a key that fits on her clutch of work keys that carries keys of such great number and variation she could be mistaken for a locksmith. Using the spare key, soon I am in her car probing for concealed compartments that could secret away a key. Hoping that through their open bedroom windows that face the driveway I will hear the boys if they cry out for me, I am virtually dismantling it, but am at last rewarded with the find of two small keys taped inside a deep recess in a way that clearly suggests they were not meant to be stumbled upon.

Back inside, I kneel down and unlock her bedside table and pull everything out of it and then re-pack them with care. I come across a handful of books I had not yet seen; two of them about shame and guilt, one bold enough to entitle itself such. My heart goes soft. This is how it always was for me—the pendulum swing of deciding her behaviour was unbearable for me, then realizing how she was besieged by her demons.

I pick one up, attracted by the deformed curvature of its cover. The dull serrated steel of the steak knife she seems to use as a bookmark slithers to the carpet. I cannot bring myself to touch it, so I lean forward; it has dark stains on the jagged cutting edge. Then I open a thin A4 notebook, otherwise unremarkable except that it is similar in appearance to the journal I had months ago, when seeking evidence to counter her denials, found in her car. That one stashed in her car was current; it covered just a few weeks, and I had randomly scanned one or two paragraphs before closing it and deciding that I did not want to read it. This one has her handwriting flowing across the unlined pages, and I do want to read it.

I flick through it; lots of pages covered edge to edge in her often difficult-to-read script, interspersed with lots of blank pages and others graced with beautiful, colourful 'mandalas' she had created. She would start with an inverted coffee cup-sized circle of about ten centimeters in diameter, then begin filling it with symmetrical shapes and colours. I know she used this as a form of therapy, of meditation, which she occasionally had interpreted for her. I was at a loss for what they might reveal about her psyche. This journal starts mid-April, of this year I assume. I flip to the back of the book and find a smattering of pages written much more recently, a few dated October and November, which confirms that she is busy with at least two journals. I stand up and page through from the beginning, scrolling rapidly down each page with my finger, looking, I suppose, for something referring to him, as this records her thoughts a few months before I had interfered with their cozy arrangement and made known my awareness that she had another man in her life. I smile wryly; little did I know the extent of it when I confronted her.

Of her breakdown and hospitalisation and the horrific deeds that preceded it, there is no mention. Instead, most of it seems to be about how she is feeling each day; an altercation with me, or last night's dream-premonition to which she attaches such meaning, then something about a difficult night's sleep and how the boys are doing, that kind of thing. I am not reading it, just scanning to pick up key words; my scrolling slows only when I pick up something that seems of interest. There is a lot of stuff about us and me, one part saying how clever and manipulative I am in putting her into a corner and using what she has divulged as information to later catch her out. And she often wrote of how I scare her, how I frighten her whole being, and I am horrified at how she thought of me. The way she describes it hints of paranoia; an obsessive fear of being found out, of being vulnerable if her secrets are unveiled, or of dreadful childhood memories being evoked and relived.

As I take some of this in, it occurs to me that nothing she writes about me sounds promising or even wishful, like I am evil personified and at pains to destroy her, and it reminds me that she recently said that the negative far outweighs the positive. There is also a lot of inner turmoil reflected in these pages, being upset with her dark side, her ugliness, her past, her 'white trailer-trash' family. Not all the pages are dated, and when they are it is not always chronological, as if she sometimes simply opened to a blank page of her liking and started writing. This is the sort of tormented self-disgust I read:

SARA-LEA'S JOURNAL

I think I'm crazy, and this insatiable longing for something I cannot define eats away at me. I am always scared to get close to anybody in case they discover I am bad and disturbed. So I keep lots of friends and don't get close to any of them. If they think I'm weird or find out too much, I simply move on. Finally I found one person who could take this pain away. But with Clive, having one person mean so much, the stakes are so high. I need him to stay with me, be with me day and night. Watch me, want me, listen to me, adore me and only me. And never see through me . . .

I claw at him, I throw tantrums and jump up and down to get his attention. I hurt him so he notices me, so he feels me, because I cannot feel myself. But now he resists me; he never used to. I used to see his confusion at what I'd thrown at him, then watch him wrestle with himself, and how he would give in, but now he is stronger and it scares me. He wants to go out, see a friend, get some exercise, read a book. And then I feel there is nothing. Then I feel he might never come back. Only the distraction of the boys keep me sane, keep me from having to gaze into that bottomless pit.

Clive makes me feel this way. Why can't he be here? I let my guard slip, let him see me, and then he's gone. See, I told you! I knew it—he would find out what a completely unsound person I am. My ugliness. My emptiness. My shame. It's his fault. I hate him. He's so horrible. How dare he do this to me! How dare he go out rather than be with me? Doesn't he know what I've been through? . . .

When he comes back, I am so angry with him for making me feel like this. I rage, I scream, I hurt him. I despise myself. I hide my embarrassment by hurting him more. Can't he see I'm vulnerable, I'm scared. Look at how he treats me. Explaining himself. He thinks he's so reasonable it sickens me. He's really just putting me in a corner from where I cannot escape. Then he walks away again. Please don't leave me, I need you! When he comes back, I can't show him how relieved I am. I need to show him he is wrong; he abuses me . . .

The mandalas seem to end in June, the last being inserted just before an entry dated June 21, the Winter Solstice, the day I confronted her about the affair. I read every word of the pages that follow. It is as though it is penned by another personality, detached and observing; gone are the disjointed, flowing ramblings about daily ordeals and reflections of self, replaced by a stony, punctilious, blow-by-blow descriptive account of our true-life drama.

It sweeps me back to that time as if it was yesterday . . .

Sara-lea's Journal

Thursday, July 1, 2010

Clive nearly caught me on the phone talking to Calix last night. We had just decided to risk another meeting today, somewhere we have never been before. Clive was putting the boys to sleep and as usual I crept outside, with a cigarette and made the whispered call, and suddenly he was there at the kitchen door. He merely stared at the phone I tried to hide in my palm and looked away, saying that Jack is thirsty and he was just getting him some water and was worried that the security gate was open. I don't know how long he was standing there and whether he overheard anything; he did not let on. His silence was worse than his violence; it is his preferred form of abuse.

Today, greeting Calix feels awkward, the energy between us is different. Somehow that simple, pure knowing and comfort that came from our deep connection, deeper than any I have known, as if ordained by the planets we so often talked about together, is endangered. Has he already pulled away from me, knowing that things have changed forever by this moment that seems frozen in time? Or is it me? I sense his sadness, no, deeper than that, almost a fear. I become tearful, and I reach for his hand, touch his face.

He smiles at me. 'It will be okay, Sara-lea,' he reassures me. 'I love you no matter what happens.'

During the last week, ever since Clive found out, he kept telling me he loves me and has emailed me pictures of hearts, knowing well my penchant for collecting heart-shaped amulets of any natural material but particularly stones and leaves. Now his hand empties into mine two stones which are, once I swivel them around, immediately recognizable as two halves of a roughly formed heart. Their jagged inner edges fit perfectly together, like the continents once had such that a whole heart comes into being when they are placed together. I am overwhelmed as I read the handwritten message that accompanies them.

Sitting here, so close to him, looking at him, I so badly want to rock in his arms, give myself to him. But I must understand what to do next so we talk about what we think Clive knows and I am horrified at the chances we took as we run through all the possibilities. Then Calix voices the conclusion I have already reached, 'You will have to tell him.'

Sara-lea's Journal

Friday, July 2, 2010

And now the day has arrived. I want to die.

I feel sick to my stomach. Is he going to abandon me the moment I say, 'Yes, it's true'? I feel so scared.

Today I say I am going to work until our appointment with Vincenzo. For some time, it had also been the day I would meet with Calix, and I would tell Clive I was working late. But actually I have no clients today; in fact I haven't been working at all this week; I just couldn't give my strength and energy out to others who so trust that I am completely devoted to their needs, when I am in such a state. But each day I pretended to go to work, and sometimes, struggling to disguise his curiosity and anxiety, Clive would ask what I was doing or how my day went and I would just tell him that I was at work.

This morning I sit in my consulting room, surrounding myself with all the sources of energy and peace I can think of. I am beside myself with anxiety and uncertainty. I light candles, burn incense, place stones on my body and work with my chakras, in an attempt to access the healing energy. I visit the bathroom more often than I need to. Each time I come back into the room and close the door I panic and immediately go back outside again and pace up and down the short passage that links together the consulting rooms of my colleagues, eavesdropping on their consultations, and I am perturbed by what they may have overheard when Calix was here in my rooms. I am feeling so unsettled; I keep glancing at my phone, checking my emails and text messages. I compose a text to Calix, then delete it, then try again. Finally he calls, although we had agreed it was best we don't speak this morning before the tribunal I will face with Vincenzo and Clive in therapy later. When we put the phone down, I realize I was hoping for a sense of containment, that everything will be okay, but I don't feel it.

I keep glancing at the clock. The minutes pass by excruciatingly slowly. I rehearse for the umpteenth time what I am going to say, what I am not going to be drawn on, and how I will respond to the inevitable pressure to divulge all. I imagine where I will sit in Vincenzo's consulting room, what Vincenzo will say, how Clive will react. I try to write these thoughts in my journal, but I can barely translate the thoughts and feelings into words and consign them to paper. So I try and read some inspirational words, the kind of things I often share with my clients during a session. I do breathing exercises, seeking peace, calm and tranquility, when all I feel is in contrast to this. I am suddenly aware of how easy it is to work with others, but not so with myself. After a while, I realize that my mind will not be stilled, and my body will not stop exuding . . . what? I think it is fear. Yes, that's what it is. Fear . . .

. . . So I am going to talk only about why I had an affair. I am going to talk about Clive, about why the person he is has driven me to this. So I

phone Clive and tell him that whatever has taken place is not my fault; I am not to blame, it is both of us. But he says he expects to hear the details of what has happened in therapy.

'Sarah,' he says, 'we are both jointly responsible for what our relationship has been like and what path it has trodden as each decision we have made and everything we have said and done has meandered it to the place it is now. But we are each responsible for our own choices at each moment, and the choice to have an affair rests with you alone.'

But I am adamant, 'It's not about what happened, but why. I only want to talk about why.'

I check the time again. It's only mid-morning. Time is moving too quickly and too slowly. I want to arrest it. In a futile gesture I toss the desk-top clock onto the floor. All of a sudden I feel claustrophobic, the walls of my small room and the slanting ceiling seem to be leaning in on me. Objects on counter-tops seem to be spinning, floating. I cannot quell the panic attack that threatens to overwhelm me. I want to vomit, but am rooted to the spot, as if leaving this room will expose me to catastrophic annihilation and that staying here is my last refuge of procrastination and avoidance, of holding myself together and preventing life as I know it from never being the same again. Finally, the feeling seems to recede. Frantically, I pack my bags and go to the gym, hoping to empty my mind and let the oozing sweat secrete my fear.

1st session with Vincenzo: 13h00

Once seated, we don't quite know how to start. We'd been seeing Vincenzo most of last year, trying to fix what seemed so broken. Clive forced me to make this appointment, and Vincenzo seems to assume that we have come to see him because we are in some sort of crisis. But it soon becomes clear he doesn't know exactly why we are here. We go around in circles for a while, as he tries to gently move us into it.

Clive appears outwardly calm, but I can feel his impatience growing. Suddenly, he feels he needs to help explain how we got here. To Vincenzo he says, 'About two weeks ago, I told Sarah I know that she has been involved in a relationship with someone else. She said she has nothing to say, then denied it. She said there is only me, I am the only person in her life. A day or two later, she said she needs to talk to me about it, but will only do it with you, Vincenzo, as she is afraid of how I might react. And that's it, we haven't discussed it further till now.'

I just cannot bring myself to say anything in the vacant space after Vincenzo opens the floor to us. My head spins and my heart leaps into my throat, then . . . 'so yes, I have had an affair,' I hear myself saying.

Vincenzo seems to be unsure of what he has heard. 'You have had an affair, Sara-lea?'

I feel like the whole world is looking at me, with mouths agape. As Vincenzo assimilates this, he tries to convince me that I need to talk about it, that Clive is going to want to know stuff, but I say I want to talk about why—why I had an affair. Vincenzo is unmoved. He says it has to be unpacked, that the questions may stay for weeks, or months, or years.

My voice croaks when I say, 'Like what?'

'Let's start with who it is,' Vincenzo leans forward. 'Do you know who it is?' looking at Clive.

I feel immobilized, absolutely stricken. I cannot say his name. 'Yes, he does,' I interject, 'so he can say.'

'I need to hear it from you, Sarah,' Clive seems to come to life and turns in his seat to face me. I feel like disappearing into the chair.

'It's Calix, but you know that.' Then, 'It started off as a friendship, then became sexual in the middle for a brief while.' I hold my hands together, then raise them to show how the relationship peaked. They seem to be working on their own, detached from me. 'Then we became friends again.' Oh, God, is this me I'm talking about?

Clive goes straight for the jugular, so like him: 'When were you sleeping with him?' I can feel the heat in him mounting. He looks straight at me. I look at the bookshelves, and count the books to see whether any are missing; it's the only way to still my mind. Vincenzo has more books than he had last year, and some have been moved, not replaced where they came from. Three books are missing, possibly in circulation or on his bedside table.

I plead with Vincenzo, 'This is not okay. I am not going to tell all, to confess. Clive has played a role in where our marriage is today. I am not the only one to blame for this.'

But Vincenzo is unyielding. 'Sara-lea, I have dealt with this kind of situation many times in therapy, sometimes it's the husband, sometimes it's the wife,' he says, as if this makes it easier, or right. He tries to buy me time by saying how difficult this must be for both of us, but that irrespective of what happens to our marriage as a result of this, it needs to be pried open and dealt with.

While Vincenzo speaks I let my mind wander, seeking the tranquility of patterns and structure as is my habit. I add the number of books on each built-in shelf to the left behind Vincenzo, convert the sum to numerology and condemn the bookshelf to a 13/4 and automatically anthropomorphize its characteristics by this label. Then I take in the titles on the spines, and reorganize them in groups more suited to their subject matter.

'Sara-lea?'

'I won't go there, Vincenzo. I won't talk about it. I want to talk about 'why'.'

'What are you most afraid of, Sara-lea?' A nice, psychoanalytical question. It had seemed so reasonable and useful when he said this last year, sitting here together, working at our relationship. I remember that at some point I had asked to burn a candle during our sessions. Clive bought it, a beautiful large dark grey one with three wicks. I am suddenly struck by the symbolism of that. Calix was right here in the room with us, burning bright. But after a few sessions, one of the wicks would no longer burn, drooping into its wax bed. Clive will soon figure this out. It will torment him. He will hate me, and I hate him.

Vincenzo asks the question again. I cry out, arms flailing, every sinew in my body straining, suddenly angry at Clive, 'Of losing my marriage, of losing my children, of losing everything.' Is he stupid? I'm afraid of facing me, of admitting to myself what I have done, of being like my mother. I am engulfed with shame. But the tears won't come, hardened and dried by the impenetrable barrier that encases me.

Vincenzo looks at me, then at Clive. 'What are you feeling, Clive? What do you need?'

But Clive seems to want to appear benevolent. He seems to want to show me that he is not keen to annihilate me. 'Sarah, it is not useful to me if you are left feeling awful with this. I need you strong, for me and for the boys.' This was just to soften me up, to get me to drop my guard, because then he says, 'I need to hear more about it. Is it over?'

I can't really say, can I? 'It ended about ten months ago.' I regret saying this almost before it is off my tongue. Give an inch, they will take a mile. Clive has that look on his face, and I can almost see his left-brain working all the permutations, seeking more information with which to bury me, to catch me out. Strange how I see them as working together as a team, Clive and Vincenzo. They push and push. I keep telling them I am confused, that I can't remember.

Then, seeming to warm up to the conversation, if that's what you call it, Clive says, 'So when did it start, the sexual relationship?' His voice coaxing and inviting me to take him into my confidence. I stare at the ceiling, the wood-grain patterns take on the forms of wild animals and form a story for me of a cruel hunt, the lure unable to escape its tormenters, helpless and restrained it seems by invisible tension wires which recoil and reel it in when strained to the limits, pulling it back within reach of slavering jowls, its claw-nails screaming deep ruts into the surface.

Unable to bear the image anymore, I gaze at Clive's shoes. 'Actually, it was also in the beginning, when you went to work in the Middle East,' I say, looking away. Shit, caught me. That was over two-and-a-half years ago. 'I really can't believe it's been so long.'

Clive is trying to roll with the blows, to absorb them lest they knock him out cold. Logic and words are his safe haven, rational and objective deduction his defensive cover. 'So that makes it more than a year and a half, nearly two years, if it ended ten months ago,' Clive calculates, seeming pleased with himself. It feels like he is just stacking up the information necessary to obliterate me. This is why I give everybody just a little part of me, so they can never annihilate me.

Vincenzo looks like he is enjoying this, in a perverse way, and I wonder for a moment if his wife has had an affair. In fact, I am convinced she has, as his energy feels unprofessional and judgmental; he cannot conceal his anger. From the moment we arrived, I could see that he was not himself.

I have to pull this back, I am getting myself caught up in an inquisition. 'No, it was very brief, just for a short while. It's really just a friendship.' I really can't believe it has been going on for so long, that I have known Calix for all this time. I'm feeling confused about the time period. I tell them I can't remember when it happened.

And so it goes on. Clive is exasperated; his face is pallid, his fingertips massaging his temples leave blotches where blood has drawn to the surface, and the scowl is now permanent. The less clear I am in answering their questions, the more persistent they become, like hounds finally locating the rabbit in the warren, tails wagging so hard and voices barking so loud with imagined justification and self-assurance that they are about to be victorious, they have their prey cornered. I back deeper into the inadequate hole, thinking if they can't see me maybe I can knock them off the scent and they will just go away, but my back's against the wall and it's dark and I'm alone. I suddenly feel so very alone, like a child unable to detect the locus of her family. I think of making a dash for it. What would my chances be? I glance hopefully at the clock.

Vincenzo notices this and announces, 'I have an extra half-hour,' apparently trying to be accommodating. I could kill him, by just looking at him. Why would I want to sit here in my lair of no return, with you baying for my blood? No, it's easier to kill myself. I've had those thoughts before, even tried it a few times.

The extra half-hour does nothing for us really, except cost us money we don't have. Platitudes spill from my lips. 'It's been over for a long time, we don't even see each other anymore. We just speak on the phone. He is just a great friend.' It sounds weak and feeble, even to me, and I know it is not entirely true. It's complex, my relationship with Calix, not just some arbitrary, regretful affair that came and went long ago. There are things about it that are just too hard to face, absolutely too hard to tell. And too much for Clive to bear; that this was not the only time this has happened. How much does he know? He said he was told things by other people, people who have seen me with Calix, and others who seem to know about the affair.

'And where does he live?' Shit, does he know? Is this a test?

'He has lived in various places around here, like Little Rock Estate.'

'And now?' he asks, sensing my vagueness.

'He moved to Mount Mpumalanga about one year ago.' That's where we live. So it seems there's a lot that Clive doesn't know. He does not know what to do with that information. I can see the pain and disbelief in his eyes as his mind struggles to assimilate the implications of it.

They are both looking at me, waiting for me to divulge more. 'We did not say things like "I love you",' I offer into the void, trying to explain myself. But we had.

I know I am looking for things to say, things that mute the reality and divert from the truth. Now Vincenzo is incensed with me, and he takes me on about avoiding the real issue, that I am not giving Clive what he needs most now, my frank response to some of the questions he has. It appears that Vincenzo is trying to verbally surrogate for Clive's suppressed fury and indignation, and is dismayed at how reasonable and understanding Clive seems. I hate this part of Clive; just like my step-father was, moments before he exploded with unrestrained abuse. I feel like I am six years old again, and that by tomorrow I will be shipped off to a 'place of safety' with the secrets of what really happened the night before buried deep within me forever. In the same way my relationship with Calix will remain; it's well-honed now, this survival skill. So I excuse myself to go the bathroom, and I overhear Vincenzo asking Clive, 'Where is your anger?'

Eventually we leave with a suggestion from Vincenzo to come back on Monday or Tuesday. He offers to see us together, or that I come alone, to help me prepare myself for a subsequent joint session. To continue the onslaught? Does he think I'm crazy? Strike that, he does think I'm crazy. To balance things, it seems, he also offers to see Clive alone. We say we will think about it and let him know. I can't wait to get out of there. I hear Vincenzo say, 'Good luck' to Clive.

I wish we had done our usual thing and arrived in two cars, but we hadn't. We drive home in silence. When we turn into our street and drive

past the security boom, Clive says, 'Show me where he lives.' I shake my head.
'Come on Sarah, tell me.'

We get closer and closer to our house, now only a few doors away. Clive
is driving slowly, as if we are running out of space and I am not going to
divulge the answer to his question before we turn into our driveway. With
my heart in my throat, I say, 'There,' pointing to a house diagonally opposite
ours. Clive's car has almost come to a halt outside Calix's house. But he
says nothing. I guess numbness has set in to preserve his sanity for the time
being.

Sara-lea's Journal

Saturday, July 10, 2010

This evening, it seems strange not to contact Calix while Clive is putting
the boys to sleep, and I hold my phone in my hands for ages while I fight
the temptation. After the boys are asleep, we get into a conversation about
the affair. We are sitting in the lounge, facing each other on the same couch,
almost touching but with our backs against the couch arms and our legs
pulled up in front of us as if this can protect us or fend off an attack or act
as a barrier to deflect something we really don't want to hear. I don't want
this, but Clive wants to know stuff. We have not mentioned it all week, but
he picks up where we left off in therapy, clearly not satisfied with what he has
heard so far. He tries again to get a handle on when it happened.

I repeat myself. 'It ended a long time ago.' I can hear it sounds
ridiculous, and it just causes him to get more specific and to the point with
his questions.

'What exactly is a long time ago?' He is infuriated, and the conversation
has just begun.

'Look, we hardly see each other at all anymore. Maybe just a couple of
calls each month, and we seem to bump into each other at workshops or
functions sometimes, by accident, that's all. We bump into each other a lot,
I guess.'

'Hardly any contact,' he persists. 'And he's following you around.'

I wonder what he knows, and think of all the times people have obviously seen Calix and me in public. 'No, but sometimes when I walk on the beach or the mountain, somehow he is there. It just happens that way. Other than that, this year I have only seen him as a client, for treatments.'

That seems to stun him for a moment. He apparently doesn't know how I met Calix for the first time in my therapy rooms. He seems so close to breaking point, going over the edge. Then, incredulously, 'You treat him professionally and you're sleeping with him? How long have you been sleeping with him?'

How had I answered this with Vincenzo? 'That was only for a few months, when you were in the Middle East,' I say, annoyed now, with myself as much as with him. I can sense that I have told him too much, and he is picking up the inconsistencies. I can no longer remember exactly what I had said earlier in therapy about when the affair took place. In fact, I can hardly recollect anything I had said. Truth is, I am in such a state that I am still really confused about what happened, and when.

'But you said it ended ten months ago. I was in the Middle East two-and-a-half years ago. Which is it?' he demands, wound up like a tightrope. Will he ever let it go? It wasn't about the sex, it was much more than that.

So I say, 'It isn't his body, it's his mind that attracts me,' as if I imagine this will make him feel better.

'Don't you understand,' his voice is strained and cracking, 'that's what's killing me.'

In unison, the dogs, lying at the foot of the couch, raise their heads and wag their tails and seek out Clive's hand as if to console him. He can feel that he is losing me now. He appears to engage in some internal dialogue with himself and after a while he seems to try a softer approach, and tells me that he understands just how difficult this must be for me. Then he tries to reason with me, how he just wants to know the basics, the high-level picture of what happened, as he calls it. He is pleading with me; it sounds awful—pitiful, weak, spineless. It is palpable to me how he is melting down inside, disintegrating, desperately trying to find things to hang onto to cease or slow his descent into an imagined oblivion as his world comes crashing down around him.

'Was he in the house? Did he come over here?'

I thought that was obvious as he now knows that Calix lives next door, but maybe not to him—it seems like the reality, the enormity, is slowly appearing to him in measured doses, just enough to intoxicate but not kill. Just how and when does he think we saw each other while I was managing life like a single mother with three young children, unless it was late in the evening when they were safely tucked up in bed? That it also happened when he was around, and all the close calls that we'd had? I remind myself that he probably knows very little. Despite my resolution to do this my way, to not divulge the details of what has happened, something in my desperate desire to ease his pain and misery persuades me to respond to his question. But I down play it. 'Yes, a few times.'

'When I was away, you slept together in the house.'

It's a statement. He is trying to bank some facts he feels he has tied down. The satisfaction of getting an answer seems at war with it being an answer he would prefer not to hear. He probes further, gripped in the misconception that this will help. 'Where? Where did you do it?' he invites the options by waving his hands around expansively and looking around. Perhaps because we are sitting in the lounge and his gestures are suggesting 'somewhere in this vicinity' (and because I just can't bring myself to say it), I raise my hand imprecisely towards some vacant space of carpet behind the couch and tell him it was here, in the lounge. 'Where? Right here, on the couch, on the floor? Come on Sarah, it was in our bedroom.' His voice is raised, tense, frustrated. It panics me, the hint of aggression and abuse. It's such a direct line for me, from the expression of anger to violent behaviour.

I feel so dirty, like tainted goods, guilty of everything, worthless. I find myself replying in a voice leveled with intense effort, 'No, never.' I instantly regret saying this, as Clive's anger flares. No, it's pain in his eyes, at the image this creates in his rich imagination of the exchange of body fluids, or Calix moving inside me, his loving whispers, my ecstasy? Incongruously, I am there now, deep in that fantasy-memory that is so recent, moistly rising inside me, like the horror and guilt of a woman being raped who discovers she is lubricated and aroused. The heat rises, my face is flushed and I imagine it is obvious to him.

He says, 'I just don't understand how you could do that.' I have no
answer for that.

This brings me to my senses and I pull back. I tell him it's enough now,
I'm not going to say, he does not need to know this kind of detail. 'You can't
do this to me, Clive!' He holds his head in his hands, looks at me, then gets
up and disappears down the passage. Perhaps it's the frustration of getting
nowhere, of not getting the answers he thinks he needs, or perhaps it's the idea
that he is sitting in the very place that I say I shared myself with another man
that sickens him. I take the opportunity to get out of the situation, away from
the conversation, and step outside into the courtyard and light a cigarette.
But within moments he has cornered me there, with his own cigarette in
hand, and picks up the cross-examination as if nothing has happened . . .

I remember how my initial compassion and understanding for her
situation, which was based on an assumption that she would be open to
talk about things, had evaporated soon after meeting with Vincenzo. I
wanted to discuss things, but when this did not pay dividends, my fury
and heartache spilled over and things quickly deteriorated into piercing,
closed questions, the truthful answers to which were appalling for
both of us. In these weeks the insecurity and distrust was evident from
both of us, and frankly, it has never recovered. My frustration at her
vagueness and indignation at subsequently finding out some of the facts
she was hiding had boiled over and my anger had erupted into verbal
abuse and this aggression would have driven her to the edge, given her
history—little wonder she tried to do away with herself and the boys
when I raised the affair again in September. I now recall the reason I
had left home so suddenly soon after this—I just did not know how to
deal with her ongoing untruths, denials, vagueness and, ultimately, her
non-negotiable refusal to say anything further about the situation. I had
felt justified in my pursuit of truth. But mostly, it was the impact that
our constant bickering was having on the boys.

Sara-lea's Journal

Sunday, July 11, 2010

. . . I wonder if I should just give up now; there is no way to salvage our marriage, no chance that he will stay after this, so why go through all this? I should just walk away and never look back. I say again that I have had enough, I am going to bed, but there is no escape from him and he stands behind me in the bathroom and there is no way to evade his 360 degree panorama of me courtesy of the wall mirror. In this moment it feels like he can see right through me and know every secret I have. He says, 'If the affair started when I went to the Middle East, or perhaps just before that, was that pregnancy you terminated his baby?'

'No,' I say, reflexively, perhaps too forcefully, and not sure what I was saying 'no' to.

Clive can sense it and says, 'I have never understood how you could phone me after I had been away for about a month or six weeks, tell me you are pregnant and that you are going to terminate it. No discussion; nothing. You would not even let me speak. You would not even hear what I had to say. I just could not comprehend how you could end a pregnancy without a second's thought when we have had, what, maybe ten lost pregnancies. And I have never really forgiven you for that.'

But I know with relief that he is on the wrong track. Relief, because as much as I had little doubt about whether to terminate that pregnancy, it was the termination some months later, when Clive was back from the Middle East and on one of his week-long business trips, and Calix and I had tried but failed for the first time of many to end our love affair, that was the tougher. I have assumed that Clive has by now concluded that I would not have sex with him for all those months because I was with Calix, though at the time I claimed it was because I was bleeding persistently from the blood-thinning drugs to clear the blood clots. And I hoped that he would recall the tampons I was using for weeks and the occasional evidence in the toilet bowl and that he would congratulate himself for the conclusion he has drawn. And that he will never find out how close I was to having Calix' child. Cutting myself there brought painful relief; I felt purified. I have yet to find a better way.

But Clive said 'ten lost pregnancies'. And the unwitting prophetic accuracy of this torments me. I'm sure he just chose a round number, though we have always been precise about this—twelve pregnancies, nine failed or terminated, we have always said. Only Calix knows I have had thirteen pregnancies and produced three boys. And Clive still does not know that of those only two are his, and how I have churned inside every time when he has jokingly said that they all look so different he wants to have a paternity test. I am in shock, in denial. I know now that I can't tell him anything. Nothing is safe to reveal. He will not stop digging away . . .

Sitting here on the carpet of our bedroom, I suddenly feel like my world is falling apart, again. Even if she was to arrive home at this moment, I think I would be incapable of doing anything. It's not just the revelation of the pregnancy and termination—what a deceitfully euphemistic word—that does it, nor is it the hint at previous infidelity. It is the confession that one of my boys is not my own. I fold at the waist and lie down on my side, with my knees tucked up, and sob tears which drip onto the pale carpet in dark blotches.

Then the memory of a brief conversation surfaces, one I had with Sarah about a month ago, just before Roxanne had her breakdown.

Sarah had said, 'Roxanne has broken up with her man.'

'Again? Why is that?' I was not particularly enamoured with Roxanne, not just because she had been an accomplice to the affair and continued to lie to me about what she new, but because her fiery relationship with her sister meant that her weekly visits were tiresome in the extreme and left Sarah upset each time and me pissed off with their childish arguments steeped in decades of humiliation and embarrassment off which they seemed to feed with relish. The animosity would literally start when Roxanne parked her car in the driveway and Sarah still inside the house and the two of them riled each other through the closed front door before they were even face-to-face. When I saw how the boys, who loved their aunt dearly, noted how these adults interacted and the distress they displayed as sugar-high delinquent behaviour while she was there, I asked Sarah to desist and if necessary to stop inviting Roxanne over until they could sort out their stuff. I had not entirely succeeded with this and my fallback was passive-resistance and the best I could conjure up was to make my excuses to not be present when she came over.

'Seems he was with another woman when he was overseas recently,' she said.

I thought, 'So he slept with another woman for a couple of weeks, and she calls off the relationship, but you have had a deep relationship for two or three years, and here I sit, carrying on regardless.'

I said, 'Did he tell her?'

'I don't know how she found out. But anyway, she won't be coming over today because she is really sick with a chest infection.'

I was not disappointed she would not be coming over. When I said nothing, Sarah said, 'Energetically, it's the grief. Lungs are grief. That's why she is sick.' I could go along with that. When I had found out about the affair, I had abused my lungs twenty-four hours a day, smoking through the sleepless nights and exercising excessively and the wheezing and lumpy sputum that I produced at will was a constant worry. It must have been grief, and I felt exonerated. 'I know this,' she said, 'from when I had pneumonia.'

'Oh, when was that?' I could not quite remember, but this felt like a double-edged sword: I could sense I would not like the answer.

'In 2008,' she said.

I was impressed. She was never so sure of the timeline, or pretended not to be. I waited, but she said nothing. So I said, 'What were you grieving?'

'One day you will know.'

So she was going to leave me with a riddle to solve; how uniquely manipulative. I took a deep breath, and considered my options. I could say nothing, or ask her to tell me now. After a few moments I said, 'Sarah, I respect your need for silence on it, but this just leaves me hanging, so I am not sure why you have dangled it in front of me.'

I think that was the end of the conversation, and I now remember that I had assumed she was referring to mourning the end of her relationship with him after I returned from the Middle East, and this thought was bitter-sweet as it was a relief if it had ended as she had once claimed but left me jealous that it had meant so much to her that she had fallen ill as a result. But here I have her riddle solved. And my gut is perversely reassured that this must be the thing that I intuitively knew was missing from the picture of her.

I need something to feed the pain, so I read on . . .

Sara-lea's Journal

Monday, July 12, 2010

This evening, Clive says he is leaving in the morning and asks me whether I have had enough time to think about it.

'There is nothing else to talk about,' I say. Every sinew in my body strains.

'Let's start with clarity about when it ended and whether it is over?'

He is rolling a twirly-whirly, and it sounds deafening as an industrial machine. I pause, trying to decide whether or not to respond at all. Then I say, 'I think it was before I started seeing Catherine about eighteen months ago. Since then I saw him just as a friend and a client.'

Clive sits bolt upright. 'This is unfair, Sarah. That's another different answer. You have to give me something to hold on to, an answer that does not move.'

'Catherine says it's my personality to close down when confronted with something tough.' I am just trying to gracefully protect myself and the truth is just too overwhelming.

Clive leans forward, as if he is about to get up. 'You are not volunteering anything, I have to keep asking. It's not fair, and it is my frustration at not getting clear answers that drive me to these questions.'

'You will never be satisfied,' I say. 'You will always have more questions.' And I don't want to hear myself give the answers . . .

. . . I find him smoking a cigarette in the kitchen courtyard, and join him there and light a cigarette. 'Sarah, I desperately need two things right now. I need to give myself permission to express my ugly thoughts and feelings, get really angry in ways I have never allowed myself to be. And I need your honesty, no matter how bad it might seem. At this point, when things are so fragile, when our relationship seems so broken, we really have nothing else to hold on to.'

I stare into some vacant space on the retaining wall. This is not the conversation content I want or expect. I feel hounded; he feels frustrated; nothing can quell the pain he feels. I hold up my hands and step into the kitchen and Clive talks to my back. 'It's not so much about the truth of the past three years, but really about being honest now. No more lies. If you don't think it's fair to disclose something, then just tell me so, but please don't lie anymore. I am desperately trying to believe you, but I am finding it difficult to pick out the true parts from the untrue when I get conflicting, vague information from you that changes every time you say something.'

Clive follows me inside and tries again to clarify when the affair took place, and I say, 'Did you go to the Middle East in 2007?'

'This is the kind of vagueness that makes me want to get up and walk out the door,' Clive erupts, his anger flaring.

'And that's exactly the kind of person I don't want to be with. You have no compassion.' He doesn't like that; he is so desperate to be perfect he forgets to be who he really is.

Clive lights a cigarette, and I tell him to get out the kitchen; he knows he can't smoke inside! He looks up at the rocky ridge above us, and I know what he is thinking.

'I think I want to move from this house,' Clive says. 'It is no longer a sanctuary and Calix lives next door.'

'This is our home and I don't want to leave it,' I say from the kitchen. 'Anyway, I think he is moving soon.'

And on it goes, this interrogation . . .

. . . Clive lights up again, to calm down a bit I suppose. Then he comes inside and stands over me as I sit on the couch. I tell him to stop threatening me; that he is abusing me. He tells me that he knows Calix has been living

next door since the beginning of the affair, or soon after. I am appalled. 'I just can't believe you would do that, check up on this with estate agents. You can't do that!'

. . . It is time for bed but he just won't stop. 'Sarah, this is hardly the time to attack me. You lied about how long he's lived there. I feel like I am constantly on high alert for more information from places and people other than you, while it is you who should provide this for me. It will make the story I have so far and want to believe in more complete, so that I can deal with it and put it away somewhere . . .'

I say, 'It's unfair of you to do this to me!'

'. . . You have had this affair right under my nose all this time. I can deal with the reality of that, with the truth of the affair, but my power and integrity is undermined by what you hold back and lie about. It is prolonging my healing and the sure footing of our relationship, and I am finding it difficult to be fully in this marriage without the truth.'

He is shouting at me: I hate it, but want it. I close my eyes and let his abuse flow through my pores.

'Why are you doing this to me, when you know I am so traumatized that anything will inflame me, yet you bait me? You say you wanted his mind and not his body; can't you see that is what is so threatening to me. Don't you get it? That's what will always be there for you both. You carry this desire for him in your heart. That's why you gave him the rest of you. How do you end almost three years of that overnight? For you, I'm just this man you say abuses you. So why would you want me?'

'You're abusing me now. Get out! Get away from me!'

. . . Later, I stand there in the courtyard, smoking one last cigarette and looking at him. In my heart I feel he is behaving like that person I do not want to be with, and in this moment he stands in stark comparison to the person I think Calix is.

Calix just won't let go either, he won't accept that it has to be over between us. I see him disintegrating at his core, just as Clive is; these two men I love.

Infuriated, perhaps by my silence, Clive stage-whispers at me, 'You fucked the neighbour.'

I ask him to stop, but he shouts it out again, goading me, trying to break down my resistance to answering his questions, frustrated by the feelings welling up inside him.

I can't take it anymore. 'You can't say that to me, you fucking bastard,' I scream at him and push him and pound my fists on his chest, but he just stands there, arms hanging at his sides, with this malicious grin and struggling to keep his balance. Why won't he hurt me back? I need him to hurt me back!

His eyes open in panic and he extends his palms towards me when he sees me standing at the kitchen door with the knife at my throat and he says, 'No, Sarah, stop.'

'Got your attention now?'

'Sarah . . .'

'Another word from you and I'll do it!'

He steps forward—'Give me the knife.'

'I said another fucking word and I'll cut myself and it'll all be over. Explain that to the boys, how you made me do this!'

'Sarah, please, you're bleeding.'

I cannot feel it, but I know it; that peaceful rush, that rich cleansing warmth that brings serene rapture.

I am in control now, and with nowhere to go and looking humiliated, he says, 'Okay, Sarah. I am freeing myself from the need to know the truth about what happened the last three years. I will just live with what I know and imagine,' and he grabs his coat and walks up the stairs and takes the dogs around the block. And those words swirl round and round my head—if only I could believe he will let it go now.

Reading her rendition of that time suddenly feels too much for me, and I come up for air. I have been completely spellbound by her recording of the events in the weeks following the revelation of the affair. It's pretty much how I remember it, except that in her characterization of herself she appears to be much more reasonable than I recall. Her written words simply don't carry the emotional tone of her evasive disparagement nor my weeping heart and bleeding ego. It seems she stopped recording our conversations in her journal when I moved out the house and she decided to no longer allow me to broach the topic, as if she had cut herself off from herself and what we were dealing with.

I want to hide it all away and lock the cabinet and pretend none of this happened, but in my rush to pour the disturbed contents of the bedside table back into their hideout some things fall from my grasp and collapse in disarray on the carpet. A floating waft of unlined A4 paper seems to disgorge itself from one of the guilt-shame books and tempts me to prevent its inexorable pendulum-descent into the chaos at my feet.

From its resting place atop an array of jumbled books and papers and small jewelry boxes, it seems to want to leap out at me. As I bend down again I see that it is decorated with Sarah's handwriting and before I know what I am doing, I pick it up. It is titled 'I feel shame because . . .' followed by a full page of about thirty one-liners and its frayed perforated margin suggests that it was torn from a book, most likely her journal, I presume. My conscience screams, 'Put it away,' but with the guiltiness of a greenhorn peeping-Tom and a metaphoric look over my shoulder I actually find myself listening out for her footsteps coming down the passage to catch me red-handed. Glancing down the list, I see that most of the confessions seem fairly ordinary, at least to someone not afflicted with whatever horrors she experienced, and while they reflect a troubled mind privately tormented by self-blame and self-hate they mean nothing to me.

But about two-thirds of the way down I read two lines that cause me to sit down heavily on the carpet:

I feel shame about my sexual desire for another
I feel shame that I dream about us being together one day
And further on:
I feel shame when I come home after I have been with him
I feel shame when I fantasize about our beautiful lovemaking
I feel shame when I lie in bed next to Clive and can still smell and feel him

The idea that she fantasized about him, perhaps when she touched herself or was in rare intimate embrace with me, wrenches at my gut.

I visualize her longing for him between times, waiting impatiently for my next trip out of town, telling him on the phone that she is touching herself and thinking of him and can't wait to be with him again—this fantasy I have because it is what she had done with me all those years ago when we had started out. It had sickened me so and was the subject of many a tormented midnight stroll around the garden, her visualizing him when we made love, imagining it was him and not me under whom she writhed and sighed and moaned, wishing it brief and over soon with me so that she could sneak away and surreptitiously phone or text him in bitter remorse and silent apology for being unfaithful to him and craving and yearning for his touch. Years ago, before I withdrew from her body, she used to hold me tightly afterwards and look deeply into my eyes and say—'Oh, how we dance together,' or 'How our bodies sing.' That I haven't heard again for years.

And those occasional sensual dreams she had and I so envied as I heard her moan and watched her face in the glow of the dimmed passage lights we left on at night for the sake of the boys' nocturnal meanderings? The innocence and beauty I had once attached to them evaporate in an instant as I imagine they were all about him. I am mortified and flushed with rage, tortured all over again by these words, in the same way I still from time to time suffer from all the rich imaginations of my mind about certain details of what went on or might have gone on.

I scramble around for her journal, and flicking through it I look for perforations which will reveal to me when the outpouring of this litany of shame-filled thoughts and acts took place. I soon see the tell-tale signs of a page untimely ripped, its margin left strangely vulnerable and exposed, which suggests it was written just before she cut herself and possibly on that very night.

I pick up the 'list of shame'. For a while I am transfixed on this page, reading those five lines over and over again. Then I run quickly through the list once more convinced there must be more declarations of guilt of similar ilk, silently reading them with emphasis, almost willing them to appear. And I flip through the other books and files that spilled out of the cabinet, frantic now, looking for hidden revelations between the pages of impersonal soft-covered self-help books, but I don't find any.

And then I come across one last half-page written entry towards the end of the journal which stops me dead in my tracks. I read it over and over. I now no longer need to doubt any of my assumptions about the termination of their relationship, as this last journal entry discharges its bilious verification that their sexual relationship persists.

Sara-lea's Journal

Undated

It seems like an eternity since I saw him last. But that's what days seem like now, drawn and interminable. When he phoned and asked to meet, there was only one answer I could give him. We both wanted it, desired it. It needed no explanation, no justification, we both knew it was to say hello and goodbye.

We meet at the usual place, where we always felt safe, cocooned in an existence that was ours alone. Where it was always just us, and it felt that nothing else existed.

We say goodbye the same way we had said hello, with the deepest connection and knowing. But this time, it is different. There are no words, no preliminary interplay, no careful seduction. It is immediate and carnal, more animal-like than human. Frenetic and feverish, as though we seek to devour each other, yet not feeling rushed nor borne of lust; our passion the pure energy of love. Our dance is flawless, and we move as one, clinging tightly to each other, as if this will ensure we live forever within each other. Though we know we already do, and always have.

We do not say goodbye. We say nothing.

Deeply buried feelings erupt as I realize that while I cannot locate the exact date, what is portrayed happened very recently, conceivably during this week. I had always wanted to believe her when she said that they were just friends and it had ended long before I found out last June or that they had agreed to end the romantic relationship and stop sleeping together from the day she confessed in front of our marriage counselor. This despite what I had heard from others and regardless of the intimate content of the emails and text messages I had furtively uncovered while she denied the existence of an affair, both of which seemed to confirm that they were deeply in love right up until the day I confronted her, and a love that deep does not vanish overnight. With a perverse hint of self-satisfaction, I now know it did not. Denial is an interesting tool.

Resentment congealed sickly with unexpressed fury rages thickly in my mind as I stare at these words, and a desperate wrath which cannot be inflicted on an appropriate source threatens to consume me as I pace the perimeter of the double-volume bedroom with the offensive manuscript flapping in my hand as if glued teasingly to my fingertips. It will not let me release it, let it fly away, let me consign it to another life, another time. Individual words and letters blur and move and swim around the page as I watch, and resettle to form new deriding statements and ridiculing phrases and goading words and mocking megaphoned insults and sneering sexual images, and I helplessly wish them back into tidy order. The reality inscribed by her own hand jeers and taunts me with the fact that I can never take this away from them; no matter what I do or how I convince myself to think it will always be so, they will always have the memories of their bond and what they experienced of each other.

Tears of rage and frustration smudge her writing as they drip noisily onto the perfumed notepaper which takes on the form of a tabloid front page garishly declaring this truth for all to see. I stoop and put the paper under my shoe and withdraw my hand as there seems no other way to detach it.

Tormented all over again by these latest unsolicited messages which cascaded from their hiding place today, anguish floods in and fights for air with rising self-disgust that I am still so easily plagued and tortured by these old thoughts. In an instant, I feel I have gone back ten paces and lost all the sense of self-worth I have fought so hard to regain. I stop myself. This is my life-script, my habit of perpetuating the past and letting it keep its grip on me. But I cannot easily escape its grasp and so I adopt the luxury proffered by therapist Julia to give myself permission to be angry and hurt, but to talk it through in my head and observe how I am feeling and then let it go. So I give my feelings words; I write them down. I write them to her. The first few sentences are jerkily staccato'd from the pen in my hand as I try to portray my feelings without inflaming her, ridiculous as that is now.

Sarah,

You have been involved with another man for more than three years. This truth is hard for me. Coming to terms with your sexual affair is extremely tough for me. That you have lied and deceived and kept secrets is difficult for me to forgive. Having him next door is still so hard for me. That you have made love with him is hard for me to accept, more so as you brought him into our home and into our bed. Not really knowing what happened and why is unbearable for me. That you won't be honest about it destroys me. That you fell in love with him . . . and that I now know there is no end to it.

I feel that you have violated me and my love for you. I feel that you have betrayed my trust in you; you have acted selfishly; you have dishonored our relationship and marriage, and put our children at risk; you have violated my body by having unprotected sex with another man; you have welcomed him into our home eroding the safe haven of this sanctuary we have created with our love and family and memories and dreams; you have exposed our children to him during the most intimate stage of your relationship, and encouraged his interaction with them as a 'friend' of yours—so you have deceived and betrayed them too; you have deluded me

for years while you continued seeing him; you have looked me in
the eyes and lied to me.

I pause and stare at the page I have filled with my scrawl. I am incensed and I wonder if the bile-filled resentment will remain forever. The scribble is illegible but I know it does not matter as she will never read this. Even if I tape it to her hands and glue her eyelids open she will not glance at what I have written. She does not want to know my feelings and never has.

I take another page:

What you see
is not really what you see
but who you are.

I put that page aside, planning to stick it on the mirror in the bathroom. Then I grab another page, now furious with myself, and ineligibly inscribe a flurry of short quotations I committed to memory months ago when I sought wisdom and consolation and trawled the internet for information and articles and chat rooms on infidelity and betrayal and pain and forgiveness.

I stop only when I run out of space on the page. On a fresh page I write:

S-L
I am sorry
I have struggled so
With your affair
With you
With our combative relationship
With all the secrets and lies
But mostly with myself—my ego, my doubts, my fears, with who
I really am

I take another page, and write boldly:

SECRECY
CORRODES
EVERYTHING

I scrunch up the pages I have already written and wrap them in this page and grind it into a ball as if sealing the thoughts forever.

I need to see her, right now, as if for the last time, and I wonder what time she will come home and what she is doing. I am convinced she is with him, that they stepped out of his car when I scampered home and are milling around in public at Phakalot, the juices of their intimacy still lingering, pervading the room and creating sensations in the people around them and lubricating the sensual energy in others' conversations where before there was none.

I have enough sense about me to remember to return the keys to their hiding place in her car, and stuff the balled papers into my bedside cabinet.

It is late, but there is no sign yet of Sarah. The sound of 'Fuck-a-lot' ricochets off the bedroom walls.

My synapses fire tormented flashes of her in ecstatic rapture with him in this bed then of her pleasuring him in his car; of today's goat horns and cornuted cuckolds, rusty phalluses and manipulated springs and clenched fists with ball-and-chain. I am heavy with the sense that nothing changes, and my emotions are screaming for air . . . .

And in this moment I am conscious that I think I wish her dead. If being married to her feels like a miserable existence, getting divorced will produce venom and spite and manipulation beyond my imagination. I had a taste of this when I moved out last August. I feel trapped. Not that I could kill her, not by my own hand, but perhaps by some unfortunate incident that would spare me the guilt and the guts required, but get the job done nevertheless. I am not exactly startled by this gruesome notion as I realize it is not the first time it has formed in my mind.

Though I don't know how I could live without her.

KILLING-OFF CALIX

20

If the desire to kill and the opportunity
to kill came always together, who would
escape hanging?

(Mark Twain)

Tuesday, 28 December 2010

Last week a devastating bush fire took hold on *my* mountain, and I took the boys along the service road for the adventure of watching the fire trucks pumping water and the helicopter buckets dropping their water-loads and offer the exhausted fire crew some refreshments. My intention was to get an eyewitness account of whether we needed to take heed and prepare ourselves to evacuate, but fortunately, the prevailing gale-force winds whisked the furnace away from our house and over the ridge, once graced by sand dunes, and down towards the rocky shoreline on the other side. I was actually disappointed as I reflected whether 'razed to the ground' was not a fitting way start a new life. For our efforts, as the danger subsided, we were proudly treated to a tour of the latest technology and equipment housed in their newest tender.

The daily media implores citizens to conserve water in the midst of this prolonged summer drought. Living high up on the mountain side has its drawbacks, and it is reported that there are, on any given day this time of year, more than 100 runaway bush fires in and around the city environs, and we are always potentially at risk. Ten years ago, the ancient looming mountains, which encircle our village and where I hiked with the dogs not two weeks ago, were engulfed in flames for weeks on end, and we had to evacuate friends living just across the valley and many homes were lost. The world-renowned scenic mountain pass was closed to vehicular and pedestrian traffic for a few years thereafter, while the authorities sought a solution to stabilise the sensitive slopes and install catch-nets and carve tunnels through the rock to prevent the frequent rock-falls from claiming motorists' lives, which had happened on occasion.

As we strolled back down to the house that day, it suddenly occurred to me that as the sole responsible adult, I need to be more mindful of the boys' security and safety. And so, looking for our emergency spare set of security gate keys, I have tried to climb into Sarah's organising logic and envisage where she might have put them. I have looked everywhere I can think of and am frustrated with her as this is a reminder of how she did things as if she existed on her own.

But about an hour ago, little Jack, in a malevolent rage, slam-locked the internal security gate to our bedroom, designed to keep us securely caged in the event of a nocturnal intruder, and incarcerated me and the two older boys. He was too short to reach my set of car keys I thought were languishing out of reach on the key holder alongside the front door, and to our cacophony of instructions, he had manoeuvred a chair and proudly ran down the passage with each bunch of keys hanging there, which ended in disappointment. I must have set them down somewhere else. Jack's anger quickly turns to apology and then fear, and now we cannot convince him to let us out of his sight. He hangs on to the security gate and cries out for his mother to come and rescue all of us, and this sets off the older boys. The search takes on a very real urgency.

I eventually manage to calm them all down and make a bit of a treasure-hunt game of it. Jack, clinging to and peering through the reinforced bars of the security gate like a jail bird, is given the role of gang leader with the task of supervising and telling us where next to search while we, his prison gang, obey his commands, and we have upended and emptied just about everything in the double-volume bedroom and en suite bathroom. Running out of hope and places to look, and aware that Jack's attention span is at its limits, I get the keys I now keep next to my bed and throw everything out of Sarah's bedside table.

My heart flickers as I am reminded of her journal and books on shame and guilt. Just two or three weeks ago I had read those words and wished her dead! I grope, unsighted, around the inside corners of the drawers and gratefully withdraw with what I have been looking for between my fingertips and release all of us with much fanfare. Free, at last, and temper-tantrum long forgotten, the boys tear down the passage towards the lounge.

Before me, amongst the books and jewelry boxes, there is a silver metal container, rectangular, like a vanity case or jewellery box. I try the latch, but it is locked. I pick it up and shake it; it is lighter and flimsier than it looks, and it sounds like papers or envelopes rustling inside and a small collection of harder, solid items crack against the internal casing as I jiggle it more vigorously. I have no doubt what lies therein and that the second key I had unearthed from her vehicle weeks ago fits the lock.

I unlock the case and read the perfumed note that glares at me:

Sweet One
The stars know it . . . we both feel it . . . and somewhere out there
on the mountain, I saw it . . .
You know this picture . . .
You and Me . . . a perfect snug fit
I love you, no matter what, Sara-Lea
xxxxxxx
10 November 2010

Attached is a photograph of them, unclothed, standing coiled together against a mountainous backdrop. And with it lie two rough stones which, together, form a heart. Eleven-two are her numbers, and I think there is no coincidence about the date.

I could not take it anymore, and so Sarah is 'gone'. But rewarded with the discovery of this souvenir and words of enduring love, I know that it is not over for me unless he, too, is 'gone'.

Even now with her gone, when preparing dinner in the kitchen I picture him there chopping and chatting and laughing with her, and sometimes I cannot settle on a choice of couch in the lounge as I visualize the indentation of their bodies intertwined where I sit. I feel I walk in his footsteps down the passage to our bedroom and even imagine I am sleeping on traces of stains on the mattress from their lovemaking. When having a shower, the stream of water cascades down their naked bodies, not mine. He is everywhere, and I cannot get them out of my mind's eye.

I open her journal to a blank page and write:

> *The only view I can take of you, Calix, is that you have acted with complete disregard for us, including the potential consequences for Sarah and the boys, and certainly without concern for me. I feel that you have intruded on, violated and abused our lives, our home, our love, our marriage, our children, Sarah and me in so many ways, and continue to do so.*

It is weak, but it is a start. And now it flows as the source of my anger has shifted to him. The backlog of words and phrases long ago constructed in the dark of night, some previously thrown at her but likely not absorbed, others scrawled in my journal in a futile 'out, damned spot' Lady Macbeth way, flow from my hand:

> *I have to guard fiercely against the power I bestow on you, Calix—that your actions have gutted and castrated me, by assuming my rightful role, by trespassing on my territory, and by taking my manhood. You have invaded my psychic space, my physical, emotional and spiritual being. You have penetrated me by literally penetrating her. While I was away from my castle, providing for my family, you raided my territory. You have*

possessed my wife, invaded my castle-home, and usurped my role as her lover and friend.

You have destroyed my life, you fucking cunt!

I now understand why I described the feeling I experienced as 'so gutted' and 'so broken'. I have felt completely a non-person.

So I am wondering how I take back my power and potency.

I try to imagine how the ancient warriors may have dealt with this dishonour. I suppose they might have found out the simple truth or even a suspicion of it, flown into a rage, guillotined their wife, raided the offender's kingdom and savagely killed the transgressor, raped his wives and daughters, pillaged and plundered their possessions, and burnt everything to the ground. Literally wiped them out—any memory or legacy of them and everything associated with them—to restore their dignity and manhood and obliterate all the terrible feelings and concerns they may have.

Then they would simply start afresh. A new life, with a new woman!

So how do I kill off Calix?

I lift the pen from the paper. With this last sentence, I am now writing to myself.

'What the fuck am I doing?' I say to myself. I need to let go of this. I need to relinquish everything. I need to start living again! I have sat with and observed the situation long enough to understand exactly the nature of what I am dealing with, and after 'scanning', everything converges at a single point, a distinct energy, a solitary figure. A man dressed in red on 'my mountain'. And I know what I have to do to help myself with this. I will start right now.

That thought returns me harshly to the present. The joyful sounds of the boys playing together down the passage hovers in the background in stark contrast to the repugnant truth that permeates my heart like wisps of white cirrus clouds above the ominous imposing darkness of cumulus nimbus storm clouds which envelop me.

Suddenly conscious that I have no idea what the boys are up to, I gather all the loose papers and stride purposefully down the passage. They have rearranged the lounge furniture and appropriated bedding from other rooms to construct a reasonable facsimile of a tent, and they discovered the borrowed-and-not-yet-returned camping equipment that was neatly stacked in the atrium. Where items are not available these have been creatively invented by them, and I see that they are busy preparing dinner over an imaginary (thank god) camp fire, in honour of our much-promised camping holiday 'one day'. Harry and Sally seem to have a role in the whole exercise, which I cannot fathom at first glance, but they seem like willing volunteers. Then I notice the pan with the doggy biscuit treats being 'cooked'.

It makes me think that it is so much easier to make-believe than to make your biggest desires a reality. Feeling that they can see right through me to my darkest thoughts, I flit right past them and on my way to the kitchen door, I say, 'I love you, each one of you, so much.'

I receive a cacophony of proud, excited responses to join them.

'Wait for me,' I say. 'What's for dinner?'

Before I join them, I hurry outside and burn the papers in the courtyard fireplace.

21

Three may keep a secret if two of them
are dead.

(Benj. Franklin)

Thursday, 30 December 2010

The view from here is stupendous, as always. Here, near the southernmost tip of the African continent, in the southern hemisphere summer, the Atlantic Ocean stretches west to eternity. I can make out the curvature of the horizon, or am I imagining it? From this elevation I almost feel I am looking over the edge of the world where monstrous waterfalls and ghastly sea monsters once lay in wait for seafarers ahead of their time who insisted the earth was round; their last thoughts as they met their end—'Shit, I was wrong!'.

As I shorten my gaze, I have a bird's-eye view of the beach below me encased in an amphitheatre of huge boulders fringed by trees and bushes. The pure white sands are blemished with sun lovers determined to absorb their share of the last glowing embers of the sun as if it is setting on the year that nears an end. Here and there solitary walkers stroll with heads bowed as if searching for hidden treasures or inspiration between grains of sand, some with their dogs bounding along or racing to catch the crashing waves. To the left and out of view is the beach unofficially reserved for nudists, which I, on occasion, visited in my twenties.

I look away from the sun towards the north and trace the west coast which seems to stretch forever; it must be more than 100 kilometres as far as the eye can see. Sleepy villages and coastal resorts—I should really take a drive out there one day, just to get away from here. Behind me, more mountains in the distance; in the foreground and beyond my house, the valley still largely greened by beautiful trees and small holdings. This is the place I have called home for almost twenty years.

It took less than forty-five minutes at a brisk pace to walk-run up the steep incline from my house to where I now sit, on 'my mountain'. As was my habit, no matter whether I felt like exerting myself or not, I had jogged at warm-up pace up the gradual incline of the tarred service road leading to the start of the trail, the dogs alternately bounding ahead or sniffing in the long grasses that bordered the road until I was nearly out of sight ahead of them and then tearing past me as if to taunt my mid-forties human inadequacies. 'Just wait,' I thought, 'your time will come.'

Then I ran, arms pumping, up the steep incline of the mountain track, fighting for traction on the loose fist-sized stones until my thighs could take no more of the exaggerated lifting needed to maintain forward momentum and propel the torso attached to them up the incline, and I stopped gratefully just before the steepest portion leading to the first lookout point, lungs heaving and bending forward at the waist to stretch the early signs of cramp from my calves. How many more years of this type of exercise would my damaged knees handle before they refused to do it any more? Thankfully the occasional pain and swelling I endured usually subsided with a few days' rest or gentler walking. I was mindful that I was likely reducing the total lifespan of moderately intense exercise they still afforded me, but I stubbornly refused to deny myself the short-term exhilaration I experienced.

I moved on again when the dogs reached me; Harry was stronger, though heavier, and always made sure he kept ahead of Sally. For some reason, they always took it easy up this steep section, either because the loose stony terrain was awkward for their paws, or they just could not see any point in this mindless physical exertion. I thought, 'Neither can I,' but even as I said it I knew that the challenge of it brought joy to my soul. From there it was a walk-run to successively higher levels, depending on my stamina, and at each level, I had to slow down and clamber up a few metre-high rocks.

This evening, when I reached my chosen turnaround point, I left the path and scrambled about ten metres along the same contour and climbed down to shelter in the leeward side of a small cliff for a few minutes in order to get out of the gusting wind, which until then was pleasantly cooling, but as my body temperature would quickly plummet after I sat and watched the ocean waves for a while in my sweat-drenched shirt, I knew I would soon get uncomfortably chilled. And although I would later run back down the mountain and all the way home, the evening would have cooled and the breeze would leave my body shivering. Harry and Sally drooled on me as they watched me curiously from above until I returned to the cliff-edge where I now sit.

I need to reminisce to surround myself with happier times. Before I met Sarah, I came up here with my dogs almost every evening at sunset, no matter what the weather. Those three dogs, the last of which died during the time I was working in the Middle East, always seemed to enjoy as much as I did the adventure of scrambling up this mountain just in time to watch the setting sun from this ledge, which was most frequently our turnaround point, about two-thirds of the way up. Any further, and you encountered a number of difficult passages before you reached the summit, and we only treated ourselves to this challenge when time and inclination allowed.

To reach the summit, you have to negotiate a number of sheer cliffs up to four metres in height, assisted by heavy chains bolted into the rock face and footholds fit for able-bodied humans. Not so for canines. The Border collie was always first; he was the most agile, keen, and obedient to commands. I would hold him tightly to my chest, with his front legs gripping my shoulders, and hoist the two of us up. Safely deposited at the top, he could barely contain his excitement and would jump up to lick my face and bark elatedly, teasing his two companions who had not yet made the treacherous (for them) journey. They were less keen and, of course, much heavier, and I always dreaded the inelegant task of carrying the ungainly bulk of their mixed breed bodies up the rocks. But with much smiling and encouraging words, more mind than matter, we would do it, and afterwards, it always seemed worth the effort for all of us. Getting back down was a challenge we always ignored until the time came as this was awkward and mostly accomplished by sheer force of gravity and a fervent desire to not spend the night alone on top of the mountain.

I think fondly of them now, these memories sparking a jumbled rush of other humorous moments with them, bringing a small smile to my lips. From time to time, the boys enjoy visiting their graves at the bottom of our garden, sometimes preparing a little tea party for them or talking to them and wondering why they do not appear out of their deep holes to playfully dance around with them. This helped us to introduce the concept of 'gone to god' and yet never entirely lost to us by being omnipresent in our thoughts.

So here I sit on the ledge at which we had most often paused to gain our collective breaths and take pleasure in viewing the setting sun all those years ago. There is nothing in front of me: just free, endless space. Harry and Sally lie panting beside me. Fully grown, they are much too heavy to consider hauling up the chains, even if this was my desire, but it is not.

Christmas day was a particularly difficult time for us all. As usual, we spent the afternoon with my family, already emaciated by family members who have passed on or are living overseas, with Sarah's absence gawking at us and nobody brave enough to mention it. The boys had wanted to buy their mother a present, and they convinced each other that this would herald her return.

'What would you like to get her?' I asked.

The inspiration was unanimous. 'A stone-shaped heart.' They meant a 'heart-shaped stone'.

I tried not to let my feelings about this idea get in their way, but I had noticed some new additions displayed for sale on the walls of the deli I frequent which I thought were a fair facsimile that would appease both them and me—a set of three small canvasses smothered in the burnt umber hue of Namib Desert sands on which lay seashells in the shape of a heart. My initial intrigue was sealed when I noticed that the artist was the blond haired woman whose soul danced in her eyes. The accompanying dedication extended 'immense peace and bliss during a most painful time' and invited you to accept into your heart an abundance of joy, peace, passion, humour, love, beauty, open-heartedness, prosperity, ecstasy, and an unconditional acceptance of life. It seemed quite appropriate as the artist, according to the accompanying brochure, was a mother who had lost her teenage son and in her grief had travelled the coastline collecting artefacts from which she fashioned these dedications in tribute to him. And we undoubtedly grieved Sarah's absence and sought to rejoice in life. I would have gratefully accepted just one of these blessings. I asked each boy to choose which of these they would like to feel on Christmas day, but this only led to confusion as I struggled to define them for myself let alone a pre-schooler.

'And you give Mommy that one, Dad,' said little Jack, pointing to a huge canvass adorned with driftwood stacked together in the form of a heart. Beneath it, the label simply declared: 'Truth'. And so that is what we did, but Sarah did not return to open her gifts, so we had a little ritual and spoke to her, and I banged picture hooks into the wall amid our tears.

So, still feeling raw, today I have come here to sit quietly, as I used to do, my mind vacant and receptive, free and absolved of the past and future. But this sublime state seems difficult to replicate. Calix's energy saturates this lump of rock. Today is the tenth anniversary of our marriage, an occasion I had frequently romanticised for a number of years, imagining where we would go and what we would do, who would be with us to share the moment, and what I would want to say. Seems silly, really, to attach so much to this number 'ten', though when I could not defend why it was so magical, I would silently remind myself that my birth date is a master number, 28/10, and to others, I would simply say it was as good a number as any to aim for.

Since the affair was exposed six months ago, I had been extremely anxious about this day, as whatever I had imagined it might be seemed no longer appropriate. For a while, I had planned to call it off, to delay a true celebration of our togetherness till such time as it felt right. But it seemed this would make too big an issue of it and simply show that I was still hamstrung by the betrayal. The safer middle road, I had decided, would be to mark the day with some time alone together but to make it fairly ordinary in order to reduce what would almost certainly be heavily mixed emotional content. Contemplating this had saddened me tremendously, and I had hoped that we would have sufficiently worked through the issues resulting from the affair to wake up on this day with unrestrained feelings of joy and celebration or, at least, pretend to. But now I am spared these reservations; Sarah is not here, and this is the one option I had not considered.

The boys are at home with Roxanne, so there is no rush to return, other than a nagging anxiety about how much of their boisterous playfulness her fragile, but much improved, mental state can tolerate. She seems to be holding up after another month in hospital on a special programme for addicts and depressives, and I remind myself that the challenge and distraction of playing with the boys is the greatest medicine of all, as with Sarah gone they are probably all Roxanne considers left of her family.

I crane my neck and look over my shoulder, and I can just make out the rooftop of my house and imagine them there. I had asked Roxanne to stay with them a bit longer than usual to afford me the privilege of watching the sunset before I return and put them to bed. Before I left, we had a late afternoon barbeque, something we now do about twice a week in the glorious summer holiday weather, and the boys loved to help prepare the coals and turn the meat. But today, it had an alternative motive for me; I sacrificed my journal to the gods of fire. For a moment, it had hovered above the coals, unperturbed, but eventually it blackened and curled in the heat, then erupted in a ball of flame, which seemed to lick at my heart. It had felt good and right, but when all that remained were the remnants of the ring binder I had welled up with emotion and burst into tears, not for the journal condemned to ashes but for a relationship which had not yet come full circle, suspended for the time being in the mystery of her disappearance. Then I stood in the shower and let the chute of water wash it all away.

The sun appears to distort and flatten as it eases itself into the ocean, like a person getting into a hot bath with some misgivings. I think of how the mind's eye deforms reality, or the truth (whatever that is?), twisting and disfiguring it to suit one's own warped and partial perspective. Is it realistic to expect to understand everything? Is it even possible to comprehend everything about one single topic? I wonder what was Sarah's view of what happened and how that differs from mine? And what is the 'truth'; what actually happened?

I am sitting with my legs hanging over the sheer drop, trying to bring myself into the present by contemplating 'what is happening now', when the dogs are suddenly alert, their ears up and tails wagging. I glance down and trace the steep path I had climbed and see him coming up fast from below, bedecked in a familiar red sweatshirt. With a wry smile I think that this is a great example of conscious manifesting, since I had thought this moment into being when I had set out on my walk-run this evening. I had thought, though not for the first time, that it was highly possible I would bump into him up the mountain this time and while still jogging on the tarred road I had wondered what I would do or say to him. I had not managed to formulate any plan by the time my thoughts were overtaken by the intense focus brought about by the exertion of running up the steeper path.

He is walking up the path, head bowed in concentration, his long legs carrying him briskly and apparently effortlessly. I force myself to look out across the ocean, not sure of what to do, perhaps needing him to initiate an interaction. I am sitting about twenty metres off the trail, and I am not certain whether he sees me, but when he comes level with us, the dogs run over to greet him and so he must know I am here. As quickly as he came into view, he vanishes, evidently opting to walk to the summit, or at least, a little further than where I sit. I suddenly feel unsafe and risk a quick paranoid glance behind me as if I imagine he will shove me off the cliff.

I tell myself, 'You are being silly. You talked to him just a few weeks ago.' But this time feels different as it is the first time I have seen him on the mountain since she disappeared, and I am not feeling confrontational. Today I want my space. I am determined to spend this time here as planned and to leave only when the descent will become too treacherous in the fading light. But I am now unsettled, and I feel the apprehension fill my being and realise I am holding my breath. It has been tough enough to drive past his house every day and occasionally encounter him on the street in the past, but now he seems to be following me up here—up *my* fucking mountain. Next he will be sitting at my dining room table, talking and laughing and drinking a glass of wine. Then I remind myself: he has already done that, and more.

I swallow the tight lump in my throat and force air into my lungs, but the tension that comes with impending hostility remains. I can feel his energy at my back even before the dogs stir again, and I turn around. He is standing a respectable distance away as if not wanting to intrude.

'Hi,' he says.

'Hey.' It's about all I can muster, and I turn back towards the ocean. I want him to make the first move. Maybe he already has?

'Extraordinary evening,' he says, conversationally. Small talk with a stranger, a fellow hiker, your neighbour? Is that what I am?

'Yes, in many ways.'

It feels rather like a game of chess, neither of us wanting to commit ourselves and show our hand. I don't want to engage with him in another polite chat. I want to get up, to stand over him or above him, to get some leverage and reclaim some of the power deficit I feel when I think about him. I am extremely tense, but strangely enough, the space between us does not seem to resonate with the same tautness as if the apprehensive energy dissipates somehow en route or he simply refuses to receive it and reflect it back to me. Maybe it's the dogs? What can I say or do to not feel at such a disadvantage? I want him to leave, and I want him to stay. I need to find out what he knows.

'Is she with you?' I say, before I can stop myself.

Uninvited, he moves closer and crouches on his haunches, like he is not intending to stay for long. He pats the dogs and scratches them behind the ears, and they dutifully sit down to try and prolong the pleasure. I want to tell him, 'Don't you dare touch them! You have touched everything else. Now fuck off.'

Then he says, 'She has gone away.' The accented inflection on the last word is ambiguous and leaves me uncertain whether this is a question or a statement.

'Yes, she has gone away. Have you seen her? Is she okay?' Being the one to ask the questions leaves me feeling vulnerable and at the mercy of his chosen response.

'I am sure she will be. But you don't understand her. You understand nothing.'

'Fuck you,' I say under my breath. How can he say such things without sounding derogatory? I want to hear him insult and belittle me, and then the game can really begin. Then I will be free to tell him exactly what I think of him. Only then can I truly kill him off.

'And what do you think it is that I don't understand?' I say.

'How to give her what she needs most. Then you will find her to be the most remarkable person in every way. And you will have everything you need in her.'

'And what is that, this thing she needs?'

Is he letting me know that he has achieved this state of nirvana? I know what it is; he talks her love language. She appreciates gifts of love—the love letters, heart-shaped stones, and all the other things she wears and keeps dear to her and acts of service—unsolicited offers to help, to do things for her, and to be available in an instant and on demand. These are not my natural inclination, so I had gone out of my way during the last few years to surprise her but to no avail. I had read somewhere that if it does not seem to bear fruit, then do not get despondent. Just keep doing it and so that's what I did. But I had ignored the footnote as it had not seemed relevant at the time—reading like a disclaimer, it said rather mournfully that if your partner is emotionally and/or sexually involved with someone else, this will frustrate your efforts.

'These things cannot be explained or taught. You either have it in you or you don't. You can't pretend it,' Calix says cryptically.

For fuck sake, is this the being that Sarah described as so conscious and without ego, these things she said she admires so much in him and why the thought of life without him seemed so unbearable? How does a conscious being sleep with another man's wife, in his house, in his bed? It seems clear that to him I am not yet enlightened enough, and I feel like it is tougher getting a straight answer out of him than out of Sarah. My mind tries to convince me that I should deck him right there, but that is not my style, or at least, confront him about the affair or tell him what I think of him or appeal to him with my pain, raw and exposed, and tell him how this has affected me. Something, anything, that I have recited in my head for six months and have imagined saying to him one day or written in my journal overwrought with the insult I believe he has dealt me. But nothing comes easily to mind, and this all feels too humiliating. Too much time lapses due to my indecision, and I don't quite know what to do next.

'Before you ask again,' he says, 'no, I don't know where she is.'

That's it, then, I decide, you are no longer useful to me. Are you not my nemesis? The one I have brooded over for six months? I have obsessed about how to kill you off, and here I sit on my mountain and joust with you. The dogs seem to pick up my feelings, or just get bored of his attention, and come over to me and paw at me and drool on my legs which I have now tucked under me prepared for the offensive, I guess. They look thirsty.

My mind is made up. 'My dogs need water,' I say. 'I need to go.'

I know what I need to do. I get up, too slowly, I think, to impress anybody. My rapidly cooling body feels stiff and sore from sitting here for so long and from the sapping heaviness I feel these days. For a moment, I am struck by vertigo and have to steady myself as I am very close to the edge of the cliff. A scene from a distant time and place flashes through my mind—rowdy, smoky, fires burning, groups of filthy, drunken men in celebratory mood in what looks like a tavern of sorts; someone has his arm around my shoulder, laughing with me, I turn towards him, and it's

Calix. Then it's gone, and I think, 'This is not good.' And I pretend to check my pockets for keys or something. Trying to appear satisfied and unrushed, I drink some water, but tossing my head backwards makes me even dizzier. I think it would be a good idea to look out to sea again in a show of calmness, but I am worried I might float off the precipice.

Harry and Sally play along. With a bark they head for the path, but I have to first walk towards and then past him to get back to the trail. I hesitate. I am beyond the precipice now, and the idea of jumping down to the stepped descent crosses my mind. It would certainly impress an observer, if only it wasn't for the inconvenience of looking silly lying there with a twisted ankle or worse. Would he carry me down in his arms? The question becomes rhetorical as I am now beyond him, and I scramble down at a half-run. I don't look back until I have reached the lower ridge, where I know I am out of sight from his vantage point. I know he has not followed me down, and I turn left and double back, off the path and along the contour where I tell the dogs to sit and wait in the shelter of a small cave peppered with animal droppings, grateful for the obedience I have installed in them in order to keep them safe and disciplined as they are with me every day in public places.

It is dark enough now to see nothing more than shadows hinting movement, and this is helpful, but I have to be careful nonetheless as I clamber back up through unchartered territory and edge above the looming precipice where I left him, that sheer-drops into the ocean below. I emerge exactly as expected, above and to the left of him, and I gloat that perhaps I know this mountain better than him; it is my friend, perhaps it *is* my mountain after all.

He is sitting precisely where I had been—what the hell is that about?

I pause to still my breathing from adrenaline as much as exertion. For a moment I take in his silhouette, appearing legless as he is precariously perched on the precipitous overhang, legs dangling in free space beyond. I wonder what he is thinking about; her perhaps?

Then it would seem that this is an appropriate moment, and I exhale a silent breath and close my eyes. Nothing else matters right now but this moment. Nothing before and nothing after—the term 'living impeccably' floats freely across the emotional void of my mind. I steady myself for the final act. This is when I let everything go. This is when I kill off Calix.

A little while later, as I jog with easy vigour the last kilometre back to the house, the dogs loping behind with tongues flapping, I decide I am going to start having sex again. It is not clear to me what type of sexual experience I am thinking of: purely physical enjoyment, transactional and without emotion, erotic and sensual, or loving and sacred, spiritual even? This seems to be the weirdest thought given what I have just done; how I got there I don't know. But I feel at ease and confident in this pronouncement, as if released from the puritan ideals born of the commitment of marriage. I think that this resolution is symbolic, that I am saying to myself that I want to be more me or to more fully experience myself for who I am; to accept my needs and desires and embrace my dark side, free of guilt and shame, and to live my life for me and what is important to me.

WHAT IS, IS

22

Pain has its reasons, pleasure is totally
indifferent.

(Francis Picabia)

Saturday, 29 January 2011

Jim has me in stitches.

In the middle of last winter, communing over a cappuccino and not quite sure how to broach the topic, I cautiously and somewhat obscurely asked him whether he has ever had an affair. I needed to talk to someone about Sarah's affair, someone I could trust, but was not quite sure how to broach the subject. He leaned back in his restaurant chair, stretched his legs, and looked into the middle distance. 'Well, now,' he said, 'that's a very interesting question indeed.'

And slowly it trickled out of him. He has been married almost twenty-five years and has children. Turns out, he has had a number of one-night stands, usually out-of-town on business trips and boosted by alcohol. But he considered none of these escapades as unfaithful to his marriage. 'They mean nothing to me,' he said. 'They happen entirely below the belt,' and he gestured with his hands as if he was unsure of whether I could locate his belt and fathom what nestled beneath it. With a wry smile I wondered if he thought I needed a refresher course given the extended drought I have experienced in that region. 'However,' he said, relishing the opportunity to build suspense for his revelation and still without any inkling of why I had raised the topic, 'I think I am now having an affair.'

I was frustrated that the news I wanted to share with him was being deferred by his self-absorbed disclosure but felt a tingle of relief as I was not yet sure what to say to him or how to say it as I had as yet disclosed my circumstances to no one. Turns out, he believed he has been in love with a woman for a year or two, somebody he has known for more than ten years. They have touched, kissed, and held hands once or twice and, according to him, had the most amazingly engrossing chats, but the biggest thing was the way he felt when he was with her or just thought about her, which he said he did almost all the time. Problem was, they almost never saw each other.

He said, 'When I sit with her and we talk, it feels like we are enclosed in a bubble, and the rest of the world doesn't exist. It lifts my spirits for weeks, which, come to think of it, it has to do because it is sometimes months before we see each other again. She offers endless promises of "let's meet for coffee again soon", but then, I don't hear from her for months, or she has endless excuses for why we cannot meet. Some of the reasons are legitimate, like her teenage kids are always around, but it's really starting to frustrate me.'

A sexless affair? I thought. That sounds more like a marriage to me—hardly see each other, repeated broken promises, and no genital contact.

'She's driving me mad,' Jim said, with uncharacteristic passion, finally able to speak with someone about his dilemma. 'I can't get her out of my mind. I can't focus on anything else. I'm completely in love with her. I've been trying for ages to get some real time with her, you know, like a weekend away or something so we can test this thing out, whether we connect at this level,' he said, pointing again to his nether regions languishing beneath the table cloth and providing part answer to my silent question.

Belatedly, and with relief that was palpable as the burden of this impasse rolled off his shoulders after sharing it with me, it occurred to him that I must have asked the question for a reason. So I had confided in him, and we talked about his situation and mine. When I told him about Sarah's affair, he was astounded that our marriage was not automatically over. He felt that if Sarah had been that deeply involved for so long, that it was not just something brief that happened and was over, that it would always be there for her and, therefore, for me.

Then he decided to tell me that some months earlier he had seen Sarah with a man walking on the beach. In the distance, it was clear to him that this couple was involved, although he had not immediately recognised her from afar. This couple suddenly separated when they came close, and Sarah had greeted him. Sarah walked on with Calix, then came back and caught up with Jim and repeatedly told him how she doesn't like walking alone on the beach. He had found it strange how she kept repeating it, and to him, this was a clear indication that she was trying to hide something. We had argued a little about whether, as my best friend, he had the responsibility to make this known to me, as in 'I think your wife is fooling around', but I was not sure myself what I would have done had it been me.

My desperate state in the aftermath of the affair had consumed our conversations for months, and I often felt embarrassed about this, but he seemed endlessly intrigued and concerned about me initially and that his friend of thirty years lived under what he called 'this tyranny' and more recently trying to help me make a decision even if I didn't have the guts to follow it through. Last year he kept saying, 'No one else but you are responsible for your own happiness, and when you are lying on your death bed one day, you need to at least know why your life was so miserable. (Fuck you, Jim.) So you need to have absolute clarity today why you should leave but that you have made at least a conscious decision to stay for whatever reason, like for the sake of the boys, and a plan in place for how you are going to cope with it in the meantime, otherwise you are just drifting and you lose control of your life because you lose your power to another.'

I always found his black-or-white approach too literal, too cause-and-effect, too linear; but sometimes I wondered if he was right. Even since Sarah disappeared, whenever we met, he rambled on in loud self-justification of his view of her and was not shy to make it clear just how disappointed he was that I had not been brave enough to make the decision 'while you are still in the driving seat'. He said that the outcome we now have as a result of her 'disappearance' is by default, through my inaction, and that my potency will forever be denied as a result. Eventually he grew weary of patting himself on the back, and for weeks now, our chats have been pretty pointless in the absence of the usual fascinations, plots, and deceptions which he always approached with gusto like some reality war game, but a small revival came of late as he is about to go overseas for a while and our last few exchanges have been hijacked by his predicament over what to do with his pseudo-affair.

So here we sit today in post-exercise euphoria on a still and sticky day, and as always, his opening words, preceded by a yawn and a stretch, are 'So what's news?' But he is not really interested in whether I have any news; he wants to tell me his. I silently hope it is not more of the same about his love frustrated, but I am feeling so agreeable chilling in the tree-shaded restaurant courtyard as is our ritual after playing beach bats or chasing a flying disc across the sand that it does not really matter to me.

Just to frustrate him, I say, 'I'm thinking of releasing this tiger from my board shorts and letting it loose on the women of the village, in an "I love everyone, and you're next" kind of way. But I haven't used a condom in years; what brand do you recommend, oh master?'

'Actually, that's a good lead in,' he says, and he surprises me by admitting they finally did the wild-monkey thing, he and 'herself'. My silent congratulations sour as his story takes shape.

'It was awful,' he says, and then in explanation, 'We had to go around the house, locking all the doors and setting the alarm in case her children came home. Then we went upstairs to her bedroom and had to close the windows and the curtains because the gardener was mowing the lawn and it was so noisy and she was paranoid that he or a neighbour would see us. I put on a condom, a brand I had never used before. It was thirty-eight degrees centigrade that day, and in this darkened fortress, I was sweating so much I just could not get any traction. Within minutes, it was like a sauna in the room, and we were floundering around, slipping off each other.' That actually sounded rather appealing to me. 'After a while, I wanted to change positions, you know, the way you need to after a while.' He looks at me, and I nod knowledgeably, then reassuringly, sensing he is about to need help with this, as his face has creased in tormented recollection of the scene he is describing.

Reliving the nightmare, he switches to present tense. 'So I turn her over to enter her from behind, but suddenly I can't feel anything. I think I'm inside her, but I'm not sure. I look down at my dick, and there it is, still willingly standing to attention. So I start thrusting, poking away, trying to get it in, and I can see I'm touching her, but I can't feel it. There's no sensation at all. So I reach down and grab it in both hands, but I have to look to see whether I have it because my hands feel they are holding something, but my dick can't feel a thing, and my vision is blurred by the sweat burning in my eyes, and she swivels her neck around and says, "Are you okay?"'

He is so meticulous and business-like by nature, that I know the imprecision of this maladroit unmanly moment would have hurled him into unfamiliar bewildered territory, and I want to reach out to him and tell him, 'It's okay,' but sense that this will offend him so much he might clam up.

'Then I get really scared, so I smack it a few times and then toss it from left to right, but nothing. It's there, I can see that, and it's not limp, but it's like a huge strap-on dildo dangling in front of me. I decide I have to quit, but I will give it one last herculean effort.' I consider whether Hercules fits the image of Jim and come up negative. 'So I lift her sweat-drenched arse up towards me and make ready for a final assault.' I raise my eyebrows, and suddenly uncomfortable with his choice of words, he gives me the lazy eye and says, 'You know what I mean.'

'Just keep going,' I say.

'So I ram it home. Bulls eye; I can see it disappear, but I can't feel anything and the moment of victory is short-lived as I see to my horror that I have visited the neighbour.'

'Who?' I say, confused, as I hadn't picked up this was a threesome.

'The neighbour,' he says, and when I shake my head in incomprehension—'I'm up to the hilt, shit-deep in her arse, you idiot. And she screams in pain and catapults off the sheets like a thoroughbred out the starting stalls and hits her head on the wall as she scrambles to get away from me, and she screams at me, "What the fuck was that?"'

I can't speak. Trying hopelessly to suppress a full-blooded guffaw I am squealing embarrassingly, causing him to look around at the other tables to see if I am drawing unwanted attention.

'And she huddles there, sobbing, with the sheet pulled around her, blood oozing from the cut on her forehead and running into her eye and yells at me to get the hell out of her house.'

I am almost comatose, not sure of whether to feel sorry for him or her, even if in this moment I could get myself to feel sympathetic while I hold my sides to prevent myself from falling about. He looks at me, looking boyish and still frowning, as if imploring me to rewind the clock, or to reassure him that it is all right, it could happen to anybody, that it happens from time to time with me; but he knows I am not having sex. He sounds so genuine in his distress, after waiting for so long to consummate his love. The picture that emerges as his story took shape leaves me somewhat discomfited. And I fleetingly wonder if this is what I have to look forward to, if I bring into reality the promise I had made myself to indulge in carnal pleasures once again.

'Anyway,' he says forlornly, once I get a grip on myself again and needing something to say. 'I think she came twice. Maybe.'

'Oh, good,' was all I could manage, and followed up with, 'And you?'

'I don't know.'

'What?'

'I have no idea,' he says, suddenly mortified. 'But the point is, I Googled it, and there are these condoms that seem to anaesthetise your dick, probably to prevent premature ejaculation. I threw the rest of the box away.'

'Shit, I was going to ask you if I could use them.' I do my best impression of a seated Michael Jackson crotch-grab. 'This monster is rearing his ugly head and won't take "no" for an answer.'

23

Acceptance of what has happened is the
first step to overcoming the consequences
of any misfortune.

(William James)

Monday, 31 January 2011

I have left it to the last minute, I know. But even under normal circumstances, it is not a task that one relishes, and these are not normal circumstances. The owner of the health store where Sarah has her consulting rooms had left a number of voicemails. His text message was the least ambiguous, professing that while he is sympathetic to my situation, rental for two months is now outstanding, and he will be compelled to clear out Sarah's stuff as he needs to rent out the space to another consultant unless I am prepared to cover the debt and pay in advance for next month. When I phoned him and offered to pay, he did not seem particularly keen on that option anyway as he said he needs an active practice to be operating above his pharmacy to generate business for the products that sit on his shelves.

At first, I felt immobilised; I wanted to keep things the way they were, and I tried to convince myself that as luck would have it, she might return no sooner I have given up her room. But I saw the folly in this thinking and that I would likely be faced with the same problem again next month.

How different can this be? I try to reason with myself, with the clean-out I have embarked on at home. I have spent many evenings, after the boys were asleep, familiarising myself with the contents of drawers and cupboards, which sounds like a strange thing to do, but that is the way it was. I reorganised stuff so that it made more sense to me and made those things I thought I would regularly need more accessible.

In the process, I threw out lots of items, the most rewarding of which was setting aside boxes of children's clothing and toys destined for underprivileged kids, which I delivered to the local care facility on the first day of school. I selected from this stash some of the almost-new-but-too-small clothing and managed to finally make good a promise I had made to two of the waiters at the deli and the gentleman who makes my cappuccinos to perfection, who have children of Jack's age but smaller in stature. The smiles this produced warmed my heart, and the other day they brought their boys to work to proudly show me they are wearing the clothing. And a wonderful bond has formed as we have twice now invited these boys with us to play on the jungle gym around the corner from the deli.

Reorganising and clearing out unneeded things helped me to feel more in control and that life was manageable as a single parent, just the way it was. I reclaimed my study and found that it was truly possible to have some surfaces around the house free of clutter. There were so many bits and pieces that belonged to Sarah amongst all this stuff, and at first, I did not know where to put them, but in the end, I converted the room downstairs, meant to be her study-office but which she never used, into a storeroom walled with boxes containing her possessions stacked to the ceiling. It did not stop me thinking about her and what had happened, but it kept me sane.

So I collected cardboard boxes from the supermarket, and here I stand in her consulting room, after dropping the boys at school, not quite knowing where to start. The cops have been here, the remnants of their dusting even more repugnant than the shambles they have left behind, not at all like the organized chaos Sarah created by choice. Enlisting the help of an assistant pharmacist, I start with the biggest items, the massage bed, the desk and swivel chair, computer and microscope, and load them in the trailer attached to the Jeep. And I scoop her crystals and oils and magic potions and an assortment of indescribable paraphernalia into boxes and label them as best I can. Laminated charts and photographs and the boys' artworks all find a home.

By lunchtime I have left one bookcase and its contents till last. Its open front is covered with a beautiful cloth perhaps to neaten the overall appearance of the room, but I have a sense that it is a sacred space, and I have avoided it for some reason. I remove the cloth and fold it neatly, and it reveals shelves brimming with books and folders squeezed to make them fit, as if the shelves would expand when necessary to accommodate an infinite quantity. It feels just too much to contemplate, and I stare out the window while I consider if I can defer it till another day, but the thought of returning is unappealing. My back aches, so I stretch towards the ceiling and bend to touch my toes and windmill my arms around my waist in an effort to release the muscle spasm that threatens to take hold. I check the time, mindful that I have to collect the boys mid-afternoon, and I wonder whether I will be done by then.

Looking for a way to avoid tapping into what I feel standing here, I am suddenly aware of how thirsty I am, and I go outside and light a cigarette and drink a bottle of mineral water after carrying two boxes down the stairs and past the staff members who are pretending not to watch and loading them into the vehicle en route. As I yet again mount the stairs leading to her room, I feel like I am floating up the staircase and recognise the queasy numbness that has set in and which I have not encountered for weeks; at least, not since we embarked on our camping travels a few weeks ago and I was anxious that Sarah would return home to find us gone. Not that I haven't felt strange and uncertain, even panicked and terrified at times, but this is distinctly dissimilar to those feelings of longing and aloneness. It is the eeriness of being in a space steeped in Sarah's energy. Suspended there, and clinging to the handrail, Sarah's closest friend at work approaches me and asks me how I am doing and whether there is any news, and I say I am doing fine, and there is no update on Sarah's whereabouts. She starts to say something about it being so weird but then is called away to attend to a customer, and this interlude puts me in motion again.

Back in her room, I close the door and kneel down in front of the bookcase. There is a beautiful, heavy tapestry draped over the top ends of the bookcase held in place by the assortment of heart-shaped stones, which cover the uppermost shelf. It hangs out of sight behind the bookcase, shielded by the books and files, and I wonder why she did not make it more visible perhaps on one of the walls in her room. I stare at the heart-shaped stones and wonder which of them are infused with their love. I start to touch some of them until my hand recoils reflexively resonating with the energy of an electric shock. I push down the ancient thoughts which menacingly surge out of the sealed box tucked deep in the recesses of my mind, which I cannot discard but know I should never again open.

I methodically start to remove the books, beginning with the top shelf, and stack them into piles of approximately equal size on the carpeted floor to accommodate fitting them all into the three boxes that remain. When I get to the items on the bottom shelf and remove the last of them, the tapestry billows as if gusted by a draft from a hidden window, and the momentum of it shifts its centre of gravity. It begins to slip, dislodging some of the stones which had secured it. I watch this with my hands full and mouth agape as the critical point is exceeded and in an instant, the tapestry concertinas upon itself, tumbling all the stones on to the carpet.

There is a moment of total silence, like when an unsafe, disused building doomed for demolition folds in upon itself in front of your eyes before the sound of the sequenced detonations responsible for its demise reach your ears as you watch from the middle distance. The belated discharges which shock my auditory senses pale by comparison, but it stuns me nevertheless because it is so unexpected, or perhaps because of the significance of the items now exposed and sprawled before me.

Because in front of me lie Sarah's journals, each quite different in appearance but unmistakably her journals, without even needing to open them, brought into light from behind the tapestry where they were somehow lodged and which concealed their secrets. I suddenly feel quite heavy, as if the load is too arduous to bear, and realise that I have expelled air from my lungs and have not refilled my chest cavity. I gather them up and put them aside and then turn my back on them and carefully pack all the other books, in a purposeful act of denying gratification. I seal the boxes and record their contents on the sides and top of each.

Only then I turn my attention to the journals and open the one that happens to lie at the top of the stack. The first words at the top of the first page spell out 'Feb 25th' but no year is noted. I close the cover quickly and find myself on my feet at the far end of the room as if propelled there by some unseen force. In this empty room, behind a closed door, I have in front of me access to potential information that I could only have wished for six months ago as I searched for the truth about their relationship.

Written on these pages is probably a detailed account of her feelings and experiences over the past few years, and hidden in those words there must lie reference to how she felt about our relationship and her other man, either clearly and unambiguously acknowledged or obliquely insinuated. Either will surely be useful to me, I think. Reading such incriminating words will be self-indulgent and re-ignite those feelings of betrayal that still linger such that they can override the throbbing tenderness of grief which pervades me, and for a moment this feels like my preferred option as the process of clearing out her room is acknowledging that she has gone and has left me engulfed in sorrow akin to the mourning of the recent passing of a loved one.

I stare at the journals with a feeling I think is repulsion, take two paces towards them, then turn left, open the door, and sneak into the bathroom down the passage where I wash my hands repeatedly as if trying in vain to remove any trace of sinful thoughts and deeds. The voices in my head of respect for privacy fight a pitched battle with the pain of deceit and betrayal. Then I return and lock the door of the consulting room with its narrative contained in those volumes that I cannot bear to engage yet cannot understand why they have been presented to me like this.

I sit cross-legged in the passage, leaning my back against the closed door as if guarding a sacred tomb. Why would she record this period of her life and then leave it to be discovered by me, in the same way that the password to one of her email accounts was left on the system for me to access? Is this her way of feeding manageable bits of information to me when she felt the time was right? Or perhaps they contain clues to her whereabouts or what has happened to her, or at least, what was going on in her mind that led to her disappearance?

This thought almost gets me to rise, and I dig a fist into the floor to lift myself up, but I sink down again. There was a time in recent months when I would never have let up an opportunity like this, but I know if I regress now to that state of paranoia and distrust and 'the need to know', there will probably be no return for me, and the availability of such information will compel me to search for more.

When we met, I had told her that I want our bond to be pure, by which I think I meant wholesome, innocent, and untainted; I even had this silly notion that we should not sleep together until we were married or at least, until our previous/existing relationships were well and truly something of the past as I had always begun my relationships with sex. So this is the moment I must turn the corner and start confronting my biggest fears and stop feeling that all is lost because our relationship is not pure. Silent tears parade self-consciously behind the hand that covers my eyes.

I now understand that when I embarked on this marriage, this committed relationship, I brought my own assumptions of love and romance and marriage that were just as pungent and confining as the shackles of organised religions once were. These expectations conspired to create a love that was unfree of my preconceived notions and beliefs. I then compounded this with aspirational assurances of devotion and loyalty for the future, pledging allegiance and duty and expecting the same from her when we had no idea what we would encounter on the way or who we would become, binding ourselves with vows and promises we barely understood. And thus I had become constrained by the fears inherent in the commitment of marriage.

And this is only a part of it, the portion that she and I are responsible for. The other ingredient, I contemplate as I sit here, is even more treacherous, more so because it is clandestine but omnipresent and nobody alerts you to it. It is what is embedded in the social construct of the institution of marriage, and without giving permission, you take on the fears and expectations of others—present, past, and future. And in this way Sarah and I have been living out a fantasy, not of our making, rather than choosing a love that is ours. And sprawled against the door with these thoughts, I feel I am able to distinguish between love and all else. Love is what it is; it is not concerned with what was or what should be.

So now I have to reinterpret what 'pure' means to me, and I realise that life, love, and marriage is not what I had hoped and dreamt it would be; life is real, it is messy and has presented me with ugly twists and turns which were carefully designed for me to grow, to teach me the lessons I need to learn. Now I must take my ego to task for making me feel obliged to react in these ways. Now I must learn to observe myself in a situation, honour myself by acknowledging how I feel about it, and give myself the power to decide what to do with it: whether to be held hostage by it, or to take the opportunity for it to free me—to know love. So when these moments come again, as they will, I shall persuade myself to take a deep breath and then release it, always ensuring that the exhalation is longer than the in-breath to expel all the clutter that clouds my vision. Then I will say, 'It is what it is, and it is exactly the way it should be' and ask myself how best I can not only love her but also take care of myself right now.

It is time to write the final chapter, to click 'save' on the final version of my manuscript. To put all this behind me, forever existent but no longer in the grip of it, and to release my ego from bondage and let my spirit soar. So I close my eyes for a long time and then take a deep breath and exhale slowly, my chest concave and protesting against the vacuum that is created. And after the new in-breath I say, 'What is, is.' And I know what I need to do. I unlock the door and step inside. I kneel down, hold each of the journals for a moment to my heart, and say, 'It is exactly the way it should be' as I consign each one to what may be its final resting place, their contents known only to the writer. Then I seal the last box and write, 'Sara-lea's Journals' with the marker pen. I will ask someone I can trust to keep them safe; in fact, I will ask someone she would trust to keep them safe.

24

Forgiveness is almost a selfish act
because of its immense benefits to the
one who forgives.

(Lawana Blackwell)

Thursday, 10 February 2011

Days become weeks, and it is now two months since she vanished.

Every story needs closure, and I pen these words with a lightness, an elation, filled with a sense of abundance and potential in this moment. Azura will be proud of me. It was with a numbing trepidation but a deep conviction that last week, as a gift to myself, I embarked on a personal journey, my own vision quest—seven days of solitude in the wilderness, just three or four hours' drive from the city.

I had not known what I expected to achieve, but I thought that setting about it with nothing in mind was the best approach. I had even searched for some way to name this experience but failed; it was something about gratitude and appreciation for life, but I soon understood that I might only know this upon my return, if at all. I was concerned that the boys would worry that I may not return, just like their mother, but I had convinced their grandparents to stay at our house so that they would at least be in familiar surroundings and with the dogs and cats. I planned to walk and paint and take photographs, no writing permitted, and then spend the last three days in deep contemplation on a cleansing fast. I carried a yoga mat, a sleeping bag, and fifty litres of water and rat-pack rations as the intention was not to starve, and I reckoned three days of fasting was sufficient for my purposes, but I would need sustenance before the long drive home.

The first day was filled with getting to my destination. After three days, I sought out a suitable shaded ledge under an overhang, within a few kilometres from my vehicle, and then I made multiple return trips to complete the laborious task of transporting the five-litre water bottles and meagre belongings to what was my home for three nights. When I sat there, it was not long and the mantra on which I would meditate came to me—truth—I did not bother whether it was about *the* truth, *my* truth, or to *be* truth. I just knew I wanted to *see* truth. For the next three days I meditated on that ledge, working with the limbic system using four in-breaths, four out-breaths, easing into a rhythmic sine wave heart beat unlike our natural 'heart monitor' spike. When I returned home, I found myself drawn for the first time to the driftwood that clung to that artist's canvass and noticed she had named it 'Truth'.

Each night in the wilderness, I had the same dream. In the dream, I am walking up the mountain with a group of people. I seem to have a woman alongside me, and it is not Sarah. We reach the rocky section. It's barren, with very little fynbos, a couple of forlorn trees here and there, and we start clambering up. The light is poor, and I suddenly notice that everyone is inappropriately dressed. The women are well covered in flowing layers, the men in hooded cloaks—almost medieval dress. When we reach a small plateau, we halt and seem to be hanging around, somewhat spread out, doing nothing much, and suddenly I start dancing. It's just spontaneous, and it becomes a real wild man, Iron John, let-my-hair-down thing. I am completely absorbed in it, totally unselfconscious. While I am dancing, some of the people seem to float off the edge of the plateau, one by one, until just a handful remain. When it is over, this guy comes towards me and tries to kill me. Then the scene abruptly shifts, and I have no hair, as if there is no longer anything between me and everything else. There is nothing around me and yet everything I need.

And while in contemplative state during awake time, swimming before my eyes I kept seeing myself or Calix or both of us sitting on the ledge on 'my mountain'. When one of us sat there, it was not long before the other swam into view, and it seemed as if we sat on top of or within each other, ethereally transposed wraithlike without any apparent discomfort or awareness of each other. At first it felt eerie rather than bothersome, and I tried without working too hard at it to observe it and allow for it, and soon it was associated with a sense of comfort.

Apart from that, there were no mystical inspirations, no flashing insights, no clarifying revelations, and no purpose-filled visions, just a sense, a deep inner knowing of peace and tranquillity. And since my return from solitary contemplation in the mountains, the world around me suddenly unveils colours and sounds I never before experienced. I notice people gravitating towards me, selfishly seeking occasion to siphon off a momentary dose of well-being, of peace, of a space where 'contentment' neither exists nor is absent. In its abundance this takes nothing from me; it actually seems to boost my potency. Those around me make unsolicited comments on how my energy and aura has changed, and they seem at once relieved by this and in awe of it, but only I know from whence it comes. I mull over what Sarah would say if she was to appraise my energy field now with her divining rods.

I wonder fleetingly whether the cops have pieced things together and will soon pay me a visit with an 'everyone is a suspect, including you,' introduction, which could either mean that they haven't got a clue or that they have decided that there actually is something suspicious about her disappearance, but the thought does not linger and has little apprehension attached to it.

Before we left on our vacation last month, I thought I should notify the detectives, from whom I had heard not a word, that we would be away for a while. I left messages for them for three days and eventually, on the road to our holiday destination, I found a bored voice on the line, which was attached to an apathetic mind apparently still reminiscing about his family vacation, or am I being harsh? His voice sounded unfamiliar, but then I established that the detective heading up the case was on indefinite sick leave, and this was his replacement I was talking to. For a moment he seemed to have a different missing person case in mind, but eventually, we found each other. He said that, 'according to the notes on file', the case is still open, but for now, they are taking the view that she left of her own volition, which I thought was a big word to use, because there was no evidence of foul play or suspicious circumstances and nothing untoward had come up when the team-of-two had come to take photographs and dust the house, her consulting room and her car and mine for good measure, which produced a hopefully inaudible sigh of relief from me, which proved premature. They had stashed her cellphone and laptop computer into evidence bags, and he said conspiratorially that they were 'busy with these' as well as her phone account records and bank statements but that nothing of interest had revealed itself so far regarding the week prior to her disappearance.

I am conscious that I no longer actively search for her and don't have that gnawing feeling that I should be. After the initial frenzied preoccupation with it, that guilty need to do something each day to try and understand what had happened to her probably came to an end many weeks ago, but what had lingered was imagining that I saw her in every other person that came into view, and these mirages caused me no end of heartache and anxiety. This smiling, long-legged woman with the purposeful stride coming towards me that made my heart stop till she came near enough for me to confirm it was not her, that tall woman with a head of rich and thick, waist-long dark hair infused with tones of copper and light the envy of all females, who just disappeared around the corner of the building in front of me and who gave me cause to quicken my pace, or the laughter coming from the young women at the table behind me which so disturbed me I moved to another table.

At times I had imagined her in the kitchen, ferreting away or flushing the toilet or coming down the driveway at the end of the day when I heard a vehicle and the dogs barked in excitement or warning. Even the occasional silver car flashing past me, driving too fast as she always did, had sometimes caused me, feeling foolish but not able to stop myself, to do an illegal U-turn and catch up with it, just to be sure.

It was only since coming home from the wilderness a few days ago that these hallucinations receded entirely, and my mind seemed to accept that I could not invoke her presence by sheer willpower and delusion. I am no longer concerned that she has harmed herself; Sarah would have prepared a much more public and dramatic sending-off. But I know now that I cannot 'will' her back; my mind has made her gone and she will return if she chooses to, when she is ready and if she wants to.

Of course, I haven't seen Calix for weeks now, not since we encountered each other up the mountain that evening, and the splendour of knowing that I was the instrument of this release is liberating and empowering beyond measure. That I had acted forcefully and decisively has discharged a sense of masculine potency that washes over me and permeates everything I do and how I present myself to the world. I have walked up the mountain a few times since then, to keep up the routine of it, not always as far up the rocky outcrop as I have sometimes taken along the boys whose eager liveliness for the adventure of it starts out fresh but can wane suddenly and unexpectedly and which I have to manage carefully and remind them that they need to conserve energy as we still have to walk all the way back to the house. The mind being a funny thing, by turn of habit, each time I set out along the service road towards the rocky ascent, I am on high alert imagining that we will encounter Calix, but I now know that he, too, is not around. And I am grateful that it seems he led a fairly solitary life ensconced in his cottage hideout deep in enemy territory—'the embedded lover' is a nice turn of phrase.

When I drive along the street towards our house, I often wonder what the other residents think of his whereabouts. If I was one of them, blissfully unaware of the intimacy that has taken place between two of my neighbours and what has transpired since, I would probably think nothing of this. If I was inquisitive about the goings-on in my neighbourhood, and it occurred to me that I had not seen him and his little car reversing out of the garage for a while nor greeted him as he purposefully strode in the evenings up the mountain we share, I imagine I might conclude that he has gone away for the summer holidays.

So that is what I would think, that he is enjoying a long summer holiday somewhere.

If someone asks, I can comfortably and honestly respond that I am pretty sure he is with her, also 'gone'.

And if they are together, there is nothing I can do about it now.

PART II

The Other Woman

This is (also) not the truth . . .

But who knows what really happened?

**Part II: The Other Woman—This is (also) not the truth . . .
But who knows what really happened?**

Rainbow promise

Recoil

The good man

Strange attractors

Chinese Bamboo

Falling apart

Equifinality

Epilogue

End of Part 2

RAINBOW PROMISE

25

The art of love . . .
is the art of persistence.

(Albert Ellis)

Wednesday, 23 February 2011

We had arranged to meet last Friday for coffee at the restaurant, which I came to discover, was a brief stroll from where she lives. That day Harry and Sally gave her a greeting far in excess of their standard open-faced, tail-wagging repertoire reserved for just about anyone without criminal tendencies. 'Your dogs are truly amazing,' she said, once they had settled down. 'I'm more of a cat person, and I brought a kitten back from the East Coast with me last month. It's the first time I've taken on responsibility for another since my son, Wade, died. His name is Pi-shu. It's an ancient Chinese name for panda. It means "brave".'

I could not stop thinking about her and wanted to meet with her, or so I had thought, to understand grief. A couple of years ago she had lost her teenage son and more recently her father; this much I knew from the information that accompanied her artwork, and I have come to realise that I am grieving the loss of many things. When I told her this, she said, 'I don't think I am an expert in grief.'

Then followed an easy outpouring of where we found ourselves to be in our lives. There was a mirrored experience in almost everything we talked about, some beautiful and stirring and some poignant and disquieting. Every story she told me I could respond to with my version in which the facts and circumstances differed, but the emotional theme, whether wounding or inspiring, remained the same. The realist in me thought that this would be true for anyone you meet and get along with; there would be many instances of hopeful common ground and comparable life experiences. But that day I felt like I was inside her stories, as if I have lived through them. Somehow, I recognised her, and it was a joyful recognition, like we had struggled in vain for centuries to escape our linked destiny perhaps due to some karmic impediments. It was a pure connection of two souls that had known each other for aeons, as though we have lived in 'parallel universes' and finally the male and female incarnations have been brought together again and made whole. And I wondered whether we had met before?

But when I told her this, Jade said, 'Are you talking about twin flames or soul mates?' I looked at her, uncomprehendingly. 'People think a soulmate is your perfect fit, and that's what everyone wants. You may meet in many incarnations, but I think a true soulmate is the person who shows you everything that is holding you back. They may even be the darkness in your life that causes you much pain and suffering and shows you your light. I think at times they make you so desperate and out of control that you simply have to transform your life. But you have to learn many lessons of love and loss and forgiveness and compassion from which you have to heal before you can recognise your twin ray, your other half, as the intensity of facing your mirror can be daunting in the extreme.'

'That doesn't sound like a peaceful, nurturing coexistence,' I said, wondering whether the golden white orb of light I experienced in the ocean that day I first saw her was a measure of this intensity. I have felt incomplete, abandoned, adrift, and barren—until this moment.

'It's not meant to be,' she said. 'A true soulmate will lift your mask and provoke you to attend to who you are so you can change your life or become who you truly are. They help you evolve and dissipate karma. Only once you are ego-free can you meet in the spiritual dimension with your twin flame, and you are likely to recognise them immediately because you really are 'one', like two sides of the same coin. You will feel whole and love unconditionally and without expectation; no game playing and manipulation. But your unconditional love will be tested because if they are in another physical relationship, you will have to respect and honour that bond. And sometimes it's difficult to know, as someone can carry the near-frequency of your twin soul.'

I was quickly getting confused. If not my twin flame, then perhaps Jade was a catalyst, carrying the near-frequency of my twin. 'Look out for synchronistic moments and the spiritual master numbers eleven-eleven,' she said, in the mistaken assumption that this was helpful. 'The eleven carries the vibrational frequency of balance, and signifies male and female parity, left and right, yin and yang, sun and moon, all these things, yet holds them both separate.'

Was it in *The Alchemist* that I read about 'solve et coagula'—meaning to separate and bring together?

'But I often hear people talking about their soulmate as a life partner?' I said.

'Live with a soulmate forever? No way!' Jade seemed astounded. 'Relationships come with expectations and conditions, and that is not divine love. No, I think it's too painful because they challenge who you are to the core. They unsettle you, bruise your ego, peel open your wounds, and reveal your agendas. They fracture your heart so new light can expose the best of you.'

I could not imagine her ever doing these things, but it was early days, surely. 'Only your last five words sound rewarding, Jade. Are you saying they come into your life just to reveal another layer of yourself to you and then leave?'

'And they give you access to your angels, your spiritual master . . . ' Jade said.

Five hours and a lunch later, we extricated ourselves from a hug that seemed to last for eternity while my whole being quivered through my body, and it surprised me that it did not feel like lust. In fact, my body was trembling throughout our time together that day, and I was sure it was apparent to her, so with some embarrassment I told her.

So we have met at the deli again each day this week, simply unable not to, and aware of the watchful eyes of the other regulars at the restaurant who know us both. Each day the conversation ebbed and flowed easily, so effortlessly, in fact, that it felt like I had known her for many lifetimes. Except for the first one, the subsequent exchanges contained much hypothesising about what exactly was going on here between us. When the vocabulary escaped her, Jade conjured up some magic, and it produced the words 'rainbow promise'. After just a few days, she spoke of the gift that meeting me had already presented her and the hope she felt as a result: of how she has woken up pain-free these last few days, and how she knows she should seek out more than she is currently allowing herself to expect in her life.

Anyhow, 'her man' Gino is out of town for the week, and he seems to be giving her an unusual level of attention these past few days, she tells me, and she believes this is because he can feel that she has turned away from him in some way, but I get the sense this was already happening before I came into her orbit. Last night he texted her and, uncharacteristically, asked her whether she still loves him and said that he feels sad, and now she is explaining to me why this might be so by filling me in about what happened the other night.

'Samantha was a bit pissed that night,' Jade says, 'and I was surprised she was saying these things in front of him and others. It set off his jealousy, but she did not mean to do that. For her it was just the most amazing thing that she felt she needed to share with me, how you had come to her last week and told her what had happened while you were swimming in the sea.'

Samantha owns the deli. 'What did she say?'

'She said that while you were speaking to her, you were moved to tears as you described watching me walk towards you in the water while you were swimming with your dogs beyond the breakers, and how you felt this light radiate from me as I came closer and that this moment seemed to last forever. Then I said to you, "Hi, Clive" as if I knew you. And that you said we spoke for a few minutes and figured out that you had bought my artwork. And that you needed to meet me, so she gave you my number.'

'Is that why you chose to meet with me?'

'I was intrigued to hear that you could see my aura.' I didn't know quite how to express it to Samantha, but I recall I had said something about a gentle glow of light. But I had not mentioned those flashes of another time and place created by the proximity of the triad of life forces in the water that day. I still don't know how to describe it; I simply understood that we have known each other before and that something will become of this moment. Treading water in the ocean that day, I did not feel overwhelmed by Jade's presence, in awe of her beauty out of my league, or sexually aroused by her. I felt completely at ease and connected. After a minute or two, I introduced myself to Gino, who had been pretending to ignore our conversation, and took the next wave to shore.

Perhaps not brave enough to call for a couple of weeks after that magical moment in the ocean, I caught a glimpse of her arriving at the deli as I was leaving on a windy Thursday last week, and this had compelled me the next morning to send her a text asking if we could meet for coffee. She said she had already come by the restaurant where I spend much of my time writing to find me. An hour later, we were sitting there together, with a cappuccino for me and a double espresso for her and the dogs at our feet.

Today we are walking through a forest, made all the more magical by a thick mist the vapours of which seem to permeate my being and enclose us in the surreal moment in which we find ourselves. We had decided that meeting at the same place again would be foolish, given the awareness growing in us as we realised how meaningful this connection was. The dogs are covering much more distance than us, darting around and sniffing and digging and chasing squirrels just for the hell of it. Her artwork was the apparent catalyst, at least, the identifiable one, which brought us together. For her livelihood, she produces representations of hearts using seashells or driftwood and other natural materials arranged on canvass, and heart shapes hewn by nature was Sarah's obsession. They are displayed at the deli, and it was these that the boys had chosen as

Christmas gifts for their mother. I guess it was them that brought us together.

'Gino wanted to know whether you are married and if your wife is beautiful and whether you have children, those kinds of things. All base, physical things, bits of information that would put him at ease. So this is why he was texting me last Friday, when you and I met here for the first time and chatted for so long. He had figured out that we were together that day, or perhaps he drove past the restaurant and saw us; it's the type of thing he would do.' She is talking about her ex-husband with whom she seems to still have an on-off relationship. Earlier she described his previous jealous rages in response to her close but platonic relationships with men, and I am feeling more and more concerned for her and mindful of my true agenda here.

We are quiet for a while, then, still thinking of the moment we met in the ocean, Jade says, 'In fact, Gino made a comment about you when you walked out of the sea that day. It seemed completely out of context, or rather, it just did not seem to resonate with the energy I felt from you, and I didn't take much notice of it.'

'What did he say?'

'I'm not sure I want to tell you,' she says.

'Okay.'

But she says it anyway. 'He said that he was told you are aggressive and violent with your wife.' This, it seems, he had found out before I had made any contact with Jade, and I instantly feel wary as I cannot imagine how and why this is so. Unless it was a chance comment, based more on his own behaviour than mine, then he already knew who I was and Sarah's view of me as an abusive husband has somehow found its way to him, and if so, surely after I knew about her affair as this was when my anger was apparent and Sarah seemed to be building a case against me in preparation for a separation when I had moved out of the house. Or perhaps he knows Calix, who had evidently said that he can't believe I am the person Sarah made me out to be?

'He didn't say anything else about it over the weekend,' Jade says, 'but when I dropped him at the airport on Monday morning, he looked me in the eyes and said, "Be good". And in a text the other day, on Friday, when he seemed to have figured out that we were meeting, he said something like "I am sure his wife would not like to know", and it was obviously a threat.'

'It seems he is not aware that Sarah is not around.' Or maybe he knows where she is?

Jade says, 'He was so concerned about me spending time with someone that is so moved by me. I just wish I could see myself in that way, but mostly, I feel so ordinary and dull.' I want to tell her she is everything but that, but it feels a bit limp, and she says as if embarrassed by what she has shared, 'Oh, I meant to tell you, I believe you know Francois, with the ponytail?'

'Yes.'

'He came to me in a dream months before I met him, as a grey wolf and then a horse, and now we are close friends. Anyway, I saw him the other day and asked him if he knew you. He said that he was one of the whistleblowers who told you about the affair.'

'Amongst others.'

'I thought that it was very courageous of him to not keep it a secret as he may have felt more obliged to be loyal to the friends he was with that evening he found out.'

I say, 'I imagine that Francois has read something into whatever was shared between you and him the other day, and that this connection I feel with you, no matter where it goes, is finding its way into the minds of people who come across it. Francois would have told Azura, and she saw us together at the restaurant yesterday. Then you introduced me to that close friend of yours, and she said she knows me, but I don't know her. What does she do?'

'Lucy? She's a kinesiologist.'

That would put her directly in Sarah's social and work circle. 'Where does she live?'

'Little Rock Estate,' she says. That was where Calix lived before he moved in next door. The synchronicity, the meaningful coincidences, abound. The interconnectedness of the people in this village strikes me because I have the strange sense that Lucy was at the dinner party when Francois found out about the affair. This energy between us, that we haven't acted on yet, but in truth we are, is already coursing through the social network. And I am anxious that if we evolve our connection to that level, we will be found out. I am irritated that I feel committed to a marriage with a woman who is not even here, and this voice in my head that knows that I have overstepped some line is in attendance. Why can't I just move the line, after all, it's my line, isn't it? And do the unusual circumstances in which I find myself not allow for it?

'I had a dream about you last night,' Jade says, with a smile. 'You were driving a Kombi, like a campervan. Our four boys were in the car, and they were all about eleven years old. We had made love for the first time the previous day, and I was not quite sure what to do, whether to come to you or put suntan lotion on my child. I was stuck in this indecision.' I am waiting for more. 'And that was it, nothing else happened in the dream.'

The last two days, at the restaurant, Jade had laughingly invited me back to her house, and I think we both knew that if we did this, we would not even get as far as the bedroom, so intense was our desire to be drawn into the other. She kept asking if I would like to come over and see her kitten, then 'see' became 'hold' and then 'stroke', and we giggled childishly at this, but I always shook my head. I don't feel ready for that yet, but I can't really explain why, except that I want her to be back with 'her man' this weekend and have her feet firmly grounded and see where that leaves her. And, in all honesty, I am concerned about what he knows or suspects and how he may react. So far we have been quite public with our meetings, which could be explained away to the curious, but being caught entering her house or in her bed would be a different matter altogether. Yet as we walk together in the early morning through the forest, the mist sitting thick and still around the nakedness of the lower de-branched extremities of plantations through which the jeep track snakes, I desperately want to take her and hold her close, stroke her face, brush her lips with mine, and lose myself in her. I look for a way we can leave the main path along which we stroll and scramble up the slippery slope away from prying eyes, find a secluded spot in the mist, and act out this fantasy.

Just then my phone rings, and I immediately think it is Sarah intuiting that something is going on, and I laugh at how silly I am; she's gone. It is the school; little Jack has had an accident and has a large gash on his forehead and needs to see a doctor urgently, and the moment is broken as we reluctantly turn around and quicken the pace as we return along the path to our cars.

Jade is pensive. A little breathless from the pace I am forcing on us in my anxiety for Jack, she says, 'I do wonder about small disasters that prevent precious time together. Is it the universe or is it our own fear that causes such a thing to happen? I mean, if we have a set of values that are ingrained and programmed as strongly as yours are, and they are, because you have held them despite your enormous challenge in your marriage, a contract that we have made with ourselves, with God and with other beings, then surely, if one starts to act against it or even has intention to, it's quite possible that these things can happen. Especially if there is uncertainty, doubt or guilt, or other disruptive energies.'

As we hurry back along the path, the mist now lifting as if reflecting the broken moment, Jade and I try to figure out what exactly this thing is that we feel: this energy that emanates between us. 'When I am with you,' I say, 'I feel like I'm a teenager. My hands are shaking and my lips are quivering and I feel like a complete idiot. I feel stuff I haven't felt in more than a decade.'

'I also don't know what is going on here between us,' Jade says, 'but I know it's something I need to hide from others because I can feel my integrity is not entirely intact. So much stuff came up for me after we met last Friday, I spent the whole weekend processing it. On Friday I kept asking myself whether you don't just want to get laid, and this is just some game you are playing. But when we said goodbye, and I felt the energy from you when we hugged, I felt something totally different. I felt your raw emotions. And now I am here with you, and I don't want to leave. It feels like this will erupt like a supernova, and I am afraid it will then just fizzle out.'

'I think I'm also waiting to see if this feeling fades,' I say, 'and I keep asking myself whether I don't just want to sleep with you. I suppose I've had a few opportunities to have a brief fling or a one-night stand since Sarah's affair, but it just didn't seem to interest me, and I walked away from it each time. I think what prevented me, mostly, was a determination not to break the faithfulness I had managed to keep for ten years. Maybe I wasn't ready or needed to be holier-than-thou for a while, I just don't know.'

'For ten years you have practised honesty and integrity. And I have to ask myself, if I want the outcome for my life that I want, am I really willing to be the one who plays a role in you breaking that code in your life? And then if this is what it looks like it could be, what kind of foundation has been laid for something new to be built upon? Or am I just being idealistic in a Calvinistic kind of way? Who says what is right and what is wrong really?'

'Jade, I don't know why we have found ourselves in this space where neither of us has resolved our current relationships.' I don't feel we are any closer to an understanding despite all our talk, but maybe that is the point. 'All I know is that I desperately want to hold you and be in your space, and if part of that expression includes, can I call it, sacred sex, then yes, I want to make love with you. But I can't know for sure yet, if we close the door to that or do it and get it out of the way, whether I will feel any different about something that just has to take place between us: something we just have to pursue here.' I can't help but recognise how these words of mine resonate with how Sarah described her connection with Calix.

'I see your heart, and it's beautiful, brimming with qualities of real love and goodness. I realise I don't know you yet, Clive, but I sense you. I trust you more than I trust myself.' I cannot think of anything to say to that. 'And the day I walked into the water and met you, I was at complete peace with myself and the world, feeling clear and connected. I was feeling detached from Gino as I have been feeling for some time, but not available to another, so I feel whatever was exchanged with you from my side was pure and without intention. Your response to me was not obvious, and I was surprised to hear Samantha recount it.'

I say, 'I moved coffee shops after I found out about the affair and since then I have been going to the deli. I am struck by how we have been in each other's presence there so often in past months but never connected. I guess that magic moment of recognition of souls had to wait until the right moment. I accept that this is the right moment.'

She goes quiet for a while, and just as I start to think the pace is getting to her, she says, 'Maybe it is about courage?' I am not sure whether she is talking to herself or me—the courage to have made contact with a stranger, or the courage to leave a relationship? 'The courage to walk away,' she clarifies for me. 'Ideally, of course, one should walk away for the true reasons, but we are all human. Did we come to offer each other help with that, or some kind of support maybe?'

'Perhaps it is about hope?' I venture that word because Sarah had stuck it on walls around the house, hopeful that our relationship would improve without doing much tangible work, at least, not together with me, wishing for a miracle. Or perhaps that she could flee her demons.

'That things will work out or get better?' Jade says. 'Then you have to include forgiveness and look at what you've been through. This kind of thing can usually not be followed through without a fair deal of pain to all involved both directly and indirectly. And there really is no such thing as a secret.' She pauses and then sounding gloomy, 'I know I am making him sad because my heart is not with him. Even worse, it is elsewhere and he feels it. I don't like making him feel sad.'

'You sound more concerned for him than for yourself.'

She thinks about that. 'You're right. I should really say that I don't like what I am doing to myself by staying in the comfort zone of a relationship which is not good for me.'

The secretary from the school calls again, sounding a bit anxious that I am not yet there to take Jack to the doctor. Feeling a little guilty, probably as much because of what I am doing as because I am not yet with Jack, I think that the injury he has suffered might be worse than I imagine.

As our vehicles come into view, Jade says, 'The one thing I do feel sure about is that there will be some healing for both of us in this. I am amazed at my energy increase since last week. I have been almost completely pain free for days because of your lovely energy coming towards me and my mind that is full of possibilities and mildly euphoric. Maybe it's really just the Vitamin B injections and raw-juicing?'

'Probably a bit of all,' I say, and we laugh together. We have reached our cars, back in full view of anyone who may be interested in noting our interaction, and there is no time for the kind of goodbye I would like to have. 'This, what is happening here,' I say, 'is scaring the shit out of me too, partly because I am thinking of the consequences. It is not just us involved in this, there are others too, but I am in no rush to figure it out right now. I will see you again soon.'

As I say it I hope it will be tomorrow, and I hope that tomorrow is already here.

26

Marriage is against nature. You can be
certain only of this moment that is in
your hands.

(Osho)

Wednesday, 2 March 2011

Today Jade has brought along a chaperone, one of her closest friends, to make legitimate our meeting at the deli. As we sit and chat, I wonder if Linda is there to check me out, to give Jade a second opinion. When Linda excuses herself to go to the bathroom, Jade says, 'It was different to experience you in your head yesterday for the first time, mostly out of your body, away from your feelings and in your rational mind. I think this is why I kept pushing the idea of backing off and stressing that I felt you were not being as open with me, because I could not really feel you.'

I look around, aware that others sit in close proximity to us, and I know just how easy it is to tune into a conversation at another table in this confined space, but it seems that nobody is paying us unusual attention. 'But I enjoyed my time with you all the same and loved the ideas you shared with me about three different types of affairs, and I am so glad I am not type one or two, neither a loveless one-night-stand, which has less emotional content than, you said, enjoying a good cup of tea, nor having a fling with someone you find sexy and is just a lot of fun. And what you said about purity and wanting to hear me scream. I could not stop thinking about that last night alone in my bed.' Jade does her best impression of looking coy. 'And I must confess, as a result I was a little naughty with my . . .'

Linda returns from the bathroom, and Jade stops mid-sentence and without missing a beat, as if we were having an entirely different conversation, she says, 'That was awful. While we were walking down the beach to the sea, Gino asked me what I am looking at, and I said I was looking at him. Then he said, "No, you're not. I'm looking where you're looking".'

She is referring to Monday, when I was playing beach bats with Jim and purely by coincidence, if there is ever such a thing, Jade and Gino walked past on their way to a mid-afternoon dip in the sea. I hadn't seen them at first, but Jim was quick to come closer and say, 'This should be interesting.' He seemed to be thoroughly enjoying being party to this evolving story and all its intrigues.

'And then he pulled me close,' Jade says, interrupting my thoughts, 'and kept holding me in the water as if to show that I was his. He kept asking me if I still loved him, and I didn't answer. He said he was sad that he can't be the person I need him to be. And the day before he asked me, "How is my writer friend?" But he is leaving it at that, and he is on his best behaviour. It was pitiful. I really did not know what to do, and I could not help glancing at you. While swimming with him, with you so close, I felt like I was being unfaithful—to you.'

I really am feeling for him. I am aware that Linda is watching me intently.

Jade says, 'When he wanted to make love over the weekend, I just could not and eventually I asked him if he really wants to, and he said no. When I put my arms around him, it felt so wrong, like it did not fit. Just from my hugs with you, I know how you feel. I have been getting up in the middle of the night, and sleeping on the couch, I just could not be next to him. And this morning he texted me to say that he is really looking forward to making love with me when he gets back tomorrow. I know he is testing me. It made me want to find an excuse to suddenly have to go away for a few days just so that I would not have to face that situation.'

Linda says, 'What are you going to do when he comes back tomorrow?'

'I think I am going to be loving and gentle with Gino. I am going to time jump back to a few weeks ago and approach my relationship with him as if Clive had never come into my life.' She looks at me. 'The all of me that wants to be truthful will reserve itself for you for now. Somehow I know I can trust you with the truth, even if the truth is that at the moment, because of circumstances and in order to prevent catastrophe, I am lying and pretending. Over time, I'm sure I can end it for all the reasons I wanted to before you came along.'

She goes on to reveal stuff about him and their relationship over the years, and how she feels about things. And she keeps saying that this is just one part of him and that he is really a nice guy and everybody loves him. These personal and intimate details about him surprise me because Linda is sitting here, and I wonder why she is disclosing these things. Jade sees me looking at her friend for a reaction and picks up my concern and goes on to say that when Linda stayed over at her house last night, they chatted about everything. And then, as if on cue and occasionally encouraged by Jade to tell more stories, Linda talks about how she has known Jade all her life and the huge role she played in Jade's son's youth, and they banter back and forth with each other as if reminiscing about old times and more recent years. And maybe they are, but I soon realise that this is partly for my benefit, to show me that Linda is an ally or to let me know indirectly more about Jade and the type of man she needs in her life. In-between sharing such stories, there are friendly questions from Linda about me and my family, my parents and sister, but nothing about my marriage.

Then it's time for them to leave. No sooner have they gone, I receive a text message from Jade: '*She said . . . I love him. I wish you guys were together ;-)*'. I think I have been thoroughly checked out, and it seems I have passed the test, if that's what it was.

Later, Jade phones me and says, 'Linda and I always have this competitive thing going on with our men. It's so bad that she often won't introduce me to someone she is interested in because she says that these men always have eyes for me. And she has this way with the men in my life, and they start to give her a lot of attention. But she said she did not see this in you, she could not divert your attention from me, and what was in your eyes when you looked at her or spoke to her was pure.'

She really needs to talk, so she speaks and I listen. She is thinking about what to do as a result of this connection we share; what to do now as she feels that we are going to take this to another level. She is wondering what to do about the relationship she is half-in, and how, if at all, meeting me had impacted on this.

I say, 'I think it does, in the way that everything influences everything, but you are already spiritually much further down the path you are on than the physical decisions and actions you have yet to take. And because of this, you will act when you feel the time is right. Emotionally, you have already left the relationship.'

27

It's impossible to be loyal to your family,
your friends, your country, and your
principles, all at the same time.

(Mignon McLaughlin)

Friday, 4 March 2011

For some reason I choose not to take the first available parking space as I turn into the street where the restaurant is situated, then I curse myself as I drive past the restaurant entrance as there are no other vacant spots, and so I drive around the block and try again and that's when Jade comes past in her car, and we stop alongside each other in the middle of the road.

'How are you?' she says, after winding down the window.

'I'm great,' I say. 'But you're not.'

She looks away. 'It was really tough last night.' She wrings her hands and stares ahead of her through the windscreen. 'I went to Lucy for a kinesiology session yesterday in anticipation of Gino's return. When I asked her what she thought about the fact that he had always falsely accused me of having other men, and now something seems to be happening, she said that he had perceived this connection between you and me in my energy field all along. And when I talked of leaving him again and my fears around it, we more or less established that I have not always been able to sustain my fire walk because of the pain of accumulated loss.' She is tearful, and I have to read her lips because her voice keeps disappearing. 'I'm going for a walk on the mountain. I sent you a mail.' And she drives off, probably afraid of being seen talking to me by him or others. I have not seen her like this before; she is in such a state.

The waiters spotted my vehicle circling outside, and my cappuccino and a bottle of still mineral water are waiting for me at my regular table before I sit down and log on to the Internet to read her mail. The dogs are sniffing around in the grass alongside the deli courtyard and will push their way through the gate and lie at my feet when they are ready. When Jade left the restaurant yesterday, I forgot to tell her that what is happening between us has changed my life, or has changed me, forever, that I hoped she would be okay when Gino arrived home later, and that she would know what to do and what to say and how to be. It seems like she did this, and so, last night, after confronting Gino about their on-off relationship, she wrote this to me:

> *When Gino came back this evening, I could not pretend. There is no way I could be physical with him any more and still feel okay with myself. He kept asking me if I had something to tell him, and I told him I had felt for some time that although I love and care for him, I don't want to be in the relationship anymore, that I can't reconcile being back in the same pattern with him, and that my body and energy are not happy. He was very hurt and angry . . . and nasty. He honed in on you as being the reason for this.*

> *I denied having spent any more time with you other than the first time; that kind of information would just be abused. So at least, you know the story if he confronts you; I somehow think he won't. But what he may do is try to talk to you, get empathy, and then tell you stories about me. He has done it with a couple of people when he has considered them a threat. He said he knew something was going on and that it will all come out in the end.*

I wish I could just say, 'Yes, I'm sorry that this has been hurtful to you, but it has happened, because it was meant to.'

I also feel anxious and agitated because I want to know that what I have with you is somehow miraculously protected from the potential damage that could be done by angry partners.

I wish it is possible to be with her now, just for a short while, to know that she is okay, to tell her again that she was brave last night when she ended her relationship with Gino. But as a poor substitute, I risk sending her a short text message telling her to breathe in the pure mountain air to feed her cells and exhale long and completely and that it will be okay—it is exactly as it should be. Jade responds that this was exactly the instruction she had received from her kinesiologist yesterday and that after her walk up the mountain she feels really peaceful and centred.

In the late afternoon, she joins me for coffee at the deli, saying she really needs to talk, and I am grateful to be together with her even if it is just for a few moments. I convince myself that it is best to keep up the established pattern anyway, to keep up appearances, if nothing else. The hounds sense her long before they can see her and arouse themselves from the blanket I have remembered to drag from the car and nudge open the gate and wag their bums towards her. Looking strained but smiling, Jade sits down and explains that she is struggling with her integrity and the concept of truth, and that she is debating with herself whether your truth is perhaps not the same as honesty. I listen intently as this is my dilemma, my preoccupation, too.

Eventually, I say, 'It sounds like you are defining integrity as being true to yourself and others. Though it's really about "wholeness" so I guess that fits. But you also come close to my understanding of authenticity when you speak of your thoughts and actions and words being congruent, or living according to your values, so that you appear real or genuine to others. Either way, I guess this begins with self-awareness or honesty with self.'

'I'm just starting to discover who I really am. Integrity, for me, is about being true to what you believe in and making this known to others. Being true to others too is impossible.'

'So when you speak or act, should it be with sincerity and frankness?' I ask. 'And openly disclose everything? Isn't that what we call honesty?

'Is honesty just about lies? What about keeping secrets?' she says.

'What do you mean?'

'Must you volunteer it?'

'What?'

'Information that is relevant to the other person, even if they haven't asked,' she says. 'And even if you know they will abuse it.'

'Now I think you're talking about lying by omission or commission. And being economical with the truth.'

'You've lost me. I'm still reeling from my conversation with Gino last night, so you really have to spell it out for me.'

'Let's just say that some people feel there is nothing wrong with omitting relevant information, like stealing and only being guilty if you're caught or only being guilty of an affair if found out.'

'What do you think?' she says.

'Well, I think it's deceitful to hide pertinent information.' This is a general belief of mine, but I'm not sure I always stick to it.

'You make it sound like you are beholden to another, to voluntarily declare everything.'

'I said it's deceitful. I didn't say it's wrong or that you shouldn't do it. And I don't know what expectations you have of each other around close friendships with other people.'

'But I'm thinking about living my truth and allowing others their truth.'

And I say, 'Okay, let's argue that the only obligation you have is to be true to yourself and that trying to fulfil a commitment to always be true to others is not only difficult but unfeasible. It's surely the same with honesty. Nevertheless, I don't think you can get around the deceit in it. But I guess some relationships get by with this collusion.'

'Please, not another big word.'

'All I'm saying is that people collude with each other for selfish reasons, to protect their relationship and themselves. It's the game we all play.'

'Like when you allow your partner to have affairs as long as they don't leave you?'

'That's an extreme case. Usually people collude in very subtle ways, to whatever degree they privately feel is an acceptable level of tolerance. Implicitly, they agree to disclose some things, but not others, and they continue to do this because there is some sort of pay-off for them. But this means there are always secrets, and trust, in its purest form, must take a knock along the way.' I am thinking about myself. 'But coming back to truth and honesty, what I understand about karma is that there is an imprint or a residual impression, at a deep cellular level, of every thought, word, or deed we have, whether virtuous or non-virtuous. It's even carried through from past lives. But the point I want to make is this: I read somewhere that it is the karma of action that has more significance than the karma of thought. So if your intention of lying to Gino comes from a positive space, it is more pure than if your motivations are harmful.'

'So being dishonest with him is not the point? Is it about how and why I do it?

'Something like that.'

'Nothing makes sense to me right now. Let's rather pick this up another time,' Jade says, frustrated with the semantics.

28

Saturday, 5 March 2011

In the morning, I take the boys and the dogs to the beach where a sandcastle-building competition promises to while away part of the day. It is a lovely day, lightly overcast and mild. We arrive well after the festivities are underway and meander along the waterline while the boys splash water and laugh hysterically at Harry, who seems to have an endless fascination with the trajectory of water molecules, while Sally herds the ankles of people wading in the surf. Jack follows the lead of his older brothers but decides to end his first experience of body-surfing when his sand-grazed tummy is red and raw. When they get weary of throwing balls for Harry and Sally, we go take a look at some of the teams' handiwork as they race against the clock. Then we are invited by a friend of Jeremiah to join their depleted team as they labour to create their masterpiece in the confines of the cordoned-off patch of sand allocated to them amidst all the teams of hopefuls. At some point, I stand aside and light a cigarette and look around at our immediate competitors to see how they are doing and spot Gino working with the team immediately adjacent to us.

I marvel at how the universe conspires to create such moments of intersection when there are more than 200 demarcated plots on the beach from which we could have chosen, and about 1,000 people. For a moment, I doubt it is him; it just seems too coincidental, and as it becomes clear to me that no amount of self-delusion will change things, I become concerned about what behaviour this might provoke in him as I remind myself how he stole glances at me as he sauntered slowly past the restaurant where I sat writing yesterday morning. By walking past the way he had, along the path that skirts the restaurant used only by residents of the apartments overlooking where I sat, it felt like he was trying to intimidate me or decide what his chances would be if he took me on in such a public place. Or perhaps he came to check whether Jade was there and with whom she was spending her time.

A little while later, he had passed by again in the opposite direction, and this time, I was more keenly aware of the scowl and a little unnerved by the sheer size of him, which gave me cause to gauge the distance between me and the flimsy timber gate, which serves as the access from the pavement where he ambled to my table in the courtyard of the restaurant. He was oozing testosterone. A not-too-pleasant image of the man, a male friend of Jade's, he had caused to be hospitalised flashed through my mind, and I thought with irrational concern that if he knew what I was busy writing about, he would certainly vault the fence and be upon me before I could click 'save'. I wondered what Harry and Sally would make of it. In the past, I had witnessed the transformation of their peace-loving cuddliness into a ferocious protectiveness that, quite frankly, stunned me too. How might they respond to the indignity of their owner being pulped?

But that was yesterday, and the proximity we found ourselves in at the sand-castle event was this morning. This afternoon he is at it again, this time on the beach while I am playing beach bats with Jim. Long into the game and somewhat fatigued, I dive to reach the ball, and the feeble return of mine leaves me sprawled on the sand and the ball looping enticingly towards his forehand. Jim senses an opportunity to be awarded double points by actually hitting me with the ball. This intent would probably be considered unsportsmanlike in any other context, but it is how we like it, and it focuses the mind considerably. Just before I dig my bat in the sand to leverage myself into a half-upright position and use my free hand to return my sunglasses, askew from my impact with the sand, to the bridge of my nose, I can see the whites of Jim's eyes as he steps forward and his bat-arm arcs behind him in preparation to execute the shot.

In that split second I am convinced he is actually smiling, and I decide I will take this up with him afterwards over a beer as I feel that it may be overstepping the implicit boundaries of our friendship, never mind our loose rules for this game. The term 'barbaric' comes to mind as I hear him hit the shot, his grunt and the unmistakable crack of his bat making contact with the ball, but I can't see it as sweat has smudged the sunglasses I have adjusted into position and obscured my vision. But in his eagerness to reap the rewards of his intended winner, more the self-satisfaction than the extra points, it seems Jim has a rush of blood and misjudges, and the ball flies off the wedge of his bat and beyond me, and the only way I can locate its far-flung destination is to follow the noses of the dogs loping towards it in the hope of retrieving it first. Jim is squinting skywards using his bat to shade his eyes from the sun, signalling that he intends to blame the yellow orb for his misfortune.

I look back over my shoulder at Jim as this is worthy of having a good-natured dig at him for the ball he skied. I turn my face to the heavens and cup my hands to my mouth and loudly yell, 'Ground Control to Major Tom—incoming.' Then I turn and trot towards the ball and almost collide with someone. I pull myself up short to avoid this person that suddenly comes into my field of vision as my downcast eyes are hidden behind smeared sunglass lenses and a peak cap and are watching the sand a metre or two in front of my running feet to avoid stepping on sharp shells or broken glass. This part of the beach is practically deserted, and he is walking diagonally across the width of the beach towards the water's edge, on a trajectory I calculate puts his starting point at the place where my vehicle is parked.

In an instant I take in Gino's self-confident streetwise swagger. He is shirtless and deeply tanned, weight-lifting muscular and hardened in that way that suggests a street fighter, who knows his way around a brawl. Tattoos cover his chest and shoulders. He says in deep baritone, 'I'm watching you.' Harry drops the ball wet with saliva into my hand, and I turn my back on Gino and walk back to the scuffled patch of sand which is my allocated spot in our game of beach bats, with as much confidence as I can muster.

After the ball goes to ground ending the next rally and now rests in tail-wagging Harry's vice jaws, I have an excuse to convene with Jim at the invisible 'net' midway between us to confirm whether that actually was Gino, and I know I don't have to ask him to watch my back while we are there on the beach after he says, 'Okay, you're right. He is big. Much bigger than I realised.'

A few minutes later, Gino cruises past again, in much the same way he did at the restaurant, in a parabolic arc from his turnaround point at the water's edge towards his beachfront property and comes within metres of my back and stands there, waiting, as I concentrate on keeping the rally going so that I do not need to turn around to face him. Jim has his poker face on, yet I would not put it past him to purposefully hit the ball beyond me towards the prowling hulk to provoke another interaction, just for its entertainment value, but he does not. Then Jim lets me know, as I am facing the sea, that Gino has moved off and hoisted himself on to the wall just beyond the parked cars from where he can watch us, and I realise that this is where he lives, right next to Jade.

When the game is over and we return to our cars, I look for signs of malicious damage to the bodywork, but there appear to be none. Gino has disappeared, but Jim has a smirk on his face, and it is a dead giveaway. He had seen Gino coming up behind me on his first 'drive-by', and had purposefully hit the ball beyond me to set up the encounter. 'You're a dick,' I say, as this dawns on me.

'I thought it would be a good test case,' he says, not feeling he really needs an excuse. 'If you can't bear the heat, get out of the kitchen. I think his intimidation tactics need to be confronted head-on. Somehow you need to break it down and get it over with. Otherwise he will keep this going, and you will always be on edge, never knowing when he is going to strike.'

'Do you mind if I decide how to do this? Or at least give me fair warning?'

Jim shrugs.

'You're still a dick,' I say.

29

Do nothing secretly; for Time sees and
hears all things, and discloses all.

(Sophocles)

Monday, 7 March 2011

Jade is telling me about the group reading she and a small group of girlfriends attended last night. The spiritual medium, she tells me, in a trance of some sort and speaking with a voice unlike her own, talked of three paradigms.

'Speaking through her, the entity said that there are those who think everything is in God's hands,' she says. 'They believe that it is God's will and that the universe will decide and they are just puppets without free will, so they have no responsibility or agency in a decision or action they take. They have not located their own source of meaning, of what is "okay" for them, and they don't have the conviction to act on this. It's as if they buy a doctrine off the shelf.'

I am so unsure of myself that I wonder if she is referring to me, how I have not been clear about what is not okay for me in my marriage. When I had tried to set out for Sarah the things I needed for our relationship to work for me after the affair, like honesty and openness, I had timidly retracted them in the face of her stubborn refusal to even engage with me in conversation about these issues.

I say, 'So it's the belief that some higher power has plans for you and you just need to follow a set of commandments?'

'Then the entity spoke of those who believe they are students or scholars and they have to keep learning lessons.'

'Wait, sorry for interrupting, but I just want to say something,' I say, waving my hand to disperse the cigarette smoke wafting her way.

'Don't worry,' she says, her eyes softening. 'I like the smell, and I like to watch you smoke. And your two-day growth.'

'The other day you used the words "truth" and "honesty" and it made me think of guilt and forgiveness, and that's what this philosophy, the first paradigm, seems to me to be based on—guilt and forgiveness. I think this is what organized religions, in fact, followers of any dogmatic beliefs, have done—made us feel guilty and somehow less than what we are. So that we feel lost without someone to lead us, and we need to follow some creed, to hide our guilt, even our collective guilt, as we are led to believe we are sinners always needing to repent. We have to hand our choices over, because we cannot forgive ourselves for what we think are sins, when in fact they might just be very human desires. It's as if we expect ourselves to be godlike rather than human. And we don't trust ourselves to act independently, because we judge ourselves against a version of pureness we were never meant to be and are therefore unsure of the goodness of our choices or our decisions and actions.'

Jade says, 'Are you saying that we condemn ourselves, rather than the mistakes we think we have made?'

'Yes, and others for theirs. So we don't try to understand why we did it and learn from it to become wiser or less ignorant. Instead we try to hide it out of shame. We suppress it, and maybe this is what we call our dark side. But surely mistakes are in your acts, not in you. They are in your doing, not your being.'

I recall Sarah's complete shutdown, her refusal to engage in anything reminiscent of her affair, and her flaring anger at anything that was linked to it, like driving past Calix, and her crushing fear that I would divulge the situation to our mutual friends.

'You are now talking about learning from our mistakes, which is the second paradigm,' Jade says, wanting to get back to what she was saying. 'The medium said these people often choose to stay in relationships or careers or other situations because they feel that there is something to learn, something they haven't yet learnt. They may be more accepting of their mistakes, perhaps even take ownership of it. But sometimes they stay in unhappy and challenging situations and they don't move on because they feel they will just have to learn the same lessons elsewhere if they don't learn them where they are. Even if they are happy with how things are, they feel they are stagnating, and they feel the need to create change or be presented with another difficult dilemma within that relationship or situation.'

While she talks, my mind wanders. Sarah was always on about learning lessons. She often spoke of believing that wherever she was at any given moment was exactly where she needed to be, and that she was being given exactly what she needed at that moment, that the challenges presented to her were for her growth. I wonder now whether this was just some ploy she had learnt over time to convince herself to accept whatever situation she found herself in. And when things turned sour after the encouraging interlude of last October, by way of explaining she said that she had come to realize she was 'not happy with happy' and that she was never contented, and that she was always in a constant state of craving for something or pushing something away. I thought that she was so afraid of unhappiness and of her needs being unmet, that she went to extraordinary lengths to try secure from the outside world what she thought she needed to be happy. I think this was mostly her need for love and affirmation, represented by appreciative acts and gifts of love, assuming, I suppose, the obvious basic needs of food and security that were so elusive in her childhood were assured.

At the time it had occurred to me that her life experience had been an endless struggle with harrowing events and that she could not imagine living a life without traumatic episodes. This was her life script. It's as if they justified her existence and vindicated why she felt or behaved like she did. It seemed to me that over the years she had lost the ability to 'be okay' or the expectation that she deserves 'normality', dull and unfamiliar as it might be to her, though she often claimed she sought it out. And the more I provided that opportunity for the consistency of a 'normal' family life and a place where she felt she belonged, it paradoxically freaked her out. It seems she simply did not know how to give herself over to it and embrace it.

And so I think of how sensitive we all are to initial experiences we have as children, how we introject the ideas and beliefs learnt from our parents or significant others, and how we replay the feelings, thoughts, and behaviours from our own childhood. It seems that even tiny details from our past can have an enormous and unpredictable influence on our life-view in adulthood and also have a tremendous impact on how we act and think.

'I think I might be stuck in that paradigm,' Jade says, superseding my reverie. 'Are you thinking you are?'

'What?' I say, the image of Sarah sitting next to me at this table still in my mind.

'Are you listening to me?' she asks, feigning annoyance. 'I asked you whether you think you are stuck in that paradigm.'

'I don't know. I'm just aware of my apparent stuckness. Why I could not leave even when things felt intolerable with Sarah, for both of us? I know I had lots of excuses, and one of them was that I felt I had something to learn. That it was me who just had to see things differently, or handle things differently, or respond to her behaviour in a different way. But for months, I was stuck in my old belief system and I just could not break free from its shackles.'

'Well, then, this may be useful,' she says. 'The third paradigm is one of co-creator, when God or spirit, the universe, and all things, are within you. And your thoughts and actions and those of others together create the reality.'

'Is this about finding your purpose in life?' I say.

'There's a not-so-subtle difference, Clive. The entity made it clear it's about co-creating your *own* purpose rather than finding it. *Finding* it suggests that it already exists and you just have to fulfill that which is already present.'

'Okay, so let's say you can create your own future from all possible futures. But you are saying that the idea of co-creating it suggests that it is not pre-ordained?'

This is the part I think Jim misses with his 'aim-ready-shoot' approach: that you alone cannot determine how you will evolve and that you certainly cannot pre-determine the outcome. It is co-determined. I silently throw another term at Jim: you forgot about 'holism', Jimbo. Oh, you don't know what it means? Well, before you submerge yourself under the water again, I'll tell you—all the parts of a system work together, and a change in one part changes the others. And I make a mental note to raise it when I next see him.

'Yes,' Jade says. 'The idea is that we are responsible for our own worlds or at least how we choose to experience it. That is very humbling and empowering, and the growth lies in navigating that. And relationships happen to fulfill some purpose. When that purpose is no longer there, it is time to move on. I did not know it at the time, but for me the purpose of my first marriage was to give earthly life to Wade, and then it was time to move on. Wade was mature beyond his years, and I believe he was a liberated being who chose to be reborn to help me and others purify our minds and open our hearts. In Buddhism, these beings are called Bodhisattvas. He was my teacher.'

This all sounds a bit new age to me. I am not sure if she is trying to build a case for herself, to convince herself that her defunct marriage and on-off relationship with Gino had served its purpose, or whether she wants to help me see that it is okay to move on from Sarah if the relationship has lived its course; that perhaps to raise three boys was why we came together?

'My karma was that I lost my child, twice,' Jade says. 'First he turned his back on me; then he died. He was spared the agony of an adult life marred by the scarring I had created, clever and lucky soul. I have looked this truth squarely in the face and been filled with complete acceptance of it. And when I became free to be able to admit that I had created the most unspeakable loss in my own life it was the most liberating moment I've ever experienced.'

'Are you saying that it was perhaps not your child that died so young and tragically, but a great Bodhisattva taking the body of a child? That he was born to you, loved by you, and now grieved by you, all for the purpose of opening your heart more deeply?' My tone is teasing, but Jade is not offended and just looks at me, as if to say, 'Oh pitiful, unenlightened one.' But I remain puzzled by why we choose life partners, and I say, 'Then why do we make this commitment, this contract of ownership and togetherness and expectation that comes with marriage, if it seldom allows for the changing flux of life and the inexorable likelihood that we all change and grow. Especially as it places an extraordinary burden on your chosen partner to provide, over time, all you need in an intimate relationship for your growth.'

'I think it's ego,' she says. 'And habit, tradition, or insecurity.'

Prompted by the affair and especially Jim's persistent questioning of me, each time I recognize that I am assuming something is a fact or a reality but really it is locked into the lens of my current belief system, I have been trying to update archaic memories which hamper my growth, and give myself permission to see it differently. To see it for what it is, rather than to project my preconceived ideas on to it. Like the tremendous struggle I have had accepting that the commitment to love someone 'till death do us part' was an illusion and that the promise to exclusively love one person only was a fantasy of those who gathered around us on our wedding day to bear witness to our vows. It was foisted upon us and we bought into this misleading chimera to satisfy their collective need and perhaps reassure our own egos. I have written it down to use as a mantra: 'I am in the process of releasing myself from the commitments, inherent or stated, in our marriage vows, and all promises, expectations and contracts whether psychological, spiritual, emotional, or physical, which we made or assumed or imagined or intended in our relationship.'

So I say, 'Yes, it's probably a hunt for security, which we disguise as commitment. But does the term "secure" imply "safe to grow within" or "reliable and consistent", which really suggests no growth or change as that would upset the status quo?'

Jade says, 'Maybe that's why an "intimate marriage" is an oxymoron, because isn't intimacy a never-ending quest for love of self and other? And if a marriage or relationship keeps you stuck, if it does not help you become wiser, more mature, then the marriage becomes dysfunctional.'

'But you see wholesome marriages, Jade, with both people at ease with themselves and each other,' I say, making a case for something that seems beyond my grasp. 'Those couples don't seem to fight over trivia.'

'But they do encounter serious challenges. It's just that they focus on those things, real problems, they don't avoid them. They are honest about things and open about their desires. So for instance, they share and openly discuss the dream one of them had about making love with somebody else, but don't argue about what to have for dinner or which movie to watch. I must say I tried this with Gino, both of us disclosing all, but it felt to me like he did not come from a place of love. Maybe it was just too late in the day. He struggled to accept the real me, and I discovered something about who he really is that I realized I did not want to be part of.'

'This sounds more like where we started the other day, when you were asking about being true to yourself and being real or authentic, which I have to say I haven't been with Sarah,' I say, wanting to share with Jade that I had never been as brave. 'In the early days already, if she noticed that some woman had caught my eye she would point this out in an accusing way, I suppose coming from her own insecurity. But I guess I now see that this was my guilt, hearing it as an accusation as if I had done something wrong, rather than a normal desire or appreciation which did no more than threaten her ego. And being aware of her wounds, I foolishly tried to demonstrate my love for her and preserve her feelings and could not be open with her. But she felt it, and she knew it. It felt like I was keeping secrets from her, so I gradually withdrew from friendships with other women and then I held this against her. Even more so once I learnt that she had regular contact with her ex's and quite intimate friendships with lots of men. Isn't that ridiculous? And a waste of energy?' I can hear the frustration in my voice.

Jade does not respond, probably thinking I have answered my own question. So I say, 'Eventually it seems we came to live together as intimate enemies, begrudging the other for constraining our growth and happiness. Especially when we were attracted to others, and could have learnt and grown from being in some sort of relationship with them. We simply could not be honest and open and respectful.' I am thinking of how this lack of openly sharing had affected my ability to trust Sarah, more than the infidelity itself. I can hear the sour resentment in my voice. And I know that it is also me I am talking about.

Jade says, 'I find that people meet different needs in me, they give me joy in different ways. If I was free to be with someone else, in whatever form of intimacy which may be emotional or physical or spiritual, then I would come back to my core partner enriched, with new insight. And hopefully he would find something in me, something better, he has never found before.'

Is this what Sarah meant when she had described how she profited from her connection with Calix, and which I found so difficult to accept? But Jade is right, it was my ego. I had felt rejected, not good enough, my role usurped; so small and frightened. Maybe I still do?

'Are you talking about absolute and total freedom in relationships?' I say. 'A society without marriage contracts?'

'And, for that reason, one without divorce and bitterness and children suffering the consequences of acrimonious separations.'

'So what about children and the benefits of family?'

'Get with it, Clive,' she says, leaning forward and sounding frustrated. 'The nuclear family is dead. It's now all about community. We are all linked together. Children spawned out of a relationship are everyone's children, everyone's responsibility, and everyone's gift. Africans have understood this for aeons.'

'So we all sleep around?' I say, my mind full of the possibilities and the drama that would ensue.

'Now you're being silly. If you do find you need to move on from that relationship, you can do so with love and appreciation for what you had, and gratefully take it with you. It may hurt, but that is just ego. Only with the freedom to fall in and out of love and experience the gift of knowing another, can we consciously decide that "this is the one".'

The astringent taste of regret lines my throat. 'Are you saying that if being connected with someone like Calix made Sarah happy or spurred her growth, that I should have rejoiced in this and honoured it? Then I would have had no need to get rid of him? Or her?'

'All I'm saying is that if you love somebody, then freedom should be the connecting link between you.'

30

```
We are shaped and fashioned
      by what we love.

(Johann Wolfgang von Goethe)
```

Wednesday, 9 March 2011

This time he walks slowly past the restaurant where I am sitting at the table speaking with Azura about her latest love and how I am holding up and other things. She avoids raising Sarah's absence, other than to ask how I am coping with the boys. I have always been honest with her about my life and feel a little disturbed that I am not able to be open about what is happening. I say something about Sarah's affair and how I am coming to terms with a lot of things, when Gino walks past. Azura waves a greeting but by the time I look in his direction he has looked away, and I wonder when this intimidation will stop or escalate into a confrontation.

'Who was that?' I say.

Azura says, 'He is in a relationship with that woman you were sitting with here the other day.'

Azura is one of those people who tends to know the latest news and gossip and has seen Jade and me in frequent deep and intimate conversation these past few weeks and it is useful to hear her say this. She may suspect something but is waiting for me to reveal it, and I try to read if anything lies behind her words.

When Azura leaves, I log on and am reading Jade's email when she arrives at the restaurant with a friend, and they sit down at a table diagonally opposite me. It is lunchtime busy, and for reasons that have now become obvious to us both, we cannot be seen spending too much time together here.

Feeling her loving energy as she sits so near to me, I read what Jade wrote last night:

> *I don't think I have ever seen myself more beautiful than this evening. I have tears streaming down my face as I write. To be completely in love and be completely loved is a first experience for me. It's always been unbalanced, usually me loving more. It is the first time I am experiencing something that feels mutual and equal. I am in awe. Again.*
>
> *I loved today with you. It was perfect. I told you before about that psychic I met years ago who said that Gino does not love me and told me there was this man, a poet, a writer, who would come into my orbit? You are so beautiful; I can't believe you picked me. When we were driving home today, you said something about needing that so much—in a way, although you referred directly to your desire for me, I felt it may be a general need. In the moment that you said that, I felt that even if this all ends today, even if we discover that it was just sex you needed and all the feelings evaporate, I feel privileged to have been the one to have given that to you. And with that came the realization that it comes naturally to me to love you.*
>
> *When I got home, I was called to the bookshelf, to a particular book. Inside, I found something I had written some time ago:*
>
> *'A soulmate is someone who has locks that fit our keys, and keys to fit our locks. When we feel safe enough to open the locks, our truest selves step out and we can be completely and honestly*

who we are; we can be loved for who we are and not for whom we're pretending to be. Each unveils the best part of the other. No matter what else goes wrong around us, with that one person we're safe in our own paradise . . . When we're two balloons, and together our direction is up, chances are we've found the right person. Our soulmate is the one who makes life come to life.'

And so it is, with you . . .

You said some things to me during our lovemaking yesterday. As I sat down on you, you said, 'welcome home' and 'I'm yours' . . . as in 'the flip side of my coin'? My twin ray?? I believe you . . .

Thoughts of yesterday and reading her words create tingly shivers that course through my body. My eyes are moist and the words on the screen blur and melt. I don't know what brought this on, this rush of mixed emotions, but it feels like she just gets me, that she owns her stuff and I feel no judgment and no need to be someone other than who I am. Again, I am aware I might be under some sort of illusion of pareidolia; the misconception that I see myself in her, that I recognize these qualities because I am intimately acquainted with them as it is how I see myself. But I am swept along on the crest of its wave with no intention to review or judge it as I am feeling so good being in her presence. I think of just how beautiful, how easy it is to spend time with her, allowing our conversation to weave and leap wherever it went. Even yesterday it just felt right, when it could so easily have been awkward and anxiety-provoking, it being our first time, but more so it being the first time that I have broken my vows of faithfulness. I have no regrets, not last night and not this morning, and I want her to know this.

I look across at her and we mouth to each other, 'How are you?' and 'I'm great'.

Then she texts me, *'One month of magic'*. How time has flown since that day I saw her light up the ocean around me and our souls sang and danced together and said, 'I see you'.

A little while later she looks around anxiously, then comes over to me, greets me with a kiss and leans on my table and says, 'Yesterday, while driving home after our time together, I asked my father, "Dad, you know how cynical I am. If you brought this magical experience to me, if you and Wade were behind it, why is it that this man is married to somebody else?", and he said, "Because you need time, my love", and he proceeded to tell me the work I need to complete without any more procrastination.'

I hesitate because I know we have only a minute or two and can't decide what to say. Her father died a few months ago, her son Wade nearly three years ago, but she communes with the spirit world and although I have had no such supernatural experiences, I never doubt that for her the conversations are real. She glances around again, so I hurry because there are things I want to say to her, 'Yesterday was sublime in every way and every moment. I so wanted to hold you last night, and to tell you how much I appreciated your open sharing about yourself and your past, and I think we both wondered at the time whether this level of disclosure was good for us and why it was happening. I am okay with it. It keeps everything in perspective and makes you whole and real for me and the comfort and honesty is inspiring.'

Jade says, 'I think it also makes those things that are often hard to deal with, like our past sexual experiences and relationships, seem more okay. At least it works like that for me. We already know each other in the deepest way, the verbal disclosure is just confirming our comfort with each other. And my ego feels no need to possess or own you, no negative jealousy or such things. If I did, what's going on here is not what we think it is.'

All the while she is talking, I look around for signs of Gino's ominous approach and accusations, just beyond the perimeter of the half-wall and fence that encloses the courtyard, where we talk under the canvass tarpaulin that shades patrons who prefer fresh air and mountain views or to smoke while drinking their coffees. I guess it will be like this for a while, maybe a long while, until he finds his way through the pain, perhaps with the help of the loving arms of another woman.

'Your ego's feelings are natural,' I say, 'but you said something so vital for me to hear as we drove home about your love for your sisters on this earth and that one of them is Sarah and I know you would come from that space if she was here no matter what happens. One of the things I have been aware of for a while is that if I was to leave the marriage, or before I should leave, I need to love and embrace her first, at a practical level for the sake of the boys and at a deeper level for the sake of Mother Earth. And it seems you keep reminding me of this.'

'I realised something magnificent happened to me yesterday,' Jade says. 'And when I got home, I looked at the list of invocations I had written long ago and deleted all of them and wrote, "The abundant life and love you have dreamed of will manifest to the last detail". I love you, and I have joy in my heart that I thought you into my world and recognised you. Now that is an exercise in conscious manifesting!'

'I have never really bought into the concept that if you really want something, you can imagine it, visualize it into your life. Sometimes I wonder if that third paradigm of co-creating our world, where the freedom to love and to express it with others, or to give it a label, polyamory, isn't just a writing-desk fantasy. I've never actually seen it, so I don't believe in it.'

'But if course it's not possible if you don't believe in it first ,' she says. 'I really want you in my life. I am drawn and attracted to and filled with hope by your patience, long-suffering and devotion to your family. But there is a part of me that wants to put a bomb under you too.'

She is moving fast, constantly working on herself and challenging herself by making brave changes in her life, and my inclination to linger in onerous circumstances seems dramatically atrophied by comparison. 'I haven't felt it that way,' I say, as she looks around, knowing we have risked spending too much time talking together. 'Not pushy. So it's funny you see yourself like that. And it was me who had the bomb.'

This reminds both of us what happened yesterday. We had spent the day together out of town, feeling safe and secure away from prying eyes and threatening glances. Although we had not yet consummated this connection we felt, I was sure we both wanted to, and I knew that if we had allowed ourselves that privacy it would already have happened. We both knew that what we were experiencing was indefensible against any accusation that this embryonic relationship has already overstepped the line, for that it had, and few partners would feel comfortable with the energy that vibrates between us. So on the way there we spoke about our doubts, about whether this connection we felt was real or just infatuation or projection or the desperate desire to have unmet needs fulfilled. Then we talked of our feelings of guilt a propos starting a clandestine relationship which was unfaithful to my current commitment and our concern for the consequences of this on others dear to us if we did not end it now before it progressed any further. For that is how we felt—two lovers knowing this would not end by our design but only when and if it was ready to.

We spoke about more things, personal revelations, in those few hours than I have cumulatively discussed in many years at home, and then we wandered around the sleepy seaside resort, feeling like two teenagers with ever-increasing desire for each other provoked by the intimate disclosures we had shared over breakfast earlier at the quaint restaurant on the water's edge. We walked bravely hand in hand for the first time in the belief that here we were anonymous and free to express our bond, and for a while without being explicit with each other, we searched for accommodation where we could share a private moment, but laughed together when we saw how embarrassed we both felt at the thought of walking into some establishment and asking for a room for a couple of hours. So we sought out a secluded spot to express our love and the magic and uniqueness of the moment and the half-built house we finally found will forever be embedded in my heart. At one stage before we came across the house, we had to hurriedly adjust our half-removed clothing behind a rock on a hitherto deserted beach as fishermen came into view and strolled towards us and we giggled like children as we ran up the sand dunes back to the car with unfastened belt-buckles flapping and underwear scrunched up in our hands and grains of sand in uncomfortable places discovered and partially removed later in the house under construction.

Before we departed that now-sacred place, decently clothed again, I had stood atop a half-built wall on the upper level and cast my eyes south towards the range of mountains around which our city sprawled, and once I got my bearings, I thought I could make out the pointy outcrop of 'my mountain' and imagined myself on the precipitous ledge which had been my sunset sanctuary for so long, and which now carried so much meaning for me. My mind saw Calix floating off the edge.

While driving home yesterday, Jade said, 'Perhaps we should not see each other for a few weeks?' and before she had even completed the sentence I said, 'No, I can't do that.'

In tune with what I am recalling of yesterday, she massages her neck and stretches her back which must have taken some punishment against the unyielding half-finished concrete floors and walls in that house. I am about to remark about it, perhaps apologise, when she shows me the tiny fresh scabs that have formed on her knees overnight in tribute to her kneeling over me on the rough unfinished floor before I understood her facial contortions were grimaces and not entirely pleasure-induced, and we stood up, still locked together, her legs wrapped around my hips and her ankles locked together behind my back and I could support her fully as we rocked gently together and then violently as she shuddered, abandoning herself to me while I held her through it and searched her face, her eyes screwed tight and her teeth tearing at her lip.

31

Wisdom is knowing what to do next;
virtue is doing it.

(David Star Jordan)

Saturday, 12 March 2011

We interact briefly at the restaurant while I am reading her latest mail, in a way that hopefully appears platonic to the casual observer, but they are not the people we are concerned about at the moment. She comes up behind me and puts her arms around my neck and kisses me softly. The dogs rouse themselves and wag 'hello' and lick her hands and face, and for a moment I wish I could be one of them. Then we talk while I remain seated and she stands, afraid that joining me at the table is too risky.

'Yesterday Gino was at home next door and I thought he might see me looking at you and Jim playing with the flying disc and so I was overly-conscious of doing it. Given Gino's head-space yesterday afternoon, as always, it was perfect that I did not come down. But then you drove past me down the road afterwards, and my heart fluttered.'

'How has he been?' I say.

'I have had some heartbreaking text messages from him, about how torn up he is and how this is going to get worse for him. He is taking terrible strain. The anger has subsided for now and the pain is coming through. I interacted with him gently re-affirming my stand, reassuring him that there was no malice intended, and that this has been coming for a long time but that he just was not listening, that he did not want to see it. And he told me that Pi-shu was with him all of yesterday and even went to the beach with him. I am astonished at this little animal and the space he is holding for me. It was like he provided a layer of protection for me yesterday, and comfort to Gino. Then he took the gap and wanted to know the truth, and asked me if there is anyone else at all? And I thought of what you said about guilt and forgiveness. I know he will not see it as truth and work with it. He will abuse it. So I am not going to fall for it, he is just trying a different tack, so I said "No". I detest lying.'

'I understand the honesty dilemma, I am living with it too,' I say, wondering whether I abused Sarah's tentative disclosure, her initial confession about the affair, and whether she perhaps had full right to clam up if she felt I was throwing it back at her in bold print—you're despicable, you're untrustworthy, you're this, you're that. 'But I remind myself all the time that when you give someone a gift, it has to be both given and received unconditionally and with grace, otherwise the transaction is flawed. And it is so with honesty.'

'Yes'. And then, 'Deep down below all the layers of ego and human failing, I just want to love you and give you all of me completely and unconditionally. I want my walls melted and to be opened up. Somehow I just know you are the man to hold me through such a melting and opening.'

'You're a princess. I am just aware of the intense emotion I feel with you. Why don't you sit for a few minutes?' When she looks doubtful, I say, 'I sense it will be okay. And I want to quickly say, as I think about the words your dad spoke to you about you needing time, that our connection, the karma of it, is paramount to me right now. Something is being worked out for me here. All else is secondary, the physical attraction, the sex, an affair, thoughts of a possible future together and all those things will find their own time and place, and however they work out it does not change the meeting of our souls.'

I can't find the right words, but this will have to do for now. She seems to accept what I am trying to say with a knowing smile. We both feel it is time to end the conversation, and Jade returns to sit with her friend and continue their chat while I try to ignore her but sneak occasional glances in her direction. Sometimes they are returned. I take Harry and Sally across the pavement to the patch of tree-sheltered vacant space alongside the car park as they need to stretch their legs and take a leak.

I am back at my table when Jim arrives, on that strange post-exertion high but sweaty and exhausted, from the gym next door. 'Do you have a fresh shirt for me?' he says. 'Then I will sit with you and have a quick beer.'

'No, to both your question and statement.'

'Okay, I will sit for a few minutes anyway. I need to tell you something.' Beer in hand, he says, 'Look, you guys are insane. You have to be more careful. From over the road where my car is parked, I could see you guys and it was so obvious you are together.'

'That's ridiculous,' I say, 'we spoke here at my table for about two minutes.' But I instantly recall that about a year ago he had seen Sarah and Calix walking on the beach together, from over a hundred meters away, and without even knowing it was her, he could see they were a couple.

'I'm telling you, it's so noticeable. You have to stop meeting here.'

Trying to keep my voice low and disguise the alarm that I feel, I say, 'Don't look now, but there he is. He is walking past.' This time Gino is walking quickly, with purpose. 'Okay, he's gone. Now he's at the curbside. Shit, he has turned around and is coming this way.'

I am unnerved when Gino stops just in front of the gate leading to the deli courtyard where we are sitting, and cups his hand over his eyes to shield them from the glare and pretends to look around. The outside area of the restaurant is packed with patrons, and he seems to hesitate, perhaps not sure now that he sees Jim sitting with me or trying to locate Jade inside the restaurant. I am wearing sunglasses, so he probably can't be sure just where I am looking, and I don't want to move my head as he might interpret that as looking away. He seems to make up his mind and walks back to the curb and across the road.

'Okay, he's gone,' I say.

Jim points skywards towards the gym that overlooks this area. 'From the treadmill at that window in the gym, I can see everything here, and he came past twice in the last hour already.'

I had not noticed him come past. I am only listening to Jim with half an ear. Gino walks past again on his return trip back to his house, and seconds later, Jade comes outside and stands next to me at the table. 'He has just walked past again,' I say through unmoving lips, still looking at Jim rather than her.

'I had better go out through the other door then,' she says, and off she goes.

'That's what I mean,' says Jim. 'A minute or two either way and we would have had a script for a good movie. And something interesting to report to my wife tonight.'

'He is like a slinky walking down stairs,' I say.

'A what?'

'You know, a slinky. Those colourful spring coil toys that kids play with. Once set in motion, they walk like a worm with legs only at each extremity, end over end, down the stairs until they reach the bottom. I think that all he needs is the slightest push to get him going, and then I don't think he will stop till he gets to the bottom of this.'

A minute later, I get a text from her: *I need to be in your arms tonight.*

And I send: *I will hold your hand while you sleep.*

32

For it was not into my ear you whispered,
but into my heart.
It was not my lips you kissed,
but my soul.

(Judy Garland)

Monday, 21 March 2011

We are sitting together at the deli, when Jade says, 'The promise of the relationship I always wanted, be it with you or eventually somebody new, gives me the inspiration and motivation to walk through the fire. You have no responsibility to me or us beyond anything other than what is completely true for you. The love I have experienced in a short time has healed me in so many ways. My only saboteur is self-doubt, and I have friends who remind me when I feel the doubt. If it feels draining or heavy for me to be leaning on your love in this, just be true to you and remove yourself. I don't believe it's your only purpose though. I still believe there is something more between us. I believe in what we have.'

'Yes, I do too.'

I want to hold her and kiss her and make love to her—again. This morning she had invited me for a massage, saying she needed the therapy, and I went to her without a second's thought even though I think we both knew that we would again transcend this artificial boundary we had tried to keep in our journey together. I walked the dogs around the long way to her house in an effort throw off any would-be interested parties, strolling along the beachfront promenade, past Gino's house and then Jade's front entrance, and around the circumference of the adjacent restaurant. The dogs and I slipped into her kitchen courtyard through the security gate she had left unlocked.

We talked while we kept the massage table between us, four hands resting palm down on the white leather, but I was afraid of what would happen when I undressed. When I could not take it any longer I came to her, and we peeled off our clothes, slowly at first, one-for-you then one-for-me. I knelt down and my tongue and lips and teeth teased her through her lace knickers until she raised herself to sit on the table, and her heels massaged my back. Then she undid my belt and I stepped out of my jeans and inexpertly, laughing, tried to use my teeth to remove her panties. Taking in the fine vellus hair that cut a trail from her navel to the sliver of fair pubic hair she had left to point the way, my lips traversed the pale bare, smooth curvature of her mound of Venus until my tongue plunged into the rosy valley of full, engorged, parted lips. With some difficulty, sound waves reverberating between folds of skin, I said, 'Did you choose the discount option at your last wax?'

'That's your landing strip, oh neophyte,' she said, lying back on the narrow bed and smiling as my craft's undercarriage touched down and lingered on the narrow, trimmed runway stripe.

'No landing lights?' I said.

'Need them?' she said, using a hand and adjusting her hips. 'And that . . . there . . . that's your aircraft's hanger.'

'Stop co-piloting,' I said. 'He's a veteran. He can do this with his eyes closed and without your guidance.'

With a sigh, 'Well, it must be really dark in there.'

'And he's only got one good eye. But he never complains.'

'Didn't he bring a rain jacket?'

'No, he's heard too many numbingly alarming stories about rain jackets lately, so it's just his helmet and two very full suitcases.'

'Well, there's no point banging that overfull luggage against the doorframe.'

'Don't worry, I'll unpack the contents shortly, but I'm warning you, I'm a messy housemate. I'm just admiring the interior decorating for now. Shame, somebody left his cellphone in here.' That's one of the things I love about Jade; nothing said with love offends her.

Her eyes rolled back, 'Well, you'd better warn him to don a lifejacket, because I'm expecting a downpour any moment now . . . Oh, god.' Her nails dug into my back.

'Not another religious orgasm,' I said. 'Fanatics under every bed, there's just no getting away from them. That was just light precipitation, anyhow, no more than a drizzle at best.'

'Stop it,' Jade said, her smile filled with so many meanings. 'I'm busy here.'

'Oh, don't mind me, I'll just lie here quietly and watch,' I said. 'But I hope you don't rain cats and dogs, that might be tricky.' And she pinched my bum and shuddered, but this time with laughter. She straightened her legs beneath me on the narrow bed. Then I anchored my whole body on her by matching our body parts, her ankles, thighs, and hips bearing most of my weight. We were instantly harmonious and entirely dependent on each other for motion. This curbed our movement, and the sensations became excruciatingly exquisite as I rocked in unison with her. Her blue eyes searched mine while I watched her face change like the seasons, until flushed with summer heat, her cloudburst drenched me with torrential rain and converged with the surge that welled up from within me.

Autumn tints blushed her face as the fervor subsided, and I said, 'That was unseasonal heavy rainfall. I hope your massage bed has ample storm-water drainage to cope with the deluge.'

Jade held my face and said, 'Your smile is totally different.'

'How so, Princess?'

'It's there. It's wide. It feels like you own it, and you are completely comfortable with it.'

'Post-coital euphoria, I guess.' No, that's not it, but my smile widened anyway. And I told her how I felt released from so many things in that moment, and that if it had been with somebody else I would never have felt this way. Somehow I knew it had to be with her. 'Don't laugh,' I said, 'it lasts a long time with me. I get it so seldom.' Harry growled a warning, and we both paused for someone to burst into the house, but nothing happened. It prompted us back to reality, though.

Showered and dressed, I had one last question, 'By the way, cat person, what is the name of that breed of cat that has no hair?'

'It's called a Sphinx.' She sat on the floor and pulled on her boots, tucking her jeans inside them.

'Why would someone shave their kitten bald? It's cruel and painful, not to mention cold.'

'They're born like that, silly. It's in their genes.'

'Well, so is yours, now, but barely. But you say it's genetic, then? Females only, I guess. Does it skip a generation, anything strange like that? You really should have mentioned "alopecia" on your application form.'

Her airborne boot bounced off my shoulder. 'I'm not a mutant,' she said, 'just rare, very expensive and sought after.'

Jade glanced around warily before she let me out the security gate. We could not kiss goodbye there in the open; even a hug seemed like it would be a dead giveaway. 'Was that the first time, you know, that you've been with someone who, um . . .'

'Exclaims loudly? Cries out in wonder, and expresses herself freely? Oh, you mean "ejaculates"?' I said through unmoving lips, in case someone out of earshot was watching. 'I'm not telling.'

As I walked away from her house, I heard her say, 'So did I get the job?'

It was a very gentle experience, I think for both of us, even if it was not as we might have wished it to be in a neutral place and with all the time in the world. We discovered unique moments in our loving, things neither of us had encountered before. And for me it was free of the anxiety borne of the negative energy which had taken up residence in my marital bed.

Our cappuccinos arrive. 'Clive, what I have had with you in a few weeks I have never had in my life. It is very, very special. I have had magic and miracles and an experience of love that is new and completely unique. You have given me back my body. I am in touch with it again, and it is responding to the physical challenges I am giving it. This morning I jogged for seven kilometers, when a month ago I could barely walk the length of the beach without pain.'

She credits me with much of how she feels, so marked and sudden is the improvement in her well-being. The physical rejuvenation is but one aspect, perhaps just a visible sign of what is happening to her. The real shift is in her spirit, her desire to live again, for the first time since Wade died; to believe in and seek out what she needs in her world and bring it into reality. Mostly, it's about how she sees herself. She feels worthwhile again.

'This earth is going through catastrophic change, Clive. What we know is true today, is not so tomorrow. And who knows how long we have on this planet as it is now? Watching some of the TV footage by chance yesterday afternoon of the huge earthquake also gave me the impetus to go back to the big picture and not to be bogged down with worries about small detail. That is all taken care of by powers greater than me, without any interference needed from me. My spirit guides will show me the way, if I just open my eyes and have no fear. The only thing that matters is obedience to spirit, the voice within, and love. Today I feel sure that you and I are doing that and are totally on track.'

I would like to believe in what she says, but I am not so sure that I am any good at locking into my gut and doing what is right for me. 'I think I am too tentative, too unsure of myself, and I don't trust my gut,' I say. 'I worry so much about the possible calamitous consequences of my choices, especially for the boys.'

'I am with you on avoiding catastrophe, on building a picture where nobody is harmed, but who knows if we are really in charge of such decisions?' she says. 'Samantha gave me a pep talk yesterday, and it was incredibly sobering. Her main point was that I have had my heart so badly broken and only recently have I started putting myself back together. I have found myself and started loving myself and life again and she sees me setting myself up for more heartache because she can see I have gone in much deeper in the past week or so, more immersed into us. Her other point was the hurt that the deceit could cause to others, though she also said she has no doubt that Sara-lea, wherever she is, has Calix on a string, at the very least waiting in the wings if not actually continuing her affair with him.'

Jade never inquires about Calix and what happened to him, and I am distracted by her point about 'Calix on a string'. Samantha has also told me that the emotional bond and sexual energy that she and others observe is overwhelming and a lot of people are talking about it; people who know us have come to her and asked, 'What the fuck is going on there?' and one patron even said, 'Do you have rooms here, those two need a bed.' We laughed and I said, 'Now that's a good angle for your restaurant.' Then I asked Samantha what she thought was going on here, and she said that she and people who have spoken to her were aware of the deepest connection and energy they have ever experienced around them.

'I have a strong feeling something is coming to an end soon, for either you or us,' Jade says. 'I have lots of insecurities about this situation, this triangle, I have allowed myself to get involved in with you. Even if one apex is a dotted line for now, I know she will come back. And then there's the triangle with Gino and over the years in our on-off relationship, we have always had these triangles, and I need a clean break. No more magnetism between him and me. I am trying to focus on my power. I don't want to lose it, and especially not lose it in my need to be around you. For me this year is about magic and miracles and its manifestation.'

'It is me who has lost my power,' I say, 'and I have been fighting to regain my potency for the last nine months.'

Wondering about Julie's take on constructive masculine energy, I am reminded about those groups of castrates, religious sects allegedly found in Siberia and elsewhere about one-hundred years ago but also more recently, who self-mutilated the 'key of the devil', that stick that sprouted from their loins, in horror, I guess, at the evil destruction and hatred they believed it spawned. The atrocities of the First World War were probably fodder for their cause. And I think of how it seems that men, males as a group, seem to be presenting now with more personal behavioural problems and conditions than before, manifesting in OCDs and addictions and other destructive behaviours and brutal testosterone-driven conduct if they engage life without a deep consciousness. I think it is because they feel they have lost their potency, their masculine energy. And it does not pass me by that I may be one of them.

'Jade, we are in a situation we could choose to see as messy and undesirable, but that view would keep us trapped. I wish to free myself from the confines of old expectations and rules and judgments and shame. Come with me, learn with me. Let's create our own rules and our purpose. Help me to do this, use your magic. You will only lose your power if you choose to.'

'Clive, I think conscious people realize that the heart is the source of our connection to a consciousness greater than the ego. The heart, not the mind, is the seat of consciousness. And it's because of you that my physical and energetic heart is healing and I can move forward with my life and rely on my body again.'

'You really do open your heart to your own presence and all the situations in your life with unconditional love. How do you do this?'

'I draw breath into my heart,' she says. 'What's so painful is approaching this with an open heart because sometimes I feel overwhelmed by tenderness and sadness and regret—and just so vulnerable—but it feels cleansed, like I'm healing it of past hurts and blockages. I just have to witness them, these emotions. But I felt sorrow this morning. I really cried, suppressing sadness. I know the ending has been pre-mourned, and this is just an ending. But I have been in silence for two years.'

I wonder if she is referring to mourning the son she has lost, or her reticence to finally extricate herself from a relationship that abused her spirit. And then we identify that we both feel sad, and realize that we have felt this entirely independently for days now, waking up to a gnawing sadness, a heaviness that does not truly lift with the distractions of the day. I wonder if it is heartache; anguish for what is about to happen or sorrow for what has happened to us over the years, or maybe part of the collective angst of past or impending pain and misery that permeates pockets of the world and its peoples, and whether this is a necessary catalyst for change.

'When you are really hurting,' I say, 'then change is ready for you.'

She ponders that statement, then says, 'That's a weird way to put it.'

I think of how people, conscious people who see more than what is apparent, have become more conscious of how we are all connected and are still working feverishly at it; like the noticeable groundswell of people around the world migrating and congregating and pooling their energies with others who are also searching for meaning, co-creating their purpose, and finding a new way. They seek harmony and love, a world in touch with Mother Nature. They would argue that to express our love is right; that there is no judgment when you embrace what is real.

'I think you are struggling with yourself, Princess, with what you expect yourself to be rather than who you are. That's the sadness,' I say, 'because you are now staring at your true self, without pretence or façade, and there's a lot that you see that is difficult for you to acknowledge and own. You need to forgive yourself, in the sense of accepting all of you and all of what has happened before—all the depraved things you think you've done and all the flawed decisions you think you've made and believe that your life is kept in balance, in equilibrium. Nothing is ever lost. Everything happens for a reason. You just need to see the gift in it.' I pause, feeling like I am lecturing her on concepts I don't even understand. 'I'm sorry, that sounds like I know what I'm talking about.'

'That's all right. I think you have a point.'

'I'm probably talking about me, really. But your despair may also be because you are connected in, because you feel things, you soak up what is going on around you more than most people do. You absorb the collective energy. Conscious people, like you, know they can no longer rely on tradition and in this void there is uncertainty. They have to craft and follow their own path.'

Jade says, 'Is this not true of relationships, especially those formalized by marriage and then constrained by the notion of "what should be?" Such that when the delusionary promised vows are disturbed, we feel compelled to act forcefully to put it right, because we have been wronged and the conventions have not been adhered to, rather than choosing to embrace "what is" and integrate it into a conscious, loving relationship.'

'Even if it doesn't work out?'

'Even if you choose to part ways in the end,' she says, keeping it within the realm of choice.

'I hate it when you do that.' She question marks her eyebrows. 'Remind me that I have a say in the outcome, that I have the power of choice to create it or create how I see it, like my circle of influence is extensive.'

'There's very little you can claim to not have influenced.'

'Maybe, but getting back to what you were saying, it resonates with my dilemma last year, which I have not yet really resolved in my mind as I still vacillate in weaker moments, when I am uncertain of myself, unsure of who I really am. That's when the dark thoughts would come, of how I have been wronged, of how I am owed something by him and her. This was when sorrow would come and overwhelm me, and I wallowed in self-pity. I was unable to control the extent of what I was feeling; intellectually, yes, but more pain than I could withhold invaded my emotions and I couldn't close the vent on my enraged expression of it. I just could not forgive, though I thought I had. It was debilitating, but it felt like a safer place to be than to have to own my feelings and take responsibility for my choices and acknowledge my role in it all. I simply capitulated to circumstances. I became a victim. Then I felt compelled to do something, to assert my rights. It was all ego. And Sarah's reaction inflamed me. When she did not respond in the way I thought I needed her to, which I suppose meant to be remorseful and compassionate and do absolutely everything in her power to show her total devotion to me and me alone, I felt betrayed once again. The double-betrayal was too much for me, and the only way to prevent myself from falling apart was to do away with her. I mean, to wish her out of my life. But I sometimes think I will never regain my sense of self and that I will never truly recover from it.'

'Don't be too hard on yourself,' Jade says. 'It's a lifetime's work to liberate ourselves from the bondage of the ego. And this work helps to release others from the bondage of their ego. It is our egos that separate us from achieving "one mind" or a God-consciousness.'

'Like "universal love"? And only once liberated, what I understand
of the Christian term salvation, are we free from the effects of karma
and rebirth?' I am still bothered, for reasons I cannot fathom, by Sarah's
rendition of our alleged past-life relationship.

Jade is about to respond, but then points towards the road and says,
'There he is, driving past and staring at us. Fuck off, Gino, how dare
you do this!' The fury and fear from yesterday is finally being vented.
I reflexively look in his direction, and immediately regret it as I want
to pay him no obvious attention, and I wonder what sort of energy he
picks up between us in his anguished state. 'He can't do that, can he?
Intimidate us like this. I've even thought of getting a restraining order
like I did before when he cracked my ribs.'

'You don't want to do that. It's a last resort,' I say, silently wishing it
was that easy.

Jade leans back in her chair, and I mirror her action, as if the physical
distance this creates between us will minimize any evil thoughts and
perceptions, and our whole mood changes.

'My frustration is that while the time I spend with you is beautiful,
the intimidation we are both experiencing does not allow for that kind
of freedom.'

She is referring to the desperate arrangement we had made yesterday
to try and get some private time together and perhaps a sandy cuddle
to release the desire building between us, and how Gino had followed
her to the secluded beach where she waited for me and glared at her
from atop a large boulder. She had to text me quickly not to come but
I was already there, just meters from her, winding my way between the
boulders. I texted Jade to leave immediately and, taking the only option
I could think of, stepped out onto the exposed sands at the water's edge
and strode purposefully toward his vantage point but by the time I
reached the lump of rock he had disappeared and I kept going until I
had reached my vehicle. The fear-reaction came later.

'We are putting a lot of pressure on both of us,' I say. 'Let's give this time
to settle down and take fewer risks, so we don't have others' shit to contend
with as well. Let's just marvel at and enjoy what we are experiencing.'

'How do we do that?'

'We could start with more platonic interaction in public, especially here at the deli. And make good use of special moments we can create. We know what we feel, let's protect it with everything we have. We would be crazy to let it go.'

'How do you do "more platonic" when the way you feel is the way you feel and there is so little time together? It's not as if we are groping each other. Well, sometimes,' she laughs, slipping her hands under the table.

I say, 'It's all in the eyes and the energy, I guess.'

It seems that Jade feels we need a change of pace and scenery. With Gino apparently heading off somewhere, she cannot resist the window of opportunity and says, 'Hey, we haven't had any private, intimate moments to sustain us.'

'Right, it's been ages.'

And so that is what we do late in the afternoon and just across the road from the beach where Roxanne entertains the boys. I feel unsure how she would respond to my overpowering desire for her but our first embrace in the privacy of her home, of the kind we cannot enjoy in public, is electric and then for a minute all flustered and urgent we comic-like run around the house making it secure and private, then lock ourselves inside a room she has created just for us to share this loving intimacy, in case her tame and supportive housemate arrives home (no more than mildly embarrassing for us), or someone not-so-tame and compassionate towards our cause comes knocking (catastrophic). We tear at each other's clothes which are removed in seconds and we remain standing as I enter her. As we become one, nothing else matters. Somehow we manage to find ourselves sitting on the cushioned floor, still joined, and then we both sink our upper bodies slowly away from each other like a snake's double-hinged jaw until we recline on our backs with our heads facing towards opposite ends of the room. And lying there, like conjoined twins that share sexual organs, rapture fills us and we descend or rise, I am not quite sure which, to ecstasy which peaks again and again until pressure of time calls it to a close.

Recoil

33

The most important thing a father can do
for his children is to love their mother.

(Theodore Hesburgh)

Thursday, 31, March 2011

'Hello,' she says.

'Hi,' I say, but my tongue and lips seem to be half a second behind the sound that emanates from my throat which has constricted and the vibrating sound waves meant for her ears fall hopelessly short as they trip over my lips.

'You look like you have just seen a ghost.'

'It feels like that.'

'You thought I was dead.' It is a statement.

'No. Yes.'

'Well, as you can see, I'm not.' And with hands clasped above her head, she pirouettes as if this will confirm for me that what I see is not a hologram.

'But you were', I say, 'dead to me.' Sarah's reappearance injects dread into my heart. I want to ask about it, to break the silence that follows, but already anticipating that I will not receive a lucid or unambiguous response, I just say, 'How have you been?'

She does not answer this, but instead says what she has come to say, 'There was no way out of the place we had got to. I could not stay, and I could not go. Neither of us could. And I was beyond the limits of my ability to deal with the situation. I felt the only option was to do away with myself. So this is what I did, just not in the conventional sense. No more of that silly stuff I did before. How about you?'

It comes out smoothly as if well-prepared, without emotional sway, her neurological feeling centres neutered. I wonder what dosage of medication she is taking. And I wonder whether she needed the time to terminate a pregnancy.

'Here all the time, waiting for you to come back. Never quite knowing if you would.'

My mind can only deal with simply structured phrases and clauses, as if it fears it will lose itself and forget what it is trying to say. I feel like a mime artist as each short sentence is accompanied by a different hand gesture. I stand there, unable to move my feet but wanting to turn away and come back to this moment to confirm for myself that this apparition before me is not real.

'Well, I think I'm here now,' she says.

'You needed time to do what you needed to do?'

'And you,' she says.

I am shaking. As much as I have imagined this moment countless times these past months, played it over and over in my mind in the dark solitude of endless nights, I know I am in shock. It is too soon, I think to myself. I am not ready yet; there is more work for me to do with Jade. Or is this the next step? Sarah steps forward and holds me. It immediately feels like she is intruding in my space. My arms move to enclose her, but they don't feel as though they really belong to me, and my elbows brush against her waist as my arms disappear behind her, and as I look past her shoulder, I see two hands suspended, afraid to hold her as they might pass right through her.

Jade was right—the ending has arrived. I recoil and step back from Sarah.

I have never been comfortable in the presence of the dead.

34

Love is not love that alters when it
alteration finds.

(William Shakespeare)

Tuesday, 5, April 2011

'Yesterday must have been hard for you,' Jade says. 'I admire your courage and honesty, and I cannot meet you with anything less. But as a result I have been on quite a journey in the last two days. As I walked past you just now and through the deli, I felt my guard come up and I could not really feel you because of this. And the minute I sat down with you now, I felt so uncomfortable I just wanted to get up and leave straight away. A couple of times during your story of your Friday night with her I felt the same way, but I stayed, because I am not willing to jeopardize what I know I have with you by being emotionally reactive, not now or ever. Even though my heart feels closed, I would like to keep the lines of communication open and the respect and the trust.'

Jade is working towards something, so I wait for her, leaning forward and attentive but careful not to invade her space, such is the fiercely protective barrier she carries around her as she speaks. Besides, she is dressed today like GI Jane, in camouflage trousers, a khaki T-shirt, and peak cap pulled low over her eyes, with squadron-pilot Raybans to complete the picture, and I am not sure I should mess with her as I cannot see her eyes, and her chosen attire is surely no coincidence. She is dressed for battle, perhaps with herself or with me or with the world in general, and I am rather foolishly unprepared for this. But what she is saying, or rather how she is saying it, is so unlike what I am used to at home; no barbed accusations and flashing anger. I can sit and listen to her own how she is feeling.

She says, 'Because I went into fear mode yesterday and my wounds were leaping in front of my face, my heart was closed and I could not feel you, I did not "believe" you. I walked away from you at the deli feeling that this is bullshit, that you are bullshitting me. I felt I had seen some of your shadow and felt unsure about you, that you were just the same as all of them. Like I have swum in the crystal clear warm water and it has been blissful, but I have been too brave by swimming out too far with you, and now I can feel the rip tide and it's time to swim back to shore quickly before I drown.'

She is on about what I had revealed to her yesterday, the first time we had been able to create an opportunity to sit together and talk since Friday night, the evening I went out with Sarah. That Friday evening had started off tense, at least for me. I was feeling uncertain and she seemed to approach it with a bubbly enthusiasm I could not match. I did not want to go anywhere in particular, anywhere special which came with high expectations when my feelings were so mixed up with dark forebodings of a rerun of evenings out together a lifetime of months ago. Worried that the evening would end in disaster, and worried that it would not. But we did not speak about us or our relationship, and I knew better than to raise any questions about what happened when she went away, where she went, or who she was with. With immense gratitude to Jade, I felt that I had moved beyond expecting, patiently, for these particulars to emerge one day. I truly felt that it simply did not matter to me anymore; I had no need to know.

Sarah and I met when it was still early so we had a few drinks, but we were both hungry so we ordered food at the bar and sat outside under a darkening sky and drank and ate and talked about nothing in particular; just inconsequential stuff aroused by the happenings around us as sunset revellers eased themselves out of the workweek and into the weekend's festivities. I was trying to be aware of what I was feeling so that how I made myself present was authentic and my intuition could guide my responses, but the moment felt so surreal as if I had ejected the DVD of the life I was living and inserted another into the tray that I felt I was having an out-of-body experience witnessing myself being there with her. At times I wondered whether she sat next to me courtesy of my imagination and if other patrons wondered why I was talking aloud to myself and what exactly was in the beer glass I nursed. It was a most disturbing feeling, and once or twice I touched her to try and reassure myself that she was real.

In her easy way Sarah flitted between donating to the bits and pieces of our conversation and reaching out to diners sitting at other tables with friendly comments which sometimes found traction around a common interest and became short exchanges. It was her anxiety, and her need to see herself reflected in others. This seemed to invite still more strangers and acquaintances into our space and this initially filled the awkward gap between us before the alcohol helped all topics, no matter how superficial, seem marginally interesting if not meaningful, and in this way we massaged the chasm into a crack. By the time we left the hotel restaurant, it was easy to slip our arms around each other and amble lazily along the sidewalk back to the car. On the way, we heard some music and in unison trailed the sound and found ourselves in a coffee bar soaking up the jazz-blues as if nothing had changed. Conversation was limited by the loudness of the music and this was a blessing as time passed without awkwardness. We got home after midnight and, after a courtyard cigarette we held each other in bed until we fell asleep.

The boys had spent the night at their grandparents, so in the morning we had awoken to an empty house and in the same bed, and we made love. It was brief and unspectacular in that it did not achieve the purpose of connecting us in vulnerability, and was vaguely disappointing for me as it had been for years though for different reasons perhaps. I had retrospectively concluded that it felt this way in recent years because she was with another man, and wondered whether it felt this way now because I am with another woman. Then I made tea and we lay in bed together not saying much. When she said, 'We have about

an hour before we have to go and fetch the boys,' we made love again
and this time the strips of peeling wallpaper-memories and doubt-filled
questions that still clung shredded and encrusted on our bedroom walls
came away and it felt like we met in a fresh room still wet with plaster
and the anticipation of new memories still to come.

It was this that I had shared with Jade yesterday, and she had leaned
back and pulled her cap down over her eyes and I could feel her bristle
as dark thoughts filled her mind until she got up to leave and didn't look
back to smile and wave goodbye in the way she always did. So today I
listen to Jade as I try figure out where this is going to land. So far, it does
not look good.

'I started to categorise you in my head in a way that enforces a belief
system about men that does not serve me and that never has, one that I
cannot go forward with. I may even have started to see you as a wolf in
sheep's clothing. And I am afraid of telling you where I went to in my
mind about you, because it may scare you, chase you away. But this is
an exciting process for me to learn something about myself and I know
you can handle it.'

She has more confidence in my resilience than I have, it seems. I fish
for a cigarette as this is the only resource I have at my disposal to appear
relaxed and unflinching and able to handle whatever it is I am supposed
to handle. Busy with the fag in my mouth and twirling a used sugar
wrapper between my fingers, I hope to appear thoughtful and don't need
to respond immediately.

'Where's Pi-shu?' I say. She had brought him with her, as she often
does, but after he greeted Harry and Sally, he disappeared over the wall
and I haven't seen him since. Hearing his name, the dogs immediately
file out through the gate and within seconds stand beneath the huge
Oak tree in which Pi-shu doubtlessly shelters, tails wagging, and Jade
does not have to answer my question.

She is still creating the background to what she really wants to say,
'My soul knows our love is real, and that this is meant to be so. This is
a repeat of a theme for me, but it is different, because of the deep stuff
we both feel. So this is an opportunity for more healing and growth. I

know you are a good man, and obviously you have a shadow, and I look forward to meeting it. But today I woke up determined to exit because I am starting to feel grubby about the whole thing. I don't like the deceit. I don't want to play the role of scarlet woman and carry the projections which that archetype carries. I don't want to be a lonely old lady with too many cats. I don't want to be the woman who broke up your family. And I don't think I want you inside me after you've been inside her.'

I say, 'What happened to the idea of freedom and open relationships and the expression of love?'

'This is the human-me speaking. It has not evolved yet. My soul has a different view.' Then she puts up her hand to stop me responding, and says, 'Wait, there's more.'

I wonder which one of these is the real issue for her. Coming just after my confession of sleeping with my wife, it seems obvious that this has provoked her doubts, but all the other stuff inherent in our circumstances she has surely known since the start. Perhaps it is the return of Sarah, her presence, the realization that she is a real person? On Sunday they had bumped into each other in the check-out queue at the local health store and if Jade had thought for a moment of avoiding Sarah, she could not have done so without it being obvious. Jade told me Sarah had said, 'You're Clive's friend,' and Jade responded in a way she afterwards regretted by pretending at first to not be sure who Sarah was. Then Sarah said, 'What is wrong with your voice?'

'Oh, it's been like this for years,' Jade said.

To which Sarah recommended that Jade make an appointment with a particular acupuncturist she has relied on extensively these past years. And so the conversation progressed while they waited in the queue with lots of questions and concern and touching by Sarah and guessing (incorrectly for a change) Jade's star sign and Chinese birth-year and her relationship status and so on, until Jade emerged if not shaken then stirred and Sarah later commented to me that Jade dresses so revealingly and that the kind of woman I am attracted to is so unlike herself.

While these thoughts cut across my mind, Jade is still talking to me, ' . . . and since yesterday, I thought of the time I was happiest with

Gino, and realised that I may have stayed forever if his other woman had accepted my place in his life and if he had been a good man, which he is not, not in the way that you are and truly loved us both. His motivations came from fear where I see yours come from love.'

She pauses to put her hand on mine, and I feel somewhat reassured because I was starting to think that she is about to trash me, to tell me what a stereotypical bastard I am to have a loving wife at home while I am sleeping with her and that she is going to call it off; that it has been devalued to 'a fling' and no longer has the soul bond of which she was once so certain.

'I love you, Clive,' she says, 'in the way I love Wade. With the deepest knowing that we are one, and I never want to lose you. But I am not desperate. I just know you will never abandon her nor your children, and I love you even more for that. The options of breaking it off or entering into a long-term affair as the secret other women are both undesirable to me, the second option being both undesirable and disempowering.'

I am now thoroughly confused. I had suspected that the news of my intimacy with Sarah would throw up issues for her, but I am hearing mixed messages here. I think to myself, 'Okay, here it comes, brace yourself.' Then she seems to go off on a tangent, and I have to wait for her to come back to her point.

'Yesterday I made an art piece that I did not know if I loved or hated. When I was done I saw that it's just like where I am right now. To me it looked very masculine and stiff like a shield or a coat of arms. The heart shape is made of a double layer of pumpkin shells, the inside is dark tiger's eye pebbles and in the middle is a white pansy. What does it tell you?'

'Not sure. All I can say is that a coat of arms is something that is adopted by a tribe or a group of people who feel they have something in common. It's a symbol of power and identity; of unity. The dark and light in the heart are probably also significant as you have made a point of mentioning it.'

'Yes,' she says. 'This morning I named it the "Shield of Truth".' I am trying to work out what message she is giving me with this description, when she says, 'For many years I have wondered if this was my path, my truth. I don't know, but I am willing to give it a try, but only because of who I believe you are. By the way, you know me as Jade, but my real names are Jacquieline Daja. JD for short, and by the time I was a teenager, it became Jade. Jacquieline means supplanter, a replacement or understudy.'

I am still grappling with where she is going with this. Silence and pretence of self-composure seem the best options for now, and she only releases me from this vagueness when she says, 'It is time for me to move away from the heart-shutting old paradigms. I want to love you, to be in your life openly, to love your children, and to embrace her too. I don't want you to give up your home, your family or your devotion to that. So if you really want me to remain in your life, tell her about me.'

'Yes, I've been wondering about that. Just not sure what it is yet, what to say to her. And how.'

'Tell her you won't abandon her, tell her she is free to continue with whatever she is busy with, and assure her that your family will not disintegrate. Ask her to meet me. Maybe we really can be sisters. Perhaps given the assurance that you will not abandon her and knowing that you have me will give her the freedom to be more open about Calix, and she will not have to choose between the two of you. Your heart is in the right place in how you have chosen to treat him. You are already a pioneer, so now I am agreeing to be a pioneer with you.'

'Are we co-creating?' I say, trying to buy time.

'Whatever,' Jade says, not interested in theorising. 'Obviously all the low vibration ego stuff is going to come up, as it did yesterday with me. It is how we handle it that matters. But don't let her bully you. Let her see that throwing her toys is the reason that she is losing you. Stand your ground and decide for you. Own your truth, but only if this resonates as your truth of course. I'll stand with you. She does not have a good argument against this, as she has experienced and justified if for herself for years, and she is not "wrong". You are simply adding the elements of honesty and openness to it a little earlier on in the process.'

35

I tended to place my wife
under a pedestal.

(Woody Allen)

Monday, 11, April 2011

'Today I feel I could hold you through anything, including any baggage you may bring with you to me,' Jade says. She looks beautiful to me, eyes shining and smiling with ease. But the beauty I feel and the love that surrounds me are from her energy, her presence. 'I know you, you are honest. You will always know when it's your shit. You don't need to get any more perfect than you already are.'

I look at her blue eyes, which gaze intently at me. We are sitting very close, both leaning on our elbows on the table that barely keeps us apart, our knees, partially obscured by the tablecloth, touching and occasionally rubbing against one another in a way that is reassuring rather than sexual, like when you touch someone on the arm when they are having a difficult moment.

Jade says, 'The other day you touched very briefly on how fucked-up you are feeling from your recent times with Sara-lea. You hide this mostly, and I want to know more. I know all about it. I was feeling like that this time last year.'

It is as if she knows. Less than an hour ago I had extricated myself from a tirade of insults by fleeing the house and I think the overwhelming feeling, as I sit here at the deli with Jade, is of embarrassment, fearing that if I told her I would face questions like, 'You deserve it; why on earth have you let her back into your life?'

'You think you know,' I say, 'just like I think I know and understand you. You might have an idea of what I have been through, because you think you have had a similar experience, but it's not possible to know how it feels for someone else. Never.' I am surprised at how emphatic I sound and how grumpy I feel.

She seems to ignore what I have said and my dismissive irritation, and says, 'The idea that our relationship may have a positive effect for you at home now that she is back, in that she may pick up on it and come back towards you, left me a little ragged emotionally. I have some pretty lofty ideals and ideas about life—you have heard me on my soap box, right? But in reality, my ego is not jumping for joy at the thought of playing that role in your life.'

'Jade, for years I believed that Sarah was right in how she described me. But one of the unexpected gifts I have received from her affair is that some friends opened up and told me what they observed, unsolicited by me—that they have seen how she treated me and that it was awful. It was always the same theme, and they said I had grown smaller and more withdrawn, anxious and ill at ease. When I ventured a few of Sarah's perceptions of me, they said . . . Well, I won't tell you exactly what they said. It was all about her manipulation . . .'

'Emotional blackmail? What really happened last December?' Jade says.

I could say out loud what it used to be like with Sarah, but not what it is like now. 'I felt trapped. I could not vent or deal with, in any way, my feelings about the pain of her betrayal, given her unstable mental state. It was just too risky. But even without that, I would have found it to be unmanageable. Her behavior, that is. At some stage I began to feel that if I continually gave in to these fears of hers then I was actually stoking it, intensifying her dependence on me. But any resistance by me to her demands was to her evidence of a flaw in my personality or that I did not love her, and the accusatory labels that flowed left no doubt of that. She conveniently diminished my contributions to the family and household and child-minding, and I could never do enough in her eyes. Negative comparisons were rife—'why can't you be more like him', knowing full well that any reference to Calix, no matter how oblique, tore me up.' Actually, this is what happened this morning.

'I'm hesitant to say this but given the hurt you were dealing with, that she caused, that kind of behaviour was heartless; it's sick.'

Sally comes to nudge my hand and I point her to the bowl of water behind my chair. I extinguish the smouldering filter of my cigarette and roll another twirly-whirly. 'Actually, she often resorted to outright 'pathologising' my behaviour, actually claiming that I was sick and mentally unstable, and even when she fell short of this at the very least she left a strong message that I was deficient in my roles as friend, husband, provider, father, or lover. The ferocity of her fear-based manipulations made little sense until I realized that she was not reacting to the current situation, which often appeared benign or insignificant to me, but to a flood of past fears which it symbolized.'

Jade says, 'To her demons from another time and place—perhaps from another lifetime?' '1303' reverberates across my mind.

'But this insight failed to take the edge off it and make it more bearable. And when her negative labels, the most prevalent probably being "you're selfish", found their target, it gyroscoped my values and disoriented me and dismantled my perspective of what was true and fair.'

How dizzy I felt an hour ago, whirlpooling in Sarah's orbit, without this fulcrum, and how disappointed I feel in myself as I thought I now sat firmly in the cradle of my values, my personal boundaries, of 'this is who I am'.

'So you internalized her perceptions of your character, your worth and desirability and values.' It is a statement; she knows this all too well from her time with Gino.

'What I felt in response to this, I think of as 'unwarranted' guilt, a paralyzing self-flagellation as I assumed total responsibility for all her ills and unhappiness and unmet needs and even her childhood pain. I took it on like it was all my doing. I rationalized and justified her behaviour and let it define me. But it sucked trust out of our relationship—I felt unsafe because of her unpredictability. The more self-doubt consumed me, the more I wallowed in shame and inadequacy. In my ambivalence I lost contact with the knowing parts of myself and violated my integrity. So the deepest betrayal was of myself, as I sacrificed bits of my wholeness. In the end, I just could not take any more of it.' Her hand, resting on my arm, squeezes me gently. 'And I fear it's escalating again, her behaviour, or perhaps it's just that I'm floundering. Sometimes I really feel I am driven to the brink of madness; it just gets too much for me and I feel like I'm about to lose it, like I did last year. It's just that while intellectually I can disown some of her impressions of me, I have yet to regain a sense of "I'm okay".' This is more detail than I expected to share, and we have never spoken at such length about my relationship with Sarah.

'And what about Calix?' she says.

'For me, he no longer exists, or what he represented and the anguish it brought, no longer exists.'

'Live and let die?'

'Something like that,' I say.

Jade has so much ground she wants to cover she starts another conversation topic, at least that is how it feels to me, unless I just haven't caught up yet with how all these things fit together. Perhaps sensing my mood, she says, 'I completely love how you look. There is nothing that looks wrong to me. Every feature, sound, gesture, and look is familiar and attractive to me. Nothing irritates or bothers me, or needs getting used to. Nothing is out of place, everything fits. This is another unique experience to me, and I feel blessed to be seen and loved by such a beautiful man inside and out. You are the other side of my coin.'

I absorb this without comment, thinking, 'That's more like it.' My spirit is soaring. She says, 'Why do you call me "Princess"?'

'I really don't know. It just came out. It's what you are to me.'

'Well, I haven't told you this, but a little while ago I "travelled".'

'You went away?'

'No, silly, to a previous lifetime.' She looks at me. 'I never know whether you're teasing me.'

'If you put on those panties again,' I say, 'I'll show you what it feels like to be teased. And then you will never wonder.'

We laugh at the recollection of those shared moments now forever ours. 'I sleep with them at night, soaked in your DNA, under my pillow—each one, even from the first time in that derelict house.' I pull a face, wrinkle my nose. 'Actually, maybe your DNA provoked it. I never thought of that. It all happened in a split second. There you were, and the reason you now call me "Princess". I was royalty and you looked after my horses, and our love was immeasurable but forbidden by the norms of the day. And so I learnt that we have done this before, been in a situation where we were prohibited from being together. I married a much older man of nobility with wolfhounds and thoroughbred horses. He had a ponytail and was kind and gentle and loved me and I lived a long and happy life. But each day I saw you and how your heart was broken because of something that could never be.' Jade smiles and says, 'I wonder if you still know how to shoe horses?'

'And I wonder if your aristocrat husband is Francois?' I say. 'You know, your dream of wolves and horses?' Will I ever be gifted a lifetime as the wealthy aristocrat who spreads his seed with his choice of beautiful women rather than yearn for the unreciprocated love of the woman of my heart?

I am so done with past lives and bad karma and violence and unrequited love. I want to turn around and walk, just keep walking, over the mountains I so love, through the city, beyond any hint of humanity and civilization, and further still through barren and desolate wastelands to where there is no future and no past; to where my spirit is boundless and my soul has no desires, and infuse my being with the drifting sands.

Jade says, 'I often get this picture of us sitting naked, you behind me with your arms around me, my legs are crossed and yours are around the sides of mine and your chin is on my shoulder and we are beautiful together—radiant, earthy, authentic, ageless, timeless, a match. Like heaven on earth.'

While she speaks, her eyes soften and her laughter-lines crease to emphasize the downward tilt at either extremity of her eyes. Her nose leads my gaze to her parting lips, which appear uncertain whether to devour me or say something. Then her half-moon smile erupts across her face, and her eyes glisten, and she says, 'You are utterly beautiful to me in every way.' And then with a laugh, 'I want to have your babies,' and she throws her head back and reclines in her chair with her palms open on her thighs as if inviting me to make the next move.

The love and safety I feel right now takes me back to yesterday. Yesterday was chilly and I had ventured with some trepidation to her house and we talked while we sat on the carpet in the lounge near the fireplace that warmed us while clothed and later unclothed on the blankets and cushions she produced from somewhere. Slowly and effortlessly we made love before the fire, growing uncomfortably warm under the shroud of blankets until Jade tossed them aside and rolled me over and straddled me, and I could watch her as she caressed herself and gently rocked on me as I touched the deepest core of her. Then she leant forward to kiss me, holding my face, and resting the tip of her nose on mine. 'I'm ready,' she said, looking into my eyes. 'I want to share all of me with you, somewhere nobody else has been.' She closed her eyes and with the slightest adjustment, she coaxed me slowly into virgin territory, undulating her hips until I was deeper than I would have imagined possible. Her face contorted and she bit her lip and threw her head back. A reddish rash spread across her neck and breasts, then in sudden frenetic motion from somewhere deep inside her a primordial scream swelled to match mine and filled our ears until I felt my head would burst, and it knew no end until I discharged myself inside her. Then she lay against me, the princess and the cobbler, as salty tears from her eyes and mine, trickled and mingled.

Here at the deli, perhaps she can read my thoughts, as her eyes move from mine to my mouth and back again, and it feels like she wants to fill my mouth with her tongue. She says, 'I keep thinking of yesterday after we made love how you said that you found it difficult to fathom my age, that you saw me as thirty, and I told you that I often feel timeless. Apparently the age we go to heaven is thirty, all of us. Thirty is the eternal age, as is our connection. It's no wonder you see me at that age, as I see you. And I do feel beautiful with you. I believe I will just get more and more beautiful with you. Funnily enough in the reading that crystal did long before we even met which fell on your birthday, she said "this man of status, with the combined heart of my son and my father, who would feed me with the energy of love, was not into looks".'

36

Bigamy is having one wife too many.
Monogamy is the same.

(Oscar Wilde)

Thursday, 21 April 2011

Soon as she sits down, Jade wastes no time with an update for me on how she is feeling.

'Your words yesterday affirmed me in a way that helped me to understand that I am exactly where I need to be, even though my inner child is wreaking havoc at the moment and has done so for many, many years with the constant anxiety and tension, no breath and the constricted muscles from my jaw to my diaphragm so my words are lost in my throat, and the heart palpitations and all that stuff. I am no longer feeling shattered. The "triangle" and yesterday's lovemaking has brought up stuff which has been raging inside of me and yet all I can think is what a wonderful space this is in which to grow up, such a loving space with other loving beings, where it is safe to be everything. I realise that at my core I am okay, because the foundations I have built through years of work are strong. And I see this because you lovingly mirror it for me.'

Although I am impatient to tell her something I am grateful for these words as they seem to indicate that she is in just the space I need her to be to hear me. I am sitting with Jade, as usual and in the usual place. The deli is full, most people sitting outside around us as the weather has cleared up and everyone seems to be enjoying the mild weather after the early seasonal rains these last few days reminded them that autumn has arrived and the rainy, stormy winter months lie ahead.

At least one of the couples sitting two tables away from us are on to us and have been asking some questions, and they glance over at us every now and then and sometimes I catch them staring at us while pretending to be engaged in their conversation or listening thoughtfully to a point being made emphatically by one of their friends. Jade spent some time at their table in conversation before joining me, and before she did this she walked past me on the way to the bathroom and whispered, 'Don't look at me like that.' So we are careful not to touch each other and every now and then I lean back and make a conscious but futile effort to create the impression of a dispassionate, platonic interaction.

As Jade gets busy with the jewelry items she has laid out at our table, preparing them for some customer by polishing the heart pendants and cutting and threading the leather thongs through the holes she has drilled through the accessories that will eventually adorn someone's neck or wrist, I say, 'She had a bad day yesterday, at least in her interactions with me, and I had assumed this was because of the conversation the previous evening and that she has taken it in her head to the worst case scenario. I had also left her with the boys all afternoon. She was exhausted and tetchy but settled down with me there and was not ugly with me.' When in close proximity to others, here at the deli, I use words like 'she' and 'her' and 'herself' instead of Sarah, and 'next door' with eyes raised towards our house on the distant mountainside when referring to Calix or a glance to the left and a jerk of my head to indicate Gino who lives next door to Jade just a long stone's throw from the deli. 'She did not want to talk about it when I got home. I think rather waiting for her therapy today to process it further. Turns out her period arrived early, she said because of the shock.'

'She just needs time, Clive. Don't push her. I consider it an act of love towards me that she is allowing me access to you. She may not say it, but I can feel that she knows me and understands this contract clearly. She is being a sister to me and honouring her path. And I see you doing the same for me as you have done for her. Part of your purpose perhaps?'

The other evening, as we were preparing dinner, Sarah said something about my two wives, and this had kicked off a conversation that continued after dinner and late into the evening as we lay together in bed. 'Sarah,' I had said, latching on to this opener with as much tongue-in-cheek as I could muster as I was uncertain where she was going with this, 'we both know monogamy does not work. In fact, it does not exist, and we now know that for a fact.' She accepted this dig at her without immediate retort. 'Polyamory is much more realistic, and is fast becoming a way of life that more and more couples are exploring. I think we should be free to love.'

Sarah said, 'Before I came home, I did a cord cutting ritual to set us both free and sever the emotional dependence.' But a moment later, when she mentioned Jade by name, I was not quite sure how to respond, and I neither confirmed nor denied the relationship that has formed between us, trying to maintain a fine balance between being honest and open without giving her a focal point to attack or become enraged about. I needed time to gauge how she was taking this. She kept herself busy with dinner preparations while we talked about having other significant people in our lives and when she turned away from me and said, 'Do what you need to do' I thought it was time for an exit strategy and thankfully we were interrupted by hungry boys calling for their food. But when she picked up the topic afterwards while we had a cigarette in the courtyard before I put the boys to bed, I realized that tongue-in-cheek had become serious and real. By the time we lay in bed, she armed with the distraction of the cats curled up between her knees and a book resting on her lap as an outlet she could enlist should the conversation get too tough, me lying on my side next to her and holding her while we spoke, the conversation had gone further than felt comfortably safe for me, but we kept at it.

It dawned on me that she had been back for about three weeks already, and we have settled, if that's the term, into a daily pattern that keeps us apart as much as possible. We are in an awkward phase with school vacations, and pass by each other like child-minders changing shift. We have not yet placed any disgruntled pressure on each other about needs unmet, but the frequency of antagonistic confrontations seems to be escalating. For the moment I have mostly succeeded in being firm with my limits and when Sarah tries to deposit her pain with me I am often able to return it dispassionately for her to deal with, but with growing unease I expect I will erupt sooner than later and don't feel comfortable with the arrangement. And it seems that Sarah is starting to join the dots around Jade. Struggling to convey my thoughts to her, I resorted to telling her how I felt our relationship still hovered in mediocre territory and I realized that this was not very aspirational and that we both deserved more. It felt like strange language to use and that I was oversimplifying a complex matter, but I cannot fault her for how she responded.

'I have noticed a change in you since I returned. You have turned away, you are looking outward. And when you open the door, other people fill the space,' Sarah said, and I imagined she knew what she was talking about.

'I don't think it can be just anyone,' I said, thinking that Calix and Jade were carefully selected, so to speak, to come into our orbits at just the right time.

'Just be careful, you don't know what you're getting yourself into. And don't fall in love.' I thought—'Is it too late for that?' This warning reminded me how she was still suffering from her love for Calix, her desire to be with him more often, and experience their togetherness doing the enjoyable things that lovers do in public, but unable to as she will not disclose the relationship. I struggled to erase these thoughts, mostly due to the secrecy, the deceit. Is the love and healing I am experiencing also about embracing them? At some point late in the conversation, her biggest fears of abandonment reared up and she told me to remove my hand from her shoulder, and it was time to close the topic, but when we switched off the light and she turned away from me to go to sleep, she let me hold her and tell her that I love her to which she mumbled a response which seemed like she accepted that. Thankfully, the boys had the good grace to sleep through the night and with the sunrise we woke up together, skin warm and cuddly. It was a promising start, I thought, to a new way of being.

'So last night,' I say to Jade as we sit together at the deli, 'she fell asleep in Joshua's bed with him. I left her for a few hours, sat outside and thought about the situation, whether I was feeling like a bastard to both of you and all the traditional takes on my role in "an affair", but this feeling did not really seem to attach itself to me, and then I went inside and brought her gently to our bed. Despite everything, including us and the recency of yesterday's loving with you, I surprised myself as I held her and felt her fall asleep in my arms and accepting of it. I think I could feel a no-bullshit, no-ego love, non-possessive, non-fearful, or self-protective, the highest form of love with capital letters. And it did not stand in opposition to or competition with my love for you. Like my heart was open, bigger.'

Jade says, 'You asked me, reminded me really, in my closed-off state the other day that I had spoken about embracing Sarah as my sister, and I really for a moment did not know what you were talking about. Your question woke me up to it, and I was able to access her heart last night and I felt myself embracing her. I cried my eyes out for her. I can't imagine how painful it must be for her to fear she is losing you and knowing that she had created this. And it's not even her fault; her early life did this to her.'

Then Jade rests her hand on mine and says, 'I had a dream last night. You were sitting behind me and holding me and she was massaging my feet. You are both part of my healing.'

'Talking of dreams,' I say, 'at about four o'clock this morning she awoke in a state from a terrible dream, and I lay behind her and held her while she related it to the built-in cupboard towards which she was facing. I could not hear her words clearly as she was speaking softly and I did not want to interrupt what seemed like her need to speak it out and recognize it as a dream that spoke of her fears. It seems that, in her dream, you were in our lives, maybe living in our home, but I did not want her and there was competitiveness between the two of you. She felt that I was leaving her, and towards the end, maybe as a last-ditch effort to get me back, she decided to do away with you.' With every sentence, Jade gets more horrified and gasps silently to my last words and turns away and holds her head in her hands, and I immediately regret telling her but also know that this is exactly what our relationship demands—complete disclosure and to tell it like it is. She looks at me through her parted fingers still partially covering her face, her head at an angle and her mouth agape. But I cannot stop now, and say, 'She poured paraffin over you and burnt you. She said something about a person locked up in a room who could not help you, and I guess that might have been me. But even with you gone, she said I still did not want her.'

'This is raising all her worst fears, losing you, abandonment.' With this she covers her mouth and sits back in her chair to compose herself and remove herself not just from me but from what she has heard me say. Then, 'She must not try her magic on me because it won't work.'

Magic? Has Jade been weaving her magic on me? And I remember that some time ago Jade had said that there was a time when people like her and Sarah were burned at the stake. And she often refers to her supernatural experiences, as she calls them. Is this about burning witches at the stake? I feel a shiver down my spine. I need to move on to a more positive scenario, this future that I believe I have been trying to co-create, and say, 'So this morning on the phone I asked her where she is at, and she said something about knowing that I will need to experiment by which I think she meant explore by opening the door to someone or something else, which I have always kept firmly shut and locked because of my vows and my fears, my smallness, and she said that she accepts that this time has arrived for me. She said all this in a way that sounded accepting of it, that something has to play out for me.'

Jade says, 'I think she is saying that it is all about you, your growth, which of course it is, but I hope she recognises that she will learn and grow through whatever is happening here.'

'Months ago she told me that what happened between her and Calix was a Karmic connection, which she seemed to define as "there was work to be done". Personal work, life lessons, growth.' I am trying to access a previous conversation I had with Jade, but I understand these things no more now than I did then. 'She said that the experience somehow left her with the realization of her value, that being authentic raised things for the people around her that was useful to them, even if they did not want to hear it or felt that she was being rude or ugly. And maybe she sees this in the same way, or am I being too optimistic?'

'She seems to be accepting what I can only describe as "love" from you and the universe.'

'Maybe, but she seems a bit puzzled by it, as in expecting me to want to leave her when I don't love her, not the reverse. Despite her worst fears, I think she feels the love from me and from you too, thank you, and this is beautiful for me to see.'

'I am in awe of all of this,' Jade says, 'I can't find words to embellish further, perhaps they would just detract. All three of us are acknowledging and demonstrating love and I don't know how to say this without sounding patronising, but I feel so proud of you. I honour you for the work you have done and your choice for love in all of this. You are on the home straight.'

'Jade, do you believe in Pleiadians?'

She looks at me, blinking slowly. 'I don't know.'

'Are you one?'

Jade laughs. 'That would be telling.'

'What about Sarah? Is she?'

'Did she land in a spaceship?' I am not sure whether her lilting smile is ridiculing or a knowing one.

'Who knows? Sometimes I think she must have, as she's so . . . different.' Jade does not ask what I mean.

'Look, Jade, the stuff that I've been experiencing confuses me the minute I try to understand it. Like the way I seem to think and feel since I met you. Also, Sarah's apparent acceptance of us and what she has set up with Calix. And months ago a psychic clairvoyant told me Sarah's a Pleiadian. Whether it's true or not, I just think the principles are valuable.'

'This is simply what you're experiencing,' Jade says. 'It's your own. Make it yours.'

'They apparently come to teach us, to help us become more conscious and move towards a purer source of light or love. Or something like that.' I am certain Jade has had this effect on me. 'But perhaps all our perceptions of what they are like are warped; you know, as higher consciousness beings, always soft and kind and ego-free, resonating with love and acceptance and gentleness. I'm not so sure they appear that way to us, and maybe our perception centres just cannot "get" them and their ways. So I wonder if they present us with ways of dealing with our wounds, and to do this they sometimes appear scathing and hurtful rather than soothing and caring?'

Jade waits for me to say more, or perhaps she is processing what I have said. 'Anyway, the part that tickles me is that apparently they relate through unabashed sensuality and sexuality.'

Jade says, 'You're referring to "polyfidelity"—their acceptance of multiple simultaneous love relationships?'

'Something like a group marriage?'

'And they are free to move between loves. They don't have that sense of physical and emotional possessiveness. Love is in their hearts, limitless. It cannot be so without freedom to pursue their desires and their oneness with the love-light.'

We sit in comfortable silence for a while, and I let my cells soak in the pool of conversations we have had. Nothing jumps out at me. Nothing resonates, or maybe everything does.

Then I say, 'Coming back to Sarah, she said something that made me realise that she does not yet grasp how far it has gone with you, or perhaps she just does not want or need to go there, which raised for me the question of honesty and integrity. Because of who I am, I had wanted to know all about her other relationship, so I had asked her to tell me. When she didn't, I had asked more specific questions. Then I went to find out for myself what the truth was. I wanted to hear the answers, whatever they were. Initially I was prepared to welcome him into our lives, for their relationship to continue in some form, to find an outcome that was best and positive for all of us, but that was undone with her continued lies and vagueness.'

'But from what you're saying it's difficult to grasp exactly where she is at with this,' Jade says.

'Exactly. So only when she indicates she is ready to hear it, I can choose to tell her more and choose how much to reveal based on what is useful to all of us, but until then further details of us are of no use and will just torment her and distract her from the real issues.'

'What are the issues?'

'One, that there is stuff missing in our relationship and whether we can find in each other what we need there is uncertain, and two, that my door to love and healing has opened.' Jade accepts this without comment and I can't read what she is thinking. Perhaps she is still reeling from my recollection of Sarah's dream? So I say, 'I know that I have an almost pathological aversion to emotional pain, mine and others, and I often imagine that this is unresolved grief from other lifetimes as I have experienced little in the way of emotional anguish this time around. So I hugely value the opportunity I have had to experience her betrayal last year and I have had to transcend this these last nine months. And I have seen in the last few days my concern for the hurt the situation may cause for all of us, and so I desperately seek another way as I understand that surviving her affair just brought the relationship back to neutral territory and that this is no longer good enough for me. This is why my door has opened, but before now it would not have been with love, just ego. And only then could I see you in my orbit, and if I had denied myself seeing you, I would have remained trapped in who I was, smaller than I really am, and not able to love.'

'I feel nothing but love for her,' Jade says. 'She is brave, and I'm sure the question in her mind is "at the end of this will I still have my husband?" More than likely the answer is yes. You are a powerful couple and now you are both accessing something even greater and more powerful. I'm sure her cord cutting was to set you free of her oppression that comes from her fear, nothing more. I have been thinking of her a great deal, how gifted and powerful she was born, but also how she has become more fully that with you at her side. You have held that space for her, like a true stallion in his full power. I see too many marriages where women cannot become their most powerful selves because their partners are too threatened by their strength or too demanding of their energy. You have set a standard for me that I will never compromise on and if and when the time comes for me to choose differently, I will have had living experience of something I did not know existed.'

THE GOOD MAN

37

Love all, trust a few, do wrong to none.

(William Shakespeare)

Friday, 22 April 2011

When I came home yesterday and told Sarah we were invited at-the-last-minute to go to Samantha's deli for a ritual of purification and abundance and healing, meant for Samantha but actually for the benefit of all present, and after Sarah said, 'Why don't you go because it's a school night and we don't have a babysitter?' I decided to go. Partly, I think, because this would fit that picture of having other people in our lives, and I thought it was an opportunity to reinforce it. Thinking how brave she was being and whether I knew what the hell I was doing, I showered and said goodbye to the boys ('I will kiss you goodnight when I get home' followed by 'Okay, but don't wake us, Dad.') and shouldering my camera bag, I made my way to the deli with her parting words echoing in my mind, 'Just don't flirt with her.'

Earlier Jade had changed her mind. At first she had said it would be too difficult for all of us to have Sarah there, but later she recanted saying that the purpose of the ritual included so many things like forgiveness and acceptance that she was okay for us to be there. But for a brief moment when I walked into the deli, there was a look of concern on the faces of her and Samantha, and a peering over my shoulder to see who trailed in my wake, and the relief was palpable when they saw it was only me.

As I make my way to the deli today with my laptop and camera bag to share the photographs of last night's ritual with Jade and Samantha, these thoughts fill my mind seeking traction, some sort of conclusion I can draw upon to make a decision and retain my power of choice in this situation and be a master of my own destiny, and this anxiety rages on in violent contrast with my natural tendency to work with the fluidity of what evolves in the combined hearts of all involved.

'Thank you for being there last night,' Jade says, when I get to the deli. 'Your energy was beautiful, gentle, unobtrusive, so easily blended with the female, yet so male. I loved your awareness and observation. You were so there, so present, so tuned into the authentic and that which is true, and it was amazing to see how you connected with those who feel like family to me. Other than Samantha, Martine is the closest woman to "sister" I have, and Fee is right there too.'

'It was lovely, and I am glad I came,' I say. 'And thanks for letting me stay on the fringe and not feel obliged to participate in the way that you all did.'

With a wicked smile Jade says, 'I must tell you, Martine so blocked me. Towards the end of the evening, she came right up in my face and asked, "So have you kissed him yet?" I lied and she said, "Move your arse, girl, for god's sake, invite him over tonight and fuck him. How old are you for god's sake? You are not going to know if he is any good for you unless you fuck him. What if he is crap in bed?" And I said to her, "But he is married", and she then told me that Sarah was married when you met her, that your relationship with her began as an affair.'

'She said that?'

'Yes. Is it true?'

'Not to my knowledge,' I say. 'But I do sense that there is something else about her, something that has happened before or during my time with her, that I don't know about. Something that is material to me, but I don't have any idea what it is.'

'Martine really pushed the issue. Even after you left, she kept saying, "There is nothing wrong with anything, everything is right, there is no judgment. You are never going to know until you sleep with him. The guy looks at you with absolute love. Hurry up, Gino is only away till Sunday" she told me, knowing that he will watch me like a hawk. "Make sure it happens tomorrow". I found this so hilarious, I just had to share it with you.'

We are laughing now, both wanting each other and both knowing we wanted each other last night. I say, 'It seems to me that Martine was saying that there are not good or bad beliefs, only the beliefs you wish to experience and the beliefs you prefer not to experience. Anything you choose to be or do or believe in is okay.'

Jade understands that I am thinking about how we are trying to co-create a possible future here unshackled by 'how things should be or must be' and sometimes we feel that we are succeeding and sometimes not. 'And you can create an experience of yourself as the source or creator of your beliefs,' she says.

I say, 'Do we really have a natural ability to create or dis-create any reality at will? To restructure our lives according to the blueprint that we determine—like an Avatar?'

'I believe that I am busy doing that,' she says. 'I believe that what we believe in is less important than the fact that we believe it.'

This is too deep for me, a topic for another day perhaps.

38

Do not believe in anything simply because
it is spoken and rumored by many.

(Buddha)

Sunday, 1 May 2011

I have spent quite a bit of time with the boys lately as it has been school holidays, and in their infinite wisdom due to the plethora of public holidays scattered disruptively over a six week period, the education authorities had decided to stagger the holidays for different schools. Which means double the workload for parents and caregivers, as little Jack has just completed a three week break and now Jeremiah and Joshua's school is closed. The burden is no greater, I tell myself, than the long summer holiday I endured somewhat unprepared as a single parent and the period of her hospitalisation before that, but somehow with Sarah's presence, it now feels different—somewhat less satisfying for me. I have adjusted quickly to the amount of time I needed to devote to them, but I feel I would like to make myself available by choice and make other arrangements for them if I feel like it. I think it is the constant pressure from her of 'it's your time to take the boys, I deserve a break' and 'your time is your own, you have nothing to fill your day, so why can't you take them?'

So I sit here and reminisce about that time, the long summer holidays and my time with the boys without Sarah, wondering if it is me who is different or feels different, somehow overshadowed or overwhelmed in her presence, or is it just the puerile mix of our personalities that stir up this frothing, spluttering void that consumes us? After the initial few weeks of adjustment after her absence last year, and overwhelmed by daily panic attacks and a sickening anxiety that permeated my gut, things really took on a different flavour. Before the long summer school holidays came to an end, the boys and I had managed to have a few adventurous outings, which the boys took to as these were exciting escapades of exploration where only brave boys could venture, or so they thought, and I think it kept their minds off the absence of their mother which was still raised every so often but perhaps less frequently.

It made me realize how well children adapt to change, and I wonder whether this is how they managed my extended absence when I worked in the Middle East. We rode quad-bikes, little Jack helmeted and perched precariously between my thighs, the older boys full of pride on their own machines, something Sarah would have prevented with a long story about how dangerous it was and with her eyes flashing a message at me, 'Don't you dare take them.' And afterwards we argued over who had more mud on their clothing, and agreed to declare it a draw. Inspired by the exhilaration of speed this evoked in all of us, we had designed and built a go-kart which they proudly took turns racing down the slope of the tar service road above the house which then prompted a spin around a race track on motorized go-karts which they have not stopped bragging about and both Joshua and Jeremiah have chosen it as the venue-attraction for their next birthdays. We had even added an extension to the tree house and I wondered whether I would ever have done this if Sarah was around. But this fun time was not entirely without its casualties; little Jack cracking a bone in his wrist and adorning his face with yet another scar, this time on his cheek bone.

Just as I was running out of fresh ideas and energy towards the end of that school holiday period, the universe smiled at us and offered us a last minute invitation to go on a camping trip to Namibia with another family whose children were at school with the two older boys, and whose intended travel companions had to pull out at the last moment. Sitting here and waiting for Sarah to join me, I look over at the boys now, playing on the jungle gym at the restaurant, and remember how ecstatic they were at the news when I put it to them as this had been their oft rehearsed dream holiday adventure in the Jeep and I had always promised to fulfill this dream one day, probably as much for myself as for them. I had wanted to feel the heat and energy of the Namib Desert sands for myself as what lay glued to Jade's canvasses on the wall now seemed somewhat neutralised. So I did not hesitate for a moment, even though we had only three days to get ourselves prepared for the trip, and the enormity of this proved almost insurmountable even though we were helped by the existence of a pre-planned itinerary and accommodation reservations, the loan of a fully-equipped camping trailer and a list of required items, courtesy of our travel benefactors. And while we were away, I wondered often about her and I imagined that she would return to find us gone and was anxious that I was missing opportunities to discover her whereabouts or petrified that she was trying to contact us as she was in danger. More than once it had taken a monumental effort to not return home prematurely and sometimes it was only a promise I had made to myself to take my lead from the boys and how they were coping that prevented this.

On the upside, all three boys seem to have adjusted by now, in their own ways, to having their mother back, and the initial flurry of needing to know where she had been has receded. But I have noticed that they still show signs of anxiety when the four of us lads go somewhere without her, or when she goes out on her own. And they have developed a resistance to going to their grandparents house on Fridays, a routine we have retained even though not all of them are at school, and their anxiety is great when I pick them up in the evening and we make our way home and I have to phone Sarah many times during this short trip to calm their fears that she will not be home when we get there. With regret, I wonder whether 'Friday' will forever take on the same gloomy connotations as 'Sunday' still holds for Sarah.

So I expected the same reaction this afternoon at our sudden departure from the house, especially as we left under tense circumstances. I have taken them to a child-friendly restaurant, or maybe it is adult-friendly as there are activities in a secure environment that keep the children happily busy most of the time. By coincidence, it happens to be a Greek establishment, and I seem to get a perverse pleasure frequenting it and hearing Sarah inquire of patrons with Greek heritage what their name's day is and other cultural things that she seemed to become conscious of after meeting Calix. I had discovered this restaurant purely by chance just a few months ago, where I could sit outside under the trees, which meant I could smoke yet enjoy some shaded respite from the summer sun, and engage in some adult conversation usually with other parents while the boys did their thing supervised by a child-minder, who wasn't very good. The food is lovely and the cappuccinos just made the grade.

This early evening the place is packed, and I chat at times superficially with other parents and other times in depth with parents I have come to know and the restaurant owner and highly entertaining staff members and drink a cappuccino and from time to time play with the boys. It seems to be a preferred destination for single parents, often fathers now divorced or enduring the ugly period of separation that precedes dissolution of their in-tact family dream. I fell into neither bracket, yet, but must have come across as having similar characteristics as a single father, and I have been the recipient of many partly disclosed but clearly heartbreaking stories these past months, which I think I filed away in my mind in a 'recent-documents' folder called 'Next Project' under 'Risks: Probability and Impact'. As they often left in a flurry, I have always felt sad for them, father and child, especially when I noticed the Dad repeatedly, with growing anxiety and irritation, glance at his watch and heard him say, 'Come on, we have to leave now, I have to get you home to your mother'.

Sunset is ever earlier these days, but it is a glorious light that beams off the rocks near the summit of the surrounding mountains as the day fades and I am obliged to climb into my jacket due to the sudden chill, which I am not sure is only the result of the yawning sun now shielded by 'my' mountain to the west. For Sarah has arrived and now we sit together and don't have much to say to each other.

The boys rush over and whisper in my ear, 'Can we give it to her now?'

Earlier, on our way to the restaurant, the boys and I had stopped at the outdoor market and chosen a heart-shaped stone for Sarah, a beautiful mottled green 'Rainforest Jasper' on a leather thong, and using the dogs as an excuse, I retrieve the gift from the car and we present it to her. She seems underwhelmed by it all, and it occurs to me that she may be confused as it seems we are rewarding her for bad behavior, but the boys had been insistent. She accepts kisses and hugs from the boys but won't let me put the necklace around her neck, and hides it in her bag.

Perhaps she is still irked by the earlier visit from Roxanne, who is navigating one of her periodic downers, and it turns out that Sarah has spent the previous two hours on her own in a shop amongst rocks and crystals of all shapes and hues the energies of which supposedly heal or provide comfort or protection or guidance, to shake off the aggravation before joining us. Sitting beside her now, with the barely contained frustration still emanating from her pores, it occurs to me that she needed more time. Roxanne is much improved in general, if I can put it that way, which only means that Sarah has taken off her kid gloves and they are at it again without restraint and she does not seem to know when to take it easy with her half-sister. Earlier this afternoon, after I had passed one comment for them to 'cool it' in front of the boys which barely penetrated and there was less than a moment's pause in their bitter exchange, without further warning I hastily shepherded the boys out the front door and stuck my head back inside, 'Sarah and Roxanne,' I said, 'please get your act together.'

The boys make occasional visits to our table to check we are still here or to tell us something with excitement in their eyes or to tearfully complain about another child, usually older, who is teasing or terrorizing them or for us to hold them and tell them that the newly-acquired bruise or scrape, administered as a result of human error of judgment by one or other offensive mechanism on the jungle gym or tree house, will be just fine and a 'Mickey Mouse' plaster will cure all. Even with dinner now on the table as the sun sets, they pass by conveyer belt fashion for some water or enough food in their mouths to get them back to the swings or ladders or tree house.

Sarah's handbag bulges with her newly-purchased stones and crystals, and after a while with a—'Want to see what I got?' she shows me one-by-one the stones and accompanying descriptions of what they offer the wearer. I feign interest in each one, as I like the stones but cannot really relate to the supposed value of their vibrations, although I wear a snowflake obsidian around my neck every day. In all my travels the last few years, the single occasion I forgot it at home I was mugged. I remove each one she offers me from its bag, and read aloud its name which is sometimes difficult enough, and the attending summary of the promised gift emanating from its polished surface. The heart-shaped ones give rise to a thought which I beat into submission before it can articulate itself in my mind.

'I needed to replenish my stock,' she says, by way of explanation, 'as I have given so many away to clients who need them. That one I've been trying to find for ages,' pointing to an unpronounceable chunk which does not seem to my mind to be so special that it would be scarce. Fortunately she had managed to reclaim her consulting room, or at least to share it with another consultant on a part-time basis. All the time she is up and down from the table, giving the boys more attention than I think they need or desire. Part of her anxious energy, or her need to be needed, I think, but her inability to be attentive to our embryonic conversations which hang mid-air each time she goes and are displaced by another unfinished idea on her return, irks me because it does not permit any meat on the conversation bone, nothing substantial or meaningful to bind us; some way for us to find each other.

With the rocks tucked away again in her bag, I excuse myself to go to the bathroom. On my return, I have to sit down opposite her on the hard bench attached to our trestle table as alongside her now sits someone she has commandeered from the group of friends-clients sitting at the table alongside us, and she talks to him about life and how he is doing and she touches him, rubbing his back and stroking his shoulder and forearm and patting his thigh and laying her hand on his forehead as if checking for fever and caressing his chest as if his heart needs a massage to increase the blood-flow to the extremities. She does this so frequently while he sits next to her that I can't decide whether to be pissed off or amused by my observation. All the while her constant questions, as if she is in a diagnostic consultation, provoke further disclosure of his personal circumstances, and he never quite looks at ease. I see that she seems truly interested in his responses, fascinated as she figures out where he is at, and offering him unsolicited advice. It occurs to me that she should charge him a fee.

I sit and smoke, half-turned away from them to keep an eye on the boys but also to tune into my feelings, and absorb little of what is said. Calix cruises by, his lanky frame question-mark curved and hunched to accommodate the cramped dimensions of his vehicle, his chin almost resting on the steering wheel, his eyes searching, unblinking owl-orbs. Calix drives-by repeatedly, a queue of frustrated vehicles in his sloth-like wake, while Sarah and her muse talk nonstop for maybe thirty minutes. Not once is Sarah distracted by the boys nor is her attention diverted elsewhere. It is as if I am not even there, and I think neither of them would notice if I got up and left. It is what I seek out most; quality time together, occasional gestures of physical affection which may just be eye contact or proximity, and a sprinkling of heartening, gentle, thoughtful words. A safe togetherness. And as I wonder why our conversations are never this deep and personal and uninterrupted, I register that his wife, also a client of hers, has glanced our way a number of times, distracted from the conversation of her laughing-joking-bantering friends by the attention her husband is receiving.

A long afternoon of gradual intoxication has left them noisy and silly and, sitting there like a door-stop, my rising irritation is finally relieved when they say their goodbyes and haul Sarah's reluctant human entertainment away and they weave their way dizzily to their waiting vehicles. Although I am glad to see the backs of them, I wonder who the designated driver is and worry about the safety of the four pre-teen children they drag after them. With them gone, we sit here in silence again. And I think now is the time to ask her when we can have a serious conversation.

'Sarah, can we arrange some time together, just the two of us, to talk?'

'What for?' she says.

What for? I think. I know she meant it, rather than saying, What about? 'A lot of stuff has happened . . .'

'I'm not going back there,' she says, looking away. Her response reels in the incredibly frustrating, hurtful feelings of being summarily dismissed. She has blocked every attempt I have made to talk with her, just like she did last year, when her approach seemed to be, 'Fuck you, Clive, I'm doing this my way and if you don't like it that's too bad. I don't feel obliged to engage with you on things that are important to you'.

'No, I mean, it's not about the past, it's about the future. Or rather today. I want to be open and honest with you.' I want to be clear with her about Jade, Calix, everything. Why do I need to make explicit the open nature of our relationship?

'So that you can expect me to do the same.' It is a statement; she makes it sound like a judgment of me.

'That's for you to decide. I don't expect anything . . .'

'I am being honest,' she says, glaring at me, daring me to disagree.

I put my hand gently on her arm, and she pulls it away. 'I'm assuming that you are. It's not you I want to talk about, it's me.'

She bends forward at the hips, and says with aggression and accusation, 'It's always about you! What about me, what about my needs?'

'I only want to make time with you to talk,' I say, but she has moved off and finds someone she knows to talk to, and they are joined by another who has entered through the gate of the restaurant courtyard. This is hopeless; surely that was not an unreasonable request, or impolitely demanded? Bad timing on my part, perhaps, but it is feeling increasingly urgent for me now to risk naming the truth and force us to be explicit about our loves. Her reactions to me are so unpredictable that I wonder whether she is still taking her medication. Is it fear? Or guilt? For the first week after her reappearance, it was not like this, and hope had risen in me, but now a sickening feeling of déjà vu nauseates my gut. I feel like this is a turning point; a point of no return.

Calix seems to have gone, but his reconnaissance alerts me to Gino, and now I am looking out for both of them. A little later Sarah is sitting opposite me again, and I wish we could find something light and cheery to talk and laugh about, or something deep and meaningful that brings us together or, better still, to just be quietly and blissfully in each other's space. In the end we choose neither; she asks to see the photographs of the dance ritual. Regretting that she has noticed my camera bag, we start at the beginning; the first picture has Jade centre-frame. This serves to inflame all her insecurities and anguish voiced as, 'Of course, you had to take pictures of her' and later, 'There are so many pictures of her' (the first true, the second not). The camera flash has this annoying habit of making revealing clothing appear even more revealing, and Jade was wearing a shimmering long see-through dress and her black underwear is clearly visible, which provokes the remarks, 'What on earth is she wearing?' and, 'I now know the kind of woman you are attracted to, so unlike me,' and 'I just can't understand what you see in her?' I look around, sighing out my frustration and pretending to check on the boys who have adorned themselves in fancy-dress courtesy of the restaurant's playroom and seem to be enacting a hybrid Darth Vader-Luke Skywalker scene I don't recognize. And then I see Calix, sitting in his car just other side the palisade fencing. This is insane, but it seems too obvious to point it out to her. Suddenly I want to tell her everything about Jade, to be explicit and blunt and just lay it out there and take what comes, but I know she is not ready to hear it yet, and perhaps I am not ready to tell it. So I think of telling her some half-truth about how meeting Jade was coincidental (yet we both know there is no such thing) and that I need her now in my life and that there is work to be done between us but we are just close friends, and realize that doing so would perpetuate the lie and embed it. I have as good as told her what's going on and she has as good as said, I have just not been explicit about it, and nor has she.

And so we jostle in conversation as I flick through the photographs and I find myself trying to deflect away from the attention Jade is getting and on to the event itself, but she is not really interested in hearing about it and then she says, 'These are my insecurities, but you are not being honest with yourself.'

I think, 'No, I am not being honest with *you*.' I want to blame her for not letting me.

And as I remember Sarah's words to me, 'I abused your trust', I think that is probably what I am now doing to her. And my integrity seems to rise, ghost-like, from my body and float towards the balustrade demarcating the restaurant's perimeter, and impales itself on its spiked palisades. As I watch its demise in horror, I feel non-human, like there is nothing else to me. But I don't know how to retrieve it, so I resort to raising how we saw Calix yesterday sitting in his parked car in an obscure place bizarrely gesturing with his arms outstretched and protruding from the windows as we drove past, just as he looms like a crucifix from the pinnacle of our mountain every morning. It was the first time I have seen him this year, or chosen to notice him, and with a jolt I had said, 'That's so weird' and I now say, 'What's the significance of that place?' and she says, 'Nothing, nothing at all.' And we look at each other as we realize I have just equated or elevated my relationship with Jade to that of her relationship with Calix, and she makes this point.

I am unreasonably angry with her and mostly angry with myself for breaking my secret pact to not bring him into conversations any more, for any reason. For if I were to do so, I know that at best it will leave me frustrated and doubting the honesty of her responses, and at worst, like now, it digs a deep hole deeper for me. And now she is upset too, either from seeing the photographs or the mention of Calix, and does not talk to me until we get home except to make caustic remarks through clenched teeth.

At home I sit outside in the courtyard when everyone is asleep and have a cigarette and remember that Sarah had a dream the night I went to photograph the ritual-dance, a dream about me being there, which she told me about on waking the next morning. It was vivid and real, she said, but she did not tell me the content. Instead she said that Jade needs a mirror to reflect herself, and that this is what I am doing for her. And I think of how right she may be, as Jade has said as much to me, that I provide a mirror for her. And Sarah told me to be careful as I am looking outside of myself instead of within; that I am vulnerable right now and needy of emotional connection, affection, and sensuality and these things, she believes, Jade gives to me.

To which I had said, 'Yes, I need these things.'

Then Sarah said this is scary for her as she does not feel she provides these things for me and that she fears she never will. And then, 'You are asking a lot of questions of yourself right now. You are busy climbing mountains, figuring out who you are and what you want.'

I thought how strong and loving and understanding she was being. 'Stay with me as I climb those mountains,' I said.

At the time I had felt like this was a constructive conversation.

39

```
The art of love . . .
is the art of persistence
```

(Albert Ellis)

Monday, 2 May 2011

'For fuck sakes, Clive, you need a strategy. Or a plan, or something.'

Jim is getting really worked up and has not yet taken a sip of his prized Dunkel Hefe Weiss beer that sits temptingly within his reach. He looks genuinely worried, as if the world is about to implode and he will get sucked into a black hole. I think he feels but won't acknowledge his own desperation, yet deep down he knows he is talking to himself. I am fascinated that he has suffered with ongoing tummy troubles for weeks now. For months he has been saying that he is giving up on the prospect that his future will ever include 'herself'. I told him that he was making love-life decisions with his head but his heart was not in it, and the dissonance was revealing itself physically. He baulked at this yet something in what I said got traction and worried him. But when I mentioned chakras and the solar plexus to him, and that he should consider bringing the colour yellow into his life, he asked if I could soon do something so frightfully appalling that the influence of Sarah in my life would forever be obliterated.

'Maybe I have a strategy,' I say, hoping to sound mysterious.

'Well, if that's the case, you are hiding it well. Or else it's a lousy strategy.'

When I look away, he says, 'Well, what is it?'

I smile and say, 'To sit here and drink a beer with you and flirt with all these lovely women and be happy.' To emphasize my point, I look around and wave my hands at the end-of-weekend crowd at the hotel bar, the same one at which Sarah and I had dinner that Friday evening. The average intoxication levels are high, and the music and rowdy banter makes it difficult to hear each other. It is a beautiful evening, though cooling fast and I am grateful for the clean shirt and sweater I always leave handy in the car. We played beach bats until the sun had long gone and we were both exhausted, but I am glad to notice that with some liquid replenishment I already feel like I am recovering. Most critically, my knees are not aching. And the unexpected bonus was that Sarah seemed nonplussed when I called her to say I would like to go for a quick beer with Jim, and would she mind if I was late for dinner? Which is not always a good omen.

Jim is clearly irritable, probably because I showed no mercy and managed to hit him in the family jewels with the ball in what turned out to be the penultimate rally, and I could not restrain my hilarity after his body appeared to levitate on contact before he lay crumpled and writhing on the white sands. But it was Gino's arrival that caused us to call it a day. We carved a hasty retreat but now I am alert to the possibility that he is watching me. Frustrated by my responses, Jim actually grabs his personal belongings on the table as if he is about to leave, but then seems to change his mind.

'Okay,' I say, relenting, but just a little. 'It's an emerging strategy.' When he says nothing, wondering how far I can push him I add, 'I'm busy scanning my environment, scrutinizing my possible futures.' He looks at me as if I should urgently see a head doctor and finally succumbs to his beer.

'It's so sad,' Jim says, his nose buried in the glass. 'You were in such a powerful position last year. Well, not you personally, you were a wreck, but you had everything going for you in terms of having the upper hand and I kept telling you that you should have taken action then, from a position of strength.'

'If I had acted then and in that way, then nothing would be the way it is today.'

'Exactly.'

'But where I am today is precisely where I need to be,' I say with more self-assurance than I necessarily feel. 'Look at what I've learnt.'

A year ago I had desperately wanted to keep my life intact—the life I had known and the life I imagined my future would be. But now I feel drawn to solitude, yet so fearful of it. I am certain it is being called up for this next period of this lifetime, a period of time I have chosen to 'work on the self'. This future is revealing itself to me.

There is still a part of me that wishes I had been clear enough, last year, about what I wanted to do and brave enough to take the big step, the ache of which would torture me beyond measure at any time, bolstered by the overwhelming anger and pain of betrayal I felt at the time to carry me through it. By now I would have settled into a rhythm of sorts with my allotted access to the boys and understood whether Sarah the-now-ex-wife would approach our separation as friend or foe and already have a sense of whether it was the right decision to have made. Except for the likelihood that I would forever have been locked into her madness, her manipulations and threats, and the most brutal threat of all, to take the lives of our boys, might have succeeded. I light a cigarette. My mind is in overtime, reminiscing with regret, it seems to me, or is it that I am finally starting to internalize what we spoke about all those months ago.

While Jim natters on, saying something about, 'You may have learnt, though I'm doubtful of that, but are you any better off?' a memory breaks the surface of one of our jacuzzi-therapy heart-to-heart's last year. In his uniquely inimical way, Jim thought he was providing moral support and a framework for me to distinguish the wood from the trees while the fractals of my ego pierced my bleeding heart. Jim was trying to convince me that I needed to look at things with new eyes and we were, as usual, agreeing to disagree. Overheated, in more ways than one and dehydrating rapidly with a couple of beers already tucked away, the conversation had moved from the sublime to the ridiculous.

'Like strange attractors,' Jim said.

'Like what?' I said, my beer going down the wrong way and bringing on a froth-filled fit of coughing.

'The organizing principles of a complex system or the phase space of an entity,' he said, looking mischievous and talking into his beer. 'A human being.'

'I have no idea what you're talking about,' I said, and needing a break from his desire to lock me into a structured way to approach my situation, I perched my beer glass precariously on the lip of the jaccuzi so that I could shift position and hook my arms over the rim from where I could survey the night lights in the village below us, coming into their own as the sky darkened. The evening star was visible and the last strands of pink discolouration faded as I watched. Jim's house was across the valley from mine, with a panoramic vista, and he enjoyed a view of the setting sun. I rested my chin on my forearms so that I would not be tempted to look up towards my house and picture Sarah and the boys there, or wonder about Calix and whether he was with her.

'Never mind,' he said, trying to sound hurt. I wished he would let up for a while. 'All I'm saying is that all your behaviour is predictable and will remain within the confines of your perception of your environment or your situation.'

'Fuck you, Jimbo. Be helpful for a change.'

He drifted over to me, carrying his beer like an hour-old newborn. I told him to move over and stop cramping me. 'Look, we sit here every night and drink copious volumes of the best German beer and hypothesize and intellectualise about your situation,' he said, 'but despite all this effort and delirious inebriation, your actions will remain within the realm of your current beliefs and values.'

'Okay. So our principles, or our values and beliefs, organize how we think and act. They also impose limitations on how we think and act, on what we see and hear,' I said, in the dwindling hope that agreement will get him to move off the topic.

'Yes, but in a crisis like yours you are hovering at the edge of chaos, when the situation in which you find yourself is uncertain and unique, like you're encountering it for the first time and there are no automatic or obvious answers on how to respond to it.' Realising he had lost my attention, he then said, 'You are dissipating,' but I did not take the bait. My body and mind were overheating and I hoisted myself wearily and deposited my bum on the timber deck encircling the jaccuzi while my feet dangled in the water and steam wafted from my torso in the icy breeze. I missed the boys and the dogs, and wondered if I could get to see them all tomorrow morning. 'Falling apart,' he said, offering an unasked-for definition in words of less than three syllables. 'You are gripped by fear and uncertainty. When you are overwhelmed like this you can crumble with terror and remain immobilized like you are. Or you can change your beliefs and your outlook on life. Rebuild yourself,' he said, turning to look at me. He was challenging me.

I said, 'You mean take a positive view of the situation?'

'You always have to do this, even if you "fake-it-till-you-make-it" because the positive outcome lies a little way into the future, otherwise you may not survive the problem you face. You will get depressed and feel hopeless and powerless, like your sister-in-law and your brother-in-law, come to think of it. Or seek refuge in sex or alcohol or drugs or other addictions, which I think they are also doing. Or my personal favourite, you go mad, psychotic. That may be next on their lists.'

And on mine, I thought. I said, 'So it's as easy as practicing some positive visualization?'

'No. It's not just about taking a positive view. You have to be realistic. What you have to do is transcend your old self-imposed boundaries and limitations. Break the rules; think out of the box. Find your own truth and do what is right for you.'

'I have to change?' The core temperature of my body was finally cooling, but my mind felt like an over-heating nuclear reactor in shut down, red bubble-lights flashing a warning all over the console and that deafening repetitive siren blaring in my head and I could not make it stop. I squeezed my temples with my fists to try release some of the pressure.

'More than that,' he said. 'Change is about doing something differently, reforming your behaviour, but within the scope of what you already know or do, so that you remain stuck within your self-imposed limits of growth. But in your crisis, you have to be motivated to *transform*, guided by your personal purpose or meaning, which I think you still need to establish, by the way.'

'You're saying that I don't yet know who I am?'

'If you do, you haven't made it known to others, especially not to Sara-lea. You should re-look your morals and ethics which govern how you act or react.' He paused, but my relief was short-lived. 'You have to redefine yourself or your situation so that previously unimaginable solutions are now visible to you, and possible to make happen. If you do this, you will surprise yourself with your ingenuity.'

'Okay. Surprise me.'

'No, I'll educate you. Bifurcation,' he said, smiling widely and just avoiding the kick I aimed at his beer glass. He glided to the other side of the jaccuzi as I slipped into the water again.

'Stop taking the piss,' I said.

Still unable to wipe the smile from his face, he said, 'You are at a crossroads, right? Between transformation and death, at least of your marriage or life as you know it and imagined it would be forever. As a system, you are far-from-equilibrium.'

'I'm not a fucking machine. I'm a human being with feelings.'

'I'd get a second opinion on that if I was you.'

'We're talking about a human relationship, Jim. I don't operate according to a formula or a programme. I can't push a button to log off and stop feeling what I'm feeling.'

'Apparently so,' he said. 'But let's assume you're human, for sake of argument, a human system. You still operate by a set of rules, and your behaviour is predictable, within certain limits. Just like an open system.' I reached for a cigarette, and he accommodated this by pushing an ashtray, considerately left by his wife no doubt, towards me, and said, 'Don't let any ash fall into the water. You're a CAS.'

'Don't be uncouth.'

'No, you're a "complex adaptive system", a CAS. Look, I thought this would appeal to you, you being into the interconnectedness of all things and that things are simultaneously cause and effect and all that stuff.' No argument there—are you married because you love your wife or do you love your wife because you are married? 'So where was I?' he said to the night sky, as if the stars now becoming visible would prompt him.

'In the jacuzzi,' I said.

'Oh yes, you're complex and adaptive,' he said, ignoring me and I was convinced he would continue to spout forth even if I went up to the vacant apartment he was generously allowing me to use while my life fell apart. 'At least, you're the former and we're working on the latter, with dwindling enthusiasm and hope, I might add. So right now your relationship is at maximum instability and you face a future that is wide open. This is your bifurcation point, and everything that you thought was true and certain, is no longer so. So all I'm saying is that you are free to seek out your own optimal solution to this situation. You are in a unique space of maximum adaptability and creativity, and you can discover within yourself new adaptive skills if you get creative and free yourself up from your personal constraints that make you feel a victim to circumstance.'

Thinking that once he has had a few beers, Jim starts to enjoy his own creative thoughts a little too much, I said, 'Are you saying that my values from the past, the way I have approached my life until now, may now be constraints? That they are no longer useful, as they are limiting the way I see my situation?'

'They may be, if they are not taking into account your current context and cause you to respond in old ways. You are obsessed with trying to work out this problem from within your current paradigm and decide on an outcome where you want to end up. But before you can do this, you have to solve the problem of the problem.'

'Are you stuttering, Jim? Or is the CD in your brain scratched?' Why is it always 'problems' and 'solutions' with him?

'You have to first understand who you really are,' Jim said. 'That's the riddle that this problem has presented to you, and the gift that this problem offers you.'

'You're sounding more and more like that psychologist, our marital counsellor, who said I seek out and stay in bad relationships with narcissists because I'm masochistic, and it would take me years to understand myself before . . .'

'You don't need a psychoanalyst,' he said, interrupting me. 'You have me. And great beer and a stunning view, all for free.' Sitting here listening to you, I thought, comes with a cost; it is not for free. You teach best what you most need to learn, Jim, but I did not say it because it was not an original thought and it would only send him down another argumentative track. I swallowed the remaining half of my beer, knowing that it was actually water I needed. And inspiration. Not to be undone, Jim finished his beer and hollered to his wife who brought us each another so quickly it seemed like she was waiting for his call. I wondered how he got that to happen. He once told me that if he is happy, then she is. When she disappeared back inside, he said, 'Look, you have reflected a lot over your marriage, and no doubt in this process you have surfaced some of your unconscious beliefs and assumptions. The crucial thing now is to be open to new ideas. You need to decide what is most important to you now; the principles and values that you need going forward in your relationship. To establish order in your mind out of the chaos you currently feel.'

'I already know them. Honesty and respect are non-negotiable.'

'Not so fast.'

'Okay. Being fair and reasonable comes to mind, and a basic level of honesty or openness. Let's call it the willingness to share and be transparent.'

'No, not all the ones you believe you already have, as I'm sure this intractable dilemma you think you are in has raised what is critically important to you. Not what *should* be, that's your old way of thinking. They should reflect who you really are. And not a long list.'

'I could settle with being respectful of the other person's dignity. And honouring them for the choices they make, or honouring your relationship.'

He dismissed me with his free hand. 'I don't need to hear them. These will allow you to transform who you are while providing for you the comfort of order, of stability. You would probably use the term "centered",' he said, in deference to the different language we used and the look on my face.

'I think all of this is crap, Jim. In my mind's eye I have a long list of reasons why I should end my marriage down the left-hand column of the page, and on the right-hand side, the reasons I should stay, I have just two lines, "She's crazy, but I love her", and "the boys". It's that simple.' I did not say that I am petrified of how Sarah would likely react and the harm she might cause; that at best she would make my post-divorce life a nightmare, and at worst I would forever fear for the boys' lives; actually, that I simply don't have the guts. Jim suspects it, but if I clearly stated it, he would tear it apart with the logic of one who was not talking about themselves and their loved ones and with little comprehension of the daily rigor of the psychotic regime in which I flounder.

'It's understandable that right now your level of anxiety feels unmanageable, but it just clouds your judgment, and you cannot respond effectively like that.'

'You're patronizing me.'

'No, listen.' Jim said. 'I'm sure your emotions are all over the place, up one day, and down the next. You love her, then you hate her. You can accept what happened, then you can't. And so your behaviour, your responses to her, are inconsistent; mixed messages, which confuse her and you. These principles, what I loosely called strange attractors, will help to limit your range of behaviours and attitudes, and then you need to embody them in all that you do.' Pinching his nose, he dipped his head under the water, and for a moment I thought of holding him there, but that would be misdirected anger, unfair even for Jim. Leaving his ears submerged, he said far too loudly, 'Oh, and focus on things that govern interpersonal interactions,' and vanished again.

'I can see you have had tremendous success with this approach,' I said, also too loudly, but it caused him to resurface as he was no doubt aware that he could not risk someone overhearing this part of the conversation. With all his attempts to strategise his way through his current love affair, it always seemed that his analysis pointed him in one direction but then he repeatedly undid himself and his own carefully formulated plan by acting some other way. When I had challenged him on this his best defence was 'it's love, I cannot control the feelings'.

'Point taken,' Jim said, wiping water and sweat from his face. 'But you need to understand the most critical part of this. Both you and Sara-lea have wanted the other to change, and you live in hope of some elusive miracle which is supported by no evidence whatsoever. But don't think of what you can *do* to change her, or yourself; think of who you should *be* to transform. In fact, think of who you really are.'

The words he chose to use grabbed my attention. 'Did you just say "be"? As in "being" rather than "doing"?' Has Jim inadvertently converted to my way of thinking, or is discovering who I am part of his paradigm of 'ready'?

Jim ignored me. 'At the moment you are abdicating, and so there is a power vacuum, because you are just fighting the infidelity with your ego. Let go of what happened and look towards the future. Then she can see who you are and what you need to come from this situation.'

'It all sounds so simple,' I said, getting out of the jaccuzi and wrapping a towel around my hips. My head was spinning, from the beers, the heat, and his unsolicited wisdom.

'Then you can learn from your future,' he said.

'You mean my past?'

'No, your future. You will be fallible, and when it gets too scary, you will desire to return to a stable state, to how things were, and just walk back into your marriage even though it's bad and nothing has changed. So once you know how you need to be and what you need to do, you can check if your actions are taking you towards your goal. Hence, learning from your future. This,' he said, wagging a finger in emphasis, 'is how you learn to think differently, so long as you have your non-negotiable principles in mind.'

'What I've got in mind is a headache. And I'm tired of you. So I'm going to bed,' I said, wondering whether I was stretching too far my reliance on the fact that our friendship had always withstood not just the occasional difference of opinion but also direct insult. But I needed a parting shot. 'I've got one for you, Doctor Freud.'

'Fire away,' he said, feigning boredom. 'Or do you need to "aim" first?'

'Equifinality.'

'Inform me,' he said, but I let him linger for a while as I dried off.

'There are many routes to the same outcome.'

'So how do you know which one to choose?'

'Choose the one that fits,' I said.

'Whatever parts your hair,' Jim said, and took a deep breath and dipped his head under the water and his body melted and distorted in refraction, ensuring that he had the final word.

'Hellloooo,' Jim says in exaggerated fashion, waving his hands in front of my face. 'Earth to Clive, anyone out there.'

'What?' I say, as the image of Jim floating beneath the surface is erased from my mind.

'Are you even listening to me?'

'Unfortunately.' I wish he would submerge himself again, like last year, but this time perhaps in his beer.

'Well?' he said.

'Well what?'

'I asked you whether you have stroked the sphinx recently.' His curiosity about my love life with Jade knows no bounds. It would be so gratifying to tell him that I visited the neighbour, bravely venturing without anaesthetic-coated condoms, and that I felt every bit of it, or that I stood tall in joyous abandon in the torrential downpour without a raincoat, or that the bald sphinx is truly . . . but this is sacred and forever just between a princess and her cobbler.

'That's more information than even your wife needs to know,' I say.

'Okay. Can you at least tell me how your friendship is going with Iron Mike Gino?' he says.

'Slinky? He's still scuttling around, glaring, hounding me and playing games with Jade. It's not bothering me hugely, maybe I'm just getting used to it and will miss him when he stops one day.'

'What games?'

'He's just infantile, telling their mutual friends bad things about her, and throwing stuff over the wall that divides their properties, and immediately leaving a party when she arrives, that sort of thing. What would worry me the most is if he and Sarah have made contact. As a team, they could be a force to be reckoned with and get up to mischief.'

'He's going to blow soon,' Jim says, predicting some forthcoming entertainment to report to his wife.

It feels like it is time to go, and I am only looking forward to this as I may be just in time to put the boys to bed, and I am grateful that, while my lateness has perhaps given Sarah a target at which to direct her irritation, the bedtime routine will provide a buffer between her and me and the tension that envelops us. 'Look,' I say, getting up to go, 'I've been thinking about one of our conversations long ago in your jacuzzi, the one about strange attractions and falling over . . .'

'Strange *attractors*,' he says with exaggerated articulation. 'It's not a forthcoming movie.'

'Exactly. Those things and falling down and transforming how I see things and reinventing myself and all those good things, and I think that in the last six months, I have moved closer to being who I truly am than ever before.'

'Good student,' Jim says. 'So you were listening to me after all.'

'Except that it has not happened in the way you seemed to describe it. It was not a conscious, deliberate process that I had any control over. And try as I might to recalibrate, to progressively refine my thoughts and attitudes and behaviours, I'm not sure even now that I can generate a list of my core values, new or otherwise. Things just happened.'

'Like what?'

'Well, Sarah left, Jade came into my orbit, then Sarah returned. Even Gino and Calix have played a role. And you, regrettably.' Jim takes a long look at a beauty coming towards us with 'regret' dripping off his lolling tongue. 'And I think I am done with "why", you know, being fixated with that question. I think I'm learning it's more about "who", as in "who am I, really?" My boys seem to look at me every day with that question written all over their faces.'

'As you transformed yourself, you became open to new creative possibilities,' Jim says, his neck straining at an acute angle as this deity walks past, and I take in the scent of her, all pheromones undisguised with perfumed fragrances. 'So you really should acknowledge that you have had an impact on the outcome you observe today. Even if you want to convince yourself that you have simply been observing it, you have actually influenced it. No matter how carefully he tries to nullify the impact of his presence or the act of observation, an experimenter cannot discount the effect he has on what he is witnessing.'

'This is not a fucking experiment,' I say.

'Everything is. It's how we learn and grow.'

'Then what I'm talking about is the effect of the experiment on me, the experimenter. When you conduct an experiment, you should not study the subject while you manipulate and monitor the dependent and independent variables and all that crap, but observe the bastard who thinks he is immune to his manipulations. That would be much more informative. Do you think that if you're extracting someone's fingernails, you can go home that night without the echo of their screams reverberating in your head and seeping into your dreams? Everything's connected, Jim. It's called co-determinacy. I'll write it down for you. It's time you disinvest yourself of the belief you can act alone, immune, and sterilised. You don't have control over your future, but you do co-create it.'

Harry and Sally have had enough of hanging around and are no doubt hungry. I swallow the remains of my beer and pocket my car keys and cellphone. 'Jim, my friend, all I know is that I have a view of my way forward, and I'm sticking with it. And I'm going to be open to all possible futures and learn from them until I'm confident I have nothing further to discover from them, and then I will choose a different future. The plan, if you need to hear one, is to bring others along with me, to offer it to them, if they want to come, but that's up to them.

I have discarded many of my old ways of seeing things, especially my expectations, at least intellectually. It's just my ego that still gets in the way, so it's not entirely authentic, I guess. And perhaps this is why Sarah in particular cannot see that she has nothing to fear by being real with me.'

40

At the touch of love everyone becomes a poet.

(Plato)

Tuesday, 3 May 2011

I say to Jade soon as she sits down, 'I came across a quote towards the end of last year, when I was trying to understand how to deal with our tenth wedding anniversary and was thinking about love and betrayal and pain and doubt. It was from Mother Teresa and went, "I have found the paradox that if I love until it hurts, then there is no hurt, but only more love". You started that idea of "the good man" and it helped me recognise that so many people are saying that. I even remembered that people have said it before, I just did not take it in. It has an arrogant aftertaste to it which I could not accept. But I don't think they meant "perfect" or "wonderful", and it's only when I am with you that I have a notion of what it might mean to me. It's something about acknowledging and accepting each other, being okay with both myself and you. Assuming a perspective of "I'm okay, you're okay". I think the way you say it, is when you think I come from love, not ego. You helped me to see it in myself and believe it, to believe in myself.'

'Yes, it's how I see you, and it's in stark comparison to Gino.'

'Slinky?'

'Stop that,' she says.

'Okay,' I say. 'Isn't it just the way you choose to see us both?' She is silent and digs her hands into her pockets. 'Anyhow, the biggest part

433

of my pain this past year was around honesty or dishonesty, which we have talked about lots, and so although nerve-wrecking, I am glad I have started this process with Sarah. Anyhow, you are a real Princess,' I say, 'but I have the wand,' and she gives me a lazy-eye smile.

Then I tell Jade about the weekend with Sarah, her response to seeing the photographs and the argument that followed, Sarah's dream and apparent awareness of what connects me to Jade that she feels she cannot compete with.

'This goes a long way to dealing with some obstacles in my mind,' Jade says. 'My main question when I woke up this morning was, at the place you are with Sarah now, easier, softer, more loving—is there still space for me, or do I feel you backing away gently?' I am surprised that Jade has this favourable view of what it's like at home.

I say, 'It may come as a surprise to you, but none of that stuff seems to have dramatically changed over these past few weeks. There is not any intimacy to speak of, except that one time, and I do not sense a real change in our closeness and affection, even though I know my love became fuller and I could express it and she had seemed to respond to this quite positively which excited both you and me as it started to feel that anything and everything was possible.'

'Where do I fit in now that she is back and it is better there? You have, sketchily, answered some of those questions.'

'I have become more outspoken or assertive, and she reacts very defensively to this. Much of the old dismissive and critical behaviour is coming to the fore again. And there is always that premonition of imminent aggression and violence, of manipulation and abuse of her power, power that she undoubtedly has but should be used with love rather than coming at me barbed with her wounds and brokenness. And our lack of physical intimacy came up the other evening and she said she would only want to share herself with me in that way when my love is more consistent, but she has said that for years. It always seems to be about me, not her, and I can't remember a time when I was more consistent than these past few weeks.'

Our conversation is disrupted because Jade is late for an appointment. Later I text her saying that I miss her and the joy that she gives me when she is in my orbit, and she writes back immediately saying, 'I was just reading from a book called "Dear Lover" . . . *when a woman remembers her Glory, a man of Goodwill can barely contain his joy . . . his Real Self arises in the presence of her own*" . . . so it's astounding that you should use the word "joy". And do you remember when you asked me my instant gut feeling about you, I said it was that you are good.'

This thing about "the good man", those exact words, have been repeated by Jade often in these weeks. It started months ago, when Azura said these words of me, but I did not absorb them. And I remember now an interesting interlude that evening when Sarah and I went out together, the evening before we made love. She had started a conversation with someone she recognized. They were sitting directly behind me, and I had to half-turn in my seat and twist my neck to acknowledge them. I took in his companion who sat back in his chair who quietly listened in and drank his beer, as if the conversation being had was too deep for him. I had the sense he was not from hereabouts, probably a foreigner or a traveller; his lanky hair seemed in need of a wash and cut, his jeans were soiled. He had that air of the occasionally employed, someone who worked with his hands, perhaps a mechanic or a builder by trade, definitely not intellectual or self-aware or emotionally intelligent. I think he must have said something, which drew Sarah's attention, and she started to tell the 'traveller' what she saw in him, from his eyes and the lines on his face and his hands and his ear lobes and his astrological sign and numerological numbers. I was waiting for him to tire of it or voice his dismissal of her prognostications as claptrap, when out of the blue he offered to read her palm. He took her hand in his and I wondered how she would react as I thought he was going to ridicule her. But it seemed genuine enough and I realized I had erroneously prejudged him.

He said, 'You have had a difficult and complex life, but you have a strong character, a tremendous spirit which you draw on to overcome life's challenges. Your magic truly inspires people, you reveal hidden forces and secrets to those who heed you, and you exert an influence on your surroundings far beyond your stature.' This was her kind of language, and at first she seemed to get a real kick out of this experience. She was watching his eyes, observing how he was working as much as absorbing what he was saying. 'You have great faith in the humanness in people, that nobody is inherently bad, and you are interested, no, fascinated by people, by how they think and feel, from the basest emotions to the purest of highly evolved individuals.'

He paused, and murmured to himself before continuing with his insights. I got bored quickly and paid half-hearted attention to their interaction and drank my beer while I tried to access what I was feeling about being here with her. When I tuned in again he was saying, 'You are a good judge of other people, but you are too judgmental at times, condemning others too readily. You demand approval and allegiance of those close to you because you lack self-assurance. You are convinced of your own rightness, you have a strong temper and are very confrontational and don't easily back down which is sometimes a problem as it may amount to . . . to a kind of mania. And you struggle with guilt. You want to repent but you cannot forgive yourself.' His monotone voice revealed no hint of value judgment and not once did he look up at her, and I was waiting for a dismissive 'you're a crank!' yet she remained impassive. 'You are searching for what is real and meaningful, not false or illusionary. You struggle with your authenticity. Your greatest challenge is to find and follow your spiritual path, from which you have often strayed.'

Then, fixing his eyes on her open hand, he said, 'You are a player,' and she said, 'No way,' her only verbal reaction to his reading, and withdrew her hand. And it is only now, as I recall this, that I understand how her feelings of guilt extend way beyond her infidelity and stretch back further than any shame she feels in her childhood deprivation or complicity in the sexual abuse. It is embedded in her cellular memory, compounding lifetimes of atrocities. And this is why not even she can truly understand it.

Later that evening I had later asked her why she said this, and she said she did not like the connotation. His dogmatic assertion left me feeling uneasy, as a few friends had made comments along this vein. One person recently said that when Sarah interacted casually with people, she did not know it left them feeling that she was 'looking for sex', which I took to mean needing some acknowledgement of herself as attractive and desirable, or perhaps to tap into her sensual being and for her to feel 'I'm okay'. And I had begun to see Sarah in this light since the affair or at least doubt the purity of some of her interactions.

Anyway, then Sarah had asked him to read my palm, and after venturing a few inconsequential insights that were close to the mark but could also have held for half the patrons at the restaurant, he said of me in various ways in his accented, broken English—this is 'a good man'. And then he looked at her and said, 'I see this in your face, not your hands. You are anxious, hiding, protecting yourself.' His arms swept left to right and back again, smudging a rainbow. 'You are over here then over there. And you are losing this man because of this. You . . . you . . .' and as he struggled to locate the words he took hold of my leather jacket with both hands and kneaded and pulled it with his finger tips, clinging, yanking, tugging, and controlling my arm, ' . . . do like this, and he . . .' and he looked at me and walked his fingers across the table-top away from her. And with that he had left, and he had left her thinking hard. It clearly had an effect on her and she held on to me and sat next to me and kept asking why she was so fucked up and saying that her behaviour was pushing me away as if this occurred to her for the first time, even though both of us had often raised this before and I had told her this in so many ways recently, sometimes directly in conversation and at other times more subtly.

While deeply enmeshed in these thoughts of that evening, Jade phones me.

'I'm telling you it works, this thing, this looking within to attract what is without. "Make room for love and it always comes. Make a rest for love and it always settles. Make a home for love and he will find his way there". I love this. I used it as a mantra last year. The same friend who told me this said she read about a personal growth guru who has a very simple formula for working through any crisis. He calls it "The Myth of Forgiveness and How to be Sexy".'

I have an aversion to gurus and self-help crap. 'Did it work?'

She ignores me. 'He reckons we never need to forgive anyone anything, we just need to own it. This will have the ripple effect of making one very attractive.'

'I need help with the second part.'

'Mmmm . . .'

STRANGE ATTRACTORS

41

Leave in concealment
what has long been concealed.

(Seneca)

Monday, 16 May 2011

The boys have, gratefully, fallen asleep quicker and earlier tonight; the two older ones exhausted from swimming lessons and riding their bicycles in the park down the road, and they were overtired and playing up so it seemed like the best thing all round for our sanity. So I come through to the lounge, and Sarah is watching television as usual, her favourite programme—the food channel, which is of little interest to me but this time I sit with her for a while just to be there. It is particularly cold this evening, and she is wrapped in layers of furry clothing and a beanie. I guess I want to talk with her, as always, and I sit there trying to become aware of what it makes me feel to be unheard. Just to feel it and acknowledge it. I need a reason to help explain why I am feeling so frazzled, edgy, and disconnected again, so despondent and rundown, when I had felt so strong before she had returned. To justify why I smoke incessantly and cannot sleep through the night again and still have to take these damn tablets that seem to be doing nothing for me.

Without any preliminaries, Sarah says, 'So what's the book about?'

I am not quite ready for this. 'It's, um, about us. You know, what we have been through, after the last three years.'

I have noticed that recently I try to avoid using the words affair or relationship, but always get a little tongue-tied when I refer to that period or what happened. I don't know why I do this; I just haven't found a good enough substitute. I try to convince myself I want to be gentle, to not use a word that triggers a sense of blame or guilt or resentment just by the act of saying it aloud, as it has had such negative connotations for us. But I also wonder what it says about whether I have progressed in dealing with it and putting it away. Then I try to retract the impression I realize I have created. I say, 'In fact, it's not really about us. I mean, it's based on what has happened and it sort of starts off like that. I am not even sure I would call it a "book", it's really just something my journal morphed into. Anyway, it is a novel, fiction, which just includes some of what took place, in the same way that any author really writes about their own experience or expresses their own views or opinions.' Why am I watering this down? The reality is that I have bled almost five-hundred thousand words of my heart and ego and now I don't know what to do with it. It is my story, the whole story as I see it, chronicled and painstakingly wordsmithed, but the plot keeps unfolding and it just won't come to an end. I say, 'What it's really about is "me understanding myself", using the context of our relationship.'

'It just seems like such a negative topic. Why would someone want to read about it? And I am not sure I want other people to read about us.' Well, that's clear enough an explanation, I think. She looks at me for a moment, then says, 'Anyway, who are you writing it for? Is it for you or are you going to publish it?'

Is this the issue for her? Is this what she thinks is getting in the way? To publish it would need a rewrite, a complete overhaul, and probably a change of names and places, that sort of thing, mainly to protect the boys. And I would have to let go of 'my story', save it and lock it away and start again, so that I could freely delete paragraphs and chapters without fear that I would forever obliterate 'what actually happened', the acknowledgement of which my soul so depends on now. I say, 'I don't know. I would like to publish a book, but I just don't know yet if

I am going to be brave enough, and I don't know how it will turn out because, frankly, the plot is still unfolding.'

'But we have to move on with our lives,' she says. 'I still think you have to stop writing and living with this thing every day in your head.' I can see she does not like the direction this conversation is taking.

'Sarah, what happened and how I have dealt with it last year is already written, so I am no longer dwelling on it, really, by still writing the book. That part just needs some editing at some stage, that's all. What I am busy writing now is probably no different to what you and I might write in our daily journals, or talk about in therapy.'

'I talk about what's going on in our relationship today, not the past,' she says.

'Yes, so long as you are talking about you, not me,' I say.

'You need to set a time when you are going to finish it. Because you will never get over what happened while you are still writing about it.'

But we are still living it; that is the part I am not really 'getting over'—the real-life deceit. 'What has to happen for you to feel we have put it behind us?' I say, trying to put the ball in her court.

'Stop writing about it! I can't keep on feeling like this.' The other option, I think, is to stop seeing him, an even better option is to be open about it, with each other. Then we can be whole, true, loved and loving. 'When can I read it?' she says. 'Other people can't believe you haven't let me read it yet.'

'I have no problem with you reading what I write. But I think we should just think about this carefully, as it divulges some of your past.'

'How dare you write about me!'

'Look, I wish we had the type of relationship where it felt safe enough for both of us, but I think you will react strongly to parts of the book, things we haven't even talked about yet. And I fear it will provoke the tough stuff that sits between us, rather than constructive and objective criticism. So maybe when the time is right for both of us.'

'And when do you think that will be?'

'When it's done,' I say. She looks at me, long and hard, then gets up to make more tea, or maybe just to keep moving, and I follow her into the kitchen and say, 'It is not just because I am writing a book, or because he lives next door, that it still lives with us. So what is more important to me is how I experience our relationship on a daily basis. I remember that month, October I think it was, that felt so peaceful for me, when I felt so together with you that it was easy, or easier, to let the pain of the affair recede, sort of, into the middle distance. For a whole month, I did not experience the anxious, critical part of you that I find so difficult to manage, and after that we came together, it seemed, around Roxanne.' In fact, for a few weeks she had put me on a pedestal, called me 'my Greek God' and produced a flurry of wondrous descriptors of me. Then, just as abruptly, I was demonized again.

'What do you mean?'

'I have come to realize, or maybe just to name it for myself, some of the moments and interactions with you that I struggle with so much. And before you say anything, this is not about you, it's about me. It's really about my need to connect. Simply put, I need eye contact, and I need conversation, that sort of thing. I can't bear it when you won't hear my thoughts, when you block your ears or walk out the room or put the phone down on me.'

I grab a jacket and scarf and we step into the courtyard and light cigarettes. I want to talk to her about my childhood, my upbringing, and how I think my learnt behaviour comes to play in our interactions. I am trying to own my part of what we have become. Harry and Sally implore me to throw their balls for them, but I don't want the distraction so I hide the balls in my jacket pockets. After a few minutes I have not said much and already I feel like I am talking to the retaining walls and pot plants. I'm not sure if she is taking any of this in. All the while I am looking at her, at her long dark hair, really, which has fallen forward across her face and caresses the paving as she sits cross-legged on the ground, bent forward, head hanging, eyes hidden and possibly closed. I so wish she would look me in the eyes again.

The cats wonder into the courtyard; they have put on weight. We often don't see them all day, and I suspect they have extended their territory to include the neighbour below us who, rumour has it, feeds other people's cats until eventually they are persuaded to take up residence with him. He now has thirteen cats living with him, none of which are his. I start to wonder if Sarah is still listening, but then she glances up at me. Her eyes are dulled, like she is somewhere else in her head. How can eyes not reveal that a living, breathing, feeling mind lodges behind them?

She says, 'I have had a horrendous life.'

'What has that . . . ' I stop myself. She is back, at least tentatively, and I understand why she has been so quiet while I spoke to her. She is not absorbing the things I said a few minutes ago that were to do with my behaviour, and now it seems she is defending herself.

She says, 'I feel that if I allow myself, or acknowledge to myself my weakness, that I will dissolve in a heap on the ground. My past is just too much for me. I have had to be strong all my life, and just move on to the next day.'

'That may be so,' I say, 'and I really believe that I am sympathetic to that. I keep trying to tell myself that the things you say to me, those things I find so difficult, are just your way of expressing yourself and protecting yourself.'

'This is the way I am. It is you who needs to adapt your response. Why is it so difficult for you?'

Because you are impossible and unreasonable, I think, but her comment again sows a seed of doubt, that maybe our troubles are all about me. 'That is a good question,' I say, 'and you are right, I need to keep improving how I respond to you.' I am trying very hard to not get hooked by these situations, but I can't pretend that I am not tired of it, that I don't wish for a home life that is free of this constant tension and apprehension I feel of imminent friction and hostility. But there is another question I ask myself: Why do I need to keep responding to it? Do I want to be with someone who makes me feel this way? No, that's the wrong way to see it. What I mean is, this anxious person that she says she is because of the life she has had, has a huge impact on me.

I say, 'This is not a value judgment, Sarah. I'm just trying to explain myself to you. I feel tense all the time, and if I am true to myself and want to say what I really think or do what I really want to do, what is right for me, I risk setting up this thing where I feel you get angry or blaming or controlling, and then I feel bad and guilty and manipulated.'

'Clive, our relationship is based on criticism and confrontation,' Sarah says. 'That's what we are learning here by being together.' Does this confirm that she is in the 'scholar' paradigm? Is this her justification for denigrating and vilifying someone by annihilating their spirit with dubious accusations and sweeping derogatory labels? Better surely to nurture and encourage them with fair criticism that they can actually assimilate? At least put your arm around my shoulders when you punch me in the stomach, Sarah.

I say, 'Perhaps I have struggled to accept that as it seems relentless, at least for the personality I am, and that when it gets too much it has catastrophic consequences, like the end of our marriage or the start of an affair.'

'Those are your fears.'

'That's right,' I say, thinking that the occasional feelings I struggle with when thoughts of the affair are sparked off for some reason, are amplified dramatically when I encounter that critical, fault-finding side of her that I find so tough to bear. 'And to avoid this, I often relegate my desires and don't express them. Then I feel humiliated and resentful, so I become morose . . .'

'You're dark, Clive. Very dark.'

' . . . and unaffectionate or choose to spend more time away from you, which pushes all your buttons from your past.' I can sense this is not the stuff she is interested in hearing.

'You've lost me,' she says. Yes, I think, maybe in ways other than what you mean right now. But she is right, that was a mouthful of negative emotions. These descriptors that have just rolled off my tongue packed into one or two short sentences are the words and feelings that orbit my head relentlessly.

'I'm just trying to describe what I think happens here, between us, for me, at least. For me, the amount of emotional energy I have to expend on this is exhausting to hold my fragile self together and try and avoid putting you off balance.' And I don't feel like a whole person, who is valued for who I am, and who can be and do the things that make me happy. 'It's what I was saying earlier about how I felt as a child. When it's put together with the stuff you struggle with within yourself, it's a terrible combination and we end up pushing these buttons in each other that leave both of us feeling like we will lose ourselves unless we defend ourselves to the hilt.'

'What is this tension about?' she says, pulling another cigarette from its box. Sometimes, she seems so reasonable. For a moment, I am irritated with her, as she seems to be off at a tangent again. But she is right; this is the key issue for me at the moment, and I am grateful to her that she has seen it. I struggle to access an answer to this. I embark on sentences, but they all seem to be saying the wrong thing and don't ring true. I had thought it was obvious; her behaviour leaves me tense, because of who I am. But the nature of this tension is 'fit'. I hunt for the right words.

'It's about congruence,' I say, 'or incongruence, really. Like when one's words and behaviours are incongruent, it feels like things are hidden and there is a lack of integrity. We find it difficult to see each other, to meet somewhere, and we have too many secrets between us, Sarah, eating away at our bond.'

In the hiatus, as she does not respond, I think of how irritated I get when her account of some event does not ring true to me. It does not seem authentic, because she goes into a much longer explanation than is necessary, justifying and explicating and raising details that seem tangential to the issue. But I know that sometimes this is because we process things differently. I think and speak things while she feels energies and vibrations. I seek out clarity and understanding by tossing about information that I can see and touch and feel, and I join the dots and consider the relationships and patterns between them and may take a long time to draw a conclusion but then stick with it—my pledge, my commitment is unbending; she senses energy and intuits feelings and sees pictures floating, shifting, blurring, and makes instantaneous decisions which she is comfortable to overturn.

These disparities test the integrity of our relationship, our fit with each other, like there is no backbone, no foundation to hold it together.

I say, 'So the integrity of the structure that joins us, the bond between us, is undermined, like a bridge that collapses because what started as a small fault-line, unnoticeable at first, now permeates our every interaction and gets to absurd levels at times.'

Sarah says, 'We're different, Clive,' as if she knows my thoughts.

'Yes, as you always remind me, we are so different; your bridge to me is cantilevered, mine is a suspension structure. These are constructed using different engineering principles.'

'I have no idea what you are talking about.'

'It's about how we are wired, the reinforcement in the concrete that bonds us.'

'I'm still lost,' she says. 'Try again.'

I am stymied, so I light another cigarette and offer the box to her, but she does not take it. It feels like she is being deliberately obtuse. A while ago I tried to convince myself to never embark on a conversation with Sarah of any depth and meaning, and expect to feel like it was worthwhile. So I had decided not to raise anything at all, except around the practicalities of life. And here I am, sparked by her initial queries about the script, deep into a topic for which neither of us are qualified; we don't even speak the same language. Our differences dramatically influence our ability to communicate, to see eye to eye. Interruptions distract me and leave me feeling unheard, so I listen patiently when she speaks and absorb what she says, then respond by following her trail of thought; but she needs continuous feedback and commentary while in conversation. So exchanges for me are considered moves like a game of chess, for her a two-person juggling act. I see other options and consider the other's reality, as my perspective exists only for me, whereas she sees things through her lens and believes others follow her faith. I believe in what I can verify, substantiate or replicate, and in things I can explain and put into words; she has faith in the inexplicable, in tarot cards and divining rods and pendulums and crystals and dreams and colours, and that your body speaks your mind. I live in my world and leave others to theirs, while she is fascinated by the human condition, the plethora of emotions, and finds herself by finding others. I am still, conserving, preserving, and safeguarding energy; indulgent and pleasure-seeking, living in my current experience without obvious ambition. She is dynamic and in perpetual motion of deep self-discovery, with a need to feel busily worthwhile, and approaches life as a struggle for survival. For me both the past and future are soaked up in the present moment, but for her only this present moment exists.

Is there any place at all where we can connect? It used to be in bed, sacredly joined, that we came together in the purest way. What is the reason we have fallen apart?

I say, 'I'm thinking that our core values or main beliefs, our respective views of the world and expectations of relationships, all these things, differ fundamentally. And we have never really discussed them, or understood them. When we have tried, usually arguing over some issue, we both stubbornly defend our take on life. And it troubles both of us so that we see things so differently.'

I stop and there is a long pause. We are both shivering and huddled against the cold. I know that the language I use to try and elucidate my torrent of thoughts is often incomprehensible to her. It seldom illuminates her understanding of me, nor helps her grasp the point I am trying to make. The fact that she has stayed with this conversation this far is surprising and promising. Then she says, 'I think you are busy trying to figure out whether you want to be here. Whether this is what you want to take on. For me, this is where I feel loved and where I can grow, so I have decided to be here, and take on its challenges.'

I look at her. She has cut to the chase, and I have finally run out of steam. I have no words left. 'Maybe you are right,' I say.

Her response is not the one I might have been hoping for. 'Are you finished? I want to go to bed now.' And without waiting for me to reply, she is gone.

42

When things seem to be going wrong for
you it usually is because they are.

(Molly P)

Saturday, 4 June 2011

'You bastard, I can't believe you did this. You set this up,' Sarah says as the boys sprint with glee towards the jumping castle provided for the party, little Jack wailing his protest as he cannot keep up.

Sarah had not wanted to come as she has issues with Azura and this had delayed us, but Azura had invited us to her child's birthday party and the boys were keen to go 'to get party packs' and they got their way. So late as usual we have just arrived and sluiced through the front gate and tried to keep up with the over-excited boys. We poured into the garden where the party is being hosted, a little self-conscious and feeling like gatecrashers who may never quite catch up with the vibe.

For a moment, I think she must be talking to someone else. But cued by Sarah's bellow, I turn and find myself facing an audience. Front and center, I see Jade standing there amongst the parents congregated on the patio seeking protection from the unseasonal autumn hot sun and gale force winds while anxiously watching their young children cavorting on the bouncy castle that seems to be a staple for children's parties these days and leaping clothed or not into the swimming pool just beyond it. Jade is wearing a peaked cap and sunglasses, with her hands tucked into her bomber-jacket; just standing there, looking our way, with a hint of a

451

smile, amongst the chatting, drinking adults. I am caught off-guard by her presence and so is Sarah, and the reasonableness and acceptance I have, for the most part, experienced in her lately, evaporates.

It feels like everybody is looking at us, but maybe they are looking beyond us towards their children. Uncomfortable with being at the centre of attention and angry with the accusation, I want to proclaim my innocence. It is the finger she points at me, that I orchestrated this and am therefore to blame for her pain, that I wish to disown. So I resort to my habit of explaining myself, and quietly say, 'Sarah, I did not know Jade would be here,' and I can sense pairs of adult eyes searching out the source of the heated exchange and locking on to us as Sarah shares a few choice words with me and I repeat my defence.

But Sarah is furious, and I know that nothing will stop her now when she marches over to Jade. Taller by some measure, she looms over Jade, right in her face like a prize-boxer at the pre-fight media circus professing how blood will be spilt in the ring, and says, 'This is my territory. This is my family unit and I am telling you to leave us alone today or I will hurt you.'

Hand-held drinks pause half-way to thirsty mouths, sentences evaporate mid-word, legs stop mid-stride and hang suspended, waiting to see what will happen next. Jade does not budge. Softly and without aggression, she says, 'What are you talking about?' I am still rooted to the spot, as Jade's presence and Sarah's public accusation have caught me off-balance; not for a moment had I expected her to be here, and I wonder why she has chosen to do this even though I cannot expect her to have known we would be here.

'Get out of our lives,' Sarah says. 'Your intentions are not pure and I can see what you are doing. I can see your agenda, you are here to take him away from me. But I'm more powerful than you.' Jade stands her ground and looks at Sarah from behind her sunglasses, and Sarah says, 'Stop tampering with us. If he wants to leave me, then let him. But not for you, for his own reasons.'

'What do you mean by "tampering"?' Jade says.

'Why don't you look it up in a dictionary?'

'What does it mean to you?' Jade says. I know what Jade is thinking—that Sarah has tampered with our marriage; without permission she has covertly opened it, fiddled and messed with it, and left it corrupted and mangled in disrepair. And we don't have the wherewithal, the trust-retrieval software, to recover what we have lost.

Sarah offers, 'Messing with something while you think nobody is watching and for your own gain.'

'Is that what you've been doing?' That remark stops Sarah, but only for a moment. A balanced view on a situation is not her forte. After a few more accusations and demands of Jade, I hear Sarah say, 'I will take you out,' and then she stomps back towards me and takes me on in full view of startled eyes and now also has the attention of half the children who are within earshot.

'Not here, Sarah,' I say, turning away from the crowd of adults and moving off past the jumping, screaming-with-joy children and the swimming pool towards the perimeter of the garden, thoughtfully extended with a timber deck overlooking the ocean.

'What you are doing is not okay,' she says to the back of my head, having followed me there, and I lean on the balustrade and light a cigarette, looking at the view in the hope that I can pretend the audience we now have does not exist. It would be a very pleasant moment, on the edge of this stupendous vista, if it were not for what I expect is coming. She lets me have it and it seems that her wrath knows no bounds. I glance occasionally across the manicured lawn at the others, and picking up my discomfort Sarah takes aim at it and says, 'I'm happy for them to see it. It will leave them entirely clear about what is going on here and any problem they have with it is their own stuff.'

I bat away the intended blackmail—if I don't comply, the entire world will get to know, even the stuff that is not true, so long as it casts me in a negative light. It feels so 'out there' now, anyway. 'Not without their permission, Sarah. It's not okay. And this is a children's party. There is a time and place to deal with this, and frankly I have been trying to get that time with you, but . . .'

'You cannot have a relationship with her while you are with me.'

Does it occur to her just how ridiculous this sounds, coming from her? Anyhow, I thought that was the deal. Her words are a grossly sanitized synopsis of the accusations and threats still airborne after her encounter with Jade but perhaps much more to the point. This demand I can accept as an expression of her wishes, so perhaps this is the moment for us both to openly state the truth we already know. But in a time-warped way the surroundings kaleidoscope around me and for a moment I feel like this is too much for me, this moment has come too soon. I juggle the options of full-disclosure and the blood-letting that will surely follow with a teeth-gritting sticking-to-my-story, whatever that is.

'Jade and I are close,' I say. 'Our relationship formed by chance when you were gone, but was not coincidental. For me, it is exactly what needed to happen.' My teeth begin to ache with the option I choose and my cigarette filter harbouring between my sandwich-lips is flattened in a futile attempt to intervene in the clash erupting between honesty and bullshit which have taken up residence on either lip. The debate is declared a draw; there is no clear winner.

'Then why did you not introduce me to Jade?'

'Why would I do that? You have met before and you know each other. And you never left space for that anyway.'

'Why don't you come close, hold me, and show her we are together?' she says, backing away and folding her arms.

'Because you won't let me.' I wonder whether she remembers her response to our first and only joint encounter with Calix, and how I could have done with her support, to stand alongside me and present a united front rather than flee like she had. She goes on for a bit and then says she is going to leave the party and go for a walk, but for some reason she lingers and we talk, interrupted now and then by visits from the boys and some parents, until she sits down next to me on the deck and seems to regain a semblance of composure. While we talk, our knees touch and from time to time she holds my hand and it seems like the worst is over.

Afterwards, I stay close to Sarah for a long while as we sit chit-chatting amongst the party-goers. Despite what they have witnessed and, in some cases, what they know, the people we are chatting with act as if nothing has happened. I wonder on whose side the support and empathy will lie, if these onlookers were brave enough to engage with it. I am not terribly optimistic that there will be a long queue behind me.

Then Sarah says, 'Why aren't you going to speak with Jade?' Jade has taken up her original position on the edge of the patio amongst the crowd of parents. When Sarah looks at me again with the same question on her face, I ask her whether she is okay with this, and she says, 'Of course.' So I wait a respectable time and then, after getting Sarah another drink, I wonder around a bit and then go and join the small gathering with which Jade is in conversation, which feels the safest thing to do.

Later, not by design, I somehow find myself sitting on the edge of the patio with Jade on my left and Sarah on my right but not talking to either. I can't help but think how absurd this feels perched between wife and lover, no, two women I deeply love, when pony-tailed whistle-blower Francois arrives at the party and oblivious to the recent interplay still fresh in everybody's minds as evidenced in the hushed tones and small groups that have congregated, says a smiley, 'Hi' to all of us and chat, chat, smile, chat. And I wonder about the significance of that.

The festivities are losing momentum, but everyone is waiting around for the cake and birthday song. While we are mingling, with our thoughts still spilling out, and encouraged by me that it would probably be best for some pacifying contact to be made between them before we leave the party, Jade manages to open a conversation with Sarah, but not before she has to endure the humiliation of following Sarah around like an attentive dog waiting for an opportunity to engage in private while Sarah perfects the art of keeping herself within arm's length and yet in conversation with others. Eventually Jade gets the opening she is looking for, and asks Sarah if it is okay to talk with her.

Sarah says, 'Take off your sunglasses so I can see your eyes.'

Jade says, 'I will if you do,' and Sarah removes her spectacles.

This is not a good start, I muse from my vantage point; it feels too much like 'gloves off'. It does not occur to them remove themselves from the crowd, and people shuffle their feet like playground mannequins after a coin has been inserted in their slots so they can watch them from the corner of their eyes while pretending not to. I feel like I am eavesdropping as I watch, along with the rest of the audience, the opening gambits from both sides. Jade has her back to me, and in tandem with the wind direction and her meek and sometimes indistinct voice this conspires against my clearly hearing what she is saying. But the wind carries Sarah's forceful utterances and I hear her tell Jade that she has investigated her and knows exactly who she is and what she is doing and there is a lot of labelling by numbers and birth signs and mumbo-jumbo witchcraft stuff fired with anger and underpinned by fear and jealousy, and Jade fends off most of it without outwardly flinching or obvious defensiveness, and I am in awe of her gentle love and compassion and resilience. From their body language it is clear that one of them is doing the talking and the other most of the listening. Even without the benefit of hearing all that is said, it is clearly all about power and one-upmanship and intimidation, threats and bullying and coercion. Do I have such a dearth of understanding of the female psyche? It sickens me; its toxicity invades me by association, and after a few minutes I cannot take it anymore and I move off, far away as possible, towards the timber deck.

Jack comes running over and says, 'Daddy, mommy is fighting with Jade. I want it to stop.'

I pick him up and turn him to face the view. 'Don't fuss about it, Jack. They just need to say some things to each other and they forget how loud they are speaking. Why don't you show me how you swim like a seal?' and off I go to busy myself with the children.

It does not go as I had hoped but perhaps how I had tacitly expected. What possessed me to think that Sarah had overcome her initial shock and insecurity? How easily I am taken in by her moments of reason, and ignore the likelihood that she will flip the switch to vindictive outrage in the blink of an eye. In front of everyone, as about centre-and-front stage as it could possibly be, they stand toe-to-toe and it ensues for at least half-an-hour. From the other side of the bouncy castle, I find myself watching the interaction.

At some stage Azura manoeuvres herself next to me as we look on from a safe distance and says, 'You know how I feel about you, Clive. I adore you. You are a remarkable man and have endured so much with her. Your heart is in the right place, and that is why last year I told you what I knew about Calix and Sara-lea. If I was her I would worship you, you would be my god, and then I could be your goddess.'

I smile weakly at her, quietly thankful for her words of support, and tell her I am sorry this is ruining her child's party. Together we watch the exhibition before us escalate to all-out-war, a mental sparring with neither the aggressor nor the pacifist gaining nor relinquishing ground, and with dark magic-power being voiced and abused and threats of violence from Sarah that she will not hesitate to take Jade out. I wonder how this jells with her expectation long held that I would confront Calix with masculine force and aggression and whether, in her mind, I was credited or despised for my non-confrontational approach?

Then Azura says, 'This is not okay; she is being so unfair given what she is up to,' speaking of Sarah and her belief that 'the Calix thing' is still going on.

'Why do you doubt Sarah?' I say to Azura.

'It's not just the stories I keep hearing about their affair. I saw them together a while ago, and I now regret that I didn't confront them on the spot. Then she could no longer keep up this pretence that it's all above board. And last week I bumped into her at the nursery coffee shop and we chatted and . . . I'm sorry Clive, I don't know how to say this, but there's something just not right there. She's not authentic. There is something missing, she is evasive and I find it difficult to believe her. It's just how I feel.'

Just this past week another convincing round of rumours have come past me, apparently without substance as people would not back up what they were saying when I have pushed for it, along the lines of—'People are saying things, everybody knows they are still together, but sorry, I can't say more, this is just conjecture' and—'Hire a private detective if you really want to know, it's such a simple process really, you will get your evidence, no problem,' which is where the trails ends as I just don't think I have the heart to do that so I have not wanted to follow-through. I don't want thoughts of Calix and what is going on between them to ever occupy my mind again, as I want to stay true to the insights I have had in conversation with Jade. But my resilience to ignore their relationship is wearing thin, and I stand here and survey the spectacle unfolding and wonder whether the time has come to actively pursue some of the leads as it appears I might need something up my sleeve the way things are working out.

And then Azura says, 'If I was Sara-lea, I would walk up to Jade and give her the biggest hug and tell her how grateful I am that she has been there for you and loved you when you have needed it most, that she is welcome in your space, and that she is a goddess and I feel her heart is here with love and so is mine.'

'Would you still say this if you knew we were sleeping together?'

Azura looks at me and says, 'Really? *Really?* Good. You deserve to be loved.' It would not be unfair to describe Azura as an expert on sensual healing and sexual rehabilitation. I move off to be alone at the far end of the garden suddenly aware that there is a lot of bad energy around us and has been for a long time and wonder, somewhat belatedly, what I should make of the realization that I am not in my preferred position on the outside observing this but part of it, as in—people have formed views around me over the past few months and years and are doing so right here, right now, as I am the man-subject at the centre of this performance.

I think of how I had woken up this morning heavy and depressed without knowing why and Sarah had sleepily told me she had two dreams. In the first, she is living on a farm alone with the boys. It is blissful and she is happy not being in a relationship. In the second dream she said I go with Jade who falls pregnant and then Sarah lives with some Chinese healer-practitioner who helps her understand the source of her issues and her mental instability and from whom she learns a technique to kill Jade, which she does, and that when I want to return to her, she does not want me back. After her first confrontation today with Jade, Sarah had reminded me of this and other premonitions she feels has prepared herself for this moment. Her psychic hunches have an eerie way of playing themselves out at some point, and I wonder whether this is 'Act One, Scene One'? And I speculate how Jade had prepared herself for this moment, a moment I had once warned her would likely be confrontational, with the bonfire she had prepared the night before last in the company of close girlfriends and upon which she had sacrificed three years of unopened mail, and three decades of photographs, journals, paintings and letters, and committed her history to embers.

Then all hell breaks loose, provoked it seems by a weak or at least unsuccessful attempt to intervene by the homeowner who has taken umbrage that the chosen battleground has usurped his entertainment arena and who tells Jade she is a goddess and men are weak. When I hear this, I try not to take it personally, and wish he would leave me out of this. They were doing just fine, I thought, and I would rather leave these two equals to establish their mutual ground than to turn their joint wrath towards me. But his intrusion disturbs the fragile balance, and Sarah, perhaps suddenly aware of the world around her, lunges at Jade. Inconveniently for him, but fortunately in my view, the somewhat inebriated self-appointed peace-keeping homeowner did not consider the option of this offensive manoeuvre and takes the brunt of Sarah's undoubted superior physicality destined for Jade. It could have been comical, but nobody laughs.

I can't be sure how or when it ends, but at some point it does, and a little later as we leave the party and make our way home, Sarah says, 'You are stronger than I realized.' I think it is best not to ask her what she means by this. 'And gentler,' she says, in afterthought. I am still dismayed by the encounter and criticism of her swirls around my head looking for an exit, but it is surely the wrong time to take her on about it.

After dinner, she says, 'I can't believe you went to talk to her.' Chink, goes the folder: 'judgmental'—I hear the voice of a critical parent.

Feeling accused of something, I say, 'I didn't really. I just joined in a conversation which she was part of. Anyway, you kept saying that I should.' Adult—factual statements, I hope, except the last bit perhaps.

'I was just testing you.' The tone is filled with bitter bile. Chink, goes the folder: 'manipulative'—does this not embarrass her?

I say, 'That's so manipulative. You do that a lot, you know. And how does it fit with being authentic?' My angry child voice erupts in emotional reaction.

But she has already moved off towards the bedroom.'

CHINESE BAMBOO

43

The love we give away is the only
love we keep.

(Elbert Hubbard)

Monday, 6 June 2011

'My wife says either you're incredibly stupid, or this is all part of a plan that is so brilliant we just can't figure it out. She says she knows you're not stupid, so you must have a strategy, but I said I'm not so sure about your IQ after our last chat. I've told you before, you're behaving like an idiot doing this in full view. And once Sara-lea came back, you certainly should have taken it underground, if it wasn't already too late.'

Jim looks at me, as if expecting me to say something. He seems genuinely distressed as he chastises me. Perhaps he is re-evaluating how he chooses his lifelong friends. He has heard talk about what transpired on Saturday and has called an urgent game of beach bats as a cover for what he usually calls 'a management summary', his term every time we meet as he tries to come to grips with what I have relayed to him so he can tell his wife.

'I kept telling you that you and Jade needed time to figure out whether you're right for each other,' Jim says. 'And you can't do that while you're being harassed and accused of having an affair. I'm telling you, Sara-lea is not stupid. She is streetwise. She's busy making plans and gathering evidence to take you apart. That other goat-horn guy is waiting in the wings, and she's going to annihilate you. It's out of your hands now. You have lost all control of the situation.' And then, apparently assuming this will end in divorce—'Look, you must take what I say with a pinch of salt, because I admit I am biased. I know that what you are most fearful of is losing your boys, and that Sara-lea will make life hell for you. But based on her behaviour, you can probably have her declared unfit to be a mother.'

'I could never do that. Not to her or the boys. And anyway, my worst fear is what she might do to herself and the boys.'

But Jim ignores this. 'This has forced your hand. Jade is not going to wait around with this uncertainty and with no movement from you. You have to give her something to hold on to. Otherwise you will lose her as well.'

He says all this while we walk along the beach, and I wonder what makes him feel that Jade needs to 'wait around'. How might he respond if I told him that she has been in attendance for centuries now? Perhaps this is not the time to tell him to ditch old paradigms? There is no intention to play beach bats. We walk along the water's edge in silence for a while, then drift towards the back of the beach and sit down on a deserted embankment that borders the polluted river flowing into the sea, a mere elevation that pretends to be a sand dune. It is one of those balmy autumn days, unseasonably warm, which seems to say with ominous foreboding of things to come—enjoy it while you still can, you're in for a stormy, late winter.

Almost before we had started walking, he had said, 'Tell me.' And so I had, but just an 'executive summary', that there was a confrontation and it was pretty messy, as I was not relishing recalling the details. Now, shaking the head he holds in his hands as if trying to unscrew it from his neck, he tells me that he needs a capsule summary, something that actually makes sense as he simply cannot relate the incomprehensible garbage he has heard from me to his wife this evening, something I now realize he does after every time he gets the latest update from me. 'Or my wife will fire me,' he says.

'Be nice to me,' I say. 'Or you will have to go somewhere else for your entertainment.' I let the fine white sand pour through my fingers.

'Why can't you just have a nice old plain vanilla affair? Like everybody else has?'

'Then you won't want to spend time with me. You will have nothing to talk to your wife about, and we can't have that, can we.'

'You're incredible,' he says. 'Incredibly stupid. Look, tell me again, from the top, I need to hear every detail. What happened when you arrived at the party?' And so I tell him again, in detail, what happened on Saturday, as Gino patrols along the water's edge not shy to make it known that he is watching us.

It reminds me of what happened yesterday, when we were at the restaurant on the beach, next door to Jade's house, and therefore near Gino's, and this was a favourite haunt of his. He still persists in slinking around, stalking and bullying me with his stares to which I had become somewhat immune. This summer-time favourite hang-out for parents with young children held its own on good-weather days notwithstanding the cooler winter months. It has a huge sand-covered playground with jungle-gyms, and we sat on the trestle-tables in the sandpit from where we could conveniently play intermittently with the boys yet chat to other parents or grandparents (I doubt any sane non-parent would sit there, or if they did, remain of sound mind for long amid the madness of screaming, sand-throwing kids). It was another blissful mid-season day, warm enough for T-shirts and shorts and sunscreen and hats.

We smuggled the dogs into the children's area and I got them to lie in the shade under the table and safely out the way of other children before the manager noticed them and asked me, as he always did, to remove them from the sandpit, after which then followed the ritual negotiation to keep there. It is not as though he did not recognize us as regulars or could have forgotten that we have been through this debate many times before, one from which he had never emerged victorious, and always seemed intent to suffer the same fate time and time again.

Sarah kept herself busy chatting to others most of the time, and I seemed to be doing more than my fair share of playing with the boys, digging tunnels under the sand with Jeremiah and Joshua, tightrope walking along the perimeter wall with little Jack, or assisting him on the

monkey bars or daydreaming to the monotony of the endless parabola
as I pushed him on the swing. But with this I had no gripe. It was while
pushing Jack on the swing for the umpteenth time, pretending to be
knocked over by his outstretched legs which brought on fits of laughter
so great he often forgot to breathe, that I saw Gino swagger in with his
shaved head and sunglasses and leather jacket and a dark-haired woman
and his dog and ascend the stairs to the bar area. I wondered where
Jade was; she probably avoided coming here, or perhaps she was with
William? That was also weird, how Jade had brought him to the deli
and I went over and introduced myself and he seemed so dismissive
and since then I have seen him every day but he refuses to acknowledge
me even when we virtually walk into each other. So much for being
accepting of the connection between Jade and me.

A little later, when I really could no longer delay, I made a quick trip
to the bathroom. On my return, blinded by the sunlight after the dark
interior, I did not immediately take in the scene and I practically walked
into them standing at the foot of the stairs. I saw Sarah first and stopped
next to her, and then I saw Gino; actually I heard him first. They were
giving his dog lots of attention, but I was sure that was just a cover for
the topic of their conversation. I nodded 'hello' to him, but he did not
respond. Assuming this was a chance meeting, and that they did not
know each other, I knew that this moment would seal it and recognized
that a pact may be spawned between them.

As we whittled away the afternoon, their connection bothered me
more and more, though I tried to rationalize that nothing would come
of it. It seemed obvious that Sarah had not yet pieced it together, as she
would not have been able to resist the opportunity to point out who he
was. I risked another glimpse towards the bar. The woman with Gino
was Amelie, and they seemed to be looking directly at me. I imagined
them talking and scheming about us now from their vantage point
beyond the upper-level balustrade.

I was sitting again at the table, Sarah standing a few metres away from
me, in the same way she had kept her distance since we arrived. I wanted
to ask her who that man was and what they were talking about. No

doubt provoked by my mounting apprehension, I said to her, 'Do you know someone called Amelie?' It was out of my mouth before I realized it, and I had no idea where I wanted to go with the conversation.

Her anxiety peaked straight away. 'Why do you want to know?' The way she said it I had to convince myself to not apologise for asking.

I said, 'She is vaguely familiar and I think she has a daughter at school with Jack.'

She swung into attack mode, and coming towards me, said again, 'Why do you want to know?'

'Sarah . . .'

'This is what you do, Clive. You manipulate and control me. You are trying to catch me out.'

'It's just a simple question,' I said, struggling to contain my anger. And suddenly it dawned on me: Amelie was the conduit through which Sarah was fed information about Jade. Sarah and Gino are in cahoots, of this I was now convinced.

So I sent a text to Jim: '*The eagle has landed. Targets have made contact. Raise status to 'orange'. Extract me—repeat—extract me!*'

In seconds Jim responded: '*Who are you? I have no knowledge of you or your situation.*' And added a smily face.

'*I won't be the fall guy, I'll take you down with me,*' I threatened.

Later, I sit at the deli, writing, when Jade arrives and says, 'It's probably not a good idea to sit with you, but I need to talk briefly, it's long overdue.'

'Okay.'

Jade says, 'Clive, my commitment to you and us is to complete openness, nothing less.' I love the sentiment, but as an opening line, given what has been going on lately, it troubles me. 'And we have not had the chance to talk this through given what's been happening here.' I watch her for signs of stress-reaction to the altercation with Sarah. 'I've tried writing to you, but I am worried that the words don't contain the

right meaning and that it is unfair to dump it on you without dialogue.'
I am not yet sure what I can contribute until I know what this is about.
Is she referring to us, or to Sarah and the confrontation? Stop deluding
yourself, Clive; you know it is about William.

'In the past month, I have been presented with what feels like a
choice. It feels like an intervention from spirit in some ways, and once
again I find myself deeply moved and it feels real. You know that I don't
believe in 'the one', and I find myself in a place where my relationship
with William has developed and deepened and I feel his love abounding
towards me as yours did. I think of you and I realise there is a possibility
that you are completely in the dark about where I am at unless you
have been able to feel it.' I was right. 'It is unhindered by ego in that he
knows full well the depths of my love for and connection to you, but
he is standing there with a wide open heart and he is saying "Jade, you
are the one; my heart, mind and spirit are certain of this. I have thought
about this for six months and I have chosen you. Now all you need to
do is choose me, but that is up to you".'

I reach for my cigarettes.

'I have been in quite a state these last few weeks,' Jade says, 'with all
that has been going on and being harassed by Gino, almost unable to
function at times.' Since Sarah returned, I had assumed, but apparently
there is another factor hitherto undeclared. 'And I've had days of deep
sadness and mourning as this overlaps with my love for you and my deep
desire for you and my feeling that what I have experienced with you
has been sublime and more special, healthy, blissful, and conscious than
anything I have ever experienced. I long for what could be or could have
been, but I am now challenged to make the right choices for me. And I
am feeling today, in my free empowered state, that I would love to have
the experience of that love, free of complication and drama.'

She stops and looks at me, as if she needs to hear from me to get
a sense of how I am taking this. I am not sure I want to tap into the
real feelings that are deep but wriggling noticeably, let alone share them
with her. 'I am looking for a gentler way of speaking that truth, but
cannot find it. William is coming down to visit again this weekend, and

I strongly desire to reciprocate him with what he offers me, to meet his commitment with mine, as if that is the next step here for me. If I don't take that step, I feel divided and unsure and hesitant and in that state nothing works or flows in my life at all.'

Jim, help—I think I am in the process of dissipating, and my possible futures are about to be wide open, but empty. Maybe you were right, others seem to be making decisions apparently in their own best interest and hurtling headlong into the consequences of their choices. Am I the only one not getting any sensual loving these days?

So I say, 'Remember, when you told me that you communicated with your father and asked him why you have met me yet I am not fully available, and the message you received from him was because you need more time to do the things you need to do?' I don't wait for her nod. 'You said to me that you felt you will be ready towards the end of the year, November in fact. And I then told you that I have recently discovered that my life has clearly identifiable cycles of seven years, but that the fifth year always seems to present a specific personal predicament, an event so personally catastrophic, that it changes forever the path of my life. In it are all the lessons I need to learn, and I'm overwhelmed. Then it seems I get closure on it, this apparently tragic setback, by the seventh year, in which another, usually related challenge reveals itself. It's like these intervening two years allow me to internalize and absorb the lessons. It's equally as daunting, this seventh-year shift, but if I have learnt the lessons, it makes way for a joyous new cycle.'

Jade says, 'Clive, in the Far East a so-called "crisis" is viewed with promise, in fact, the direct translation is a "dangerous opportunity".' I say nothing. 'So what happened in the last cycle, if you don't mind telling me?'

'We need more time to discuss that. The point is that this year, 2011, is year five. It's so weird, as if nothing seems to happen for five years, then all of a sudden I'm overwhelmed by change and growth.'

'Just like Chinese bamboo,' she says.

'Please Jade, join the dots for me.'

'Oh, I read somewhere that for five years nothing happens, at least nothing visible above the surface, while an extensive nurturing root system is being prepared underground. Then suddenly the culm grows . . .'

'The what?'

'The culm, the stem. It suddenly emerges from the soil and can grow at a rate of up to one metre per day, though I'm sure that's an exception. And each individual bamboo apparently has a five-to-seven year lifecycle, so perfecting the time to harvest is critical. So perhaps you should accept your natural cycle, that this is the time to grow and harvest all that you have learnt but not yet assimilated or digested in a way you can consciously use.'

'Okay, so I'm a newly conscious Chinese bamboo.'

'You can joke, but this is helpful to me. Perhaps it explains why it's appeared that you were so stuck, and why you didn't make the big move last year when everything, absolutely everything, was screaming out loud and clear and seemed to point in one direction and the outcome for your marriage looked so patently obvious, at least to others. It was not yet the time to harvest. Somehow you knew this, and I am in awe of how you stay true to yourself, how you are not persuaded by others. I told you before I can sense that something is about to radically change, but I think I have misinterpreted how I experienced you recently. I thought you were withdrawing, stuck, scared, and holding on. But I can see now you are actually making yourself ready.'

'Jade, you always see a good side to me. Truth is, at times I feel I am sure-footed on my path and at times I am shit-scared, but I'm trying to let go. So when we spoke about "November", I told you that I had a clear sense that in three months, which would make it just around the corner now in July, the transition that awaits me will take place or at least begin to show itself. I am still unsure exactly what it is and I'm pretty sure it's not the obvious; I just need to be ready for it. And we never challenged those statements, we have just accepted them. So I accept that we both have things to do now, and when November comes, we will see where we are at. But before you go, I need to tell you one last thing. I don't yet know who you are to me—a soul-mate, a twin flame, a love that transcends many lifetimes? I don't know. But I'm starting to understand that you are an angel. My angel. One of those angels I never acknowledged.'

What I am really wondering is whether she is Angelique.

44

If you remain angry at someone, then who
is suffering?

(Tristan J. Loo)

Tuesday, 7 June 2011

I was sitting with Jane when Jade arrived. She chooses to sit inside the deli today, working on her laptop. I just half-smile a hello when passing by her on my way to the bathroom. We don't sit together and don't speak to each other.

I had confided in Jane last week for the first time about my marriage, quid pro quo I guess after she told me that she has struggled with bipolar episodes for decades and she seemed to have a good understanding of the condition. Her manic-depressive husband, afflicted by a concoction of related personality disorders, eventually killed himself. So we sit here talking about it as it is also on my mind. And I wonder if this is some sort of epidemic.

Getting a bit lost in the midst of Jane's extrapolation of the various drugs and treatments and conditions that appear similar but are not, and how more damage can be done by misdiagnosis or an inappropriate drug regime, and the high percentage of successful suicides that are people with borderline personality disorders, and what it was like for her to live with a philandering psychotic husband, first ex and then dead, for almost twenty years, I had stopped absorbing the information. Then, almost mid-sentence after getting tongue-tied with an almost unpronounceable name of the latest specialized drug, Jane says, 'How are things going?'

I know what she is referring to and it is relatively easy to pick up the story and fill her in about what has happened over the last few days. She is horrified, and what she says next, stings me the most—'Clive, remember when Sara-lea caused a scene here a week or so ago?' I nod and light a cigarette. That day, Sarah had pounced without warning, even though we have a long-standing agreement that she will call ahead before she dumps the boys with me in case I am busy working. I had introduced her to Jane, who was sitting in conversation with a friend at another table and Jane became the brunt of some disparaging words from Sarah.

Jane is a bit wacky, with a conservative and affluent background yet with an arty flavour that must have caused a rumpus every so often in the social circles she once graced. She sometimes comes and sits with me and talks about things, mostly arbitrary, and I wondered how the ordinary looks of mid-fifties plain Jane could possibly provoke such jealousy. Or perhaps it was irrelevant; anybody else, male or female, was a threat?

'Well,' Jane says, 'my friend I was chatting to that day knows you. She has a child at the same Montessori school that Jack goes to. She was so upset by Sara-lea's disparaging remarks that, after you all left, her tongue loosened, and she spoke about the bond you have with Jade and that the cord that binds you is obvious. Then she told me some dreadful stories, and she said something like "Clive is an awesome man, but he is never getting away from that one. It's been bad and wrong for him for a long time and he's known it, but she is cooked and he is trapped".'

Jane lights a cigarette and waits for a response from me. I break open another sugar wrapper and pour the contents into the ashtray we share. Jane leans forward and all but whispers, 'I just don't know how you keep going, Clive. How do you manage to be in a relationship with a woman like that? Someone who abuses her power and in my view has no consideration for the humanity in all of us.'

'It's a complex situation, Jane. She's a complex individual.'

'You mean complexed? Tell me what went wrong in your marriage, Clive?'

I look at her: I'm not going back there. But in my humble opinion the superficial answer is that we cannot 'see' each other, and the root of this lies in inauthenticity born of the fear that we will expose to ourselves who we truly are. The motive—shame for past abuse and atrocities, and the modus operandi—all bound to ego—is secrecy and denial. The real reasons lay deep and go back a very long way; longer than imaginable—'The secret wound still lives within the breast', I muse. Clandestinity or furtiveness, call it what you like, it pervades and saturates everything, even what you think it will not blemish, until its host is decayed by its corrosiveness. Africans greet each other with—'I see you' because they believe they only exist in relation to the other. And when a human system seals itself off in this way from whom it really is, shuts itself off from the notion that we are in everyone and they in us, or refutes the notion that we co-create our existence and our experience of that existence, I wonder how soon the inertia becomes noticeable in entropic self-obliteration.

As if to rescue me from this topic, Francois and Azura arrive at the deli, and sit uninvited at our table. Not without their own personal troubles, those two. Azura is one of Jade's closest friends, and knows of our love. Probably with the public exhibition at the party in mind, she says, 'How is your friend?' hooking her chin in the direction of Jade.

I know who she is referring to but feel compelled to say, 'Who?' And she looks past me through the open door of the deli and I say, 'Oh, you mean Jade? She's fine.' As if called by the fact that she is in our thoughts, I can sense that behind me Jade is moving. As I am sitting with the others, this presumably gives Jade the cover she needs to come to our table and say, 'Hello,' and after brief hesitation from both of us it seems permissible to hug. Azura asks her if she is okay, and she says, 'Not really,' and goes back inside. As Jade's friend she could ask her that question privately, but chooses not to.

My three companions look at me. I look back. 'Okay, enough of that,' Jane says, not to be put off by the new arrivals. 'At least tell me how your sex life is?'

I say, 'It's phenomenal. How about yours?'

Picking up the thread, Azura says, 'Did having children have a huge role to play?'

'In what?' She just looks at me. 'Okay, it just feels like it was during that time that things fell apart.' Actually, in my own mind I can be more specific; it was after we 'untimely plucked' Angelique from Sarah's womb. Over the years we never used contraception because we always assumed she would struggle to conceive after the string of losses, but strangely, after Angelique she fell pregnant quickly and easily and produced three live births on the trot, two of which are apparently mine. Until little Jack arrived; then the problems started all over again. What is it about him that punctuated this run of good fortune?

'Are you even sure they are yours?' Francois says, not to be left out, and I wonder whether this is a dilemma of his own.

'No, and I always used to joke about having a paternity test for little Jack, he just seemed so unlike me in every way,' I say, not really wanting to think about it, that revelation in her journal. 'I haven't really answered your original question, Jane, but you know what our circumstances were like. Sarah would agree with most of what I've said about the sleep-troubled stress and exhaustion, but further than that she has a totally different view of our shared experience. She felt I was never around to support her and never helped her manage the children, and she says for that reason she had an affair. She seems to still feel that way.'

'Perhaps both of you are right?' Azura says.

'Of course we are,' I say, 'but surely the core of any unhappiness comes from within us. The nucleus of this is "feelings", not facts. We judge things and take decisions and make choices based on how we feel about the so-called "facts". We are not good at considering all the evidence objectively and afresh.'

Azura says, 'Do you mean emotions or feelings?' I look at her, exasperated. 'Look, Clive, feelings are real and normal, even the dark ones. They're sort of like the weather, bright and sunny one day, gloomy and miserable the next and you just need to face them.'

'I carry sun-block and a raincoat with me every day,' Francois says, with a self-congratulatory smirk.

Azura stares him down. 'But emotions, they are created by your thoughts; they are in your head—the stories you tell yourself. So they are self-inflicted, and I think you have poisoned yourself with them.' I am not sure whether this is directed at me or Francois.

'Let me see if I've got this,' I say, irritation rising. 'Needs are okay, as are feelings—like the weather, sunny one day, rainy the next. So it's okay to whine and pout a bit, once in a while.' And then, to appease Francois, who I think is on a hiding to nothing here, 'I'll just put on sun-block one day, then my raincoat the next, and I will ride the wave. But expectations and emotions, not so? Expectations you throw at the other, without their permission . . .'

'And try to control them,' Francois speaks above me.

' . . . and judge them with disappointment if they don't meet a promise they never made in the first place, yet it was just in your head. But emotions are what you carry when your mind chooses to interpret a situation in a particular way, because of who *you* are, *your* unresolved wounds perhaps.' Azura's head is nodding up and down.

Francois's head is bobbing sideways, like one of those nodding toys on a spring. He fiddles with the cutlery and says to the fork, 'It's not okay to try and make another person the target of your unmet expectations and emotions.'

'This is so confusing,' I say. 'Apparently it is good to express what you're feeling, and what your needs are, but not to get emotional about it?'

Jane injects herself into the banter, 'But in a conscious way, by owning them and not attaching them to the other. So if you feel manipulated, disappointed or blamed, those are your emotions, and I guess you should ask yourself why you feel them, as it's not because of Azura.' Jane lifts her eyebrows at Francois. 'Of course you can choose to label her as manipulative or misleading or whatever, but this will just keep you stuck.'

Francois is not buying this and turns to Azura, who has folded her arms. 'Invective and obscenity and labels are some ways of trying to shake them away and velcro them to me. Your angry outbursts, making assumptions as if you truly are able to know my motivations, as if you can see what I see through my eyes, it's all just a self-gratifying jerk-off, and I see little respect and compassion. I'm half expecting you to soon explain and justify and excuse your behaviour, as you have frequently done before.'

What you see is not really what you see, but who you are, and it amazes me, when you get down to the core, just how similar everybody is. And what I see going on here is very familiar, very close to home. They have come here to talk to each other, through my situation. I should be enjoying this, but I am not. It is funny how things can 'turn' in a moment.

I say, 'You are reminding me of the games we play, Azura,' hoping that she realizes she is not immune to this. 'And I can label so many of my interactions with Sarah in this way. So to get back to your point, I guess I'm talking about perceptions, the labels we attach to feelings or emotions or whatever.'

'It is part of the human condition, this "whatever",' Jane says, sounding a bit pissed off that her conversation has been annexed. 'We usually filter out information that doesn't fit with our preconceived notions when we actually should update our beliefs such that we take a fair view of the current situation. She is stuck in her life script, and I think that because of who you are, you are keeping her there.'

'Who?' Francois says, not quite keeping up. Azura gives him a look.

I say, 'Something like that, though we all are, Jane, stuck in our life script. Mix this together in a brew of assumptions and expectations and add a sprinkling of fear from old wounds unresolved, and you have a powerful cocktail. That's my answer, the superficial version anyway, to your question about what went wrong. I think I'll call it the "communication calamity cocktail".'

Jane says, 'I know what you mean. Right now I am so frustrated with my partner, who is such a wonderful man in many respects, that I often think of leaving. Our individual differences, our personalities, are such a struggle, especially when provoked by a challenging situation.' She talks directly to me, cutting the others out, and I realise this is what she came to talk to me about.

'I have come to learn that in situations of extreme stress, three things come into play.' Francois again, wanting to regain a foothold on the conversation.

'Tell me,' Jane says, with more challenge than inquiry in her voice.

'The extent to which you can make sense of what is happening to you is crucial. And to do this, you need someone to share it with, test it out, and hear their experience of it. If it was at the time of your first child it's quite obvious, because it is unchartered territory, and it's so difficult to comprehend what is happening. You need to get a handle on the rollercoaster of your emotions and find a way to understand the impact of the stress and exhaustion and all the constraints that have suddenly changed in your life. And how you negotiate your relationship with your spouse is everything.' Azura's first child was sired by Francois, and she has that look of 'so there is stuff you have not told me about yourself, Francois?'

'Well, we had an antenatal group,' I say, helpfully, 'most of whom are still close friends, and this helped, but not much else. Sarah's family was not around at all. I guess what we needed most was to share more openly with each other, which would have helped us accept that what we were experiencing was normal. That it was not just me, the other was also struggling. Perhaps we just needed more support?'

'No. You needed more sharing, deep and honest chats, and more opportunities to understand what you were going through, together,' Jane says. 'That's what was missing then, and now. The distance between you and Sara-lea is now vast and is fed by secrets and imagined fears and self-protection. Simply put, unless you share openly you can never make sense of your struggles.'

'Yes, support, I think, that's the next factor,' Francois interjects, trying to seize back control and looking my way to show who he is talking about. 'In fact, just believing that you have access to the help you might need is enough for you to hold yourself together.' He glances at Azura. 'And I guess your core partner is your first port of call.' I can sense Azura lining up her questions to be lobbed at him later.

I say, 'Okay, so zero from two so far. I think Sarah felt she was on her own because outwardly I didn't show my inner turmoil as she did. And Sarah's script that life is a struggle came to the fore and I fell right into it, feeling like I was constantly under siege and should dig deeper into the bunker and keep my helmet below the ramparts.' Jane smiles, and I say, 'No, not that helmet, oh wicked one,' just as Gino swaggers by with his playful hound, the totem-pole of his testosterone-filled helmet figuratively pronounced in my mind, and I resist the urge to swivel around and check whether Jade is still sitting inside.

Azura says, 'Your helmet was below the ramparts because she was disinterested in it?' Her eyes flick down towards my belt and I wonder whether she is about to invite me for a session of sensual healing? I am not sure I like the way this conversation is going.

'After all the failed pregnancies you had, didn't the joy of a new baby carry you through?' Jane says.

'You know that wears off quickly, especially with severe post-natal depression, from which I think we both suffered, by the way.'

'That's a good question,' Francois says, retrieving the thread of points he wants to complete. 'Because I think that the last component that determines how well you handle intense strain or trauma has to do with "why?"' What a wonderful word, I think, and regret that Jim is not here; he would hate this.

'Is it a question of whether the challenge is worth the effort?' Jane says.

Francois says, 'Some things I gave up on quickly, other times I hung in there against all odds, and how I coped in the end seemed to be about how much it meant to me.' Azura is noting all this down, so be careful what you say, Francois. 'If you can find meaning in your suffering, and perhaps imagine a light at the end of the tunnel, a belief that it is worthwhile and will come to an end or a promise of a better place one day, I think that provides the motivation you need to get through it. And actually come out the other side better, stronger.' He is embittered that she left him, I know that much. Why does he not just say this directly to Azura? That he feels she gave up too quickly when the going got rough.

Amid thoughts of soot-blackened faces and equidistant tracks tunneling through seemingly impenetrable mountainsides, the challenges and hurts of life, I say, 'That sounds too much like the reason religion became so popular when life on earth seemed so intolerable, like in the Dark Ages, and it gave hope to the downtrodden masses if they could believe that they would benefit from all their suffering.'

Suddenly his ally, Jane looks at Francois and says, 'So it's almost as if you experience the obstacle as eustress, a positive, motivational stressor, rather than distress.' She has thrown in 'big' words as if in a tussle of intellectual superiority with Francois, and it has served its purpose as Francois goes quiet. Then, looking at me, Jane says, 'Which makes you sick in one way or another.' But my thoughts are of railways tracks . . . I am in a train, steaming into a tunnel . . . 'Too theoretical for you?' she says, no doubt seeing that my mind is elsewhere.

'Yes.'

'Okay, Clive, then discard it. But if you take nothing else from what I've said just hold on to this,' as if neither Francois nor Azura have contributed anything of value. 'You need to move forward now, so stop trying to make sense of what has happened, there's plenty of time for that.' Strike one for Jane, and Francois falls down a peg or two. 'The same goes for regrets, for what you think has gone wrong. And it doesn't mean you have to stay in the situation you have stoically endured, thinking that if you leave now, you will not be rewarded for your pain.' Is this tacit support for Azura, or self-justification for why she left her manic husband after years of abuse? 'So stop questioning yourself. Don't look for meaning in why this is happening, look for meaning in your future.' Strike two for Jane. 'But live in this moment, and right now, you need to make sure you are strong so start looking after yourself and be judicious with the support you choose to surround yourself with.'

'That makes some sense to me,' I say, looking at all of them in turn to acknowledge their contribution. 'It certainly seems to be a better approach than to do what I think Sarah calls "hope", and she has that word plastered all around the house.'

'What happened to "honour" and "glory"?' Azura says.

'Sounds full of ego to me. Just trust in your dream, your future you are creating. Infuse every cell in your body with it. It should be enough, no?' Jane says. Fuck off, all of you, enough of your silly one-upmanship.

'We create our own hell, Clive, but forget to take responsibility for it.' Someone has climbed into Jane's face, it has changed, along with her energy and her voice; a veil descends across her features and it seems like she is talking from another time and place. Her lips are moving, but it is not her speaking. 'It is so easy, and it is the strategy of the ego always to blame others and find causes somewhere else, because then there is no need to change.' Francois goes rigid; I am sure he is making the sign of the cross. 'Instead you choose to suffer, to bear the burden of what's not okay, and then you have to learn how to tolerate. In fact, that's what people have been doing for centuries, learning tolerance. And that's what you've done. You have tolerated the most intolerable. And you think people admire you for it, for enduring and suffering? Well, I don't. I don't respect you for it, and you can be sure she doesn't either. So it sounds to me like you need to stop tolerating and learn to transform.'

That word again. Where are you, Jim?

Are Jane's words further confirmations that 'who' is a more constructive dilemma to busy myself with than 'why'? 'You reap what you sow?' I say, glancing at Azura and Francois and wondering whether I have been suitably admonished and whether Jane needs help to come back from wherever the hell she is.

Azura says, 'Frankly, people are tiring of it, your endless relationship problems, and you and Sara-lea have become the object of extreme distaste.'

'And it's rife,' Francois says, pouncing quickly to keep me the subject of this discourse and prevent Jane from further alarming him. 'I've heard people express their embarrassment for you and how you turned their stomachs with the airing of your dirty laundry. Jane's right, they have lost all respect for you.'

'Sara-lea's been telling people that you're sleeping with prostitutes,' Azura says. 'That you've had lots of affairs, and that you beat her; she's showed people the scars.' I stare at her. Perhaps I should write a textbook on psychological disorders? 'Toxic relationships eventually become alienating, and everyone who has had to listen to this stuff over and over eventually avoids you at all costs, especially when a week later they see you all wrapped up in each other again.' Then I wonder why they have come to sit with me and ask me how it is going but talk about themselves?

'And you are left alone with your terrible twin in the mess you have co-created and then finally have to face the tragedy of fucking up the lives of the children in the middle, and all the consequences that come with that,' Francois says, and Azura flicks a glance at him again. I feel like a conduit for their conversation with each other.

Not quite finished yet, someone says through Jane, 'Watch, Clive, just watch how you have created your own hell. If you become aware of it, it will be the greatest moment in your life, because from there your transformation can begin, and it's clear you need to start a new life, a new phase of this lifetime. So watch carefully each step you take and be a little more conscious. In fact, just by watching, it will simply start disappearing.' Jane pauses, then seems to come out of the trance-like fuzz.

I say, 'Jane, what's concerning me is travel.'

'You want to go away somewhere?' Francois says, with relief in his voice that Jane's trance is over.

'No, I think I've been somewhere, that's the thing. It's me who's been doing this for centuries. It's happened a couple of times now, when I feel as if everything converges into this moment – all my past lives and my future lives, as if we have a concept of time which is entirely false. The first time it happened, or at least the first time I became conscious of it, was the night Sarah disappeared, you know, last year. Images, places, and people scrolled behind my eyelids, and I was scared shitless but I thought I was just strained and confused.' Francois pushes back his chair, as if fearful this is contagious. 'Actually I think it also happened once on the road above my house, when the energies of Calix, Sarah, and me came together. I hadn't even met Jade nor her ex, Gino, but they were there, flashing by – even the both of you, Francois and Azura. Somehow we are all connected in time.' Jim would be so freaked-out by this, I really should tell him just for the fun of it.

'No kidding?' Azura says, smiling, I imagine at Francois' discomfort.

'I'm serious. And I think that Jade is the reincarnation of the unborn baby we lost, Angelique.'

'What?' Azura and Jane say together. Francois looks away.

Why am I confiding this just because they are waxing lyrical about me and my marriage? Is their audacity borne of the fact that they think they blew the whistle? I already knew about Sarah's relationship with Calix when they came to me, but I have never bothered to disinvest them of this view. Or are we all connected such that none are unfamiliar outsiders?

'Never mind. All I'm saying is that something is being played out here. It's already written, in fact, it's already happened, in the future. All I need to do is take note, or "watch" as Jane said.' Francois finds sudden interest in the soles of his shoes, looking surprised that they have soles. Perhaps he and Jim can console each other over a beer or two?

Then Jane says, 'I really have to go now, Clive, but from personal experience, all I can say is don't be kind and gentle in your divorce discussions. It's in your nature, but you'll regret it. You can always be generous later, by choice,' but I am only half-listening. When Jane leaves, I excuse myself from the table and walk the dogs alongside the deli. Jade walks past towards her house with the live fur of Pi-shu wrapped around her shoulders. She does not acknowledge me, like a Princess might disregard her cobbler. When I return to the deli, Francois and Azura have gone.

45

Do not believe in traditions because
they have been handed down for many
generations.

(Buddha)

Friday, 10 June 2011

I am mulling over her text message she sent me last night when she joins me at the deli. It says:

> *'I am so in love with you. I'm not sure this is mutual in the way I feel it and have been feeling that for some time now. I'm sorry I could not contain you this week in the way that I find usually comes naturally to me. It was good for me to hear you express your doubts about me too, whether I could be committed to a long-term relationship. Are you referring to William?'*

'I love you completely,' Jade says the moment she sits down, her baby blues searching mine. Since I have known her, she may lean back to create some distance but I have never seen her turn her gaze away from me, even in the most difficult part of a conversation, and I have so valued this trait as I cannot remember when last Sarah has looked me in the eyes except in jaw-jutting anger. In fact, I don't think I can remember her smile or laughter. 'And I had a taste yesterday of feeling needy and not being able to have those needs met.'

'What were you needing?'

'Simple things, really.'

'Tell me. I'd like to know.'

'Things like . . . needing to be held gently by you, and being able to express my love openly. And feeding you my chicken korma while we sit together on the couch. Couple stuff, I guess. And I had a taste of the resentment that a prolonged period of that could bring. By early evening, I felt drained and was not feeling good with myself, and I realised this is only going to get harder on a human level.'

'Sarah has given me an ultimatum of sorts,' I say, 'to stop seeing you. I told her I would talk with you and clarify our boundaries. I kept telling her that what we should be focusing on is our relationship, hers and mine, not what's going on between you and me. Which I suspect has run its course, really, at a physical or romantic level at least, though I didn't say that to her.'

Jade does not respond to my last comment. Instead we speak briefly about what had happened on Saturday, and it leaves us hopeful that it was the unexpected public nature of it that set Sarah off.

'I think we are in denial, Jade. She will never make the leap to what we are hopeful of creating here.'

'You need to believe before you can bring it into being,' Jade reminds me.

She leans forward and runs her fingers lightly across my forearm and says, 'My soul will always be in awe of what goes on here between us. My dreams last night were affirmations of who I am despite my shaky exterior. It was really beautiful. Linda slept over and while I was sitting chatting to her, warmth suddenly spread though my body and I felt a deep sense of my worth. You really started something, Clive, and I had another first of many recent firsts—my very first experience of my own worth without my beautiful new mirror sitting in front of me. Today I feel worthy of twenty-seven bright, clean, pure pumpkin shells.'

This sounds good, just the stuff I would hope to hear from her if I was inclined to impose my wishes for her on her. To see her beautiful and energized, waking in the morning without her body in pain, feeling good enough to dance again and take up jogging, ready to re-enter life again since Wade's death nearly three years ago, to emerge from her self-imposed reclusive lifestyle and internal journey of self-discovery and moments of wishing herself away when it all became too much.

'But where there are gifts, there is always potential for damage too,' she says. 'This is the nature of duality. And suddenly the triangle is not an option for me anymore. In fact, it's the triangle that created the shaky me in the first place. Memories of Mom and Dad, either fighting or loving each other behind a locked door, and me going "what about me?" and always feeling left out. Do I want to perpetuate the shaky me or do I want to shine?' Harry needs to take a leak; someone closed the gate to the courtyard and he has almost gone squint. So I ask Jade to pause that thought. I am sure she is aware of the other triangle she preserves with Gino and is establishing with William. When I come back, she continues where she left off.

'You asked me the other day why I never had good men banging down my door. I know this is about to change, you have raised the bar and I have made a choice to act honourably on my own behalf because I have a new experience of myself now, thanks to you, precious, beautiful man. William arrives later today. You know that I met him about six months ago and this thing has been simmering between us. And that a while ago, he said he had been dreaming of me every night for many weeks, some of it quite sensual as I mentioned, but in a spiritual or sacred way. I had engaged with him in conversation because I felt comfortable to, and my initial gut feel about him had been good. And whenever I went to see him, we connected well. So I have decided that I am going to take a closer look at it and see for myself as I sense that there is learning there for me. I have told him the depth of us, you and me.'

Okay, this sounds not so good. Not the stuff I would like to hear from her if I was inclined to impose my wishes for myself on her. She keeps talking about it, repeating things; it is not going away. Our recent conversation about William escapes from its little box neatly stashed in one corner in the attic of my mind away from all others and hurtles through my mind like a captive beast. I resort to another cigarette and fashion a twirly-whirly.

Jade says, 'Clive, I am letting my dream of you-with-me go to the universe and surrendering to co-creation though love. For you and for myself. So I wish you well with your marriage and I pray that this time will catalyse the change that is needed for you to be powerfully in love together and that you start to get your needs met in a more meaningful way.'

My mind is reeling. I'm a little confused by what she has said. Was her confrontation with Sarah just too much for her? Is this a 'Dear Jonny'? I disguise my feelings behind a smile and ask, 'Is this a "Dear Jonny"? I don't think I've ever had one before.' She smiles at me, sad but self-assured. I say, 'Look, I think we should just leave this now and come back to it in a few days. I know that what happened at Azura's party has really shaken you up; me too. I am expecting something to happen, for someone else to do something, something that is not in my control and is not part of the dream.'

'Like what?'

'Like divorce papers.'

'I feel like you have withdrawn from me this week,' she says. 'The week before Azura's party I felt we were at a pinnacle. I felt so abundant with love when we met that day, and I had that awesome connection with your boys. I felt I could embrace Sarah and everything that comes with this situation. But since then it feels like the bubble has burst.'

The boys have met Jade a number of times, usually at the deli, and sometimes her ginger kitten was with her, which the boys have adored, each in their own way. But what astonished me was the connection they had forged with her in Sarah's absence. She had no pretence about her when they interacted; she did not pretend to be anyone other than who she is, and she never feigned to replace their mother in Sarah's absence.

'It feels like that to me too,' I say. 'And I understand that it can feel like I have pulled back, at least from our deep conversations, because I have, for reasons I have explained,' and then realize she is waiting for me to recap them. So I say, 'I am feeling skittish, on high alert, and very wary of people who might be watching us now, so my behaviour with you has changed in public, to protect both of us. Even now, I am watching out for Gino or Sarah or someone who might see us together and jump to conclusions about us even though our paths have begun to diverge. So I'm not even looking at you while you speak, and I am so guarded about how our interaction may appear to others. I just don't want to incite something when it is so combustible. And I can feel you are scared, and I don't know how to protect you.'

'When Debi was massaging me yesterday,' Jade says, 'she said that one of her friends Natalie was observing us at deli the other day. You may remember a blonde girl I greeted at the table next to you on that very busy Sunday. She had seen Debi later and made a comment that I was there with a family, but I greeted a guy first, that was you, and there was something not okay with you. She is gifted in discerning energies, so I decided to call her. I did not lead or prompt her at all. I asked her what she saw, and she said she saw a black cloud over you of both suppression and oppression, as if you are suppressing something like the shadow emotions of anger or rage, and that there is an energy in your life oppressing you. And she said your kindness and goodness were clearly visible and she wanted to make eye contact. She said your eyes showed pain. It's amazing what people observe in a few minutes. And I think my sadness around you lifted when I allowed myself to voice what may have seemed judgmental and which had become a frustration to me and I had wanted to retract it.'

I say, 'What are you talking about?'

'Your long-suffering in your marriage. Every time you've had enough, she throws you a few crumbs, and that keeps you going. I have told you this is one of the things I so admire in you and why I think you are a good man, but as I listened to the elaboration of what Natalie saw, that you are under someone else's oppression and that it is making your soul "sick", it helped me to understand the long journey you have to embark on to get yourself back.'

If she is intending to lift my spirits with this, she is going about it the wrong way. 'Let me tell you what has been occupying my mind lately,' I say. 'I'm feeling exasperated because she just won't connect with me. And I am so disillusioned because I have realized that what I thought a committed marriage or relationship meant to me has evaporated. I feel like I could not have been more wrong, and the problem is, I'm not yet sure what has taken its place. I have been floundering around trying to create my future, hoping Sarah will be part of it. But I have not yet discovered who I am. I haven't yet invented myself.'

I had been saying for months that after Sarah's affair I was recalibrating my assumed views of all the concepts inherent in love—trust and honesty, sharing and openness, respect and privacy—but I am not sure yet whether I have settled with a significantly different perspective on any of these issues. And the railway tracks that appeared in my thoughts while in conversation with Jane and the others, linger, troubling me. I suppose I thought that the way we were together when our relationship started is the way we would stay, entities rolling along on perfectly equidistant channels forever, like railroad trucks I read about somewhere on the 143.5-centimetres distance between two tracks of a standard gauge railway line, that measurement precisely because of history and tradition and expectations cast in stone and taking into account neither the modern day requirements of rail transport nor the unique experience of the individuals and the context in which they find themselves. That thought brought on the uncomfortable feeling of being in a rut.

And I imagined, as changes happened and challenges arose, like having children, that the terrain might transform into a treacherous winding mountainous ascent to be negotiated together with care and effort-induced steam, working as a team in support of each other by shovelling precise amounts of coal and ensuring that too much pressure does not build up. And that even in the darkest moments, we would press on through gloomy tunnels burrowed through mounds of seemingly insurmountable distress and, exhausted, find a light at the end of the tunnel where we would turn our sweat-drenched soot-blackened faces to each other, produce a reassuring smile, and breathe a mutual sigh of relief as our marriage-train steams on towards the easy meanderings of old age together. But would either of us be better people as a result? And, anyway, this presupposes that we both had the same growth needs, and experienced the same stressors and in the same way, and that we would respond in similar fashion. But of course we had not, and if the space between your mutual life-paths also varied, as our tracks had, presenting unexpected kinks in the rails, would that derail the train? This is sort of what it felt like; trying to put the wrecked train back on the track all the time, only to be derailed at the very next turn, because we never attended to the core problem with the railway tracks. We never got round to fixing it. Or is it the train?

I think now of Sarah, and how she said she had chosen to be with me, to stay in our marriage despite loving Calix, to return to me or not to leave me, depending on how you view things, because of the challenges I bring her as a result of being the type of person I am. It all felt a bit selfish really; I wonder what happens once your partner has decided they have learnt all they can from you. Can they really know when that moment has come, as relationships ebb and flow and people grow in spurts and lulls, seldom in sync with each other? How can I be sure of this moment?

Jade puts her hand on my shoulder, wondering where my mind has gone. 'So this scholarly approach,' I say to Jade, 'to learn and grow through a challenging relationship, really tested my idea of commitment and marriage.'

'You're learning some tough lessons about life and love.'

'But I think it is because we are immersed in trivia, stuck in old, self-defeating paradigms, never getting to address real issues, like who we really are. When being true to myself and honest with her made me feel too vulnerable to her retaliation, I was no longer able to truly see her and I defined my worth as how she saw me. I could see this happening before my eyes, but I did nothing about it. And that's what saddens me now.'

Jade says, 'But I think you are more real today than before, even if you feel you cannot locate it or name it.'

And she leaves without saying goodbye.

—◦◦◦—

The weather is fair to middling and there is a smattering of occupied tables both inside and out. I am thinking that this is not one of my best days, and wonder not whether but when it will get worse. Seconds later Sarah arrives with the boys, and I think that at least my angels are smiling down on me today by choreographing this so smoothly, just one woman at a time.

'Shouldn't the au pair be with you?' I say, then realize it is probably not the best opening line. But to tell her she is unofficially no longer welcome here, after accusing Samantha of being an accomplice to my relationship with Jade, would surely have been a worse option. We have just settled down when Stilla arrives with her son and they sit at the table next to us and I introduce her to Sarah. I had met Stilla a few years ago, in another coffee shop, and we had a couple of conversations about the work we have in common. At that time she was in a long-distance relationship of twelve years, and the man in her life was about to relocate and move into her home and she was excited but rattled by what this might mean for them. At one point Stilla had said, 'I must tell you I am attracted to you, but I don't know why. I feel I want to mother you,' and we had both laughed at this. I never saw her again until now, as the last two days she has come to the deli for coffee, yesterday with her man, today with her grown son.

Sarah not-quite-mumbles how disgusting this woman is; I can hear it clearly and I feel that everybody else can, and I wish I had been firmer about her not being welcome here with an attitude. She has a habit of doing this, expressing aloud her repulsion of someone, and it infuriates me. I wonder if all the women somehow connected to this moment will descend upon this poor restaurant today.

'Oh, so you're the woman Clive is so attracted to?' Sarah says, as Stilla politely gets up and comes towards her to greet her properly, and this stops Stilla in her tracks. As if expecting one of us to answer her, Sarah looks aggressively at me then at Stilla and back again with an 'isn't that so' accusation on her face. Last year, fearing I would leave her after I found out about her affair, Sarah had asked me about 'other women' I was friends with. There weren't really any significant enough to speak of, so thinking hard I had mentioned my infrequent chats with Stilla amongst some others. Now I feel indignant; she is abusing a confidence I had shared with her.

'Look, boys,' Sarah says, 'this is daddy's girlfriend,' and I can see their confusion as she usually tells them that Jade is my girlfriend. Stilla tries to brush it off with some over-friendly remark and a shaky smile. I look at Stilla, who looks at me then at Sarah, and excuses herself to go to the bathroom. I suggest to the boys that they play for a while on the jungle gym.

Sarah is bristling, and I concentrate on not being impaled by her porcupine quills. 'Sarah,' I say, leaning close to keep it private, 'that was awkward and unnecessary, to say the least.'

'If you are offended by it, you should ask yourself why.'

I ask myself that question often, I thought, so I will tell you why, Sarah. 'What you're feeling actually has nothing to do with Stilla and you don't need to lay it on her. I just think it's confrontational and unnecessarily embarrassing for her, and confusing for the boys.' It is more in the tone of her voice than what she said.

'It's the truth. And that's my gift to the universe. I say the truth, things that people don't want to hear, and it gives them something to think about.' This is likely what Calix convinced her of, that she adds value by being authentic. If only that was what she did, or was; a whole person presenting all of herself, it may be received as a gift, untainted by her own stuff. Can't she see that she does or says things to other people without their permission, out-of-context remarks that may hurt or confuse them?

'Sarah, you do this with all my friends and acquaintances, especially females. Neither Stilla nor I feel better nor wiser because of what you have said. She and I have discussed it long ago, so I think you have used what I told you for your own ends, not for anyone else's benefit. There is no value in what you have done.'

But Sarah is already out of her chair and on her way inside the restaurant before I finish the sentence. Little Jack follows her, and as I light a cigarette I peer through the open inter-leading doorway and I see her, arms folded and head leaning forward somewhat aggressively, talking to Samantha. Jack turns around and smiles broadly and makes as if to go somewhere but Sarah pulls him back and I hear her admonishing him and the look of self-reproach on his face. Samantha's voice suddenly carries to me, and everybody sitting inside must be able to hear their conversation. 'You need to let that go, Sara-lea,' Samantha says. 'As far as I know Jade is deeply involved with another man.'

I see Sarah's lips move again, and then hear Samantha tell her to 'Fuck off.' Sarah follows Jack outside, and Jack shouts to me, 'Mommy won't let me say hello to Jade.'

Her eyes spitting fire at me, and with as much hurtful and malicious intent she can garner, Sarah says, 'Now I know why you are here; because she is. It must really hurt you now that she has a boyfriend.' Jade must have returned without us seeing her. Perhaps she forgot something here.

Jack has a guilty look on his face and casts his eyes downwards and says, 'Daddy, you are not allowed to speak to Jade.' I am so angry with Sarah that she has left Jack feeling like this.

'Sarah, please. Don't involve the boys.' I have not said this before, but now I feel it is overdue. 'I'm surprised that someone with your experiences in childhood, of parents whose horrific actions and words so affect you still today, is not more keenly aware of the impact you're having on them. If you have issues with Stilla or Jade or with me, for that matter, don't lay it on them. Let them interact with Jade and talk about her.'

Just then Stilla returns from the bathroom and Sarah grabs her stuff to go. 'He is attracted to blonds like you,' Sarah says, with her back to Stilla and her head half-turned. Why is it that I never quite know what to do in these situations?

'You have beautiful hair,' Stilla says, with a half-smile, trying to hold her own but looking quite uncomfortable and unsure of how to deal with this.

Sarah steps forward and stands toe-to-toe with Stilla, and says, 'Oh, I know I'm beautiful inside,' and then she leaves through the gate of the courtyard.

I put Jack on my lap as he wants to play a game on my computer. Stilla waits for a while, absorbing what has happened. When Jack wonders off to play on the jungle gym and is out of earshot she says, 'I can see you have a real problem there, Clive.'

'I'm sorry about that.'

'No, that's okay. I'm not taking it personally. I understand it's her stuff. On the surface of it, in EQ terms, that was just a lack of self-regulation, and probably a lack of empathic and social or relationship skills. But I can see she has some deep-seated stuff, and I really should not say this, but there is definitely some psychological condition behind that.' Stilla might be blond but she is insightful and perceptive and is not referred to as 'professor' in other circles for no reason, so I know this is coming from her professional observation. 'Those wounds are deep, Clive, much too deep for you to believe you can rescue her. And I can see it's taking its toll on you.' Stilla is speaking without malice, but with concern, slowly and pausing between each sentence for me to respond and continuing because I don't. 'If you are not happy at home, you will find someone else, and she can probably see this coming. She is acting with jealousy, but not with love, as if she picks up things are suddenly not just about her anymore. It's quite narcissistic, actually. Her focus was entirely on herself and she was reacting solely on the basis of how that situation affected her. You need to watch how that affects you.'

Stilla waits for me to signal if I want to hear more, but I say, 'We are in a tough place at the moment.'

And she says, 'She is hard, Clive, she has hardened herself, and you are soft. So be careful. Prepare yourself for the worst, she is going to take you apart.'

FALLING APART

46

You are in a pitiable condition when you
have to conceal what you wish to tell.

(Syrus)

Wednesday, 15 June 2011

I have been thinking a lot about secrets and secrecy lately, how I felt it had destroyed me and our relationship. That it silently eats away at your integrity, corroding the essence of who you are, and that when the rust and decay reveals itself, it is too late to repair, it has to be excised. What is the antioxidant?

Something happened this afternoon which I have not yet raised with Sarah. At lunchtime Joshua was playing games on the computer, and when I thought to check on what he was up to, I saw he was in Sarah's email. I wanted to close it down but something caught my eye, an email from someone called Michael, and before I knew it I had scanned it and was gripped by its content. So I scrolled through the thread of messages and read from the beginning, more carefully this time, while my stomach twisted and my hands quivered and my heart bled. Starting a few months ago, it traced a forming relationship; his words at first wondrous and appreciative of her finer qualities and their invigorating times together, then syrupy sweet and provocative, and the penultimate one lamenting the times they cannot be together, cuddling on his couch, drinking red wine before a roaring fire and such things. She sent brief responses from time to time, but they were fairly innocuous, cheery and encouraging words of appreciation for him—not incriminating, but perhaps she is more cautious than he needs to be. The latest email from him, the one that had caught my eye, is much more explicit, describing her remarkable breasts and sexy stomach and the enticing trail of fine hairs at the base of her back which lead to mounds of the softest skin which encase the target strip of his desire, or vocabulary to that effect. Then his words boldly declared that it was her fault he finds her so kissable and how he simply cannot keep himself at arm's length from her, such is the impact on him of her perfection.

I was astounded. Was this for real, or just his fantasy?

In that post-dinner, pre-bedtime for boys, we are leaning back in our chairs at the dinner table while the boys irritate each other in an overtired frenzy. My mind is awash with secrets. Low vibration ego jealousies surfaced and challenged what seems to me a more respectable petition for honesty, a plea for integrity and openness, where love and acceptance can shine. As I sit with her now, jealousy, thinly masquerading as truth, flares up and overpowers any good intent. I should raise my concerns with her and give her a chance to help me understand the true nature of their relationship, but I know she will deny everything and pick a fight with me or simply stick her fingers in her ears and refuse to talk about it.

At times I am convinced Sarah knows all about us, but I need to have another go at explicitly declaring the full truth about my relationship with Jade and what it has meant to me in order for us to go forward together. I need to warm her up to it, and gauge her receptiveness. This time I try a circuitous route to gently ease into the topic. I look at her and put my hand on hers.

'Hypothetically, if you could be guaranteed that your worst fears would not come true, that there would be no unpleasant consequences for you, would this free you up to be more honest and open with me?'

'What are you talking about?' Sarah says, pushing my hand away.

'I just think that we hide stuff because we are worried about what might happen if we don't keep it secret. I know I do it.'

'Are you talking about yourself?'

'Of course. But this could be anyone, including you and me.' She looks at me and folds her arms in self-protective mode. I need to be judicious; if she thinks I am leading somewhere with this that will put her in a corner and she will come out spitting fury or throw in the towel and walk out of the conversation before it gets any traction. I do not know whether her anxiety and vigilance stems from the fear of potentially losing me or the fear that I know what is really going on in her life.

Precisely how Calix transitioned from client-to-friend-to-lover is being played out again with 'Mr Arms' Length', and I beat this delinquent thought away with such vehemence it ricochets off the lounge walls. We get up and take the dishes to the kitchen; a helpful relocation as I ward off the indignation I feel that rises like a tidal wave and washes over me, and I was about to confront her head-on about this guy, Michael. The boys sink into their allotted couches to watch the end of a wildlife rescue programme on television, and while we tidy up in the kitchen and out of earshot, we continue the conversation.

'There is nothing going on,' Sarah says, as if she knows where my thoughts are going, and steps into the courtyard and lights a cigarette, and I follow. There was a time that this action was a bonding experience.

The need for integrity has swept all other fears and values out the way. 'I don't really care if there is, Sarah.' Can't she understand that her affair, past or current, is not the issue? It's about how we relate to each other, our dysfunctional communication, our fear-ridden reactions, our sparring interactions, our critical labels and assumptions. 'The issue is about trust and openness in our relationship, for us to confront real issues, not trivia. It's about being authentic and real with each other because, outside of myself, I need you to be my source of truth. And when you say those words they fall into the "I-don't-know-whether-this-is-true" Calix block.'

She goes quiet, thoughtful. It will soon be time for me to put the boys to bed and it is too late to open the topic of Jade. I feel frustrated, again, that we cannot name our truths knowing that it will be absorbed and integrated into whom we are. And I'm rattled about what happened

earlier today. 'But let's rather bring it into today, Sarah, because that's all
that matters. Whether it's Calix or this other guy, or in my case, Jade, I
think that we walk around with unnecessary guilt.' She has gone rigid,
petrified, but in response to which name I am uncertain. Perhaps it is
all three? 'And the need to be clandestine about these things must be
exacting a terrible toll. I certainly feel it. And the chasm . . .'

'He's a client who became a friend,' she says, throwing her cigarette
into the pot plant. 'How dare you be so disrespectful? You have no right
to raise him!'

'Sarah . . . ' but her fingers are in her ears as she disappears inside.
How does she even know who I am talking about?

Later, when she is getting ready for bed, she says, 'What did you
mean when you said the other day that I have kept words from Calix?'

I am lying in bed, reading, and really want to avoid an argument to end
the day or give any opportunity to reopen the events of Saturday at Azura's
party, so I say, 'Nothing in particular, it just seemed obvious to me that you
would keep what he has written you given that you keep other stuff.'

'But I only got letters from him at the very beginning.' That she has
received letters from him, and much more recently, of that I am now
certain, because I have seen them or at least some of them. And she is
afraid I know this, perhaps even know the content. She is not wrong that
I know what is going on, but has no need to be anxious about it.

'Uhuh,' I say, feeling it is the safest response.

'So how . . . What are you . . . What I mean is I don't understand
why you brought it up?' She is stumbling over her words and it is so
unusual for her to open any conversation about him that I am alerted
to the possibility that she is sounding worried and this feeds my doubts
related to the stories I have recently heard.

'What are you concerned about?'

'Nothing,' she says. 'I trashed some of his letters long ago and the
rest I left with someone to destroy for me,' which I find difficult to

believe but we leave it at that. She is clearly shaken. And now so am I and I cannot fall asleep after she has raised this issue which inflates for me the spectre of doubt inspired by the stories that have washed over me these past few weeks. I really thought I had moved beyond these feelings, but lying here I have this intense desire to get away from it all, from this house, this street, and this town. I do the next best thing.

'I'm going to have a cigarette,' I say, and leave her to her thoughts, wondering why her reaction to these things seemed so ominous to me, so anxiety-ridden and defensive.

I sit outside in the cold night air and think about what is bothering me. I have been really pissed-off since the confrontation, and not just because of what happened at Azura's son's party. This morning Jade had told me what had transpired while walking on the mountain when she bumped into Lucy, her homeopath/kinesiologist, the one who said she knows me. The only person Jade says she has told the full story about us during a treatment, and a person I was immediately wary of. And when I told Sarah a month ago that I thought Lucy was part of the grapevine divulging rumours about her ongoing relationship with Calix, Sarah had been furious and worried in equal measure, saying that it is not acceptable for Lucy to disclose information given in confidence during a clinical consultation. Lucy had told Jade this morning, 'It's still going on, you know,' referring to Calix and Sarah, and this is why I thought this is the time to offer Sarah the option of being open about things without fear of negative consequences. Lucy had also said, 'Perhaps now she knows just how Delia felt.' Delia and Calix had ended their marriage in 2007, perhaps just months before Sarah said she had met Calix.

Jade said to Lucy, 'Can I tell Clive what you have said?'

'Yes.'

So Jade told me. And then I phoned Lucy, after much debate with myself, and I am still not sure why I did it but to be honest I was starting to think that I might need some ammunition of my own. And because last week someone in the health store where Sarah has her consulting rooms, saying that she hates doing this but is 'concerned about it' after what happened last year, told me that she thinks there is something going on between Sarah and one of the other healthcare practitioners, and she mentioned the name of a man with whom Sarah regularly 'talent-swops'—treating him free of charge in return for the speciality or preference he can offer in return.

'Why are you telling me this?' I said to her.

'I just thought . . .'

And I said, 'If something is concerning you, why don't you speak to Sarah about it.' But it threw me. The situation with Calix I think I can work with; it is somehow familiar. But I have been completely blind to the possibility that there is someone else. My obsession with Calix has put me right off the scent. I now know she was referring to Sarah's 'arms' length' client-friend. The thought of it has left me jittery and uncertain and rational argument with myself cannot settle me.

But Lucy was disappointingly wary and not as forthcoming as I had expected, and she told me to decide whether I really have a marriage and to leave Jade out of it. When I pushed her, she told me it was just conjecture. I pushed her more, and she told me to hire a private detective and I will find out all I need to know. Not the first time I have heard that.

So I said, 'If you are hesitant to talk to me, this is how I feel. It seems that Sarah or Calix has confided in you in a confidential session and you say you have heard stories from others and this you have passed on as "it's still going on". Not only have you broken a professional confidence, but if you are saying this to people then I ask you to tell me what you are basing this on as this is my marriage you are talking about.'

Lucy put the phone down without responding, but shortly after sent a text message:

> *'I am sorry for your confusion in your marriage, Clive. I am usually very confidential about what has been told to me in my therapy room, and I deeply regret my slip-up with telling Jade and I know it will never happen again. I only confirmed this to Jade*

to give her peace of mind as Sara-lea was threatening her with
violence. As to telling you details of what I know, that will never
happen. The state of your marriage, well, that is for you to decide.
Please consider this our last communication about this topic.'

Irritated with her and feeling unsettled, I had started something in my mind and was unable to let it go. I had inadvertently set something in motion, which was not the problem, but it came from a place deep within me of fear and frustration, not love and acceptance. I imagined the worried, conspiratorial conversations taking place across this beautiful valley of which I am not aware. I was alarmed that there was stuff going on here that I knew nothing about, and that there were people and relationships involved in this that were way beyond my comprehension. I felt completely out of the loop and out of my depth. Being honest and open suddenly seemed like it was more likely to put Jade or me in danger than sort things out and clarify relationships. Expecting others to be candid and upfront with me seemed daft, and I didn't know whose game to play now.

As I replay the day's events through in my mind, I light another cigarette and stretch out on my back in the courtyard and look up at the night sky, searching for guidance in the stars. But they twinkle back at me with a message I cannot decipher, and I wonder whether this is all just a huge cosmic joke and I am the only one who has missed the punchline.

My conscience likes to leap forward and explore possible futures and return to report in and in this way I find my peace, my path. But the stealth-drones disappear into the ether and none return, lost to the cause. I think of peoples who, in history, have collectively established a cause, a Notion—in my case, to create my future, or polyamory, or something like that; I'm not even sure what it is anymore and maybe that is the problem. And at some point, the Notion becomes so powerful, it holds sway over the people. I guess no one can identify how and when this transition happens, and some of the people are martyred to the Notion which has become omnipotent, a power in itself. This is how I begin to feel, buffeted around. The plot, the dream, the 'great idea' now has a life of its own and for its own ends, and as much as I like to talk it up, to go with the flow, now that I stare at the reality of it I am petrified.

My back aches from lying prone on the unforgiving courtyard paving. It must be well after midnight, and I am getting a bit chilly. The stars have simply reflected back my thoughts, but without the benefit of useful illumination. For some reason, I start recalling Jim's words all those months ago; what was that term he used—'strange attractors'. And that if I could pin them down, I would be able to hold onto my core and be at my most creative. Would 'co-creating' count? Because of 'bi-something or other', that there are endless possibilities, many possible futures I could choose from? I can sense that the situation has escalated, and have perhaps been anticipating a change of pace, but the swiftness and the shifting balance of power has not rewarded me with enlightenment. If I understood Jim correctly, I should expect things to fall apart and then rebuild, anew. But I might have got that wrong; it seemed so contradictory to his 'I am the master of my own destiny' approach.

Wanting to shake these thoughts from my mind, I go inside and see a pack of cards on the kitchen table; Sarah's horse cards. I take them outside and sit in the courtyard and close my eyes and think of Jade. The card I draw is the 'White Horse: Rasa Dance' (card number 38, adds to 11, signifies life path for me) and I read about it in the accompanying booklet, recalling Jade's reference to the significance of the number 'eleven'. I learn that Rasa is the shortened name for the Mare of Linda actually called Tabula Rasa (clean slate). This card, it says, is about authenticity in action, co-creation, and the music of connection. I read it:

> *A swirl of energy connects two beings dancing in spontaneous flow. Freed from the limitations of species, roles and expectations, they move in timeless communication where thought becomes form and open hearts lead the dance.*

The Gift

Here's where we put all the pieces together, where new concepts and conventional methods fuse and expand, creating unexpected possibilities. Authenticity in action draws on responsiveness, assertiveness, discernment, physical collection, mental, and emotional agility, fluidity of consciousness, imagination, nonverbal communication, subtle body awareness, intuition, consensual leadership and the paradox of boundaries and oneness.

The Challenge

When two beings move in synchrony, a greater consciousness arises and with it a feeling of ecstasy. Can you stay present and focused during these moments of intense joy? Can you accept the gift of expanded awareness without becoming addicted to it? If the next moment offers frustration, indecision, conflict, performance anxiety, or miscommunication, can you dance with that too?

How weird is that? I put the booklet and the cards into my pocket, and walk from the courtyard down to the garden dimly lit by the shy moonlight and the distant glow of city lights reminding me that I am not alone. I walk around the pool marvelling at the jiggling reflections which disappear just as I am tempted to grab them and make them mine. I feel compelled to sit down on the grass, heavy and damp with dew, and try to absorb the beauty of the silhouetted mountains and the twinkling lights in the valley below me.

I close my eyes and think of Sarah lying in the bedroom behind my back and draw a card. It is the 'Black Horse: Boundary Dance' (card number 18, adds to 9, for me signifies completion). It says—negotiating personal space, holding your ground, anger, frustration or incongruence. I am astounded. Consulting the booklet, I learn more:

Two horses approach each other, ears pinned slightly and tails swishing in anticipation, they begin the tenuous dance of respect and connection.

The Gift

When anger shows up, it signals that someone has invaded your physical or psychological space, perhaps unconsciously, perhaps with the intention to control or take advantage of you. Either way, the surge of energy that accompanies this emotion helps you stand your ground when someone pushes your boundaries.

The Challenge

It takes courage and awareness to use anger judiciously. You must be willing to tell someone to back off when he or she steps over the line, even if the person has 'authority' over you. If anger is expressed appropriately it does not need to come out sideways directed inappropriately at an innocent party.

So the number of the white horse card, which I extracted with Jade in my mind, signifies my life path; thinking of Sarah conjured up the black horse which denotes completion. Needing help with this, I turn to the introduction at the front of the booklet, which offers the following insights. Horses teach that anger in its pure form is indicative of a boundary violation. Frustration, which may look like anger, comes when we are doing something that no longer works and both intensify to rage if they are not dealt with appropriately and immediately. I know it well. Reading on, it says 'Rage turned inward leads to addictions, depression or illness. Agitation, which seems like anger or irritation, is present when we are facing someone who is incongruous; in other words, what they are presenting is not what they are truly feeling.'

It is a mouthful, and I think it has just left me more confused than ever. Anger, frustration, rage, agitation—I know these feelings, I know them well. I don't like them, never have. They repulse me, whether it is me feeling them or I feel them in others, I always want to get out of that space. They are not my friends, and I don't know how to use them. I am not even sure I know how to distinguish between them. But I do know that things feel incongruous; that was the tension I felt and tried to describe to Sarah, and I feel it now. And I do know that boundaries have been crossed. Consciously and unconsciously, physical, emotional and psychological or psychic boundaries are being tampered with, and there are few people in my orbit who feel okay, fully intact and centred.

I climb on to the small jungle gym we erected for the boys, and lie on my back looking up at the stars. Still they do not grace me with insight; or perhaps they have, but I am not sure I like what I am thinking. Forces are coalescing, and I appreciate that the next move is mine to make. My future is at hand.

In the end, does it all rest on the draw of a card?

47

Do not believe in anything merely on the
authority of your teachers and elders.

(Buddha)

Monday, 20 June 2011

Last night I made my move.

It is early, long before sunrise. I had got to bed late and enjoyed perhaps two hours of uninterrupted sleep before I woke up and lay there for hours with persistent but fuzzy thoughts and a throbbing headache, before I surrendered the warmth of the duvet. Harry and Sally were less inclined to do so; though they were lying on top of the duvet, or I could say on top of me without too much exaggeration. In the darkness I first patted the bed around me to make sure there were no other Homo sapiens curled up there on whom I may inflict damage. Then it took all my willpower and repeated nudging and whispered instruction from me to encourage them to relinquish the plush comfort of a spring mattress and body warmth and pleasant doggy dreams for what they knew was to come—the bitter cold and damp drizzle and unyielding paving outside. And to make matters worse, experience has shown that there would likely be one or two other occupants in this bed when we return, freezing and tired, such is the musical-chair extravaganza that seems to increase in pace as the night wears on.

So I sit here on a hard, wet, all-weather patio-and-garden wrought-iron chair, ankles crossed, and calves resting above hip-height on the matching garden table, and feel my lower back go into spasm in protest against the ungainly position I have assumed for the last hour. I am wrapped in a marginally weather-proof jacket, but the persistent light rain is starting to seep through the outer layers of down feathers and the cold has set up residence in my bones. The dogs put up with it for a few minutes then wondered off together to sulk under the slight warmth of the night-lights beneath the cantilevered balcony overhanging the pool, where they still lay in the bitter cold and on the unyielding paving but would at least stay dry. Every now and then, they raised their heads to check that I had not sneaked inside without them. It occurs to me that if I wished to rinse away whatever it was that clung to me and brought me to this state of mind; it would be much quicker and more effective to hop in the shower. Self-flagellation might even be preferable, but it seems I have chosen the route of the wheel or the rack or some such barbaric contraption.

Mostly I think of last night. Sarah had been pushing me about Jade and our marriage all week, wanting feedback on her ultimatum, and after I had put the boys to sleep and wondered drowsy and yawning into our bedroom, I found her propped up against a continental pillow sowing the hem of one of the boys' school trousers, the cats curled up next to her.

'Do you want anything from the kitchen before I come to bed?' I said.

'I'm ready to have that conversation now,' she said.

'Let's rather have this conversation in the lounge, Sarah, not in our bed.'

'We will have it here or we won't have it,' she said. 'I feel safe here.'

She wanted to control this moment, and in my head a battle ensued about whether I should take her on or relent. So I told her I will come back when she is ready, and I let the dogs out for a leak and tried to gather my thoughts. Last year I swallowed my dismay and felt I had to accept her stance, her approach to repairing our bond after her affair and her dismissive behaviour towards me. But last year broke me; it broke my heart. It would have healed, scarred but beautiful, had our souls met in loving, vulnerable honesty. And now I felt comfortable that I have given us enough time to show signs of doing this. With hindsight and a new-found sense of self, I think I now know who I am and won't do that again. For me, therefore, un-judged sharing and disclosure are minimum requirements of a relationship. And in this moment I feel with certainty that it is time to move on. I acknowledge that our marriage is over, the spiritual contract is broken; I know that with every part of me. What remains is a sham, an illusion, a fear-based pretence of togetherness. And for what? Ego, security, tradition? All fakes and charlatans, those. We just need to sign a paper, and move on to new beginnings. I know this choice will present me with a vacant future as William has extended his stay and romance is clearly in the air and they have made no pretense at disguising their affection. And that is why I can act now; the timing is right and this is for *me*, unfettered by others' expectations and unclouded by others' needs.

The dogs returned all-too-soon. The wet shine on their coats and blinking eyes reminded me just in time to stop them at the doorway and encourage them to shake outside before I let them in, and with them happily ensconced on their couch in the entrance hall, I walked unenthusiastically and stiff legged down the passage and sat down on the corner of the bed. Sarah was peeling an apple with a steak knife, and after waiting for a while, I asked her to please stop what she was busy with.

'I will stop in a moment when I am done,' Sarah said.

So I waited, and when she was done I said, 'We can't go on like this. Our marriage is not working.'

'That means we will get divorced,' she said.

'Is that what you want?' Why don't I leap at it?

'The only thing that prevents me is that I can't imagine being without the boys,' she said. So it is true, what I heard, and that she has felt this way since she met Calix. 'We will start by separating.'

'I just don't think that a separation will help. We're either in this or we aren't. But first I would be happy to think about how else we can do this and explore any alternatives.'

'There's nothing to discuss.' Sarah skewered the apple core with the knife.

'I would like to renegotiate the expectations we have in our relationship, to reach an understanding between us and agree how to be as parents and with each other in a different way, whether we are married or not.'

'There is nothing to negotiate,' she said, 'other than how to separate. That's what we will discuss with a mediator.' About a month ago, she had raised the option of mediation; probably after Jade appeared on her radar. Now it seemed she was fixed on the idea.

I tried again—'That seems like the obvious next step if we can't find another way. For me, this is not about what the outcome is, or at least it's not about the form of the outcome, but the substance.'

'What the hell does that mean?'

'It's important what's in our hearts as we go through this process. I want to do it with the right intention. Then we will be in a good space, wherever it ends up. So it may seem unconventional, but if it's a question of how we can still satisfy both our needs to be with the boys every day, I would like to speak with you first, with the support of a professional if you like, who can help us see if there are any options we cannot even imagine.' What am I thinking?

'Legally I don't have to say anything.'

I was certain that everything she has said so far has been a non-negotiable demand, a decision she has already taken, a stance she is defending; is she incapable of conversing without adversity?

'This is not about "legally" this or that, Sarah. It's about accepting the point we have reached and looking forward, together. To do that, we don't have to approach this from positions of adversity, like intimate enemies, and ruin or negate all the beauty we have experienced. There really is another way.'

Somehow my approach opened the door just a crack, and then we really talked. She told me how she was broken when we met, just weeks after her 'foster' father, the man she had met when she was six years old and had chosen to call 'Dad', had died and a few months after she had been attacked in her apartment. She said it had seemed to her that I was the person who would make life okay for her again, and in the years that followed our marriage, she started to feel whole again, despite all the lost pregnancies, and she was feeling more herself again and had come out fighting for her needs ever since then. But that after we terminated Angelique, everything went awry, and she spoke a little of her behaviour, of it at times being out of control, of how nasty she can be when she felt the need to protect herself, and of how she withdrew from intimacy and lived 'like a nun'. And I thought—'Who or what was Angelique to her? Why had she never truly recovered from that experience? It seemed to have an indelible impact on her sanity.'

When she spoke of how she withdrew into herself after all those lost pregnancies, I understood that although she launches barbed accusations at me for being the cause of her unhappiness, the pain really lay deep within her, profoundly deeper than I could ever access. I felt that I actually understood it, and her; that's why I am so close but too near for her sense of comfort and safety. My need was always to be closer to her, receptive, but she could not tolerate that for fear of annihilation from horrors exacted and received in this and other lifetimes. If I am her soul-mate mirror, then with me looming before her all the terror of self-revulsion is presented in stark relief. So when all else failed, in the last few years she ensured this distance in the starkest way possible by being with another. And her withdrawal from emotional and physical intimacy was the deepest hurt she could inflict on me and the most successful.

The conversation went well for a while; by that I mean it felt like it came from the heart yet not without vulnerability and pain, and that it was honest, candid, and without bullshit or vindictiveness. I listened carefully, and now and then shared with her some of my experience of us. Before I understood any of this, when I first chose to be with her, I remember the words 'payback time' echoing in my mind, and assumed it meant that it was my time to carry someone through their walk of fire, for her to lean on me as I had on my previous partners. Now I was aware that only she could work through the timeless guilt from past atrocities, but what I don't understand is how to approach life with her on this physical plane, this lifetime.

Then, unexpectedly, she ripped the knife from its juicy bed and pointed its tip at me and said, 'It's you who wants to dissolve our marriage!'

It was not the words so much, but the dark, malevolent energy that scorched the air. It was like she had flipped a switch and a different personality had come to the fore. Suddenly we were adversaries again, and I said, 'Sarah, I did not say that.' I should have just walked away with my new-found wisdom, but I always get caught off guard by this façade of reasonableness and sharing. And the insight I now had was happening before my eyes—we got too close for comfort in our conversation and she needed to repel me.

She leaned forward from her reclining position and the serrated blade nicked my chin as I flinched. I kept my arms at my side and it took all I had to resist grabbing her hand that held the knife.

'You did! You said you want to dissolve our marriage! And my name is Sara-lea!'

Yes, I could see that as her voice had changed; in fact, her whole face took on a different shape, like it lost personality, and seemed to be that of an entirely different person from just moments earlier. I was conscious that there was more to this name change than I had assumed.

But I was slow to catch on. 'What I said was I think we should renegotiate our marriage, relook the expectations we have in our relationship, with the help of . . .'

Sarah screamed, 'No, you didn't! You said you want to dissolve our marriage.'

' . . . a mediator if necessary. Then we can go our separate ways, and we can go with an appreciation of what we had and look to new beginnings with joy in our hearts.'

'No, you didn't!' she said again, and this time the knife-point hurt, and I thought I might soon look like Jack. 'I have taped the conversation. You're devious and deranged! You're mentally unstable!' she yelled.

This morning, sitting outside, I can hear the projections, but last night I lost it. Not outwardly so much, although my voice was strained and my body language was no doubt more aggressive as I sprang off the bed and stood up. But inside, deep inside my heart, I was repulsed by this person she becomes and thought that this short sentence of hers encapsulated who she was and was confirmation of all my feelings that my heart was not safe with her. She made no attempt to follow through with the knife but, now standing, I started shaking as fear coalesced with outrage and pumped through me.

'If you have taped this conversation, then show me the tape.' A more meaningless request I could not have made. It gave her an opportunity to feel fully in control.

'No.'

'It's not okay to do that, Sarah. Show me the tape.' I could hear the filing cabinet that exists in my head screech open on its rails and supplementary annotations were added under 'judgmental,' 'temperamental,' and 'manipulative'.

'I don't have to, you bastard!' Her tongue curled towards her chin in that unconscious habit she has when she was being spiteful and vindictive.

I started to walk away from her, towards the bedroom door, and said, 'People have warned me about this, about what you are most likely doing, that you are streetwise and vindictive and will approach this not with your heart. I told them I don't believe them, that they have you all wrong, but it's just that I didn't want to believe them.' Harry and Sally must have picked up on the change in my voice and stood still as statues, just other side the threshold with concern etched on their faces.

'Why are you so upset? What are you afraid of?' she said, goading me, challenging me. While she waited for me to respond, again her tongue extended from her mouth and beyond her lower lip.

I paused in the doorway, seething with a feeling I knew all too well as I lived with it almost every day—a chronic impenetrable hopelessness only surpassed by the flaring indignation at the emotional manipulation of the moment. Slowly and without emphasis, I said, 'Actually, after this I am no longer afraid of anything.'

As if to prove me wrong, in the most alarming way she seemed to disembark from the mattress without employing the use of her arms and had covered half the distance towards me, her knife-wielding hand outstretched, while she hissed, 'Don't walk out in the middle of a conversation,' needing the target to remain within range.

But this was not a conversation; it was a set-up. I slam-locked our bedroom's security gate, and I was gone, down the passage and out the kitchen door, cold coffee and cigarettes in hand. She shook the security gate, and then had to retrieve the keys hidden in her bedside cabinet, and this diversion seemed to release something and she did not follow me outside.

I sat in the courtyard with canine company. How that tirade had not disturbed the children, I don't know. I don't think I had said anything that could obviously be used against me if things got ugly, though I had no doubt a greedy lawyer would find something. What infuriated me was that she had done this, that this was her approach to our predicament. How many other conversations had she recorded, and what else has she been up to? My computer, my cellphone, and my journal? Has she found the script? And when she had said to Jade that she has investigated her, perhaps that was just the tip of the iceberg? And even worse, if she has not taped our conversations but was pretending that she had, then she was playing with my emotions, with my intention to work this through together. It was that manipulative exploitation that drove a stake into my heart. The stainless-steel saw-toothed violence I could not even contemplate, it was so foreign to my mind.

So I sat outside for an hour or so in the intermittent drizzle and gusty wind, trying to convince myself that this was a blessing, that being so plainly reminded of why I cannot stay in this relationship was so necessary just when my heart softened and led me astray. I realized I need to get advice on how to broker a separation in a way that avoids the catastrophic consequences of last year, given her reaction. Then I walked around the block with the dogs, who must have thought I had amnesia and revelled in the bonanza of a second evening outing. Twice I passed Calix's house, and looked up to see that his lights were on and his shadowed silhouette paced what I assumed was the living area with his cellphone against his ear, and I wondered whether he was being updated on what was going down in the life of the person he loved.

48

We trust our secrets to our friends, but
they escape from us in love.

(La Bruyère)

Tuesday, 21 June 2011

Sarah just swept in, dumped a couple of bags and dropped the boys
with me for a couple of hours at the deli and they are already arguing
over who should use the computer first. She arrived without a word but
with a glare, and when my mouth opened but my mind could not think
of something appropriate to say, she departed without a word.

Five minutes later, Roxanne phones to say she is in the area and
asks if she can come by for a coffee and a chat, as she is very concerned
about what is going on. It almost seems choreographed. I am reluctant
to see her now but minutes later we sit opposite each other at the deli
and the last time she arranged to have a 'serious chat' all those months
ago erupts, when we walked along the beach and she had told me all she
knew about Calix and Sarah and apologised for her part in not telling
me about it at the very beginning.

While this memory flashes at speed through my mind, she examines
my face and asks if I am okay, and without waiting for a response she
then tells me that Sarah mentioned that I want to dissolve our marriage
and I try not to let this irk me. Joshua and Jeremiah are having a race to
see who can finish their milkshake first, and Jack wants to sit on my lap,

but I don't want him to hear this. And I don't want to talk here at the deli, not with those recollections.

I say, 'Let's walk along the beach, rather. We can chat more privately there.'

We walk along the promenade where the dogs can enjoy some free space and new smells as we near the beach. It is chilly, with an on-shore breeze, and I feel compelled to break into a jog along the beach. Joshua and Jeremiah head for the distant river, now in full flow, which bisects the crescent of beach. We amble along and are halfway to the river without a word yet spoken, Jack shrieking with delight as he teases the dogs with sticks and sand tossed gleefully into the air and like wonderful au pairs they keep him entertained.

'How are you doing, Roxanne?' I am mildly irritated already. This does not feel like a good idea.

'I've been okay for a while. You know, up and down, still, but much more stable. The peaks and troughs are not as unmanageable, so I think I've got the medication right by now.'

'So what has Sarah told you?'

'Nothing much,' she says. I know this is not true, but it does not matter anymore to me. So many things just don't matter anymore. 'What happened to your chin?'

'Nothing. Shaving with a blunt blade.' So Sarah has not told her everything, just a skewed version to favour the impression she wants to create.

I tell her briefly about the conversation I had with Sarah and what transpired at the party, to which she responds just how unacceptable Sarah's behaviour is, especially in front of the boys. 'I can see what has happened to them, and I know why they beg me to stay longer with them when I come to visit.' I am not sure that I agree with her reasoning, but anyhow. She also speaks about how she struggles with Sarah's behaviour towards her and that the only reason she visits our house is to see her nephews. Her stopovers are brief, and she says that each time she nonetheless feels she has been knocked ten steps backwards. 'Sara-lea has become so moody and critical. I feel that she criticizes everything I say or do, and she always tries to control and interfere with my interaction with your boys.'

You don't know the half of it. 'It's at its worst when she's not feeling okay with herself,' I say, 'when things feel out of control for her. You should just ignore it,' knowing well just how I struggle with this.

'Clive, I'm so used to it now that it just flies right over my head. But every time I leave, I breathe a sigh of relief and have to tell myself that I am a beautiful person with a good heart and I am not all the things Sara-lea has dumped on me.' We walk on further, then she says, 'You know, Clive, Sara-lea's actions seem to suggest that there is still something going on with Calix, otherwise she should be able to let go of the stuff she holds on to, and if she really wants to rebuild your relationship she should be prepared to talk openly about anything and everything. Anybody knows that is the only way to deal with this. And she should do everything she can to put you at ease. Given the type of work she does, it's ridiculous that she cannot see this. I'm sure she advises her clients to do it. I'm not sure if it's because she is entirely self-centred or that she is so guilt-ridden and ashamed that she simply cannot go there. Or maybe she holds it against you that she cannot be with him?'

'Let's not get on to Calix,' I say. For some reason I pause and look behind me. Gino is about twenty paces away, tracking us. He falters, hesitates, then calls his dog. I wait, as he does, now just ten paces away.

Jack runs towards me, 'What's the matter, Daddy?' and I scan for the other two, now far ahead of us near the river. A group of four strollers are closing in fast, their dogs already with us and busy with a tail-sniffing routine which irritates Harry no end and he pirouettes in a futile attempt to restore his dignity as evading one interloper simply positions him for the other.

'It's okay, Jack. Stay with Rox,' I say, and take two paces towards Gino which unnerves me as it has the effect of immediately enlarging him. His dog upsets the tentative understanding between Harry and the two Rottweilers by attempting to mount a distraught Sally and Harry loses his gentlemanly demeanor and all hell breaks loose. Turn your back and your girl gets screwed, I think. Strangely none of the dogs seem intent of inflicting grievous harm; it is all about territorial domination—so human. But there is much screaming and gesticulating and running into the fray from human owners which incites them as they absorb our terror and feel the need to defend their owners.

I have picked up Jack. 'Come away, leave them,' I say. Reaching sudden telepathic agreement that there will be no winners here, there is a bristling standoff, as much between hound as human. It takes me a little while to convince everyone to walk away before calling their hounds.

I wait for Gino to move on and watch Roxanne for signs of recognition, before saying, 'I know that I cannot expect you to say anything about it to me, even if you did know something. And the issue now is not about him and her. Although I guess it is in the mix if their relationship is still in play as it is bound to affect her behaviour with me especially if attack is her best form of defence. All I know is that how we have dealt with it has been hopelessly inadequate.'

'But this is how she deals with everything, she pretends it never happened,' Roxanne says. I want to turn around but Gino is heading towards Joshua and Jeremiah and with anxiety growing we follow in his footprints. 'All the stuff she experienced in her early life, I experienced too, the abuse, all of it, but I wear it on my sleeve and talk-talk-talk about it until it no longer gets in the way of who I am.' I am not so sure about that. 'Anyway, the problem is, Clive, I really don't know any more what is going on there. I told you all I know. She does not share those details with me, not since I told her months ago that I had heard that they were still seeing each other and she went absolutely ballistic. At times I think it started just because you were away and she was alone and looking after three young children.'

I am tiring a bit of the conversation; it's really just more of the same. And I am not prepared to let on what I know about Sarah and Calix, in case this is what Roxanne is looking for. It feels like she is intent on trying to persuade me of something, but I don't yet know what it is. Gino has walked right between Josh and Jeremiah, and seems to say something to them as they look up at him. I want to turn around now, and as if on cue, both dogs come bouncing over and bark their excitement and establish wet and sandy contact with my hand. Jack throws sand in the air, and they are off again as we retrace our footprints in the wet sand. Keeping an eye on Joshua and Jeremiah, who seem to be challenging each other to break off the largest chunk of hard, wet sand that cradles the river water without falling in, I say, 'I really don't know what else to say to you, Roxanne. I have told you what is happening and how I feel about things.'

But she does not seem ready to let it go yet, and says, 'I have never seen her worse than she is today.'

'Well, it's useful to hear that, because I have been trying to understand for myself whether things have always been this bad. I mean, whether I have always experienced her like this.'

Roxanne thinks about that for a moment, then says, 'In fact, you're right, she has been like this for the past three years or more, I'd say. Or maybe since the children came, I don't know. She was never this bad before that. And when she hurt herself and the boys . . . ' Her voice trails off. 'She had never done that before, far as I know. It's as if she has dealt with absolutely nothing and she cannot bear to see the impact her affair has had on your relationship.'

'Well, all I can say is what it feels like for me. I am not clever enough to understand why.'

'I don't know how you put up with it. After what she has done to you, her relationship with Calix, her disappearance for months, and how she still treats you. I would completely understand it if you were to have an affair. It's what I would do if I were you.'

She looks at me as if she has asked a question, but I don't respond to her. Perhaps this is the reason she is talking to me? So I say, 'Maybe it's because I keep thinking that she can't help it, that she has a psychological condition from her childhood experiences.' Or her soul seeks exculpation from another lifetime?

'What do you mean?'

'I wish I could speak to her psychiatrist, but she would never let me. I think she has some sort of borderline disorder. It would be awful if she has but it remains undiagnosed and she gets no help for it. That's negligence.'

'She's probably bipolar like me,' Roxanne says.

'No, I don't think that's it,' I say. 'It's more like a severe anxiety disorder, and certainly OCD, maybe even something like Aspergers—you know, with her apparent lack of empathy and how she recalls all the prices at the supermarket and plays with numbers on vehicle registration plates. How she seeks patterns and how small things bother her. It's on the spectrum of autism, a mild form I think, and that certainly fits a range of her symptoms.' I am not going to tell her what I really think. 'She keeps saying, "Am I crazy?" but I think this is why she is so brilliant, it's part of her genius and why she is so good at what she does. Look, I'm a layperson, but think of her excessive reaction to stimuli, her senses go wild and she has absolutely no ability to reign herself in. She is on constant high-alert and her anxiety levels leave her dysfunctional, or at least she seems to freak out at things that are quite manageable.'

I stop myself, not appreciating the labels I am throwing out and thinking of how likely it is she will tell Sarah everything I say. I had wanted to throw Roxanne off the scent, but I don't know how to undo it. 'Look, Roxanne, I don't like the label, but I've been told that there's little doubt it's BPD.'

'What?'

'It's just a collection of unsavoury behaviours, probably provoked by her history and extremely high anxiety levels. If you prefer the shorthand, some call it Borderline Personality Disorder, though not everybody would be happy with such a diagnosis. Some don't even believe there is such a thing and, frankly, I'm not sure myself.'

'Yes, I've noticed that thoughts race around her head all the time and she feels she is going to be cornered by me if I raise the most arbitrary thing. Perhaps she's just feeling bad and guilty? She's repentant? But I think her behaviour is narcissistic,' Roxanne says. I am about to protest. Narcissist—such a damning label. But it strikes a chord and my irritation surfaces nonetheless. 'When she needs something to happen in a particular way, or she is feeling freaked out about something, she will do exactly what she wants to do and to hell with the impact on others.' Roxanne is getting worked up. 'Even afterwards, she cannot see what she has done or that what she has said has dramatically affected others in her space. And she won't listen to reason. She has the most infuriating habit of creatively explaining away a situation or simply discarding something that seems like it's so obvious it cannot be contested. What's infuriating is that I don't see her behave like this with other people. When I've told them how she is with you and me, they don't believe me. Not even my therapist believes me!'

Gino sweeps past again, all too slowly for my liking, with a glare that Roxanne either does not notice or ignores. Harry stands stiff and erect until the threat has gone.

'She just believes that she is right, Roxanne, to point out your faults or to blame another. It's like a preemptive strike because she feels guilty, even if she shouldn't. Perhaps she has needed this defence since childhood?'

'It's worse than that,' she says. 'She remains convinced that she is right, that what she did was okay, when to others it is indefensible. Or if you want to tell her later how you felt about it, she doesn't want to hear it; she seems to just dismiss your feelings. She seems to have no appreciation of consequence and no remorse, and she is incapable of having a conversation about anything that she thinks will threaten her or get in the way of what she needs in that moment, so much so that she gets wildly agitated and abusive when this happens. But you know all this.'

We walk in silence for a while and the boys catch up with us. I do know I am talking with someone who is diagnosed with bipolar, who flips between excessive drinking and drugging, excessive shopping, excessive meaningless sexual experiences, and debilitating depression—someone who at the moment can barely get out of bed to go to work. It occurs to me she is here because she needs to hear herself say these things.

'I've seen it all, Clive,' Roxanne says. 'And I see myself so much in her. In fact, she's exactly like my father, her stepfather, excessively controlling and then she erupts with abuse. And also like our mom, that's what really scares me. We used to plead with mom not to rile him, but she would do it until he couldn't take it anymore. Just like Sara-lea did to you that night she locked you out the house.' She looks at me as if wondering whether I can recall that time. I look out to sea and make out the speck of a boat, probably a fishing vessel, just below the horizon, and wish I was there. 'Sara-lea, well, as a child she was like a Barbie-doll.' It is her oft-repeated descriptor of Sarah. 'She would play along with him to get her way, manipulate him around her little finger.' Yes, I understand this now; in an Oedipal way she has always wanted to sleep with her father or father-figure. And I wonder whether Calix was that for her, in some way? Was I? 'Me, I challenged him and got the whip. My brother also had it hard, but he would always find a way to make us laugh afterwards. For some reason he was not removed from the family as we were and I shudder at the thought of what he had to endure. Little wonder he has also been treated with ECT for chronic depression and suicide attempts, isn't it?'

'At the home for the bewildered.'

'Where?' she says.

'Sorry, it's meant to be a joke, but it's completely out of context. That was insensitive.' I know it is my awkwardness and rage at what they went through.

'What worries me the most, Clive, is that you will end up like him,' Roxanne says.

'Your brother?'

'No, like Sara-lea's biological father. He slowly killed himself, do you know that? Because he could not deal with our mother's behaviour and her affair with my dad, the neighbour, and how she treated him all the time. Jeez, it's so fucking obscene how this is playing out again. It's been coming for a while, but I've watched you this past year in particular, and I think I can see you doing that. I've seen you reach breaking point too many times. You are not the person you were a few years ago. Please look after yourself better. Your boys need you.'

We have arrived back at the deli, and stand on the pavement near her car. I realize I've never asked Roxanne about the abuse; it had always felt like I would be prying. 'Did, um . . . were both of you exploited, you know sexually, and physically assaulted, and all that.'

Jack runs up to me and whispers in my ear, 'There is Calix's car.' I am instantly on high alert; Calix's unmistakable vehicle is parked in the bay alongside mine and I look around for him. He has never been so bold before. My mind tries to find reason in the unreasonable. Perhaps it is just coincidence? But there are other vacant parking bays scattered about. Maybe he wants to speak with me, found my car but not me? I am spooked—Gino and now Calix. I feel as if I am being squeezed, like a boil, about to pop. I just don't know what is real and what isn't.

Roxanne has not noticed his car as she is looking the other way. Or does she know what is going on around us? 'We went through exactly the same stuff, Clive. But we have never really spoken about it to each other. She won't go there.'

We hug goodbye. Then she gets into her car, and I look at her, feeling for her as I have always felt for Sarah. The experiences they have had that I cannot possibly comprehend. And then, as if it has just occurred to her, she says, 'She said something to me the other day which seemed out of context. She asked me whether I would consider moving in with her again. I told her no way, under no circumstances. I could never live with her. I don't even like her.' She waves goodbye to the boys. Before she drives off, she says, 'Clive, you need to end it. It is best for the boys.'

49

Sing, muse, of the wrath of Achilles.

(Homer)

Saturday, 25 June 2011

I am sitting with Jade at the deli, chatting mostly about my conversation with Sarah and trying to figure out where it may go as Sarah seems to be avoiding meeting with the mediator, when I hear the boys' voices, 'Dad! Dad!' and they scrambled over the half wall demarcating the restaurant's perimeter.

This is immediately followed by a whirlwind of dark energy and Jade leaps out of her chair and says, 'I'm gone,' and in an instant she disappears inside the restaurant to exit, I assume, through the front door on the other side just as Sarah's shrieking accusations reach our ears before her upper body protrudes over the wall enclosing us. Jade is clearly not keen on another public confrontation, and I can't say I am either, but I have nowhere to go nor any reason, I think, to go anywhere. Nor do the other patrons, who I suddenly observe are not regulars and I catch myself thinking that this must look comical to the casual observer. It is very Jerry Springer.

All this takes place in a matter of seconds, but time slows down as it often seems to do in such moments, and I am able to scan my 3D-goggled-eyes across the scene of the deli courtyard, the wide-screen motion picture of this moment of my life, and take in the excitement of the boys left stage as they vault the wall, feel the joy in my heart as I see them, the wrath-filled energy of Sarah centre stage fighting for my attention, the exit gate right stage left ajar as if hinting to me of my next move and possible future, the unseen but imagined flight of Jade behind my back, and the background-filler reactions of the bit part patrons scattered around the scene and all playing their part as the drama unfolds. My senses are filled with home theatre 7.1 Dolby surround-sound, and it occurs to me that I should adjust down the volume level of the centre speaker of Sarah's accusations but I cannot momentarily locate the remote control. My only conscious thought is what is she doing alone with the boys, especially in this state?

I sit back in my chair for a more panoramic view as one does when you are seated in the front row of a cramped home theatre basement and too close to the wide-screen you, in a moment of debt-burdened amnesia, purchased to show off to your friends hoping that some would actually come visit you for a change. I barely take in what she is saying, but there is little doubt it is not nice. I notice words like 'marriage' and 'affair' and lots of 'you this' and 'you that', but I am more concerned about the boys who come rushing up to me and I greet them with a tight smile but genuine delight. Some of the deli customers, enticed to sit outside on this day which is warm although the skies are overcast, are trying not to notice, pretending to carry on their conversations or suddenly busying themselves with the food on their plate. But a few of them can't help themselves, and they seem to achieve something I have never seen before—keeping one eye looking straight ahead of them or perhaps at Sarah but the other turned in my direction. And suddenly my smile is real at the absurdity of it all. Sarah seems to run out of words for me, at least for the moment, and with her long skirt billowing in her wake, she lurches menacingly past the gate which gives access to where I sit and towards the front of the building and the boys run inside the restaurant behind me and I sit there absorbing the relative silence while I wonder whether this is actually happening and what is actually happening.

The other customers continue as if nothing happened, looking a bit resigned as if they heard 'cut' bellowed from some concealed megaphone and are getting ready for the cameras to roll for 'take two' because we got something wrong in our first attempt. Only one woman keeps staring at me, the distaste on her face seeming to suggest that it was me who cocked up the scene but as I am the lead actor in this comedy-drama she fears she will be fired if she actually expresses her irritation at me. Maybe she thinks I missed my cue or fluffed my lines, or maybe her husband had an affair. A voice in my head quietly tells her to 'Fuck off and mind your own business' and reminds her that she is not indispensible in this true-life drama and she should pull herself together as there is no script for this; I am making it up as I go along, and the problem is that the other star actors seem to have their own ideas and interpretations of how they want things to go. I have never been any good at improvisation theatre, anyway.

It seems that Sarah has been delayed somewhere en route, probably taking little Jack to the bathroom as I cannot see him either but both Jeremiah and Joshua are now sitting with me. I am sure they heard the initial interaction, but their emotions are confused by the excitement of being here. A minute later, little Jack comes running, screaming towards me along the pavement between the parked cars and the gate, now closed, imploring me to intervene.

'Stop them, Daddy. Mommy is hurting Jade. She grabbed me and pushed me over.' He is holding his forehead, and I can see blood.

He clambers panicked and wide-eyed down the half-wall alongside the gate, courtesy of the elevated ground level on the other side, employing the table and three-person bench at which the woman glaring at me sits to descend to ground level. In the process he deposits her meal on her lap but she is guilty of knocking her own glass of red wine over. She tries to stand up to escape more damage. Her knees get locked under the heavy table so she tries to push the table away from her but she succeeds only in shifting the centre of gravity and next thing three women are lying on their backs, knees hinged over the upturned bench as if doing a set of 'tummy crunches' and presenting their underwear to the tarpaulin and everyone fortunate enough to be sitting this side of them. It is one of those moments when you just know it is indiscrete to stare but impossible not to. They seem unsure whether to cover up or get up first, and without agreeing the first step wrestle with each other in the cramped space which makes matters worse as it requires a coordinated effort to extricate themselves. None of the spectators move, frozen in the uncertainty of whether to help or spare them the indignity of their exposure. Whoever pressed 'Pause' please press 'Play', I thought. You could hear a pin drop; until a woman at the table alongside me covers what I assume is her husband's eyes with her napkin and says 'George! Stop that!', but not before I catch the wide smile on his face. I think she should wipe the drool off his chin.

Even little Jack, huddled in my arms, freezes during this pantomime, but now he is crying again and pleading with me to stop them while I use a napkin to dab at the graze above his eye. I look up and see Gino and his cohort, Amelie, standing just inside the gate waiting innocuously for a table. He is wearing sunglasses, as always, and I can sense he is looking at me. I half-expect Calix to make his appearance. I cannot protect my flanks and perhaps he is inside already and I extend my neck and look for his car.

Next thing Sarah is at my table with fire in her belly and venom in her words. She is talking on her cellphone while spitting her rage at me and reacting to the boys' questions. From time to time, I offer some placating words in a half-hearted attempt to soothe her and the boys who have gathered around, or probably myself, and remind her that the boys are absorbing everything but nothing seems to penetrate her fury. The strange inner calm I feel seems to come from years of experience that when she is in an irrational state, having a psychotic episode as Vincenzo once said, there is nothing I can do. I have just never felt it so clearly, and I think that this is because what is happening is exactly what needs to happen. This thought is at war in my mind with the idea that this whole transition was supposed to be orderly, or at least work to a plan and a timeline encased in love and gratitude, and I have to reconcile the two voices by promising that I will come back later to this raging debate and so manage to bring about a tenuous ceasefire in my head. I reason that the universe or my angels have had a hand in this, as if to say,

'We can see you need help to jump, so here's a push to help you along. But don't expect us to do all the work for you.'

Sarah is up and down from the table, talking on her phone. I wonder where Jade is and whether Gino saw the altercation. All the while the dogs nuzzle us for attention and have that quizzical eyebrows-raised and head-tilted look and try to get in-between us to break the tension, which does not help matters and serves to inflame her and give her an illegitimate target for a few choice words. While the boys eat a promised snack, I hear her leaving phone messages that she wants to be hospitalized, probably talking to the voicemail service of her psychiatrist. She also phones other people, asking for help.

I realize this charade has drawn the attention of customers and staff within the restaurant as well, when Sarah disappears into the dim interior and accosts Samantha, who is standing legs astride, hands on hips, and mouth agape. I can't hear the conversation but I imagine she is telling Samantha that this is not okay and trying to get information from her. Twice I crane my neck to look in their direction, and Sarah yells at me, finger wagging, arm flicking dismissively at me to go away and her neck stretching forward and only just managing to still remain attached to her head that she wants to aggressively stick in my face but it is hopelessly ineffective as she is so far away from me. Waiters waft ghost-like between tables with plates of food, but no attempt at normality can distract from this moment. So I sit in my chair and interact with the boys and sneak a few drags of nicotine while I try to keep the carcinogens from blowing in their direction by extending my arm to the sky. It is not a cigarette I particularly enjoy while I let the plot unfold like reading a novel slowly and deliberately and turning the pages without much rush or passion or intrigue but also not entirely without interest.

Gino and Amelie have been seated behind our new lady-friend with the underwear, and he has shuffled the chairs around so that he can look directly at me, as Amelie does from time to time. Done with Samantha, Sarah comes back outside. Shards of glass cascade from her as she sits down at the table again busy with her phone. I wonder what I can or should do for her, just how I can support her in this moment, but come up with nothing. Then she gets up and stands by the jungle gym behind me and phones Jade, and to my dismay Jade actually engages with her in conversation and I think it would also be quite acceptable to tell Sarah to leave her alone, or even threaten to open a case of intimidation and violence as Jack imparts to me what happened. I cannot hear the conversation; I'm not even trying to. But when she shouts at Jade, 'I will take legal action if you come anywhere near him,' followed by 'I will hurt you,' everybody hears her, and I glance over at Gino for his reaction. He is smiling, but maybe Amelie has said something funny.

All the while Jack sits on my lap and the two older boys are expressing their concerns about why we are fighting and why we can't stay married. So she has told them about our conversation. When Sarah ends the call with Jade, she returns to the table and gathers her stuff together. For someone to whom tears come easily the look in her eyes and the angle of her mouth and her purposeful actions portray a more calculating and self-satisfied mind than an anguished one.

I say, 'Sarah, don't go, you need help. Let me get you help,' but she leaves with a show of hugs and kisses for the boys and a promise that she will see them soon, in that way that people say such things when they are about to be incarcerated and you actually won't see them for a long time, other than with their head shaved and ankles shackled in a cold cramped room with a bright, bare bulb swinging from the ceiling. If she is leaving the boys with me then it probably means she is planning to go to hospital or away, maybe in the way she did before, and the sense of déjà vu guts me. How am I going to take the next necessary steps if she goes away or if her mental state is unstable? I think—so it's just me and the boys again.

Although the violent and angry behaviour they have witnessed has temporarily abated, I can see that it lingers with the boys in an age-appropriate way; little Jack more clingy than usual, Jeremiah and Joshua questioning me about all sorts of things and trying to persuade me to make everything all right again and looking over their shoulders at me for reassurance when they should be distracted and fully engaged with the games they are playing when they venture briefly to the small jungle gym tucked away in the corner of the deli courtyard. But it is not long before they return to my side, seeking surety which I cannot bestow.

I smile at the woman still staring at me, and she looks away. She has placed a napkin over her soiled blouse. The red stain on her short skirt will be embarrassing when she stands up to leave, and I wonder if I should offer to buy her some tampons, but realize that I am probably pushing my luck. I am sure she wants to cause a fuss but Sarah's presence probably spared me that displeasure, and perhaps she thinks I have taken enough punishment and she cannot possible match or better Sarah's wrath. I don't want to open that door for her, so I make no apology for the incident. She is a welcome distraction for me, the comedy in the drama, and it amazes me how okay I feel despite what has happened, how I am able to sit here without a desperate desire to get away from the energy that surrounds this moment and the glares and dark thoughts and whispering voices that pepper the conversations around me. I wonder whether it is because I feel safe at the deli, or because of Jade's love and astonishing capacity and willingness to withstand this onslaught, or just because it is right.

Like a jagged, splintered mirror, Sarah reappears at our table. All conversation stops in the courtyard, and Jack hides behind me and clings to my shirt. To me she says, 'Well, done, you have actually made it happen.'

Then Jeremiah says, 'I like Jade.'

'Why do you like her?' Sarah says, sticking her face in his, which causes him to swallow his tongue.

Joshua says, 'I like her cat,' as if Jeremiah has confided this to him and he can speak on his behalf.

Then little Jack, always wanting to contribute and with the memory of a recent incident etched in his mind, says, 'Daddy, you are not allowed to see Jade again.' He wraps his arms around my neck and buries his face under my chin, sending his condolences.

I say, 'You boys can decide for yourselves how you feel about Jade.'

Sarah says again, 'Daddy is going to leave us and marry Jade,' and she makes a show of taking off her wedding rings. She tells them all

sorts of things that occur to me to be things you simply don't say to
children in the heat of the moment. I have a meaningless pep-talk with
myself—if anything, you sit them down later and explain things calmly
to them, and then you should not exaggerate but tell them the truth,
and help them understand what this means to them, and so on. I don't
look at her when I think—'What vicious, soul-destroying, spite-filled,
manipulative wrath.' But I say nothing. I wonder how much of this is
carrying as far as Gino.

'You have no idea what I am capable of,' Sarah says loudly to anyone
who is listening. She grabs the knife at the table setting and pierces the
table cloth repeatedly. 'I will kill her.' I look around for Samantha, who
will not take kindly to the mutilation.

At this, Jack climbs under the table, sobbing. She reaches for him,
but he is so shocked by her behaviour and now these words, that he
won't let her touch him.

'That's enough, Sarah,' I say, and she heads inside the deli still
gripping the notched blade point-down. Jack lets me pick him up
again and I cuddle him on my lap while I offer him reassuring words. I
realize I need to get them away from her—why have I been so slow to
see this? I have enough of my wits about me to recite some words the
psychologist-lawyer recommended for such moments, or a reasonable
proxy for them: 'Sarah, I am taking the boys until things calm down
again.' I doubt whether she hears me, but I have at least fifty witnesses
in the packed deli courtyard, some of whom I have offended with
my too-loud voice. More quietly I say, 'Come on, boys, let's go to the
aquarium.'

Gino stands up as we near his table and, carrying Jack, I am at his
mercy. He edges around Amelie to cut me off at the gate, but something
makes him hesitate. As I unlatch the gate to make good my escape I come
face-to-face with William, who looks right through me with brown stony
eyes as he squeezes past. Surely Jade would have told me that he was in
town? Unnerved, I hurry the boys and dogs into the SUV. It is raining
now, just a light drizzle, or had I not noticed it before? Sarah runs over
from the front entrance and grabs the driver's door and opens it.

'Please, Sarah, not now, the boys,' I say and shut the door, but she yanks at it again, shouting at me. So I shut it and lock it, and she stabs at the door handle and then the window with the glinting steel before storming off to her car.

'Legally you have to be back at four o'clock!' she yells as I reverse the Jeep. I hear her shriek, 'You can't go so far as you will not be back in time!'

What on earth is she talking about? Legally the au pair should have been with her. I am catapulted ten months back to a time I would rather forget, but all the attendant emotions of that time come rushing in. My skin itches and I start sweating; the pungent feverish odour of panic and pain too much to bear. The boys are struggling with their seatbelts, and I pause and twist in my seat to help sort it out. I should also check my wallet for the aquarium cards, as I think that the ones in my wallet have expired. Sarah makes use of the delay to drive up and park me in, at an angle across the front of the Jeep; full of aggression, intimidation and control.

I look across towards the deli and see that Gino has swiveled his neck to watch, and he seems suspended in indecision. William seems to be standing alongside him, unsure of himself, perhaps looking for Jade. Some of the deli customers are actually standing up to get a better view. Behind me the boys are watching all of this in terrified immobility. Then, speaking on their behalf, Jeremiah says, 'What's going on, Daddy? Why is Mommy so angry?'

'It's all right, boys, mom is just having a rough time. We are going to have a nice time together at the aquarium and you will see her later.' My voice belies what is going on inside. I know I cannot let her take the boys later; not in this state, not in any state. What I need to do now is just get them away from her—I can later build a case around the 'legal' element, but I know that right now she will be immune to that and any other reasonable argument.

The rain is coming now without reserve, and Sarah's clothing starts to blotch as she shouts something through my car window and then goes back towards her car, and I quickly do a three-point-turn in confines I am convinced will never cater for the extra-length of the SUV. As I swing the behemoth tank left, she runs over and tries to grab the door handle, and I imagine this either wrenches her shoulder socket or nearly leaves her ringed fingers amputated and clinging, bloodied, in the nook of the door handle. And I recall how Sarah once told me that her stepfather used to drive off like this in a rage and after hurting her mother. 'Broke her arm once,' she had said. Sarah tries to jump on the bonnet and grabs hold of a windscreen wiper, and it tussles with her, determined to perform its job, and the point of the knife gouges ugly streaks across the windscreen. Her wet hair falls across her face, and I can see the water droplets clinging to her eyelashes, her wide eyes demented. As I accelerate away to the left, she loses her grip with the arcing momentum and slips down on to the blacktop leaving the hint of her trajectory etched by the knife on the bonnet. The last thing I see is Gino, running across the road.

I drive off with the boys, playing soothing classical music much to 'hard-rocker' Jack's dismay, but after a few minutes he settles with it. Sarah repeatedly tries to reach me on the cellphone, but I just won't have a conversation with her in this state in front of the boys. I expect she will chase after us, as she has done before, but it seems she doesn't. I decide to take the circuitous mountain pass rather than the more obvious coastal road that passes by the security booms leading to our house, in case Sarah was more aware than I realise and is in pursuit. Gino, certainly, might have overheard me mentioning the aquarium. I am driving too fast in the unwieldy SUV on the narrow, winding roads through the village, frequently overtaking taxi drivers and lazy shoppers hunting for a parking bay, and the boys complain of feeling nauseous and that the seatbelts are cutting into them. Through the village now, we meander under tree-lined curves beyond which smallholdings sprinkled with horses flash by. We make good time, and before each kink in the road when my line of sight is greatest, I glance in the rearview mirror and there is no sign of Sarah's car in hot pursuit. But when we hit the start of the mountain pass, hinted by the sudden increase in gradient, I am forced to slow to a crawl behind a construction vehicle with a trail of cars in its wake. This stretch of road is dead-straight, before the series of hairpin bends begin, and I have a clear view for some distance behind me.

Vehicles concertina in frustration ahead of the Jeep, and then, one by one, behind it. Seconds feel like minutes. Looking anxiously ahead, I realise I will make little headway even if I risk an overtaking manoeuvre. And then I see Sarah through the curtain of rain, or at least what seems to be her car, coming up fast six or seven vehicles behind me. And behind her, what looks like Gino's unmistakable cross-over vehicle.

'Fuck it,' I think, 'how is this going to end up?' I am hemmed in now, as a stream of traffic comes towards us; overtaking is suicidal. Behind us, a silver vehicle veers across the solid double white line into oncoming traffic, then it cuts back into our lane, forcing evasive action from the stream of traffic coming at us, and now I am sure it is her. Gino has less courage, or perhaps a modicum of self-preservation, which only emphasises Sarah's madness. She hangs out of her window, shaking her fist and mouthing what I can only assume are obscenities and abuse.

One vehicle at a time, Sarah gains on us. Now only three cars separate us, and she tries again as we near the first blind curve with fresh flowers and a white cross a permanent reminder of someone's loved one who tried this in the dead of night not so long ago. But it seems she cannot get back into our lane, as we are almost at walking pace and the cars behind me have closed ranks as the tip-truck driver ahead of us slips a gear and grinds to a halt.

'Come on!' I say, too aggressively, and turn up the volume to distract the boys. I can hear the gears crashing, and in horror I watch as an eighteen-wheeler negotiates the s-bend just ahead and passes by us and I see the whites of the driver's eyes, one arm yanking at the horn and the boys block their ears as the tone changes and the Jeep shakes as it is sucked into the air tunnel as he passes my window, now open. Then his vehicle fills my rearview mirror and Sarah's car disappears from view and my mind fills with mangled metal and compressed flesh being dragged against its will. I listen for the sound of it, and when the horn stops its desperate warning I stick my head out the window, but I cannot see her. Suddenly we are moving again, through the s-bend, and I lose sight of them, which means they cannot see me. Without thinking, I swing into the oncoming traffic, horns screaming their outrage, and turn into the first excuse for a road.

The tarred side-road ends almost immediately, barely longer than our driveway. A stony and overgrown path points the way up the mountain. I stop when the front wheels crunch on the gravel.

Jack says, 'Where are we going, Daddy?'

I say, 'Hold on, boys, it's time for an adventure,' and engage low-range second gear as we tip and sway over the rocks and fallen branches. Perhaps we can conceal the Jeep in the overgrowth?

It is slow going. The track is steep, no more than a hiking path or perhaps a long-forgotten fire-break, leading straight up the mountain. There is not much mud, the rainwater running quickly over the rocks and down the slope. Branches screech down the Jeep's flanks, sometimes obscuring my view through the windscreen, but the brutish motor takes no strain.

I can still see the tarred road behind us, which means we are not yet safe. I am willing the overgrowth to present us with a veil of greenery and shroud us from sight. Then my heart sinks when Sarah turns in, followed by Gino, and her low-slung silver sports car jumps around in my rearview mirror. Her car surely won't get far on this path; no driver of sane mind would allow those Pirelli tires off the tarmac. But in this moment, this prolonged psychotic episode, I remind myself she is not rational. Without any apparent deceleration, she crashes through the undergrowth partly flattened by the Jeep, and I am astonished as her vehicle is carried onward by sheer force of momentum alone. If she had her wits about her, she would commandeer Gino's soft-roader, but her single-mindedness works in our favour and I find myself wishing the path to get still worse as it is only the capabilities of our vehicles that keep us apart. If this turns out to be a cul-de-sac, I will never be able to outrun them with three boys. I quicken the pace, and each time it seems our path seems blocked by the dense foliage and we cannot go on, I try to forge a plan for that eventuality, but then we smash through the undergrowth and are granted a reprieve. The track quickly gets very rocky and the Jeep's sump takes a pounding as I break all the rules of off-road driving. We cross-axle through a set of deep ruts, testing the Jeep's articulation, and I send silent blessings to its engineers. Surely she will never get through that? Then the sickening crunch as the Jeep's front overhang hits a rock, but momentum carries us over.

Jeremiah says, 'You're going too fast!'

'This is exciting, just like our off-road camping trip, guys.'

'Wait for Mommy,' Joshua says, looking back down the track.

It seems only Jack has an appreciation of our circumstances. 'Don't let her catch us!' he says, with genuine terror in his voice, and I can see her vehicle losing traction and kicking up dust as it comes to a standstill, the front wheels buried in a donga and the undercarriage resting on exposed rock.

Sarah tries to get her vehicle moving again, but the rear wheels which power the car hang suspended off the ground. Behind her, Gino's vehicle slews off the track and comes to a halt half obscured by the vegetation. I wonder if that was covered in its marketing campaign? And for a moment I allow myself a sense of relief, and we put some distance between us and our pursuers.

Then suddenly the track conjures up an obstacle we cannot cross and I stop. I run to the front of the car to take a look. In front of us is a gully, the length of the Jeep, with some boulders and rotting tree trunks once placed to aid a pedestrian crossing, but almost too treacherous to walk across, and certainly not intended to carry a load in excess of three tons. Beyond that the track seems to continue until it bends to the left. It taunts me, 'Get across, and you're safe.' But I would be hard pressed to negotiate the gap even if guided by the expert hand signals of a navigator standing on the other side. A fraction either way, and the Jeep will topple into the gully.

I look back. Anxiety becomes panic. Sarah has left her vehicle, and is running awkwardly up the steep slope towards us. I can hear her screaming, and she is holding something in her hand which my mind convinces me is the knife. Beyond her, I can see Gino coming at a run. I might take my chances against one of them, but I have no chance of protecting the boys from both of them. There is no other option.

'Get out the car,' I shout at the boys. 'Now! Come, come, come.'

I ignore their protests and haul them out, and carry them one-by-one across the gully.

'Now, see that tree up there at the top of the path? We are going to have a little race. But the rules are, you have to get there at the same time. The three of you are one team, and you are racing against me and Jeep. So you must help each other. Don't leave Jack behind.'

'I don't want to,' says Jeremiah.

'Boys, please . . .'

'I'm getting wet,' says Joshua.

'If you can hide away from Mommy, there's a treat for you.' It is called 'live to see another day'.

'There's Mommy,' says Jack. 'Run!'

Gino has overtaken Sarah and is coming up fast. Panic is quickly, desperation. Everything in me screams to run in the opposite direction together with the boys and dogs up the hill, away from the threat, in a frantic attempt to ward off the inevitable for just a few moments longer. But I have to leave the boys and reduce the gap and return across the gully to the Jeep, and I feel like I am abandoning them to their fate. Beside the Jeep once more, I take one last look at the contorted, makeshift bridge. There will be no room for error. I will have to start a little to the right. Standing in front of the right-side headlight, I set my sights on a blackened tree trunk without branches, and imbue it with a sense of promise and hope it can carry the burden of faith I place in it. Suddenly fearful for their safety, I let the dogs out and set them in pursuit of the boys and they scramble across the gully. Maybe they will sense the madness and protect the boys?

I look down the track once more and imagine that Gino's hulk is slowing, his chosen form of physical training now working against him.

Wordlessly I urge him to stop, to give up, to come to his senses. But he can see that we are stranded, and surely this eggs him on. Behind him, Sarah hobbles and curses, and it is the thought of the horrors she may inflict that set me in motion again.

Then I am in the car and it crawls forward. Within seconds, the Jeep is committed, suspended above the gully. It lurches sickeningly as stones dislodge and the tree trunk that was the mainstay of my chosen route gives way, and suddenly I cannot see the boys on the track ahead of me but only the peak of the mountain as the rear wheels sag into the cavity. The SUV loses momentum as the wheels spit out debris, fighting for traction. But I resist flooring the accelerator. I talk to my angels and guides, and apologise for not having kept in touch. For a long while, it seems, nothing happens; then the wheels find solid ground and it feels like I am boosted across the chasm by an invisible hand.

I nearly collide with the boys and dogs. Frozen in fear or wonderment, they had stopped, huddled together in the rain, to watch.

Gino crosses the gully as we drive off, too exhausted to carry on running, and as the reality of our escape dawns on him he throws stones at us which bounce off the roof. He was so close, just seconds away.

'One crazy, one stupid,' I think.

Then they disappear from sight as the track veers to the left, still climbing steeply. The boys are laughing with nervous excitement, but Jack starts crying with relief. The wet-dog smell of Harry and Sally permeate the confines of the Jeep as they lick each other dry.

Then I have to stop the Jeep. Not that it is unwilling, but a boulder twice its size blocks our path, scowling at us and arms folded in stubborn refusal to budge. Beyond it, I suspect, the disused firebreak continues, but that is of no further use to us now. For a moment, I imagine it is not there, or that if I simply continue with sure-footedness we will defy gravity and the Jeep's approach angle will make light work of it. No matter how much I will it to change shape, its vertical face leers back at me as if to say, 'I have been this way for centuries, and you think you can make me change?'

Another voice says, 'You have created your own hell!'

I look for a way around the boulder, but there is none. Bushes, small trees, and large rocks border the track. The boys are subdued, rigid in their child seats, brought on by my indecision and the hopelessness that I am trying to fend off. Harry and Sally stick their faces between the headrests behind the boys' child safety seats, and look expectantly at me for instruction. Think, damn it!

Still no sign of Sarah nor Gino. Our only hope is that they have given up. Or come to their senses. I have faith in neither of these options. And if they hear us, they will come. How do you outrun two people propelled by rage and madness? They must be walking up the path, only seconds away from the curve that will bring us into view. And if they see the vehicle, they will know we are on foot, and they will know that they have us. There is no time to seek out a hiding place, not with three unwilling boys. She is after Jack, of that I am now certain.

'We are still playing hide-and-seek,' I say, feeling like I am sacrificing two children to save one. 'And from now on, we can only whisper. Get out of the car, quietly.'

'It's raining,' Jeremiah says, pointing out the obvious.

'That's why you're going to hide under the car with Josh.' The most obvious place to hide, is the most unlikely. 'Quick, climb under. And don't talk or move until I come back for you. Not for anyone, especially not Gino or Mommy.'

I post Harry and Sally, like sentries, at the rear of the vehicle. Harry goes ballistic and won't let anyone come within reach of the Jeep, if any of us are in it, and Sally follows his lead.

The rain stops, and I wonder whether this is not to our detriment. Carrying Jack, I round the boulder, and then I hear Gino's voice, shouting back to Sarah, 'There they are! They're stuck!'

He must have come around the bend and has the Jeep in his sights. Sarah will not be far behind. I don't have to work hard to make a noise as I crash through the undergrowth, wanting to draw them after us and away from Joshua and Jeremiah. Once they are convinced we are ahead of them, I will pick up the pace, suddenly confident I can outrun Gino even with the burden of Jack if I keep heading uphill. My knees have the rest of this lifetime to recover, and I promise them I will forever forego the bliss of foolish jaunts up 'my' mountain if they just hang in there.

Then Harry barks a warning, and I stop dead in my tracks and listen. Now I know exactly how close Gino is to the vehicle. Seconds pass. Then Harry goes crackers, and Sally joins him. Either Sarah or Gino is too close to the car, or trying to get in. I can't bear this, I have to go back.

Jack says, 'Go, Daddy!'

Misunderstanding him, I start to retrace my steps.

'No,' he screams, 'run away.'

His voice must have carried to the Jeep, because I hear Sarah shout, 'They're up there!'

Moments later I can hear them crashing and stumbling up the hill. They must be this side of the boulder, and I turn and go, at a half-run. After fifty paces or so, I stop to look back for them. Gino says something which sounds like, 'I see them,' and now I know the race is on. Jack and I need to put enough distance between us and them and get them away from the Jeep and two wet, frightened boys.

I misjudged it slightly, but maybe it was the best I could do.

Trying to stay hidden, so that they would track us by sound and not notice that two boys were not with us, took its toll as I often had to avoid the easier route and beat our way through thorned thickets. I shifted Jack between hips and used my free arm to ward off the brambles and branches as best I could. But it was not long before Jack had become a dead-weight and, without my arms for balance, I stumbled a number of times. The loose stoned path up *my* mountain felt nothing like this terrain. I could seldom see through the undergrowth to the ground where I had to place my feet, and I lost precious time when I had to detour around boulders and when there seemed no way through the dense flora. If Gino was keeping an eye on our progress, he could anticipate my movements and take the short side of the triangles I had to negotiate, and gain on me each time. For Sarah, no doubt in his wake, it was even more straightforward. I reckon my pace had to double his, just to stay ahead.

Aching for the pump-arm assist of my arms which clutched tightly to Jack, just when I felt I could no longer go on up the relentless incline, or at least that I could no longer confidently outpace Gino, we took a bad tumble. Holding onto Jack to try and cushion him from the impact, I could not break my fall and took the brunt of the landing on my elbows and knees. He clung to me and I just did not have the energy to get up. Then I heard Sarah cry out, followed by, 'Wait, I've twisted my ankle!' and I was astounded how the sound of her voice travelled to us; they must be really close. Gino must be a bit ahead of her if she felt the need to call out so loudly. For a moment, I wondered whether this was a ruse, a deceptive ploy to fool us into slowing down.

But that gave me the motivation I needed. I gathered Jack and said, 'Just a little further,' and on we plundered until we came to the hint of a contour through a forest of trees, and I was sure neither Gino nor Sarah could see us as we diverted from our upward trajectory. As we staggered, crouched and quietly as possible amongst the trees, I counted off the paces, wondering when they would pick it up and what they thought my next move would be.

When I judged they would have reached the contour, I adjusted Jack on my back and with a 'Hold on as tightly as you can,' I plunged recklessly down the slope. Suddenly I was calling on different muscle groups, and my thighs felt like jelly as they struggled to brace us as we slalomed between the trees and slipped on wet leaves and slid on my bum down steeper parts, holding Jacks hands clenched around my neck whenever I could. Brush tore at my face and branches pierced my windbreaker. Now that we were committed, there was no margin for error. We had to reach the Jeep before they did.

We hit the track just below the Jeep, and I had to scuttle a little way up the path, my knees complaining vociferously from the strain of the high-impact down run. I offloaded Jack in the passenger seat, and whispered to the others as I peered under the chassis. Where the fuck were they? Harry? Sally? In the stillness, I could hear our pursuers thrashing and cursing as they came down the path towards us. I could not see past the mammoth boulder, but they seemed very close, and I panicked.

I clicked my tongue, in the way that meant 'Come.' And the dogs, then Joshua and Jeremiah, cautiously ventured out of a hollow they had camouflaged with branches.

Reversing blindly towards the kink in the track, I see Gino edge around the huge boulder. Now he comes at us in huge moonwalk leaps and I fear he will reach us unless I can turn the Jeep around. Then Sarah comes around the boulder, and I realise it is her I dread the most. Gino gains on us, then recedes as I become less cautious, and I know it is now or never. At the curve in the track I swing into the bush and the Jeep shudders to a violent halt as we crash into a rock or a tree or something hidden by foliage and the dogs cascade with a yelp into the tailgate. Gino is nearly upon us and, frozen in time, for a moment we seem to stare at each other, him optimistic and me helpless. I engage 'drive' and the mud-terrain tires fight with the underbrush as I accelerate too strongly. The rear bumper seems to be caught on something. Piercing screams emanate from the little people behind me, and I am convinced we are destined for our last stand. I lock the doors.

Then the rear bumper detaches from the car and we catapult out, dragging dislodged debris clinging to the undercarriage. It is hard to say whether we hit Gino or he hits us, but I hear his grunt as he folds at the waist and first his torso then his head leaves an imprint on the bonnet and he bounces off and falls to the ground. Before we careen downhill, I see Sarah shaking her arms at us in rage and frustration.

The Jeep slides to a desperate standstill. I have forgotten about the gully which looms before us. But it seems less imposing from above, or perhaps I am more reckless now. I choose a different line, avoiding the splintered timber beam and the cavity it once spanned. It is incautiously calculated; my only goal, the tarred road. The front fender dislodges on the way in, not helped by the gradient, and then we pitch and tilt and are across the other side before the trench can even think of claiming us.

The clinging fender screeches its disdain as we lurch down the track, and the dashboard flashes dire warnings I ignore. When we reach Sarah's stranded car, which blocks our escape, I barely slow down across the ruts, and the Jeep shunts it out the way. But that is its last contribution to our progress and we deposit the mangled fender in the makeshift vehicular graveyard. Gino's car, we edge past, with a nudge for good measure.

Back in the traffic again, I only slow down once over the ridge of the pass. Some other road users peer curiously at the SUV, then at me, the driver, wide-eyed or shaking their heads, either judging my inconsiderate haste or my off-road driving skills. I remind myself that Sarah is resourceful, and while both their vehicles may need recovery assistance, it is a short walk for them back to the tarred road.

All three boys seem traumatized and anxious, and I can be of no more help against the truth they witnessed than to mutter, 'We're okay now, they've gone.' Jack tells me he is not feeling well and that 'Mommy hits me and shouts at me', but I mention the puppet show at the aquarium and this seems to distract him from his anguish. Their emotional needs are my prime concern and I need to gather my thoughts and don't really know where else to go other than to seek the relative safety of a crowd.

We leave a bedraggled looking Harry and Sally at the entrance, needlessly chained to a pole just to appease the security guard who glares at us. I have done my best to make myself look more respectable, exchanging my torn, muddied clothing for the track pants and sweater I keep in the Jeep in anticipation of a spontaneous bout of exercise. Once inside, we wash our faces and hands. We are just in time for the feeding of the penguins. The boys have removed their sodden sweaters, but their damp, soiled board shorts are irritating them and they soon grow tired of watching the sharks and rays and giant turtles and are causing such a commotion in the otherwise morgue-like hush that I take them to the play area and make models of sea creatures out of putty and play with them in the sandpit. In my apprehension, I keep them within arms' reach which is not that difficult as they are clingy, and the intended distraction of other laughing, playing children does little to ease their minds or mask their recent terror. I can see they are just not themselves, and I realize they are deeply shocked and distressed by what they have witnessed. I wonder whether I can still afford to dismiss the notion of therapy for them.

——◦◦◦——

Later, when we are driving home, the boys are very quiet, unusually so; not even Jack asks for his favourite music. Sarah would have come down from her psychotic high by now. While traipsing around the aquarium, I left messages for Sarah's psychiatrist and got hold of Catherine who had little more than platitudes to offer.

To Catherine, I said, 'If you don't believe my version of events, that's fine. But there are witnesses, at least of what happened at the deli, and I think you and her psychiatrist are being negligent. For fuck sakes, Catherine, she's now a direct threat to the boys!'

'On what grounds are you saying that? What has she done to them?'

I said, 'My next step is to remove the boys from her care,' and I disconnected.

I thought of life for Sarah without them and a life for the boys without their mother. And of life for me if something happens to them. Then I left a voice and text message for the psychologist-attorney we had consulted on the matter last year, hoping for expert guidance on how to deal with such eventualities, but he has not responded yet. All those signed papers listing rights and obligations and constraints and 'what ifs' bear no relevance to this moment. I resisted calling the police services and child welfare, as I was sure that surly woman would delight in removing the boys. I reach behind me to give each of them a squeeze on the thigh. I cannot think of someone who won't berate me for these decisions. The option of a minder, a private detective, to guard the boys, keeps floating about, but it seems wrong—I don't want to set that kind of energy in motion.

When we get close to home, Joshua utters the first words, 'Please, no more of that nonsense with Mommy.'

'Don't worry. We will avoid that, my angels.' We cannot go inside if she is there.

'Why do you call us "angels"?' Jack says.

'Because you all are. You are my angels. You guide and protect me and give me reason to be.'

And you, little Jack, truly are, because you are Angelique. Not Jade, but you; I now know this. This is why you try to stop your mother from repeating her endless cycle of violence. This is why you stab and thrust at her, just as she inadvertently allowed you to be hacked and plucked from her womb. And aeons ago, she chopped and slashed you from my womb; this is why you protect Jade and me from her. This is why you are accumulating all these physical scars. This is also why you are prone to violent defensive outbursts yourself—you're saying 'No! No! Get away' as if still screaming silently from your amniotic sac as first the outer chorionic membrane and then the inner amnion is pierced by blade or an amnihook or fingercot and you are excised and ripped from your cushioning amniotic fluid and life-giving placenta. This is why your tummy is your weakest link, Jack, and all your little illnesses seem to stem from there. This is why, when you were younger, you vomited blood every day for three months from a non-specific or undiagnosed illness that perplexed the top medical minds in the country. Your stomach is mirroring the bloody invasion of mine, all that time ago, and when you were wrenched in fragments from her belly just a few years ago. Life promised you protection and shelter until you cried out and inhaled with your own lungs, but neither your mother nor your father could carry out this sacred duty, not in either lifetime it seems.

Now I know who you are.

50

Anyone who says they have only one life
to live, must not know how to read a book.

(Unknown)

Saturday, 25 June 2011 (continued)

After the boys fell asleep, I wandered aimlessly around the house for an hour or more before phoning Jade. I don't know where Sarah is, but while we visited the aquarium she has been on a rampage through the house and it is a mess. I have no idea where to start, except to clean up Jade's artwork which lies in tatters in the passage. I don't feel safe in this house and certainly the boys are not.

Now I am sitting in the paved courtyard outside the kitchen. This time, Harry and Sally don't bother me with their tennis balls but lie listless and concerned a few meters from me as if uncertain whether they want to be seen to be associating with me. Jade is appalled to hear my description of the car chase. Then, at my request, she describes what happened when Sarah grabbed her outside the front entrance and pushed her around on the pavement between the tables and wide-eyed patrons until she had her pinned against a vehicle and this was when little Jack started beating Sarah on the thigh and tried to push her away from Jade, and Sarah had flung him aside and then shoved Jade to the ground, hurling abuse at her. Jade says that despite the physicality of it, she is not reeling in the same way she had after the war of words at Azura's party. But as she speaks, I can hear she has wiped her hands of

Sarah and sense that she no longer believes in the possibility of 'the third way', in which we all, maybe William and Calix included, would be in each other's lives—with love and respect, and without fear.

Jade says, 'What I think of now is you and how you find your way towards the outcome you need and deserve – not her, not me, just you and your beautiful boys. Of course, I want us to be in each other's lives one day in some way, but right now I am letting all of that go.'

'Just how does that help me?' I say, although I know I need to have my own answer to this question.

'The same person who gave me that reading on your last birthday, before I even met you, told me last week that you will keep going back to her, even if you got divorced. The full realisation of that has hit me like a ton of bricks and any inner conflict around the choices I now make are somehow resolving and I have a sense of gratitude towards myself and a gradual dissolving of self doubt or wavering around these decisions. I have my gift from you to treasure always, a most precious one. You helped me release myself from the last strand of my toxic addictive karmic relationship, even if I could not return the exact same favour. Thank you for that—you helped me to save my life. But I see with alarming clarity, despite the gift that you brought, that I have felt toyed with, manipulated at times. And something has leveled for me just now, somehow I've seen a more balanced view and I no longer put you on a pedestal. I'm not looking up at you anymore. This is a profound learning for me.'

'You're angry, with me? That's okay.' It hurts, but I am relieved I am no longer on a pedestal.

'Fuck it, Clive. Can't you see she's a split second away from doing something you will never be able to reverse? How will you forgive yourself? You have to take steps now to protect your boys!'

I say, 'That aggression, that explosive anger, as I understand it, is like post-traumatic stress.'

'I know where I'm coming from here, Clive. And I know what is in your heart. But she is so damaged by her wounds that she is not coming from love but from an entirely selfish place of survival and to hell with anybody else.'

'Jade, she has accumulated her fair share of harrowing incidents in her life and her survival literally depends on it, this overpowering fear and offensive verbal hostility which sometimes spills over to physical assault. For this reason she has learnt to extinguish the memories of all her yesterdays because without this coping mechanism, she will collapse. That's why she always lives outside of herself, why she can't stop for a moment for fear she will sink into her own thoughts and feelings. And that's why her anxiety levels are permanently so high, and keeping her mind busy with her obsessive-compulsive behaviour is the only way she can stave off psychotic moments when she completely loses it, like she did earlier. If you were a student impassively watching a case-study movie of what transpired at the deli, you would have observed just how all this was working.'

'Clive . . .'

'Jade, please understand, all of what I've said really just touches the surface. These are just the outward behavioural manifestations of something much more fundamental. And this is what maddens me so; it's why I just can't let go of her. The abuse she experienced when she was a child? She no doubt feels it was her fault, so she hates them and she hates herself because she thinks she deserved it. They touched her body, but actually they deformed and blemished her soul. And so I think she learnt to hate everyone who comes really close to her. Last year she asked me for forgiveness, which at some level she always had, but she really needs to forgive herself, to stop hating herself, for all her lifetimes. So if only she could forgive the men who unconsciously tried to annihilate her before she even had the chance to know life.'

Matisse and Picasso have wandered into the courtyard and sit inches from my ankles looking at me, a gesture neither offensive nor needy. Their presence feels unlike the act of solidarity I feel from the dogs; neither siphoning nor offering emotional energy; just being. 'But the abuse she feels she has invited into her life, even the abuse she exacts on others . . . Don't you understand! The knife . . . It's the infanticide, Jade, or whatever the hell you call murdering unborn babies. How on earth does a soul deal with that?' My forehead is cradled in the palm of one hand and the tears are flowing freely. I am talking to the cellphone and to Jade and to the universe. 'She needs to "travel", she needs to return to a previous incarnation and somehow undo things, or receive forgiveness for her atrocities. Or maybe she doesn't have to "travel", but she needs to free herself of all the hatred she feels or she will continue for the rest of her life to destroy all the men who come near her . . .'

I am sobbing and I don't quite know what I'm trying to say, but I can hear in the long silence that follows and then in Jade's tone of voice that she has heard some or other version of this all too often from me, and when she speaks again she is resolute.

'Clive, I'm sure you have shared this with her, in some gentle way . . .'

'She . . . Jade, I even told her that I am with her so that she can stop hating.'

'And that's all you can do, the rest is up to her, and I think you are doing her a disservice if you stay for these reasons. So yes, I will say it just once—I think you should get divorced. But you may choose not to, and I have detached myself from wishing an outcome,' and I hear this as her genuine concern for me and not herself.

'I fear that she is in meltdown, just like last year . . .'

'Listen to yourself, Clive. She is ill, and she needs professional help. You can't do it for her. I am feeling angry at you for getting her so wrong, and I know that's not fair as you have tried to tell me in so many ways what she's really like and what she's capable of and why you have been petrified to leave her. But for what it's worth, Clive, I think she has to hit rock-bottom, feel abandoned, face all her worst fears, forgive herself, or whatever it is she needs to do. And only then will she truly look at herself and feel strongly enough about changing her behaviour and attitude. That will be the biggest learning, the biggest gift you can give her.'

'Intellectually I understand it, Jade.' I have my emotions back under control. 'And if that outcome was guaranteed, I might even be brave enough to martyr myself to that end. But it feels like there's a part of me that is dead to her. She said the other evening that she thinks I don't love her anymore and she threatened to kill herself, but I felt no compulsion to challenge her, to say of course I do, even though recently I felt I could say it and feel it in my heart for the first time in ages. But actually I think I meant that I was with her, dealing with the situation with love. Gentle, tender, understanding, caring, whatever you want to call it.'

'Are you surprised? You undermine yourself in order to placate her, and then she annihilates you again. It's clear you don't feel safe with her. You can only take so much. And staying with her is just feeding this side of her, and you have become co-dependent. I thought you could not leave her because of love, and the other reasons like the boys and how she would make your life hell and the damage she might inflict on herself or your children. Those reasons may still stand, though I now think you stay because there is something in it for you.'

'We've been through this before,' I say, not wanting to acknowledge this stark judgment.

'Just look at how she behaved at the deli earlier,' Jade says. 'I'm not even talking about her attack on me, that's beside the point. It's what she did to her children, in front of her children. The knife . . . and chasing them up the mountain. You cannot get more selfish than that. There was not an ounce of adult perspective there, and she always gets away with it. And you have helped her to do that, for ten years, with love in your heart and with all the right intentions, but you cannot fix her. And while I wish that for her own sake she learns from that, I no longer devote any energy to that hope and I no longer anticipate it or expect it. My angels are no longer attending to her. As for Gino . . .'

The exchange goes on for a while, until Jade says, 'Sara-lea asked me to get out of your life. It was not just a demand to stop seeing you, what she is asking me to do is to get you out of my thoughts and out of my heart.'

'Jade, you need to know that she threatened to kill you. And that William was there.'

After a long pause, she says, 'Nothing surprises me anymore, Clive. This is going to conclude in the way it has to, that future is already written.'

Afterwards I sit with my back resting uncomfortably against the sloping retaining wall and my legs outstretched and crossed at the ankles, a cappuccino and cigarettes within arm's reach. The dogs have come to a decision, and as usual it is Harry who leads the way, voting with his feet, and now they lay either side of me against my legs as if to support me. I light another cigarette and look ahead with some foreboding to what might happen next, wanting to see Jade and knowing I cannot or should not.

The dogs bark, and I look up to the road and see Calix strolling past. I don't bother to greet him. Yet I have this strange affinity for him. He too, can see what's coming, and I know he is hurting.

51

When a secret is revealed, it is the fault
of the man who confided it.

(La Bruyère)

Monday, 27 June 2011

Sarah did not come home again last night and is not answering her cellphone. I have no idea where she spent the night.

Earlier I received by email a brief synopsis on the process of mediation from the lawyer-psychologist with whom Sarah has apparently made an appointment for this coming Friday. So Sarah wants to control this process, I thought, and opened it. It did not seem to be a process that accommodates exploring alternatives to divorce; it seems to be about how to get divorced in the most agreeable way possible. So I texted Sarah to ask her to bring it forward or postpone it until next week, arguing that I don't think it is wise to have this meeting on Jack's birthday and the day before his birthday party; yet this sounded weak even to me. Actually, I was just trying to trace her, to get her to reveal herself. Not knowing where she is has me on tenterhooks. It is as much about knowing she is okay as it is about knowing the boys are safe. Sarah's psychiatrist will not speak to me—she is concerned for Sarah's state of mind but unwilling to be drawn into the fray as that is a legal matter, she says. The attorneys from last year's post-suicide attempt are 'looking into the matter' of tightening future restrictions, but said that if she is not with the boys right now there is little they can do unless she reappears and there is evidence of a direct threat. I will have to lay a formal complaint against her, they said. It's 'dead ends' every way I turn.

The boys have gone with their grandparents to the theatre this morning, and I grow more and more concerned about their safety. I dropped them off at the theatre, and will collect them all in a couple of hours. I came to the deli to pass the time, writing, not knowing what else to do with myself, hoping that Sarah will take the opportunity to confront me without the boys present. I keep looking over at Jade, but she never looks my way, though I sense this is difficult for her to do. I am sure she feels the heat of my eyes. Although I felt strong and resolute over the weekend, being in her presence like this saddens me beyond measure, perhaps more so than the imminent collapse of my marriage and intact family, and I cannot understand why it seems to mean more to me. It feels like a hole in my heart that I cannot sit with her and just talk. That is what she has been to me; someone who feels like home, my most comfortable couch, my tastiest cheese cake, my favourite blend of coffee, an exhilarating run up the mountain, a beloved pet snuggling up close. Comforting; where I can lose myself, where I don't have to be anything but myself. Where I am loved and held and appreciated. My twin flame? I look over at her again, and it looks like she has been crying. I can see she is absolutely devastated, and perhaps for this reason I keep avoiding her as she sits at the large inside table working on her computer, or pretending to. In the end we do share a few words, Jade and I, when I squat next to her table.

She says, 'Clive, my heart swells with love for you, but I need to do what is right for now. I sense deeply that in order for you to go through what you need to go through and get where you need to get to, that safe and peaceful place beyond the enormous turmoil of today, requires me to remove my energy from your orbit entirely, my every thought, though I'm not sure how to do that. She is still in my dreams too, all the time, and I don't know what to do with that. But I know that if she senses it there, if she does not believe that I have gone, she will crucify you because of me.' When she pauses, I don't know what to say, and I briefly look up at her.

'I cried this morning talking it through with Samantha. I love you so much, but these are my fears and I need you to hear this although I have expressed it before. I fear that removing my thoughts and energy may leave you feeling abandoned and lost, or at the very least believing that I'm gone for good. And then I may lose you and have to say goodbye to being in your life in that special picture where everybody is okay. And that you may seek to fill the void with someone else. These are my fears.' I can't bring myself to look at her, and she is speaking so faintly that without the benefit of reading her lips and feeling the expression in her eyes, I have to tilt my head towards her. 'But the wisdom deep inside me knows that there is only one way. I have to step into the emptiness beyond your beautiful love with faith that if this is what I think it may be, then it will become that one day and we will return to each other more whole and ready for something spectacular.'

I feel an intense physical pain emanate from somewhere in my body I cannot locate. I am crouching uncomfortably on my haunches alongside her table, not feeling safe enough to sit down next to her. The spacious interior of the deli, once our sanctuary, leaves me feeling exposed, and I am aware of the eyes of the staff upon us as they glide tentatively around us going about their business. Even those who were not present on Saturday would be apprised of the situation by now and what went down and have observed the two of us over the months.

Then she says, 'So I will leave town soon and do some business up the coast. I leave with a bubble of excitement and joy under the sadness and unease, knowing that on this journey is learning and experience which is going to continue to heal me to completion. Should this road lead us fully back to each other, what I will bring to you will be even more beautiful than what you experience now. I know this and it reverberates in a deep resounding "yes" in the deepest part of my soul. I love what you have made me, what you have revealed in me to me, how I have been able to practice being the fullness of who I am with all the conflicts and emotionality without rejection. You have made me feel safe and loved to just be me. I am so much more of me because of you.'

I suddenly trace the source of the pain. The ache comes from my knees. I place my hands on my thighs and lever myself into an upright position to ease the stiffness and immediately regret it as the delinquent crystals my knees now house grate in protest. They took a real pounding the other day. In fact, before that they were hurting more than usual since my last run up the mountain, not because I have been overdoing it, but because I have not been keeping it up lately and the thigh muscles are a bit lazy. So the working parts don't slide smoothly in the groove, and I am reminded of wayward railway tracks.

Then Jade rests her hand on my arm and leans closer to me and says, 'I cover you and your beautiful children in gentle light and I see you clearly on the other side of this smiling and unscathed. My prayers are with you as a constant mantra. Use your angels, your guides. They do not work without our request and we need to acknowledge their existence. Keep asking. You are loved and supported.'

I turn to go outside again, and she says to my departing back, 'I love you so much.'

I sit alone outside under the awning as I need to absorb what is going on and what she has said. Apart from the fact that Jade fears losing me, her concerns seem to be all about me—whether I will be crucified, whether I will feel abandoned and lost, whether I will be okay as I negotiate my way through this turbulent time. She just stated her fears but otherwise said very little of herself and this is so refreshing. Even when I had spoken to her for those few minutes and felt her heart bleeding on the floor and asked her how she is doing, all she did was look at me and ask me if I am okay.

I wonder where I will find the support that I need to get through this time. Jim, bless him and his crude patriarchal ways, is a steadying hand and he will intercede again when it is meant to be. Matthew, I think, is still out of the country. Perhaps Jade is saying that she has fulfilled her purpose to support me, and I like to think that perhaps she has done all she can and should do to shore me up and bolster me and authenticate my 'goodness' while I come to this resolution and embark on the route of consciously manifesting it. It is good that it is done, as it makes way for our bigger purpose, and perhaps the opportunity to see one day whether we will be in each others' lives, without drama but rather in the way she so eloquently speaks of it—what were her words?—'smiling and unscathed'.

Yes, Jane, I created my own hell. So now I must follow through, and do this alone. This is my shit, not hers, not anybody else's.

I'm not even sure I can grasp what I am dealing with here. Yet I have a strong sense that I am about to choose a future; I'm probably already in it. It does not feel forced, nor does it seem I have to forcibly pry it open. My future is wide open, and so is Sarah's. In fact, I have many possible futures I can create and from which to choose right now. This future is appearing, showing itself, inviting me. It feels familiar to me, as if I have imagined it before or lived it long ago or it has already happened. Though I cannot describe it; it is not of a nature that it can be defined and held and evaluated, feared facets excised and discarded, and supplemented by more desirable aspects. It is an all-or-nothing package, and all I have to do is move with it. While this moment feels about as unstable as life can get, if I embrace it consciously, willingly, is it not a moment of ecstatic potential?

Can I find 'meaning', the motivation to push through?

What else had Jane said? Oh yes, just 'watch'.

EQUIFINALITY

52

The right to swing my fist ends where
the other man's nose begins.

(Oliver Wendell Holmes)

Thursday, 30 June 2011

It is Thursday night or technically Friday morning. It is bitterly
cold and an icy wind worms through every ill-fitting timber slat of the
disused security shed in which we sit, huddled and cramped. It was
erected, carelessly but no doubt with good intent, to straddle the narrow
paved walkway intended to distinguish roadway from beach and prevent
the ever-shifting beach sands from encroaching on the tarmac, but the
paving was a laughably deficient barrier against the vagaries of nature.

The beach sand that was scuttling around the floorboards when we
climbed up the makeshift stairs with gaps where planks should be and
opened the rickety half-door now rests motionless under cover of the
blanket on which we half-sit, the residue of it wrapped around us like
a toga. But the wind continues to give wings to the top layer of beach
sand and there is already a film of gritty grains covering the blankets and
the balaclava pulled over my head, for which I am eternally grateful.
The stilts and cement blocks on which the cabin rocks like seaweed in a
swell are intended to elevate it above occasional spring tides which roll
across the beach and flood our beach bats' court and breach the narrow
raised promenade to swirl around the wheels of any vehicles unlucky
enough to be left in the faded white demarcations of diagonal parking

bays that front Jade's property. Owners of these vehicles usually sit at the beachfront restaurant across the way and bemoan the forces of nature and order another round of drinks while they wait for the defective storm drainage system to slowly siphon away the foamy waters. Tonight is one of those nights, but the late-night revellers are long gone, asked to leave no doubt long after official closing time.

The door threatens to come off its rusty hinges in the wind, and Jim, who is getting grouchier by the minute, closes it. I open it again and say, 'We need to be able to see.'

I look towards Jade's house and imagine her in bed, every inch of which I know. I hope that she is restful, getting some sleep despite the turmoil and evil intent compressing us. Perhaps I should have told her I would be here? From where we are holed up, we have a great view of Jade's front garden and artist's studio over her half-wall and timber gate, courtesy of the stilts on which the cabin is perched, and clear line-of-sight for fifty metres of the roadway either side of her property, dimly lit by the outdoor security lights of surrounding residences. Most importantly, we probably occupy the darkest space along the street.

'You had better start explaining real soon,' Jim says, trying to sound commanding but not quite carrying it off.

'Keep your voice down. And sit still. The whole idea is that nobody sees us or hears us.'

The stilts creak and sway as Jim tries to stuff more of the blanket I have provided behind his neck, but every time he resettles himself, it seems to drop off his shoulders again, and I wonder if our combined mass exceeds the recommended load for this rickety structure. Jim has removed his sodden shoes and socks and rolled up his trousers and has not stopped complaining since we got here, so I hand him a beer from the six-pack for his troubles. I try to ignore my squelching Timberland boots as I prefer to put up with the discomfort rather than face the agonizing embarrassment of trying to pursue someone barefooted.

'Is there something you need to disclose to me?' he says, refusing to lower his voice. 'You've brought some cosy blankets, beers to get me pissed, and that security stick that looks like it can do some real damage.

You been talking to her, plotting revenge? I've told you, it was an honest mistake, really it was.' He swings the torch by its leather strap, and its oscillation irritates me, quelling the mirth that rises from the ashes of his confession all those months ago. 'Or do you swing both ways?' he says. 'It's okay, I'll still be your friend, just not after dark.'

'Shut up, Jim.' I take the torch from him and put it down at his feet.

I had texted Jim before midnight, 'Pick you up in ten. Wear all black and bring something to keep you warm, beers are on me'. We had parked my vehicle down a side street some distance away. When we opened the doors he caught sight of my ruined face in the glow of the interior lights, but said nothing until we had waded through the ankle-deep sea water and ensconced ourselves in our hideout.

'I was dreaming about herself's nether regions, about to attempt a re-entry.' He always refers to the object of his desire as 'herself'.

I hush him with my palms, and whisper, 'Then you should thank me for saving you from a repetitive nightmare.'

'Tell your dogs to move up, and to stop farting. Did you really have to bring them with you?'

'That's uncollected trash and stagnant storm water you're smelling, or the seaweed and detritus and dog poo, the council workers have been clearing from the beach. And you will thank me the dogs are here if things go as I suspect they will. So leave them be, they haven't moved once, and at least they'll keep quiet and won't get pissed.' Harry and Sally, with chins mounted on their forepaws, watch this interchange with raised eyebrows.

'I thought you were taking me to a strip-joint or an S&M dungeon given the all-black attire, otherwise I never would have agreed to get out of bed. But this will be more exciting, I'm sure. So which naked woman are we going to spy on through her bedroom window?' he says, peering hopefully at the three or four properties within range. 'Did you bring night-vision binoculars?'

I ignore him, and he says, 'Look, I hope this doesn't take long because I have to get up in the morning and pretend to work.' Jim picks up the torch again and shines it in my eyes, 'If I stay here all night with you, will my face look like yours?' I grab the torch from him and switch it off, and pour some coffee from the flask. 'What the fuck happened to you, anyway?' he says. 'Your dear demented wife finally had enough?'

'I think she has. But it wasn't her.'

'Are you going to keep me in suspenders?' I have the sense that Jim really thinks he is being original with these malapropisms. I am embarrassed to recall that I had introduced him to this expression.

I take another long look around and wish I had night-vision binoculars. 'Okay,' I say, 'I was at the deli . . .'

'Where else would you be?'

I ignore him. 'Slinky was there.'

'No, you're kidding me. Old slinky did this to you?'

'Well, not exactly. The table did.' Slinky finally got a crack at me. The threatening undertones and clearly mounting aggression of recent weeks, even the car chase, had not quite prepared me for this moment.

'Let me see,' he says, and I hood my face with a blanket and close my eyes and shine the torch to a count of five. He takes in my face, incredulous, then looks at the stitched gash just above my swollen, purple eye, and I can imagine him gradually register the full picture as he slowly takes in the other tell-tale marks on my face. It hurts to talk, to move my jaw, but not because of the eye. 'Couldn't this wait till tomorrow, at the deli? This deserves to be told over a cappuccino in more luxurious surroundings. I want to survey the crime scene while you tell me what happened, to get a really good feel for it. Maybe you can even walk me through it. Perhaps one of the waiters, that really big one, can be a stand-in for Gino.'

'Fuck off, Jim.'

He looks around as if we are in public, then leans forward, relishing the details he is yet to hear. 'So?'

'He was sitting at that front table by the gate . . .'

'Who?'

'Keep up with me, Jim, I am only telling this once. Gino, he was right there by the gate, with two women, having breakfast. One of them was Amelie, who I told you was the one who spread the rumours that I abused my wife. The other was a client of Sarah's, her name is Sophia. Probably just a coincidence,' I say to his raised eyebrows I can imagine more than see. 'Knowing that we were leaving, the dogs scooted off for a pee, and I had to walk right past them to get out the gate . . .'

'Speak up a little; I can't hear you properly with this fucking wind.'

' . . . and Sophia recognized me and called me over and started talking to me.'

'You're fucking crazy, after what happened on Saturday! What did he do?'

'Nothing.' Stage whispering is a strain, so I opt for low volume, hoping the wind will make it inaudible beyond the hut. 'I think he was looking down and away from me. So I stuck out my hand and said, "Hi, Gino".'

'Why can't I witness these things?' Jim says, bemoaning his ill-luck. 'I always have to hear it second-hand.' For a split second a light passes across us, in the way spotlights sweep suspiciously around prisons or concentration camps, and we reflexively try to shrink ourselves into the blankets. Then above the rain and wind, I hear the rumble of an engine, and within seconds a light delivery truck passes by.

'I bet he is not alone in that truck and is looking for some privacy,' Jim says, watching the brake lights disappear around the corner of the restaurant. 'His boss would probably not appreciate the fact that he's using company assets for his nocturnal adventures.'

'It's as good a time as any to take a commercial break before I go on. Remember when I spent those days in solitude meditating on the mountain? Each night I had the same dream.'

'Oh, come on,' he says, rolling his eyes and throwing his arms in the air, spilling some of his beer on Sally, who takes it good naturedly and licks it off her fur and then nudges him for more.

'Bear with me, I think it's important.' I pass him another beer. And I tell him how in this dream I danced with wild abandon on a mountain plateau while my companions, one by one, seemed to float off the edge until few remained. I work my tongue around my teeth, but all it does is spread the uninvited sand grains and other less appetizing airborne flotsam around my gums. 'Anyhow, then the scene shifts and I have no hair. There is nothing around me, and yet everything I need.'

'Yes?' he says, needing more; perhaps a neatly rounded conclusion, a definitive outcome or clear direction, or at the very least, something that happens.

I say, 'And that's it.'

'That's it? You're a skinhead just like old slinky, and that's it?'

'You're so literal, Jim.' I swirl coffee around my mouth and spit out the offending liquid, hoping it misses the blanket. 'I think it's saying that in the end I'm free, at one with myself, my thoughts and my whole being unrestrained and directly connected to the Great Spirit.' I can almost imagine the hairs on his neck standing up and the shiver rumbling down his vertebra. That reminds me, I must introduce him to Francois.

'You're so weird, anybody told you that? Are you on medication for this?'

'Actually . . .'

'Don't answer that,' he says, more careful with his beer this time and choosing to raise his free hand. The blanket it held in place falls off his shoulder. 'Anyway, what did this guy look like?'

'Nobody in particular. He was faceless.'

'Well, it seems obvious to me who he is, but anyhow, I hope there is some relevance to this that will no doubt be revealed in good time.'

I pause to take another look at Jade's studio and along the road before I continue. 'So back to yesterday, I'm being introduced, okay? And you know how sometimes the eye sees something, but the mind just won't recognize it, like its scuttling through its internal corridors trying to find an appropriate folder with a similar past experience, so that it can decide how your body should react?' My eyes have readjusted after my night vision was ruined by the torch light. Jim looks at me with his head cocked to one side, a doubtful expression on his face. 'Well, it was like that. There was this delay, and now I see it in slow-motion. Gino's hidden arm, on the far side, started moving up and towards me, but there was something wrong. I could feel it but not figure it out. It was moving too fast in an upward trajectory. I'm not sure if I realized that his fist was closed, but I can picture it now. I can also see now that his head should have turned towards me first, to locate my hand if he was going to shake it, but it followed his arm. Anyway, thank god for instinctive reflexes, as his fist only glanced across my cheek, but I stumbled on a fucking umbrella stand and caught my eye on the corner of a table before a bench halted my fall. Rather painfully, I might add.'

'Was it the same bench?'

'No, not the same bench those women fell off,' I say, not too sorry that he cannot get a thrill from pointing out the karmic payback.

Rubbing my back, I say, 'Yes, you may as well laugh,' and then I have to rearrange the blanket again.

'Then what happened?' Jim says, not the least bit concerned about me and my discomfort.

'I was stunned, concussed I suppose. Nothing seemed to work properly and for a moment I could not get up. Next thing, he was on to me, pummeling me and shouting obscenities. Just as Harry and Sally came crashing over the half-wall, the waiters pulled him off and ushered him out. I guess the women went with him. The only thing I remember is he yelled out something about my boys while I was still busy trying to restrain the hounds.'

'What?'

'I couldn't make it out. But it sounded like a threat to do something to them.'

'That deli is becoming the entertainment centre of the universe,' he says, this time carefully stretching his arms up towards the sky as if offering his beer to the gods. 'If only that gorgeous owner and I might add the-now-single Samantha got her act together and broadened her offering, so to speak. Say, a weekly reality show in which you could be the star attraction. Wouldn't that be a blast? She would make a killing. Sorry, I'll rephrase that when I'm more pissed.'

'Help yourself to another beer,' I say, worried that we will run out long before sunrise or he is saturated.

'Now here's something I can tell my wife, finally, something of substance worth reporting. I will get a promotion, I'm sure. Maybe I'll even get to sleep with my boss tonight.' He pretends to look at his watch. 'Or make that tomorrow night. With me on top, for a change.'

'Yes, sleeping with your wife probably does make a change for you.'

He ignores me, and says, 'What did you tell Sara-lea?' Everyone else uses her preferred full name, and I wonder whether I should too as she is now no longer the person I met and fell in love with.

'Well, I haven't seen her all week. I just told the boys that you accidentally hit me with a beach-bat, I hope you don't mind. I could not exactly say that Jade's ex-husband took a crack at me, out of the blue, and that it was apparently not the first time he has threatened a male friend of hers. With all that's going on the last thing they need is to hear about more violence. I am sure Sarah would be underwhelmed by it all, because she already knows.'

'She is not doing herself any favours, if this comes out in the divorce proceedings,' Jim says, predicting only one possible outcome for our marriage and I am at a loss to contradict it.

'I refuse to bring the boys into it.'

'You'll be surprised what you will do, especially when you see what she uses against you. You're putting up with this in addition to the fact that she's still fucking that goat-head and threatening violence. She's playing with your boys' emotions, and yours. You need to insist, just don't accept it.'

'Easier said than done, Jim. She is very clever with it.' Jim starts to throw him arms in the air but, mindful of his beer, stops the upward trajectory and glances with deep concern at Sally.

'Anyway, how were things before Saturday?' And I tell him of Sarah's manipulations with the boys, being obtuse and spiteful and putting horrid thoughts into their heads, almost as though she was squeezing me out.

'You should've said "no",' Jim says, when I describe another double-bind situation that Sarah created. 'An arrangement is an arrangement.'

'You would have said "no". Me? I said "okay".'

'It's just a set-up, Clive, so she can hold something against you. Damned if you do, damned if you don't. She has been doing that forever,' he says dismissively.

'Anyway, as if in dress rehearsal for Saturday, last week's madness ended with her accusing me of having an affair with some woman whose name I didn't even know right there in the sand-pit restaurant, and going on about legally this and legally that in full view of everybody, and brave little almost five-year-old Jack was screaming and hitting her and refusing to get into the car.'

'He has anger issues, that kid of yours. Just like her.'

'A right spectacle, it was, and I made as little effort as possible to stop him. He's got this uncanny stabbing motion with his arm, it's unnerving.'

'Why didn't you confront her about her behaviour, right there in front of everybody?' Jim says.

'Now why hadn't I thought of that? Idiot!' I hit myself on the side of the head. 'Jesus, Jim, you're so fucking frustrating, you make things sound so simple. Think about it. She's either deranged, or has such deep-seated issues that you'd easier understand quantum physics. Neither option is promising.' This is not the time to extrapolate what I think is really behind Sarah's apparently unhinged behaviour. 'The boys were so upset already, and they've seen enough hostility, I just could not take her on in front of them. I also know that when she's in that almost-psychotic state there's really no point. At any rate, a few minutes later she was back, shouting obscenities at me over the wall at the beachfront restaurant, that one right over there,' I say, leaning out the doorway and pointing vaguely towards the restaurant adjacent to Jade's property. 'I think her parting words were—"You nasty piece of work".'

'Please, this is too much for me,' Jim says, holding his face in his hands, and we recede into our own thoughts, Jim with his beer and me with my coffee. The wind shows no sign of abating, and carries on its wings intermittent squalls which not only flurry through the flimsy walls but seem to defy gravity and seep up through the floorboards and have soaked the seat of my jeans. The more I wriggle, the more irritated my butt becomes. But it is strangely comforting to me, these water-laden gusts, as it whisks away my sickly revelations almost before they are swallowed by Jim's auditory canal such that I don't have to hear their echo and contemplate the sick reality of my words. Sitting motionless lets the cold creep right into our bones, and I wonder how much longer we will last before our teeth start chattering. Jim shifts position again. 'I'm getting so fucking stiff,' he says.

'Steady, Jim. That's more information than I need. You want the baton? I'll show you how to use it on yourself.'

With a—'Fucking dog,' Jim shoves Harry's head, which has found its way to his thigh, and Harry gives him a look.

Wanting to bring my recollections of what transpired last week to a close, I say, 'That's not all, Jim.' But first he wants me to retell him in more detail about that bruising confrontation last Saturday at the deli, with the death threats and sangoma–witchcraft curses that kept the deli regulars enthralled until little Jack panicked and caused those three women to upend their bench and display their underwear to whomever cared to peek, ending with the car chase.

Jim says, 'So you've got me here to watch kinky Slinky attack Jade? Jesus!'

'Not sure. But let me fill you in about the crazy voodoo stuff that Jade and I have experienced this week. That's why we're here, watching her place.'

'I don't want to hear it.'

'You have to, as I may not be around soon to tell the tale, and I might need your help tonight.'

Jim is not too sure if I am being facetious or not, but I can feel the tension in my voice and I guess I am doing a poor job of hiding the fact that I am shaken by these events. I want to light a cigarette. I take a second empty sugar wrapper from my pocket so I can keep the fingers of both hands busy by twirling to a frenzy, a habit that grew in the wake of discovering her betrayal while I paced about outside in my feverish midnight anguish.

'I can't believe this,' Jim says. 'I'm sitting here shivering in the dark of night, and an awful one at that, with someone who thinks he will suffer a premature demise perhaps in my presence and before sunrise. And he's telling me this story because he wants me to bear witness to what really happened so that the perpetrators can be brought to justice. Fuck it, Clive, I'll be a target by association. We're camped deep inside enemy territory with a flood outside and no back-up. Where are the fucking cops? Sorry to offend your dogs' sensibilities, but what use will they be? Can't this wait till daylight and familiar surroundings?'

'Jim, someone's been into Jade's studio the last three nights. You can see it from here, it's that shed buttressed against her bedroom.' He does not care to look. 'She only told me this morning. Nothing was taken during the first break-in on Monday night but some personal items were mysteriously left behind with a "Kilroy was here" tone to it. When we spoke about it this morning she said she was initially unconcerned about it as she thought it was some homeless people looking for shelter. The second night some of her personal items were tampered with and displayed around the studio – photographs were pinned on the walls and spread across the desk, her artworks defaced, and letters strewn about on the floor.' I hold out the nearly depleted six-pack. 'Want another beer?'

Jim shakes his head, but I can see he is enthralled by the mystery of it when he says, 'That sounds like the work of a vindictive and deranged mind.'

'You like the idea of that?' I say. 'It fits your thesis? Then wait, the worst is still to come.'

'Why don't you shine this torch under your chin like a campfire ghost story; really give me the shits?'

'Listen up, Jim. Jade was blasé about it and refused to act even after the second incident. All she did was install a motion detector with a security light. What happened last night was more menacing. Without doubt it's witchcraft stuff, and so she mentioned it to me this morning and I can see she is scared. She has not yet figured out the meaning of the symbols smeared in red on her walls, yet other items carefully placed about leaves little doubt of the black magic at work.'

This provokes Jim to look out towards Jade's studio. 'This is insane. I'll have that beer now.'

'No, I'll tell you what's insane. I have experienced the same vandalism, or that's what I thought it was until this morning.' Ignorant of what had taken place in her studio, first thing this morning I hurried down to the deli to tell Jade my news.

'Don't tell me the same things happened to you?' he says, reaching over for the beers I was too slow to supply him. And I tell him how, in a one-plus-one equals three way, this morning Jade and I grew evermore appalled as we related our discoveries to each other and it dawned on us that we were under a concerted two-pronged attack—for we learnt that on the same nights we had experienced the same pattern of intrusion with menacing messages escalating in intensity.

'In my case, Jimbo, on the first night the pot plants at the front door were upturned and their content emptied. Mischievous kids, I had thought. The second night, which happened to follow the day our gardener was there, stepping into the kitchen courtyard to have a pre-dawn smoke and pace around, I discovered the pitchfork and garden shears left on the courtyard wall, and thought how uncharacteristic that was of him. But I thought nothing of it. My thoughts yesterday morning were no more ominous than that, and I simply opted to lock the tool room door from then on, as it just occurred to me that these doubled as dangerous weapons, especially in the hands of boisterous boys, and I remembered that a few weeks ago Jack had a temper tantrum and was about to hit Jeremiah without realizing he had a pair of scissors in his hands and I had to dive-tackle him to prevent . . .'

'Now you know why I never come to your house,' Jim says, needing to contribute something but fresh out of mystery and mayhem in his life. 'It's safer to read about these things. At least then I survive long enough to read the sequel.'

'I'll send you a complimentary copy of my much-awaited novel. You won't have to wait long for it to be published as I think we're nearing the climax now, perhaps the penultimate chapter.'

'You'll be famous—post-humorously.'

'That's posthumously, Jim. It's more like a psycho-horror, not a comedy-drama. In fact, the only amusing bits are when your character takes centre stage, and even those parts are not that witty—more like funny-peculiar than funny ha-ha. Anyhow, at least you will have something else to tell your wife, that you knew a blockbuster author who is now deceased.'

'But then who will play beach bats with me? There will be nobody on whom to inflict body-blows anymore,' he says, which reminds me to take another look outside.

'When I have two good eyes again, I suggest you suit up in full protective gear. I will have no mercy, Jim. Anyhow, there's always Gino.' The balaclava is irritating my face, strands of wool catching on the freshly-formed scabs.

'So that's it?' Jim says, reeling the conversation back in. 'Pot plants and garden implements?'

'There's more.' Jim fake-gestures that he has had enough, but his ears have practically detached themselves from his face and impatiently climbed down my throat to pull the story out. 'This morning, as I let the dogs out and turned to close the front door behind me, I saw blood-red streaks and spatters on the double-doors.'

'For fuck sakes, you too?' Jim is horror-struck. He does not believe in this stuff, but I think it is because it sends shivers down his spine and makes his hair curl. He wriggles about and gets fidgety and starts to scratch himself all over, dislodging the blanket again. Harry and Sally lift their heads to watch him, and I imagine them saying, 'Why don't you grow your own, Jim? Look at us, our furry blankets never leave our sides'. Jim says, 'Real blood or, um, just really red?' He does not wait for confirmation. 'I think it's time to leave town. And I'm talking about me. You're on your own, buddy. And don't think that decades' of undeniably dubious friendship guarantees my undying loyalty and protection. The feudal system is no more,' Jim says, dredging up a conversation we had six months ago just before Sarah disappeared the first time.

'No, yours is an undying love.'

'And no amount of beer in lieu of danger pay will bribe me to sit here any longer in this lean-to and listen to this shit. Just give me the juicy bits and we can go home.'

'I no longer expect your valiant devotion ever since you set up that run-in with that Neanderthal Gino on the beach, and look where that got me.' I touch my face, at least the balaclava covering it, which will soon be rainbow-coloured. 'I'm after your brain, not your brawn.'

'So why exactly am I in this hell-hole with you and your canines tonight?'

'So I can chase the bad guys while you work out a strategy.'

Jim tries to smile but it is not convincing. 'You need to involve the police now,' he says.

'You're probably right, it's just that I don't have any proof it's her. I took photographs of the front door before making my way to the deli to show Jade and we checked whether it matched the symbols in her studio. I could not see any pattern to them, but she's been working on it.'

Throwing together a synopsis for Jim, of all that has happened the last ten days, has left me feeling acutely uneasy and I am certain this churning angst is not entirely influenced by Jim's overstated impressions and at times melodramatic reactions. I feel it as tightness, a constriction in my chest, not queasiness in my gut, and it has been swelling in proportion all day. The theme of the last week, albeit dissimilar in content, has an eerie correlation with the pattern of escalation that preceded Sarah's disappearance last year and was the precursor to the horror she inflicted on herself and the boys before that. I now think there is no way back for her. Feeding Jim's insatiable appetite for intrigue might have passed the time but does not take the edge off the reality of why we are sitting here in the dead of night. I think this tension will only be relieved if my worst fears are realized tonight, which means we will see action and I am suddenly aware of not being cut out for it.

Jim says, 'So to hone in on the deranged heroine of this sordid tale for a moment, where is Sara-lea these days? Moved in with your arch-rival, Calix, yet?'

'I don't know. I haven't seen her since Saturday. But she kidnapped the boys yesterday.'

Jim's jaw hinges open. I pour some more coffee from the flask, spilling half of it, and wonder how to tell Jim what really brought us here tonight. Sarah has not responded to the daily voicemail and text and email I have been sending her since she moved out and disappeared. But today, which is now yesterday I guess, she somehow managed to persuade the au pair (summarily fired) to let her take Joshua and Jeremiah from the nursery playground, while I was attending to a lengthy ablution with Jack, whose tummy was upset, yet again. Frantic phone calls produced no leads as to their whereabouts. So by mid-evening as I paced around the kitchen courtyard and Jack dozed in front of the television, my mind was all over the place and swimming with dark forebodings. Our cats, Matisse and Picasso, sat apart on the parapet wall that overlooks the courtyard, tails neatly wrapped around them, the tip tucked in between their forepaws, and I made a note to check if they always lie with their tails on the same side. Even Harry and Sally had tired of 'fetch the ball' and lay near their empty bowls hoping for amnesia to set in so that they might get a second evening meal. It would not be the first time I had done that in the disarray of the last twelve months.

My mind was having great difficulty accommodating what was happening. It was used to conducting reconnaissance missions into possible futures, scanning various paths forward and returning with intelligence of what it had seen. But now my imagination dispatched emissary after emissary ahead down the only possible route and none of them returned. I knew it was Jack she wanted, and believed the others were safe until she had him in her grasp. Feeling hemmed in within the confines of the kitchen courtyard walls, my thigh muscles started twitching and trembling first, as if trying to pull me in different directions, but each option seemed to be counteracted by an equal and opposite force; the appeal of each alternative I considered was offset by a contradictory negative consequence or diluted by a prohibitively off-putting downside risk. Then one additional variation of a thought plummeted into the cup already filled to the brim and, too heavy to contemplate, it broke the calm surface tension that belied the barely contained agitation within my head, and fear spilled into my body. Pure, unadulterated terror. Though my whole body spoke to me, warning me that all was not well, I speculated whether it just needed me to take some sort of action; to do something, anything.

Then my cellphone showed that Angela was calling. 'Hi Clive,' she said as if we were not living in unusual times. 'Is Sara-lea with you?'

I said, 'No,' and my blood froze. 'Not since Saturday.'

'Well, she's not answering her phone.'

'Yes, I know. When last did you see her?'

'She left the boys with me this afternoon, saying she needed a break. I did not . . .'

'She . . . You . . . Josh and Jerry? She left the boys with you? You've got them?' Why would Sarah go to the trouble to snatch them, only to dump them within reach, if not to show just how easy it is? Because she wants Jack?

' . . . press her on what time she would return, but now it's after dinner and I'm getting concerned. The boys are asking for you and I can't placate them any longer. Come to think of it, she seemed pretty spun out this morning.'

'Angela, do you realize . . . Never mind. Just listen to me.' In an instant, deep concern became alarm, then horror—that icy dread when the indescribable monster has you and it will soon be over, but 'soon' will persist to infinity. 'Listen Angela, wherever you stand on this stuff that's going on between us, please listen carefully to what I'm going to tell you.' And running up the front steps to the car with Jack complaining in my arms, I related, headlines only, what has transpired since the weekend. She listened quietly, and I could not fathom what she was making of it. But if she was silent, I reasoned, then she was worried.

'I know none of this, Clive, except that she seemed angry with you. It just seemed like there was some unpleasantness, but she didn't go into any details. I didn't think it was unusual, given the circumstances. I don't think . . .'

'There's more, Angela,' I said, reversing out the driveway. 'For three nights in a row our house has been vandalized.'

'That's nothing to do with Sara-lea.'

'For fuck sakes, Angela, just listen to me. She's a danger to herself and the boys. She cannot go anywhere near them, do you understand? If you see her, let me know.'

'I don't believe she will do that . . . She told me not . . .'

'Angela, I'm coming over to fetch the boys.'

'You can't . . .'

'I can. It's not negotiable.'

That is what happened around sunset, but to Jim I just say that Sarah took the boys and I got them back. He does not ask for more detail, and I think his brain is oversaturated and struggling with how to condense this all into a synopsis worthy of reporting back to his wife.

'And you think all this witchcraft shit is her?' he says.

'I don't know.'

'Could it be her lover-boy, the one who has a fetish for horns?'

'I don't know him well enough to say and I can't find him. But he has motive and is into the esoteric side of things. Maybe under her expert tutelage . . .'

'What about Slinky Gino?'

'It's not his style, it's too subtle and psychological. And that brutish oaf would never delay the instant gratification of his explosive aggression.'

'Okay. So what's Jade going to do now?' he says, looking out towards her place.

'Leave town, it seems, probably later today, until we figure this out.'

'You should too.'

'Not without the boys.'

'Then take them with you. Where are they now, anyway?'

'At their grandparents' house.'

'Are you mad?' He spills his beer again. 'How can geriatrics ward off a crazy lady?'

'It's the only place they feel safe away from me, and there's a security guard patrolling their street. Now that she is bold enough to kidnap them, the boys can't stay at home because Sarah has a key for the security gates.'

'Then change the locks, or move out, or something, but you're not staying at my house. Shouldn't they be under some sort of protection now? You've surely got enough to justify that?'

I have changed the door locks, but new security gates will take three weeks to manufacture and replace.

'I don't want some welfare agency getting involved and removing the boys. It will destroy them. It's exactly what happened to Sarah, isn't it, and look at the damage that caused? And anyway tomorrow is Jack's birthday and . . .'

The dogs raise their heads and their ears prick up, and I tell them it is okay. Then above the whine of the wind I hear what they had; shuffling feet wading through water. I feel around for the security baton, but cannot find it, and it occurs to me it should have a beeper or a flashing light or something.

'What is it?' Jim says, murmuring softer than he has all night. 'Can you see them?'

'Stay calm, Jim, or the dogs will pick up your anxiety and react,' I say, and think how ridiculous this sounds until I realize I am talking to myself. As I screen out all irrelevant noise, above the din of the whistling wind and the creaking of the rotting structure, murmuring voices carry to my ears, and Harry growls. I can just about make out a single figure, wearing what seems to be a trench coat, coming towards Jade's property from the far side. I grope around in the blankets. 'Where's that fucking baton?'

'Oh, is that what you're looking for?' Jim stage-whispers. 'Think I'm going to give it to you and rely on my non-existent kung-fu skills?'

'Then you tackle the intruder, and I'll run for help.'

'Here, you take the baton,' Jim says, his mind quickly made up.

Something does not fit. The shadow-shape is lilting and zigzagging through the ankle-deep waters, and making no attempt to conceal itself as it nears Jade's gate. 'He's wearing a hood,' I say. 'No, wait, I think it's a blanket over his head.'

'Give me intelligence that's useful,' Jim says from just behind my ear, trying to get a look for himself.

I wait a few more seconds, then slump down into the blanket, laughing. 'It's just a homeless guy, talking to himself. One of the regulars around here. I think I recognize his outfit. Talking about split personalities, he always argues with himself and loses.' Harry and Sally sink their chins on their forelegs with a barely audible whine, looking disappointed, and I wonder if they relish the thought of combat tonight.

'Jesus,' Jim says, knocking over his beer. Perhaps he is not very thirsty. 'I think I just dissipated.'

'Better than constipated and other vile words that rhyme.'

'Your sense of humour is only exceeded by your personal charm.'

And we lapse into silence, listening to the wading boots fading into the distance. My heart is still leaping out of my chest and my muscles tremor as the surge of adrenaline seeks an outlet. We sit like this for a long while, then Jim says, 'What was that term you kept using when we were chatting last year?'

'Probably, "fuck off, Jim," or some variation of that.'

'No. Something about "no matter what you do, you'll end up with the same result"?'

I don't correct his slight misinterpretation. 'Equifinality.'

'What?'

'Equi, as in "equal",' I articulate with exaggerated care. 'And "finality", which is self-explanatory, even for you.'

'Then I will concede that I think I get your point.'

'You're so gracious in defeat, Jim.'

'But don't think I'm withdrawing anything I said last year, when you just could not see the writing on the wall, not even when she used her own blood to put it there,' he says, referring to Sarah's inclination to self-mutilate and graffiti her internal pain on our walls by way of greeting my homecomings until I managed to coax her into professional help after I found her lying in a cooling, pink-stained bathtub. I hope this is not the start of another of his beer-inspired ramblings of 'life according to Jim'. 'I'm still standing by it, every word. You should have left her then with your body and mind still intact, partially at least. By now you would have reinvented yourself and your three boys would have known sanity for the first time in their short, sorrowful lives.'

We both fall silent again, and I can hear Harry snoring until Jim nudges him. I imagine lighting a cigarette and wonder if I could get away with it. Jim's eyes melt into the middle distance, deep in thought. After a while, discarding our hitherto hushed tones, full voiced he says, 'After she tried to take her kids' lives last year, I had hoped that you were finally free of her when she disappeared. But no, you wanted to be a fucking hero so you let her back in and I for one would hold you responsible if anything happens to them now.' He looks out towards Jade's house. 'I reckon that's all the action we'll get tonight. And for what it's worth, I would say Sara-lea seems to be self-destructing, in complete meltdown. Not only is she making her ongoing affairs so public, but from her recent violence and this latest madness it seems she has lost all reason, and to bring the kids into it is shocking. I won't remind you of my view.'

'No, you won't.' But that does not stop him.

'My view is that you have fucked yourself, big time. But it doesn't matter now, as I think we have reached the endgame.' He has heard enough and seen enough to prophesize. 'I reckon in the next couple of days, in fact before the weekend is over, your future will be mapped out before your eyes. She's going to blow. Or her hit-man will.'

'Got enough to report to your wife and justify your absence this dreary night?' I say.

'Yup,' he smiles. 'Just do me a favour. This time give me advance notice when the final scene is about to take place. Front row seats please, as a member of the inner circle. I would hate to miss it.'

For a moment I think I am defibrillating or the cabin is about to collapse, but then I realize it is my cellphone lodged in my shirt pocket vibrating against my heart. I look at my watch; it is a quarter-to-four. I use a corner of the blanket to conceal the glow from the screen. It's the neighbourhood watch security team. I had asked them to check on our house as often as possible through the night. 'Has the alarm gone off?' I say. 'Which zone is it?'

'It's not the alarm, sir,' says the female voice. 'Your password, please?'

My mind goes blank for a moment; then it comes to me.

'Please hold while I connect you to the officer on site.'

'What's happened?' I say, suspiciously looking around our claustrophobic quarters wondering whether I am on candid camera. My mind is instantly awash with horrid thoughts about the boys.

'Bear with me, sir, you're going through.'

A male voice, heavily accented, says, 'We are outside your house, sir. We don't see your dogs. Are they inside?'

Christ, is that all this is about? 'No, they're with me.'

'Anybody at home, sir?'

'There shouldn't be. Why?'

'Are you able to return home right away?'

'Why? What is it?'

'Sir, there are two cats nailed to the front door. Lots of blood or red paint, it looks like, splattered around. And what seem to be the words "This" and "That" with arrows pointing to each cat.' This and That were the nicknames of our cats before we rescued them as eight-week old kittens, the only two survivors from the litter abandoned in a cardboard box alongside the road. I gag on the bitter bile that rises. 'That's not all, sir. Below the cats, the word "Next" is written. Does that mean anything to you? And there's an arrow pointing to a drawing of some stick figures with the numerals "567" . . .'

'How many stick figures?' But I already know the answer.

'Three.'

Joshua, Jeremiah, and little Jack.

'567'? I can't immediately think what that means, except that Joshua is seven years old, Jeremiah is six, and Jack turns five tomorrow.

'I'm on my way,' I say.

53

But after observation and analysis,
when you find that anything agrees with
reason and is conducive to the good and
benefit of one and all, then accept it
and live up to it.

(Buddha)

Friday, 1 July 2011

Around the deli, dampness hangs thick in the air from last night's storm, and I should be exhausted from the night spent with Jim in the hut but I am not and I realize that it will set in later, when it is ready. The cappuccino tastes awful, my gut still churning from the unappetizing early morning clean-up of what remained of 'This' and 'That'.

Something makes me look up and I see Gino pacing up and down the pavement, talking on his cellphone and looking around as if he is trying to locate someone. With his arrival, my face spontaneously throbs and above the eye it feels raw like a scab that has been picked, the wound oozing blood again and sensitive to the rush of air it has exposed. I feel conspicuous as no other patrons seem willing to withstand the chilly early morning air, but for some reason I don't feel particularly vulnerable to another attack. But I do startle when, through the door behind me a woman steps into the courtyard where I sit and says, 'Oh, hi.' It is Amelie.

Feeling flanked, I say, 'Hello, Amelie,' my level voice belying my feelings.

She pauses alongside my table, smiling at me and looking around. Maybe she is not sure where to sit, given she has so many choices as there is nobody else here, but she is lingering in the way people do when they are about to say something but don't quite know how to start. So I start it for her, and say, 'I think we know each other, but haven't formally introduced ourselves.'

She smiles and just looks at me, as if she does not know what to say without incriminating herself. 'You borrowed my cigarette lighter the other day,' I say. I thought this a better option than to remind her she was here the other day when Gino decked me.

I extend my hand, and she says, 'And you are?'

'I'm Clive,' I say, and wonder why she is playing this game. I think of what I really want to say to her about the rumours she is spreading about me, and that she is a snitch for Gino and/or Sarah, and there is this frozen moment between us, bodies immobile, smiles painted, eyes locked, as we both seem to be unsure what the next best move is. The moment is broken only when Gino appears from behind me. He ignores me and greets her and they sit at a corner table behind me with him facing in my direction. Far as I know, Jade has described this as her space and said that Gino never comes to the deli, but here he is again today, together with his closest female friend, staking his claim on territory that we have assumed is mine and Jade's and ours. It is cloudy but he is wearing sunglasses, I saw that much when he entered, and if I turn my head and risk a glance in his direction I will not know if he is meeting my eye, so I keep my eyes focused on my laptop and wonder—what is the meaning of this?

My heart leaps when my cellphone rings; it's Matthew, he must be back from overseas. It's not like me to be this jumpy, is it? Or is this the new me?

'How are you, brother, it's been a long time? Don't you love me anymore?'

'Hold on, Matt, you got a few minutes, I need to talk to you?' And I seek some privacy under the guise of taking the dogs for a stroll on the grass verge adjacent to the deli. 'This is early for you,' I say. 'You still in bed?'

'Yes, still shagging the secretary.' I doubt it is true. Matthew has a directness and innocence about him such that he is always forgiven for these remarks. Sometimes, even by his wife. I think of asking him what brand of condom he is using but, picking up on my tone of voice and instantly sounding awake and serious, he says, 'What's up?'

I recap the last few days to put him in the picture, and then say, 'I found the two boys at Angela's house last night, so I dropped them all at their grandparents with strict instructions about security, and then I staked out Jade's place.'

'You what?'

'I took that security guard baton I have and some blankets and we, Jim and I and the dogs, hid in a little unused security hut outside Jade's house. It wasn't so easy to conceal my car, it's so distinctive and the only one of its type in the area, so I had to park it miles away. There's access to her kitchen back door from the other street, too, through the driveway gate where her car is parked, and I couldn't cover that side but her studio was in clear view of where we sat.'

'You should have called my brother. You know his background, he loves that stuff.'

'Too late for that now. It's proved to be a good way to reduce my nicotine intake. Anyhow, nothing happened and about two hours before sunrise, I got a call from our security guys. I'd better come home, they said, because there are two cats nailed to the front door with the words "This" and "That" painted in red and a whole lot of other stuff which turned out to be the previous markings from Wednesday night. Are you still there, Matt? . . . Matt?'

'Yes. Go on.' In almost any adverse circumstance over the many decades I have known him, Matthew seldom gives away his true feelings. But at that moment I could feel the hairs on his neck stand up.

'Anyway, when I got there, I had a good look at it. There were also three little painted stick figures lying horizontally at the bottom of the door, with the word "next" and an arrow pointing to each one. What do you make of that?'

'Same thing you do,' he says.

'So I cleaned up the mess, I can't let the boys see that. It was awful. Harry and Sally acted all strange, at first they wouldn't let me near the cats, and I had to lock them up in the house while I did it, and they wouldn't stop whining and scratching at the front door. Anyway, then Jade phoned to say all her tires have been slashed.'

'But weren't you outside her house all night?'

'It must have happened just after we left to go back to my house, or someone managed to get over the driveway security gate on the other side of the property, which is not impossible. Even from Gino's property next door, it's really just a hoist and a leap over the wall. Jade was upset with me for watching her place, or for not telling her, or both probably. Said she doesn't need that kind of energy around, but what was I to do? I managed to distract her by getting her worried about *her* cat. If she can get the tires replaced in time, she can still leave town today as planned. She was ambivalent about it all week, but I think this has settled it for her.'

'Maybe you weren't as well concealed as you thought?'

'Or maybe it's more than just one person, acting in concert,' I say. I tell him who else I think could be involved; the same names I gave to the 'good' cop.

'Called the cops yet?'

'Because of the cats, yes, and got hold of that same tame detective we had before. Frankly, I was not sure what to make of Saturday's events, and I may have slipped up by not taking firmer action there, but I was advised earlier in the week that there was not much I could do about Sarah as the boys were safe with me and she hadn't infringed on any of the court's stipulations.'

'Jeez, you're not serious? Does there have to be a homicide for them to pull their fingers out?'

'Practically, it seems. Besides, nobody knows where she is. But now, well, we might have trouble proving a case of kidnapping, but I'm sure she has breached the court's requirements in some way. Anyway, I'm hanging around now for the police to let me know when they can come take a look and then I can go fetch the boys. I had to concede that there is no direct evidence to connect it to Sarah, and it took a while to convince him that it's not a dull case of vandalism but a real concern I have for Sarah and what she might do to herself and the boys.'

'Not to mention you and Jade.'

'I had to dig deep and reveal more than I would have liked, because I can't risk them taking the boys away. Between the lines I think he understood this, but it means he has to instigate things unofficially. But because of the history and the unusual circumstances, I think he eventually understood the urgency and they will investigate it, keep an eye out for her vehicle, try to locate her cellphone position, that sort of thing. Not sure what help it will be, though.' I have kept moving while talking, aimlessly, following the dogs, really, and now they are outside Jade's driveway gate, sniffing and barking and wagging their tails and looking back at me as if to say, 'Here's a place we could call home'. But for me, it is also tainted now, and I call them and head back towards the deli.

Matthew says, 'What's your gut say, Clive?'

'I have to consider the possibility it's her, the risk is too high not to. Whoever it is, I would have thought the dogs would be next, but maybe they're too difficult to get to being with me all the time.'

'And even if it's not her,' Matthew says, 'I think you have to find her quickly, within twenty-four hours, for her own sake. How can we help? Where did she go last time she disappeared?'

'She never said. I've driven around this morning, up the mountain passes, past her favourite haunts, anywhere I could think of, but I really don't think she's in the area unless someone's helping to conceal her. I've also gone all the way to her workplace, the two gyms she goes to, and I've called a number of her friends. This time I was more open about it and asked them to keep a lookout for her. A couple of them offered to drive around the village side streets today. And I plan to have a go at her psychiatrist, if she is courteous enough to return my call. The confounding thing is, Sarah is typically so confrontational and impulsive, know what I mean? She always acts in the moment. She will walk right up to you and speak her mind or push you down or whatever. It may be brash and reckless and tactless, but that's her style, and at least you knew where you stood.'

'But this,' Matthew says, 'this seems premeditated. From what you've told me the last four nights were planned to perfection, steadily escalating.'

'When we got back from the aquarium on Saturday, I saw she had destroyed Jade's artworks, those four pieces you've seen. And I mean destroyed, canvasses shredded, shells crushed to sand-grain smithereens, even the frames wrecked.'

'So there's no reason to think it will end here?' When I don't respond, Matthew says, 'I've kept much of your saga from Jordan at your request, but I'm going to tell her everything now, okay?'

'Yes. My concern, if it is Sarah, is that those cats meant so much to her . . .'

'She's gone over the edge?'

'And she's gone underground. Nothing's beyond her now, Matthew. My main concern now is the safety of the boys. And to flush her out.'

'How are the boys?'

'I called my parents really early because I was anxious after what happened, and they are fine. I spoke to each of them, and wished Jack "Happy Birthday" and promised to be there soon as I can.'

'If you need a place to stay . . .'

'Thanks, I haven't decided yet what to do tonight, I'll let you know. But I think I need your presence tomorrow at Jack's party.'

'Shouldn't you cancel it, and get the hell out of here?'

'I've thought about it, Matt. Sarah could disappear and be untraceable for months, and we will live in perpetual fear. It almost feels like that's her intention. The boys won't be able to go to school or participate in sport and extramural activities and they'll have to be under constant guard. Their lives will be severely restricted and I can't do that to them. I refuse to. I've had enough of this now. I want to end it, flush her out, and get her the help she needs.' Not to mention, get her irrational dark energy out of my orbit. 'And for reasons I won't get into now, I believe she is after Jack, so I think it will all go down at his party.'

And Matthew says, 'Okay. Let me think about what you've told me, and I'll call you later. And if you're going to hang around, ask the police services for protection.'

When I return to the deli courtyard, I find Gino and Amelie still sitting there. Back at my table and keenly aware of their presence, my mind leaps around trying to locate where things have got to and how I am feeling about it. I am sitting here because I just don't know where else to go; the revulsion I had felt once I had cleaned up the mess at home was all too much for me to stay there. Today was meant to start with our scheduled appointment with a mediator, and I don't know whether Sarah cancelled it. I have the mediation forms on my laptop which I should have filled in by now and sent back to them, but I keep opening them and then minimizing them, as I have now done, and eventually closing the files. It is as if I know it is a needless exercise, or I need an interim step to get me there; what is it?

And tomorrow is Jack's birthday party; now there's a disaster just waiting to happen. Am I being stubborn by not calling it off, or will this really be the opportunity for her to resurface? I plan to call on Jim and Matthew's loyal physical presence after all. Oh shit, it dawns on me that there are things to do for the party. I try Sarah's number again, as I have every hour, and disconnect when I get her voicemail. There was no sign of Calix at his house early this morning and he has not responded to my voicemail, so putting faith I don't necessarily feel in his sagacity I text him, trying a different tact—'Sara-lea is unstable. Please help her.' I do the same for Catherine, her psychotherapist. Then I phone Granny again, just to still my anxiety over the boys, and to tell her I will be delayed as I have to get my head around refreshments and decorations and party packs and a birthday cake, which Sarah was going to bake.

'I could try my hand at baking tonight,' I say to my mother, 'but the promised fire engine cake is probably beyond me.'

'I'll do it,' she says. That sorted, I start making a mental checklist for the party. Even though it is just us three sitting in the deli courtyard, Samantha keeps popping outside with her 'the customer is always right' smile firmly locked in place, like an overly anxious parent checking up on the kids playing too quietly in their room. Perhaps it is pre-emptive damage control. I wonder if Jade has updated her on the more sinister happenings.

Jane strolls by, looking all funky and ten years younger with her grey hair cropped short and spiky. She waves and says, 'I've had a few thoughts. I will stop for a cup of coffee with you later on my way back.' But for some reason I just know I won't see her later. I dispatch a silent wish to her retreating back—be safe.

Then Francois walks in, flustered, and shakes my hand, and I laugh inside at my slight hesitation. 'Glad I caught you. My dad's really ill,' he says, and I wonder how he manages to always be smiling so broadly, especially with that kind of news? 'I'm leaving today for Johannesburg to see him. I'm planning to stay there for a while, see what the work opportunities are.'

'Sorry to hear about your dad. How's Azura doing? What's going to happen to Marcus?' Marcus is the child they share.

'Sorry I gotta run, I've got lots to do still.'

That's so uncharacteristic of him. I have never seen Francois in a rush before; panicked, eyes wild, like he is high. It is as if all the central characters are paying a quick grim reaper visit and it feels ill-omened rather than a blessing. I have a deep knowing that when the day closes, my life will have changed. It feeds my growing disquiet, and all the while I am preoccupied with these thoughts, I can hear Gino's voice in the background at the table in the far corner. It sounds smooth and easy, and then suddenly my reverie is broken and I look up to see Amelie standing next to me. Gino, it seems, has gone. I think she has said something to me, so I say, 'Excuse me?'

'I would like to say something to you,' she says. 'Do you mind if I sit down?'

'Okay.'

We both light cigarettes. She looks earnest and sincere, rather than sounds it, but I listen to her as she proceeds to apologise to me for saying to Jade that she thinks it was me who may have broken into Jade's studio. That is news to me. I tread a fine line between gushing my acceptance and refusing her act of contrition. Without giving too much away, I manage to let her know that I am aware that she has heard stuff from Sarah and that her name also came up associated with ugly comments about my alleged aggressive nature some months ago, and more recently that I frequent whorehouses and deal in drugs and sleep with teenagers and cut and burn Sarah. I am very wary of somehow linking this to Jade. I excuse myself after just a few minutes saying I have a party to organize. That should do the job of alerting Sarah; it is practically a personal invite. The detective has not called yet, but I cannot wait around any longer. I pack up my gear and make my way to my car, while the dogs make a quick detour for their ablutions to the adjacent patch of grass to which they are drawn, and I am grateful I don't have their acute sense of smell. I look up to see Gino leaning against the bonnet of my car, one booted foot perched against the shiny grill in the absence of the ruined fender, arms folded across his chest. And I wonder if Amelie just stalled me so that Gino could get into position? I say, 'Hi' and smile from behind my sunglasses, my good eye trying to watch him while scanning the immediate vicinity for his reinforcements. I open the tailgate and the dogs jump inside and then, feeling decidedly bolshie, I walk up to him and say, 'Need help with your car?'

I intended to back this up with the appropriate nonchalant demeanour, trying to appear reposed, but I strike what feels like an awkward pose, as the tension within me seems to contort my limbs. Gino is about to say something, or do something, but then looks beyond my shoulder, and I can feel rather than see two of the male waiters standing behind me, one of them as big as Gino. I must remember to bring them more giveaway children's clothes and tip them better next time. Gino hesitates, then takes the two steps he needs to reach me and hisses between clenched teeth, 'Next time,' and as he steps past me, he firmly nudges my shoulder with his. He is expecting to meet with resistance, but my cowardly flinch turns my shoulder and assisted by the uneven paving which catches his heel, he stumbles. It is probably not the most graceful shoulder charge he has ever executed. Fucking jerk!

Confused emotions course through my veins, and I need to walk it off before I go to the supermarket and visit the boys and wish Jack happy birthday. So when Gino has gone, I let the dogs out the car again and take them for a stroll around the block, past Jade's house, where the dogs run ahead and wait expectantly at her gate again as if that's where they really want to go or think I should go and I have to call them to get them to come with me. On the way back, I think about Jade's last email and how she is coping as she prepares to drive away from town and this mess. As usual, I need my time with her to talk things through, hear her wisdom, and feel her energy.

Her email of last night went:

> *I dare not let the thoughts of today pass my lips—what do we do with the unspeakable?*

> *I'm about to embark on a journey of serious commitment. But I have two loves and I don't know what to do with that—so I go with what seems right. I want to be loved and desired exclusively too. I want to judge myself for this duplicity. I hate that I cannot tell him. I have to live with it and be okay with me, but I would hate to be in his shoes. I realise only in hindsight that I got pissed off with you for no sign of forward movement for 'us'—actually backward once she started to cotton on; for what looked like apathy. I was open to a new way of loving—but realised once I saw her character and personality and her dangerous nature that it would be impossible and would be fraught with drama and ugliness—no love can withstand too much of that. I think I*

always believed you would never leave. So into the calculator of
my three perception centres—mind, heart, and gut—went this
information; heart stayed strong—the other two calculated low.

In the car I phone Jade to tell her what happened and warn her to be careful as Gino is apparently willing to continue overstepping the physical boundaries, and she hits the roof, both because Gino had chosen to ruffle me with his proximity and threats and because she does not trust Amelie's motives.

'It infuriates me that I cannot speak to Sarah about what's going on,' I say. 'The potential threat of violence from her is just an extension of her control. Anyway, she is such a hypocrite. She was so friendly when she borrowed my lighter the other day.'

'Who? Amelie? And a gossip,' Jade says. 'She is still spreading stories that you abuse your wife, and when I bumped into her yesterday evening, she asked me whether I had established who had broken into my studio three times this week because she thinks it is you, as she put it—"that weird guy with the dogs that I sit with at the deli".'

'How did she even know about it?'

'I don't know, but I think they want to pin it on you.'

'What do you think?'

'I don't entertain the thought. I told her, like I told Gino months ago, that I don't believe you are aggressive with your wife, that I know you are not that person. When Calix and Sara-lea seemed to disappear without trace, that fuelled the suspicions around you. There are things I have wondered about you, things that would bother me like pornography, drugs, and other women, that are partly my issues and partly because I have heard the stuff being spread around about you, but we have spoken about these things and I believe I know who you are. We both know who did it, Clive. And I now fear for my cat and your dogs.'

That lingering doubt about my character clarified, at least for now, I say, 'I don't know what Sarah was up to at night this week since she moved out of the house, and in theory it could be him or her or their accomplices, for all we know. But we can't be sure who did it.' I imagine the look on her face, doubtful, or perhaps it is pity or frustration at my denial. 'And I think you're turning a blind eye to another possibility.'

'What's that?'

'It's "who". William.'

'That's absurd.'

'Disinvest yourself of your personal attachment to him for a moment,' I say. 'It's disconcerting that he came to the deli that day, and apparently did not tell you he was in town. He is in touch with things like psychic space, and you have told me that despite his apparent initial acceptance, it turns out he struggles so with our connection and with your love for me. And how difficult it is for him that we are in close proximity here at the deli and how he has psychic dreams about it and seems to know when you dream of me. And I fear that you are not being true to yourself by accepting his conditions, his views on love and relationship, that you are building your love house out of straw, but that conversation's not for now, if ever. I'm just asking you to accept that it's not beyond the bounds of possibility for him to team up with Sarah and divulge all about us, perhaps even add that we are still seeing each other and other nonsense. Maybe even bring Gino into it. In fact, the three of them working together would be formidable.'

'Why would he do that?'

'To wedge forever a no-go zone between us.'

'No,' Jade says.

'I'm just saying what's possible, Jade. The other day, the last time he was here, he uttered the only words he has ever said to me—"You have no place in our union," and off he went.'

'Then we must consider Calix too.'

'You're right, but let's leave it at that for now. Breathe, Jade, breathe. Bring yourself back into the present with breath. Calm down, you need all your senses focused right now, on the here and now. Just keep Pi-shu close, and when you leave, drive safely.'

54

Do not believe in anything simply
because you have heard it.

(Buddha)

Saturday, 2 July 2011

When I arrive at the deli this morning, I see Jade's car with pristine discs of black rubber treads on each wheel rim, and am confused enough to check my cellphone to see what day it is as she was supposed to depart yesterday. I smile, as by her own admission Jade finds it difficult to get things together, to organize herself around a task. So I sit outside and log on to the internet. I know that when she is ready, she will come and talk.

I had argued that I cannot prepare a surprise party with Jack around, so the boys are with their grandparents and my mother has come to the rescue and enlisted their assistance to bake a cake. It is not long before Jade detours past my table on her way to deposit a load of artwork in her car and slowing down, she says, 'With all his faults, this is one thing Gino always did for me. He packed all my stuff and made sure I was good to go,' and I wonder if this was what she had wanted or was it for his own gratification, one of the ways he exerted control over her.

'My house is in disarray, and I'm so not ready to leave,' she says, as she passes by again and carries another two canvasses she has removed from the deli walls where she displays them and dumps them in the boot of her car. Most of the items are delicate and she can only carry two or three at a time, and I cannot even help her as this will be too risky.

When she returns, she stops by my table and I say, 'Where's Pi-shu?'

'In the car, getting cabin fever. And he's still pissed at being locked up in my bedroom last night.'

'You haven't left because you weren't ready to?'

'In more ways than one. Yesterday completely threw me, and I just could not get it together. It took all day to get the tires replaced, anyway. And this is a big day for me.'

'I know it's the anniversary of Wade's death. I will never forget it, as it is also the day that Sarah confessed her affair.'

Our eyes soften in unison. I get up and we hug, and I hold on to her a little longer and tighter than is polite. As we disengage, she hesitates and scans my face, then touches it gingerly. It looks worse now than when she saw me briefly on Thursday morning, a veritable rainbow of colours. If she notices I am favouring my left knee after gashing it open to the kneecap, while attempting a theatrical dive chasing a flying disc with Jim the other day, she says nothing. I feel edgy, incomplete again in anticipation of her imminent departure, and look for something coherent to say. I think she is justifying her decision to flee town with—'I really have to visit my stockists up the coast,' but we both know why she is really leaving. And I don't know if or when she will return. I don't want to ask her, because I might not like the answer.

'Remember how upset you were when I told you I had raised Amelie with Sarah, because this could be linked back to you? You were afraid that Gino would abuse this information, and that Sarah would hurt you. I think you want to get out of here now because you feel this has started.'

'Well, look what's happened the last few days,' she says. 'Her mangled mind is toying with me, Clive. It's sick. It's worse than a full frontal attack, which is what you got. I find I am now carrying my mace spray around with me wherever I go, and I know that means I am not okay.'

She had thought after last Saturday's menacing altercation that it was a good time to get away for a while, but the incidents this week had really spooked her. Not just Gino's vented aggression, but also the break-ins to the art studio leading off her bedroom on her property, as the personal nature of what was done had escalated each time and its clear message spoke louder than the wanton destruction that took place. What happened to 'This' and 'That', Matisse and Picasso, has left no doubt in her mind.

'That reminds me,' I say. 'Given the confrontations and the threats and the break-ins to your studio, I was wondering whether you should not get legal protection and keep her a few hundred meters away from you and your home?' I think I say this because we both feel we are abandoning each other to our own devices and therefore cannot watch each other's backs.

'I don't want to do that. I don't want that energy here. I want to do this with love. And I can take care of myself. It's you I'm worried about. Gino is a loose cannon, and to think he actually attacked you after all this time means there's definitely an escalation, or he finally has confirmation about you and me. What's scary is that she got to him and they're working together now.'

Although we can talk without being overheard as we are alone in the courtyard of the deli, someone who knows Sarah well steps into the restaurant and I say, 'I think we should continue this later.'

'I don't have time,' Jade says, 'and I really need to ask you something.' She folds her arms and we place ourselves either side of one of the poles that supports the tarpaulin above us, as if this creates a more respectable picture to an observer. To add to the illusion, I half-turn away from her and look out towards the parked cars, hoping to create the impression of an impolite or half-disinterested conversationalist. 'Tell me if I am wrong,' she says, lips barely moving. 'Tell me if this is my stuff because this is what I heard from you. A week or two ago I heard you say if you had done this differently we could have continued like this indefinitely, and this is not what I would want to hear from you, I suppose. I think I heard most clearly that you are not ready to consider the end of your marriage, that you persist with the dream picture, and as willing as I have been to entertain the dream picture I realise she will not. What I have heard from you is "I want my marriage, I want myself" which is completely acceptable and fine but once again makes me ask, "where does that leave me?" Given the two confrontations and all the rest of it and the space I am in as a result I think what I would prefer to hear is that you see you are not getting your desired outcome and need to make different choices now.'

I think Jade has got a point. Not because she heard me right, but because I have not been clear with her. I have not made promises to her, which I think she might now be in need of because of the recent escalation and the uncertainty that leaving town brings and the choices she will face while she is with William. I had thought that anything I said, in the vulnerability of the past few weeks, would interfere with her path, with what she needs to accomplish by November. Besides, I don't yet know my own possible future, so how can I expect her to commit to 'ours'.

Jade is not yet done and says, 'Then your discussion around revealing all about us in the mediation as all you feel you have left is your integrity, felt like another blow . . .'

'Jade, she already knows about us.'

' . . . I feel very much on the back foot too now and edging towards selfishness from the standpoint of when the shit hits the fan, I'm going to be the only one watching my back, especially when you come clean with Sara-lea. It seems to me that revelation is not going to be about us and how precious this is to you but about either preserving your marriage or preserving your integrity. So I am feeling this is not okay for me at all anymore.' She looks at her watch. 'I'll come back just now to say goodbye.'

It may be the last minute rush to depart that has set her off in this panic, or her way of justifying what she is doing; or perhaps it is fear for her safety. But I think I now have another possible answer to why she is leaving. I sit and wait for her, and I hope she is not going to be long as

I need to leave shortly to do last minute preparations at the party venue I have organised.

Then the moment arrives.

'I'm done,' she says. 'I am just collecting some stuff from home. I will come by here when I leave to say goodbye to Samantha as she has popped out for a while and I promised to give her a squeeze before I leave.'

'I might not be here then. I have to go now to prepare for Jack's party.'

'So I probably won't see you later before I leave.' She looks haggard, as much physically as emotionally. I get up to hug her goodbye. She seems fuller, rounder, as if her body has stored fat reserves in anticipation of a period of impending stress and deprivation. We hold each other tightly and she whispers into my ear, 'The other day I realised just how good you are for me. You so gently and compassionately and without any hint of criticism or judgment, light my dark corners for me. Thank you for showing me where I still hold anger and resentment, where I am not dealing with something quite honestly. You are a blessing and an angel. I value my relationship with you above anything I have ever had.'

From within the deli, watchful eyes are upon us, but still holding me tight, she says, 'I began a difficult conversation with you a few weeks ago. I had wanted to continue it and then Saturday happened, taking us into a state of emergency again and putting you at the rock face of possible divorce and on top of it I am going away, so I thought perhaps this was not the time. I have written to you, but I also want to say it.'

And she goes on to tell me more about William. She is talking quickly now, maybe because she has run out of time or maybe because it is a difficult topic or else she is feeling my anxiety or worried about her own safety. Most of this I already know, some of it intuitively, but it feels much more laden with possibility when I hear it now. I keep my chin firmly buried in the saddle of her shoulder because I don't want her to see my eyes; they will reveal too much. I want to shake her, to scream at her—'No! No! No!' and to tell her not to go away or ask her to wait because I am coming with her. But I say, 'Thank you for telling me. I have known this and was waiting for it to happen.'

'My sense of loyalty to you, to us, and my dream make me feel that to engage with this could feel duplicitous and incongruous,' Jade says. 'My fear and judgment of myself is about what if I take my focus off us by looking at something else that is potentially threatening, as opposed to a non-threatening focus like work? How will that affect the November outcome? And then I have to remind myself that I have been given no option but to take my focus off us and detach from ideas or outcomes, and given no alternative but to leave because I am under attack.'

'I think you should go now, it's not safe for you here. Get yourself out of harm's way and on the road. Give yourself time and space to think about things. About you, about this, and about us.'

She arches her back and extracts her face from my jersey, such that I cannot prevent her eyes from searching mine. 'You are so amazing, Clive, such a great and good man and my thoughts go always to your lightness and wit, your authenticity and presence. I never see you slip behind a mask. You inspire me to be the absolute best me I can be.'

Her soft lips brush my neck, and I feel rather than hear her draw one last deep in-breath to take the smell of me with her. Our minds convince our bodies to disengage with each other, and her hands roll down my arms and for a split second squeeze mine, and she has to use them to push herself away from me. I don't look towards her when she leaves the deli, but I glance around for signs of Gino, and watch her until she is safely through her security gate.

55

But that I am forbid, to tell the secrets
of my prison-house, I could a tale
unfold whose lightest word would harrow
up thy soul.

(Shakespeare's Hamlet)

Saturday, 2 July 2011 (continued)

I leave shortly after she does and rush to collect the boys and two of Jack's friends for his birthday party. The venue is the local fire station, where we have arranged for a part-education, part-fun-filled demonstration of fire and rescue services for the kids. As we enter the premises through the remote-controlled gate, my skin crawls and I can feel Sarah's presence. But her vehicle is not here. Jim is waiting, looking uncomfortable with his hands pocketed and pacing between the fire tenders. Matthew has just called to say he is five minutes away. He is always late.

The station commander shakes my hand and says, 'Your wife dropped off the cake and said she will be back shortly.'

The extravagant proportions of the fire station suddenly seem to close in on me. My skin is cold and clammy. I want her to show herself, but fear leaps into my throat and lodges there.

'Oh, good. Where is it?' I hear myself say. 'Come with me, boys.' I take Jack and Joshua's hands. 'Jeremiah, hold Jim's hand.'

Slowly, I lift the lid of the cake tin. As promised, it is a fire engine cake, meticulously bedecked with a pretzel ladder and licorice fire hoses and red sucker flashing lights atop the cabin.

'Wow,' Joshua says.

Jack reaches for it, then stops and says, 'Dad, what does that say?'

He can read, but it does not make sense to him. It says, 'Happy Birthday—next.'

'Why does it not say "Jack"?' Jack says.

'Where's mommy?' Jeremiah says.

'Let's go,' Jim says. 'Now!'

'No.' I use my cellphone to take a photograph of the cake and send it to the detective with the message—'*What now?*'

He calls straight away and needs little convincing after witnessing the graffiti on the front door yesterday. He says, 'I'll do what I can but it's short notice and we're short staffed, so it's likely I can organize protection by this evening, perhaps only tomorrow.'

'Tomorrow is too late,' I say. 'We'll be gone by then, one way or the other,' and I place the cake in the SUV with Jack crying in protest.

Every time I hear another vehicle pulling in to the station, I rush towards the entrance expecting to see Sarah, but it proves each time to be just another invited family arriving and I hope they don't misread as disenchantment the expression on my face and my furtive glances over their shoulders, as if anticipating the arrival of more important guests. I tell those people who ask after Sarah, that she is not feeling well and may arrive later, and note the let-down evident on their faces. They look at my battered face, but few mention it. Only one of the fathers asks me what happened to the Jeep. When it seems most have arrived, I suggest to the station chief that we may as well get going.

'What about your wife?' he says. 'She said don't start without her, so shouldn't we wait?'

I glance at my watch: it is 11.11. 'It's just a number,' I think, and shake my head and the demonstration gets going. The children sit on a carpet in a demarcated area with big eyes and full of concentration, looking smart in fleeting ownership of fire helmets and jackets, and I

envy the senior fireman's ability to hold their attention while they learn
how to crawl to an exit in a smoke-filled room and roll themselves over
and over to extinguish the flames if their clothing has caught alight.
They set off the siren and the kids count down from sixty and watch
spellbound, while a fireman slides down the pole and gets equipped in
his gear, boots, mask, oxygen tank, and all in record time.

Under these circumstances, I realize just how porous these premises
are. Much to his dismay, I shove our beloved baton, yet to see action,
into Jim's hands, and send him to watch the road access gate and direct
Matthew to the rear of the station building, open to the mountain. I am
half-expecting to be sucked into another lifetime. My heart lumps my throat
and the tension is unbearable. Is it the foreboding of her simply making
an appearance, or the anticipation of a surprise attack? Just where has her
crazed mind gone with this? If she is going to strike, I surmise the primary
target will be Jack, but will she attempt to neutralize others first? Or will
it be some sort of Blitzkrieg, a saturation bombing with little concern for
collateral damage? And what role will she have assigned to Gino?

I pretend to hide myself behind my camera near the building's
entrance so I can keep a lookout for Sarah, while the children queue
up in single file in anticipation of sliding down a single-story fireman's
pole. Then the siren goes off again, and the team-of-eight firemen seem
to forget we are their guests and dash around and within one minute the
fire tender in which they now sit races from the building, siren blaring.
For a while we stand around nonplussed, and it takes us adults a while
to realize it is a real call-out.

Jim is quick to call a caucus in hushed tones. 'Boykie,' he says, trying
to soften me with the affection of the nickname he has assigned to me
for decades, 'this is the excuse we need. Tell them the party is over due to
unforeseen circumstances beyond your control . . .'

'Jim,' I say, not looking at him but over at the children, trying to
keep all three boys within range, 'we'll stick with the plan.'

'What plan?'

'My brother will be here soon as he's done with his meeting,'
Matthew says, caught between understanding my need and not liking

this one bit. I turn away from Jim's grumbles and we try to placate the disillusioned boys and girls by telling them we could not have organized it more perfectly had we tried. We hang around devouring party snacks and someone finds a football to keep them busy and I have a tough time keeping an eye on all three boys. Harry and Sally stick to me like Velcro, clearly perturbed by the nervous energy, and I wonder what their minds make of this. My mind, meanwhile, is playing paranoid tricks and I begin to suspect that Sarah could have orchestrated the call-out as it has left us alone and vulnerable, so I assign myself to watch Jack and Matthew and Jim to each of the older boys. Matthew fixes a half-smile to his face and carries out his child-minding with grim determination; Jim however, looks irate and visibly uncomfortable around all these children, and broods on the fringe by the main gate near his parked vehicle.

I am just about to tell him he is neglecting his duties, when the fire truck reappears and the fire crew waves both a smiley-greeting and humble-apologies. It was apparently a false alarm, and for their patience, the kids get a chance to tinker with some of the specialized equipment and roll out the fire hoses, and for a moment I am fully in the present and my heart smiles from behind my clicking camera at the squeals of delight as they each take a turn and water jets from the nozzle under pressure and a few of them take the opportunity to scamper through the spray. With the interruption nearly two hours have elapsed, and I wonder just how much more of this I can take. Then the fire chief tells me that they have permission to break regulations and will transport the kids in fire tenders to the after-party venue despite it being just beyond the range of the traffic roundabout demarcated for such 'educational' trips.

Jim marches up to me as the barely contained tension spills over and says, 'Fuck it, Clive, you're fucking crazy!' I notice the affectionate nickname has been ditched.

'Fuck it, Jim,' I say, not to be outdone by his overindulgence in expletives. 'Get into your fucking car and keep your fucking eyes open!' I think the score is three: two.

I send Matthew ahead in his vehicle to cast his eyes around the next venue before we arrive. When I arrive, I scan for any signs of Sarah's presence. The second venue is a restaurant, one half of which is devoted to the children's playground, a maze of covered, elevated boardwalks and fun activities, and I wonder what possessed me to think that we could manage this but I really had not considered it would get this far. It suddenly occurs to me how many people and young lives I am putting at potential risk. It is filled to near-capacity with squealing, laughing, crying, running children, and I can imagine Jim's blood curdling with the prospect of our complement to add to the mayhem. Parents of young children have a look about them that distinguishes them from 'normal' adults, and I imagine that even if we had plain clothed minders here, hulking at a corner table, sunglasses and all, Sarah would identify them within seconds. And that's assuming they would look like normal adults to start with.

Dogs are not allowed inside this venue, so Harry and Sally sit like sphinxes either side of the entrance door, looking quite proud of themselves though I am sure that tedium will set in and this will wear off, and for a moment the word attached to this thought triggers visions of other, more enjoyable pastimes. I try and picture how far out of town Jade may be by now, but I cannot get a sense of it. And by divine synchronicity, in that moment I receive a text from her—'*Salty liquid fills my eyes*'. She and Pi-shu must be finally on the road, two sentient beings I don't have to watch out for right now. After the children have disembarked and been ushered within, I rally my unenthusiastic troops.

'Gentlemen, assume your positions,' I say, shooting hopelessly short of achieving levity.

'Bulge under armpits? Check! Dark glasses? Check! Moustache? Check!' Matthew says, seeing where I am trying to go with this.

'Where the fuck is your brother?' Jim says too loudly, sounding right on the edge and a number of patrons of this 'family venue' cast questionable looks at him. This is more than he had bargained for.

Matthew does not take offence. 'He's been delayed at his meeting. He said he will be on his way shortly, but he is a couple of hours out of town.' The disappointment of the hoped for back-up from a man with the reputation of a marine and the skills of a professional hunter, drain the colour from Jim's face as if it was only the imminent anticipation of his arrival that kept the plug in place. Jim does not know the full story, but Matthew and I share a knowing glance that says his brother's presence is sorely missed.

I wander around a lot but mostly position myself near the entrance, belatedly concerned that perhaps Harry and Sally will be the next targets after all and they are completely exposed where they proudly sit. I ask Matthew and Jim to stay within five meters of the three boys, which is a mathematical impossibility. But this instruction serves to keep other adults entertained, and there is much hilarity and finger pointing at these two grown men on their hands and knees, bums in the air, trying to negotiate, good-naturedly in one case only, the playground of elevated roofed structures and tunnels too narrow for their girth, and their creative excuses after being repeatedly told that adults are not allowed on the equipment. To their relief, it is eventually time for cake and birthday songs, which is when Sarah normally takes over with her creativity and sense of what will work for the children. Surely this is the last opportunity she has?

It is the type of venue where it is difficult to say when a party ends, but bit-by-bit our invited guests bid farewell and others melt into the masses. As it is no longer 'Jack's party' I can feel the tension in me subsiding but it still needs an outlet. When I want to call it a day, Jack says, 'Where's Mommy? You promised she would be here.' I hadn't, but he wants it so. The boys still seem to have endless reserves of energy and beg me to go to the deli, just a long stone's throw away, for their favourite milkshakes, and this feels more appealing than going home to a place which no longer feels like home.

Matthew has to go but pledges to return in a couple of hours 'if necessary' and Jim thinks about it but cannot find a ready excuse to leave or perhaps he is afraid of missing the action, again. I think his brain has putrefied, so I say, 'Come on, I'll buy you a beer, it's the only compensation you're going to get.' So I sit with Jim at our regular table at the deli, and download the photographs of the party on to the laptop and start to put a picture-book together just to give me something to focus on.

'Boys,' I say, 'please stay close, and after all that cake, let's wait for half-an-hour before we have milkshakes.'

Jim says, 'What happened to the nannies they promised?'

'The detective's trying to organize something for us from tomorrow, something about paperwork and the formal process they need to follow.'

'When will you leave?'

'In the morning. It's too late to leave now.' The trailer is ready, bags packed, and waiting at the door. I just need to load it.

'I still think you're fucking crazy.'

'There's no other way, Jim.' He lapses into his own thoughts perhaps, like me, too anxious for idle chatter and his mind too full with the horrors of this week. Just ten days after the winter solstice, darkness has abruptly descended around us, bringing with it the oppressive reality that we still don't have closure, the unrequited release I so longed for. Eventually I light a cigarette. Then my cellphone beeps a notification; it is an email from Jade.

Is it you, Clive, who has been preparing me for him?

If I consult with my rational mind, I can come to a conclusion that this has been presented to me to spare me the agony of the triangle that 'may always be' and my most recent repetitive dream which tells me there will be little change with regard to my place there even after the race is run. I can go to the rationale that despite the love and depth we share, if I look at all the factors and put them into my mental calculator, Sara-lea being the greatest factor, the odds of a peaceful conventional life together seem slim. And I need that, I want that.

I sometimes wonder if a total commitment to something else is the only thing that would take me away from you completely—as we discussed, and as I knew would be necessary for you to complete what you need to do on this leg of your journey without me playing any part at all. It does not detract in any way from the love or feelings I have for you which leaves me in a quandary.

This is where I am today. It could change tomorrow. I can only hope that there is no serious or permanent damage to us should the time come for us to be together in a real way, and that if that time comes we will have perspective on why this needed to be here now. Yet I am sure that will be hinged on the choices I make.

I realise that this is going to raise as many questions for you as it has for me and a whole lot of emotions too.

So I'm going to ask you to release me to this, if you have not already.

So Much Love

I gather the boys, and with Jim hanging back a little, we take the dogs for a short walk on the patch of grass alongside the deli and down past Jade's house while I think about things. I cannot help but peer through the driveway security gate to see signs of her car, even though she must be well clear of the city limits by now. What is this need she has to keep saying these things to me? She seems fixated on this other man; perhaps not sure of what will happen when she sees him, how she will feel, or what the consequences will be of how she chooses to handle it. I am startled by how much it seems to overwhelm her. I realize I had considered it a small issue in the greater scheme of things, just a brief moment of crossing paths with him because he is conveniently en route, perhaps a day or two in his presence and then off to wherever she is going. Whatever the level of intimacy she chooses or has already shared with him on previous visits, I had already decided is of no consequence to me and we have never raised it. But reading that email, it dawns on me that it seems more like a destination, perhaps the sole purpose of her going.

When we return to the deli, it occurs to me that I have not seen Samantha around since we arrived, and I want to ask her what time Jade left and warn her about Sarah. Frankly, I don't have a plan for tonight; I had hinged everything on her showing herself before nightfall, and now doubt fills my mind. Sitting here, waiting, starts to feel unbearable, and I decide to reply to Jade, if just to let her know that I am here, to feel me. So I log on with the laptop for ease of typing. I want to tell her how I feel—fragile and emotional, but I know I have to stop burdening her with what is happening here and how I am feeling. I know that the time for that has long passed, but I really don't know what to say to her. I try to explain where I am at without imposing on her, but my emotions are all over the place and it all comes out in a jumbled mess and in the end, I compose a long and rambling response which reads like a dispassionate discourse, a considered opinion of some matter far removed from me. It feels nothing like what I am really feeling, so I delete it.

Then Jim says he needs to 'relieve' himself.

'Why don't you just say "I want to have a shit"?'

He gets up, and says, 'I'm in polite company. If I'm not back in three days, send in a search and rescue team.'

'More likely search and recovery by then,' I say to his departing back, and note how our frazzled brains can do no better than this mindless banter. I ask one of the waiters for two bowls of water for the dogs. Jack sits on my lap, wanting to play with my cellphone. I can hear Joshua and Jeremiah behind me, sitting at a table just inside the open doorway through which Jim sauntered like he has been sitting in a saddle for a week, and playing some or other card game. All within easy reach. An image crosses my mind of trying to cram my sleeping bag into its carrier, supposedly custom-made for it but I am convinced designed to be marginally just too small for it to fit. That is how I feel. Now that I am sitting down, I can barely move, and my knee throbs. I can tell my body is digging into its last reserves after the ever-mounting angst of today, which has been stuffed into the fragile vessel of my body, and I have this intense desire to close my eyes. My mind, I think, has long ago given up, saturated beyond recovery. My brain translates the message from my body, and decides the best way to put it is to remind me that I have had only four hours' sleep since Wednesday night.

'Just give me a moment, Jack,' I say. 'I just need to send a message quickly.'

'Can I have a milkshake now?'

'Okay, and please check what your brothers want and order for them too.'

I hear Jack asking his siblings what they want while I key in a few lines to Jade:

Hey, Princess

You will know what you need to do. For you.

With love and respect, I wish you on your way.

May your spirit soar . . .

I press 'Send', fumble the cellphone into its belt clip thinking surely be now they should have designed something less cumbersome. When she reads this, I hope she feels released.

And then it happens.

56

Saturday, 2 July 2011 (continued)

It all happens so quickly.

A commotion breaks out from somewhere inside the deli. I am so distracted by my thoughts and numbed by exhaustion that I do not pay immediate attention to the furore. Favouring my injured knee which protests whenever flexed, I only look up and peer in through the window but cannot make out clearly what is going on; just people in motion and looks on faces that alarm me. I have got my own problems, I remind myself, so I will leave them to it. Then Harry moves. To a degree it is the uncharacteristically swift pace at which he gets up, but more so his manner, his emotional energy, which alerts me. It shouts 'emergency'. In the next instant, someone yells, and then I hear Jack's piercing scream.

Next thing, I am inside, every cell of my being seeking out the form of Jack, but without success. The laser focus of energy and eyes inside the deli limelight a figure straddling something on the floor, its arm arcing sickening blows. My mind is struggling to register it; it is Sarah atop Jade. I scream out for Jack as Harry crashes his massive frame into Sarah and then she is on her side, outstretched arm still clinging to Jade's clothing, with Harry between them and the knife I now see clutched in her hand, metal gleaming red, scythes and hacks at Harry until I get hold of Sarah. For a moment I see her eyes: how can gateways to the soul indicate the presence of a living being behind them and yet be so without life? Then, like an upturned tortoise, I am lying on my back clutching Sarah, holding her wrists and pinning her arms across her stomach and wrapping my legs around hers. But now I am defenceless as Gino's knuckled fist finds its mark and splits my skin with a rush of blood which fills my eye as my cheekbone fragments, and I fight against the darkness that envelops me.

He has me in a neck hold, trying to drag me away. Sarah's legs break free of mine, and still hanging onto her I scuttle like a crab and twist my body to undo his vice-like grip, and think of Sumo wrestlers. But I can feel the life-force draining from me while I thrust and convulse, trying to dislodge him. No, it's Harry, who has him by the shoulder and is hauling the combined weights of the three of us across the floor, trying to yank Gino off me, and I hear Gino scream in my ear as his flesh tears. With what feels like my last conscious effort, I whiplash my neck and the back of my skull makes contact with his nose with a crack and a spurt of blood and I feel his grasp loosen and I can breathe again. But I hang on to Sarah until someone wrenches the knife from her hands and lifts her, kicking, biting, and screaming from me. This person, firmly holding onto Sarah, looks like Calix. But that is not possible, is it?

Then a cascade of images consume me and come to rest at a scene: I dismount and gather into my arms a deep-red robe which conceals the form of a woman, near-dead it seems and almost weightless. Then suddenly I am, again, inside the deli crawling over towards Jade and yelling at Harry, 'Harry, yonder!' but not caring too much if he obeys me, and the words sound garbled.

I scream, 'Jack! Jack!' I know he is here, I heard him scream. Jeremiah is crying and saying, 'Please, Daddy,' over and over again; Joshua's emotions seem masked by a catatonic stare. It is amazing what inconsequential things one absorbs in a moment like this—that deathly hush; perhaps it is because a calamity focuses the mind tremendously. I can hear the music piped through the restaurant's speakers and a car alarm going off in the middle-distance, and I see three or four people standing in a shabby half-circle a fixed radius from Jade with lips syncing yet hear no sound emanate from them. I take in some overturned chairs and a table, and some stuff scattered around on the floor beside her that may be her artworks or table settings—it is just a peripheral blur.

Harry is going berserk, making frenzied attempts to paw at his wounds. I call out again, 'Jack! Where are you?' and kneel over Jade. She is quiet and still; her eyelids are closed. There is blood everywhere, or so it seems, as the area immediately surrounding Jade telescopes; the whole universe becomes a black hole concentrated on the orb that encircles her. It is as if everything that matters converges at this point. She lies in a very unnatural position, as if something uncomfortable is beneath her. She is clinging to a tablecloth, and when I pull it aside, I see that her white fleece top is a mess. But when I lift her left hand still protectively resting on her stomach, what I see and touch there is slippery and rubbery and feels nothing like the material of a garment. She has what appear to be multiple stab wounds, mainly to her abdomen, and defensive lacerations to her arms and hands.

'Jade? Jade, please!' I hold her face in my hands. Her cheekbone and temple are spliced and oozing. Blood mats her blonde hair and pools on the floor from the wound in her head; the bump I feel for already prominent. I think I feel a faint pulse, very weak and irregular. But I can't be sure.

My vision blurs, my tears are warm. 'Princess . . . Not now . . . I'm not ready . . . What do you need? . . . ' I am confused and I realize I am talking to her, but in my head—'Go, if you wish . . . *may your spirit soar . . .*'

One arm is awkwardly twisted behind her back, and I wonder if it is broken. I lift the tablecloth, and then I see him. Her arm is holding Jack, shielding him behind her back. I am indecisive; I don't know what to do as I don't want to see what I am sure I will see. The wheel of time grinds to a halt, heavily scraping and groaning as it rotates in my mind with a repetitive sequence of thoughts, over and over—'I have killed my son; I, Clive, have sacrificed him from cowardice and dread and procrastination and the stubborn, selfish need to do this my way. I have lost my love, my protector, my angel; my laughing playful tempestuous essence of a boy, for the longing of a sick fantasy of freedom to love. Nothing will bring him back but to undo time. God, what have I done?'

Then Sarah's satanic screams set me in motion again. But I have to push Jade, move her a bit to pull him free, and it's startling how heavy she is; in an instant I know I have carried bloated, deadweight human bodies before, and how in uncooperative angular repose they appear grotesquely heavy. Now I am talking to Jack. I am trying to be careful, gentle with him, but one of his limbs remain wedged beneath her and I cannot lift Jade and extract him at the same time. Behind me someone gasps in horror.

'It's all right now, Princess,' I coax her. 'I have him. You can let him go. You saved him. It's okay, give him to me now.' But I am not sure she succeeded, and I am afraid to take my eyes off them for fear both Jade and little Jack will not be there when I turn back to them. Perhaps if I keep looking at them, they will never be able to leave me? 'Help me, someone, please. Jim, where the fuck are you?' And suddenly Jim is there and Jack is free and I hold him close. He doesn't feel right. He is also heavier than I am used to—so much for the notion of losing twenty-one grams at death.

Standing next to me now, Joshua says, 'Stop Mommy.'

'It's okay now, Josh,' I say. 'It's over. It's okay. Everything's okay. Where's Jeremiah?' I cannot see what is wrong with Jack, just smudges of blood but no obvious signs of injury. 'Jack?' but he is non-responsive. I want to shake him back to life. I feel for a pulse, but I think it is mine I am feeling, fast and loud, and I can feel my heart drumming in my chest, my blood coursing through my veins.

'Jim, get the boys to the Jeep, now.'

'Someone has called 911,' he says. 'Wait for them.'

I put Jack in his arms. 'Don't let them out of your sight.'

'Boykie . . . ' But I already have Jade in my arms and she feels light as a feather as I carry her to the car. I have little doubt she is bleeding out and I cannot sit there and watch her go. She lies bleeding all over the rear seat with her head cradled on Samantha's lap, tablecloths pressed to her belly to staunch the bleeding and hold together what seems determined to spill out and haphazardly covered with my jacket and the dogs' blankets for warmth.

As I start the car, I feel an incongruous sense of relief because they are all with me and not within reach of Sarah. I cannot see through my left eye; yes, it is the same eye, closing fast, and I struggle to judge speed and distance. While I weave and jerk through the lazy inebriated weekend traffic, hazards flashing, Samantha talks gently to Jade.

'How's she doing, Sam?' I say.

'I really don't know . . . I mean, it looks . . .'

'For fuck sakes, just hurry,' says Jim, preferring not to hear what it looks like.

By some stroke of luck, the third row-of-seats are still in place after carting children to the party earlier. In the rear-view mirror, I can see Joshua and Jeremiah sitting wide-eyed in the back. Jim sits uncomfortably erect in the front passenger seat holding Jack, both of them bouncing and swaying around as Jim has not had the opportunity to reach for his seatbelt. Jack's little body is rag doll limp, the usual sheen of his olive skin seems pasty and blotchy. I place my hand on him whenever I can. Jim says, 'There's a bump coming up on his forehead, right here, it's bleeding a little.'

'Yes, I see it now. Blunt force contusion, not the knife, thank god. Let's hope it's a good sign, that he's just out cold.' Jim's expression is a mixture of distaste and horror as he seems to contemplate the reality of what he holds in his arms. 'Hold him close, Jim. Give him all the life force you've got. I'm counting on you,' and for once he can find no retort.

I had no time to check on Harry's wounds. Sally was trying to do that for me, and I had a moment to notice that so long as she kept away from his neck for the most part he was letting her. Although he was still whining, I am sure he would have collapsed by now if he was in serious danger. He will surely later let me know that he is not impressed with my nonchalant disregard after his heroics. I can still picture the perplexed expression in their eyes as I accelerated away from the deli without them.

To nobody in particular I say, 'That was a helluva time to take a shit.'

EPILOGUE

I am starting to think that none of this really happened.

I have not been back to the deli since. Samantha has called a number of times to see how we are doing, the boys and me, and once she relayed to me what she knew until I told her, 'Please stop. I don't want to hear any more.' But it is her need to verbalise away the trauma, and I listened for a while as she said, 'Clive, I was in the kitchen arguing with the chef, in fact, I had called all the staff off the floor to shit on them, when Jade stuck her head around the door and mouthed that she wanted to say goodbye. I was surprised because I thought I had missed her, but it seems she just could not leave town without connecting with me.' Samantha only has a partial account, as she did not witness the first few seconds. 'I was following Jade out from the back-office and heard her shout, "Get away," and Jack scream, but by the time I had reached the top of the stairs and rounded the corner, the first thing I saw was that she seemed to be trying to shield Jack from Sara-lea and then Sara-lea knocked her down . . .'

I wonder what will happen to Sara-lea? I call her that now as I cannot think of her as the same person she once was to me. When I close my eyes, I can clearly picture her even now. The strength of her was phenomenal; it frightens me still. And I have awoken to it, taut with panic and distress, every night since then; this unbearable, silent, malevolent force pressing me into the mattress. She has been committed for thirty days of psychiatric evaluation, or will be soon, ironically at the same state-managed institution where Roxanne was incarcerated, but in high-care. People will no doubt wonder if it was premeditated, and whether Sara-lea arrived at the deli to see me or to confront Jade, and I am sure the previous confrontations and threats have informed this perspective and will play a role in how her actions are judged. I know she was there for her own darkest motivations, and that her target was Jack, but if her legal team can focus their argument around Jade and our relationship, perhaps they will plead 'temporary insanity' or 'self-defence', I don't know. Do they still talk about a 'crime of passion'?

How on earth will I convey to the honourable court what this is really about without signing her death warrant? They cannot pass judgment on a murderous atrocity from a previous lifetime. Raising it in her defence as mitigating circumstances will surely be considered absurd, and in more barbaric times would have left her accused as deranged or evil, a 'nature worshipper', and consigned her to the torture of the wheel or the rack or the bed and sealed her fate to be burnt at the stake to release and purify her soul and prevent forever her earthly form from inflicting such carnage again. This would surely be insignificant compared with the anguish she is no doubt experiencing now?

What I do know is that my life will be a living hell for months to come. It will be picked apart, and there will be nowhere to hide. I might as well just give my manuscript to the judge to save the court's time; perhaps I can present him or her with a complimentary copy at my first book signing? Things will be said about me that I don't even know about myself, some true, some not, but even the falsehoods will become their truth if people choose to see it as such. What actually happened will not matter.

Perhaps I will finally know who I really am?

I wonder if what I heard today will prompt me to write the final chapter and close this book. I have not been able to access my feelings since it happened. My sense are numbed. For a while I felt culpable, that she was driven to act in this way as she was tormented by my love for Jade, or Jade's love for me. I felt repentant that my action or inaction had brought such horror to Jade's world, and accountable for the gruesome undignified deaths of 'This' and 'That'. And a deep remorse, wretched, for what the boys have endured. And for weeks now, while I know beneath it all I felt a crushing 'sadness', above that, when I searched for a word to fill my being, I encounter a real sense of release. Like I have been breathing in, in, in and am now finally exhaling. I have transcended the bifurcation point and chosen a possible future. I have fallen apart and begun to reinvent myself. Jim should be proud of me. But strangely, at least to me, he seems angry and distant, and I'm trying not to jump to conclusions what that's all about. Not yet. I will wait for him to tell me, if he wants to. Perhaps he will choose to say it's because he missed all the action.

What keeps me going each day are the boys, and Jade, of course. I spend a lot of time trying to gauge what they each need most right now. I don't know exactly what they witnessed, but it was probably everything, and they will live with this for the rest of their lives. They have attended a few play-therapy sessions with a child psychologist, where they role-play with figurines and toys, but just because it is the thing to do rather than because I have any faith in it. How the psychologist describes the violent scenes they recreate has horrified me. Joshua, who like me has always lived in his head, I worry about the most as he seems even more remote and reclusive. Jeremiah, as always, appears balanced and has taken on the task of moderating between them on my behalf, but the toll this exacts from him is palpable.

Little Jack has yet another war-wound, and he seems destined to carry this life's experiences etched forever on his face, but I now understand why. I do not know how he will choose to respond in future to queries of—'And how did you get that one?' One day he could write a story about his face; in fact, maybe one day there will be the technology to just scan in his face and touch-screen your way by scar to transport yourself into a virtual-reality experience of defining moments in his life. He yearns for Matisse and Picasso even more than the other boys and once a day we venture together down the steep slope beyond the swimming pool, treacherously sliding down with gifts in hand, to talk with them at their graves alongside the Border Collie and the others. Almost before it begins, the ritual usually degenerates into one or another playful game and I am comforted that it brings them peace and joy and togetherness and adventure. Jack says he wants to get another kitten, but we are looking after Pi-shu who has an uncanny affinity for Jack and in this way I stall his demands for now.

Jack is even wilder than before seeping with uncontrollable anger, and is consumed with acting out sword-fights even with the most inappropriate furry toys, but at least he is expressing it. But it is his heart I worry about; he keeps coming to me and whispering in my ear, 'I am happy my soul chose you to be my family, but I made one mistake. Please, no more fighting, Daddy.' How on earth does he understand this stuff?

Harry, ever by my side, will be just fine. I think he has forgiven me. He looks weird, bald patches all over where they shaved his coat to clean and suture his wounds. When the veterinarian suggested we shave off all his hair, I said, 'You mean like a sphinx?' but I decided against it due to the midwinter chill. Unlike Jack's face, regrowth will soon secret away the evidence of what happened and no one will insist he tells the story. I wonder if he bears his own emotional scars.

The need to see Jade, to let her know that I am with her, for her to sense my presence and feel my love, is the other daily constant that keeps me going. And during that critical time when it was touch-and-go whether she would make it, to remind her that her life was worth living, and that her son and father would wish it so. And I imagine that during that time as she lay there, apparently still and peaceful to the eye, motionless in an induced coma and through the agonies of multiple invasive operations, she was in deep conversation with them both while she decided whether to stay or cross over.

I am sitting on the ledge up the mountain, with my thoughts. Harry and Sally lie panting just behind me. The prospect of walking on the slopes of the mountain, just one more time, also encourages me to take my next breath. So I have done this every day without fail since it happened, and the thoughts are seldom different, except that today they are. What makes today different is the news I heard when Jade's surgeon rounded on me earlier today. He had bounced, smiling, into her hospital room and called me aside and said he had great news for me—that she will make it, but she will carry horrific scars, emotionally and physically.

'She's over the worst of it now, and barring any unforeseen events; we can safely say she will be okay. We have saved what we could, and full recovery will take a while, but she should be able to live a normal life.' And I concurred.

But the next thing he said I heard, yet I could not quite register it. I accepted it nonchalantly with an—'Oh, thanks for telling me,' but my mind just could not assimilate it: 'Jesus, Sarah,' it said. 'What have we done?'

What he said to me was that the baby, or in his words the foetus, did not survive. It was a little girl. 'We estimate she was sixteen weeks pregnant,' he said. I did not know. Jade never told me. I haven't been with her in that way for quite a while now, and bulkier winter clothing could conceal anything . . .

When the surgeon left us alone, I sat in the reclining chair in the far corner of Jade's hospital room and wrote the digits '1303' over and over and over again on the notepad resting on the arm of the chair, pressing so hard I eventually broke through to the cardboard backing, but that did not stop me. Will her soul ever find peace?

'Angelique,' I thought, 'you chose yet again to be in my life. You have been here all along. I don't know what to say to you, Jack.'

'Hello, Clive,' says a voice just behind and to the left of me. I swivel and look up, and then have to look higher because Calix is taller than most. 'I'm sorry if I'm disturbing you, and if this is not a good time . . . I just . . . I would like to talk with you.'

Neither of the dogs move, not even their tails are wagging; they just look at him. I say, 'I've been expecting you for a while now.'

He sits down next to me, and a minute passes in silence. Then he says, 'I was not ready to speak with you before, even when we met here on the mountain and chatted. But the time is right, now, for me. I have moved on, and I need this for closure.'

I cut in, 'Why now? What in particular has prompted you to talk with me now?'

'Lots of reasons, I guess. I am seeing someone else now, Tasmin, as I'm sure you know. She has been a close friend for a few years, but she is not convinced that I have moved on.' I have heard that Calix is 'seeing' Tasmin, previously our next-door-neighbour on the south side and recently divorced, and I wonder idly whether he had a role to play in that. Her character is not unlike that of Sara-lea; they even look alike in many ways, tall, long dark hair, gorgeous and mesmeric, and it did not surprise me. The story goes that it started a couple of years ago and has been on-and-off ever since, so maybe Jim was right? But somehow it does not fit. I had always assumed that when Sara-lea said she had pneumonia, grief-induced, that it was connected to his 'other woman'. But now I am persuaded that it was at the time she lost the pregnancy with Calix's baby—I'm going to assume a cause-effect connection; I deserve to believe I have at least one question answered.

Calix says, 'And this has raised concerns for Tasmin, after Sara-lea confronted her a week before the attack and she also told me "it's too close",' and I don't ask him what that means. 'Then she tried to attack Tasmin, in full view of everybody. She had grabbed a knife.' I don't want to know. Surely I cannot help him deal with Tasmin's issues? 'And just before that Tasmin spoke with you.'

I say, 'Yes, I think I put my foot in it when I congratulated her on your upcoming marriage. She was indignant, she nearly fell out of her car.' And now I remember that Tasmin, too, had felt compelled to tell me 'it is over between them', and I realize she was convincing herself. It was clearly bothering her, and I had inadvertently sharpened her anxiety. I think I had said something about 'after three or four years together' and she frowned and said, 'It wasn't that long, was it?' And I saw the look in her eyes.

Calix says, 'Out of the blue, a month ago Sara-lea told me she had a dream that I was going to marry Tasmin in February next year.'

'Oh. She told me you phoned her to tell her the news. She backed it up with—"see, you have nothing to worry about". I even wondered what it will be like to attend your wedding.' And we both laughed, that punctuated chuckle that surrogates for words that would be needlessly spoken, in the shared knowledge that this is simply Sara-lea. Creating her own reality, Sarah was. She has a good grip on the theories of complexity and chaos—intervene selectively at just the appropriate moment to remarkably influence the system of which you are a part. But not such a good grip on herself.

Calix skirts around for a while, then offers, 'What I did, it's been done before. It happens all the time, and I am certainly not the only one.' Is he asking for redemption by normalizing it?

'Yes, it happens all over,' I say, 'but that doesn't make it okay, and you will have to make your own peace with it. This is not the first time you've done it.' He appears to take no offence and surprises me by briefly describing the circumstances of one of his other affairs with a married woman, one I already know about, and the way he puts it leaves me thinking that it is always the same—a marriage that is not fed and nourished, the chilly indifference between a wife who feels discontented and resentful and a husband who feels unappreciated and withdraws, and the arrival of a third party to pick up the slack. But actually I am thinking about another incarnation, as I see clearly now what connects us. But Calix still has things he needs to say.

'What happened between me and Sara-lea,' Calix says, leaning away from me as if to distance himself from what he is saying, 'without trying to extricate myself from my part in this—I really believe we are co-creators and that you have had an equal role in this.'

'Is that what you've come here to tell me?'

He does not respond.

It is a beautiful afternoon and not entirely surprising for two young residents in our street to pass by us on their way to the summit and wave a greeting. I guess it is only fair that this moment is witnessed by others, in case one day we are unsure of whether it actually happened. I never bring my cigarettes with me up this mountain, but I feel like one now. Sharing this sacred ledge with me, Calix confides how devastated he was when Sara-lea tried to end it after I found out, and how at the brink of despair he felt that life could not go on without her. So he wrote her letters, he says, beseeching, pawing at her, decanting his misery and desolation. 'I think I've caused you a lot of trouble,' he says. With a start, I realize that at the time of her breakdown last September Sara-lea's burden of guilt was not reserved for me, as she was battling on two fronts, witnessing two men she loved and who loved her fall apart before her eyes, one who lived with her and the other who lived next door. And perhaps when his attention turned to Tasmin, and she realized she was losing both of us, that was all too much for her? Love, betrayal, rejection, and bloodletting—it seems like a potent cocktail to me. The insight that I alone was not the cause of her self-destruction does not soothe me. On the contrary, it evokes intense feelings of resentment towards Calix for discharging his needs once again in our family home with the luxury of not having to pick up the fallout.

Before I can find the words to express this, he tells me how the reawakening gradually, insidiously, began through occasional interactions after she returned from hospital. Calix says again, 'But I have moved on,' as if it sounds more convincing when he hears himself say it out loud. And as much as he may wish to believe that he has indeed moved on, I do not have faith in that possibility; not from a love of that depth, abruptly ended but not quite, while you languish in such propinquity. I do not tell him that it was the most painful experience I have ever encountered and above which I had to rise—that this was the gift from this ecstasy of betrayal so profound.

Then Calix tells me about when they first met and how he shared his feelings for her as early as their second consultation, and how he came to be our neighbour and when their affair began and a few other things. With the tease of information that might fill in the gaping holes for me, I feel the spark of curiosity flicker and tinge my heart. But I know if I open this door, I will enter a house with many rooms and not want to leave until and unless I have examined every inch of it—the embracing bedroom of vulnerable intimacy, the darkened basement of deceit and lies, the sunny attic stacked high with boxed-memories of a glorious love shared, the creative kitchen where a mutual passion was shared, and on every surface and wall their heart-love ornamentally displayed. That is not my house.

'It was an unfair situation,' he says, as if this might help, 'the illusion of a relationship lived through an affair that contained almost only moments that were wondrous. It's not real, and you could never compete with that.'

Nothing I have heard so far suffices as an act of contrition or an outpouring of regret, and I ask myself again if this is what I expect to hear from him. But I realize that the content of our conversation is practically irrelevant, the words themselves less important than the simple truth that it is taking place. Details of what actually happened, what he or I feel about it, confessions and apologies and admissions of wrongdoing from him, anger and indignation and accusation from me, none of these would hold much meaning. What connects us, is all that is of interest to me now.

'What I don't understand is if your love was so perfect, why she did not leave me for you?' I say.

'Why she couldn't leave your marriage? I often reflected on what it would be like to live with her, and to this day I still wonder. She was up one moment, down the next, but that's Sara-lea. But she said she still had work to do with you, whatever that meant.' As an understatement, I could not better that. She had told me of her 'karmic connection' to Calix, and I think that Sara-lea already understood what connects us all and was trying to work out her karma, but had to wait for us to 'see' it for ourselves. 'Each time she told me,' Calix says, 'even early on soon after you returned from the Middle East, that you suspected she was having an affair, I begged her to put it on the table. But she wouldn't, she just couldn't. I guess it was insurmountable for her to consider the impact on your boys given her own childhood.'

'If you had done that,' I say, 'all this would have been different, at least our experiences of the future path we would have travelled. But I'm not sure we would have ended up in a different place.'

I wonder if until now I have dishonoured him as an opponent, not an adversary or a foe, but a warrior-challenger, by not looking him in the eye before now and telling him where I stand, that these are my boundaries. I have no doubt he would have stood firm and told me his. I don't regret it, I just acknowledge my observation. I guess I had imagined that if I perfected the art of non-resistance my energies would flow to the end, like a river to the sea, victorious while he exhausted himself with each thrust and parry. But if that was so, at that time it would have been driven by ego, an attempt to assert my masculine potency. I had arrived at my 'sea' some time ago; now it looks as if he too has arrived. It seems we each chose our paths of least resistance and cut through the cliff-rock towards the sea of life; at some stage our tributaries crossed paths and often meandered within sight of each other, even on the physical plane. And the sea of life at which we now assemble, of this present moment which contains all moments past and future, is boundless and abundant. There is nothing to contest or impugn, nothing to acquire and possess and deny the other.

I try again, more directly this time. 'What connects the two of you, Calix? Or, for that matter, the three of us?'

'I don't really know, but I remember an experience I had early on, soon after I met her. Perhaps it was a dream. It seemed to take place in ancient Roman times or Early Middle Ages. I was on horseback accompanying my consort; that was her. Then I was drawn into battle, leaving her at the mercy of whoever came across her. I don't know if I ever returned, perhaps I was lost in battle, though I did not see that part. Then you, a legionnaire of sorts, gathered her up and cared for her.' The burgundy-red cloak lying out of place in the field in the midst of a war . . .

'I took your woman, centuries ago,' I say.

'You rescued her.'

'You came back, I'm sure of that, and you wanted her back.'

'I imagine you were beholden to care for her in my absence.'

'But then I couldn't let her go.'

'You saved her. But I couldn't do the same for you this time round.'

'Well, you gave her back, sort of.'

And now I know, with certainty, why he has been following her, or me.

I half-expect him to raise Sara-lea's present predicament, and somehow link it to me as co-creator of the pain that gave rise to her pathology, and add that to his perception of my role in Tasmin's angst. As a pre-emptive strike, I tell him that I am uncomfortable talking about Sara-lea as she is not present, but that I recognize that this moment is unique and I sense in the intentions behind our words a deep respect for each other and the love we share for her—yet I want us to be cautious of this.

So we sit on this ledge, talking about nothing in particular, with lots of quiet space in-between. There are many things in the present that we don't talk about; not Jade, the boys, nor what happened just a few weeks ago. This ledge, this mountain, has witnessed it all before: two entities, two energies engaging in dispute over a third that must be preserved or conquered. And it has been this way right here in our village since the early settlers arrived and confronted the indigenous peoples. Yet this rock, with wisdom of the ages, is patient. For four years now, it has observed this particular case, even though for much of that period it looked on as the clandestine manoeuvres were obscured and undeclared to some of the protagonists. Duty-bound to destiny, or if you like, the grand plan which is beyond ordinary human understanding, it has faithfully kept this secret knowing that when change is ready it will reveal itself. It has only given us this knowledge now that we can truly 'see'. For it knows that nothing is ever lost, not even the sum of all love, and that the ebb and flow of intimacy—intimate friends and intimate enemies—is forever constant. It also knows, surely, that it does not take very long for the third party to become superfluous while those two duelling forces discover an affinity of sorts as they learn why a set of circumstances have come into being so that they could reconnected.

And I think—'You understand life backwards, but you live it forward.'

At some point, Calix decides that he has to go. And I am amazed at how tranquil Harry and Sally have been, not entirely disinterested and very much part of it all but leaving us to do what we needed to do. 'I'm going to hang around here a bit longer,' I say. I need to empty my mind. I wait until he disappears below the ridge, and then I close my eyes again and let the memorized words of a poem Jade had written and sent to me many weeks ago scroll before my eyelids.

> *The road cradles me*
> *Like the devoted lover of my soul*
> *And its joy*
> *Steadfast and Tender*
> *Allowing me all the rhythms of creation*
> *Contracting and expanding to bring beauty to form*
> *Breathing in perfect sync with me*
> *As I give birth to my Truth*
> *He whispers 'you are free'*

When I open my eyes, I can still see Calix in his burgundy-red sweatshirt, smaller now and almost at the tarred service road that leads back to our respective homes. Then I hear the others coming down the rocky path. They pause behind me, and then one says, 'Was that your brother?'

I smile. 'No, hardly. Why?' but my response is not well-enough considered.

'I just thought you look similar, or maybe . . . ' he says, gesturing with his hands for the words he cannot find to describe what he felt.

'Actually, maybe you're right,' I say. 'He is my brother.'